Jilly Cooper is a well-known journalist, writer and media superstar and the author of many number one bestselling novels. Her novels include *Riders, Rivals, Polo, The Man Who Made Husbands Jealous, Appassionata, Score!* and *Pandora*. She and her husband live in Gloucestershire with several dogs and cats.

SCORE!

Jilly Cooper

CORGI BOOKS

SCORE!
A CORGI BOOK : 0 552 15059 2

Originally published in Great Britain by Bantam Press,
a division of Transworld Publishers

PRINTING HISTORY
Bantam Press edition published 2000
Corgi edition published 2000

7 9 10 8 6

Set in 10/11 pt New Baskerville by
Phoenix Typesetting, Burley-in-Wharfedale, West Yorkshire.

Corgi Books are published by Transworld Publishers,
61–63 Uxbridge Road, London W5 5SA,
a division of The Random House Group Ltd,
in Australia by Random House Australia (Pty) Ltd,
20 Alfred Street, Milsons Point, Sydney, NSW 2061, Australia,
in New Zealand by Random House New Zealand Ltd,
18 Poland Road, Glenfield, Auckland 10, New Zealand
and in South Africa by Random House (Pty) Ltd,
Endulini, 5a Jubilee Road, Parktown 2193, South Africa.

Printed and bound in Great Britain
by Clays Ltd, St Ives plc.

To Ann Mills,
dearest of friends,
with love and gratitude.

CAST OF CHARACTERS

JAMES BENSON	A very smooth, extremely expensive private doctor.
BETTY	One of Rannaldini's pretty maids.
TEDDY BRIMSCOMBE	Rannaldini's head gardener, renowned for his green fingers and wandering hands.
MRS BRIMSCOMBE	Rannaldini's long-suffering housekeeper.
MR BROWN	An Australian racehorse owner.
MISS BUSSAGE	Rannaldini's PA – a gorgon.
RUPERT CAMPBELL-BLACK	Multi-millionaire owner/trainer, ex-Olympic show jumper and Minister for Sport. Director of Venturer Television. Still Mecca for most women.
TAGGIE CAMPBELL-BLACK	His adored second wife – an angel.
MARCUS CAMPBELL-BLACK	Rupert's son by his first marriage, recent winner of the Appleton International piano competition.
TABITHA CAMPBELL-BLACK	Mistress of the Horse for *Don Carlos*. Rupert's estranged daughter from his

first marriage. Serious wild child and event rider.

XAVIER CAMPBELL-BLACK   Rupert and Taggie's adopted Colombian son.

BIANCA CAMPBELL-BLACK   Rupert and Taggie's adopted Colombian daughter.

EDDIE CAMPBELL-BLACK   Rupert's father, five times married and raring to go. A sexual buccaneer of the old school.

BRUCE CASSIDY   Beleaguered press officer for *Don Carlos*. Inevitably nicknamed 'Hype-along'.

CHLOE CATFORD   Mellifluous mezzo soprano, and compilation queen. Sings Princess Eboli in *Don Carlos*. Significant Other Woman in several marriages.

GIUSEPPE CAVALLI   Capricious Italian bass, the ghost of the Emperor Charles V in *Don Carlos*. The inamorato of Granville Hastings, he sings like an angel and drinks like a fish.

LADY CHISLEDON   A pillar of Paradise.

CLIVE   Rannaldini's sinister leather-clad henchman.

MISS CRICKLADE   Paradise village busybody.

HOWIE DENSTON	Artist's agent and ghastly creep who runs London office of Shepherd Denston, toughest music agents in New York.
DIZZY	Rupert Campbell-Black's comely head groom.
DETECTIVE SERGEANT KEVIN FANSHAWE	Rutminster CID smoothie and new-style catcher of villains.
FLORENCE	Hortense de Montigny's ancient retainer.
CHRISTY FOXE	Indefatigable PA during recording of *Don Carlos*.
DETECTIVE SERGEANT TIMOTHY GABLECROSS	Old-style catcher of villains.
BERNARD GUÉRIN	Battle-scarred veteran. First assistant director, *Don Carlos*, Tristan de Montigny's *droit*-hand man, who so acts as sergeant major keeping order on the set.
DAME HERMIONE HAREFIELD	World-famous diva and Rannaldini's mistress. Seriously tiresome, brings out Crippen in all.
BOB HAREFIELD	Her charming, mostly absentee husband, long-term lover of Meredith Whalen.
LITTLE COSMO HAREFIELD	Hermione's fiendish nine-year-old son. Could give

	lessons to Damien in *The Omen*.
EULALIA HARRISON	A frumpy feature writer.
GRANVILLE 'GRANNY' HASTINGS	English bass, singing the Grand Inquisitor in *Don Carlos*. Outwardly cosy old pussy-cat.
LYSANDER HAWKLEY	Formerly a man who made husbands jealous, now happily married to Rannaldini's third wife Kitty. Rupert Campbell-Black's assistant.
THE REV. PERCIVAL HILLARY	A portly parson, who confines his pastoral visits to drinks time.
GEORGE HUNGERFORD	An extremely successful property developer, chief executive of Rutminster Symphony Orchestra. Live-in lover of Flora Seymour.
JANICE	Rannaldini's head groom.
JESSICA	Ravishing production secretary, *Don Carlos*.
BEATTIE JOHNSON	A seductive, totally unprincipled journalist.
SEXTON KEMP	An extremely fly East End film producer. Chief Executive of Liberty Productions, who are making *Don Carlos*.

LUCY LATIMER	Make-up artist on *Don Carlos*. Still centre and agony aunt to entire cast and crew.
CLAUDINE LAUZERTE	Actress and Gallic goddess, married to a French government minister.
DETECTIVE CONSTABLE LIGHTFOOT	Eager young constable, traumatized by steamy stint at the 1991 Valhalla orgy.
ISA LOVELL	A brilliant, obsessive jump jockey. A Heathcliff of the gallops.
JAKE LOVELL	His father, ex-world show jumping champion. Now National Hunt trainer.
TORY LOVELL	Isa's mother and Jake's wife – loving and super-efficient, a hard act for a daughter-in-law to follow.
MARIA	An ace cook.
DETECTIVE CONSTABLE DEBBIE MILLER	A pulchritudinous policewoman.
COLIN MILTON	Once-great tenor now playing Count Lerma, the Spanish ambassador in *Don Carlos*. Old sweetie, eminently bullyable.
ÉTIENNE DE MONTIGNY	France's greatest painter and national hero.
ALEXANDRE DE MONTIGNY	Étienne's pompous eldest son, a judge.

HORTENSE DE MONTIGNY	Étienne's sister – a blue-blooded battle-axe.
SIMONE DE MONTIGNY	Étienne's granddaughter and Alexandre's daughter. In charge of continuity, *Don Carlos*.
TRISTAN DE MONTIGNY	Étienne's youngest son and Rannaldini's godson. Director, *Don Carlos*.
DETECTIVE CONSTABLE KAREN NEEDHAM	The belle of the Bill.
OGBORNE	Chief grip, *Don Carlos*.
LORD (DECLAN) O'HARA OF PENSCOMBE	Recently ennobled television megastar, managing director of Venturer Television and Rupert Campbell-Black's father-in-law.
VIKING O'NEILL	Golden boy and first horn of Rutminster Symphony Orchestra.
OSCAR	Deceptively indolent director of photography, *Don Carlos*.
FRANCO PALMIERI	Vast and vastly famous Italian tenor, playing the title role in *Don Carlos*.
MIKHAIL PEZCHEROV	Lovable but rather base baritone, playing the Marquis of Posa in *Don Carlos*.
LARA PEZCHEROV	Mikhail's adored wife.

DETECTIVE CHIEF INSPECTOR GERALD PORTLAND	Admin king and limelight hogger, Rutminster CID.
ROZZY PRINGLE	Exquisite-voiced soprano playing Tebaldo the page in *Don Carlos*. Worn down by overwork and importunate family.
GLYN PRINGLE	Rozzy's husband – an accomplished drone.
PUSHY GALORE	An ambitious and irritatingly good-looking member of the *Don Carlos* chorus. Real name Gloria Prescott.
CECILIA RANNALDINI	Italian soprano and world-famous diva. Rannaldini's feisty second wife.
SIR ROBERTO RANNALDINI	Mega maestro and arch-fiend, with musical directorships in Berlin, New York and Tokyo. Co-producing *Don Carlos*.
LADY (HELEN) RANNALDINI	Rannaldini's fourth wife and Rupert Campbell-Black's first wife, devoted mother of Marcus and less so of Tabitha. A legendary American beauty.
WOLFGANG RANNALDINI	Rannaldini's son from his first marriage. Little Hitler exterior hides heart of gold. Former boyfriend of Flora Seymour.

SALLY	Another of Rannaldini's pretty maids.
FLORA SEYMOUR	Soprano and viola player and former wild child, traumatized by teenage *affaire* with Rannaldini, now living with George Hungerford.
ALPHEUS P. SHAW	World-famous American bass, singing Philip II in *Don Carlos*. Splendid-looking, but pompous sexual predator.
CHERYL SHAW	Alpheus's justifiably jealous wife. Great tree and social climber.
DETECTIVE CONSTABLE SMITHSON	A very PC DC.
BABY SPINOSISSIMO	Dazzling Australian tenor and sexual buccaneer of the modern school.
CHIEF CONSTABLE SWALLOW	A Rutshire god, and friend of Lady Rannaldini and Dame Hermione.
SYLVESTRE	Sound engineer, *Don Carlos*. Man of few words but countless deeds.
SYLVIA	Glyn Pringle's housekeeper.
VALENTIN	Charismatic camera operator, *Don Carlos*. Oscar's son-in-law.

LADY GRISELDA WALLACE	Wardrobe mistress, *Don Carlos.* Nervous-breakdown van always on call during production.
SERENA WESTWOOD	Record producer of *Don Carlos.* Cool, competent beauty.
JESSIE WESTWOOD	Serena's four-year-old daughter.
MEREDITH WHALEN	Set designer, *Don Carlos.* Highly expensive interior designer. Known as the Ideal Homo, because he's so much in demand as spare man at dinner parties.

THE ANIMALS

THE ENGINEER	Tabitha Campbell-Black's event horse.
GERTRUDE	Taggie Campbell-Black's mongrel.
JAMES	Lucy Latimer's rescued lurcher.
PEPPY KOALA	An Australian wonder horse.
THE PRINCE OF DARKNESS	Rannaldini's vicious and generally victorious National Hunt horse.
SARASTRO	Rannaldini's cat.
SHARON	Tabitha Campbell-Black's yellow Labrador, later has walk-on part as the Grand Inquisitor's guide dog.
TABLOID	Rannaldini's Rottweiler.
TREVOR	Flora Seymour's rescued terrier.

DON CARLOS
THE INITIAL CAST OF THE FILM

PHILIP II, KING OF SPAIN	Alpheus P. Shaw
DON CARLOS, INFANTE OF SPAIN	'Fat Franco' Palmieri
ELIZABETH DE VALOIS, PRINCESS OF FRANCE	Hermione Harefield
TEBALDO, ELIZABETH'S PAGE	Rozzy Pringle
PRINCESS EBOLI, A SPANISH LADY-IN-WAITING	Chloe Catford
RODRIGO, MARQUIS OF POSA FRIEND OF DON CARLOS	To be filled
THE GRAND INQUISITOR	Granville 'Granny' Hastings
THE GHOST OF THE EMPEROR CHARLES V	Giuseppe Cavalli
COUNT LERMA, THE SPANISH AMBASSADOR TO FRANCE	Colin Milton

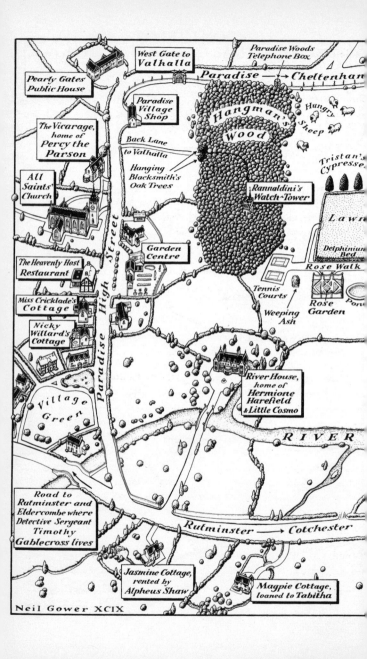

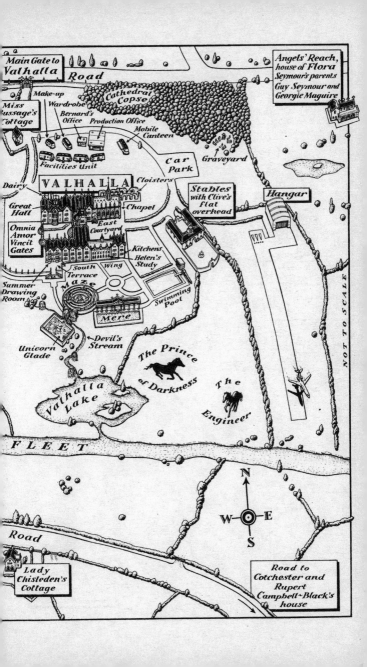

Main Gate to *Valhalla*

Road

Cathedral Copse

Angels' Reach, house of *Flora Seymour's* parents *Guy Seymour* and *Georgie Maguire*

Make-up

Miss Bussage's Cottage

Wardrobe

Bernard's Office

Production Office

Mobile Canteen

Facilities Unit

Car Park

Graveyard

Dairy

VALHALLA

Cloisters

Stables with Clive's Flat overhead

Hangar

Great Hall

Chapel

Omnia Amor Vincit Gates

East Courtyard

Kitchens

Helen's Study

South Wing Terrace

Maze

Swimming Pool

Summer Drawing Room

Mere

Devil's Stream

NOT TO SCALE

Unicorn Glade

Valhalla Lake

The Prince of Darkness

The Engineer

FLEET

N
W ⊙ E
S

Road

Lady Chisleden's Cottage

Road to Cotchester and Rupert Campbell-Black's house

OVERTURE
1977

Many men hated Roberto Rannaldini. Many women, after loving him passionately, hated him even more. To be regarded at twenty-eight as the most exciting conductor since the war had necessitated brutal trampling on the way up. But at least Rannaldini could count on the unqualified love of his ten-year-old godson, Tristan de Montigny. To Tristan, the dashing maestro, with his suave, catlike smile, his deep, caressing voice, and his recklessly fast cars, was the most glamorous person in the world.

Most importantly Rannaldini had been a friend of Tristan's mother, who had died when Tristan was a baby, and was the only person prepared to satisfy the boy's craving for information about her.

'She was so beautiful, so sweet, so proud of you, Tristan, and she love you so much. Her death happen in moment of madness, when she feel she cannot cope, and was unworthy of your father.'

Tristan's father, Étienne de Montigny, was France's most illustrious painter. He was revered for his portraits and landscapes but most famous for his erotic paintings, many of which, *Salome's Ecstasy*, *The Rape of Lucrece* and more recently *David and Jonathan*, hung in the great galleries of the world, elevating near-pornography to an art form.

Étienne, outwardly a laughing giant of a man, had spawned a pack of children from three wives and numerous mistresses. Twelve years ago, when he was sixty, he had met Rannaldini, newly arrived in Paris to make his fortune as a conductor. The two had struck up a rapport, and Étienne had taken the handsome, impossibly precocious teenager under his wing. In return Rannaldini had not only milked Étienne's contacts but also posed for him.

Part of the fun for collectors of what became known as Étienne's 'extremely blue period' was to identify Rannaldini in the paintings as everyone from Apollo to the head of John the Baptist. Rannaldini had also provided beautiful young models to titillate the old goat's palate and palette.

The most beautiful had been Tristan's mother, the sixteen-year-old Delphine. Even Étienne's staunchest supporters had been horrified when he had made this exquisite child his fourth wife and within a few weeks impregnated her.

Nemesis moved swiftly. A proud, delighted Étienne was busy sketching his newborn baby, Tristan, when he heard that his fourth and favourite son, Laurent, a young army officer, had been blown up in Chad. Laurent had always been a rebel, and rumours persisted that he had been taken out by his own side. Too crazed with grief even to call for an inquiry, Étienne promptly lost interest in baby Tristan, and hardly seemed to notice when, a few days later, Tristan's young mother committed suicide. She had been suffering from post-natal depression. It was left to Étienne's sister, Hortense, a rusty old battleaxe, to organize Tristan's christening, at which, as one of Delphine's last wishes, Rannaldini was a godfather.

Étienne's indifference persisted. Tristan was the only one of his children he pointedly ignored and never praised. The boy had been brought up with the rest of Étienne's gilded pack in Paris or at the château in the Tarn, but he was always the wistful calf which grazes away from the herd, longing for yet shying away from love.

Which was why his godfather was so important to Tristan and why on that wintry November evening in 1977 he could hardly contain his excitement as, in his first dark suit, his gold hair slicked down with water, he peered out at the galloping black clouds and frenziedly thrashing trees of the Bois de Boulogne for a first glimpse of Rannaldini's Mercedes.

Although Rannaldini got a Machiavellian kick from singling out Tristan for attention, knowing it irritated the hell out of Étienne, he was genuinely attached to the boy. He had also been a wonderful godfather: writing from all over the world, never forgetting Christmas or a birthday, taking Tristan to concerts whenever he swept through Paris. For his confirmation he had even given him a Guarneri cello, valued at thousands, which Tristan had been practising for days hoping Rannaldini might ask him to play. Tristan had also painted him a water-colour – not too much like Degas – of polo players in the Bois.

There was Rannaldini's Mercedes. Tristan hurtled downstairs, beating the housekeeper, slithering on a rose-patterned rug across the floorboards, shyly shaking his godfather by the hand, before submitting to a warm, scented embrace.

As usual, Rannaldini was in a hurry. As a tenth-birthday present, he was taking Tristan to Verdi's greatest opera, *Don Carlos*. The curtain would rise in an hour so they were cutting it fine, but first he wanted to hear Tristan play and whisked him into the library.

Here Rannaldini paused only to admire himself on the cover of *Paris-Match*, and clock any new artists on the dark red walls. Over the centuries, the Montignys had increased their fortune buying paintings ahead of fashion. Rannaldini had considerably bolstered his coffers by using Étienne's eye to build up his own collection.

Opening the piano score of *Don Carlos*, at the great cello solo at the beginning of Act IV, he placed it on Tristan's music stand.

'Try this.'

Even though Tristan was sight-reading, he played with total concentration and the sad sound blossomed as his long fingers vibrated on the strings.

'Excellent,' cried Rannaldini in delight. 'You work very hard. And this is excellent too,' he added, putting Tristan's watercolour inside the piano score. 'I will hang it in my study. We must go.'

'I hope you will not be bored,' said Rannaldini, man-oeuvring the Mercedes through the pre-theatre and dinner traffic at a speed that astounded even the Parisians. 'It is long opera but very interesting. I will briefly explain story.

'France and Spain are ending long, bloody war. To unite the two countries, Elisabetta, the French king's beautiful daughter, is to marry Carlos, the son of King Philip II of Spain. Understand?'

Tristan nodded. He loved the way Rannaldini never talked down to him.

'Young Carlos reach France in disguise, wanting to see if he has been lumbered with ugly cow, but when he see Princess Elisabetta out hunting in the woods,' Rannaldini gesticulated at the Bois de Boulogne, 'he find her utterly beautiful, with dark hair to her waist. When he reveal he is Carlos, her future husband, she fall in love too. They will live 'appy ever after.' Jumping a red light, Rannaldini made a V-sign at an outraged crone in a Volvo.

'Then awful thing 'appen. Carlos's father, Philip II, decide he want Elisabetta for himself and marries her instead. This is very selfish because King already has beautiful girlfriend called Eboli.

24

'Poor Carlos, however, cannot stop loving Elisabetta even though she is now Queen of Spain, married to his father, and she still love him. But everywhere in Spanish court they are spied on. I won't spoil the ending.'

They were approaching the opera house.

'Rannaldini, Rannaldini,' shouted admirers, surging forward.

A group protesting against nuclear tests was also lurking. One, a handsome but ferocious blonde, banged on the Mercedes window, which Rannaldini lowered a fraction.

'How would you like your testicles shrivelled by radiation?' she yelled.

'Sounds interesting,' murmured Rannaldini, closing the window as her furious face disappeared in a tidal wave of fans.

'I'm getting a bodyguard,' he complained, as a couple of doormen finally dragged him and Tristan through the stage door.

Tristan was unfazed, particularly when Rannaldini, while donning the splendour of white tie and tails, offered him a birthday glass of Krug. All down the passage, singers could be heard warming up.

A white gardenia in a glass box for Rannaldini to slot into his buttonhole was delivered to the Maestro's dressing room. Most of the flowers arriving were for Cecilia Rannaldini, his second wife, who was singing Eboli, and who now could be heard screaming, 'When will people learn I only like *red* roses,' as she hurled everything else on to the floor.

Chic and svelte for a diva, Cecilia had done much to advance Rannaldini's career, not least by changing her famous name to his. Having barged into the conductor's room and smothered Tristan in kisses, she started rowing with Rannaldini in Italian.

Carlos was being sung by a plump, good-looking Italian, Franco Palmieri. Rannaldini's latest discovery, an unknown South African called Hermione, was making her début as Elisabetta.

The packed audience was too old to interest Tristan but, with his chin resting on the front of the red velvet box, he gazed down in wonder at the glittering instruments in the pit. Opposite him were the cellos and behind them towered the double basses, red-gold as beeches in autumn. But once the action started on stage, and hunting horns heralded Hermione as Elisabetta riding in on a real grey horse, Tristan hardly noticed the orchestra. Hermione's thick brown hair did indeed curl to her waist and he couldn't take his eyes off her cleavage, which seemed to part like curtains whenever she hit a high note – and how gloriously she sang!

Rannaldini's black hair was drenched with sweat, as his dark eyes sent laser beams to singer or musician so they responded almost without realizing it. Now he was smiling at Hermione, magicking increasingly beautiful sounds with a twitch of his baton.

Cecilia Rannaldini had a pure, clean voice. But, not realizing that shouting and crying all night can harm the vocal cords, Tristan thought she sounded very rough. She was, however, a great actress and, as she glared at Hermione, put him in mind of the wicked queen in *Snow White*. King Philip, on the other hand, was so stern and cold with his son Carlos, he reminded Tristan of his own father, Étienne.

Alone in the big box, he was also terrified by the Grand Inquisitor, blind, hooded, bent over his sticks like a black widow spider, and when the flames began to flicker round the poor bare feet of the heretics, Tristan leapt to his own feet screaming, 'No, no they mustn't burn,' which was luckily drowned, by orchestra, church bells and chorus loudly praising God and the Inquisition.

Every role in *Don Carlos* is demanding, but it was the young Hermione who drew the most rapturous applause. Tristan clapped his hands until they were as pink as the carnations that cascaded down on her.

After more champagne and hugging, as people poured backstage to congratulate them, Rannaldini, Cecilia, Fat Franco, who'd sung Carlos, and Hermione swept Tristan off to the Ritz, where he still couldn't speak for excitement. Everyone was sweet to him because Rannaldini made sure they knew both of his birthday and of his famous father.

The management presented him with a frothy fruit cocktail filled with coloured straws. Rannaldini, who never minded what the boy ate, allowed him to have lobster Thermidor with sizzling cheese topping, followed by blackcurrant sorbet.

Hermione, who'd changed into low-cut dark blue lace, presented him with one of her pink carnations. Then a birthday cake arrived with ten candles and he opened Rannaldini's presents: a red leatherbound copy of Schiller's play *Don Carlos* on which Verdi had based his opera, and a video camera. Tristan couldn't stop saying thank you.

'He already play cello very well,' boasted Rannaldini.

'Are you going to be a musician?' asked Hermione.

'No.' Tristan blushed and stroked the camera. 'I'm going to make films.'

He was too happy to absorb the tensions around him. Singers are often so fired up after a performance, they want sex instantly. Franco's machismo was clearly dented because Hermione made it plain she was interested only in Rannaldini, which didn't improve Cecilia's temper either. She and Franco muttered that Hermione had deliberately hung on to notes to make them run out of breath. Nor would she have got such applause in the middle of Act V if Rannaldini hadn't made an artificial pause. Fortunately Hermione didn't understand Italian.

She was like one of his sister's old-fashioned dolls, Tristan decided, who opened their big eyes and said, 'Mama,' although in Hermione's case it seemed to be, 'Me, me.'

'Was it really twenty call-backs?' she was now asking Rannaldini. 'Pinch me, so I know I'm awake.'

She screamed as Rannaldini pinched her hard enough to leave white marks on her arm. Then he dropped his sleek dark head and kissed them better. Cecilia stormed out, pretending that their daughter Natasha had flu.

'My wife is more neurotic than the horse in Act One,' grumbled Rannaldini. 'You should be specially interested in *Don Carlos*,' he added to Tristan, 'because one of your Montigny ancestors visited Spanish court during Philip II's reign. And the Inquisition kill him, thinking he is spy. I wish I had smart relations like that,' he went on fretfully.

'I cannot imagine you not being smart, Signor Rannaldini,' said a soft, dreamy voice, and they were engulfed in the sweetest scent, as though a bank of violets had bloomed behind them.

It was the only time Tristan had ever seen his godfather blush. Pausing at the table, in floating chiffon as violet as her eyes, a gently mocking smile playing over her full pink lips, was the most beautiful woman in France: Claudine Lauzerte, the actress wife of the opposition Minister for Cultural Affairs.

'Madame Lauzerte!'

Jumping to his feet, Rannaldini kissed her hand. Then, clicking his fingers at the wine waiter, he beseeched her to join them.

'I am leaving. I hear your *Don Carlos* is wonderful, with a sensational new star.'

Bowing and scraping like a brothel-keeper at the arrival of a royal stag party, Rannaldini introduced Hermione.

'And this is Franco Palmieri who play Carlos.'

Leaping up, Franco sent several glasses and a vase of flowers flying.

Claudine Lauzerte had such impact that for the first

five minutes people talked gibberish in her presence, so she turned to Tristan.

'This is my godson, Tristan de Montigny, Étienne's boy,' explained Rannaldini proudly.

'Ah.' The violet eyes widened in amusement. 'Your father often ask me to sit for him, but we are both always so busy.' She glanced at the video camera. 'You are obviously destined to become a director. With those looks, every leading lady will do exactly what you tell her.'

Noting Tristan's pallor, his deep-set eyes mere hollows, she chided Rannaldini. 'This poor child's exhausted! Take him home.'

'I will send you tickets,' Rannaldini called after her.

'I cannot believe I've met Claudine Lauzerte,' babbled Hermione. 'She must have had several facelifts to look so lovely.'

On the drive home, having jettisoned a furious Franco, Rannaldini pointed to a round white moon, retreating behind a lacing of dark clouds.

'She is upstaged by your beauty,' he told Hermione.

From the back seat, Tristan noticed Hermione continually holding her throat as if it were some precious jewel. Tomorrow he would take his new metal-detector, a present from Aunt Hortense, into the Bois and find her – and perhaps Claudine Lauzerte as well – a diamond ring.

Hermione was now complaining about lecherous conductors.

'I was doing Rinaldo last week and Sir Rodney Macintosh, who must be over sixty, asked me to his room for a nightcap and greeted me wearing nothing but a pair of socks.'

Rannaldini wasn't remotely shocked.

'Eef you knee conductor in groin, he won't give you more work. You must invent fiancé, preferably black belt at judo.'

Even such a fascinating subject couldn't stop Tristan dropping off. Later he never knew if he'd dreamt it, or whether Rannaldini's hand really had vanished into Hermione's dark lace dress, and a moonlike breast emerged.

He did wake screaming, however, as Rannaldini pulled up outside the house and Étienne, still in his painter's smock, loomed huger and blacker than the Grand Inquisitor in the doorway. Although his father cheered up when he saw Hermione, he curtly dispatched Tristan to bed.

'And no ducking out of school tomorrow.'

'Good night, little one,' called Rannaldini, then, to irritate Étienne, 'I'll be up in a few minutes.'

In fact it was an hour, and Tristan again woke screaming from lobster-induced nightmare as another broad-shouldered black figure loomed over him.

'It all 'appen four hundred years ago,' said Rannaldini as he tucked the boy in. 'You mustn't 'ave bad dreams.'

Looking round the bleak attic room, seeing the video camera, the red leatherbound copy of Schiller's *Don Carlos* and Hermione's carnation in a tooth-mug on the bedside table, he picked up the silver frame, containing the only photograph of Tristan's mother, Delphine, in the house.

'So beautiful, a little like Madame Lauzerte, don't you think?'

'Will she sit for Papa?' asked Tristan hopefully.

'I doubt it. She is very pure lady – her nickname is Madame Vierge.'

'Did they really burn people alive in those days?'

'They do today with electric chairs and bombs. That's how your brother, Laurent, died,' said Rannaldini.

But the terror in Tristan's eyes was in case his father walked in and heard the forbidden name. Such had been Étienne's heartbreak, no allusion to Laurent was allowed in the house.

'Why didn't King Philip like Carlos?' Tristan asked wistfully.

'Fathers and sons.' Rannaldini brushed back the boy's hair. 'Philip was jealous, Carlos had whole life ahead of him – to pull the girls.'

'Can I work for you when I grow up?' murmured Tristan.

'One day we will make great film of *Don Carlos* together,' promised Rannaldini.

1

Eighteen spectacularly successful years later, on a wet, windy, late-October morning, Sir Roberto Rannaldini gazed down on the valley of Paradise, often described as the jewel of the Cotswolds.

Rannaldini owned many splendid houses, but the brooding, secretive Paradise Abbey, which he had somewhat hubristically renamed Valhalla after the home of the gods in Teutonic mythology, was the one he loved most.

From his study on the first floor he could admire, albeit through mist and rain, his tennis courts, swimming-pool, hangar for jet and helicopter, lovingly-tended gardens and racehorses, grazing in fields sweeping down to his lake and the river Fleet, which ran along the bottom of the valley.

To his left, coiled up like a sleeping snake, was the famous Valhalla Maze. To the right, deep in the woods, lurked the watchtower, where he edited, composed and seduced. Beyond, disappearing into the mist, was the ravishing mill house, belonging to Hermione Harefield, his mistress for the last eighteen years.

But even as Rannaldini gloated over his valley, the dying fires of autumn seemed to symbolize his own decline. For the first time ever, his massive royalty cheque was down. Last Sunday, when he was conducting at the Appleton piano competition, his favoured candidate and latest conquest, the ravishing Natalia Philipovna, had been beaten into second place, despite intense lobbying, by Rannaldini's detested stepson, Marcus Campbell-Black.

The same evening, Rannaldini learnt he had failed in his bid to take over the Rutminster Symphony Orchestra, who had accompanied the finalists. As an ultimate humiliation at the party afterwards, the first horn had hit Rannaldini across the room – his fall had been broken only by the pudding trolley and the flaccid curves of a grisly crone from the Arts Council. The newspapers had had a field day. Rannaldini shuddered.

Like Philip II of Spain, who had exhausted himself and his nation's coffers trying to hold his Habsburg Empire together, Rannaldini was also learning by bitter experience that his vast kingdom could be maintained only by the crippling expense of waging war on all fronts. He was currently engaged in law-suits with orchestras, unions, sacked musicians, mistresses and ex-wives.

Nineteen months ago, merely to spite his great enemy, the very rich and arrogant Rupert Campbell-Black, whom he believed had orchestrated the break-up of his third marriage, Rannaldini had made a catastrophic fourth marriage to Rupert's neurotic ex-wife, Helen. In return for his habitual infidelity, Helen was now busy squandering his millions and, because Rannaldini was only five foot six, deliberately dwarfing him in public by wearing very high heels.

Rannaldini was sad that his two eldest children from earlier marriages, Wolfgang and Natasha, had left home after frightful family rows. But, saddest of all, he knew his music was suffering. Accusing Rannaldini of blandness in the *Daily Telegraph* last Monday, Norman Lebrecht had suggested he stopped settling scores and started studying them again. Rannaldini might outwardly be the greatest conductor in the world, with orchestras in New York, Berlin and Tokyo, but he was poor in spirit and horribly alone.

33

Outside, rain swept across the woods like ghost armies marching on Valhalla. Although his office was tropically warm and the windows and doors were closed, an icy wind suddenly rustled all the papers and the fire died in the grate with a hiss. On the chimney-piece, a gilt and ormolu clock of Apollo driving the horses of the sun chimed twelve noon.

Valhalla was full of ghosts. They never frightened Rannaldini: they were his accomplices in terrorizing the living. But, hearing an almost orgasmic groan, he looked up quickly at the Étienne de Montigny oil to the right of the fireplace. Entitled *Don Juan in Transit*, it portrayed the great lover, looking suspiciously like Rannaldini, humping a lady of the manor but distracted by the swelling bosom of her young maid hanging clothes outside in the orchard. It was the attention to detail – the yellow stamens of the apple blossom, each hair under the maid's armpit, the pale green spring light – that made the painting so perfect.

Rannaldini smiled at his reflection in the big gilt mirror. His hair might be pewter grey but his face was still as virile and handsome as Don Juan's in the picture. He also had two trump cards.

The first was a film of *Don Carlos*, which he was poised to conduct and co-produce. The nightmare of cutting a three-and-a-half-hour opera down to a manageable two hours for filming had not been helped by Rannaldini insisting that an overture, an aria, and linking passages to make the story more accessible, all composed by himself, be included. The plot of *Don Carlos* had been gingered up with several sex scenes and, to appeal to the pink pound, Carlos's best friend, the gallant Marquis of Posa, would be portrayed as a homosexual.

An all-star cast, who would have screaming hysterics when they discovered any of their numbers had been cut, had been assembled for some time, because singers have to be booked several years ahead. They included Hermione Harefield, who at forty would need careful lighting to play the young Elisabetta. Nor could she act, but at least she did what Rannaldini told her, which was more than did Franco Palmieri, who was playing Don Carlos and who had grown so fat he made Pavarotti look anorexic. However, it had been written into his contract that he must lose seven stone before filming started next April.

In the past Rannaldini had often given juicier parts, in more ways than one, to his ex-wife Cecilia in lieu of alimony, but she and Hermione would have murdered each other on location. As a result, the part of the seductive, scheming Princess Eboli had gone to a ravishing mezzo, Chloe Catford. The search, though, was still on to find an unknown star to play the Marquis of Posa. Having, in his opinion, agreed to over-pay everyone else, Rannaldini was hunting for a bargain.

Opera films were seldom big box office. Why, therefore, had these vastly high-earning singers committed themselves when they knew what purgatory it was to work with Rannaldini?

The answer was Tristan de Montigny, who by driving himself into the ground to win some recognition from his father, Étienne, was now one of the hottest directors in the world. With his ravishing English-speaking version of Manzoni's *The Betrothed* tipped to win several Oscars, he had spent the summer filming Balzac's *The Lily in the Valley* with Claudine Lauzerte. The word on the street was that, despite being over fifty, 'Madame Vierge' had never looked more beautiful or acted better.

Success with actors of both sexes had been helped by Tristan's wonderfully romantic looks: the model whom Calvin Klein loved best. At six foot two, he was too thin, and his gold curls had darkened to burnt umber, but the peat-brown, heavily shadowed eyes, the cheekbones higher than the Eiffel Tower, and the big mouth, usually smiling but of incredible sadness in repose, made everyone long to make him happy.

But it was a mistake to be fooled by Tristan's gentleness: he could be both manipulative and monomaniac in getting the film he wanted.

He and Rannaldini were both so successful that they seldom managed to meet except for an hour snatched at an airport or a midnight dinner after a concert, but they had retained their affection for one another and their dream of working together, which at last was going to be realized.

But, sadly, too late to please Étienne. All the newspapers littering Rannaldini's desk reported that France's greatest painter since Monet was dying but refusing to go to hospital. Rannaldini was tempted to cancel tonight's Barbican concert and fly out to bid his old friend farewell, but he'd get more coverage if he waited until the funeral. He couldn't spare the time for both.

He felt a surge of hatred as he noticed an intensely glamorous photograph in *Le Monde* of Rupert Campbell-Black embracing his son Marcus before putting him on a plane to Moscow. If Rupert was relinquishing one child, he might consider a reconciliation with another, Marcus's younger sister, the ravishing nineteen-year-old Tabitha. Rupert loathed Rannaldini so much that he had disinherited both Marcus and Tabitha for attending their mother's wedding to Rannaldini.

Tabitha, however, like Tristan, was one of the few people who liked Rannaldini – not least because, when she became his stepdaughter, he had given her a large allowance and bought her a wonderful horse called The Engineer. But within a few weeks of marrying Rannaldini, Helen had caught him leering through a two-way mirror at Tabitha undressing, and packed her off to an eventing yard in America. There Tabitha was winning competitions and was already spoken of as an Olympic possible. She was also making friends.

'I've been invited to fifteen Thanksgiving parties and I'm going to all of them,' she had announced, in her last letter home.

On the other hand, she missed Rupert dreadfully. She had always been his favourite child, the one who rode as fearlessly as he did, and, like Rupert, she had hitherto dismissed her brother Marcus as a wimp.

Knowing it would unhinge her, Rannaldini played his second trump card, faxing out all the cuttings of Marcus being outed before winning the Appleton piano competition and being reunited with an overjoyed Rupert. Rupert had totally accepted that Marcus was gay and in love with the great Russian dancer, Alexei Nemerovsky. He had even flippantly told a group of reporters at Heathrow that he was looking forward to meeting Nemerovsky, and felt he was 'gaining a daughter rather than losing a son'.

Silly, silly Rupert, thought Rannaldini, as he filled his jade pen with emerald-green ink to scribble a covering letter.

'Dearest Tabitha, I know you will want to share your mother's joy that your brother is both a national hero and reconciled with your father.'

Smirking, Rannaldini handed it to his new PA, Miss Bussage, who looked like being his third trump card. After only a month she had transformed his life, keeping track of children, wives, finances and his gruelling schedule. Nor did she have any compunction about feeding pleading love notes, demands from charities and bad reviews (after the author's name had been put on the hit list) straight into the shredder.

Rannaldini dreamed of Miss Bussage giving him a bed review:

'You were very boring in the sack last night, Maestro, please do better this evening.'

In her forties, Miss Bussage had the look of a well-regulated musk ox, with small suspicious eyes and dark, heavy hair that flicked up, sixties-style, like two horns. Her thick body was redeemed by a splendid bosom and rather good legs. Like musk oxen, she was also able to survive the arctic climate of Rannaldini's rages, and gave off a strong, musky scent in the rutting season.

Friendly one day, downright rude the next, which Rannaldini, used to sycophancy, thought wonderful, she had now picked up his private telephone, which none of his other staff would touch at pain of thumbscrew.

'Marcel Dupont for you.'

Dupont was Étienne de Montigny's lawyer. He had grown rich over the years but had had his work cut out, extricating the great man from scrapes and marriages, and preserving his vast fortune.

'What news?' asked Rannaldini, seizing the receiver.

'The worst.' Dupont's voice trembled. 'Étienne died an hour ago.'

Glancing up as Apollo's clock struck one, Rannaldini crossed himself. Death must have been at noon when the fire died in the grate and Don Juan in Étienne's painting cried out in anguish. 'I am so sorry,' Rannaldini's voice dropped an octave. 'I trust the end was peaceful?'

'Did Étienne ever do anything peacefully?' asked Dupont. 'Like Hercules, he battled to the end. He wanted to see another sunset. I know how busy you are, Maestro, but . . .'

'I will certainly be at the funeral.'

Then Dupont confessed it had been Étienne's dying wish that Rannaldini should join Tristan's three older brothers carrying the coffin.

'But surely Tristan . . .' began Rannaldini.

Dupont sighed. 'Even in death. I can trust your discretion.'

'Of course,' lied Rannaldini.

French law insists that three-quarters of any estate is divided between the children of the blood, with whole shares going to legitimate children and half shares to any born out of wedlock. Tristan, therefore, would automatically inherit several million. But the law also stipulates that the fourth quarter of a man's estate can be divided as he chooses.

'Étienne itemized everything for children, mistresses, friends, wives and servants,' said Dupont bleakly, 'but he left nothing personal to Tristan, not even a pencil drawing or a paintbrush. Why did he hate the poor boy so much?'

'Poor boy indeed.' Rannaldini was shocked. 'I will ring him.'

'Please do – he's devastated, and the end was dreadful. I hope this story doesn't leak out. Anyway, while you're on, Rannaldini, Étienne left you two of his greatest paintings, *Abelard and Héloïse* and *The Nymphomaniac*. Both are on exhibition in New York.'

Together they were worth several million. Not such a bad day, after all, thought Rannaldini.

2

Having witnessed Étienne's extremely harrowing death, Tristan had immediately fled back to his own flat in La Rue de Varenne, trying to blot out the horror and despair with work. He had been on the brink of making the one film his father might have rated, because it was with Rannaldini. Now it was too late.

Scrumpled-up paper lay all over the floor. His laptop was about to be swept off the extreme left-hand corner of his desk by a hurtling lava of videos, scores, a red leatherbound copy of Schiller's *Don Carlos*, books on sixteenth-century France and Spain, sketches of scenes, Gauloise packets and half-drunk cups of black coffee. Photographs of the *Don Carlos* cast were pinned to a cork board on the rust walls. Over the fireplace hung one of Étienne's drawings of two girls embracing, which Tristan had bought out of pride so that people wouldn't realize his father had never given him anything.

He was now toying with a chess set and the idea of portraying his cast, Philip the king, Posa the knight, Carlos the poor doomed pawn, as chess pieces, but he kept hearing the nurse's cosy, over-familiar voice.

'Just going to put this nasty thing down your throat again, Etienne,' as she hoovered up the fountains of blood bubbling up from his father's damaged heart.

And Tristan had wanted to yell: 'For Christ's sake, call him Monsieur de Montigny.'

He also kept hearing Étienne muttering the words 'father' and 'grandfather', as he clutched Tristan's sleeve, and the roars of resistance, followed by tears of abdication trickling down the wrinkles.

At the end only the extremely short scarlet skirt worn by his granddaughter Simone had rallied the old man. Tristan hadn't been able to look at his aunt Hortense. It was as if a gargoyle had started weeping. He prayed that Étienne hadn't seen the satisfaction on the faces of his three eldest sons that there was no hope of recovery.

There was no way Tristan could concentrate on a chessboard. Switching on the television, he felt outrage that, instead of leading on Étienne's death, they were showing the young English winner of the Appleton, Marcus Campbell-Black, arriving pale and fragile as a wood anemone at Moscow airport, and being embraced in the snow by a wolf-coated, wildly overexcited Nemerovsky, before being swept away in a limo.

Rupert, Marcus's father, had then been interviewed, surrounded by a lot of dogs outside his house in Gloucestershire.

'Campbell-Blacks don't come second,' he was saying jubilantly.

God, what a good-looking man, thought Tristan. If he had Rupert, Marcus and Nemerovsky playing Philip, Carlos and Posa, he'd break every box-office record.

He jumped as Handel's death march from *Saul* boomed out and the presenter switched to Étienne's death: France was in mourning for her favourite son; great artist, *bon viveur*, patron saint of vast extended family.

'Montigny's compassion for life showed in all his paintings,' said the reporter.

But not in his heart, thought Tristan bitterly. Étienne had never been to one of his premières, or glanced at a video, or congratulated him on his César, France's equivalent of the Oscars.

'Of all Étienne de Montigny's sons,' went on the

41

reporter, as they showed some of Étienne's cleaner paintings followed by clips from *The Betrothed*, 'Tristan, his youngest son, has been the most successful, following in his father's footsteps but painting instead with light.'

That should piss off my brothers, thought Tristan savagely, as he turned off the television. Dupont had rung him earlier and, like a starved dog grateful for even a piece of bacon rind, Tristan had finally asked if Étienne had left him anything other than his due share.

'Nothing, I'm afraid.' Then, after a long pause, 'Maybe it's a back-handed compliment, because you've done so well.'

Dupont had meant it kindly. But Tristan had hung up, and for the first time since Étienne had fallen ill, he broke down and wept.

Half an hour later, he splashed his face with cold water and wondered what to do with the rest of his life. He was roused by the *Sunday Times*, commiserating with him, then more cautiously probing a rumour that he was the only member of the family who had been left nothing personal.

'Fuck off,' said Tristan hanging up.

Fortunately this pulled him together. The bastard, he thought. All my life Papa noticed me less than the cob-webs festooning his studio. Looking at his mother's photograph, he wished as always that she were alive, then jumped as the telephone rang.

'Papa?' he gasped, in desperate hope.

But it was Alexandre, his eldest brother, the judge.

'We're all worried you might be feeling out of it, Tristan. You're so good at lighting and theatrical effects and knowing appropriate poetry and music, we felt you should organize the funeral. We want you to be involved.'

His brothers, reflected Tristan, chose to involve him when they wanted their christenings and weddings videoed. He wished he had the bottle to tell Alexandre to fuck off too.

Instead he said, 'I'll ring you in the morning.'

Without bothering to put on a jacket, he was out of his flat, driving like a maniac to the Louvre to catch the last half-hour, so that he could once more marvel over the Goyas, Velazquezes and El Grecos. Every frame in his film would be more beautiful.

When he got home there was a message on the machine. Rannaldini's voice was caressing, deep as the ocean, gentle, recognizable anywhere.

'My poor boy, what a terrible day you must have had. I'm so sorry. But here's something to cheer you up. Lord O'Hara from Venturer Television rang, and he's happy to meet us in London the day after tomorrow. I hope very much you can make it. And I think I have found a Posa.'

3

Hollywood in the mid-nineties was governed by market-
ing men who earned enough in a year to finance five
medium-budget films, who believed they knew exactly
what they could sell and only gave the green light to films
tailor-made to these specifications. To perform this func-
tion for *Don Carlos* and handle the money side, Rannaldini
had employed Sexton Kemp as his co-producer.

Sexton, who had started life selling sheepskin coats in
Petticoat Lane, was now a medallion man in his early
forties with cropped hair, red-rimmed tinted spectacles
and a sardonic street-wise face.

Sexton's film company, Liberty Productions, so called
because he took such frightful liberties with original
material, always had several projects on the go. As he was
driven in the back of a magenta Roller to the meeting
with Declan O'Hara, Sexton was busily improving
Flaubert.

Musically illiterate, he found the sanctity of opera
plots incredibly frustrating. Why couldn't the French
Princess Elisabetta become an American to appeal to the
US market? At least he could constantly play up the sex
and violence in *Don Carlos*:

'All that assassination and burning of 'eretics, and
rumpy-pumpy, because we're using lots of the singing as
voiceover, while we film all the characters' fantasies
about rogerin' each other.'

For a year now Sexton had worked indefatigably to raise the necessary twenty million to make the film. He had also organized distributors in twenty-five countries. '*Don Carlos* is not exactly a comedy,' he would tell potential backers, 'but very dramatical. And wiv Rannaldini and Tristan de Montigny we can offer both gravitas and a first-class seat on the gravy train.'

As a result Rannaldini's record company, American Bravo, and French television had both come in as major players. Conversely CBS had been unenthusiastic because *Don Carlos* is very anti-Catholic and they were nervous about alienating America's vast Hispanic population. For the same reason, it had been a nightmare wheedling money out of the French and Spanish governments. Sexton had promised filming in the forest of Fontainebleau to bring tourists to France and the restoration of numerous crumbling historic buildings in Spain for use as locations. But each time he neared a deal, the government would change and there would be a new Minister of Culture to win over.

Even the last Spanish minister, a Señora Mendoza, who had a black moustache, hadn't fazed Sexton.

'One bottle of bubbly and a tube of Immac and we was away.'

Unfortunately, shortly after this, Señora Mendoza had fallen from office and for Sexton, and was never off the telephone angling for another seeing-to. Contrary to Señora Mendoza's forward behaviour, there was also a real problem of filming nudes and sex scenes in Catholic countries.

A substantial sum had been promised by a group of Saudi gun-runners, who wanted to raise their profile by having their names on the credits. (Unknown to the Saudis, Sexton was busy dealing with the Iranians.)

His greatest coup, however, was to enlist the support of the recently ennobled Declan O'Hara who was managing director of Venturer Television and a complete *Don Carlos* freak. Unknown to his tone-deaf partner and son-in-law, Rupert Campbell-Black, Declan had pledged ten million towards the film's costs.

London had an untidy look on that chill mid-October morning. Grey and brown plane leaves littered the pavements and clogged the gutters. Brake-lights were reflected like flamingos' legs in the wet road ahead as the traffic slowed in Park Lane.

Excited at the prospect of meeting a real lord, Sexton was glad he, Tristan and Rannaldini were going to work out a plan of action before Declan arrived. Rannaldini could rub people up the wrong way.

Sitting in Rannaldini's exquisite flat overlooking Hyde Park, Tristan felt warmth creep back into his veins. He had just lunched on the fluffiest Parma ham omelette, sorrel salad, quince sorbet, black grapes, gently dissolving Camembert, excellent claret and very black coffee. It was the first food he had eaten in three days.

After the meeting, Rannaldini, Sexton and he were off to Prague to see the possible Posa: a Russian with lungs of steel called Mikhail Pezcherov.

Tristan was already mad about Sexton, who was now hoovering up black grapes with a big hand, gut spilling over his waistband, his face absolutely still, only his eyes swivelling in thought as he tried to persuade Rannaldini of the benefits of accepting laundered Russian money from the Iranians.

'Don't worry your pretty swollen head over that one, Ranners. The Saudis need never know.'

In preparation for meeting Declan, Tristan had whiled away last night's insomnia speed-reading Declan's massive biography of Yeats, which had just received ecstatic reviews. Declan had also once interviewed Étienne on one of his vastly watched, prestigious programmes. The two had clashed. Declan had accused Tristan's father of meretriciousness and pornography.

'That you're a genius makes the whole thing more reprehensible.'

Étienne had stalked off the set. Tristan was ashamed how drawn he was to people who had seen through his father.

As Sexton and Rannaldini were still arguing about money, Tristan was glad there was so much to look at in Rannaldini's sitting room. On the vermilion walls hung numerous portraits of Rannaldini. On every surface were silver-framed photographs of Rannaldini and the famous, dominated by one of him getting his knighthood, and another of him smiling at a very blonde girl. What a beauty. Tristan made a mental note to ask Rannaldini to introduce him: what wonderful things the camera could do with her face.

On a low table in the middle of the room beside a huge brass bowl of dark crimson orchids lay the score of *Don Carlos* with cuts and possible scenes pencilled in for discussion with Declan. As the sun appeared, casting its mellow autumnal light on the park, Tristan felt a surge of optimism.

'Oh, look, there's Rupert Campbell-Black in a morning suit,' said Sexton, in excitement, 'I wonder where 'e's going.'

An outraged Rupert was in fact coming to Rannaldini's flat. As a fellow director, having learnt about the ten million, he had spent half the night raging at Declan for such suicidal pledging of Venturer's hard-earned cash. Rupert had never before questioned one of Declan's artistic decisions, but as the last film he'd seen in the cinema had been a remake of *The Incredible Journey*, where he'd been outraged because the bull terrier had been changed to a more politically correct breed, and the last opera an amateur production of *The Merry Widow*, with Declan's wife poncing around in the title role, he couldn't see the point of *Don Carlos* at all.

'I mean the guy's in love with his stepmother,' Rupert, who had loathed all his four stepmothers, had stormed at Declan.

Despite his indignation and the insensitivity that

so often goes with social fearlessness, Rupert noticed Tristan's black tie the moment he entered the room and said how sorry he was about Étienne's death.

'Bought a couple of oils of his twenty years ago. Bloody good painter, and bloody well rocketed in value,' he added, even more approvingly.

As Rupert was wearing a morning coat, Rannaldini smoothly suggested a glass of champagne. Feeling he could use it, Rupert was about to accept, then noticed the photograph of his daughter, Tabitha, on the piano and curtly refused. The thought of Rannaldini having access to her drove him to madness.

'Haven't you grown since I last saw you?' he drawled, then, tilting his head sideways to glance at Rannaldini's lifts, 'Or maybe your shoes have.'

Trouble ahead, thought Tristan, as Rannaldini's face contorted with fury.

Étienne had always painted in a north-facing studio, claiming that the harsh light picked out every wrinkle and red vein, showing the face as it was. Rupert must be forty-six or forty-seven but, as he sat down on the window-seat looking north over the park, his beauty made Tristan gasp. The sleek, thick gold hair, untouched by grey and brushed back from the wide suntanned forehead, emphasized the lovely shape of the head. The long, heavy-lidded, rather hard lapis-lazuli blue eyes, the high cheekbones, the Greek nose, the short upper lip pulling up the curling mouth, the smooth olive complexion could all have belonged to a Latin or a statue, the face was so still. Then Rupert caught a glimpse of a portly mongrel in a tartan coat, waddling along behind an old lady, which reminded him of his wife's dog, Gertrude. His eyes softened and his mouth lifted, and Tristan wondered how any woman ever resisted him.

'Sorry Declan can't make it,' Rupert was now saying, in his light, flat, clipped drawl. 'He forgot he was taking my children, *his* grandchildren, to *Toad of Toad Hall*. He

48

always swore he'd never accept a peerage and now he has it's clearly unhinged him, particularly if he's intending to waste ten million on some crappy opera.'

Rupert then proceeded to tear the project to shreds. The only person he praised was Sexton for raising such an incredible amount to subsidize such tosh. Rannaldini immediately rose to his feet and opened the door.

'If you won't come in with us,' he said icily, 'we'd better look elsewhere.'

'We can't, Ranners,' said Sexton aghast. 'It's goin' to be a mad scramble as it is. We gotta start filming by the end of March because the first scenes take place in a forest wiv no leaves. It's goin' to be grite,' he added to Rupert, his eyes shining brighter than his gold necklace. 'Two mighty armies meeting on the skyline, and then the 'unt streaming down the 'ill.'

'Where's that being filmed?' asked Rupert.

'Fontainebleau,' said Tristan quickly. 'The French government have put in a lot of money.'

As Venturer were putting in even more money, countered Rupert, the film should be made on Venturer territory, namely in his woods at Penscombe.

'Most beautiful beechwoods in the country,' he added, haughtily.

'That is debatable,' snapped Rannaldini.

'Let's debate it, then,' snapped back Rupert. 'We can also get the Cotchester Hunt for virtually peanuts, and hounds won't have to go into quarantine. You'll never find decent hounds in France.'

Tristan had visions of drawing his sword for his country's canine population.

The reason Rupert wanted his woods filmed was to categorize them even more firmly as an Area of Outstanding Natural Beauty to scupper any evil plans to slap a motorway through *his* estate.

Rannaldini, who was determined the first act should be shot in *his* beechwoods at Valhalla, also to stop any motorway through *his* estate, said the French would never agree to it being filmed at Penscombe.

'Anyway, your house at Penscombe was only built in the late eighteenth century, too modern for *Carlos*,' Rannaldini added dismissively, 'whereas Valhalla is medieval and steeped in religious tradition.'

Seeing Rupert's eyes narrow, Sexton said hastily, 'We do need to film in a monastery-type situation, Rupe.'

So Rupert switched to the fatuousness of the plot.

'I mean, the guy's in love with his stepmother.'

'Can't agree more, Rupe,' interrupted Sexton excitedly. 'I was just saying to Ranners, why don't we make Elisabetta Carlos's real muvver? Incest is really hot at the moment.'

'Don't be ridiculous,' said Rupert, who disliked his mother even more than his stepmothers.

Tristan, who often fell asleep in meetings, was really enjoying this one, and having great difficulty not laughing.

'The plot's far too complicated,' went on Rupert. 'Needs a narrator to tell you what's going on. We'd better use Declan.'

Then, at least, Venturer's lawyers could claw back a massive fee for Declan's services. Rannaldini, who intended to introduce the opera himself for an even more massive fee, said this was totally unacceptable, so Rupert attacked the cast.

'They're all geriatrics. How can that old bat Hermione Harefield, who must be well into her forties, play a girl in her teens?'

Then before Rannaldini could reach for *his* sword:

'Or Fat Franco, who's forty-six and at least forty-six stone, play a twenty-year-old Infante? Don Kilos, that's a joke, and there aren't many of those in the opera.'

'Fat Franco goes down very well wiv punters,' said Sexton, reasonably. 'He's one of the biggest names of opera.'

'Biggest being the operative word. Here's the guy you

want.' Rupert chucked a photograph down on the table.

'Wow, who's he?' Tristan grabbed the photo in excitement.

'An Aussie called Baby Spinosissimo, not sure that's his real name.'

'Speenoseeseemo,' said Rannaldini coldly. 'He's totally inexperienced.'

'And breathtakingly good-looking,' said Rupert. 'Taken them by storm in Oz. Done well enough to buy himself several racehorses.'

'And, eef he landed the part of Carlos, would no doubt be able to afford more horses for you to train,' said Rannaldini bitchily. 'Leave the casting to us. You don't know what you're talking about.'

'How about Elisabetta becoming an American?' suggested Sexton, who never gave up. 'They adore Dame Hermione in the US.'

'Shows how stupid they are,' snarled Rupert. 'America was hardly built, like my house,' he glared at Rannaldini, 'in the middle of the sixteenth century, and Hermione would have even more difficulty in passing herself off as a Red Indian than as an eighteen-year-old virgin.'

The meeting ended in uproar.

'Who's getting married?' asked Tristan.

'Lovely girl – conductor actually – called Abigail Rosen, marrying a lucky sod called Viking O'Neill,' said Rupert, breaking off one of Rannaldini's crimson orchids and putting it in his buttonhole.

'Rannaldini knows Viking,' he added nastily. 'He's the horn player who hit him across a hotel dining room a few nights ago. Easy as a shot-putter – or shit-putter, in Rannaldini's case.'

But the gods were on Rannaldini's side. As the front door banged behind Rupert, Helen Rannaldini rushed into the sitting room.

What a beautiful woman, thought Tristan, admiring the tragic, ravaged face, as he leapt to his feet. But Helen was too distraught to notice him.

'Oh, Rannaldini, Tabitha's on the phone. She's been fired! I hoped I'd catch Rupert.'

'He's gone, let me talk to her.' Rannaldini whisked out of the room. 'Perhaps you could organize some drinks, my dear.'

He was sweating with excitement as he picked up the telephone. As he had predicted, his stepdaughter had flipped when his faxes had arrived. Tabitha had always been Rupert's favourite child and suddenly Marcus, her brother, had stolen his affection. She was shocked rigid to discover Marcus was gay, and crazy with jealousy that Rupert seemed to approve of Marcus's new love.

'Daddy was always so foul about my boyfriends, and now he's crawling all over some poofter. And there's even a photograph of Marcus and Nemerovsky hugging on the front of the *Washington Post* – yuk!'

Having read the faxes, Tabitha had ridden in a cross-country competition, hurtling over the fences as though death were the favourable alternative, before sliding off her horse, The Engineer, fifty yards past the post. The course doctor had diagnosed her as dead drunk.

Yesterday morning she had been suspended for nine months, mostly because of her appalling language and lack of contrition. Afterwards, she had gone out and got even drunker, she had only just woken and screwed up courage to ring England. How fortunate that Rupert and she had missed each other.

Rannaldini was smiling broadly. 'My naughty child! Come home so I can spank your bottom,' he quivered in delighted expectation. 'You have been away far too long. I'll send the Gulf.'

'I'll make my own way. I want to travel with The Engineer. Could you possibly lend me a couple of grand?'

4

Euphoric at the thought of Tabitha returning, Rannaldini swept into the drawing room and promptly invited her mother to join the trip to Prague. After all, Prague had been where he had first bedded Helen on the stage of an opera-house where, earlier in the evening, he had conducted *Don Giovanni*, and he didn't want her to give him a lousy press as a husband if Tabitha was coming home.

'I can't go,' wailed Helen. 'I've got to host a dinner for Save the Children.'

'Bussage will cancel it, and tomorrow I will send Save the Children a large enough donation to quell any disquiet,' said Rannaldini expansively.

'I would love to go,' Helen told Tristan wistfully. 'Prague was the place—'

'Where you and I spent our first wonderful romantic weekend, exactly one year, eleven months and three days ago,' said Rannaldini, kissing her.

'You remembered the exact date.' Helen's eyes filled with tears.

'Of course,' said Rannaldini smugly. It had not been difficult, it had also been his forty-fourth birthday.

'But I haven't packed.'

Rannaldini looked at his watch.

'You have half an hour. Serena won't be here until five.'

*   *   *

Serena Westwood was a young, ambitious record producer, who had just been poached by Rannaldini's record company, American Bravo. Her first assignment was to produce the recording of *Don Carlos*.

Helen nearly refused to go to Prague when she saw Serena, who looked like a brunette Grace Kelly. Her heavy hair, drawn back into a French pleat from a snow-white forehead, was shinier than her patent leather ankle boots, and she was wearing nothing under her austerely cut pinstripe suit.

Rannaldini had clearly been saving Serena's child as well as sending a vast cheque to Save the Children because Serena immediately kissed him, thanking him in a cool, clear voice for flying up two of Helen's young maids, Betty and Sally, for the night to look after her four-year-old daughter, Jessie.

'Bussage masterminded the whole thing,' said Rannaldini smoothly, 'and it is good for Sally and Betty to have an outing.'

'Jessie fell so in love with them she hardly noticed me leaving,' said Serena, turning to an outraged Helen. 'Oh, Lady Rannaldini, I know it's a liberty hijacking your maids, but I've been stuck in Rome with Dame Hermione and rushed home to find my nanny had walked out, so Sir Roberto very kindly came to my aid. But it's you I've got to thank.'

'We cannot cast Posa without Serena,' said Rannaldini. 'Now we have time for a glass of champagne.'

'How was Hermione?' snapped Helen, who detested her husband's mistress.

Serena waited until Rannaldini had left the room to get a bottle, then said, 'Absolutely bloody. She's recording *Arsena* in Rome next week so I spent all yesterday checking out hotels with her. They were either too hot, too cold, too dark, too light, too big and not cosy enough, too poky. I kept frantically apologizing to the hotel managers – you know how sweet and obliging

54

the Italians are. She deserves a kick up the *arsena*.'

'She does,' agreed Helen ecstatically.

'I finally flipped and shouted at her,' confessed Serena. 'So, as a peace offering, I sent her some ravishing lilies and the bitch rang up shouting that they made her sneeze. "I want yellow rosebuds in future, and I'll tell you exactly which florist to go to."'

What a lovely young woman, thought Helen, putting her arm round Serena's shoulders in an utterly uncharacteristic gesture of intimacy.

'Come and meet our director, Tristan de Montigny.'

'He's next door phoning his auntie Hortense,' volunteered Sexton.

Poor old Hortense was being extremely cantankerous and giving Tristan a long-distance earful. For the first time in eighty-five years, she was no longer Étienne's little sister. As head of the family, she was feeling old, arthritic and frighteningly exposed. Tristan so wished he could comfort her.

Oh, my goodness, thought Serena, as he wandered back into the room. He was wearing a battered leather jacket, a buttoned-down peacock blue shirt, and Levi's clinging to his lean hips. Serena immediately wanted to plunge her fingers into his shock of dark hair, and run her tongue along his rubbery jut of lower lip before burying her mouth in his. Instead, she smiled coolly, accepted a glass of Dom Pérignon, and said, 'Tell us about this Posa, Rannaldini.'

'He's called Mikhail Pezcherov. Solti call me after hearing him do the role in Russian. He's now singing Macbeth in some crappy production and making ends meet belting out songs in a nightclub.'

'And which do we have to endure?'

'If we leave soon, we'll make the second act of *Macbeth*.'

Landing in Prague, they were driven over the cobbles of ill-lit back streets to a crumbling opera-house.

Rannaldini, well known to scream at latecomers, had no compunction in sweeping his party into their seats in the middle of the banquet scene. A rumble of excitement went through the theatre and Lady Macbeth stopped singing altogether to gaze at the great Maestro.

Another wild-goose chase, sighed Serena, who'd made sure she was sitting next to Tristan. The sets and costumes might have come from an amateur operatic society's production of *Brigadoon*. Neither conductor, soloists nor chorus could agree on *tempi*. Attempting to glide through a castle wall, Banquo's ghost sent it flying.

But out of this shambles came a voice of such beauty, so deep, rich, soft, yet intensely masculine, that Rannaldini's party turned to each other in rapture. Tristan was so excited he hardly felt Serena's pinstriped leg rubbing against his.

Mikhail Pezcherov was also an excellent actor, with a square, expressive face and strong features, enhanced by a black moustache and beard, and a curly bull's poll tumbling over soulful dark eyes. More important, if he were going to play the gallant Marquis of Posa, he was of heroic stature, with long, strong legs that would look marvellous in tights.

Afterwards, he welcomed Rannaldini and his party backstage.

'My knees knock, my tongue thicken in mouth, I can only croak hello, I am so excited,' he announced, thrusting mugs of very rough red wine into their hands.

He wished he could afford something more expensive but all his money was going home to support his darling wife, Lara, and his children. Showing the visitors their photographs, he wiped away copious tears, but all would be worthwhile, if they could live together one day in comfort.

'How did you meet your wife?' asked Helen.

'I was best man at wedding. Lara was bridesmaid. I sing "Nessun' Dorma" at reception. Zat was zat,' sighed Mikhail.

'Lady Rannaldini and I had our first romantic weekend in Prague,' purred Rannaldini.

'Zat is good,' said Mikhail. 'I trust guys who love their wives.'

'I too.' Rannaldini caressed Helen's cheek.

Really, thought Helen, when he's as charming as this, I can remember why I married him.

Back at Rannaldini's suite, Mikhail got stuck into a better class of red, wolfed down his own incredibly tough steak, and polished off everyone else's leftovers.

Rannaldini, who for once hadn't made a single bitchy remark, produced the score of *Don Carlos* and thumped away on the piano. When Mikhail came to the end of Posa's wonderfully beautiful dying aria, it seemed impossible that only five listeners could have made such a noise, cheering and shouting until people in the next rooms banged on the thin walls.

'So thrilling to find him together.' A tearful Helen squeezed Serena's hand.

'You're going to give the part exactly the right ker-pow quotient, Mick,' Sexton told Mikhail. 'Tomorrow our people will call your people.'

'You better call my vife, she handle money,' said Mikhail. 'If I really have zee part?'

'You have it,' said Rannaldini, who had been particularly captivated when Mikhail congratulated him on his piano-playing. Not since Hermione had he discovered such a thrilling talent. Now, where had he put his treasured jade fountain pen? In his excitement, he must have handed it absent-mindedly to the waiter after he'd signed for room service.

'May I call my Lara?' asked Mikhail, as his glass was refilled yet again.

'Go into our bedroom,' said Rannaldini.

'Can I possibly borrow your mobile to check on Jessie?' Serena asked Sexton. 'I've got a horrible feeling I've left mine in the taxi.'

Helen had buttonholed Tristan. When she'd first moved to England from America, she told him, she had worked as an editor in publishing, which had involved a lot of research. Perhaps she could help out on *Don Carlos*.

Tristan listened politely. Close up, Helen's huge, staring eyes, ribby body, spindly legs and flesh worn down to her admittedly perfect bone structure, reminded him unnervingly of paintings of chargers dying of starvation in the Crimean War.

Across the room, trying to make Tristan jealous, Serena was chatting up Rannaldini, who was terribly sexy, but definitely not husband potential.

'We *must* have dinner one evening,' he was murmuring. 'Bussage can always find a window for special people. At least promise to sit next to me at the Gramophone Awards on Tuesday.'

Helen's face had lit up while Tristan talked to her, but it went dead as she noticed the wolfish expression on Rannaldini's. Meticulous by nature, Helen became obsessive under stress. Now she launched into a frenzy of tidying, lining up scores and magazines, plumping cushions, whipping glasses from people still drinking – anything to maintain her sense of controlling the environment.

'Leave it. We are not at home,' exploded Rannaldini, and then, remembering his role as cherishing husband, 'Go to bed, my darling, you must be tired.'

Having told Mikhail he would fix him up with a shit-hot agent, Shepherd Denston's, who would handle everything, and arrange for him to have coaching in Prague to prepare him for rehearsals starting in December, Rannaldini said he was off to bed.

'Helen and I have happy memories to relive.'

He found Helen faffing round in her nightie. She always laid out her clothes for the morrow, and she was certain she'd packed her saxe-blue cashmere and the lapis-lazuli brooch that went so well with it.

'You packed in a hurry,' soothed Rannaldini.

'I guess one of the maids has nicked it,' said Helen shrilly. 'I hate Prague! The beds are so hard, the food's disgusting, you can't turn down the heating so I'll have hot flushes all night, and finally there's no bath plug.'

'I will plug your hole, my darling,' said Rannaldini softly. 'D'you remember last time we play game of naughty doctor, taking liberties with young girl patient, and how excited you became?'

Helen gasped as he pushed her back on the bed.

'She has been very naughty.' Rannaldini locked the door. 'She deserves good spanking for not eating enough.'

'The others'll hear us. You can't, Rannaldini!'

Parting Helen's legs, Rannaldini laid his tongue on her clitoris. Not for nothing was he known as the James Galway of Cunnilingus!

Helen achieved orgasm, fantasizing about Tristan de Montigny. Rannaldini pushed himself over the edge thinking about Tabitha.

'My darling child,' he murmured, as he came.

'Why can't our marriage always be like this?'

'From now on it will be,' promised Rannaldini.

Next door Tristan and Mikhail, who was drinking from the bottle, were dissecting the character of Posa.

'He changes in the opera.' Tristan lit another Gauloise. 'He starts out an idealist, then realizes he's got to act politically to get things done. He has to put on a different face to hide the brutal facts.'

Like you'll have to, thought Sexton, with a sudden surge of pity, if you're going to work with Rannaldini.

'Posa was like IRA freedom-fighter,' announced Mikhail.

Anxious to make a note about parallels with the IRA, who were *very* hot in Hollywood at the moment, Sexton found his pocket computer had suddenly disappeared. He was distracted by Serena, who had unleashed her dark hair like a cavalry charge, and undone two buttons of her pinstripe jacket.

'Can I have a word?' she murmured.

Wildly excited, Sexton padded after her into the second bedroom.

'Is Tristan OK?' she whispered.

'No, shittin' himself about the funeral on Monday, poor little sod.'

'It's going to be like a state funeral.'

'In-a-state more likely, wiv all his dad's ex-wives and mistresses fighting to sit in the front row, and all the paparazzi hangin' abart.'

God, Serena was pretty. I'm going to score, thought Sexton joyfully.

He was about to unfasten the last button of her jacket and push the door behind them, when she hissed, 'Get rid of Mikhail.'

'W-w-what?'

'At *once*! Tristan wants to take me to bed.'

Sexton took it on the double chin.

'Don't hurt him,' he urged. 'He's on the blink.'

Mikhail was desperate to go on partying and Sexton had frightful difficulty shepherding him into a taxi.

'Such a lovely straightforward guy,' said Tristan, as he and Serena walked down the dimly lit landing.

Outside her room, she put a caressing hand on his chest.

'Sorry about your father,' she whispered, 'but a good fuck's truly the quickest way to cure the pain.'

Taking her key, dodging her puckered-up lips, Tristan dropped a kiss on her cheek. Having unlocked her door for her, however, he showed absolutely no desire to follow her inside. The trouble with new men, thought Serena furiously, was that they were so desperate not to harass women you never knew if they were gay or not.

5

The Gramophone Awards took place five days later over a splendid lunch at the Savoy. Record producers and agents in sharp suits gossiped guardedly as they awaited their illustrious artists in the foyer. Women press officers, their shiny highlighted hair and long golden legs belying the severity of their neat black suits, hooked musical big fish out from their pools of admirers and ferried them like children to the right table. The progress was maddeningly slow because it involved so much hugging and hailing on the way.

More hot and famous than anyone, but hidden behind dark glasses, Tristan reached the table of Shepherd Denston, international artists' agents, virtually unnoticed. He was delighted, however, when his host, Howie Denston, a fawning little creep who ran the London office, informed him that Liberty Productions' cast for *Don Carlos* had cleaned up in the awards.

Alpheus P. Shaw, who was playing Philip II – Howie consulted his pocket computer – was Artist of the Year. Glamorous Chloe Catford, the mezzo, who had posed naked on her winning record sleeve, was the People's Favourite. Solo Vocal had gone to Rozzy Pringle, who was playing Elisabetta's page, the Opera Award to Hermione, while Early Opera had been awarded to Granville Hastings, who'd been cast as the Grand Inquisitor. Fat Franco's *Italian Love Songs* had been voted

Best-selling Record. Most prestigious of all, Rannaldini had won Record of the Year.

'Odd that you all know in advance,' said Tristan, accepting a glass of Sancerre.

'Not at all.' Howie Denston lowered his voice. 'Singers have such monstrous egos you'd never get them to an award ceremony unless they knew they'd won.'

Nor was it a coincidence that all the cast of *Don Carlos* – except Fat Franco – were Shepherd Denston artists. This was because Rannaldini had recently wangled himself the chairmanship of the agency. He had therefore ensured that 20 per cent of the vast fees earned by the singers in the film would go back into Shepherd Denston's pockets.

Howie Denston, known as Mr Margarine because he spread his oily charm so widely over his artists, had now abandoned Tristan and bolted back to the foyer to await Hermione and his new chairman, who were probably having a bonk upstairs and bound to be late. Tristan didn't mind being left. He was always happy watching people.

Also at the Shepherd Denston table, besides the award winners, was the retiring chairman, who had an ulcer. Next to him sat Serena Westwood, out of pinstripe into clinging scarlet, acting cool towards Tristan, determined to show him what he had missed by not seducing her in Prague.

Rannaldini, who'd done the seating plan, had also sat Serena next to Giuseppe Cavalli, a hunky young bass, who'd be winning awards in a year or two. Giuseppe had been cast as the ghost of the Emperor, Charles V, who appears at the end of the opera and draws his grandson, Carlos, into the safety of the tomb.

No-one was likely to be safe with Giuseppe, who was an unghostly thug with shoulder-length black curls. Given to check shirts tucked into bulging jeans, he had a huge fan mail from women, but was in fact the lover of Granville Hastings, known as 'Granny', who could have uncheerfully murdered Rannaldini for continually fixing Giuseppe up with rich single women. Lone parents were even more predatory than loan sharks, reckoned Granny.

Elegant, tall, silver-haired, always exquisitely dressed, Granny appeared a cosy old pussy-cat. Inwardly his heart was breaking. For years he had sung Philip II, the finest bass role in the repertoire, but now, at nearly sixty-four, he had been demoted to the just as difficult but more pantomime villain role of the Grand Inquisitor. As the bigger part, Philip also got the bigger pay cheque, and keeping Giuseppe was very expensive.

Alpheus P. Shaw III, a very successful, self-regarding American bass sitting at the head of the table, was pointedly ignoring Granny because they had just sung Philip and the Inquisitor in the same production in Paris. Granny, supposed to be blind in the part, had totally upstaged Alpheus by bumping into furniture and at one moment, when Alpheus was hitting a ravishing top note, putting his finger into a candle flame and saying, 'Ouch.' Alpheus, who had no sense of humour, had been outraged.

A magnificent-looking man, with red-gold hair brushed back from a noble forehead, Alpheus looked as though he'd been carved out of Mount Rushmore. Married twenty years and the father of three fine sons, he was also a stern upholder of family values.

As he forked up a smoked-salmon parcel with his right hand, however, Alpheus's left hand foraged between the plump, white thighs of Chloe the mezzo. He and Chloe had fallen in love two years ago when they both appeared in *Aida*. Engagements had separated them, so they had accepted parts in *Don Carlos* to be together in the long weeks of recording and filming. Alas, Alpheus's wife, Cheryl, harboured suspicions, and was threatening to join him on location.

The great din of chatter suddenly stopped as Rannaldini stalked in with all the prowling chutzpah of a leopard who has no intention of changing a single spot.

No star in decline wins Record of the Year.

'It's God,' murmured two record executives, as he swept past them.

He was followed by Hermione Harefield, looking slightly flushed. The lunchers giggled as they noticed the jacket of her purple Chanel suit had been wrongly buttoned up.

'Gangway, gangway for Dame Hermione,' yelled Howie Denston pummelling aside other late-comers and sycophants, as Hermione glided across the room as stately as the *QE2*.

'I so wanted to creep in here anonymously,' she was saying loudly.

Embracing Tristan, with whom she intended having an *affaire* on location, kissing Sexton with whom she did not, Hermione totally ignored that upstart Chloe the mezzo, whom she disliked intensely, and Serena, whom she'd not forgiven for sending the wrong flowers, and Granny, who had never treated her with due reverence. Instead she turned to Alpheus, who was going to sing her husband.

'Your Majesty.' Hermione curtsied skittishly.

'Madama,' replied a bowing Alpheus, equally skittishly as he held her chair for her.

Everyone was very sad Rozzy Pringle, who was playing Elisabetta's page, hadn't made the lunch. She was singing Octavian in Budapest, but sent tons of love. Later, a delightedly squirming Howie would accept the Solo Vocal Award on her behalf.

'Rozzy's so lovely,' sighed Chloe, as Alpheus removed his burrowing hand to cut up his chicken Cenerentola. 'She's got no ego problem, unlike some.' She glared at Hermione.

'I hope,' Hermione glared back, 'that Rozzy is not overstretching her voice. I never do more than forty concerts a year.'

'Why have you never done a Three Sopranos, Dame Hermione?' asked the retiring chairman, with all the enthusiasm of one who knows he will never have to handle it.

'There is only *one* soprano,' said Alpheus.

Hermione bowed her head. 'Your Majesty is gracious.'

Conversation kept being interrupted by waiters grinding black pepper and pouring wine and water.

'Still or fizzy, Dame Hermione?'

'Still, please.'

'One would have known that you would choose only something that ran deep like yourself,' observed Alpheus playfully.

'Great big plonker,' muttered Granny.

'Amen to that,' said Chloe.

Alpheus was hung like a donkey.

'Oh, look,' she nudged Tristan, 'here's your leading man.'

Causing howls of mirth by wearing a vast T-shirt saying, 'I've beaten anorexia', Franco Palmieri, who was playing Carlos, had reached the Megagram table next door. Appropriating four buckling chairs, he waved jauntily at Chloe then scowled at Alpheus, whom he detested even more than Granny did.

'Fat Franco longs to be the Fourth Tenor,' Chloe whispered to Tristan, 'but very sensibly the others won't let that conniving shit near them. Don't worry,' she added, as she picked the fruit out of her glazed apricot tart, 'hatred always produces incredible sexual chemistry.'

'I prefer happy team,' protested Tristan.

'With Rannaldini as team leader?' asked Chloe incredulously. 'They say his dagger follows close upon his smiles.'

'He is very great friend,' said Tristan coldly.

'Good, perhaps you'll have a benign influence on him.'

Tristan was heartbreaking, Chloe decided. Those bruised eyes seemed to read her soul. 'I'm sorry about your father,' she added. 'The funeral must have been harrowing. Claudine Lauzerte looked stunning.'

'She did.'

But even Claudine's divine presence had not distracted a paparazzi frantic to find out, among other things, why Rannaldini (in even more built-up shoes so as not to be dwarfed by Tristan's three tall brothers) had carried the coffin.

Noticing Tristan's hands clamped to his thighs to stop them shaking, Chloe said gently, 'When I got my first Amneris at the ENO, I splurged on one of your father's drawings.'

'He would have loved painting you.' Tristan found he could say it without too much pain. Chloe couldn't have been prettier, he decided, very French, in fact. Her straw-coloured bob had a thick fringe, which emphasized permanently smiling, slightly dissipated eyes. Tristan had also noticed long slim legs and a black cashmere bosom, arching like a purring furry cat inside her dove-grey suit.

Glancing up, her eyes widened and held his for longer than necessary. She would be perfect to screw on location, he thought, but since Étienne's death his libido seemed to have gone into hibernation. He knew he had snubbed Serena the other night, and would have to put in a lot of spadework if she wasn't going to act up during the recording. Idly he noticed Chloe putting Sweetex into Alpheus's cup of coffee, and wondered if they were having an *affaire.*

'Carlos loved his granddad, Charles V, like Prince Charles loves the Queen Mum,' Sexton was telling Granny's boyfriend, Giuseppe, who had sunk nearly two bottles of red and was still flirting with Serena in the hope of a fat record contract.

At last Rannaldini had reached the table. Wafting 'Maestro', his famous scent, created specially for him by Givenchy, longing to goad all the male members of his cast that in Mikhail Pezcherov he had discovered the greatest bass baritone of the age, he immediately insisted that everyone swap places.

'It is crazy,' grumbled Tristan, who was now next to Granny, 'Giuseppe, who is twenty-eight like me, is playing not only Alpheus's father, but Fat Franco's grandfather, and he must be half Franco's age.'

'That's opera for you,' said Granny, in his beautiful voice. 'Although no stretch of the imagination would go round Franco's waist these days.'

'Have you met Rupert Campbell-Black?' asked Tristan.

'I would walk naked across the Arctic Circle for a touch of his nether lip,' sighed Granny.

'He thinks *Don Carlos* can't work with Hermione and Franco.'

'Then you'd better stamp your pretty foot and replace them, my dear.'

Hermione had finished her third helping of apricot tart when everyone was asked to toast the Queen.

'Most people oughta be drinking to themselves,' muttered Sexton. 'Never seen such a bunch of fairies.'

A roll of drums, and the awards started. Having accepted his gold statuette of a harpist, Alpheus proceeded to thank everyone, from the sound engineer to his wife Cheryl, his fine sons and Mr Bones, his German shepherd, ending with Mozart who had, after all, composed the music.

'How very caring.' Hermione clapped vigorously. 'I'm much looking forward to working with Alpheus.'

She was irritated that it was too dark, except on the platform, for everyone to see how lovely she was looking. Tristan de Montigny was lovely-looking too, and even seemed to be getting on with that acid-tongued Granny. As well as an *affaire*, Hermione was looking forward to having many in-depth conversations about herself with Tristan.

Rannaldini was table-hopping again. Posing for the *Daily Express* with David Mellor, he smirkingly fingered the carpet burns on his knees and elbows, acquired while seducing Serena Westwood in her new office last night. It had made him feel like a schoolboy.

'I'll have her but I'll not keep her long,' he murmured, blowing Serena a kiss across the tables. Just long enough to control her during the recording so that she used exactly the takes he wanted.

There was a great cheer as the newly married Viking O'Neill, golden boy and first horn of the Rutminster Symphony Orchestra, who had hit Rannaldini across the room after the Appleton piano competition, sauntered up to collect his award for his recording of the Strauss concertos.

'What a beauty,' murmured Granny, putting on his spectacles.

'If Polygram'll release him, I want him to play first horn in *Don Carlos*,' whispered Serena.

'Ladies and gentlemen.' A grinning Viking seized the microphone. 'Once upon a time, three dogs took part in an intelligence test at Crufts. They had to arrange a pile of bones in the best shape. The first dog who came in was an architect. He looked at the bones, built a pretty little house and everyone clapped and clapped.

'The next dog was a town planner,' went on Viking, in his soft Irish accent, 'who scoffed at the dog architect's little house, knocked it down, and rebuilt the bones as a beautiful town. Everyone clapped even more. Finally, the third dog came in. He was a tenor, and he ate all the bones, shagged the other two dogs and asked for the afternoon off.'

Such screams of laughter greeted this joke that Viking could hardly be heard thanking his record producer, the orchestra and his divine new wife, the conductor Abigail Rosen, which brought even more resounding cheers.

Returning to the Polygram table, Viking disappeared into the vast congratulatory embrace of Fat Franco on his way back from a grope or a toot or some other mischief. For a second, Franco pretended to box

Viking's ears for making snide jokes about tenors, then the two men put their heads together until Franco gave a bellow of laughter.

Seeing his chosen Don Carlos collapse on to his four gold chairs again, scooping up petit fours as though they were Smarties, Rannaldini shouted rudely: 'Unless you give up sweet things, Franco, you'll never get into Charles V's tomb.'

'You no give them up,' shouted back Franco. 'Viking tell me how you sail through air like dashing elderly gent on flying trapeze and flatten sweet trolley and member of Arts Council.'

You wait, vowed Rannaldini, as the roars of laughter subsided. I'll cook your goose before you've had time to stuff your gross belly with it.

At the announcement that Chloe had won the People's Award, the entire room rose cheering to its feet, except Hermione.

'I am clapped so often that I am not used to clapping,' she told Alpheus, as he returned, brandishing his award.

As Chloe, in her discreet dove-grey suit, reached the platform, a huge blow-up of her naked on the sleeve of her prize-winning record appeared, to even louder roars of applause, on the monitor.

As Serena put her hand on Giuseppe's crotch, he fell into the petit fours.

'Best place for him – young people need their sleep,' said Granny, who was feeling much happier after a long chat with Tristan. The boy was too sweet for words and had wonderfully revolutionary views on playing the Grand Inquisitor.

'Are you ready, Dame Hermione?' asked one of the Identikit press officers, as vast illuminated olive-green letters announced the Opera Award of the Year.

'This is the big one,' said Hermione, whipping out her powder compact.

Meanwhile, losing no time for revenge – after all, Franco wasn't a Shepherd Denston artist so they wouldn't lose 20 per cent of his massive fee – Rannaldini was talking in an undertone to Howie Denston. 'Do you know anything about a tenor called Baby Spinosissimo?'

'Making waves in Australia, heartbreaking looks, I'll check out his availability. And by the way,' Howie lowered his voice, 'we've got to watch Alpheus. He tried to get Liberty Productions, American Bravo *and* Shepherd Denston each to pick up the tab . . .'

'You will ensure cash settlements for Dame Hermione,' interrupted Rannaldini, as his mistress mounted the rostrum.

'Good people,' began Hermione, but alas, Rannaldini's mobile had rung.

'Tabitha is home, Maestro,' said Clive, his leather-clad bodyguard, silkily.

Rannaldini leapt to his feet. 'I 'ave to go,' he told the astounded table.

'But what about your award?' cried an aghast Howie.

'You accept eet,' said Rannaldini blithely. 'A family problem come up. I call you,' he shouted to Tristan.

'Most of all I would like to thank Maestro Rannaldini.' Hermione wiped away a tear.

But she had lost her audience, as every eye followed Rannaldini out of the room.

6

Rannaldini could hardly fly his helicopter home for excitement. Would days of riding out in all weather have coarsened Tabitha's amazing beauty? Would being fired so ignominiously have tempered her extraordinary arrogance, her capacity for rage?

Evidently not. Rannaldini entered the west courtyard through ancient gates, optimistically crowned with rusty iron letters spelling the words *omnia vincit amor*. Sprinting up a mossy, paved path, flanked by lavender bushes, and pushing open the heavy oak door he found Helen spitting with fury. Tabitha was showing no contrition at all. Halting her mother in mid-lecture, she had snapped that she hadn't flown five thousand miles for an earful and sloped off to the yard to settle The Engineer for the night.

'Now she's attacking the vodka,' spluttered Helen. 'We've clearly got a lush on our hands – Rupert always drank too much. And after over a year away she didn't even peck me on the cheek.'

'Where is she?' demanded Rannaldini.

'In the Blue Living Room.'

The Blue Living Room, an upstairs drawing room, which everyone else at Valhalla still called the Red Morning Room, had just been redecorated by Helen at vast expense in soft blues and rusts to complement her own hazel-eyed, red-headed beauty. The orange flames dancing merrily in the grate and the last tawny leaves on the beech outside enhanced the effect. Rannaldini's Étienne de Montignys and Russell Flints had been banished in favour of an autumnal watermill by Samuel Palmer, and a Canaletto of sea-blue Venice. An embracing Cupid and Psyche by Canova provided the only erotic note.

Tabitha sat slumped in a carved brown chair, which was Rannaldini's only contribution to the room, watching Wallace and Gromit on television. She was wearing frayed jeans and a Stop Puppy Farming T-shirt. A green toggle clung to her wrist like mistletoe. She was very thin – probably from taking those mad mood-inducing slimming pills to keep her weight down.

Her face was deathly pale, the long turquoise eyes bloodshot and heavily shadowed, the long nose reddened, the mouth clamped round clenched teeth in an attempt not to cry. White-blonde hair, used to being washed every day, hung lank and greasy to her collar-bone. She was clutching a yellow Labrador puppy as though it were a hot-water bottle.

'Where d'you get that animal?' asked Rannaldini sternly.

'Sharon? She was a stray, wandering round the docks.'

Rannaldini clicked his tongue. 'Have you alerted the quarantine authorities?'

Tab's eyes darkened in terror.

'Please don't betray me. I couldn't leave her in Kentucky.'

Rannaldini, who was never too hot, put a log on the fire.

'How d'you fiddle it?'

'I came through France. There's a boat smuggling in thirty dogs a day. The Engineer and I had to wait as it only sails when there's no moon.'

'How long have you been travelling?'

'Four or five days.'

Rannaldini filled up her glass.

'Naughty little girl,' he said softly, taking Sharon and examining her. 'Certainly she doesn't look rabid.'

He dropped the puppy gently on the floor.

'How can we punish you?' he purred.

'The American Horse Show Association's done that already, for Christ's sake.'

'So they should have done. Risking the life of that beautiful horse I gave you.'

'Engie's fine, I promise you.'

Tab's light, clipped drawl was so like her father's. Every time he heard it, Rannaldini was excited by how much he could hurt Rupert by controlling and manipulating her. Moving round the room, only pausing to run an admiring hand over Psyche's marble bottom, he pressed a button on the back of Tab's chair. She gasped then screamed, as its wings suddenly clamped round her waist, trapping her.

'What the fuck – lemme go!' Fighting tears, she clawed fruitlessly at the imprisoning wooden arms, until she nearly pulled the chair over.

'It's a debtor's chair,' mocked Rannaldini, as he closed in on her. 'Eighteenth century. Used to trap debtors like you. I've been looking for one for ages. You owe me two grand for your journey home, remember.'

'I'll pay you back.' Tabitha flinched away.

When she could retreat no further, she allowed his fingers to caress her cheek for a second, then dropped her head like a snowdrop.

'My father's such a bastard.'

Rannaldini shrugged.

'Maybe he's pleased Marcus is gay. Probably never wanted a son competing with him.'

Having left pawmarks all over Helen's pale blue Regency sofa, Sharon was now attacking a cushion Helen had embroidered of a virgin and a unicorn. Neither Tab nor Rannaldini took any notice.

Rupert's remark about gaining a daughter when Marcus had shacked up with Nemerovsky had been the one that had hurt her most, confessed Tab.

'He's got a daughter, for Christ's sake.'

'And *what* a daughter,' said Rannaldini lovingly.

'I want to make him madder than he's ever been before.'

'Let's find something really to worry him.'

Rannaldini moved fast. With his Polaroid memory, he had not forgotten four and a half years ago, his leading jockey, Isaac Lovell, and Tabitha exchanging an impassioned eye-meet in the paddock before the Rutminster Cup. Isaac had been riding Rannaldini's vicious but generally victorious horse The Prince of Darkness, who'd fallen at the last fence. Tabitha had been the groom looking after Arthur, a big grey gelding, trained by her father, Rupert.

Tragically Arthur had died of a massive heart-attack, way ahead of the field but just the wrong side of the winning-post. Slumped sobbing over Arthur's body, Tabitha had been too distraught to feel the hand of sympathy Isaac Lovell had dropped on her shoulder as he led home the unhurt but shaken Prince of Darkness.

The Campbell-Blacks and the Lovells had been feuding for nearly forty years, since Rupert had bullied Jake at prep school for being the cook's son and a gypsy with a wasted leg. Gyppo Jake and Rupert had slogged it out on the international show-jumping circuit throughout the seventies, with Jake finally getting his revenge during the Los Angeles Olympics by running off with Rupert's then wife Helen.

Later Jake had returned to his wife, Tory, Helen had eventually married Rannaldini, Jake and Rupert had both switched to training, but their feud had not abated. One reason, apart from loathing Rannaldini, why Rupert had disinherited Tabitha and Marcus was because photographs had appeared of both of them smiling at Jake Lovell, who as the Maestro's trainer had been a witness at Rannaldini's wedding to Helen.

If Helen and Jake had once fallen so passionately in love, reflected Rannaldini, might not history repeat itself? By a delicious coincidence, Isa Lovell was coming to lunch tomorrow, which would give Tab a decent night's sleep.

Unhampered by scruples, Rannaldini didn't give a stuff that Isa was already living just outside Melbourne with a tough little tomboy called Martie. They had invested in a yard that had done brilliantly its first season but which still needed capital. For this reason, Isa had come home to make serious money in the National Hunt season and also to help his father, Jake, now increasingly debilitated by the polio he'd had as a child. Rannaldini had several horses in training with Jake, and had invited Isa over to try out two mares he had bought in France and to plan for the future.

As usual Rannaldini had another motive. During the winter in Melbourne, Isa had won three of Australia's biggest races, including their Grand National, for Baby Spinosissimo, the young tenor, whom Rupert had suggested should play Don Carlos. Isa would know if Baby was sufficiently broke to accept the part for a quarter of Fat Franco's fee.

There was nothing youthful about Isa Lovell. Money had always been tight when he was a child: at six he was helping in the yard and jumping at shows, at eight coping with very public trouble in his parents' marriage, and his mother's attempted suicide. Despite having been champion jockey three times, he was aware at twenty-six that he would soon have to support his parents, and was therefore considering moving into training.

Isa had trendily tousled black hair, lowering black brows, and slanting, suspicious dark eyes dominating a pale, expressionless face. He looked like the second murderer in *Macbeth* and had a Birmingham accent you could cut with a flick-knife. But at five foot eight, he was tall for a jockey, with an undeniable brooding gypsy glamour. Not above dirty tricks on the course, where he was nicknamed the Black Cobra, he was as arrogant as Tabitha and, as champion jockey, had had his pick of the girls.

After fourteen hours' sleep, a long, scented bath and a raid on her mother's bedroom Tab, unaware Isa was coming to lunch, wandered into the Blue Living Room. She reeked of Helen's favourite scent, Jolie Madame. She was wearing Helen's new dark green cashmere polo-neck, which turned her turquoise eyes almost emerald. Her newly washed hair flopped arctic blonde over her white forehead, as she sidled over to the drinks tray to get stuck into the vodka.

'That is not a suitable breakfast and that's my roll-neck,' began Helen furiously.

'Shut up,' murmured Rannaldini, but with such venom that any further reproach froze on Helen's lips. 'We have a guest. Tabitha, my dear, I don't think you've met Isaac Lovell.'

Tab halted, tossing her head so haughtily Isa could see up the nostrils of her long Greek nose and the curling blonde underside of her lashes. But as he breathed in her scent, he was so unaccountably overwhelmed by foreboding that he found himself trembling.

Tab in turn saw a young man as dark and narrow as the gallows, and as still as the embracing Cupid and Psyche on the plinth beside him. His eyes were filled with hostility and in his hand was a glass of tomato juice as blood red as the feud between the two families.

'What the hell's he doing here?' she demanded in outrage.

'Discussing my horses,' said Rannaldini.

Everyone jumped as the door crashed open and a furi-ously growling Sharon the Labrador backed into the room frantically worrying a sheepskin slipper. Hanging on to the other end, growling equally loudly but looking more sheepish than the slipper because he knew the

76

drawing rooms were out of bounds, was Tabloid, Rannaldini's senior Rottweiler.

'Get them out of here,' screamed Helen, as a rose-garlanded Chelsea bowl *circa* 1763 smashed into a hundred pieces. 'You know those uncontrollable brutes aren't allowed in the house.'

'How did he get in, then?' spat Tab, scowling at Isa.

'Don't be so goddam rude,' shouted Helen.

Ignoring such brawling, Isa picked up Rannaldini's *Times* and turned to the racing pages.

Lunch was predictably unrelaxed. Isa, who had the conversational skills of a Trappist monk, who had never visited Sydney Opera House or seen the Nolans and the Boyds in any of the art galleries, and who had never forgiven Helen for nearly destroying his parents' marriage, turned his back on her and talked horses with Rannaldini. Watching his weight, he drank only Perrier, picked the bits of lobster out of the delectable mango and shellfish salad and had no tartare sauce or vegetables with his Dover sole. Tab just drank vodka and, horrified she was so violently attracted to Isa, disagreed with everything he said. Rannaldini watched them in delight, an evil smile flickering over his lips like a snake's tongue.

After lunch Rannaldini, Isa and Tabitha rode the new French horses and the dappled-grey Engineer round Paradise. Tab, who had put on a blue baseball cap and an indigo bomber jacket, with 'Can't Catch Me' printed on the back, proceeded to show off, executing dressage steps as gracefully as a ballerina, jumping huge fences and five-bar gates, beating Isa easily as they thundered down the long ride past Valhalla lake.

Passing the gates leading to Hermione's beautiful mill, River House, Tabitha noticed her fiendish son Little Cosmo Harefield touting for a 'fiver for the guy', who looked surprisingly like Rannaldini's fearsome PA, Miss Bussage.

'What's that obnoxious brat doing at home?' she asked, knowing perfectly well that Little Cosmo was Rannaldini's son. 'I thought he'd gone to prep school.'

'Cosmo has been suspended for bullying.'

Tab was shocked by the pride in Rannaldini's voice.

'Like son like father,' she said disapprovingly.

Rannaldini laughed.

On the village green, parents and children were happily building a huge bonfire. As the horses clattered down Paradise High Street, lights were coming on in the cottages. Seeing people companionably having tea and watching television, Tab was overcome with longing for Penscombe.

'What date is it?' she asked.

'October the thirtieth,' said Isa.

'It's Daddy's birthday tomorrow,' she said bleakly.

Mist was rising from the river as they turned right towards Valhalla. The house itself was hidden by its great conspirator's cloak of woods, but ahead in a dense copse known as Hangman's Wood, they caught a glimpse of Rannaldini's watch-tower.

The roar of a tractor taking hay to Rannaldini's horses was accompanied by deep complaining from the rooks. An early owl hooted. In the dusk, Tab kept losing sight of Sharon the Labrador as the dog plunged into a stream choked by leaves as yellow as herself.

Entering Rannaldini's estate down a little-used back lane, The Engineer stopped, and trembled violently, sweat blackening his dappled coat, his big brave eyes rolling. Even when Isa and Rannaldini rode on ahead, he refused to follow them between two gnarled oaks into a tree tunnel in which blackthorn, hazel and hawthorn intertwined overhead like a guard of honour.

In sympathy with The Engineer, Sharon raised her hackles and yapped, and when shouted at by Tab, rammed her tail between her legs, and howled.

Even when Tab uncharacteristically laid into The Engineer with her whip because she was so humiliated he was napping in front of Isa, the horse wouldn't go forward. Finally he backed, terrified, into a rusty barbed-wire fence, entangling his hind legs.

Only Isa's lightning reactions, leaping from his mare, chucking his reins to Rannaldini, gently talking to The Engineer as he calmly set him free, avoided a hideous accident.

'Could have severed a fetlock, you stupid bitch,' he swore at Tab as he bound up the horse's leg with a red-spotted handkerchief.

Tab, who'd also jumped down, couldn't stop shaking and had to lean against an equally shaking Engineer for support. After he'd given her a leg back up, Isa handed her Sharon to hold.

'The little one's gone far enough. Better carry her home.'

'Let's go back through the main gates,' said Rannaldini, swinging his horse round.

The setting sun had emerged from beneath a curtain of dark grey cloud, firing the puddles, warming the swirling silver spectres of old man's beard. As they swished home through the wet leaves, Isa lit a cigarette and drew deeply on it. Then, as Tab's hands were full of reins and Sharon, he held it to her lips for a couple of puffs, letting his fingers rest for a second against her cold face.

'Few horses like that lane,' observed Rannaldini idly. 'Sir Charles Beddoes, a previous owner, got so bored with the local blacksmith visiting his young wife Caroline, he rearranged the old man's beard cables between the two oaks. Then he surprised the lovers in bed. Escaping on his horse down the back lane, the blacksmith rode straight into the cables and – snap – they broke his neck.

'Over the years many villagers have heard the clattering of his horse's hoofs or seen him hanging above the road at twilight.' Rannaldini's smile was satanic in the half light. 'Sometimes on winter evenings at Valhalla you can hear poor Caroline sobbing for her lost love, or see her wandering the passages in a blood-stained grey dress.'

'A fashionable colour for ghosts,' said Isa sardonically, but he crossed himself quickly and spat on the tarmac, as they turned into the Paradise–Cheltenham road.

'Maybe,' said Rannaldini, 'but the trail of her little footprints comes through locked doors leaving marks on the flagstones.'

'Why the hell did you take us that way, then?' yelled Tab. Then, slipping all over the wet leaves, endangering both her horse's and her puppy's lives, she galloped back to the stables.

Once the vet had given The Engineer the OK, Tab retreated along endlessly twisting dark passages to her bedroom, refusing any supper, tempted to drown herself as she soaked in a hot bath, sobbing helplessly like Caroline Beddoes as she waited in dread for the sound of Isa's departing car.

7

Valhalla was full of priest-holes and secret passages, known only to Rannaldini and Clive, his leather-clad bodyguard. Rooms on all levels enabled people to peer out of the small mullioned windows through the creepers into other people's bedrooms. Not trusting Rannaldini, Tab drew her tattered crimson damask bedroom curtains that covered the window overlooking the courtyard but left open the others so that she could gaze south over the quiet starlit valley.

Valhalla had been a royalist stronghold during the Civil War. On one of the mullions was carved the head of a cavalier – probably Prince Rupert of the Rhine. Running her fingers over his long hair and proud, patrician face, Tabitha wished he'd gallop down the centuries on his charger and whisk her away from all this confusion.

From the Summer Drawing Room directly below her bedroom she could hear the distant rumble of Rannaldini's voice, and longed to gaze at Isa through a crack in the floorboards.

Used to owners banging on, Isa was only pretending to listen to Rannaldini's post-mortem about why The Prince of Darkness had only won by four lengths at Chepstow. To take his mind off Tabitha, he was deliberately pondering on a small, lazy chestnut two-year-old called Peppy Koala, which he'd seen last week in Australia – or, rather, not seen because, frightened by a snake on the gallops, the colt had flashed past him faster than light.

Peppy Koala's owner, a tycoon called Mr Brown, had no idea of the colt's potential. Isa didn't ride horses for the flat, but he reckoned he'd found a Guineas, possibly a Triple Crown winner. If tipped off, Rannaldini would certainly pay for the colt, and its fare to England, but would then want total glory and control. He was a difficult, demanding owner.

Unfortunately Baby Spinosissimo, the Australian tenor, who let Isa do what he liked, had run out of money. It couldn't be long before someone else sussed the colt's potential. Rupert was also serenading Baby. The racing world was a bloody jungle.

Isa was brought back to earth at the sound of Tabitha's name. Rannaldini was saying idly that he was thinking of settling a very large sum of money on her.

It wouldn't be worth it, Isa told himself. Too much blood had flowed under the bridge and, being superstitious, he couldn't defy that feeling of foreboding when Tabitha had entered the room that morning. As Rannaldini fetched the brandy decanter, Isa glanced at a letter on a nearby desk:

Dear Dame Hermione

I am sorry to suspend your son, Cosmo, but we cannot allow bullying, particularly of a much younger boy. Xavier Campbell-Black is only six and a half, a plucky little lad, who has settled in as a day-boy extremely well. The fact that he is black makes the whole business even more reprehensible. I hope ten days at home will give Cosmo the chance to reflect upon his actions.

That was poetic justice, thought Isa sourly. Rupert had bullied Isa's father at school. Now Rupert's adopted son was getting a taste of his father's medicine.

'Tell me all about Baby Spinosissimo,' said Rannaldini, filling up Isa's glass.

Later they went out on to the terrace to admire the winter stars, which Isa knew well, as he had to rise most mornings several hours before it was light. A small silver moon was sailing up from the east. As Isa breathed in the smell of moulding leaves and woodsmoke, Orion and his dog stars blazed down as beautiful, solitary and icily imperious as Tabitha. And, like the little silver moon, how much light she cast around her!

The chapel clock tolled midnight. Tab turned her sodden pillow. Oh, why had she left the latest Dick Francis downstairs? The front door banged. Isa was gone. She gave a wail of despair. But hearing distant steps on the flagstones, she hastily turned off her light, in case Rannaldini was on the prowl.

The footsteps, slow and deliberate, were coming up the stairs, getting closer and closer. In a moment of panic she felt sure she heard the door of the empty spare room next door stealthily opening and closing. As the boards creaked outside her heart stopped.

It must be Rannaldini. She wanted to scream, but who would hear, with her mother locked in Mogadon-induced stupor at the other end of the wing? Sharon, asleep on the bed, was no protection.

The floorboards creaked again, as if someone were deliberating. Then there was a knock.

'Who is it?' gasped Tab.

Shutting the door behind him, Isa leant against it. In the moonlight his eyes were a skull's black hollows. 'I've been brought up to hate the name of Campbell-Black,' he said wearily, 'but I can't help myself. You are the most desirable . . .'

But he didn't have time to finish. Tab had belted across the room, tripping over a still unpacked suitcase into his arms.

'You're as *verboten* as a cream bun in a health

farm,' she gabbled, 'but I can't help myself either.'

For a second, he put his hands round her white throat, so slender that he could have snapped it in an instant, telling himself he could still escape. But her breath, which came in little gasps, smelt so sweet and her mouth, shyly testing his, was so soft, that he found himself gently sliding his tongue between her perfect white teeth.

But it was the last gentle thing he did. Sharon must have thought one of the blacksmith's oaks had landed on her as they collapsed onto the bed. Ripping off Tab's striped pyjamas, scattering the buttons of his shirt, jamming the zip of his jeans, leaving on just his gypsy earrings to ward off evil, Isa appreciated her true beauty only when he held her naked and quivering in his arms. Kissing, often biting his way downwards, he found a little seahorse tattooed just below her left breast.

'You're in for a bumpy ride, fellow,' he whispered mockingly, as his exploring fingers crept between Tab's legs.

'Oh, bliss, you mustn't, oh, please go on,' gasped Tab, then, worried that he might be bored by such a wonderful but extended foreplay, 'Oh, please come inside me.'

As Isa brought her to extremes of pleasure with the same pelvic thrusts that drove winners past the post, she knew exactly why he had been nicknamed the Black Cobra. It was as though constant lightning were being unleashed from his body, and she never seemed to dry up, as if a Cotswold spring was constantly bubbling between her legs. As their breathing grew quicker and the four-poster creaked like an old tree in a high wind, she thought she had never known lovemaking like it.

As he watched them through the two-way mirror, which kept misting up, Rannaldini realized he had never seen anything like it either. Silvered by moonlight, they were so transported by their passion, it was as though Canova's Cupid and Psyche had sprung to white-hot life:

constantly changing positions, they coupled with snake-like frenzy.

Now Isa was kissing one of Tab's small, amazingly high breasts, biting the nipple until she cried out. Now he was lying sideways his dark head and stabbing tongue buried in her blonde pubic hair as simultaneously her lips and tongue teased and caressed his cock, which Rannaldini was furious to confess looked bigger than his own. At least the little blighter couldn't hold out much longer.

But, exulting in his control, Isa drew himself out as proudly as Excalibur. Then swivelling round, he plunged inside her once more, his pale murderer's face triumphant, his hips a juddering blur. Only when Tab arched, went rigid then cried out, did he finally let himself come, kissing in ecstasy her long white throat, her damp forehead, her loving mouth, as for a fleeting moment his defences were down.

Frantically wiping a peephole in the steamed-up mirror, Rannaldini thought he would explode – and did. He must install a video camera so he could gloat for hours over the playback. Reluctantly he had to admit that Isa was as good at riding women as he was horses.

'I love you,' mumbled Tabitha, when Isa finally removed his mouth from hers.

'Thank God you've washed off that bloody awful perfume.'

'It's Mummy's. Jolie Madame. She never wore anything else until this summer when she switched to Organza so I thought I'd help her use up the old stuff.'

In horror Isa realized he must have smelt the same scent on his father, when Jake had come upstairs to tuck him in after stolen meetings with Helen.

'Never wear it again,' he snapped, and rolled off her on to his back.

'Buy me something else, then. God, you're a revelation, I've always been *soixante*-nervous before, but with you it was unbelievable.'

Isa couldn't believe it had happened. How could he have betrayed his parents like that?

'I'd better go,' he said.

Hearing the rusty creak of drawbridges being pulled up, fighting desolation, Tab scooped a drowsy Sharon into the warm place left by his body. Then she caught sight of the bedside clock. 'It's October the thirty-first now,' she said insolently. 'Happy birthday, Daddy. Sleeping with the enemy is the worst present I could give him.'

Isa glowered down at her, his arms trapping her like the debtor's chair. 'Is that why you went to bed with me?' he hissed.

'Not entirely,' said Tab.

For the next week, they devoured each other, making love in the hayloft, on the wet autumn leaves, knowing they were playing with fire but unable to stop themselves. Aware of the difference in their backgrounds and temperaments, Isa was the more detached of the two. But within three weeks Tab was pregnant.

Isa, who had a strong sense of dynasty and a smouldering eye for the main chance, hoped that Rannaldini would settle money on her as hinted, and insisted they got married. There was no way a possible Lovell heir was going to be terminated. Anyway he couldn't get enough of Tab.

But he was worried sick about Martie, his Australian girlfriend, to whom, in explanation of his absence, he had considerably exaggerated Jake's illness. In junking her and consorting with the devil-led Campbell-Blacks, had he lost all his principles?

Terrified of trapping him, Tab would willingly have had an abortion.

'I've never looked after a man,' she gibbered. 'I'll probably give you hay for dinner.' But she loved him so passionately, she was only too happy to get married.

Events were much bowled along by Rannaldini, who not only agreed to pay for the wedding, which – because of his overflowing diary – could take place only on a late afternoon in the middle of December, but also offered them his latest purchase, Magpie Cottage, just across the valley, rent-free.

Helen had mixed feelings. Tab could have done infinitely better and it would mean the press raking up her *affaire* with Isa's father, Jake, but she'd enjoy showing everyone at the wedding how much better she looked than Tory, the wife Jake had gone back to. She must book in for a few days at Champney's.

Finally there was undeniable pleasure in how much the whole thing would enrage Rupert, and at least it meant that Tab, who had draped a banana skin on Psyche's head only that morning, would move out. And Rannaldini wouldn't run after her any more if she married Isa, who looked capable of knifing any competition – or so Helen thought.

8

Meanwhile, rehearsals for *Don Carlos* were supposed to have started in a defunct WI hall in North London. Tristan, however, grew increasingly frustrated when all his stars, headed by Fat Franco who was singing Otello at La Scala, failed to turn up. This meant that poor Mikhail, whose hotel bill was being picked up by Liberty Productions, had no-one to rehearse with except his voice coach, who found it a great strain having to squawk Hermione's and Chloe's parts, let alone growling like an old bear pretending to be Alpheus. The reason for this mass absenteeism was that top singers hate rehearsing because they don't get paid for it. 'Why should we roll up because Mikhail Pezcherov hasn't sung the part in English before?' they chorused. 'We're only going to be reading our parts at the recording anyway, and could be whizzing round the world avoiding tax and making fortunes elsewhere.'

'Franco and I never met when we did *Tristan and Isolde*,' protested Hermione, on a very crackly call from a Florida beach. 'I just put on cans and recorded the entire opera from the orchestral track.'

'That's why it was so lifeless and boring,' yelled a furious Tristan, but Hermione had hung up.

Tristan also spent a lot of time on the telephone shouting at Rannaldini.

'How the fuck can I direct individual rehearsals when there aren't any individuals to direct?'

'I am shocked at them all,' lied Rannaldini, and to placate Tristan, he invited him down to Valhalla the following Saturday. 'Then we iron out every problem. I also invite that Australian tenor, Baby Spinosissimo,' Rannaldini added airily. 'He's coming down to see his jockey, Isa Lovell, who by an extraordinary coincidence happens to be my jockey. Why don't you drive down together?'

Rannaldini rubbed his hands in glee. What frisson it would add if Tristan, and particularly Baby, were present at the wedding! Thank goodness, Clive, his bodyguard, had discovered that on the big day Rupert would be out of the country with his son Xavier.

Poor Xav had not only had to endure Cosmo's horrible bullying. Rupert had also found his little son sobbing his heart out because he'd been scrubbing his face for hours trying to get it as white as Rupert's. Rupert had struggled not to weep too. Instead he decided to give Xavier some sense of identity by taking him back to Colombia. Here, Xav could meet the nuns in the Bogotá convent in which he'd spent his first two years, and see something of the ravishing surrounding countryside. Taggie, Rupert's wife, and Bianca, Xav's younger sister, would have gone as well if Bianca hadn't caught measles.

At midnight on the eve of the wedding, therefore, an unsuspecting Taggie was at Penscombe, filling up the deep freeze for Christmas. Bianca, whose temperature was down, was fast asleep upstairs. The six dogs, except for Gertrude the mongrel who always kept an eye open for scraps, slept in their baskets. Two huge moussakas for the staff party were complete, except for the cheese topping which was bubbling on the Aga.

Having laid the big scrubbed table for the grooms' and jockeys' breakfast tomorrow, Taggie had left space at the end to wrestle with her Christmas cards. Very dyslexic, she found proper names a nightmare. She was dickering over whether to send a card to Rupert's ex-wife, Helen, to heal the breach, and make it easier for Rupert to see Tabitha again, but she wasn't sure how to spell 'Rannaldini'. Hearing the strange strangulated croak of a fox's bark she glanced out of the window. A car was lighting up the trees as it sped along the opposite side of Rupert's valley when the telephone rang.

Oh, bliss, it must be Rupert. He hated her working late. She must remember to sound sleepy.

'Is that Taggie?' asked a slurred voice, so like Rupert's. 'Look, I'm getting married to Isa Lovell at five o'clock tomorrow – no, today. Will you come? I'd like some family there, apart from Mummy.'

'Oh, no, Tab, you can't.' Taggie collapsed in horror on the window-seat.

Tab burst into tears. It was several moments before Taggie could elicit the fact that her stepdaughter was having Isa's baby and Rannaldini, being angelic, had masterminded the wedding and that Tab was madly in love with Isa.

'But he's so busy race-riding five days a week and helping Jake' – at the dreaded name, Taggie jumped as though she'd been stung – 'with his yard that I don't see much of him. He doesn't need me as much as I need him.'

As Tabitha was obviously getting cold feet, Taggie beseeched her to postpone the wedding.

'You don't have to marry him, darling. Have the baby here. We'll all help you look after it.'

'Daddy wouldn't allow that,' sobbed Tab.

'Of course he would. It'll kill him, Tab. Anyone else but Isa! You know how he feels about the Lovells – and not having the wedding at Penscombe will break his heart. He was just about to ring you and make it up.'

'Put him on, then,' demanded Tab.

'He's in Bogotá with Xav.'

Immediately, Taggie knew she'd said the wrong thing,

as Tab, who was as jealous of Xavier and Bianca as she was of Marcus, slammed down the telephone.

A disgusting smell of burnt cheese sauce brought Taggie back to earth, as Gertrude the mongrel wandered over stiffly and laid her head on her mistress's knee. 'Oh, Gertrude, what am I going to do?' sobbed Taggie.

'Is your name really Spinosissimo?' asked Tristan, as he edged his navy blue Aston on to the M4.

'Course not,' said Baby. 'I got it out of a rose cata-logue. My real name's Brian Smith. But you can't have Smith alongside the Pavarottis and Domingos on a record sleeve.'

Outrageous, incredibly glamorous, Baby Spinosissimo had burnt-sienna curls, thickly lashed debauched grey eyes, a beaky little nose and a pouting, but wickedly determined, mouth. Slightly plump already, he finished a whole box of Quality Street on the way down, chucking his sweet papers out of the window. He also spent a lot of time on Tristan's telephone talking to his bookmaker.

Responding to Tristan's ability to listen, Baby was soon telling him about his sex life. Women ran after him in droves, but the only person he was remotely interested in was his trainer and jockey Isa Lovell.

'He's got such a capacity for menace. I can't sleep at night for imagining him gripping me as he grips those horses.'

Baby also confessed that buying horses for Isa to train had screwed him up with the taxman.

'Jan one, and the debtor's prison looms.'

In return Tristan told Baby about his problems with *Don Carlos*.

'Fat Franco won't rehearse.'

'He's got half Colombia up his nose, for a start,' said Baby dismissively. 'And he hates the part of Carlos. Thinks it's very difficult and not important or sym-pathetic enough. Domingo feels the same. He dismisses Carlos as a wimp with one solo.'

'What d'you think?' asked Tristan.

'If the part was decently acted by someone hugely attractive . . .' Baby smoothed his curls. 'What else are you up to?'

The Lily in the Valley was nearing its final cut, said Tristan. Tomorrow he was nipping over to Paris to re-do some dialogue with Claudine Lauzerte.

'Are you pleased with it?'

'Yes,' admitted Tristan, 'but one has no idea what will happen when it faces an audience.'

'Claudine Lauzerte,' Baby rolled his eyes, 'is a terrific gay icon in Oz.'

They were in deep country now. The sun hadn't appeared for days, probably singing Otello in Milan. But despite bare trees and lowering skies, the winter wheat spilling like a jade sea over the rich red ploughed fields gave a feeling of spring.

Driving through the russet cathedral town of Rutminster approaching some traffic lights, they drew level with a black Mercedes driven by a young girl. She was wearing a Stop Puppy Farming T-shirt but her pale blonde hair was fantastically garlanded with pink and white flowers like a Botticelli angel. A Labrador puppy as yellow as her hair lay across her thighs. Her seat-belt was undone and she was unashamedly taking slugs out of a vodka bottle. Tristan, who knew he'd seen her before, nearly ran into the car in front.

'Ke-rist on a Harley-Davidson!' gasped Baby.

'Oh, Don Fatale,' muttered Tristan, because the girl had one of those faces that makes everyone else's look commonplace.

'Where are you going to, Mademoiselle?' shouted Baby, lowering his window.

'It'll be Madame in an hour or two,' shouted back Tabitha, lifting the vodka bottle to her lips and driving on.

At the edge of town, she gave them the slip.

'That's one for the divorce courts,' said Baby. Then,

to Tristan's surprise, he admitted he had been married briefly when he was twenty-one. 'My brother had such a beaut stag party I wanted one too. So I had to get spliced. My stag party was so great, I only just made the wedding, passed out as soon as I got to the reception and didn't wake up till next day. My mother-in-law never forgave me, and nor did my wife. It only lasted a few weeks.'

Baby told the story so wickedly that Tristan couldn't help laughing, but neither could he stop thinking about the girl at the traffic lights. Then he remembered. He'd seen her in a silver frame on Rannaldini's piano.

Across the world in Bogotá, Rupert had returned from a marvellous day out. Xavier had totally captivated the nuns, who had not seen him since Rupert and Taggie had adopted him four and a half years ago. He was so tall, straight-backed and confident now, and proudly showed them photographs of Taggie, Bianca – who'd come from the same convent – Bogotá his black Labrador, Gringo his pony, already covered in rosettes, and finally of his big brother, Marcus, winning the Appleton.

'We read about Marcus in the papers,' said Mother Immaculata. 'You must be so proud – and what about your sister Tabitha?'

'We don't see her any more, thank God,' said Xav flatly.

'She's in America, eventing,' explained Rupert hastily, vowing to telephone her the moment he got back to England.

Returning to the Hilton, he found a message to ring Taggie urgently. When he heard the news he went berserk.

'What time is it in England?'

'About three thirty.'

'We've got to stop it. Rannaldini's set the whole thing up in revenge for Marcus winning the Appleton and the rows over *Don Carlos*. Gimme his number.' Then, for once forgetting his wife's reading problems, 'For Christ's sake, move it.'

As Tabitha breezed in from the hairdresser, a purring Rannaldini told her that her father was on the line. For a second her face lit up. Then, picking up the telephone, she was scalded – even thousands of miles away – by the lava of Rupert's rage. If she *really* went ahead and married Isa, he would never speak to her again, never allow her back to Penscombe, never give her a penny.

'So what else is new?' screamed Tabitha. 'You said exactly the same thing when Mummy married Rannaldini. I love Isa. It's not just because I'm having your grandchild.'

'Won't be any bloody grandchild of mine! It's spawn of the devil!'

'Bollocks! You're the devil. I know what you got up to – terrorizing Jake at school, and Tory when she was a deb, making Jake's life a misery on the show-jumping circuit, pinching Revenge from him. I'd no idea that Revenge started off as Jake's horse, or the reason Macaulay wouldn't go for you in the World Championship was because you'd beaten him to a pulp in the past, just as you beat up Mummy.'

'I bloody fucking didn't!'

'Yes, you did! You're the biggest bastard that ever walked.'

'You ain't seen nothing yet!' howled Rupert. 'I'll destroy your marriage and bring down Rannaldini and the entire Lovell family.'

'Oh, go screw yourself!' A shattered Tab slammed down the receiver.

Rupert was straight on to Taggie. 'I can't get back in time to stop the marriage but I'll get it annulled tomorrow, and I'll strangle you if you go to the wedding.'

The moment Rupert hung up, Tabitha called Taggie and begged her to go.

* * *

'Christ! Look at Hammerklavier House of Horror,' shivered Baby as, after extended drinks at the Pearly Gates, he and Tristan drove towards Valhalla. Rooks rose out of a shroud of mist, thickened by bonfires of wet leaves. Sinister, conspiratorial as its owner, the great grey house lurked behind its mighty army of trees. Its tiny deep-set windows, thought Tristan, were like the eyes of medieval scholars grown small from poring over learned texts lit only by a flickering candle.

As Rannaldini had wanted maximum publicity without alerting Rupert, he had waited until midday to invite the leading gossip columnists, who had dropped everything to be there. The rest of the paparazzi, in black leather jackets and dark glasses, tried to storm the electric gates, as they opened to admit Baby and Tristan. Remembering Étienne's funeral, Tristan ducked in horror. Baby, on the other hand, waved happily.

At the end of a long drive through dark woods and deer-haunted parkland, Tristan and Baby were directed through the *omnia vincit amor* gates. Rannaldini's all-devouring smile welcomed them at the front door. Inside they found Tabitha. Except for the puppy-farming T-shirt and the flowers in her hair, she was unrecognizable, her swollen eyes redder than carbuncles, her face grey, except where it was covered in blotches. Despite having thrown up after her terrible row with Rupert, she was still attacking the vodka.

Delighted by the turn of events, Rannaldini was about to introduce her, when Tab gave a cry of relief, and shoving Baby and Tristan aside ran towards a dark girl, who had followed them into the house. 'Oh, Lucy, thank God you've come!'

One glance at Tab's blubbered woebegone little face told it all.

'Has your dad been horrible to you again?'

'Horrible, horrible,' sobbed Tab, as she led Lucy upstairs.

Lucy Latimer was Tabitha's greatest friend. They had

met when they became involved in animal rights. A vegetarian and a make-up artist, Lucy was very careful not to use cosmetics that had been tested on animals. Extremely successful because she combined a painter's eye with a sympathetic, soothing nature, she fortunately had a spare day between filming to make up Tab and provide moral support.

'Come on, Latimer.' Tab gazed at the wreckage in her bedroom mirror. 'This is the greatest challenge you'll ever face.'

'Don't you worry.' Lucy unpacked a roll of brushes, sponges and assorted bottles. 'I'll have you stunning as ever in a trice.'

'And talking of stunning, did you see that man in the hall?'

'Couldn't miss him, really,' sighed Lucy, 'but you'll have to put all that behind you now.'

Only a streak of saffron on the horizon gave a clue the sun was setting, but apple logs burned merrily in the Summer Drawing Room.

Rannaldini, looking very good in a morning coat, because the grey waistcoat matched his pewter hair, handed Tristan and Baby glasses of champagne, and apologized that they had run into a wedding.

'Who's getting married?' asked Baby.

'My stepdaughter, Tabitha.'

'She doesn't seem very keen on the idea,' said Tristan, wincing at his father's painting over the piano, of a leering man undressing a very young girl.

'Just last-minute nerves.' Rannaldini seemed to be killing himself over some private joke.

'Who's the lucky guy?' asked Baby.

'My dear boy, I thought you'd have known. It's your jockey, Isa Lovell.'

The colour drained from Baby's suntanned face. He seemed to shrink, like a larky March hare suddenly looking down a gun barrel.

'Christ, he can't be,' he stammered. 'What about Martie? He was talking of marrying her after Crimbo.'

Rannaldini always got a charge out of inflicting pain.

'He'll be in in a minute to tell you himself. He was irritated not to be riding at Cheltenham today.'

Tristan felt desperately sorry for Baby and put a hand on his rigid shoulders.

'This happen very quick. You told me she only came home the day of the Gramophone Awards.'

'Ah,' sighed Rannaldini. 'When one is young, love work like lightning. Like Carlos and Elisabetta.'

'Carlos and Elisabetta happen so quick because they were giddy with relief an arranged marriage had turned out so well,' protested Tristan.

'I believe in arranged marriages,' said Rannaldini warmly. After all, he had arranged this one.

'I hope you'll stay for the wedding,' he begged. 'You might even sing something during the signing of the register.' He smiled at Baby who, having drained his glass of champagne, had got a grip on himself. 'Dame Hermione is singing "Panis Angelicus",' went on Rannaldini. 'Ah, here comes the bridegroom.'

And in strolled Isa, still in old cords and a tweed jacket.

'Hi.' He smiled almost mockingly at Baby, who found it impossible to act normally as he blushed and couldn't speak. Isa always had this effect on him.

'Hadn't you better get changed?' snapped Tristan.

'Plenty of time,' said Isa coolly. 'I thought Baby might like to see round your yard, Rannaldini.'

It wasn't long before Baby found his tongue again.

'Why the hell didn't you marry Tabitha's brother Marcus?' he hissed. 'At least he's the right sex. I suppose you knocked her up.'

'This is a very nice mare.' Isa opened a half-door.

'She'll lose it if she goes on hitting the vodka. I suppose it's also for the money.'

'Rupert won't give her a penny,' sighed Isa. 'And

97

Rannaldini will only help out if it suits him.'

'Well, you're not getting another cent out of me.'

In the safety of the loose-box, Isa ran a finger down Baby's gritted jaw. 'It doesn't change anything,' he said softly. 'If you're a good boy, I'll tell you more about this amazing horse I've found. Did you know,' he added idly, 'gypsies consider it unlucky if a marriage takes place after sunset?'

Meanwhile Tristan was exploring Valhalla. Grey and spooky in the December twilight, it would be the perfect setting for *Don Carlos*. He could imagine the hunt streaming down those rides, or Eboli chasing Carlos through the maze. There were dungeons for Posa's death, and a splendid mausoleum for Charles V's tomb. Even the *auto da fe*, in which the heretics were burnt, could be staged in the courtyard outside the chapel.

As he wandered through rooms formed by yew hedges, statues of naked nymphs lurked in every corner. Tristan wished he could offer them all his jacket. To his right, the wood kept readjusting the mist like a shawl around its shoulders and, as he reached the big lawn, to the north four vast Lawson cypresses reared up, like monks in black habits with their pointed hoods over their faces. Gazing up from beneath them, Tristan suddenly felt the terror of the sixteenth-century man-in-the-street, overwhelmed by the dark, towering forces of the Inquisition.

Quickening his step as night fell, he nearly ran into a pack of paparazzi. As they levelled their long lenses like a firing squad at a new arrival, he decided they were part of some present-day *auto da fe*, destroying reputations for public delectation.

In a blinding flash, he realized that *Don Carlos* must be made in modern dress. The present English Royal Family were so similar to Verdi's French and Spanish royalty. Elisabetta was so like both the sad Princess Diana and the wistful Queen Elizabeth, married to the short-fused, roving-eyed Prince Philip, who was not unlike Philip II of Spain. And they, too, had a son called Charles, who was romantic, idealistic, longed for a proper job, had a loving nature and was terrified of his stern, critical father, as Carlos had been. Whilst in Eboli, the feisty mistress in love with Carlos, could be seen an echo of Camilla Parker Bowles, and in the noble Marquis of Posa a touch of Andrew, her diplomatic soldier husband. They could start the film with these characters in the royal box, then cut to the two armies on the skyline.

But who was the modern equivalent of the Grand Inquisitor? wondered Tristan, as he retraced his steps to the *omnia vincit amor* gates. Who terrorized people to madness? Why not Gordon Dillon, the ruthless editor of the *Scorpion*, who would shop his own children to boost circulation and who went around in tinted glasses and soft-soled shoes, scaring his staff as shitless as the public? The Inquisition bully-boys, who cast such terrifying shadows over *Don Carlos*, could be represented as lurking paparazzi or as the chinless, ruthless courtiers who spent their time spying and manipulating at Buckingham Palace.

Tristan couldn't wait to tell Rannaldini.

'Monsieur de Montigny.' A soft lisping voice made him jump out of his skin.

In his path lurked what appeared to be yet another leatherclad member of the paparazzi, with hair as pale as his bloodless face and the leer of a chemist when asked for something embarrassing. Before Tristan could tell him to piss off, the sinister creature introduced himself as Clive, Rannaldini's henchman.

'Sir Roberto was worried you were outside without an overcoat. He thought you might like a cup of tea, or something stronger, before the service starts in half an hour.'

Fifty miles away at Penscombe, Taggie Campbell-Black was still tearing out her dark hair. Rupert's reprobate old father, Eddie, had invited himself for the weekend. Having ensconced him happily in the study with a bottle of Bell's and racing on television, Taggie took the opportunity, as she hastily made up her face for Tab's wedding in the kitchen mirror, to discuss the crisis with Rupert's assistant, Lysander Hawkley. Lysander, who was married to Rannaldini's young third wife, Kitty, and who had also ridden his horse Arthur in the Rutminster Cup the same year Isa had ridden Rannaldini's delinquent Prince of Darkness, was absolutely horrified.

'Tab can't marry Isa, Taggie, he's an evil bugger. He spat at me before the race and made some seriously insulting remarks about Arthur – who, being a horse, couldn't answer back – and he gets up to wicked tricks on the course. Nearly rode me into the rails and called me "Campbell-Black's bumboy",' Lysander flushed. 'Bloody insult. Not that,' he added quickly, 'if I was that way inclined, I could think of anyone nicer than Rupert.'

'You probably could in his present mood,' sighed Taggie, as she fluffed blusher on her blanched cheeks. 'Oh, Lysander, what am I going to do? Tab couldn't have done a worse thing.'

'Poor darling,' said Lysander, who, having been worshipped unconditionally by Tab for four years, had a rosier view of her than most people. 'She's so impulsive.'

'She'll be so isolated in that camp,' said Taggie. 'Jake and Tory won't like it any more than Rupert, who'll kill me when he discovers I've gone to the wedding. But I can't not – Tab sounded so pitiful.'

'I'd come with you,' said Lysander, 'but I'd murder Rannaldini. Take Eddie – he'd liven up any party.'

Rannaldini's woods soared up like black cliffs. Trees, sheathed in ivy, danced like witches at some wild Sabbath.

'What a creepy house,' shuddered Taggie, as Rupert's helicopter landed, and she helped her father-in-law climb out.

'Why's the fella flying both the German and Italian flags?' snorted Eddie, glaring up at the roof.

'He's half German, half Italian.'

''Strordinary to be on both losing sides in the last war.'

As they hurried towards the *omnia vincit amor* gates, a lot of people were getting out of a minibus.

'Must be the tenants,' said Eddie.

'No, I think they're Isa's relations,' said Taggie.

9

It was nearly six o'clock. The little chapel, attached to the north wing at Valhalla, was packed to overflowing. Having drifted in to a rumble of approval twenty minutes ago, Helen, on her own in the left-hand front pew, grew increasingly furious. In order to upstage Tory Lovell and Hermione, she had spent a fortune at Lindka Cierach's on a ravishing smoky-blue suit, nipped in to show off her tiny waist. She had spent almost more on a fox-fur hat, about which Tab had been vilely rude. One should not call one's mother 'no better than a bloody murderer' on one's wedding day. And because Tabitha had never written thank-you letters or looked up Helen's family when she was in America, none of them had bothered to fly over for the wedding, claiming it was too near to Christmas. Even Marcus had deserted her because Nemerovsky had a first night in St Petersburg.

As a horrible result, Rannaldini had spitefully filled the relationless row behind her with Valhalla staff: Sally and Betty, the pretty maids, who'd gone to London to look after Serena Westwood's Jessie, Mr Brimscombe, the gardener, who was hopping mad because Helen had stripped his conservatories of flowers, Mrs Brimscombe, the housekeeper, who'd been allowed out of the kitchens for half an hour, and to top it the fearful Bussage in a trilby and a severe grey dress. No doubt they'd be joined soon by Clive, Rannaldini's henchman, and Tabloid the Rottweiler.

Having ignored Helen, the bridegroom across the aisle was reading the *Racing Post* and murmuring to Baby, whom he'd somehow seconded into being his best man.

As there was a limited time one could admire the white fountains of jasmine and freesias and the Murillo Madonna, which Rannaldini had insisted on hanging on the wall to the right of the altar, Helen walked down the aisle to disabuse Lady Chisledon, a local worthy, of any idea that Bussage might be a relation.

Bloody hell! Helen prided herself on not swearing, even in private, but Taggie Campbell-Black had just tiptoed in looking wildly embarrassed but undeniably gorgeous in a crimson suit with a black velvet collar and a little crimson pillbox on her dark cloudy hair. Rannaldini, who was hovering in the doorway, was all over, or under her, because Taggie was so tall, like a bull terrier courting a wolfhound.

Even worse, Taggie had brought Helen's dreadful ex-father-in-law, Eddie Campbell-Black, who was getting drunker by the minute with the aid of a hip flask and wearing Rupert's far too large morning coat, with a badge pinned to the lapel, saying, 'Old men make better lovers.'

'Ouch!' squawked Helen, as Eddie pinched her bottom.

The Lovells looked as though they'd come to a funeral, the men in dark suits, the women with too much hair sticking out under the front of their hats, except for Tory, who looked, maddeningly, much prettier in a royal blue suit than Helen remembered, and who never let go of Jake's hand.

And now, late as ever, Hermione swept in, having abandoned her usual Chanel suits in favour of a white angel's midi-dress and a gold halo hat. Psyching herself into the saintly role of Elisabetta, thought Tristan sourly.

It would hold more credence if she made the odd rehearsal.

In one hand, Hermione was clutching the music of 'Panis Angelicus', in the other, her fiendish son, Little Cosmo, who proceeded to kick the pews, crunch crisps and stick out a green tongue at the rest of the congregation.

'That's Rannaldini's illegit,' whispered Meredith Whalen, who'd taken one overexcited look at Tristan and swept him and Lucy Latimer into a back pew. 'Can't you tell from the nasty rolling black eyes? And he's twice as evil as Rannaldini.'

Meredith, who was known as the Ideal Homo because he was so much in demand as a spare man at Paradise dinner parties, was a hugely successful interior designer, whom Rannaldini had booked to do the sets for *Don Carlos*. Meredith looked so innocent and sweet all his gay friends wanted to put him in short pants and smack him.

'And did you ever see anyone so tense as Jake and Tory Lovell?' he was now whispering to Tristan. 'Like blasted oaks. I suppose it's sad when one's little acorn goes astray. And look at Bussage! She's a worse control freak than Rannaldini and she's wearing her control frock. We could film Philip's coronation in here, you know. Don't you just love that Murillo? Must be worth five million. That's why Rannaldini spends so much time in chapel gloating over it.'

Eddie Campbell-Black, who'd been ogling Lady Chisledon, suddenly spied Hermione, one of his former amours.

'Hello, Henrietta,' he bellowed.

Tabitha, who was even drunker than Eddie, swayed on Rannaldini's arm in the chapel doorway.

'You look sensational,' he murmured.

She was wearing two triangles of white silk, high at the neck and falling nine inches above her knees. She held a small bunch of freesias, to match the flowers in her hair.

'My dress is new, my knickers are borrowed from Mummy,' she informed Rannaldini. 'My toenails are painted blue, and you're the something old.' For a second she frowned at him. 'I ought to be at Penscombe, with Daddy giving me away.'

'The last thing I'm ever going to do is give you away,' purred Rannaldini, his right knuckles gently kneading her left breast.

Then he winced at the first strains of 'Here Comes the Bride'.

'Who chose this junk?'

'I did,' said Tab, then, glancing round the chapel she gave a sob. 'Oh, thank God, Taggie and Granddaddy are here.'

Striding up the aisle like a young Amazon, she paused to squeeze her stepmother's hand.

'What a vulgar dress,' said Hermione, in a very audible whisper.

'When's her baby due?' asked Little Cosmo loudly.

Lucy, who'd hardly had a second to change into a dark brown suit and black bowler, or to apply any of her make-up skills on herself, prayed that Tabitha wouldn't be sick.

'That's Percy the Parson,' hissed Meredith, as a red-faced cleric with straggly grey hair moved forward to welcome the bride. 'He's got such a plain wife, they're known as One Man and His Dog.'

Lucy fought the giggles.

'And the bridegroom is to die for,' sighed Meredith, as Isa moved beside Tabitha. 'Such a moody, vindictive little shit, pure Heathcliff, in fact, but bags I be Catherine Earnshaw.'

'Should have had a haircut. Fellow's hair's longer than Tabitha's,' said Eddie loudly.

There was an awkward moment when Percy the Parson asked if anyone knew of any impediment or just cause why the couple shouldn't be joined in matrimony and Little Cosmo called out, 'I do,' with a maniacal cackle and had his ears boxed by his mother.

'To have and to hold from this day forward,' intoned Isa.

'Chap sounds like something out of *Brookside*,' muttered a disapproving Eddie, taking a swig from his hip flask.

'I, Tabitha Maud Lavinia, take thee, Isaac Jake,' said Tab in the flat, clipped drawl that reminded almost everyone present of Rupert.

'Love, cherish and obey,' she went on, looking mockingly at Isa from under her mascaraed lashes.

'Oh dear.' Taggie blew her nose on a piece of loo paper. She certainly hadn't obeyed Rupert today.

'With my body I thee worship . . .' As she lurched over to kiss Isa on the jawbone, Tab nearly fell over. 'And with all my rather depleted worldly goods, I thee endow, although I am going to keep The Engineer,' she added, as an afterthought.

'*Tabitha!*' hissed an appalled Helen. What would the Lovells think?

Fortunately everyone was distracted by the ringing of Little Cosmo's mobile. Tab got the giggles.

Even more fortunately, Percy dispensed with a sermon. He'd been kept waiting quite long enough, and when he'd asked Helen and Rannaldini for touching memories of the bride, Helen couldn't think of any and Rannaldini's had been quite unrepeatable.

As everyone knelt to pray it could be seen that the bridegroom was wearing sapphire cufflinks as big and blue as his wife's eyes.

Followed by a smirking Rannaldini, a tight-lipped Helen, an ashen Jake and Tory, Tab and Isa went off to sign the register.

Tristan turned to Lucy. 'That is best make-up repair job I ever see. You wouldn't know she'd shedded a tear.' No Frenchwoman would be seen dead in that black bowler, decided Tristan, but Lucy had a nice face, not pretty, but kind and generous. With her dark curls, freckles, bright eyes and athletic body, she reminded him of a heroine in one of those Mallory Towers books his girl cousins were always devouring in the holidays.

Lucy, who'd spent her life studying faces, thought Tristan's was marvellous. She longed to paint out the dark shadows, bring forward the deep-set eyes and add a bit of tawny blusher to the sallow cheeks. There was also deceptive strength in the jaw. And when he smiled he had wonderful even white teeth.

She jumped as Meredith, who was now standing on the pew to have a better view, whispered that the Lovells looked as though they were signing a death warrant. 'Probably will be if Rupert rolls up.'

'Who's that beautiful woman in the crimson suit?' asked Tristan.

'Taggie Campbell-Black.' Lucy was appalled to feel a stab of jealousy.

Married to that white-hot fury, thought Tristan in dismay. He hoped Rupert didn't beat her up.

Hermione had now mounted the pulpit, her gold halo hat glinting in the candlelight, and opened her music and her big brown eyes.

'Panis Angelicus' rang out on the arctic air.

Tristan gave a shudder of pleasure.

'Could you make her look eighteen?' he muttered to Lucy.

'She doesn't look much older, she's so lovely.'

'A maestro a day helps you work, rest and play,' giggled Meredith.

Hermione would have eked out 'Panis Angelicus' for ever, if a mobile hadn't rung again.

'Hi, Joel. Who won the four thirty at Doncaster?' demanded Little Cosmo, and Hermione had to scuttle down from the pulpit to cuff him again.

Hermione was followed by Baby, who strolled up to the chancel steps, turned, with his hands in his pockets, and looked straight at Isa and Tabitha, who were waiting to return for the blessing.

'Where'er you walk,' sang Baby, and the chapel went

still because he had one of those extraordinary voices whose music goes straight to the listener's heart, and, as he sang, his face lost all its mockery and decadence, leaving only sweetness and beauty. Isa Lovell's face was totally expressionless, but his eyes were as dark as an open grave at midnight.

God in heaven, thought Tristan, he's got to replace Fat Franco and play Carlos. Glancing round he found Rannaldini smiling straight across at him, making a thumbs-up sign, as the congregation launched into 'Jerusalem'.

Isa, his saturnine face lit up, a cigarette concealed in his left hand, was whispering to Tabitha as they came down the aisle.

Oh, please let it be OK, prayed Lucy.

Helen followed, in great embarrassment, on Jake Lovell's arm. His limp was so bad that their progress was painfully slow.

Eddie tugged Taggie's sleeve.

'Wasn't that the fellow Helen ran off with at the Los Angeles Olympics?' he demanded loudly. 'D'yer mean to say the bounder's done it again?'

10

After that the Marx Brothers seemed to take over. The guests were firmly shepherded upstairs for champagne cocktails in Helen's Blue Living Room, and the bride and groom disappeared for their first legal bonk.

Seeing Lucy gazing in wonder at a Sickert of a pretty dancer, Tristan joined her and in no time had learned she was twenty-eight, had worked, like him, on a number of big films and owned a lurcher called James.

'Nice scent,' he said, scooping up several asparagus rolls.

'It's called Bluebell. It reminds me of home.'

'Where's that?'

'The Lake District.'

'Ought to be called Daffodils, then. "I wandered lonely as a cloud." How did you meet Tabitha?'

'At a Compassion in World Farming rally. We were trying to stop a lorry taking baby calves abroad. When the driver and his mate got out of their lorry because we were blocking the road, Tabitha jumped in, backed up the lorry and drove it away. They arrested her just before the motorway.'

'What was she going to do with them?' Tristan noticed Lucy refusing chicken vol-au-vents.

'Let them loose in her father's fields. We both spent the night in gaol. It sort of bonds you. We've been friends ever since. She's got absolutely no side,' she added humbly. 'And she's so beautiful. I make up so many faces but hers is easily the best.'

'You do excellent job today. Look, Lucy.'

When he spoke her name in that husky Gérard Depardieu voice, Lucy was lost.

'We start filming *Don Carlos* next April for three month, maybe more,' he went on. 'I would like to offer you the make-up job. Would you be free?'

'Yes, please,' gasped Lucy. She'd have cancelled anything.

'Singers are very highly strung,' sighed Tristan. 'They can't pack their voices away in a case like other musicians. But if you can calm Tabitha you would have no problem, I think.'

Having discovered they both shared a pathological loathing of ramblers and deliberately neglected their woods in the hope a rotten tree might fall on one, Eddie had taken an unaccountable shine to Rannaldini.

'How far d'you go?' he said, peering out of the window.

'The whole hog every time,' giggled Meredith. 'Oh, do look at the bride.'

Helen had removed her fox-fur hat because it flattened her hair but, to her horror, Tabitha had just returned in jeans and a navy blue polo-neck, which had pulled most of the freesias out of her hair. 'I was cold, Mummy,' she protested, feeding vol-au-vents to Sharon the Labrador, who had a pink bow round her neck.

'Champagne, Mrs Lovell?' said a lisping, mocking voice.

As Tory Lovell swung round, her sudden desolation that Rannaldini's evil henchman, Clive, was addressing her new daughter-in-law rather than herself was almost palpable.

'The make-up artist is most important person on the set,' Tristan was now telling Lucy, as they admired an olive-green wood by J. S. Cotman. 'She is first person an actor see in the morning. If she say, "I haven't been paid for weeks, the director's a bastard," it poison atmosphere.'

'You couldn't be a bastard,' blurted out Lucy, then went scarlet as he glanced at her bare wedding-ring finger. 'It's hard to be in a long-term relationship if you're a make-up artist. On location, you tend to slip into *affaires*. I had a boyfriend at home, but we've just broken up,' she confessed, in her soft Cumbrian accent. 'He was fed up with me being always away. Said he wanted Marks and Spencer's dinners and someone who listened in the evenings. Weddings always make you feel a bit bleak.' She must be drunk already. She could tell this man anything, and he hadn't volunteered a word about himself.

'Are you married?' she asked.

Tristan shook his head.

'Perhaps that's why I too make films – you become part of big family and kid yourself you're not alone.'

'Who gave you those gorgeous cufflinks?' Meredith admired Isa's sapphires. 'Are they a present from the bride?'

'No, the best man,' said Isa.

'And let the best man win,' murmured Baby.

Tab, who had been lighting a cigarette, looked round sharply, but as she opened her mouth to retort, Helen tapped her on the shoulder.

'Can you *please* rescue poor Tristan? He's been stuck for ages with your friend Lucy.'

'No-one gets stuck with Lucy,' snapped Tab. 'You chuck him a life-belt if you're worried.'

'Dinner is served,' announced the fearsome Bussage.

Waiters holding candles guided the guests past tapestries and suits of armour down dark, wandering passages to the Great Hall, which looked stupendous. A string quartet was playing in the minstrels' gallery. The

111

red and gold mural of trumpeters, harpists and fiddlers gleamed in the flickering light of hundreds of candles.

A bottle-green cloth stretched the length of the huge table. Mrs Brimscombe and the maids had risen at dawn to search the woods and intersperse the gold plate and the glittering armada of cut glass with beautiful red and gold fungi and the last coloured leaves of autumn.

In front of a huge organ rising to the ceiling, a side table groaned with silver dishes of oysters, giant prawns, vermilion lobster, slices of sole in cream sauce and stuffed sea bass. Carrying on the main table's colour scheme were great bowls of tomato mayonnaise, *sauce verte* and gleaming gold Hollandaise. And this was only the first course.

At dinner Lucy lost Tristan. She was stuck between a dull Lovell cousin and Little Cosmo, who she felt sure was about to slice a red-spotted toadstool into her food. Tristan was next to Helen, who bombarded him with questions about *Don Carlos*, then interrupted with her own views, 'I mean, the poor old Grand Inquisitor was visually challenged,' when Tristan tried to answer them.

She was far more tense than she had been in Prague, her hazel eyes constantly policing the room for women who might be getting off with Rannaldini, particularly the adorable Taggie, whom Rannaldini, in a fit of mega-malice, had seated between himself and Jake Lovell.

Taggie didn't know which man unnerved her more. Rannaldini was being unbelievably charming. Knowing what a great cook she was, he found her the tenderest piece from the saddle of lamb, then sought her opinion on the russet apples glazed with Cumberland sauce. Would Bramleys have added more piquancy?

Taggie mumbled truthfully that it was all delicious, but she couldn't forget the hideous way Rannaldini had treated her friend Kitty, while she was married to him. Jake, on the other hand, was like a small thunder-cloud.

'I'm desperately sorry about this,' stammered Taggie.

'No more sorry than we are,' said Jake bleakly.

Down the table, the bride sat between Baby and Isa, a cigarette in one hand, a fork in the other, her eyes crossing, hardly taking in the horse talk that flowed across her.

Poor red-eyed Tory Lovell tried to hide her despair. She and Jake had managed to patch up their marriage miraculously but now she'd have to see Helen, with whom Jake had once been so hopelessly in love, at the baby's christening and at birthday parties for years to come. She wished she liked Tab more. She shouldn't be smoking and drinking like that, it was so bad for the baby. Tory had so longed for her first grandchild.

When Tab cut her cake, she most audibly wished for an Olympic gold for The Engineer. People were beginning to table-hop. Jake joined Isa and Baby, ignoring Tab, who got to her feet.

'Musht go to the loo.'

'Aren't you going to throw us your bouquet,' called Meredith, 'so we can see who's going to get hitched next?'

Instead Tab threw her flowers high into the rafters, but as the single women and Meredith surged forward, she reached out and caught them herself.

'I'm the one who's going to need it,' she said, glancing enigmatically at Isa.

With distress, Tristan noticed the delight on Rannaldini's face then turned and caught the satisfaction on Baby's. Rannaldini was clearly as crazy about poor little Tab as Baby was about the cool, sinister Isa.

A family drama in a princely house, he thought wryly, which was how Verdi had described *Don Carlos*.

Eddie Campbell-Black was nose to nose with Lady Chisledon.

'I do wish they did soap operas about people of our class,' she was saying.

* * *

Lucy had never met anyone quite like Little Cosmo. 'What are you going to do for a living?' she asked.

'I'm going to lead paedophiles on and then blackmail them,' said Little Cosmo, who was lighting a joint.

His mother, who wished to speak to her director, plonked herself between Tristan and Helen. 'Tory Lovell is such a charmer,' she said pointedly.

Helen flounced off.

Everyone was wandering back to their seats for the speeches. Not wanting to be landed with Hermione, Tristan introduced her to Baby.

'No, we haven't met,' said Baby, 'but we share the same colourist in Mount Street.'

Hermione, who'd always sworn her rich brown hair was natural, was absolutely furious. Making a hasty getaway, Tristan sidled up to Taggie. God, she was adorable.

'I hear you adopt children from Colombia,' he said. 'I once recce'd a film there. The people are ravishing.'

Taggie melted instantly and was soon telling him about Bianca's adventures in the nativity play.

'"I love acting, Mummy," she said yesterday, "but I hate being watched." I'm not boring you?' she asked anxiously.

'Never, never,' murmured Tristan. 'My singers, alas, love being watched but hate acting.'

Taggie was shyly producing photos of Xav and Bianca when she felt a laser of jealousy from Tab and hurriedly shoved them away.

'Stop doing a number on Isa's divine stepmother-in-law, Tristan, I want to make a speech,' shouted Baby, who had clearly recovered his high spirits.

'In a minute, like Leporello,' he bashed the table with a spoon, 'I'm going to list all the men, women and kangaroos Isa's been to bed with but first I want to read out the telegrams. Here's an excellent one for Tabitha: "Are you sure you're doing the right thing, darling? love, Granny."'

After a long pause, this was greeted by screams of laughter.

'Wonderful woman,' said Eddie, who was trying to light a Gristik. 'Propose to her every Christmas, know we'll end up together.'

'Sit down and shut up, Baby,' called out Rannaldini, with a big pussy-cat smile. 'I'm the one who's making the speech.'

'Helen's not with us,' called out Lady Chisledon.

Next moment, the mother of the bride came rushing in.

'I cannot believe it. Someone has set fire to my fur hat. Tabitha!' she rounded furiously on her daughter.

'Must have been Lucy,' said Tab, collapsing on to her husband's knee. 'She's so anti people wearing fur.'

'I never!' stammered Lucy.

'Sort it out later,' said Rannaldini. 'Sit down,' he added chillingly.

Helen sat, red blotches of rage staining her neck.

'Brilliant cake, Mrs Brimscombe,' shouted Tab, taking a bite of Baby's untouched piece.

Both Jake and Tory had looked at her in horror.

'Spit it out,' Tory wanted to shout, but it was too late.

'Ladies and gentlemen,' began Rannaldini silkily, 'it is with great pleasure . . .'

But for once he was talking to air as Rupert stalked in. He was wearing a crumpled lightweight suit and must have hitched a lift from Bogotá on someone else's jet.

'Enter the Pin-up from Penscombe,' whispered Meredith in ecstasy.

Aware that Rupert was the father of Xavier, whom he had bullied so dreadfully, Little Cosmo slid under the table.

'Hello, Daddy,' called out Tabitha.

For a second Rupert glared round, taking in first the bride, his daughter, on Isa's knee, then his father, with his hand down Lady Chisledon's shirt, and finally the bride's stepmother, who was also his wife, cringing between Jake Lovell and a smirking Rannaldini. His fury was as blasting as nerve gas.

Only Hermione was unaffected. 'Rupert Campbell-Black! Just in time for the dancing!' she cried, charging him like an excited buffalo.

Stepping out of her way, Rupert chucked an envelope on the dark green tablecloth. Clive, who shadowed Rannaldini's every move, was gliding in from the right.

'Venturer are pulling out of *Don Carlos*,' said Rupert softly. 'You can fucking well survive on your own.'

'But you're the chief backer,' hissed Rannaldini, 'and the contracts—'

'Have not been signed,' interrupted Rupert. 'You should stop your Rottweiler lawyers being so greedy. And that's only the opening shot, you poisoned dwarf.'

Then, totally ignoring a frantically mouthing Taggie, Rupert turned on his heel and stalked out.

'Rupert Campbell-Black gets away with being rude because he's very posh,' announced the muffled voice of Little Cosmo.

'Penis angelicus,' sang Tabitha, and slid under the table to join him.

11

The following day Rannaldini, Tristan and Sexton, who'd been heartbroken not to be asked to the wedding, held an emergency meeting. Without Venturer's millions the film was seriously in jeopardy. They couldn't postpone because it was written into Alpheus's contract that they would finish at the latest by the end of June. Sexton was particularly gutted: he had not only regarded Rupert as a terrific gent, who was shit-hot with money, but also as comfortingly much of a musical Philistine as he was himself.

Rannaldini was just sighing that he would love to help out financially but what with the wedding and tax bills looming . . . when Tristan took a deep breath – after all he had no dependants – and said as soon as the French lawyers stopped wrangling, Liberty Productions could have the bulk of the money Étienne had grudgingly left him. Then he suggested they economize by filming in modern dress, drawing parallels between the Spanish and the English royal families.

'Grite, grite!' cried Sexton in excitement. 'Princess Di as Elisabetta – the Americans will go apeshit! And we can change Charles V's ghost into the Queen Muvver.'

'Don't be fatuous, Sexton,' snapped Rannaldini.

To Rannaldini's delight, however, Tristan then proposed they film at Valhalla, which would be much

117

cheaper. 'You have mausoleum, dungeons, cloisters, and huge state rooms.'

'And we can save on location fees, travel expenses and hotels by putting the cast up at Valhalla,' said Rannaldini gleefully, envisaging unlimited extensions and redecorating on the budget. 'Once recording's over, we'll recce Buckingham Palace to get the thing authentic.'

'If the leaves are back on the trees by the time we start shooting,' added Tristan, 'we can always send a second unit to film the opening scenes in Romania where it'll still be winter.'

'Sounds expensive,' said Rannaldini, not altogether playfully. 'We'll build in serious penalties if you don't finish the movie on time.'

Meanwhile the cast were still not turning up at rehearsals but each night Tristan and Serena Westwood spent hours on the floor of Tristan's flat, shuffling papers trying to schedule the recording. It was like wrestling with some massive seating plan, fitting in with singers' availability and keeping the difficult ones apart.

'Tricky when they're *all* difficult,' sighed Serena.

'I suppose Rannaldini will have to turn up for the recording,' said Tristan wearily.

Serena smirked because the Maestro was still finding time to take her to bed. But, to her irritation and despite heavy hints, Tristan still hadn't made a move on her.

The recording itself was held in a huge assembly room attached to Wallsend Town Hall in north-east London. As the orchestra straggled in on the first day, in early January, the temperature plummeted below zero. Snow lay thickly over the regimented beds of wallflowers and pansies. Lengthening icicles glittered from the gutters in the morning sun. Inside the hall it was even colder: the central heating had been switched off in case gurgles and clicks were picked up on the tape.

'It's going to be breathe-in time for everyone,' said a fat female member of the chorus, looking round the tiny gallery with disapproval. Down below technicians were trying to find room for all the orchestral chairs and music stands, and putting green bottles of water by every singer's microphone.

The off-stage band had ill-advisedly been sent to play in the bar where an impromptu rehearsal for soloists, who had deigned to turn up, was also under way. Hearing screeching, Sexton, who was heroically trying to get into the jargon, remarked that Dame Hermione was 'in fine voice'.

'Chance would be a fine thing! That's the chorus master,' said Serena sourly.

'Do you have a pass, sir?' asked a man on the door, as Rannaldini stalked in, chocolate brown from skiing.

'It's Maestro Rannaldini!' hissed the other doorman. 'Where have you been? Outer space?'

Within seconds, Rannaldini was rowing with both Serena and Tristan, and changing everything. Half an hour later, Hermione swept in and started yelling that her dressing room was too small and too far from the stage, and she had nowhere to warm up.

'How dare you send me yellow roses that are fully out when you know I only like buds?' she then shouted at Christy Foxe, Serena's PA, a little scrubbed-faced school-leaver, who had just staggered in with Hermione's four suitcases. 'And don't forget I always have a glass of chilled champagne at eleven.'

'No need to fucking chill it in *this* hall,' muttered Christy, making his escape.

Rannaldini was now altering the schedule. No matter that the chorus, who had been booked for the day at vast expense, would be cooling their heels, he wished to kick off the recording with Hermione's last duet with Franco. When Fat Franco didn't show up, Rannaldini dragged him out of another recording studio in Rome and sacked him.

'That's a million saved for a start,' he told Tristan glee-fully, as he put down the telephone.

When Franco's agent came on the line in apoplexy, Rannaldini countered suavely that the final contract had not been signed, again due to lawyers wrangling; and, if it had, Franco was in default for not having attended a single rehearsal or having lost a kilo of weight. 'He hasn't got a fat leg to stand on.'

'How can you fire the finest tenor in the world?'

'*Pour encourager les autres.*'

As shock-horror at the sacking ricocheted round the world, Liberty Productions called a press conference to announce their new leading man: 'The dazzling, drop-dead gorgeous, honey-toned Australian tenor Baby Spinosissimo. The most exciting thing to come out of Oz since Joan Sutherland.'

'And the same sex,' muttered the *Daily Mail,* scribbling furiously.

Aware that he was getting Liberty Productions out of a hole, Baby had played terribly hard to get. When Howie Denston, now his agent, had rung to offer him the job, he had said he'd think about it. He then went screaming ecstatically round the house, before calling Isa Lovell. He was going to earn more money in a few months than in his entire life, so he could now pay his tax bill and buy that horse, Peppy something, Isa kept banging on about.

Baby rolled up at the subsequent press conference on the arm of a ravishing pony-tailed youth in a pinstripe suit. Gwynneth, the flabby crone from the Arts Council on whom Rannaldini had landed when Viking hit him across the room, was covering the event for the *Sentinel.* Wildly excited, she whisked the pinstriped youth from group to group, introducing him reverently as 'Mr Spinosissimo's partner'.

'How long have you and Baby been together?' asked the *Telegraph.*

'Oh, he picked me up in the car park half an hour ago,' grinned the youth.

'D'you prefer guys to women, Baby?' asked the *Mirror*.

'I prefer sheep,' said Baby. 'If sheep could cook, I'd marry one.'

Over the roars of laughter, a blonde from the *Scorpion* called out, 'Who's this guy Schiller who's done the tie-in?'

'Shriller, if it's Dame Hermione,' drawled Baby.

The only obstacles ahead seemed to be that Baby must lose a stone before filming, if he were to look suitably lovelorn, and that the *Don Carlos* press officer, Bruce Cassidy, predictably nicknamed 'Hype-along', would have to try to hide the fact that Baby swung every which way including koala bears.

In another corner of the room, as the loudspeakers played Posa and Carlos's Friendship Duet, Rannaldini and Tristan told a battery of cameras and tape-machines how delighted they were Baby was taking over and how equally excited they were about their new Russian discovery Mikhail Pezcherov. Rannaldini did most of the talking, as Tristan lit one Gauloise from another and looked languidly beautiful.

'Bankable and bonkable,' wrote the *Mail*.

'You've been called the Italian stallion and the Kraut lout, Sir Roberto,' piped up the *Scorpion*, 'how come the Frog Prince is making a film with you?'

'Rannaldini,' said Tristan, in that husky, smoky accent with a slight break in it that sent shivers down every woman's spine, 'as my godfather and friend, has inspired and encouraged me. It has been my lifelong ambition to work with him on *Don Carlos*. I have every confidence in our collaboration.'

12

Alas, the recording was continually embattled. For a start, Rannaldini was only interested in the music sounding as he wanted. He would scrap even Hermione's most glorious take if he didn't like the intonation of the clarinets. Nor would he adjust his tempo to suit a singer, and had no intention of adjusting it for Tristan, for whom the timing of every bar was crucial.

Normally in films, music is added later to enhance the action, but in filming an opera, the action has to fit already recorded music. Thus, Tristan kept having to halt Rannaldini if he played something too fast or too slowly because when it came to filming the relevant singer wouldn't have the right amount of time to run to the centre of the maze or indulge in a passionate clinch.

Rannaldini detested this. He had arranged for a camera to be on him constantly while he was conducting, so that the video could be shown on a huge monitor to guide the singers on location. Such was his monstrous vanity that he required endless lighting rehearsals, and would hold up a hundred musicians, not to mention singers, chorus and technicians, all on overtime, for twenty minutes while his hair was brushed and the shine taken off his nose. Once started, though, he was reluctant to be halted except at his own whim.

Nor were his singers behaving any better. Hermione was staying at the Lanesborough, Chloe at the Capital.

The hotels were only a stone's throw apart, but both divas insisted on travelling in different limos. When she discovered that Chloe's dressing room was bigger than hers, Hermione was enraged and duly took her revenge the next day.

Singers are reputed to sing less well when they have their periods. Their vocal cords thicken and the diaphragm supporting the voice becomes sore and easily tired.

Next day Chloe recorded her great aria, 'O Don Fatale', and denounced her 'fatal gift of beauty' so gloriously, but with such controlled venom, it was impossible not to think it was part of her character. As she came to the end, however, and before the strings could tap their bows on the backs of their chairs in congratulation, Hermione had produced a Tampax from her bag, and thrusting it towards her, asked solicitously, 'Are you needing this, dear?'

Chloe was outraged.

'I can't believe you're still young enough to use those things,' she snarled back, and retaliated later in the day by dropping her handbag in the middle of an exquisite take of Hermione's aria in Act II. This triggered a five-minute screaming match, with Hermione threatening to walk out. Only Tristan managed to calm her.

'There are women, Hermione,' deliberately he made his voice even huskier, 'who Verdi claimed are "born for others, who are quite unaware of their own egos, and who rise above the petty squabbles of lesser mortals".'

Hermione was so moved she behaved herself for the rest of the afternoon.

On the other hand, she was not the only member of the cast to be worried that Fat Franco had been ousted by an unknown Australian. At least Franco would have ensured that *Don Carlos* was a commercial success. Confidence was restored, however, the moment Baby opened his mouth. The entire orchestra turned round to gawp, and at the end of his first duet with Chloe,

Mikhail put down the score he was studying, ran across the hall and flung his arms round Baby. 'You have most beautiful voice I ever hear. It will be privilege to vork with you.'

Mikhail's own voice was just as impressive: Posa's death scene had everyone in tears. Mikhail, however, was easily demoralized, particularly by Alpheus the bass who, in the great duet between Philip II and Posa, kept sighing and wearily holding the bridge of his nose between finger and thumb, as Mikhail, with his poor command of English, fluffed line after line.

Baby and Mikhail on the other hand took to each other instantly, almost as an extension of their comradely role in the opera. In the evening they went on pub crawls, rehearsing their songs for the next day to the noisy delight of the punters. They tried to take Tristan with them but, to their disappointment, he insisted on returning alone to a friend's flat he had borrowed overlooking Regent's Park. After all the rows and hysterics, he needed peace to study the next day's score.

Mysteriously with Mikhail's arrival things started to disappear. Serena mislaid some pearl earrings, Alpheus some gold cufflinks. Chloe had quite fancied Mikhail until a large topaz ring, the only decent present Alpheus had ever given her, went missing. The cutlery in the canteen had to be replaced twice in a week. Only Baby, Mikhail's buddy, remained unfleeced, which convinced Hermione, who'd made an unbelievable fuss about a missing umbrella, that he must be the thief.

'All Australians are descended from convicts.'

'I have never stolen anything in my life except thunder,' snapped Baby.

Poor little Christy Foxe, the PA, had the thankless task of getting the cast to the right mikes on time. A singer meant to sound far away has to stand back from the mike, but if, in the middle of a number, he has a love scene with another singer, he has to rush to the mike next to them.

In the ensemble numbers, therefore, it was like Waterloo in the rush-hour, with little Christy shunting Dame Hermione, like a cattle truck, in one direction, and the chorus master propelling Alpheus, like the Intercity Express, in the other. Collisions, screaming-matches, kicks on the shin and slapped faces were inevitable.

There were more rows in the control room, which was where singers flocked after a stint of recording to listen to the playback and try to persuade Serena and Sylvestre, Tristan's handsome blond French sound engineer, to use the take in which they had sounded best.

Baby, who knew he sounded best in everything, got so bored even of listening to his own voice, not even hand-some Sylvestre could distract him, so he frequently started dancing round the recording-machines, much to Alpheus's disapproval.

Alpheus already disapproved of Granny's hunky boyfriend, Giuseppe, because if Giuseppe's consump-tion of red wine didn't impair the beauty of his voice he might one day topple Alpheus in leading bass roles, as Alpheus had toppled Granny. Alpheus also disapproved of Granny, who sat calmly knitting colourful squares for a patchwork quilt for his and Giuseppe's bed, shaking with laughter at his own even more colourful asides. He hardly bothered to put down his needles when he sang, but chilled the blood every time he opened his mouth to deliver the words of the Grand Inquisitor.

Alpheus disapproved most of all of the orchestra.

'I think the brass section have been drinking,' he complained, during an evening session.

'I should be extremely surprised if they hadn't,' said the orchestra manager calmly.

In turn, the orchestra, who worked flat out at every session, thoroughly disapproved of the singers, regard-ing them as lazy, stupid, hypochondriacal, hysterical and grossly overpaid. They did, however, forgive Baby, because he made them laugh and was monumentally generous. Whenever hampers or crates of wine rolled in from his increasing army of fans, they were handed over to the orchestra. Alpheus, who begrudged giving away anything, was horrified. No wonder Baby had difficulty with tax bills.

Meanwhile, Chloe and Alpheus had worked out their schedule so that whenever neither of them was singing they could slope off to bed.

The ladies of the chorus also thought Alpheus was yummy, and whiled away long, cold hours gazing at him. Predominantly middle-aged, given to baggy jerseys and straining leggings, they were of little interest to Alpheus. One member of the chorus, however, Gloria Prescott, rose like Venus from the permanent waves and was nick-named 'Pushy Galore' because she always pushed her way to the front, nodding, gesticulating, shaking her blonde ringleted head and overacting to catch the director's or conductor's eye. She also sucked up to Dame Hermione.

'Ay am *such* a fan.'

So Hermione befriended Pushy to infuriate Chloe. Alpheus, Rannaldini, Sexton, Sylvestre and Mikhail had all clocked Pushy. In return, Pushy whispered constantly in all their ears, including Tristan's, that her greatest role at music college had been Elisabetta and wouldn't she be younger and prettier in the role than Dame Hermione? One morning she was practising one of Hermione's arias, and hitting all the high notes perfectly, when Rannaldini's vulpine smile came round the door.

'Would you like me to accompany you, my child?' Then, as he was tinkling away, 'You see, I am not such an ogre. When I say thees or that ees bad, it is because I have ears to 'ear the wrong things.'

The chorus were not booked for the following day, but Rannaldini confided to Pushy that he would specially like to send a limo for her tomorrow afternoon so she could hear the orchestra recording the overture that he himself had composed, and then perhaps they could have tea at the Ritz. Pushy was in heaven.

But if Rannaldini was histrionic when he conducted Verdi he was ten times more difficult when it came to his own music. Having reduced the orchestra to nervous wrecks in the rehearsal beforehand he started rowing with an increasingly demented Tristan.

'If you take it that fast,' yelled Tristan, 'the hunt will never have time to stream down the valley.'

'Then they must stream queeker.'

'Then you will lose magical flowing effect.'

'I must be faithful to my music.'

'First time bastard's been faithful to anything,' muttered Viking O'Neill, the first horn.

'I must be faithful to story,' shouted Tristan.

'OK, we rehearse two ways: queek then flowing.'

Rannaldini proceeded to take his overture at a breakneck speed, his stick a blur, and then at such a funereal pace that the strings ran out of bow, the wood-wind and the brass out of puff, and all got screamed at again.

Tristan nearly killed Rannaldini. So did Serena, when she saw the ringleted, beribboned Pushy Galore at the back of the hall.

'Rannaldini said no outsiders,' she stormed.

'Sir Roberto kaindly sent a limo for me,' simpered Pushy.

Tristan sat shaking in the control room, his head in his hands.

'Quiet, please, we now record,' said Rannaldini imperiously, filling the musicians with such terror they could hardly pick up their instruments. 'Remember, gentlemen, this is for ever.'

He then took his overture at a totally different, lilting, cantering tempo to which the orchestra had a mad struggle to readjust. At the end there was utter silence. Gazing at their shoes, waiting for the inevitable explosion, his musicians didn't see the tears in Rannaldini's eyes.

'Thank you, gentlemen, that was absolutely beautiful,' he said quietly. 'You can have the rest of the afternoon off.'

So he can take me to tea at the Ritz, thought Pushy joyfully.

But ignoring Pushy, abandoning the gaping orchestra, Rannaldini bounded upstairs to the control room where, for once, Serena had lost her cool.

'You cannot waste an entire session,' she yelled, as she met him in the doorway. 'What about the introductions to the other acts?'

But her tirade faltered, as Rannaldini's hand crept inside her purple jersey.

'We shall go 'ome to your flat.'

'But Jessie is there with Nanny Bratislava.'

'Tell little Jessie she must learn to call me Uncle Roberto.'

13

The next drama to rock the recording was when Rozzy Pringle finally turned up to sing Tebaldo, Elisabetta's page. A seventies beauty, the doe-eyed, long-legged Rozzy was so like Celia Johnson that everyone had wanted to have unbrief encounters with her. She was much too old for the part, but at least she'd make Hermione look young, and she had a host of fans.

Granny and Rannaldini, who'd often worked with her, admired her inordinately. Serena and Alpheus had long collected her records. On the other hand, Hermione disliked all other sopranos on principle, and Mikhail, Baby and Chloe, being from a younger generation, scoffed that Rozzy was past it.

Tristan was livid with them. Enchanted at the prospect of working with one of his heroines, he filled Rozzy's dressing room with spring flowers.

But when Rozzy finally came through the door, on a dank, grey, viciously cold morning, he was appalled. She looked old enough to be Hermione's grandmother, and was purple with cold to match the darned violet blazer she was wearing over her long, flowered dress. To combat the ageing hippie look, she had curled up her hair but it had dropped in the fog, and fell in lank straight tresses over her jutting collarbones. Everyone greeted her effusively to conceal their shock.

'Hi, Rozzy, I'm such a fan,' said Chloe, clanking

cheeks. Then, ten seconds later to Baby, 'She must have lied about her age in *Who's Who*. She'll never see fifty again.'

Having thrust a beautifully wrapped present into Tristan's hand, 'a little something because you're so kind to book me', Rozzy fled to the loo.

'Such a drag having Rozzy Pringle here, stinking out the lav again,' grumbled Hermione, half an hour later, as little Christy Foxe propelled her towards the microphone.

'You have to move to mike four, next to Baby, in bar forty-five, Dame Hermione,' he reminded her for the tenth time. Then, consulting his score, he said, smiling at Rozzy as she crept grey and shaking out of her dressing room, 'You start off standing twelve feet from mike two, then move up close to mike three, Mrs Pringle.'

'Don't worry,' Tristan put his bomber jacket round Rozzy's trembling shoulders. 'Tebaldo's just as petrified as you in this scene. Just make sure those opening "Hey theres" really ring out.'

Rozzy, Baby and Hermione were all in place, their breath rising in white plumes as Rannaldini swept in.

'Morning, Rozzy, lovely to have you with us. Shall we catch up over a spot of lunch?' he called out, eliciting scowls from Serena, Pushy and Hermione.

It was too early for the offstage band, waiting in the bar, to have got drunk. Seeing Rannaldini raise his stick on the monitor, Viking O'Neill came in with the mournful, fading sob of the departing hunting horn.

'"All is silent, night approaches, and the first star glitters on the horizon,"' sang Baby, who worked the mike like a rock star.

Now they'll eat their bitchy words, thought Tristan, as Rannaldini nodded, smiling at Rozzy, but despite her anguished face and frenzied mouthings, no 'Hey theres' came out.

Rannaldini halted the orchestra. –

'Rozzy?'

'Sorry, Maestro.'

'From the top.' He raised his baton.

Viking's horn, then Baby, both hauntingly exquisite, were followed by silence, and a dreadful, strangulated croak.

'Relax, Rozzy, one, two, three,' called Rannaldini.

Rozzy's heart was crashing, the blood pumping through her veins, but her throat was drier than the desert. Even after ten minutes of struggling, all she could produce were scraping gasps. Tristan, in the control room, felt as if he was watching a dog, whose vocal cords had been cut in the vivisection clinic, trying to cry out as the surgeon's knife went in. By the time he had run down into the hall, Rannaldini had lost his temper.

'How dare you call yourself a professional singer?' he was screaming.

'You've let us all down,' reproached Hermione, as Rozzy fled to her dressing room, her body racked as much with coughing as with sobs.

Rannaldini picked up the telephone to the control room.

'Who booked her, for Christ's sake?'

'You and Tristan did,' snapped Serena. 'We're going to have to reschedule.'

'Tebaldo was my favourite part at college,' piped up Pushy.

Rozzy's present to Tristan was a cushion, green velvet on one side, the other exquisitely embroidered with the words, 'The Lily in the Valley'.

Tristan couldn't bear unhappiness. Leaving everyone fighting, and Baby and Hermione to finish their duet, he drove Rozzy to Harley Street with his car heater turned up.

She had had a terrible Christmas, she revealed, between sobs, yelling at insolent stepchildren, placating Glyn, her idle husband, coping with his frightful mother, who kept commiserating with him for being neglected by a wife who was always selfishly pursuing a career. Matters had not been helped when Rozzy had nipped off on 28 December to sing Mimì in a cheap Hungarian production to pay a tax bill, before singing Brünnhilde, with laryngitis, in Athens three days later. Brünnhilde's immolation scene had done for her.

Why the fuck did you risk it? Tristan wanted to shout.

The throat specialist said Rozzy had thoroughly over-strained her voice. He couldn't promise that it would come back and she certainly couldn't sing in the recording.

Seated in Tristan's car once more, Rozzy cried so hard that passers-by – swept down Harley Street by the north wind – gazed in horror.

'People will think I am woman-beater,' grumbled Tristan, and drove her to his flat overlooking Regent's Park, which glittered with hoar frost in the midday sun. All round the walls of the sitting room were propped photographs of the cast.

'I like to live with my characters,' explained Tristan.

'Past and present,' said Rozzy, picking up a large photograph of Claudine Lauzerte in its own silver frame. 'I wish I looked as good as that now.' Wincing, as she glanced in the mirror she wiped mascara from under her eyes. 'People used to say Claudine and I were a little alike.'

'A little.' Tristan smiled as he handed her a vast Bloody Mary.

She looked half starved. He couldn't have her blubbing all over a restaurant. He'd been too uptight himself to eat the Chinese takeaway he'd brought home last night. Perhaps he could heat it up for Rozzy.

'I'm sorry to be such a drip,' she said, following him into the kitchen. 'Yesterday I discovered Glyn had appropriated thirty thousand pounds I'd saved for my tax bill to subsidize some dodgy property deal.

'He's also employed an incredibly pretty temporary

housekeeper called Sylvia at vast expense for the few days I was going to be away recording *Carlos*. This morning I took my mother-in-law Go-Cat in her breakfast bowl instead of muesli . . .' Rozzy started to cry again.

'You're just overtired,' said Tristan, putting an arm round her shoulders. 'I found my washing in the dishwasher this morning, and my car keys in the fridge.'

He let her run on as he got out the takeaway. The waxy topping of orange fat looked disgusting.

'I can't go home tonight,' Rozzy was whispering to herself. 'Glyn'll think I'm spying on him and Sylvia. Oh, Tristan, what are we going to live on if I can't sing any more?'

For once when his mobile rang Tristan was relieved.

It was Baby in ecstasy, and having a large vodka, because Christy Foxe, who'd been such a trooper, had finally walked out.

'He was fed up shunting Hermione around,' explained Baby, 'Rannaldini being so vile to Rozzy was the final straw. The brave little lad got up and sang "The Prisoners' Chorus" from *Fidelio*. After he'd gone, he sent Rannaldini a message on his bleeper, saying, "Stuff job up your ass, rude letter to follow."'

Tristan started to laugh.

'After Christy walked out,' went on Baby gleefully, 'Alpheus, too vain to put on his glasses and too busy ogling Pushy Galore, failed to read Christy's last pencil note on the score saying, "Please move back here, Herd of Elephant coming through", so Dame Hermione ran slap into him. Hermione is now suing for a broken toe, Alpheus for a broken rib. I think you'd better find another PA, Tristan.'

Grinning and shaking his head, Tristan switched off his mobile.

'We're in luck. You can stay on at the Capital, and take over Christy's job. You know *Don Carlos* backwards. And because you're wonderful at sewing – that is most beautiful cushion I ever have – when we go on location, you can stop Griselda, the wardrobe mistress, having nervous breakdown. And to keep you on the cast list,' Tristan chucked the takeaway cartons in the bin, 'you can have the non-singing role of the Countess of Aremberg. All you'll have to do is cry when the King sacks you, and you're very good at that. Come on, I'll buy you lunch.'

Rozzy got to her feet unsteadily. As he caught her before she fell, Tristan felt her desperate boniness.

'You are the kindest person I've ever met,' she said, in a choked voice.

Sexton and Serena, however, shook their heads at such unilateral brokering of a deal, and Rannaldini went ballistic at such prodigality: a singer's salary for a neurotic geriatric PA.

That night, in revenge for Alpheus ogling Pushy, Chloe invited Sylvestre, Tristan's handsome blond sound engineer, back to the Capital and discovered he was as good at twiddling knobs in bed as out. Afterwards, as they shared a bottle of Dom Pérignon on Liberty Productions, Sylvestre sighed that Tristan was too kind for his own good.

'We had location manager on *Lily in the Valley* so useless he couldn't find his own cock. Tristan called him into his caravan to sack him, but he spent so much time listing his good points so as not to demoralize him that the guy came out three hours later convinced he'd been promoted.'

More seriously, they were now without a page who, in Tristan's new present-day version, had become a bodyguard. Tebaldo is not a huge part, but a vital one, a larky little fellow, usually played by a charming *gamin*.

Pushy Galore came forward immediately, ringlets and ribbons flying. She knew the part, could she audition? Rannaldini, Sexton, and Alpheus were all keen.

'Give the young woman a chance,' urged Hermione, because she knew it would irritate Chloe, who longed secretly to be admired and promoted by Hermione.

Serena, however, wanted to kick in Pushy's buck teeth, because she was always making eyes at Rannaldini, and Tristan thought her ghastly and far too refined to play a bodyguard.

The argument was at full throttle in the control room when Viking wandered in. Despite their earlier differences, he had played like an angel throughout the sessions, and he and Rannaldini had achieved a grudging, if transient, respect.

'Here's one soprano who isn't working at the moment.' He chucked a photograph on the table.

The girl wore an ivory silk shift. She had a shiny dark red bob, pale gold skin sprinkled with freckles like a tiger lily, and cool, watchful green eyes.

Viking put a tape in the machine. Her voice was of such piercing, distinctive sweetness that Tristan had to hear only a few bars.

'Bravo, Viking, who is she?'

'Flora Seymour – she's Georgie Maguire's daughter, so it's in the genes. She played the viola in my old orchestra, but trained as a singer as well. She's got the most angelic voice in the world.'

'Give me her telephone number,' said Tristan.

He met a lot of opposition. Serena, Hermione and Chloe all thought Flora was a tramp, probably because she'd had *affaires* with both Rannaldini and Viking, and because they'd all three had designs in the past on the filthy rich, if slightly shady, George Hungerford, with whom Flora was now living.

Rannaldini didn't want any advice from Viking and he'd fallen out badly with Flora. But he doted on her voice, which had never been properly exploited. He was enough of a mischief-maker as well to see the potential for avenging himself on Flora's lover, George Hungerford, who as managing director of the Rutminster

Symphony Orchestra had foiled Rannaldini's takeover bid and who, as a developer, was also threatening to slap a motorway through Valhalla.

Sexton, who was watching the mounting costs in horror, was in favour because Flora sounded cheap.

'How d'you know her so well?' asked Tristan.

'I was once hopelessly in love with her,' said Viking.

Answering his mobile, he wandered out of earshot to speak to his new wife. 'Abby darling, I love you too. I've also been matchmaking,' he lowered his voice. 'I've posted Tristan de Montigny down to Rutminster Hall to see Flora.'

14

Flora sat naked on the white shagpile drying her hair. In the long gilt bedroom mirror she could see three moles on her inside thigh and soft red pubic hair, still damp from the bath. Her small freckled breast rose every time she lifted her arm, but her two spare tyres didn't shift.

Schiller's *Don Carlos* was now open between legs grown far too chunky to play a page-boy poncing about in white tights. She mustn't get too engrossed in the story, or she'd forget her hair and the sleek bob would shoot upwards like an explosion in a mattress factory.

'A hundred eyes are hired,' she read.

Surrounded by George's guards, who watched her every move, Flora identified with Carlos. Then she looked up at George's photograph on her dressing-table: cropped-haired, square-jawed, dark brown turned-down eyes, mouth set like a steel trap in the Harvey Smith/John Prescott rough, tough North Country mould – himself against the world. Only Flora knew how sensitive and kind George was behind the façade, but he was terribly possessive.

Having screwed up his first marriage because he was a workaholic, George had taken the autumn off to cement his relationship with Flora, but had returned to work because mega property companies and orchestras don't run themselves. Most of his time was spent in Germany. Flora wanted to travel with him, but she couldn't bear to be parted from Trevor, her little black and tan terrier, who was now asleep with a red ball in his mouth on the vast oval bed, whose headboard hummed with every dial. When she was away Trevor wouldn't eat, and neither he nor she would survive quarantine, so she stayed behind and missed George dreadfully.

Flora was also lonely because her great friend Marcus Campbell-Black, having won the Appleton, was now blissful in Moscow with Alexei Nemerovsky, and her other friend, Abigail Rosen, was having a baby and blissfully happy married to Viking.

Abby, a maternity dress hiding a non-existent bulge, had recently driven down for the day and chided Flora for putting on weight.

'You've never been an achiever, Flora. You never really concentrated on your singing career, and you've never stuck to a diet.'

'Too right,' Flora agreed gloomily. 'I'm the one who should be wearing the maternity dress.'

'George is an incredibly attractive man,' went on Abby. 'If you're going to keep him you mustn't let yourself go.'

Flora's hair was dry now. Thick as the shagpile inside, snow was growing on the window-ledge. Tomorrow she and Trevor would build a snow-dog. As she reached for her glass of champagne, Trevor flew off the bed, rushing downstairs in a frenzy of excited barking. Outside, Flora could see the lights of Rannaldini's helicopter bringing Tristan from London. Trevor had mistaken it for George's.

The heat of the hair-dryer had removed any need for blusher. Ringing her eyes with brown liner, Flora wriggled into a pair of black jeans, covered the flesh that spilled over the waistband with one of George's evening shirts, squirted on Coco Chanel and belted downstairs. The Frenchman who came through the front door with snowflakes in his hair was so handsome and so near Flora in age that she promptly had another glass

138

of champagne on an empty stomach out of shyness.

Tristan, however, noticed a Schubert quintet, in which he had often played the cello part, on the music stand in the drawing room and they were off, chattering *dix-neuf* to the dozen. Tristan was only too happy to tell Flora all about Tab's wedding because it gave him an excuse to talk about Tab.

'She's the most beautiful thing I ever saw,' confessed Flora, 'but crazy like a fox, and so volatile. It must be like being married to Mount Vesuvius. I gather Rupert pulled out of *Don Carlos* as a result.'

Tab's wedding took them down one bottle, then they moved on to the recording. As Flora's parents lived in Paradise Valley next to Rannaldini and Hermione, and she knew Chloe, Serena and Meredith too, the gossip on that took them most of the way down another. Tristan, who'd noticed all the burglar alarms and the grilles on the windows, thought Rutminster Hall was ghastly, but improved by George's Rottweilers stretched out in front of the fire. By the time they'd finished the second bottle, he'd ceased to worry about all the guards.

'Where are you filming?' she asked, as they tottered in to dinner.

'Valhalla.'

'Then I can't do it. George would never allow it,' squeaked Flora in horror, then shut up because two of George's guards were serving steak and kidney pie and pouring a matchless Margaux.

After they'd shut the door, Flora told Tristan how strapped George was for cash.

'He owes the Germans about forty million in bridging loans. If it were me I'd never sleep again. If I'd taken the part I could have helped out with a few bills, but truly I'm too fat. I've got a treble chin, although most trebles don't have chins like mine.'

Tristan laughed. He thought Flora utterly ravishing and said there would be masses of time for her to lose any weight before filming started at the end of March.

'But I haven't got page's legs.'

'As it's in modern dress, Tebaldo's become one of those handsome detectives Princess Diana and Princess Anne seemed to get so close to. So your perfectly OK legs will be hidden by trousers.'

'But the main drawback,' went on Flora, 'God, I hope this room isn't bugged, is working with Rannaldini. George is insanely jealous and has never forgiven Rannaldini for beating me up and trying to rape me last August. I promise you it's true,' she added, seeing Tristan's look of horror. 'Rannaldini wanted me to stay the night with him after singing in *The Creation* but I bolted back to George.'

Then, after a large glass of Armagnac, she said, 'I'll do it, if George says it's OK and if I can bring Trevor. Perhaps he could wear lifts and audition for one of Philip II's wolfhounds.'

Trevor wagged his stumpy tail approvingly.

As soon as Tristan left, Flora rang Germany. George was dreadfully torn. He felt sick at the thought of Flora working with Rannaldini again and neither did he want her anywhere near that impossibly glamorous Tristan de Montigny, exuding cross-Channel pheromones. But he couldn't stand in her way.

'You'd never forgive me or yourself if you turned down the break of a lifetime.'

'You're the break of my lifetime,' sobbed Flora, who half wanted George to forbid her. 'Nothing will ever be as wonderful as falling in love with you.'

The moment she rang off George regretted it. Flora would have other chances and he didn't trust Rannaldini. But when he rang back the number was engaged, even though it was two o'clock in the morning. She was obviously speaking to Tristan, accepting the part. George only just stopped himself ringing all the other numbers in the house.

Three hours later, Flora was slumped at the kitchen

table, finishing *Don Carlos* and a large tub of banana and yoghurt ice cream, when she saw more fireflies dancing in the window.

Having made a detour to the other side of Rutminster to drop some Roman coins into the excavations of a rival, to prevent him getting planning permission from English Heritage, George had landed his helicopter outside the kitchen.

As Flora, followed by a sleepy Trevor, ran across the snowy lawn into his arms, George said, 'I've got a meeting at nine in Düsseldorf, I can only stay an hour.'

'Let's spend every second of it in bed,' said Flora, dragging him upstairs.

In fact, George was angelic. A fine bass himself, he returned the following evening to help her learn the part.

Flora also received a call from Sexton.

'We're writing into your contract a clause to say you mustn't fall pregnant before the end of filming. Can't 'ave a private dick in the club.'

15

Before her first recording Flora spent the night with Abby and Viking, who had practically to drug and drag her screaming into his car to get her to Wallsend Town Hall, which had grown even colder, the icicles outside even longer. The red-nosed chorus, in their overcoats, looked like carol singers.

Flora was supposed to take over where Rozzy had not started: in the Forest of Fontainebleau with Hermione and Baby, but as a dreadful anticlimax, Hermione had just rung in for the second day running saying that the broken toe she'd sustained in her collision with Alpheus was much worse.

Tristan was so angry for Flora that he drove much too fast over icy roads back into London to the Lanesborough. Thundering on the door of Hermione's suite he was admitted by her excited PA. Hearing shrieks of agony, he thought he had misjudged his leading lady, but barging into her bedroom, found her having her legs waxed. To Hermione's fury, he immediately insisted she and one hairy leg return with him to Wallsend.

Flora, meanwhile, had been immensely comforted to find a good-luck card in her dressing room from Serena's new PA, Rozzy Pringle. She was attempting to get her trembling lips round a few arpeggios, when Rozzy herself rushed in with a mug of hot Ribena.

'Hello, my poor lamb, you mustn't be frightened.

You've got such a lovely voice. I've studied the role so if you need any help . . . I have to confess,' Rozzy went on, as she hung Flora's blue scarf on a hanger, 'I was prepared to hate you because my husband, Glyn, is so in love with your mother, he's got all her records.'

'I'll get him an advance copy of her next album,' promised Flora. 'We're all huge fans of yours.'

'Come and meet Granville Hastings,' said Rozzy. 'He's such a darling.'

'Why are there so many people here?' muttered an aghast Flora.

'You've turned up on the worst possible day,' whispered back Rozzy indignantly. 'By constantly ignoring poor Tristan's schedule and pulling out people to sing as and when he felt like it, Rannaldini's created the most appalling backlog. All the rest of the cast are here in case they have to do retakes. Poor Tristan!'

They found Granny regaling an audience with chit-chat.

'My dear child, welcome.' He put down his knitting to give Flora a kiss.

'Where the hell's Rannaldini?' Even the normally ebullient Baby was uptight over all the hanging around.

'Having a poke, I expect,' sighed Granny. 'He always poked the prettiest chorus girls at the Garden, bending them over the red velvet balcony of the royal box between rehearsals. If anyone came by, he used to pretend he was showing them round the opera-house.'

Granny rose, still knitting, and went into a sequence of languid pelvic thrusts. 'Down there ees the peet, where my orchestra play [*thrust*], and zat is rostrum where I perform miracle [*thrust*], and zat is proscenium arch [*thrust*].'

'When you 'ave feenish, Granville,' said a chilling voice.

The laughter died. Granny dropped several stitches.

'Dame 'Ermione soldier in. At least 'ave the courtesy not to keep her waiting.' Rannaldini glared round.

'Anyone got a Fisherman's Friend?' came Hermione's pathetic bleat.

Limping ostentatiously, she joined Baby and Flora on the platform.

'Just like the Teddy Bears' Picnic,' hissed Flora, glaring at Hermione's full-length mink.

'I assure you, this will be no picnic,' hissed back Baby.

Rannaldini just had to stand there. His cruel, cold, pale, malevolent face was enough to give a performance its special edge. He raised his stick. Viking's dying horn call floated out of the bar.

Flora was so terrified she began loud and sharp. It didn't take Rannaldini long to put the boot in. After the fifth take, when she'd finally got the notes right, he said, 'That was better, Flora, but you *are* expected to act.'

Flora flushed. 'But I thought—'

'Don't,' said Rannaldini crushingly. 'You do not have the necessary equipment,' he added bitchily. 'To be a singer you have to have a voice. To be a musician you have to have a brain. Don't confuse the two.'

There is a limited number of times you can ask a singer to repeat herself and get the words, notes and acting right. Rannaldini exceeded it. Flora was also slimming, and the rare perfect take was invariably wrecked by her rumbling tummy.

'This is hopeless,' yelled Rannaldini, calling a lunch break. 'We will finish scene tomorrow.'

The last day was even more tempestuous, particularly when George Hungerford rolled up with Trevor, Flora's terrier, and sat at the back of the hall scowling at Rannaldini. Flora got even more flustered, particularly when Trevor started howling at Hermione's rather dubious top notes, which reduced both chorus and cast to fits of laughter, so master and dog were banished from the hall.

'That nasty little dog is, alas, a critic,' said Serena, as she picked up the telephone in the control room to ring

Rannaldini on the rostrum. 'Dame Hermione has lost her top.'

'Where? Where?' said Sexton, looking round the control room in excitement.

'Her top notes, you bloody idiot.' Serena slammed down the receiver.

Rannaldini decided to take a break and listen to the playback. Tristan bore George off for 'a cup of tea and a piece of shortbread for Trevor'.

Smarmy frog even knows the name of my dog, thought George ungratefully.

'And then you can sit in the control room,' added Tristan.

'No, he can't,' snapped Serena, who'd nipped down to the canteen to grab a cup of tea, and who hadn't forgiven George for choosing to live with Flora rather than her. 'Our singers' weaknesses and how we conceal them are entirely our secret.'

'Weaknesses?' squawked Hermione, who, having clocked Rannaldini's preference for Serena, had been spoiling for a fight. 'What weaknesses? How dare you, you patronizing hussy?' Grabbing cups and saucers, she started smashing them on the floor.

'Pull yourself together, Hermione,' said Serena bossily. 'My little Jessie wouldn't behave like that.'

Appearing in the doorway, Rannaldini ducked to avoid a milk jug and frogmarched a screaming Hermione off to her dressing room. Three minutes later, he came out zipping up his flies.

'She'll be OK now.'

'But we're going to have to drop in someone else's top notes,' whispered Serena.

Tristan decided to placate George with a large whisky instead and bore him off to find one.

'Flora is wonderful,' he said enthusiastically. 'She is determined not to betray her panic to Elisabetta, but listen to the tension in her voice.'

'She's not having to act,' snarled George, 'and who's

that damn sight too good-looking boy playing Carlos?'

'Baby Spinosissimo. He's sublime, but extremely gay.'

The ladies of the chorus, who were not needed in the finale, were drifting away. Pushy's hard little heart was breaking as she knocked on Rannaldini's door.

'Ay've just come to say goodbay, Maystro.'

'My dear, can you keep a secret on pain of death?'

'Of course,' lied Pushy, wriggling inside.

'How would you like to sing Dame Hermione's top notes?'

At last the recording was over. Tristan heaved a sigh of relief that Rannaldini would now whizz off round the world out of their hair, allowing himself, Serena and Sylvestre to get on with the editing.

But, to his horror, Rannaldini went nowhere, hogging the edit suite, putting his stamp on everything, causing endless rows over which take was used, twiddling knobs so some singers sounded less good and others better than they had at the recording. Granny, getting to the end of his career, needed careful editing. Hermione, as Rannaldini's mistress and more importantly because of their mutual record sales, couldn't sound less than perfect. Sylvestre dropped in Pushy's top notes so no-one could detect the join.

Still disappointed that Tristan hadn't made a move, Serena put it down to the fact that she had supported Rannaldini on every artistic decision. She had also, reluctantly, become very smitten with her Italian stallion. It was so sweet of Rannaldini on the last day of editing, because her involvement in the film was ended, to invite her, Sylvestre and Tristan back to his flat over-looking Hyde Park for a farewell dinner.

As Serena was leaving to relieve the babysitter, because it was Nanny Bratislava's night off, she handed Rannaldini a picture her daughter Jessie had painted specially for her 'Uncle Roberto'.

'How charming of Jessie,' Rannaldini wiped away a tear, and as he ushered Serena into her minicab, promised he would call her later.

Bounding back into the house, however, he rolled up Jessie's picture, plunged it into the drawing-room fire and lit his cigar with it.

'What are you doing?' demanded Tristan in horror.

'Now the recording is sewn up,' Rannaldini inhaled happily, 'I have no more need to ingratiate myself with little Jessie's mother.'

There were more fireworks in March when members of the cast were issued with cassettes of themselves singing so they could learn the words to which they had to mime on location and time their movements to them. Then they discovered how much Rannaldini had doctored the recording. Chloe was incensed by the cuts in the 'Veil Song' and in 'Don Fatale'.

Rannaldini blithely blamed Serena.

'Anyway, those numbers don't add much to the plot, my darling.'

Baby was outraged he'd been so often drowned by Hermione. Alpheus felt Rannaldini had consistently favoured the orchestra and every other singer. It was sacrilege to cut his great solo in Act IV and his character didn't 'garner sufficient sympathy'.

Mikhail was so cross, he rang up Rannaldini in the middle of the night. 'Why did you not use my third and best take in death of Posa?'

'Because it was too slow,' said Rannaldini coolly. 'Serena wanted to get Acts Four and Five on to one CD for when the record comes out.'

'At this rate my billing will be so small and low down, only snails and mice will be able to read it,' sighed Granny, who'd also been savagely cut.

'Think of poor Verdi,' snarled Rannaldini. 'He had to drop the entire first act of *Don Carlos*, because the Parisians couldn't get their last trains home.'

'And directors have been putting it back ever since,' said Granny drily.

Sylvestre, the handsome French sound engineer, felt Hermione's performance had been so enhanced by subtle additions that he sent her her cassette with utter confidence. In a frenzy Hermione returned the tape by taxi, shrieking down the telephone and threatening legal action. 'You have rejected every single take I wanted and my top notes sound terrible.'

Sylvestre waited four days, wrote to Hermione saying he'd laboured all round the clock on a new tape, and sent her back the old one. By return of post, he received from Hermione a letter, which he framed, saying, 'You have worked miracles.' Also included was an invitation to luncheon, which lasted twenty-four hours.

There was great consternation when a hatchet job, on the horrors of recording with Rannaldini, appeared in the *Sunday Times*, written by little Christy Foxe. As Christy subsequently turned out to be Rupert Campbell-Black's godson, and the son of Janey Lloyd-Foxe, a very dangerous columnist, Rannaldini and Tristan wondered uneasily if this were the first round in Rupert's war of attrition.

16

One of the secrets of Rannaldini's success was that he knew when he had pushed those he needed too far. Immediately the editing was finished he suggested he, Tristan and Meredith, the set designer, should recce the state rooms at Buckingham Palace.

Rannaldini and Meredith went back a long way. They had done up numerous houses together without falling out. Aware that Meredith had been the lover of Hermione's charming husband, Bob Harefield, for fifteen years, Rannaldini had never outed them because he was fond of Meredith, and Bob, as orchestral manager of Rannaldini's old orchestra, the London Met, had made life incredibly easy for him.

Neither Rannaldini nor Hermione, on the other hand, had made life easy for Bob, who'd pretended he was far too stretched in Australia setting up a new opera company, to come home and organize *Don Carlos* for them.

Meredith, a hugely successful interior designer, had turned down a mass of work to create the sets for *Don Carlos*, but he intended to screw a vast fee out of Liberty Productions, and although missing Bob a great deal, he was very excited about working with such an enchanting Frenchman.

*   *   *

On the day of the proposed trip to the Palace, so many builders' lorries and cars belonging to outraged planning officers were already whizzing in and out of Valhalla that the Fancy Fish frozen foods van slipped through the gates unnoticed. Famed for his cheeky, cheery manner, which could sell shellfish à la King to a barmitzvah party, Terry, the Fancy Fish rep, had long had designs on Valhalla, particularly now rumours were spreading of a film crew rolling up at the end of March.

Harriet Bussage, Rannaldini's PA, had tipped Terry off that Sir Roberto was in rare residence. On his way to make his pitch Terry decided to pop into Bussage's cottage, which nestled in a copse half-way up Valhalla's drive, to deliver a cardboard box of sole Véronique as a thank-you present. Loading up other boxes, in case Bussage was tempted to place an order (Terry never missed a sales opportunity), he was just admiring the snowdrops and aconites in her little garden when he heard a male voice, sepulchral and terrifying:

'How dare you spell Spinosissimo wrong!' followed by a great thwack and a shriek.

'I'm sorry, Maestro.' It was a woman's voice now, quavering, pleading. 'Please don't hurt me.'

'How dare you put a comma in that letter to Lord Gowrie, when I dictated a semi-colon,' intoned the man's voice.

More thwacks were followed by even more piercing shrieks:

'Punish me, Maestro, I'm so sorry.'

Rushing to the rescue through the back door, Terry froze with shock. A naked Miss Bussage was spread-eagled face down on the kitchen table, with wrists and ankles strapped to each wooden leg.

Beside her, an equally naked Rannaldini, with an erection rivalling the tower of Pisa, was laying into her reddening but surprisingly trim bottom with a hunting whip. Watching them with indifference was a large fluffy white cat.

Next moment sole Véronique, garlic king prawns, not to mention jumbo crispy cod fingers, destined for Little Cosmo, went flying all over the kitchen and Terry had fled.

'It was the bleedin' excitement on their faces fixed me,' he told his wife that evening.

Five minutes later, Meredith and Tristan, having enjoyed a merry champagne brunch at the Heavenly Host, bounced into Bussage's parlour to find Rannaldini, immaculate in a pinstripe suit and shocking pink tie, autographing a pile of photographs.

'Helen said you were here,' giggled Meredith. 'The helicopter's waiting. What the hell did you do to that sweet Fancy Fish man? He's just taken the side off Tristan's flash car.'

Booked in for a two-hour trip round the state rooms, which was all the time Rannaldini could spare, they lunched beforehand at Green's in Bury Street. Over oysters, lobster and Sancerre, they decided they needed ideas for the Great Hall, which was going to be turned into Philip II's bedroom. They also required a set, probably the Summer Drawing Room, into which Philip summoned Carlos from the polo field for a pep talk. This was a duet composed by Rannaldini, so he didn't want a too-spectacular décor to distract people from his music. But they could go to town on the state room in which Philip had his great political debate with Posa, which had only been written by Verdi. For this Rannaldini had evil designs on Helen's Blue Living Room.

Arriving at the Palace, Meredith commandeered the red guidebook. 'That's the arch through which diplomats and heads of state enter,' he announced, as they peered down into the pink-gravelled quadrangle.

'Her Majesty lives on the opposite side,' said Rannaldini, pointing to a dark blue door.

'Why don't you give her a bell?' suggested Meredith. 'Ask if we can pop in for a brandy. You must have met her when she gave you your K.'

'And on many other occasions,' said Rannaldini icily. 'Anyway,' he added, looking up at the empty flagpole, 'she is not in residence.'

'"In 1826 George IV chose John Nash to design a new palace,"' read out Meredith, '"but he was hampered by a chronic lack of funds." Nash *et moi*. I expect he gnashed his teeth.' Rather like a child swinging between two parents, Meredith linked arms with Tristan and Rannaldini. 'You will give me a decent budget, won't you, boys? We can't stint on royalty. Oh, look, they've got Sky Television. Lovely to think of that butch Prince Andrew watching all that golf.'

Tristan was gazing up at the lion-coloured columns of the ambassadors' entrance.

'The English stole the idea for that double portico from the Louvre,' he grumbled. 'They steal all our decent ideas.'

'Well, we won both of those,' Meredith waved the guidebook at two panels celebrating the battles of Trafalgar and Waterloo, 'so boo sucks.'

'Weeth a little help from the Germans,' said Rannaldini crushingly. 'Now concentrate. Not now,' he snarled, as a group of middle-aged tourists tiptoed up reverently in the hope of an autograph.

Meredith was disappointed the tour didn't include the ballroom. 'You're only admitted', announced Rannaldini pompously, 'if you're getting a decoration.'

'Get you,' said Meredith, who was now busily sketching a grand staircase, which unfurled like the frill round a golden wedding cake.

Tristan, lost in thought, was admiring a lovely marble of a lurcher having a thorn removed from its paw by Diana the huntress. He must find a postcard to send to Lucy Latimer. Thank God he'd booked her to do the make-up and to calm Hermione and Chloe when filming started. There were dogs in every painting too, which meant he'd have to include lots in the film. Dogs, he reflected wearily, were almost more of a nuisance than children.

'This is the Green Room,' Rannaldini paused on the threshold, 'where one mingles before proceeding to the Throne Room to meet one's hosts.'

'How lucky we are to have you to initiate us,' said Meredith gravely.

'Stop taking the pees, you little popinjay,' said Rannaldini. 'How about this décor for one of the drawing rooms?'

'No good for your colouring,' said Meredith firmly. 'Green's awful with grey hair and a sallow complexion. Someone would spear you with a cocktail stick. Although we could drag the dungeons this colour to cast a sickly glow on poor, doomed Posa.'

Tristan kept having to hide his laughter by examining paintings.

'This is how I want room where Posa defies Philip,' said Rannaldini, as he hustled them into the Throne Room, which was the length of a cricket pitch. The crimson silk walls were lined with gold sofas. Huge cut-glass chandeliers glittered from the ceiling like a fleet of Jack Frost's air balloons.

'The ceilings at Valhalla are too low for chandeliers,' protested Meredith.

'Then raise them,' said Rannaldini imperiously.

Through an arch flanked by white-winged genii holding gold paper chains, burgundy red steps led up to two crimson thrones, embroidered with the initials EIIR and P.

'We must reproduce those for Elisabetta and Philip II,' said Tristan in excitement.

'And keep them permanently at Valhalla after filming's over,' giggled Meredith, 'we can unpick the E and P and change it to R for Rannaldini and H for Hermione, or Helen or Harriet Bussage,' he added slyly, 'depending on who's in favour.'

Rannaldini allowed himself a chill smile, but he could only think of a throne initialled T, with naked Tabitha sprawled on its faded damask, waiting for him to mount the burgundy red steps and her.

In every room there were beautiful clocks depicting heroic scenes. How slowly the minutes must have ticked by for the young Princess Diana, thought Tristan, and for Carlos and Elisabetta. How d'you cure a broken heart in a gilded cage, particularly when every ravishing piece of Sèvres showed idyllic scenes of young shepherds and shepherdesses in love?

'I want a scrolled codpiece for Christmas,' said Meredith, bringing everyone back to earth.

'Her Majesty enters the Throne Room through that emergency exit,' murmured an official, who'd recognized Rannaldini, 'so she doesn't have to walk through a lot of rooms.'

'That's nice,' piped up Meredith, 'so she can always retreat down the backstairs for a squirt of Diorissimo.'

'Half the big-looking glasses,' confided the official, 'despite being covered with gilt patterns of leaves and flowers, are actually hidden secret doors.'

Rannaldini's eyes gleamed. How perfect for the to-ing and fro-ing of lovers and Inquisition spies, often the same thing in *Don Carlos*, and for himself, who liked to vanish like the Cheshire Cat.

They had reached the great spine of the state rooms – the Picture Gallery – mostly Dutch and Flemish masters. Tristan was enraptured and went into a flurry of oh-*mon-dieu*s, particularly over Rembrandt's *Old Ship-builder and His Wife*, whose faces were luminous with affection and inner light. If only Lucy could make the faces of his cast glow like that.

Too much enthusiasm for anything other than himself unnerved Rannaldini, who whisked them past each masterpiece, only pausing to admire Guido's terrifying painting of Cleopatra being bitten by the asp. Etienne had been the same, thought Tristan, with a pang. As a child he had never been given time to linger over a painting.

'*Christ Healing the Paralytic.*' Consulting the guidebook, Meredith paused before a large oil. 'He ought to have a go at Tabitha Lovell.'

'Is she still drinking?' Tristan tried not to sound interested.

'Buckets,' sighed Meredith. 'She'll give birth to a little pickled walnut at this rate.'

'This is the best picture in the room.' A good-looking official drew their attention to Charles I astride a fine grey horse. 'His eyes really follow one round the room.'

'So would mine given the chance,' said Meredith admiringly.

'This is the Blue Room,' purred Rannaldini, 'where one gathers for drinks before grand diplomatic occasions.'

'This is it, glorious,' squeaked Meredith, whipping out his notebook and scribbling frantically. 'Corinthian pillars the colour of Harrogate toffee, sea-blue flocked wallpaper, masses of gold framing the mirrors and ceiling, pale turquoise sofas, perfect for the Summer Drawing Room and Philip's pep talk to Carlos.'

Diluting the gilded splendour, through floor-length windows green lawns could be seen sweeping down to a lake surrounded by willows. 'I'm going to scrap my fences and flower-beds and sweep down to *my* lake,' Rannaldini was thinking aloud.

'Take a lot of mowing,' chided Meredith. 'Teddy Brimscombe would give notice and no-one else would put up with you. I like this vermilion,' he mused, as they moved into the Music Room, 'like a winter sunset and incredibly flattering to your colouring.'

Rannaldini smoothed his hair complacently, but the smile was wiped off his face when Tristan was suddenly mobbed by a party of French tourists, demanding his autograph, taking pictures and asking after Claudine Lauzerte.

Outraged to lose the limelight for a second, Rannaldini dived under the red rope and played 'God Save the Queen' on the Music Room piano. Guides blanched, security men with walkie-talkies rushed in, the French tourists, melting away from Tristan, cheered and clapped as they recognized Rannaldini.

'I couldn't reseest it.'

'That's OK, Sir Roberto.'

Their last port of call was the White Drawing Room, which took all their breath away.

'This is answer for the Great Hall,' exclaimed Rannaldini. 'Then for Philip's debate with Posa we can restore our Blue Living Room to its former glory with reds and crimsons.'

'Isn't that the room Helen just redecorated?' said an aghast Tristan.

'Yes, poor darling,' agreed Meredith. 'We tried a hundred coats before we got the right blue. But this gilt and white is to die for. And there's darling Queen Alexandra over the chimneypiece. She was as good about fat Edward's philandering as Helen is about yours, Rannaldini, so we might placate her with a new portrait over the fireplace.'

Meredith does get away with murder, thought Tristan, as they trooped down the staircase.

Out in the sunshine, Rannaldini stalked off to the Palace shop.

'We must take Sexton a present,' said Tristan, as he and Meredith panted after him. 'He was so heartbroken he wasn't allowed to join us.'

'He'd have wanted chandeliers in the larder,' said Meredith sensibly.

'Get him a box of royal fudge,' mocked Rannaldini, who had bought a mug for Tabitha and crested tea-bags for Helen and Bussage.

'I'll get him postcards of all the interiors so he can pretend he's been,' said Meredith.

Out in the street Rannaldini announced he must leave them.

'It is Isa's birthday, I got tickets for *Riverdance*. Sadly, Isa cry off.' Rannaldini looked delighted. 'I hope Tabitha won't be too bored with just her old stepfather.'

'Dear boy.' He turned to Tristan who, for one miraculous moment, thought Rannaldini was going to ask him to take Isa's place. But with an evil smile, as if he could read Tristan's mind, Rannaldini merely thanked him for sparing the time.

'My God,' giggled Meredith, as Clive, Rannaldini's henchman, glided up in the most flamboyant orange sports car.

'A Lamborghini Diablo,' boasted Rannaldini. 'A beautiful girl deserve evening out in a beautiful new car.'

As Clive slid across into the passenger seat, Rannaldini took the wheel and roared off towards Hyde Park Corner.

'Silly old ponce,' went on Meredith. 'Talk about mutton dressed as Lamborghini.' Then, seeing the desolation on Tristan's face, 'Don't tangle with that nest of vipers, baby boy.'

17

At first Tab had tried so hard to make her marriage work, giving up booze and fags for the sake of the baby, keeping tidy the charming cottage Rannaldini had lent her, cooking – admittedly pretty disgusting – meals. But Isa was used to a clockwork mother and a clockwork mistress, Martie in Australia, who'd both provided uncritical admiration, clean shirts, tea on the table, and an impeccable answering service.

He was also as driven as Tristan, and didn't want to be distracted by jealous tantrums or grumbles about burst pipes. He was away most days, race-riding or at his father's yard, where it was made quite plain Jake didn't want Tab anywhere near his horses.

So gradually she drifted into drinking. One Sunday, when Isa had gone over to see Jake, she had downed half a bottle of vodka before starting on the ironing. Trying to watch *Champions* on television at the same time, she singed the colours of a very important owner. Isa could curse in Romany for over five minutes and proceeded to do so.

On the way home, he'd stopped at the garage to buy Christmas cards for all his owners.

'You can't send those,' said Tab, in horror. 'They're all spangly and it's horrendously naff to say "Season's Greetings".'

'Don't be fucking stupid,' snapped Isa, and handed

her a fiver. 'Here's the stamp money. Make sure you post them tomorrow. What's for supper?'

'Hell, I forgot. I'll ring for a pizza, or we could go to the Heavenly Host.'

'We can't afford it.'

And the row escalated. The following night Isa arrived home late to find Tab had gone out clubbing in Rutminster, and things went from bad to worse.

Isa was so cool, silent and withdrawn, Tab so up-front and tempestuous, she felt like a tidal wave hurling itself against the sea wall. Physical passion had drawn them together, but the doctor had insisted on no intercourse for the first three months.

'It's all right,' bleated Tab, who was terrified Isa might find a replacement from all those groupies mobbing him on the racecourse, 'I'll go down on you.'

But when she tried, she retched all over him and the bedclothes. She was suffering from morning, noon and night sickness. Her hormones were all to pieces and she was paranoid about everything, snapping Isa's head off one moment, in floods of tears the next.

Isa was sympathetic until he saw the overflowing ashtrays and plummeting vodka bottles.

'Hasn't the doctor told you to give up?'

'He said cut down because it would cause me and Baby Rupert too much stress if I stopped completely.'

'Don't call it fucking Rupert.'

Tidy by nature, Isa was driven crackers by Tab pinching his jerseys, socks, razors, and CK One, his precious after-shave. As she drank more, she forgot more: to put out milk bottles and dustbins – but, worse still, for a jockey's wife, she forgot telephone messages. Isa started putting all calls through his mobile and his bleeper, which made Tab even more paranoid about other women.

At Christmas everyone made an effort. As their daughter, Darklis, was in South Africa, Tory persuaded Jake to let her invite Isa and Tab to stay.

The Old Mill, which Tory had been given by her rich

grandmother, was big, rambling and totally horse-orientated. The only paintings on the walls were of Jake or Isa's horses, or of their various sporting achievements. There were scant carpets on the wooden floors, all the sofas and armchairs needed upholstering. Nor were the Lovells into central heating.

Outside were days of extraordinary beauty and bitter cold. The chill factor, because of the east wind from Siberia, was minus 16 and produced wonderful sunsets and sunrises, rose pink on the horizon above snowy fields.

Traditionally in racing yards, the grooms have Christmas Day off. It was a matter of pride for Jake to do the horses with Isa, just to show everyone that polio hadn't got the better of him. Outside he noticed the wind had scattered ivy-mantled branches all over the fields, clearing out the dead wood. Like me, he thought, with a shiver.

The only way he could relieve his pain-racked leg and back was to soak in a boiling bath, but he returned home to find Tab had used all the hot water. He found her in the kitchen, hugging the Aga, clean, pale hair flopping over her ashen face, her long turquoise eyes angry and bloodshot. Exactly like her father, thought Jake savagely, and as capable of causing havoc.

Poor Tory, attempting to cook Christmas dinner for the family and the grooms, was also trying to get to know her daughter-in-law.

'I have no idea how to change a nappy,' Tab was saying disdainfully.

'They use Velcro now. It's as easy as putting a bandage on a horse,' said Tory encouragingly.

Picking up Jake's hatred, Tab escaped to pack her presents, stopping on the way upstairs to pinch Tory's sellotape and a pile of newspapers because she'd forgotten to buy wrapping paper. The whole thing took ages because she kept stopping to read. There was a huge piece, in the *Telegraph* colour mag, about eventing stars destined for the next Olympics. Tab was not even mentioned, which made her feel more of a failure than ever.

Turning to the *Sunday Times* she found a lovely picture of Rupert and a piece saying how well he was doing. Tearing it out, she fought back the tears. The blue sky outside reminded her not of Mary's robes, but of Rupert's eyes. The bells pealed far more sweetly at Penscombe.

Remembering the mountains of presents, the banks of holly, the huge fires, Taggie's goose, her parsnip purée, and the brandy round the Christmas pudding, which flamed longer than the Great Fire of London, Tab forgot the earth-shattering rows with which she and Rupert had disrupted the entire household. The last one had been because Rupert had only bought her a Golf GTi convertible for Christmas, instead of paying forty thousand for The Engineer, for which Rannaldini had forked out later in the year when he'd married her mother. God, she had taken her wonderful family for granted.

'Can't you ever forget about being a bloody Campbell-Black?'

Isa had walked in and caught sight of the piece in her hand. Sharon, stretched out on the bed, scattered receipts as she waved her tail.

'Have you been ransacking my mother's tights drawer?'

'Hardly be tight on me,' snapped Tab. She'd got so thin she could jump through the hoop of the sellotape hanging from the bedside table.

'I was looking for a thick jersey,' she went on, 'which one certainly needs in this house. The only thing I could find was Pond's Vanishing Cream. Your mother could start by using it on her hips.'

She thought Isa was going to hit her.

'You been drinking?'

'Of course not. I promised.'

Isa wasn't sure. Like most drinkers, Tab went through

three stages: clinging and filled with anxiety when she woke up, incredibly cheery after the first few slugs, then punchy and belligerent when she was coming down. It looked as though she'd reached the third stage. But he didn't want to upset his mother, so he asked if Tab would come downstairs to open the presents.

'The gritters are out,' he added, gazing at the lights flashing along the horizon. 'We're in for a hard night.'

'People use them on their teeth round here.'

The Lovells were frugal, short of money and had allotted one present to each person. Tory had gone to a lot of trouble to track down an early history of eventing in a second-hand-book shop for Tab. Isa had rather pointedly given Tab some scent called Quercus, so she wouldn't nick his CK One any more, and a rather ugly gold locket.

'I'm going to put your picture in one side,' said Tab, hugging him, 'and Sharon and The Engineer in the other.'

Used to Penscombe prodigality, where everyone received presents from every dog, horse and human, and in anticipation of a fat Christmas cheque from Rannaldini, Tab had rolled up with a crate of champagne and a side of smoked salmon for the Lovells. Her individual presents were less successful and all wrongly labelled. Tory opened a red fishnet stocking of dog treats, destined for Sharon, then some boxer shorts.

'Sorry, they're meant for Isa, although I suppose Sharon could wear them if she was a boxer not a Labrador.'

Isa, thinking of their bank account, grew increasingly tight-lipped as he opened a silver-topped whip, two beautiful dark blue cashmere jerseys, 'because I'm always nicking yours', and a camera, when he'd already got four.

Tab herself was desperately disappointed to have nothing from Rupert and, even more worryingly, no fat cheque from Rannaldini. Instead, he and Helen had given her a royal blue vase edged with gold and decorated with a pastoral scene.

'Very pretty,' said Tory.

'Except Bussage picked it up at a car old-boot sale,' said Tab furiously.

She was most excited about the present she'd got for Jake and Tory. She had taken a photograph of their ancient lurcher, Beetle, from Isa's photograph album, and commissioned Daisy France-Lynch, a friend of Rupert's, to paint from it an exquisite miniature. To her horror, Jake merely grunted and put it face down on the table.

'Why are your parents so ungrateful?' sobbed Tab as she watched Isa changing for dinner, thinking how ravishingly a dark suit became his wild black hair and pale gypsy face.

'Why d'you do things without asking me?' hissed Isa. 'Beetle was the puppy my father bought for my mother, as a peace-offering because he loathed living with your mother, and he wanted to come back to Mum and he'd heard her dog had been run over. He found Mum in hospital, dying of a massive overdose because she couldn't live without him either. They believe Beetle was the talisman that saved Mum and their marriage, and you have to go and give them a flaming painting of her.'

'I didn't know, I never thought,' sobbed Tab.

'You never do,' snarled Isa, reaching for his after-shave.

She *must* have been drinking to have wrongly wrapped up all those presents. Then he twigged, as he realized he was slapping not CK One on his face but neat vodka.

Dinner was bearable because there was plenty of wine, Tory had cooked a delicious turkey, and as Isa and Tab were sitting at opposite ends of the table divided by the grooms no-one realized they were not speaking to one another.

163

The telephone had rung constantly: owners, jockeys, friends, Tory's sister Fenella from America, Darklis from South Africa, all called to wish the Lovells happy Christmas. No-one rang Tab.

Tory found the silver bachelor's button in her Christmas pudding, which caused lots of laughter. From silver charms in puddings, the conversation moved on to superstitions.

'One mustn't get married after sunset,' said a pretty redhead, making eyes at Isa.

'And never eat your own wedding cake,' said her plump friend.

'Why not?' asked Tab quickly.

'Anyone want any more Christmas pudding?' cried Tory desperately. 'Jake, do shove round the white.'

'Why not?' insisted Tab.

Even more of a chill than there was already fell over the room.

'A marriage is supposed to be doomed if you marry after sunset,' said the pretty redhead with a shrug, 'and the gypsies say if you taste your own wedding cake your child will die.'

'But I did both those things,' Tab clutched her tummy in horror.

'It's only a silly old gypsy's tale,' said Tory, in distress. 'Think of the times you see a single magpie and nothing awful happens.'

A ringing telephone made everyone jump.

'It's your father, Tabitha,' said the head lad returning from answering the call.

Tab streaked out of the room. 'Daddy, oh, Daddy!'

'My darling leetle girl,' said Rannaldini, 'your mother sends love. I just wanted to know how you are getting on.'

As Tab returned to the dining room, hollow with desolation, Jake was making some dismissive crack about Penscombe Pride not winning the George VI tomorrow.

'My father's a far better horseman than either you or Isa ever were,' screamed Tab, and fled upstairs where,

164

mistaking Jake and Tory's room for the loo, she re-gurgitated turkey and vodka all over their bed and passed out.

The next day, Isa and Jake went off to Kempton, and Tab, who had no intention of getting to know her mother-in-law better, made the excuse that she couldn't leave The Engineer any longer and drove back to Paradise.

It was lovely to come home to such a pretty place. Magpie Cottage, which was faded russet, rather than black and white, lay just across the valley from Rannaldini's watch-tower, with a beech copse behind and a stream running down one side. On the lawns, back and front, it was hard to tell where snow ended and snowdrops began.

Tab loved Magpie Cottage but she grew nervous on her own; Sharon picked up the vibes and kept barking at the wind or imagined bangs, which made Tab more scared than ever. Taking a slug from the bottle of vodka she'd bought in a pub on the way home she started brooding on the superstitions they'd discussed last night and then about one magpie for sorrow.

Finding a paintbrush and some black paint in a kitchen cupboard, she went out into the fading after-noon. The sky was a pale, silvery grey, dotted with darker grey clouds and patches of gold on the horizon. The snow was too powdery to make snowballs, but had drifted beautifully, sharp as a shark's fin against the garden wall. Sharon charged round the lawn raising spray like a skier, as Tab added an S to the board outside. Now it was Magpies Cottage – two for joy.

'I'm going to make my marriage work,' she told Sharon, 'and you can show everyone how good Labradors are with babies.'

18

The cold spell continued. There was no racing, which made Isa very twitchy and cross because neither he nor Jake were making any money. The horses grew bored and restless. Pipes froze, so Tab, who'd forgotten to stop the milk, bathed in it instead.

Rupert beat the chill factor by taking Taggie, Xav and Bianca skiing. Tab ground her teeth over their photographs in the paper.

Fighting hangovers, and sickness, she still staggered up to do The Engineer every morning because she couldn't bear him to get closer to one of Rannaldini's grooms than herself. Then she returned to the vodka, which she found increasingly difficult to buy because she had no money. Several of her Christmas cheques bounced, before she discovered Rannaldini had stopped her allowance as well.

Isa doled her out pocket money for housekeeping, but grudgingly. It would be much more sensible, he said, for her to wheedle some serious dosh out of Rannaldini, which was why she had accepted the invitation to *Riverdance* on Isa's birthday in January. At the last moment, Isa had cried off in a rage. Tab had a maddening habit of always borrowing his jackets. Grabbing his Puffa from the back of the bedroom door, he had found all the Christmas cards to his owners unstamped and unposted in the pocket.

Which was why Tab had a lone evening with an amused but utterly unyielding Rannaldini.

'Isa is a successful jockey. You have a charming, free cottage, and if you bothered to check, you ungrateful child, you'd discover the Sèvres vase I gave you for Christmas was worth a few bob. Young people should make their own way.'

He wouldn't even lend her a grand or two to appease Isa and the bank manager.

The coupling of an alcoholic and a workaholic is not a happy one. As Isa worked endlessly to keep the show on the road and compensate for lack of support from Tab, he had less and less time to spend with her, which lowered her confidence and made her drink more out of loneliness.

Isa was so cool he fell asleep in the middle of a row, and she could never tell, behind that expressionless face, what he was thinking. In fact, throughout that long, hard, cruel winter, Peppy Koala, the chestnut colt, so charming, so idle, so uncompetitive, had never been far from his thoughts.

He was just making plans in late February to fly out to Australia when Mr Brown, Peppy Koala's owner, suddenly called him. He was in England, taking over some Bristol electronics firm. Was Isa free tomorrow evening?

Mr Brown also wanted to see Jake's yard, and having read about Isa's wedding in *Hello!*, said he'd sure like to shake hands with the new Mrs Lovell, who looked a beaut, so perhaps they could have dinner at Isa's place.

Switching off his mobile, Isa looked round at Magpie Cottage. God, it was a tip! The ravishing little chest of drawers Taggie had given them for a wedding present was already covered in drink rings, like a pond in a rainstorm.

Knowing there was no way he could bring Mr Brown back here in its present state, Isa swallowed his pride and a large whisky and rang Helen. Could he borrow Mrs

Brimscombe, Betty and Sally tomorrow morning to blitz the place? Then all Tab had to do was collect some pre-cooked food from Waitrose and make herself look beautiful.

As luck would have it, in lieu of payment, one of Isa's owners had given him a brand-new Jaguar XK8, which was being delivered to the cottage that afternoon. If money ran out he could flog it. For the meantime it would impress Mr Brown.

The three-month ban on sex was now up, but the cold war seemed to have set in too hard for Isa to placate Tab by making a move on her that night. Tab had stopped being sick, but instead when she opened her mouth a stream of resentment came out.

On the morning of Mr Brown's visit, however, she was full of good intentions: no booze, and wifely behaviour. By midday a tight-lipped Mrs Brimscombe and a giggling Betty and Sally had made the cottage look wonderful and set the table.

'Why don't you buy some daffies for that lovely blue vase?' suggested Betty.

Tab had been just off to Waitrose when she went to Isa's chest of drawers to borrow a pair of socks. Rooting round under the lining paper she found a lovely laughing picture of Martie, his Australian girlfriend. He's still in love with her, she thought in terror, he's going to leave me.

When the telephone woke her, it was dark. Isa wanted to know if everything was on course. Mr Brown had been impressed with Jake's yard. They'd be back around six thirty.

'What have you bought for supper?'
'It's a surprise,' bleated Tab.
'Shall I get red or white?'
'Both, I should think. See you later.'

Whimpering with panic, Tab looked around her. How could she have made such a mess? An empty vodka bottle and fragments of the royal blue and gold vase Rannaldini had given her for Christmas littered the floor. She'd better go and buy the food for dinner; then she could tidy the place and herself while it was heating up.

Her car was out of petrol, so she borrowed Isa's new Jaguar. God, it was bliss to drive. In no time she had reached Waitrose, and loaded up with a smoked-salmon mousse, three packets of Coronation Chicken, new potatoes, ready-made dressing and a pretty red and green bag of salad. Adding banana and yoghurt ice cream, a brown loaf and runny Brie, she was off to the checkout counter, piling on Pedigree Chum and Whiskas on the way. Catering was so easy if you knew how. She even ignored a great glacier of vodka bottles. Hurrah for Tabitha the coper.

Her undoing was a white tablecloth covered in glasses, and a beaming salesman with a special offer of Chilean Chardonnay.

'Might as well have a slurp,' muttered Tab, as her trolley developed a mind of its own and veered booze-wards.

A man in a flat cap and a green Husky had had the same idea, and was soon swilling away, waggling his nose back and forth in the glass like a windscreen wiper.

'Remarkably good,' he said to Tab.

'It is,' she agreed, smiling back at the salesman, 'and a terrific bargain. Could I have another glass just to make sure?'

'What a lovely little hidey-hole,' said Mr Brown, as Isa drew up outside Magpie Cottage. 'Look at those prim-roses. I'm dying for a leak.'

Isa's first thought was that his Jaguar had been stolen, the second that his mobile was ringing. Ignoring it, he ran into the house. Chaos met his eyes. Charging into the downstairs loo, he found no bog paper and no towel. Fuck Tab!

The best he could do was a box of tissues from the kitchen, which was also a tip, with no sign of dinner and no flowers. A fire was laid in the grate but unlit. Littering the floor were fragments of the Sèvres vase and Martie's torn-up photograph. He had better answer his mobile.

'Are you the owner of car P704 HHA?'

Isa had to think twice.

'Yes. It's been stolen?'

'We're not sure, sir. It's been abandoned across the gangway in Waitrose's car park, obstructing the flow of traffic, and the alarm is causing a disturbance. No-one can get inside the vehicle.'

Coming out of the lavatory, flapping his hands, Mr Brown was rather amused by the news.

'My spouse is always locking herself out of her car, and my teenage daughters never lift a finger in the house.'

He was very happy to give Isa a lift to Waitrose. He'd seen photographs of Tab in *OK* magazine on the flight over and was looking forward to meeting her even more.

They found Tab and the man in the flat cap sitting in a little café half-way down a second bottle of Chilean Chardonnay. Not having driven Isa's car before, she had no idea that it was his number being paged with increasing urgency.

'This is Hugh Murray-Scott,' she announced happily. 'He's a friend of Daddy's.'

'Where are my car keys?' snarled Isa.

'Car keys?' As Tab rootled through the pockets of her jeans, Mr Brown and Mr Murray-Scott admired her slender hips. 'Here they are. Now, where did I put my trolley?'

The final straw was when Isa found his lovely new Jaguar had been rammed by another car with a furious owner.

'It's only metal,' said Mr Brown soothingly. 'Don't blame the little lady.'

He thought Tabitha was wildly exciting.

'I'm sorry you won't be able to enjoy any home cooking,' mumbled Tab. 'I'm not only off my trolley, I seem to have lost it as well.'

She ended up trying to write a cheque for the Chardonnay with her toothbrush, and Mr Brown swept them all off to the Old Bell for dinner. Despite Isa hissing at Tab to keep her fucking trap shut, she and Mr Brown got on famously. She was soon telling him about her Olympic hopes for The Engineer, and he was telling her all about Peppy Koala. 'Prettiest little horse you ever saw.'

'If you brought him over to Paradise, he and The Engineer could meet,' said Tab, whose eyes were sparkling at the sight of the bottle of Moët arriving in an ice bucket.

'Aren't you rather isolated in that little cottage?' asked Mr Brown.

'I'm Isa-lated,' giggled Tab, 'because my husband is always late home.'

Mr Brown thought it a very funny joke.

Isa wanted to throttle his wife, but if he could stop her doing anything frightful, Mr Brown's obvious infatuation might just work to his advantage. By the time they had all ordered lobster with moules marinières to start with, Mr Brown was talking about *when* he brought Peppy Koala to England rather than *if*.

'If you run him in the Derby this year,' Isa was saying, 'he'll get a seven-pound allowance because, as a southern hemisphere horse, he'll be so much younger than the others.'

Tab sloped off to the ladies. On the way, wondering whether to pack in a quick vodka at the bar, she caught sight of a tank of lobsters. She hadn't realized they weren't born red. Black, already in mourning, they waited helplessly, their claws tied together with elastic

171

bands to stop them killing each other so that they could be boiled alive and intact.

Tab was so distraught, she up-ended a nearby ice bucket on the floor, scooped up as many lobsters as it would hold and fled into the street. Outside, in her thin jersey and jeans, the cold hit her like a left hook. If she could reach the sea she could set them free.

Isa and Mr Brown caught up with her on Rutminster bridge crying hysterically, trying to hitch a lift. When Isa tried to snatch back the bucket, she emptied the lobsters into the river.

Although the young lady was a handful, Mr Brown admired her spirit and was horrified by the way Isa tore into her.

'Don't you understand, you stupid bitch? They can't survive in fresh water.'

'Like me,' sobbed Tab. 'I can't survive in the wrong marriage any more.'

After a week of cold war, Isa flew to Australia on the pretext of winding up the yard he had started with Martie. As March came in, bringing days of torrential rain and flooding, Tab died of every kind of jealousy. Looking out listlessly one morning she noticed the sun had broken through. The stream that flowed past the cottage had also broken away from its course into lots of smaller streams, glittering like a crystal lustre as they danced down the valley to join the river Fleet. We're free to make our own way in the sunshine, they seemed to sing to Tab.

'Your future godmother, Lucy, won't like it, Little Rupert,' Tab told the baby inside her, 'but you and I are going hunting.'

Tab had always hunted, until Lucy had persuaded her it was cruel. But so many foxes escaped, and a ropy old pack like the Rutminster Ramblers never caught anything anyway, and the poor Engineer was so bored of dressage it would pep him up to have a day out.

172

Gold catkins lit up the valley like Tiffany lamps. As The Engineer floated over the fences, Tab had never been more conscious of owning an Olympic horse. She was so enjoying herself she didn't notice a strand of wire. Next moment The Engineer turned over on top of her.

It didn't hurt at first. She was conscious only of her white breeches turning red with blood, and screaming, 'The baby! Please save the baby!' before she passed out.

By the time Isa had flown home at vast expense, mother and horse were doing well, but little Rupert had died.

Tab was utterly devastated, sobbing and sinking into despair. Isa, who loved children, was determined not to show he was equally devastated. He never reproached Tab, because he knew in his heart that it had been his fault. He had longed to take her in his arms, but such was his loathing of the Campbell-Blacks, he couldn't convince himself he hadn't unleashed some gypsy curse. Instead he had gone to Cheltenham, won a big race on a horse of Baby's and not come home that night.

Rannaldini, delighted at the turn of events, had been playing Iago. Clive, who had let himself into Magpie Cottage with Rannaldini's master key, had been responsible for putting Martie's photo in Isa's sock drawer. He also tipped off Rannaldini when Isa was away, enabling him to ring Tab and drip poison into her ear.

'Isa is finding it *so* difficult to break with Martie. She was so capable, and they were together seven years and he *is* seven years older than you.' Which was vilely hypocritical of Rannaldini, who was intending to move in, despite being nearly thirty years older than Tab himself.

He would play the same game with Isa, telling him how wild Tab was, how young and unstable, how late coming home, how not always alone, how fond of the bottle. Subtly, slowly, treacherously, the same shoulder Rannaldini was providing for them both to cry on was the wedge he was driving between them. He encouraged Tab to use his indoor school and have a cross-country course built on the estate. Her suspension would be up in August in time for Gatcombe. But he still hadn't given her any allowance. Let her beg for it.

The National Hunt season was nearly over. Isa's winnings were shoring up Jake's yard so money would grow even tighter. Playing his usual cool waiting game, Isa had not pestered Mr Brown about Peppy Koala.

Finally, Mr Brown rang him. 'I'm dead choked your little Tabitha lost the baby. How is she?'

'Pretty depressed.'

'Not surprising, the way you treat her. If you can't be nice to a pretty lady like that, how can I trust you with my little horsy?'

'That's crazy,' said Isa sharply. 'No-one fusses over horses like my father. Where were you thinking of sending him?'

'Well, Sir Roberto Rannaldini's offered me so much dosh I nearly sold to him, but in case Peppy's that good I'm giving him to your other father-in-law, Rupert Campbell-Black.'

If Isa couldn't blame Tab for losing the baby, he could, and certainly did, for the loss of Peppy Koala.

The following day Rannaldini and a suicidal Tab rode round Paradise. A big red sun was disappearing into the mist like the brake light of Apollo's chariot, putting a pink rinse on the bare trees and a rose flush along the horizon. Conscious that they were about to be invaded by far more famous singers, robins and blackbirds were carolling their heads off.

'I've had some lovely letters about the baby,' muttered Tab, 'from Lucy in Belgium, Meredith, Mr Brown, and even from that glamorous French director you invited to our wedding. He sent me a lovely poem about Little

Rupert really existing and being a plant of light.' For a second, her stony little face softened.

That one would have to be knocked on the head very quickly, thought Rannaldini.

'Mrs Brimscombe told Isa how sorry she was about the baby,' he said idly. 'Isa said, "At least it's given Tab something new to grumble about."'

'The bastard,' gasped Tab.

'I suggested you get a part-time job.'

'And what did Isa say?'

As the sun sank, all the birds that had been singing so madly went silent. As the glow in the west became an orange fire, Rannaldini noticed a little adolescent moon turning her slim back on such ostentation. She reminded him of Tabitha.

'He said you were unemployable.'

'God, he's a shit. You wait till the bloody ban's lifted – we'll show him.'

'That's how I wanted you to react,' said Rannaldini silkily.

As he moved his horse close to The Engineer, his hypnotic black eyes were level with Tab's. Perhaps he had such an impact on women, she thought, because he was small enough to dazzle them, like a low-angled winter sun.

'Filming starts the week after next,' he announced. 'I'd like to offer you a job on *Don Carlos*. As mistress of the horse,' he added sententiously.

'Sounds perverse?'

'As well as hunting, war scenes and polo during the overture, horses will be needed for Philip's coronation, and Tristan might want to film Carlos and Posa galloping across country. We need someone to organize it. We'll pay you a very good fee.'

'Won't people think it a bit odd you hiring a totally inexperienced member of your wife's family?'

'Not in the least. Tristan has already signed up his

delectable niece, Simone, to handle continuity.'

'Can The Engineer have a part?'

'A starring role.'

'Then I'll do it.'

She was flaming well going to show Isa and Rupert that she could do her bit for the marriage.

19

What Rannaldini did not tell Tab was that also joining the crew, as second assistant director, and as hellbent on proving himself, was his eldest son, Wolfgang. This had come about because Rannaldini, wildly jealous of Rupert's rapprochement with Marcus and closeness to Xavier, wanted his son back, and had ordered Sexton to employ him.

The twenty-four-year-old Wolfgang, who had just gained an excellent law degree in Germany, had agreed to work on *Don Carlos* as a filler before taking up a plum job in Berlin. He had not been back to Valhalla for six years, ever since Rannaldini had pinched from him his beloved Flora Seymour, who was then a sixteen-year-old schoolgirl.

Highly, if somewhat rigidly, intelligent, Wolfgang had read Schiller in the original, and parallels between the cold, tyrannical Philip stealing Elisabetta from his son Carlos were not lost on him.

Now a jackbooting Eurocrat with a slimline briefcase and narrowed eyes, Wolfgang was determined not to let Rannaldini bully him. His job would be to run errands, keep the chorus in order and yank singers out of their dressing rooms, which in turn would give plenty of opportunity for bullying.

I am completely over Flora, Wolfgang told himself firmly and repeatedly, as he hurtled down the M4.

The only car that overtook him was a red Ferrari. Glancing right as it shot past, Wolfie nearly rammed the car in front, for in the passenger seat, yacking her head off to a beautiful boy instantly recognizable as the tenor playing Carlos, was Flora in person.

Wolfie had to pull into Membury service station to recover.

I am not over her, he told himself bleakly.

Unaware of the havoc she had just caused, Flora was much too busy worrying about tomorrow's filming.

'You just have to hit the mark and mime to your own voice,' said Baby soothingly. 'It'll be a doddle, I promise you.'

'Hey doddle doddle, I'm sure it's going to be more difficult than any of us think.'

'There's bound to be a voice coach around to bring us in. God, I could murder a burger. Let's stop at that Little Chef.'

'You mustn't. You look fantastic. Adonis Carlos.'

After a week at Champney's, Baby had lost his double chin and his gut.

'I can wear all my jackets as wraparounds like the Queen Mother,' he crowed. 'And I adored being whipped by all that seaweed.'

Flora gazed gloomily at the yellowing verges. It hadn't rained for weeks. The motorway was littered with furry corpses desperate to reach the river. Crows hung overhead like vultures.

'George and I were so miserable at the prospect of being separated.' She sighed. 'We had a stupid row last night and slept back to back loathing each other. We were just making up when Trevor barked hysterically at some non-existent burglar. By the time I'd defied George and let Trev out and in, the mood was broken. And Trev doesn't give a stuff,' she added, as the little dog raced back and forth along the top of the back seat, yapping furiously at dogs in other cars.

'And that's the precious life blood of a master spirit you've just devoured,' she said reproachfully, as she retrieved a chewed-up copy of *Captain Corelli's Mandolin* from the back seat.

'That's a nice ring,' said Baby, admiring the row of coloured stones on her left hand.

'It's called a regard ring. Victorian men gave it to their sweethearts if they were separated as a token of their regard. George gave it to me before we started rowing last night,' she added dolefully.

'You are entering the misnamed Valley of Paradise,' she intoned half an hour later.

From the south side, they realized the immensity of the operation. Opposite lay the great abbey of Valhalla, as grey and brooding as the clouds hanging over it. Around it, all over Rannaldini's parkland, like a huge circus, sprawled lorries, caravans, tents, a mobile canteen, Portaloos and vast generators.

'God, it's a creepy place.' Flora shivered. 'Rannaldini is rumoured to have a torture chamber under the house. It's safer to walk round Brixton after dark. My parents live there,' she pointed to a large Georgian house on the right of Valhalla, 'and that's Dame Hermione's shack further down the valley. Golly, the river's low. And up that little lane to the left is Magpie Cottage, where Isa and Tab clearly aren't going to fifteen rounds.'

'Spoilt brat,' said Baby dismissively.

'Takes one to know one,' chided Flora. 'D'you fancy Tristan?'

'I certainly do. Don't you?'

'One can't not. He's so Holy Grailish, and separate. And so sad behind all that charm. D'you think he's gay?'

'Hope so, but at least we've got three months to find out. Shall we have a quickie in the Pearly Gates?'

'No,' said Flora firmly. 'We've got to behave.'

* * *

179

Valhalla swarmed with technicians, everyone obsessed with his own agenda. Meredith, determined to produce the most memorable sets, whisked about trailing comely chippies, who could transform a dog kennel into Aladdin's cave in twenty-four hours. Not only had they ripped apart the Great Hall and the two drawing rooms, but also the dining room, the entrance hall and Rannaldini's study and bedroom too.

Tristan was outraged, and having a shouting match with Meredith as Baby and Flora arrived.

'Those other rooms were not on the budget!'

'They might just get into shot,' said Meredith blithely. 'Rannaldini didn't want to risk it. I love it when you act masterful.'

Tristan stormed off, as Meredith turned to Baby and Flora.

'My dears, it's all too exciting, and wait till you see Tristan's boys. They're so glamorous, he *must* be gay.'

Tristan's boys – the crew, mostly French – were, indeed, a glamorous bunch. They all seemed to have skiing tans and lean jaws, rapidly being hidden by beards so they wouldn't have to shave when they dragged themselves out of bed at the crack of dawn. Totally professional, they had already checked and tested their equipment for the first shoot day, making sure that lights and sound gear were in working order and camera and lenses properly calibrated.

Poised to grumble at everything *anglais* and to blow Gauloise smoke in the face of any singer who played up, they were also acting bolshie because most of them hadn't been invited to Rannaldini's smart dinner party that evening.

Those who had included the wonderfully languid director of photography, known as Oscar because he'd won so many Oscars and because, with his floating scarves, dark hair flopping from a middle parting, and endlessly assessing heavy-lidded eyes, he was a dead ringer for Oscar Wilde. Oscar seldom went near a camera. He appeared to sleep most of the day, but was paid five thousand pounds a week to make sure that the sets and the singers were beautifully lit. Despite his effete appearance, he was a doting family man, who spent his time on location – when he wasn't asleep – talking to Valentin, his handsome son-in-law, the camera operator, who earned two thousand a week. They had arrived with several crates of claret, and intended to escape home to Paris on every possible occasion.

Sylvestre, Tristan's sound recordist, who'd already sampled the *Don Carlos* wares during the recording, said little because he was always so busy listening. Sylvestre's aim on location was to pull the delectable Simone de Montigny, who was in charge of continuity. Much of Simone's energy would go into proving she had not been booked to work on *Don Carlos* because she was Tristan's niece. The daughter of Tristan's eldest brother, Alexandre the judge, she was in fact just two years younger than Tristan. Having caught a glimpse of Wolfgang Rannaldini she knew exactly who she wanted to pull on location.

And then there was Lucy Latimer, who'd been working in Brussels on *Villette*, which had overrun by several days so she had had a mad scramble to get to Valhalla on time. She was cheered that Sexton had provided her with a beautiful caravan in which to work. She had already unpacked her make-up brushes and sponges for the first day's filming. Her main problem would be in persuading the cast that the camera, four feet away, saw different things from an audience up in the gods.

In the fridge were three bottles of white, plenty of veggie snacks, and a garlic-flavoured cooked chicken, for her russet shaggy-coated lurcher, James, who ate much more expensively than she did and now, in a smart new green leather collar, lay replete and snoring on one of the bench seats. Above him in the window, Lucy had already put stickers saying: 'Lurchers Do it Languidly',

181

'A Dog is for Life not just for Christmas', and 'Passports for Pets'.

Round the big mirror, semi-circled with lightbulbs, beside snapshots of her little nieces, Lucy had stuck photographs of the cast and the members of the Royal Family, or Gordon Dillon, the editor of the *Scorpion*, they were supposed to represent.

Over the door was pinned her prize possession, nicked from the BBC, which said: 'Please ensure that all spirits are returned to the spirit tank in this room.'

It was creepily appropriate in Valhalla, where every shadow appeared inhabited, and the dark cliff of wood behind the row of caravans and tents, known rather grandiosely as 'the facilities unit', seemed determined to obscure the stars. Who knew what ghosts might creep out of the cloisters or, on this bitterly cold night, the identities of the mufflered and overcoated figures scuttling by.

Also on Lucy's walls were thank-you cards from the cast she'd just been looking after. As usual there had been tears and promises to keep in touch. But for once she wasn't mourning the end of yet another location *affaire*. Her thoughts had been too full of Tristan.

She had been overjoyed to find a big bunch of blue-bells in her caravan, but slightly deflated that every woman in the cast and crew had also received flowers. But at least he'd remembered she liked bluebells, and she kept his good-luck card, which she would certainly need. Tomorrow she had to make up Baby and Flora, who would each require at least an hour and a half, and if things moved swiftly, she might even have to do the ancient tenor playing the Spanish ambassador. Thank God Dame Hermione had insisted on her own make-up artist at vast extra expense.

Fifty yards from Make Up, Hermione's squawks could be heard issuing from the dairy, which had been turned over to Wardrobe. Lady Griselda, the wardrobe mistress, big, deep-voiced, kind, vulnerable and a bit dippy, looked like Julius Caesar in drag, and had a small mouth like the slit in the charity tins she so often jangled on street corners.

As a deb Griselda had played the double bass in a pop group called the Alice Band, and had briefly been in waiting to a lesser member of the Royal Family. She now lived with a lot of cats in a thatched cottage in North Dorset, where she knew 'absolutely everybody'. The cottage was called Wobbly Bottom. Griselda tended to send herself up, before anyone else could, by dressing outlandishly. Today she was wearing a floor-length red-embroidered tunic and a purple turban.

She was also having a nervous breakdown, because Rannaldini (who'd employed her because he felt she'd know how the upper classes dressed) was being absolutely beastly.

Riding coats and breeches littered a large sea-blue damask sofa, which had recently and peremptorily been ejected from Helen's Blue Living Room, as Flora, Baby and Hermione tried on their clothes for tomorrow's shoot.

Tristan was pacing about. There were a million technical demands on him, a potentially disruptive crew, production pressures, worry that the cast would gel even less in a strange environment.

Rannaldini's beautifully manicured fingers were drumming on the table. Sexton was massaging his big face with his hand, always a sign that all was not well.

Hermione, in white breeches, black boots and a waisted red coat with black velvet facings, cut long to hide her large bottom, was preening in the mirror.

'You look lovely, Hermsie,' boomed Griselda, whose social and sartorial instincts were rapidly being sabotaged by her thumping great crush on Hermione.

'Women don't hunt in red coats in England,' snapped Tristan. 'It looks vulgar. Please try the dark blue one again, Hermione.'

'The dark blue won't show up against the trees,' argued Rannaldini.

'I want to add a cheery note to the winter gloom,' pouted Hermione.

Baby, who was supposed to have hurtled across country to join the hunt incognito, was wearing a brown herringbone tweed jacket and, having lost so much weight at Champney's, was marvelling at himself in buff stretch breeches. As Elisabetta's bodyguard, Flora was wearing a less fitted brown riding coat to accommodate the bulge of her gun.

'All of them are same colour as countryside.' Rannaldini's voice was rising. 'They'll get lost.'

Meredith, oblivious of the storm breaking over his airborne curls, was trying on the diamond tiara Hermione was supposed to wear for Philip II's coronation.

'Put on your hats for the total look,' urged Griselda.

The row escalated because neither Hermione nor Baby were prepared to wear hard hats with black chin straps to resemble Camilla Parker Bowles and Prince Charles.

'How could anyone fall in love with anyone at first sight wearing that?' protested Baby. 'D'you want Hermione to smoke a fag as well?'

'Those hats are authentic,' protested Griselda, getting up with a rattle of Valium to tap Hermione's brim further down over her eyes. 'We must set a good example to the Pony Club.'

'Fuck the Pony Club,' snapped Baby.

'Rannaldini would quite like to,' murmured Meredith.

'You can take off your hats the moment you dismount,' pleaded Griselda. 'And Hermione's blonde wig will then tumble beautifully down her back.'

'My hair won't tumble anywhere,' snarled Baby. He loathed his Prince Charles wig, complete with incipient bald patch, even more than his hat.

Meredith, who was now trying on a flower-trimmed straw bonnet, suggested that Baby's and Hermione's hard hats might look better if they were dressed up with long earrings.

'Only if I can wear my scarlet coat,' said Hermione mulishly.

'English women don't wear—' began Tristan.

'But I'm not English,' said Hermione, with a peal of merry laughter, as though she'd made a frightfully good joke. 'I'm South African.'

'Reimpose sanctions,' muttered Baby.

Valhalla, like many ancient ecclesiastical buildings, was H-shaped with the north and south wings forming the verticals of the H. Rannaldini and his family lived in the south wing overlooking the valley.

Meanwhile, in the north wing, other members of the cast and the upper echelons of the crew were bagging their bedrooms, which in contrast to the lavishness of the south wing consisted rather creepily of ex-monks' cells reached by badly lit uncarpeted staircases and long, narrow corridors.

'Bit scary,' quavered Lucy, pushing a reluctant James into a darkly panelled rabbit warren, almost entirely occupied by a big mahogany double bed.

'I don't mind sharing,' said Ogborne, Tristan's cocky and Cockney chief grip, who had a shaved head, an earring, and looked like a self-confident pig. Employed to hump equipment around and shove heavy cameras along tracks, Ogborne had had no difficulty in carrying all of Lucy's cases upstairs.

'Plenty of room for you, me and Fido in here,' he said, patting the bed.

'I talk dreadfully in my sleep, and James snores,' said Lucy hastily.

Down the corridor, Alpheus Shaw, psyching himself into the part of Philip II, was getting more regal by the second, referring to himself as 'one', and striding around with his hands behind his back. He had also demanded the biggest bedroom, which had the biggest four-poster and small leaded windows looking north into the woods and east up the valley.

However, he was deeply displeased that, unlike Tristan, he had not been put in the lush south wing, which he had admired loudly on a previous visit.

Only half the principals were *in situ*: neither Mikhail, Granny, his wayward boyfriend Giuseppe, Alpheus nor Chloe would be needed for a couple of weeks. Alpheus had come down ostensibly to show solidarity and to inspire the cast. After all, he was the principal male singer now Fat Franco had been fired. In reality he wanted to screw Chloe without having to fork out for a hotel – particularly as his wife Cheryl always went through the Amex receipts.

Looking down, he could see Tristan and Rannaldini walking towards the house, their arms waving as they yelled at one another, their shadows long and black behind them.

Inside the dairy, Meredith, like a small child comforting his mother, was patting the vast shoulders of a sobbing Lady Griselda.

'It's just first-night nerves, don't take it personally.'

Griselda gave a sniff.

'Try not to get lippy on that hunting tie, Hermsie,' she called out, 'and I'd be grateful if you'd all put your clothes back on the hangers.'

'What time's dinner?' asked Baby.

'Seven thirty for eight,' said Flora, as she wriggled back into her old grey jersey and scruffy black jeans. 'I can't be bothered to go home and tart up.'

20

Dinner began scratchily. Helen, a lousy hostess at the best of times because she never refilled glasses or introduced anyone, was clearly livid at being invaded by so much mess and so many strangers. As a final insult, drinks were being served in the old red morning room, which she had spent two years of her excruciatingly unhappy marriage transforming into an exquisite symphony of faded blues and rusts. Almost overnight, it had been reduced to a gaudy riot of cherry-red walls, gilded ceilings, floor-length mirrors framed with gold leaf, and two crimson thrones initialled E and PII at the end of the room. Worst of all, three huge glittering chandeliers, hovering overhead like Spielberg spaceships, highlighted every bag and wrinkle – an unkind contrast to the ludicrously flattering painting of herself over the fireplace in which she was portrayed as Athene, goddess of wisdom, with an owl perched on her head.

Having flown in from a wildly successful Mahler's *Resurrection* in Berlin, to ensure Valhalla's cuisine exceeded anything French, Rannaldini had unearthed the Krug and was welcoming guests, and accepting compliments on the room. 'It ees, of course, based on Throne Room at Buckingham Palace,' he told anyone who would listen.

As the crew gathered in one corner puffing Gauloise

187

smoke, and the cast retreated to another trying not to breathe it in, gossip whizzed back and forth in all languages. Everyone was also assessing talent.

'How can I tell Tristan's boys apart when they've all got beards?' said Baby fretfully.

'Jesus must have had the same trouble with his disciples,' said Meredith, 'except this lot have got gorgeous names like best-boy and focus-puller. Valentin the camera operator's heaven, but he's just back from his honeymoon.'

'Best time to turn them, before they start looking round for other women. God, he's divine.'

'Also Rannaldini's son, Wolfgang, so he's out of bounds, *very* straight and rather fierce. I'm sure he's going to insist we all have uniform willies – like Common Market carrots. He's nice.' Meredith nudged Baby, as Sylvestre, the sound man, who'd tied back his long blond hair in a pony-tail, wandered through the door.

'Even straighter and utterly monosyllabic,' said Baby dismissively.

Having grabbed a drink, Sylvestre was soon comparing notes with Ogborne, the chief grip. Flora looked sexy enough, even if she did need a bath, they decided, but those sodding great rings on her hand suggested a rich boyfriend.

'That blonde looks a goer,' said Ogborne.

Sylvestre, who'd much enjoyed Chloe's goings and comings during the recording, agreed.

Then both men choked on their drinks as Tabitha stalked in, turquoise eyes flashing, hair slicked back from her forehead like Rudolph Valentino. She was wearing a cashmere crop top to show off a sea-horse tattooed below her left breast and very low-slung black hipsters. Having filled a glass with so much vodka that the ice she added made it overflow, she made a beeline for Lucy and dragged her over to the fireplace.

'Why do the most beautiful girls always pal up with

dogs?' said Ogborne, still sour at not being asked to share Lucy's bed.

'Because their dogs like each other,' said Sylvestre, as Sharon the Labrador bounced up to James the lurcher, who went up on his toes and nearly sent a bowl of grape hyacinths flying with his long wagging tail.

Tab immediately launched into the state of her marriage.

'Isa was there when I got home from auditioning horses. Then he went straight out, saying he'd gotta go over to bloody Jake's and couldn't make dinner tonight. So I press the redial button, and guess who answered? Fucking Martie in Australia. I'm going mad, Luce.' She drained half her vodka, hand trembling.

'And what was even worse, when I ran down the garden trying to catch Isa, I saw this man on a horse, his hair white-blond in the moonlight, and for a second, I thought, by some miracle, Daddy had come to take me away from this nightmare. Then I realized it was bloody Wolfgang having a snoop. He's furious Rannaldini's lent us Magpie Cottage. And Rannaldini's given him this ace job and he's got no experience. Can't you see *The Ladybird Book of the Cinema* sticking out of his pocket?'

Lucy was about to say how sorry she was, when Rannaldini clapped his hands for silence.

'I would like to welcome you all to the Throne Room at Valhalla on this very special evening,' he said smoothly, 'and introduce my wife Helen, our daughter Tabitha, by the fireplace, and our son, Wolfgang.' He turned to smile at the extremely handsome but undeniably boot-faced young man standing by the window.

'Wolfgang, Wolfgang,' Hermione charged forward, 'I haven't seen you since you were in short pants.'

'And hasn't he turned out yummily,' sighed Meredith, to giggles all round. Poor Wolfgang blushed dark crimson.

'Tabitha, you look just laike your sibling,' said Pushy

Galore, who although only in the chorus, had somehow pushed her way into the party and, to match the décor, was busting out of red velvet braided with gold, 'but not laike your dad or mum.'

'Rannaldini's not my father,' spat Tabitha, 'any more than *he's* my brother.' She scowled at Wolfgang, who scowled back.

An awkward silence was defused by Tristan wandering in. His hair was still wet from the shower, his eyes blood-shot from late nights poring over the storyboards of each scene, which, like an extended comic strip, covered the walls of his suite upstairs.

Tristan apologized profusely for being late and for Lady Griselda who, knowing everyone in Rutshire as well as Dorset, had gone out to dinner, for his delectable niece Simone, who needed ten hours' sleep on the eve of a shoot, and for Bernard, his first assistant director, who was handling some row with Equity and couldn't make it either. He was then so charming to everyone, particularly Helen, that she soon forgot about dust, breakages and chipped paintwork.

In fact, Tristan was incredibly uptight. He always got blinding headaches before filming started, particularly after that row with Rannaldini. He needed five more hours on the score. His confidence had been jolted because his cult film *The Betrothed* had just lost out in the Oscars to a mainstream American comedy. He was also sad to see the large salacious Étienne de Montigny of Abelard and Héloïse, which his father had left Rannaldini, hanging opposite the fireplace, to Helen's obvious distaste.

Oscar, the director of photography, and his son-in-law Valentin, however, were both jolted out of their habitual languor by the painting. 'That's the look we need for the shove-and-grunt scenes, Tristan,' said Oscar, waving his green cigarette-holder in the direction of Héloïse's left breast. 'Beautiful flesh tones. Your father certainly knew about light.'

'I love that painting too,' said Hermione, smiling warmly at Oscar because she wanted him to light her beautifully, and because she liked the piratical good looks of his son-in-law. 'Étienne de Montigny was always begging me to sit for him.'

Tristan had had enough and belted off to the more reassuring comfort of Lucy, who had been deserted by Tabitha in need of more vodka, and who went scarlet when Tristan kissed her on both her already flushed cheeks. Oh, why had she worn a red wool twinset to stand by a blazing fire?

'Thank you ever so much for the bluebells,' she stammered.

'I know you love them, and I remember very good poem about Lucy.

> *'A violet by a mossy stone,*
> *Half hidden from the eye.*
> *Fair as a star, when only one*
> *Is shining in the sky.'*

Tristan reeled off the verse in triumph.

But no-one looks at her when all the other stars come out, thought Lucy. She'd never found the poem very flattering.

There was a pause.

'And this must be James.' Tristan put out a hand to stroke Lucy's lurcher, who was now curled up on the crimson throne initialled E for Excellent.

'You remembered,' said Lucy rapturously.

'Of course. He is beautiful. How old is he?'

'About twelve, the vet says.'

'Where did you get him?'

'I was on a shoot in the East End. He was running round the streets, terrified, with his lead flapping, so I coaxed him into my caravan with a bit of quiche. He was starving.'

The words were tumbling out of Lucy's big, trembling

191

mouth. 'Then he leapt on to a chair, as if he wanted me to make him up, so I took off his lead to make him feel at home and put it on the table. Would you believe it? The next moment, he'd leapt down, snatched back his lead, put it on his chair, jumped back and sat on it.' As Lucy caressed James's brown velvet ears, her voice broke. 'He was desperate not to lose the only possession he had in the world. I had to keep him after that. I'm sorry,' Lucy wiped her eyes, smearing her mascara, 'I'm boring you.'

'I would run around East End with lead trailing,' said Tristan gently, 'if it found me an owner like you.'

Squawking, like a pheasant disturbed in a wood, was coming from the other end of the room. Oscar, not recognizing Hermione, had put up the terrible black of assuming Tabitha was the beautiful young girl who was going to play Elisabetta, and loudly assuring her he would have no problem lighting her at all.

Hermione was hopping.

Touching Lucy's blushing cheek with one finger, Tristan shot off to calm Hermione, which also gave him a chance to say hello to Tab. But Tab had grabbed a bottle and, saying quite untruthfully that Lucy's glass was empty as an excuse to fill her own, shot past him going the other way.

'Who's that man who looks as though a marmalade cat's died on his head?' she hissed.

'That's Colin Milton,' grinned Lucy, lowering her voice. 'Poor old boy's been in the wilderness for years. Kept forgetting his lines and then had a nervous breakdown. He's playing the Spanish ambassador. He's really sweet.'

Meanwhile, anxious to make Alpheus jealous, Chloe was chatting up Wolfgang and, to prove she was not just a pretty face, discussing Schiller.

'In the play,' she said, 'Philip offers his mistress, Eboli, in marriage to a disgusting old courtier.'

'He also offers Carlos up to the Inquisition,' said Wolfgang bleakly, 'because both his mistress and his wife are in love with Carlos. His religion gave Philip a marvellous excuse to murder a son he hated.'

Wow, thought Chloe, you're a chilly boy, ruthless as your dad. The combination of blond, chiselled, Luftwaffe-pilot looks with Rannaldini's night-dark eyes was very disturbing.

'Oh, good*ee*!' Hermione clapped her hands. 'Here's Alpheus.'

Alpheus, who had deliberately arrived late to make an entrance, looked splendid, deeply tanned, wearing a frilly cream shirt tucked into dark blue velvet trousers to show off his T-bone figure. Helen's eyes widened with excitement as he kissed her hand.

'Here comes the Lothario from Long Island,' said Baby sourly.

'He *is* handsome,' reproached Flora.

'Like a lobster,' snapped Baby. 'Tasty body, but a head full of shit.'

'Dinner is served,' grumbled Mr Brimscombe, the gardener, who was violently opposed to Rannaldini's plan to obliterate his flower-beds in a great Buckingham Palace sweep of lawn down to the lake, and who had only agreed to butle because so much crumpet was on view.

21

As the Great Hall was being transformed by Meredith's myrmidons into Philip II's bedroom, they dined in the old Prussian blue dining room, which now had walls the tawny red of beef *consommé,* and a gold ceiling to match all the gold plate and the frames of the portraits on the walls. A brass trough filled with white daffodils stretched down the middle of the table.

'"And then my heart with pleasure fills and dances with the daffodils,"' said Tristan, who had been summoned to sit on Helen's right, but hoped Lucy and therefore Tab might come and sit on his other side. But, tossing her ringlets, Pushy Galore nipped in and stole the seat.

'How the hell did she get in here?' Chloe hissed to Flora.

'Sexton brought her. In that dress, she looks as though he ordered her from the *Past Times* Christmas catalogue. The last shall be first – she'll probably end up marrying Tristan.'

'Having cased the joint, she'll more likely become the next Lady Rannaldini. As Helen clearly hasn't thought we were worth a seating plan, shall we sit together?'

Flora nodded, clutching a furiously growling Trevor to stop him attacking James. She was actually in a state of shock. She'd had no idea her old flame Wolfie was working on the film or that he'd grown so devastatingly attractive. If only she'd bothered to wash her hair and change.

In honour of the stag hunt with which *Don Carlos* opens, they dined on the darkest, meltingly tender venison steeped in a rich red wine sauce.

'The secret of venison is that it should be well hung,' announced Hermione, scooping up most of the delicious celeriac purée.

'Like blokes,' agreed Baby.

'Sublime, Rannaldini,' announced Alpheus, determined to raise the tone. 'How d'you make it so goddam tender?'

'I eenjeck the marinade into the tissue with a hypodermic syringe,' purred Rannaldini.

'How gross,' snapped Tabitha, and fed her venison to Sharon under the table.

Colin Milton wasn't eating his venison either. '"Great Henry, the glorious King of France,"' he muttered to himself, '"wishes to bestow the hand of his daughter ..."' Oh, hell, what came next?

His hand was shaking so dreadfully that when he tried to raise his glass of Château Mouton Rothschild 1949 to his lips, he spilt it.

'Don't waste that stuff, Colin,' shouted Rannaldini, down the table. 'Eet cost a fortune.'

Bastard, thought Lucy, who was already embarrassed because she had refused the venison.

Sitting beside her, Wolfie noticed her empty plate.

'I don't eat meat,' she stammered. 'I'll be fine with vegetables.'

Wolfie stood up. 'I'll have a word with ...' he glanced up the table at Helen '... er, Mrs Rannaldini.'

'*Lady* Rannaldini,' howled Rannaldini. 'Have you lost your manners, Wolfgang?'

An ugly flush spread over Wolfie's face and his

white-knuckled hands clenched the table. Lucy felt terrible, particularly when Mrs Brimscombe hobbled in, apologizing, with the most delectable vegetable lasagne.

'I make it specially for you, Lucy,' called Rannaldini, determined to ingratiate himself with Tabitha's friend.

You're still a bastard, thought Lucy, delighted that Wolfie was now defiantly emptying tomato ketchup over his venison.

When everyone was eating the lightest primrose yellow syllabub with bitter chocolate sauce, Tristan stood up. Having thanked Rannaldini and Helen for allowing their house to be invaded, he went on to talk about *Don Carlos*, repeating Verdi's description of:

'"A family drama in a princely house", which must have been very like Valhalla. It is also a story about sexual jealousy and loneliness in high places.

'Both Schiller and Verdi were obsessed with oppression,' Tristan continued, 'the tyranny of Philip II over his family and his subjects, the tyranny of the Church over everything. Today, the Church has loosed its stranglehold, instead we – and particularly the Royal Family and the government – are controlled by the media. That is why we have set our *Don Carlos* in modern dress, with a corrupt press baron replacing the Grand Inquisitor.'

As part of her job Lucy never stopped watching faces. Seeing the rapt attention of Flora, Chloe, Pushy, Hermione, Helen and even Tab, her heart sank. How stupid to think she had a hope against such dazzling competition. Lost as a star, when all the rest are shining in the sky, she thought sadly. As if to comfort her, James laid his long nose on her knee. At least she hadn't had to go abroad this time and leave him behind.

In the flickering candlelight, Tristan's face had lost its hollows and yellow-greyish pallor. His eyes glowed with conviction.

'None of us is going to get him into bed,' murmured

Meredith to Baby. 'Like Spielberg, he only fucks the movie.'

'In real life Don Carlos was horrible person,' Tristan was now telling his audience. 'He roast animals alive, he gallop his horse to death, he assault and flog palace maids, he even bit the head off a pet lizard and ate it.'

'Ooh,' squealed Pushy.

'I could have murdered a whole lizard at Champney's last week,' called out Baby.

'You are very beautiful now, so it pay off,' laughed Tristan, then serious again. 'Tomorrow we begin filming the first act, which is perhaps the most tragic. Dusk is falling on a great forest. The huntsmen are riding home. Elisabetta and Carlos experience *le coup de foudre*, first love striking like lightning. They have few moments of ecstasy, thinking they will live happy for ever. Then it is over.'

Noticing the desolation on Tabitha's face, he was ashamed to feel a flicker of satisfaction her marriage might not be working out. He had been haunted by dreams of her lean, jeaned body and garlanded head ever since the wedding.

After he'd wished everyone good luck for the morning, there was applause, coffee and liqueurs.

Down the table Hermione was telling Alpheus that Rannaldini often lent her his Gulf IV for overseas engagements. Why shouldn't the Maestro do the same for his principal bass?

Misinterpreting the excitement on her lover's face, Chloe tried once more to galvanize Wolfie. 'Do you like opera?' she asked.

'I liked you in *Nabucco*,' admitted Wolfie, 'when the ENO brought it to Munich.'

'It's pronounced Na-*book*-o,' snarled an eaves-dropping Rannaldini.

I hate my father, thought Wolfie, I should never have come back. I hate Helen. She had always been a pain in the arse when her son Marcus and Wolfie had been at school together. And now she had put him back in his old room, which she'd obviously been using as a spare room, then expected him to rave over the chintz curtains and the flower paintings on the pretence she'd redecorated it especially for him.

I loathe Tabitha, he thought. She's a spoilt brat, worse than Little Cosmo, more arrogant than her father, and now in possession of the nicest cottage on the estate. And there, laughing across the table with Chloe, was Flora, his old love, bloody gold-digger, covered in his father's fingerprints, now shacked up with a guy as old as and probably richer than his father. He had forgiven neither her nor Rannaldini, and Flora, seeing the antagonism battling with the longing in Wolfie's eyes, found it very disturbing. As solid as Tebaldo's gun, she fingered the mobile in her jeans pocket, willing George to ring.

Rannaldini was now talking about Valhalla.

'Part of the house is twelve century. It has been owned since the beginning by aristocrats or monks.'

'Certainly by neither today,' said Tabitha sourly, as she reached through the white daffodils for the Kummel.

'Sometimes,' Rannaldini ignored her, 'on summer nights we 'ear the most beautiful plainsong from the chapel, but no-one is there. A sad, weeping lady in grey, Caroline Beddoes, is often seen gazing out of a blocked-up window on the north side. She has blood on her dress and a little dog in her arms. Sometime she glide through doors which exeest no longer. You can hear the hiss of her silk skirts on the flagstones.

'And, of course, as in many great houses, there is a legend that when the lake dries up the head of the family will die.'

'It looked promisingly low on the way down,' murmured Baby.

Everyone laughed nervously, glancing furtively into the shadowy corners – except Alpheus.

'Did you really manage to negotiate a cash settlement?' he was asking Hermione.

'Do you believe in ghosts, Sir Roberto?' quavered Pushy.

The lights seemed to dim.

'I believe, my dear,' the excited throb in Rannaldini's voice was growing more insistent, 'in a great departure lounge crowded with spirits desperate to get to the next world or to return to this one, to avenge themselves or to clear their name or find a lost love.'

'Attractive, isn't he?' whispered Chloe.

'Satanically,' shivered Flora.

'Been to bed with him?'

'Yes.'

'So have I. Brilliant, wasn't it?'

'Yes.'

'We also have the legend of the Paradise Lad, a beautiful novice,' Rannaldini's eyes gleamed, 'flogged to death by the monks for falling in love with a village girl. Sometime we hear him sobbing. Listen.' As Rannaldini held up a white hand, a moan came from the chimney and everyone jumped in terror. 'But it is probably only the wind.'

The port and brandy were orbiting like formula-one cars. Suddenly the door creaked slowly open. People screamed and clutched each other, as no-one entered. Then Rannaldini's white cat, Sarastro, padded in.

'It's the night shift come to sit on Colin's head,' whispered Tabitha.

Next moment even she had jumped out of her skin, as Sarastro arched his back and hissed, his tail thick as a snow-covered Christmas tree. But he had only seen James, who would have given chase, if Lucy hadn't grabbed his new green collar.

Helen was not happy. Tristan was perfectly charming but she wished he didn't always want his crew to enjoy the same privileges as himself, when it meant her having on her left Ogborne, the pig-like chief grip whose shaved head was gleaming in the candlelight and who had just poured himself a third glass of port.

'Got everything you need?' she asked acidly.

'Well, Cindy Crawford would be nice,' said Ogborne, adding kindly, 'but it's been a great meal.'

'Where does the name Valhalla come from?' asked Pushy.

Helen opened her mouth. At last a chance to show off, but she was pre-empted by Ogborne.

'Wagner,' he told Pushy. 'Valhalla was the palace built for the gods by the giants Fasolt and Fafner. You must remember that wonderful moment at the end of *Rhinegold*, when the gods pass over the rainbow bridge and enter the castle at sunset.'

The entire table fell silent, gazing at him in amazement.

'And who's that very handsome gentleman over the fireplace?' simpered Pushy Galore.

'She's so far up Rannaldini,' hissed Chloe, 'one can't see her toenails any more.'

'That is my great-great-grandfather on my mother's side,' said Rannaldini, smiling warmly at Pushy. 'A tremendous rake. That portrait has been known to wink at very pretty girls.'

'Bollocks,' hiccuped Meredith. 'You bought Great-great-grandpop and all your other ancestors in the King's Road in the late eighties.'

Tristan tried not to laugh, and because Rannaldini had thrown Meredith such a filthy look and he didn't want his entire crew and cast quitting Valhalla in terror, he got up to go.

'Bedtime, everyone. Thank you, Rannaldini and Helen, for a wonderful evening. It has put us in great mood for tomorrow.'

Not *all* of us, thought Flora sadly, then squeaked in ecstasy as her mobile rang.

'I'm in a seven-foot by seven-foot four-poster in

Doosledorf,' said a broad Yorkshire accent, 'and I need soomeone to fill it.'

'Oh, George,' sighed Flora, 'I love you so much and thank you for my lovely regard ring.'

Wolfie flinched.

'OK for some,' said Tab bitterly, then, pleadingly to Lucy, 'Come back to the cottage for a quick one.'

'Can I come too?' asked Ogborne, picking up the bottle of Kummel.

'No, you can't,' said Tab rudely.

Lucy sighed inwardly. 'It'd better be quick – I've got to be up at six.'

Having made a few telephone calls, Rannaldini locked his study door, pressed a button and the bookshelf slid back to reveal a wall of monitors.

'Two-way mirror on the wall,' murmured Rannaldini, 'who is the fairest of them all?'

Sadly, Tab had gone home. He must get Clive to install that video-camera in Magpie Cottage. Flora had pushed off to her parents' house, Hermione to River House. But there was poor bald Colin, without his toupee, pacing his little cell, and Tristan had fallen asleep on his chess-board, clutching his mobile. Oscar was also asleep, Valentin calling his new wife.

Ah, that was more interesting. Pushy Galore going down on Sylvestre, and Ogborne snorting with delight over a porn mag. Wolfie lay on his back, smoking. Rannaldini had so often seen the same bruised furious reproach in Wolfie's mother's eyes. Of all of his wives, she had been the first and the worst treated. She had been so young. He must win Wolfie over. In the next cell, Baby was gazing at a photograph of someone suspiciously like Isa Lovell.

Pouring himself a brandy, Rannaldini sat back to watch Chloe and Alpheus but, despite Chloe's ravishing body and flickering expertise, it was so mainline, he soon nodded off.

Even when she had tumbled into bed, long after midnight, Lucy couldn't sleep. The house, like an ancient arthritic, kept shifting its position, creaking and groaning to get comfortable. The wind howled, the central heating gurgled, James was restless, and in the next room Colin Milton was so nervous they might get to the Spanish ambassador tomorrow, he spent all night practising his lines.

Lucy tried not to think about Tristan. For once she was glad when her alarm clock went off at five thirty.

22

From six o'clock onwards a mighty army of lorries, caravans, a canteen, generators, double-decker dining-buses and a Portaloo euphemistically nicknamed the honey-wagon rumbled eastwards into Rannaldini's woods. Their destination was a beechwood known as Cathedral Copse, because its silver trunks soared to the sky like the pillars of a huge nave.

It was a bitterly cold day. In a clearing Oscar, the director of photography, his purple scarf and dark hair flapping, was eating a bacon sandwich, glancing from shivering stand-ins to light meters, and briefing the gaffer, the chief electrician, who in turn told his minions, the sparks, where to put the lights. Except in the place where the singers were going to act, the carpet of faded beech leaves was criss-crossed with camera tracks and cables and teeming with focus-pullers measuring distances, boom operators, and props men trying to look useful.

Over in Make Up, Lucy had grabbed a cup of coffee and a hot dog for James before starting on the long haul of making up Baby, who needed Alka-Seltzer, lots of blue eye-drops, concealer for his dark shadows and blusher for his blanched cheeks.

'You've got such a beautiful face,' chided Lucy. 'You should cut out the booze and get a few early nights.'

'Carlos is supposed to look pale and wan.'

'Not in this scene. That comes after his dad's nicked his girlfriend.'

'How's Mrs Lovell's marriage?'

'Fine.' Lucy drew a white line inside Baby's lower lashes to reduce the redness.

'Yeah, yeah, Rannaldini's won a peace prize. Is Isa catting around?'

'You should know. You're his friend.'

'He's not the greatest communicator, except with horses.'

'Aren't you nervous?' asked Lucy, who was accustomed to calming terrified actors, particularly on the first day.

'Not in the least. Don't change the subject. You went back to Magpie Cottage – she must have said something. She was certainly on the pull last night, flashing her sea-horse tattoo.'

'She dressed up because she thought Isa was coming with her. I don't want to discuss it. Now, what are we going to do about your green tongue? Here's a pink cough pastille, if you can keep it down.'

Next she had to cope with a sobbing Flora, clutching a furiously yapping Trevor with one hand and tugging her red hair down over her ears with the other.

Whereas make-up artists usually adjust to their subject's wishes, film hairdressers tend to impose their views on others. Flora had got stuck into the tattered remains of *Captain Corelli's Mandolin* only to discover she'd been given a short back and sides.

'George will sling me out. Oh, for God's sake, stop it, Trevor!' Flora's voice rose to a scream as the little terrier lunged at a surprised James.

'You can get away with it, you've got such a lovely face.' Lucy tied a powder-blue overall round Flora's neck. 'And it'll soon grow.'

'Not for three months, it won't,' mocked Baby. 'That gauleiter Simone from Continuity won't allow it, and

Lucy said I've got a beautiful face too. She says it to all the girls.'

'Oh, go away and annoy Wardrobe,' said Lucy, throwing a sponge at him.

'I shall go and inhabit *my* caravan. Look, it's on the call sheet – "Mr Spinosissimo's caravan". It's eight inches longer than Hermione's, I measured it – so yah, boo!'

Lucy then had to turn a quaking Flora into Hermione's private detective, thickening her eyebrows, giving her sideboards and a small moustache, and creating brown stubble with a dry sponge.

'I'm bored in my caravan. It's lonely being a mega-star,' said Baby, half an hour later. He was so turned on by Flora's new butch look, he couldn't stop pinching her bottom.

'You're wanted in Wardrobe, Mr Spinosissimo.' Standing in the doorway, his shoulders broadened by a lumber jacket, was a stony-faced Wolfie. 'Get your ass into gear, the director's waiting.'

'Treat 'em mean, keep 'em keen. Heil Hitler.' Baby goosestepped after Wolfgang. 'Christ, it's cold. If March is meant to go out like a lamb, this one's New Zealand and deep-frozen.'

Over at Wardrobe, Tristan and Lady Griselda, in a floor-length fur-lined red coat and a fake-fur hat like a tsar, had decided that as Carlos had just flown into France incognito, it would be more appropriate for him to lurk at the meet in a covert coat.

'Wouldn't a flasher's mac be more suitable?' said Baby.

He was still violently opposed to his Prince Charles wig and enraged Tristan by asking the grinning crew whether he looked a prat or not. When they voted by a show of hands that he did, he tore it off and threw it into a bramble bush.

Tristan only gave in because he and Rannaldini,

who'd just rolled up in his huge wolf coat, had been sucked into an even worse screaming match with Meredith, who didn't appear quite so young and boyish out of doors. The point of contention was a hunting lodge, which looked as though it had been exclusively decorated by Colefax & Fowler.

'We are not making fourth-rate production of *Hansel and Gretel*,' snarled Rannaldini, whose idea it had actually been because he wanted a free summerhouse, but who hadn't forgiven Meredith for last night's bought ancestors.

'Carlos and Lizzie have a love tryst in it,' Meredith stamped his little snow boot, 'so it must look nice.'

'We should have seen a model first,' said Tristan reasonably.

'It look like cuckoo clock,' hissed Rannaldini.

Meredith flounced off, muttering that his artistic input had been compromised. The cuckoo clock was banished and stood sulking near the car park for the rest of the shoot.

Because Hermione was still squawking in Make Up it was decided quickly to relight and shoot the first four lines of Baby's aria, when he expresses rapture after catching his first glimpse of Elisabetta.

There was already a crimson blur of new bud on the beeches. Bluebell leaves and green flames of wild garlic were pushing through the leaf mould. But such signs of spring were speedily blotted out by the snow machine scattering white foam everywhere, even between the cracks in the dry ground.

'Remember not to bang your chest. It sound like Beeg Ben,' begged Sylvestre as he miked up Baby.

Next moment, everyone jumped out of their skins, as music poured *fortissimo* out of speakers hidden behind two venerable sycamores.

'Doesn't it sound gorgeous?' cried Flora, rushing out of Make Up, her eyes filled with tears. 'Rannaldini's overture is simply sensational. You'd never know it wasn't Verdi.'

'You always admired him,' said Wolfie coldly.

Flora flushed. Next moment she had tripped over a sign concealed by the snow saying 'Beware of Snakes'.

'Oh, God,' she wailed. 'Trevor and I are going to invest in some thigh boots before summer.'

Meanwhile, Hype-along Cassidy, the harassed press officer, who was expecting a reporter and photographer from the *Independent*, was sidling from one bewildered member of the French crew to another, imploring them to charge forward and ask for Dame Hermione's autograph when she deigned eventually to come out of her caravan.

'Bruce Willis's press officer does the same thing,' he lied.

Tristan was taking Baby through a quick rehearsal. Valentin, Oscar's handsome son-in-law, perched on a little chair behind the camera, was following them, as Ogborne, a red knitted flower-pot covering his shaved head, pushed the camera along the silver rail tracks.

As the head of Props pressed a button, and the smoke-machine enveloped Baby in swirling grey mist, Lucy shot forward with her brushes to take the shine off his nose, and a hairdresser rearranged his curls.

'More smoke,' shouted Tristan.

'That brown velvet collar needs straightening,' yelled Griselda.

'Quiet, please, we're going for a take,' brayed Bernard, the first assistant director.

An incredible tension gripped everyone – even the birds were silent, the breeze still.

'Sound rolling,' said Sylvestre.

'Camera rolling,' called Valentin.

'Mark it,' said Tristan, and the clapper-loader jumped in front of the camera, saying, 'Slate one, take one,' and snapped his clapper.

'Action,' shouted Tristan.

Out strolled Baby into the sunlight.

'"Fontainebleau. Immense and solitary forest",' he sang exactly in time to his own exquisite voice. '"What rose-filled gardens, what Eden of loveliness could equal in Carlos's eyes this wood through which his smiling Elisabetta passed?"'

'And cut!' shouted Tristan. 'That was great.' Then, loping over to Baby, 'Could you make it a little more ecstatic? You are expecting hideous future wife and suddenly you discover you are to marry most stunning girl in world – you could even clutch yourself with joy.'

'Anything's better than clutching Dame Hermione.'

'*Tais-toi!* You're miked up! OK, we go again.'

The mournful clarinet began once more, the smoke-machine fired another swirl of mist. As Tristan called, 'Action,' glamorous Valentin, riding his camera like a jockey, reminded Baby of Isa.

'Fontainebleau,' he sang rapturously.

After three takes, each more miraculous than the one before, Tristan said, 'Fantastic! Check the gate.'

Once the clapper-loader had shone his torch into the camera to check there were no hairs or dust to ruin the picture, Tristan shouted: 'Cut and print.' Everyone cheered, because the first shot was in the can.

The rest of the aria was going to be used as voiceover as Baby smuggled himself into France and the Spanish ambassador's entourage. It was now time for Hermione. Having borrowed a tape-measure from Griselda and discovered Baby had the longer caravan, she was now screeching at Bernard Guérin, the first assistant director. 'I answer only to Tristan de Montigny or Sir Roberto, and no-one, absolutely no-one, orders me to hurry up. And in future ensure that my caravan is not parked next to the honeywagon.'

Bernard, who'd been unable to make last night's party, acted as Tristan's sergeant major. His job was to see everything ran smoothly on the floor. Any hold-up cost thousands.

Bernard also did the bellowing and bossing around, which enabled Tristan to drift about, inspiring, charming, manipulating, and still appearing as Mr Nice Guy, even when he pushed people to the limit. Bernard, who'd been in the army with Tristan's brother Laurent and held him dying in his arms in Africa, hero-worshipped the Montigny family. He also got wildly jealous and sulked if anyone got too close to Tristan.

Sadly, one of the reasons Hermione was being so gratuitously rude to him was because he had a brick-red face, the rolling eyes and big teeth of a rocking-horse, an ebony moustache covering a huge upper lip and the bray of a choleric donkey.

'When Frogs are ugly, there's no competition,' whispered Baby, as Bernard emerged from Hermione's mauling, his red face darkened to maroon and enlivened by a delta of purple veins on his forehead.

With a sigh, Rannaldini vanished into Hermione's caravan and came down the steps a minute or so later, ostentatiously tucking his shirt into his trousers. 'Dame Hermione is now on her way,' he called out smugly, so the crew could hear. 'You must learn tact, Bernard.'

Nemesis, however, was hovering: almost on cue, Hermione's young, hopelessly harassed but adorably pretty make-up artist wandered down the steps of the honeywagon next door. In her clinging orange cardigan above knitted red and white trousers, she looked every inch a star. To the rapture of the *Independent* photographer, she was then stampeded by crew members, crying "Ermione, 'Ermione!' and begging for her autograph.

Hype-along Cassidy, the Press Officer, whose brown velvet hat was knocked off in the rush, only just managed to beat them off as Hermione herself emerged in the red riding coat Tristan had vetoed last night.

Whatever happened to Rannaldini's dominance

ending at the recording? thought Flora in alarm.

Hermione was further outraged when Tristan cautiously suggested her make-up was too heavy for outdoors.

'Which, roughly translated, means it makes the old bat look a hundred,' whispered Baby to the crew, who he'd got totally on his side.

Hermione's quailing make-up artist was then ordered by Tristan to take her make-up down, which meant another hour's delay. Later, Bernard stole off to have a pee behind a holly tree, and only just missed Hermione frantically applying eye-liner.

'Her next CD will be called "Hermione goes to Hollybush".' Baby's joke was soon whizzing round the set.

Baby proved a complete natural, who only had to glance at his lines in Make Up before going from nothing to regulo ten in thirty seconds. Hermione, on the other hand, was used to having a raised eyebrow seen in the gods, and was defeated by the stillness, subtlety and control of cinema acting. She was soon driving everyone crackers insisting, 'But I always enter right for this aria,' and because she, like everyone else, had a monstrous crush on Tristan, wanting to know her motivation for every syllable.

Tristan's niece, Simone, in charge of continuity, was tiny and elfin with a glossy dark brown urchin cut and mournful Montigny eyes. Her fragility, however, belied a forceful personality. As most of the film was shot out of order, Simone's main task, apart from timing takes, was to insist that each scene blended into earlier and later ones.

'Your cigarette was only a quarter smoked last time, Baby,' she was now shouting, 'and we agreed you should carry a whip, Dame Hermione.'

'Oh, sugar, I left it at home.'

'Wolfgang can go and get it,' said Rannaldini. 'That's what he's here for.'

Having played in the first rugger team of an English public school, Wolfie was used to being yelled at under pressure. But with Bernard shouting instructions into his earpiece all morning, it was as though the Battle of the Somme had broken out. Now Rannaldini was pitching in.

'And you can pick up another thermal vest from the Mill while you're there, Wolfgang,' Hermione called after him. 'I cannot afford to catch cold,' she added, as Tristan's eyes rose to heaven at the thought of more delay.

By the time they broke for lunch, only Baby's four lines had been filmed, and everyone had such cold noses they looked like an advertisement for Comic Relief.

Aware she had a French crew, Maria the caterer, a pretty, pregnant Italian, was on her mettle and had produced baked red snapper with aromatic Chinese sauce, steak and kidney pie, sautéed garlic potatoes, a vegetable stir-fry for Lucy, followed by rhubarb crumble or treacle pudding.

Everyone piled up their plates and charged the dining bus, where Tristan, because of the cold and it being the first day, had ordered bottles of wine for every table.

'How the hell are you going to put up with Hermione?' asked Oscar, as he tied his napkin round his neck to protect his purple scarf.

'Divas are not fully balanced human beings,' said Tristan dropping three Disprins into a glass of Perrier. 'If they were they wouldn't be great.'

After lunch the rows escalated.

'What is my motivation for this scene?' Hermione asked Tristan for the thousandth time.

'You are cold, exhausted and lost in a huge forest,' said Tristan, through gritted teeth. 'Suddenly Carlos steps out from behind that tree and offers you his protection.'

'If I've just come off a plane, surely I'd offer her a slug of duty-free,' said Baby helpfully.

'Will you stop taking the pees?' Tristan's voice rose. 'As I was saying, Hermione, you're lost in a wood.'

'"Just a little lamb who's lost in a wood,"' sang Hermione, *fortissimo*, then went into peals of laughter as everyone jumped out of their skins.

'Don't you wish that pistol was loaded?' murmured Baby to Flora.

'I feel like Agent Scully. At least we've got the same-coloured hair,' whispered back Flora, who was very excited by her gun, which was a Heckler-Koch 'toy', as used by the SAS.

She was feeling spooked, however, because Rannaldini had nastily insisted she take off not just her regard ring but also her sapphire engagement ring.

'It ees almost beeger than the evening star, and much too camp for a detective,' he sneered. 'Why not lend it to Baby?'

'Look mean, Flora, *chérie*,' shouted Tristan, 'and when you see Carlos, shield Hermione and point your gun straight into camera.'

'Stand by to shoot, please,' bellowed Bernard.

Everyone moved out of shot.

'Here we go, let's turn over.'

And poor Flora was into a rat race. If she sang loud enough to have the right facial movements, the sound was too loud for her to hear the playback and she got out of synch. Alas, the promised voice coach had been sacked even before he'd started. Instead, to help her sing in time, and come in at the right moment, the video of Rannaldini conducting the score was now being relayed on a huge monitor behind the crew. This made her even more nervous.

She kept fluffing her lines, let alone remembering to look mean and shoot into the camera. Nor was she helped by planes going over, Griselda charging up to smooth her riding coat over the bulge of her gun, Lucy racing in to tone down her red nose with green face powder, Simone telling her to do up her top button, or Rannaldini continually shouting.

'I don't like hecklers, even if they do have cocks,' she muttered dolefully. Then, just as she got things right, her mobile rang.

'Oh, George,' Flora burst into tears, 'I'm a lousy actress, but I can't talk now. I'll ring you back. I'm sorry, everyone.'

Rannaldini went berserk. 'Are you going to take this thing seriously?' he yelled, grabbing her mobile. 'Because eef not Gloria knows Tebaldo's words and is only too 'appy to take over.'

'Leave her alone,' shouted Baby, who'd been crunching clove after clove of garlic in anticipation of his clinch with Dame Hermione.

There was a red glow on the horizon. The third lot of snow needed topping up, the day was running away. Blown like a dry leaf by everyone's arguments, Flora leant against a tree, got lichen on her breeches and bollocked by Griselda.

'Everyone hates me,' she muttered miserably.

'I don't,' said Sylvestre, who could hear her through the mike.

'I don't,' said Rozzy Pringle, the former singer of Flora's part, whose voice had broken down in the recording, and who'd just arrived to help in Wardrobe. Putting a little stone hot-water bottle into one of Flora's blue frozen hands and a mug of hot Ribena into the other, she whispered, 'You look chilled to the marrow, poor little duck.'

'Oh, Rozzy, how lovely to see you.'

'And you. Don't cry, darling, your make-up will run.'

'Ooh, that looks nice,' called Hermione. 'I'd like some hot Ribena too. Go and fetch me some, Wolfgang.'

Which made Wolfie hate Flora more than ever, particularly when he met Helen panting up the hill going the other way. 'George Hungerford's just called the house. He can't get through. Can you tell Flora to switch on her mobile? He says it's urgent.'

'I'm not having any of those thoogs bullying you,' were George's first words, as Flora rang him on Bernard's mobile.

'Flora,' snarled Wolfie, 'are you going to hold us up all night?'

He wants to kill me, thought Flora. Even with a hundred people milling around, he terrified her.

The next day went much better. In the afternoon, they even filmed Carlos and Elisabetta's first kiss. Baby's attempts only to kiss Hermione between her jutting lower lip and her chin came to nothing: she sucked in his tongue like a Hoover.

'Cut,' shouted Tristan then took her aside. 'As this is the first kiss of an innocent young virgin, *chérie*, I think it should be more tentative.'

'That woman could suck Tasmania back to the mainland,' Baby regaled an hysterical crew. 'God knows how Rock Hudson did it for years.'

'It's called a Fontaineblow-job,' giggled Flora, who'd regained her high spirits. 'When the weather improves you've got to bonk her.'

'That'll be a piece of piss,' drawled Baby. 'When I was a little kid in Oz my parents were always sending me up chimneys. Hermione's fanny holds no fears for me.'

23

The first weeks of filming were very traumatic for Tristan, and his good nature, particularly when large crowds, horses and hounds were introduced, was severely tested.

Extras, as Sexton was fond of saying, are more expensive than lawyers. Tristan planned to use much of the chorus's already recorded singing as voiceover, and when he employed actual crowds, to keep down the budget by packing as many of their scenes as possible into the same day.

One of his problems was that Sexton had advertised for extras in the *Rutminster Echo*, and the same lot rolled up for every crowd scene, whether as poverty-stricken woodmen and their wives or glamorous French courtiers and ladies-in-waiting or suave dark-eyed diplomats from the Spanish delegation.

This was particularly apparent because Pushy Galore, one of the few trained singers used as an extra, pushed her way to the front in every crowd scene.

If any of the extras managed to have a word with Tristan, they could claim they had 'taken direction' and charge for extra pay. If they were filmed beside any of the stars, this could be categorized as a 'cameo appearance' and they received double pay.

One of Wolfie's most important jobs, therefore, was

to keep the extras away from the cast, which was particularly difficult the day Hype-along invited down a reporter from *The Times* and was bunging anyone he could see to ask for Dame Hermione's autograph.

This was after a most unfortunate piece had appeared in the *Independent* headlined 'Dame Qui?' saying none of the French crew had a clue who Hermione was. Poor Hype-along had had to rise at dawn and buy up every *Independent* on sale at the Paradise village shop before Hermione could send out for one.

It was even harder to keep the extras away from Tristan, who was so polite, whose head was so much in the clouds, and who was so horrified by the way Rannaldini was shattering everyone's confidence that he'd speak to all and sundry just to reassure them they were doing brilliantly.

As well as bellowing through his loud-hailer to the extras to keep back, Wolfie had to tell them what expression – sad, shocked, deprived, happy – to use. Uninstructed extras always look like the village idiot. Every week, Sexton came down with money in a Gladstone bag, new readies for the extras, used readies for Hermione. Wolfie had to distribute these.

The extras made their first appearance at a stag hunt through snowy beechwoods. A very mettlesome stag had been hired, and Baby and Flora made jokes about fast bucks, particularly when the stag took off into the forest scattering rustics and was last seen chasing ghastly Percy the Parson, who'd got a thumping crush on Baby after hearing him sing at Tabitha's wedding.

Griselda, the wardrobe mistress, massive in a mauve boiler-suit, was having even more of a nervous breakdown than usual. She had spent days amassing clothes for woodmen and foot-followers that were suitably bucolic. Rozzy Pringle, her new PA, had spent hours labelling them with each extra's name and hanging them on clothes rails.

Alas, all the extras had lied about their neck size and

ended up wearing collars so tight their eyes popped out, like an old Pekineses' reunion.

Then Rannaldini started screaming that nobody looked dirty enough.

'Thees ees not catwalk at Aquascutum fashion show.'

'You OK'd those clothes yesterday,' said Griselda, bursting into tears. 'I hate extras,' she sobbed. 'Only ten per cent of the men wear underpants, and only five per cent of the women.'

'Can you tell me which five, when you've got a second?' asked Ogborne, his shaven head hidden in a blue wool flower-pot today, as he laid the tracks for the dolly on which the camera travelled down a different ride.

Lucy had loads more people to make up. The courtiers and huntsmen were fairly straightforward, but she had great difficulty with the chorus of poverty-stricken woodland folk, because none of them looked remotely undernourished.

She had even more of a problem keeping a straight face when Colin Milton, instead of removing his marmalade toupée to play the balding Spanish ambassador, insisted on hiding it under a bald skull-cap.

Flora – who as Hermione's detective was meant to shadow her during the hunt – found singing while controlling a horse extremely difficult. Tab had grudgingly lent her The Engineer because she wanted her little grey horse to appear in the film. Unfortunately every time Wolfie, who was cantering around like a polo umpire, bellowed through his loud-hailer, The Engineer bolted. Yelling that she couldn't afford to lose an Olympic horse, Tab finally insisted Flora switch to Wolfie's old pony, Audrey. This triggered off a further screaming match with Simone, because it screwed up continuity, and with Wolfie, who didn't want poor Audrey between Flora's thighs.

Tab didn't care. As mistress of the horse, her word was

law. She had already tranked the delinquent Prince of Darkness, because Rannaldini wanted Hermione to ride him in the film.

'Rather like a selling plate,' grumbled Baby.

The Prince of Darkness was fine when he was galloping across country, but he lashed out at crowds, particularly at Pushy Galore, who had shoved her way to the front of the foot-followers. Pushy was livid and promptly reported the Prince and Tab to the union. This may have been due to jealousy.

Every time Tab appeared on the set, all one could see was technicians tripping over cables and camera tracks and cannoning into each other as they cricked their necks for a third and fourth glance. Even Oscar, the director of photography, woke up.

'Talk about the return of Hale-Bopp,' he sighed, as Tab and The Engineer flew past, blonde hair, grey mane and tail flying.

After Tab, the most eye-catching sight on the set was Hype-along Cassidy, the Press Officer, who had ginger sideboards and, even in winter, whisked about in flowered kipper ties and flared pastel suits. 'Seventies is my trademark,' he was always saying. 'If you're different you're remembered.'

Hype-along knew more people than Griselda, but in twenty-five highly successful years he had never met a bunch whose vanity and caprice exceeded the cast of *Don Carlos*. Not only did they want coverage in the posh papers, but also double-page spreads in the tabloids praising their artistry but not mentioning their sex lives.

On the extras' second day, Hype-along wheeled in the *Sunday Express*, whose photographer was having an adventurous time leaping out of the way of The Prince of Darkness and snapping the hunt as they streamed down a woodland ride.

'So pleasant to have a break in Paradise,' announced Hermione, slowing down to bow to the *Express* photographer as she and Colin Milton cantered decorously past. 'It's so peaceful here.'

Colin's chestnut mare had furry legs like a feminist. It was lucky he was hanging on to her mane for grim death for next moment they were overtaken by a yelling peril.

'Move it, you fuckers!' shouted Tabitha. 'You're hunting, not pulling a coffin, and for God's sake sit up, Grandma,' she added to Hermione, 'and shorten your reins.'

Hermione turned puce. 'To think I sang at her wedding for nothing! I'm not surprised Isaac's fed up with her already. I also think she's been at the hip flask.'

Wolfie thought the same thing, and finding a half-empty bottle of vodka in the hollow of a large oak tree, emptied it on to the grass.

Tristan, meanwhile, knew exactly what space he wanted between horses and, in the politest possible way, made Hermione, Flora, Colin and the hunt return to their starting-point at the top of the ride again and again.

They were at last achieving a perfect take, galloping out of the wood with the sun shining and ivy glittering like chain-mail on the trees, when Tab came scorching across their bows, screaming, 'Cut, cut, cut.'

Horses and riders slithered to a halt.

But before Tab could weigh into them in front of a flabbergasted crew, an outraged Tristan and an apoplectic Bernard, Wolfie had hurtled up, caught The Engineer's reins and yanked him to a halt.

'What the hell are you playing at?'

With his furious, flushed face, his gleaming blond hair, and his plunging horse, he looked just like St George. But his indigo eyes blazed like Rannaldini's.

'Hermione's toes were pointing down like Darcey Bussell,' yelled back Tab, 'and Spanish ambassadors don't cling on to their horses' manes. And who let Hermione carry a hunting whip without a lash? It's *so* naff. And if she wants to wear a red coat, why doesn't she get a job at Butlin's?'

'You've just wrecked a perfectly good take!'

'My reputation is at stake,' countered Tab, who was getting thoroughly above herself. 'If this goes on, I'll have to take my name off the credits.'

'After all your forty-eight-hour experience,' said a scornful Wolfie, thinking how pale and unhealthy she looked in the spring sunshine. Then, seeing the first assistant director puffing up the hill, he added, 'And you'll bloody well apologize to Bernard.'

'I will not, you bloody Alfred Hitler.'

'Alfred?' Wolfie raised an incredulous blond eyebrow.

Realizing she'd goofed, Tab had to recover herself. 'Adolf's much more evil elder brother,' she said haughtily. 'And don't you dare take the piss out of me.'

'Can we get on?' said a chilling voice, which promptly sent the sun in.

It was Rannaldini.

'You're out of order, Wolfgang. Tabitha was quite right to halt the film. That whip', he added bitchily, 'is wrong. Hermione had a lash yesterday and The Prince of Darkness should be wearing my saddlecloth. *Very* black mark for continuity, Simone.'

'Not if he's being ridden by a French princess,' said Wolfie defiantly. 'Your saddlecloth incorporates the colours of the German and Italian flags,' and swinging his horse round, he cantered off to tell the hunt to go back up the hill again.

How truly kind of Wolfie to defy his terrifying father for my sake, thought tiny Simone tearfully.

To avoid more chaos, Tristan filmed the hounds on a separate day. The Cotchester Hunt, pulled out by Rupert, had been replaced by a splendidly sixteenth-century assortment of wolfhounds, greyhounds, salukis and lurchers. But being gaze hounds, who chased what they saw rather than what they smelled, they ignored the extra, drenched in aniseed, who'd replaced the stag, and tore instead after the camera moving on its dolly. Soon Ogborne, clutching his flower-pot hat, Valentin, in his new English brogues, and Oscar, who'd nodded off against a copper beech, could be seen belting off into the wood in terror.

James the lurcher, who'd been signed up as a hound, immediately rushed back to Lucy, where the other Valhalla dogs, Sharon, Trevor and Tabloid, Rannaldini's Rottweiler, who'd all ploughed the audition, proceeded to rubbish him out of jealousy.

'Cut down the tallest puppy,' said Flora, who was in such hysterics, she fell off Audrey.

Despite the traumas, wonderful work was being done. Hermione's long, one-noted 'Yes', when she agreed to marry Philip rather than Carlos, had everyone in tears. And at the end of two and a half weeks, the first, and probably most taxing, act was in the can, the buds could feel free to burst open in Cathedral Close, and the wild flowers to throw off their blanket of artificial snow.

Action would now move inside to the dungeons and to Alpheus's bedroom scene. Alpheus, Granny, Chloe, Hermione, Mikhail and Baby would be needed, but no horses or Flora, so she and Tabitha could have a break.

But there was no respite for Lucy. Her make-up had been inspired, except when Tristan popped into her caravan and her hands started shaking. When he watched the rushes, he realized even more what a treasure he had found. Flora with her short back and sides looked disturbingly androgynous. With miraculous shading, Baby had lost all his puppy fat – he was also acting everyone off the screen, you couldn't take your eyes off him.

The only person not ravished by the rushes was Hermione. She was in the habit of pestering her agent, Howie Denston, twenty times a day, even ordering him to ring up and tell her chauffeur to turn down the car radio when she was being driven the half-mile from River House to Valhalla.

Now she told Howie to tell Tristan she could only film

in the afternoons, when her big brown eyes were fully open. She also sacked her make-up artist and insisted on having Lucy.

Lucy was then summoned to Hermione's caravan for a glass of very cheap South African sherry as the great diva lay stretched out on a bed, a pad steeped in witch-hazel over her eyes.

'As I'm playing a beautiful young princess in this film,' announced Hermione, 'I thought it fitting at first to employ a beautiful young make-up artist, who would be *au fait* with the latest trends. While you're here, Lucy dear, could you peel those grapes, and pop them into my mouth? Now I realize I was wrong.' Hermione sounded as though she was going over to Rome. 'Far better to go for a mature, older woman, like yourself, who knows the ropes. You mustn't be fazed, Lucy. I have every faith in you.'

'I wanted to ram her bloody grapes down her throat,' Lucy told Tristan afterwards.

Although he was cross, Tristan was ecstatic Lucy could now feed his ideas into Hermione's thick skull. But realizing Lucy never finished clearing up and doing her paperwork before midnight, he promised her more help – perhaps Rozzy from Wardrobe.

'And you need more light in here.'

Lucy was so touched he'd noticed she'd have made up the entire crew. Griselda, however, was livid. Rozzy was the best assistant she'd ever had: she was determined to hang on to her.

Wolfie was also proving a great asset, checking Oscar's cigars were lit and that Tristan didn't lose his camera script. And if he found Bernard ugly and uncharming, he didn't mob him up like the others. Having been brought up with artists, Wolfie was quite used to them losing their head and their nerve several times a day, and somehow managed to get everyone – except Hermione – out of their dressing rooms on time.

Outwardly, however, he appeared terribly arrogant.

The crew, resenting this, pinned a notice saying 'Stalag Studios' on Wolfie's door and whistled 'The Dambusters' every time he walked past. Ogborne and three of the sparks had too much to drink one lunchtime and proceeded to circle the production office, where Wolfie was wrestling with the next day's call sheet. Sticking their arms out, they pretended to be Lancasters and lobbed Scotch eggs through the window.

Wolfie ignored them, but later that evening Tristan found him gazing miserably into space. He knew Wolfie's arrogance was a defence mechanism, and that beneath his reserve he was warm-hearted and thoughtful. It had been Wolfie who had told Tristan Lucy needed more light.

Tristan had also noticed the anguish Wolfie couldn't hide when an ecstatic Flora, baseball cap tugged over her short back and sides, had flown off to join George that morning.

Tristan was a workaholic but, for once, he abandoned his storyboards and bore Wolfie off to dinner at the Old Bell in Rutminster. Wolfie had always been jealous of Tristan because Rannaldini had such a high regard for him but now, over several bottles, they discussed Schiller, horrendously competitive fathers and, inevitably, the cast.

As they walked back unsteadily from the Valhalla car park, across the valley, a light like a low bright star was shining in Magpie Cottage.

'You could loosen up with Tabitha,' said Tristan idly.

'She's appalling,' said Wolfie bleakly. 'The most awful human being I've ever met.'

'The wicked stepsister.' Tristan smiled in the darkness. 'And you could stop bitching up Flora.'

'I made love to Flora in every inch of this park,' said Wolfie. His face was in shadow, but his voice was raw with pain. 'The night I took her to the school dance, my father landed his helicopter on the cricket pitch, and

223

Flora disappeared into it like *Close Encounters*. I left home the next morning or I'd have murdered him. And how can she live with that thug George Hungerford? He's knocked down more buildings in Dresden than Winston Churchill.'

As they wandered past the north wing Tristan noticed, with a sinking heart, the curtains moving in Bernard's still-lit window. If Bernard felt he was being usurped as Tristan's confidant he would give Wolfie a hard time.

24

Next day Rannaldini pushed off to New York for a week and, heaving a sigh of relief, Tristan decided to kick off indoor filming with Posa's moving death scene in the dungeons. This was scuppered by Mikhail missing the plane from Moscow. So Tristan switched to a later scene, in which Carlos and Philip are joined by Eboli and the Grand Inquisitor, with the Spanish rabble outside the dungeons all clamouring for Carlos to be set free. This meant an awful lot of people for Lucy to make up.

Her biggest challenge was to turn the silver-haired, noble-browed, patrician Granville Hastings into Gordon Dillon, the Neanderthal thug who edited the *Scorpion* and whose hairline rested on his straight-across brows. Lucy was terrified of letting Tristan down, but Granny promptly cheered her up by bitching about Hermione. 'My dear, the only reason Madam is *so* addicted to playing the pink oboe is that she's read that seminal fluid rejuvenates the vocal cords.'

Lucy giggled, then added charitably that it seemed to work.

'She showed me the marvellous reviews she had for *Rinaldo*.'

'Her mother must have written them,' said Granny waspishly.

'Oh, you do cheer me up.' Lucy was sticking on a long line of beetling black eyebrow.

'Don't take any truck from her, Lucy Lockett,' said Granny, 'or from Alpheus, who's such a wooden actor he makes that table look like Anthony Hopkins, and you're going to have dreadful trouble with his hooter.' Granny smirked admiringly at his own beautifully aquiline nose. 'Alpheus has a bigger conk than Rudolph the Reindeer.'

Lucy had just grabbed a pair of scissors to trim the ends of Granny's brows when Meredith bustled in in great excitement.

'You can down tools, Lucy darling. Hi, Granville dear. Repairing a dungeon wall, one of the set-builders has unearthed a skeleton with a rosary round its neck.'

'Oh, my God.' Lucy nearly dropped her scissors.

'Anyone we know?' asked Granny, retrieving a dropped stitch.

'Probably the planning officer,' said Meredith gleefully. 'He's been so dire.'

The dungeons at Valhalla had always been damp and chill. Now none of the crew would go in there, even after Percy the Parson was summoned and sprinkled holy water from a Smirnoff bottle.

Ever conscious of a spiralling budget, Tristan gritted his teeth. He'd have to reschedule. Mikhail had now rung in from Moscow claiming to be laid low with bronchitis, so Baby could shove off for a few days and stop making a nuisance of himself and they could switch to the Great Hall, which had been transformed by Meredith, with the help of a massive white and gold silk four-poster, into King Philip's bedroom.

Meredith's minions were already busy dusting the arctic white marble chimneypiece, and touching up gilt cherubs, who were getting up to no good in the frieze running round the white walls. The prop table groaned with priceless ornaments, which Rannaldini intended to keep after filming and which Meredith kept re-arranging, driving tiny Simone crackers.

Griselda had agonized long and loudly over what a king should wear in bed and settled for a magnificent Turnbull & Asser dressing-gown in pink and purple stripes, which Alpheus was equally determined to hang on to after filming. Having spent a duty fortnight in the Caribbean with his wife, Cheryl, he was also frantic to screw Chloe.

Filming began with the insomniac Philip's great soliloquy. Even though he had played the part twenty times, Alpheus was avid to know his motivation.

'The candles are guttering,' said Tristan. 'It is the *heure de loup* just before dawn, when man's resistance is at its lowest. You feel old and threatened because your ravishing young wife and your sexy, demanding mistress are both madly in love with your son. You are also deeply hurt and raging with jealousy.'

'Too right,' agreed Sylvestre, dropping a cold micro-phone down Alpheus's hairy chest, which had just been greyed up by Lucy. 'I would be peesed off with scenario like that.'

'No-one asked your opinion,' snapped Bernard. 'All right. Quiet, please, we're going for a take.'

'How d'you get a pompous ass like Alpheus to act devastated?' muttered Meredith.

'Show him a seven-figure tax bill,' muttered back Granny.

'Quiet!' thundered Bernard.

In the heartbreakingly beautiful cello solo, which sets the mood of the aria, Alpheus wandered dazedly round the room, then plundered Elisabetta's desk, which was rumoured once to have belonged to Louis XIV. As he riffled through her diary, scrutinized her itemized telephone and Amex bills, and finally rooted under the mattress of the big double bed for love letters, Rozzy Pringle gave a groan. How often had she done that

227

at home, praying she wouldn't stumble on more evidence of her feckless husband Glyn's infidelities?

Alpheus then sang the first part of the aria so beautifully, and with such an air of nobility and resignation, that the crew gave him a rare round of applause.

Alpheus *can* act and his nose looks fine. Naughty Granny, thought Lucy indignantly.

If only it were me singing that aria, thought Granny.

Tristan was going to use the rest of the aria as voiceover when he filmed Philip forcing himself on a young, unresponsive bride.

Suddenly at the prospect of watching Alpheus and Hermione in the sack, the number of people on the set seemed to have quadrupled. Mr Brimscombe, Rannaldini's gardener, who was always leering into the female extras' changing room, was pretending to trim back the famous Paradise Pearl wisteria so that he could peer in through a high stained-glass window depicting St Cecilia at her organ.

The weather was still bitterly cold and the cost of heating the hall alone was putting Liberty Productions over budget. There was no way, however, that Hermione was going to risk turning blue in a shove-and-grunt scene.

Howie Denston hadn't quite screwed up enough courage to tell Sexton and Tristan that she wouldn't be filming in the mornings any more, but she made him ring in now to say that she had a cold. Everyone was less than amused when she promptly whizzed off to sing in an arena concert in New York, except Rannaldini who was already there and was taking a fat percentage of her hundred-thousand-pound fee. Far from chiding her, he sent the Gulf to collect her.

A demented Tristan was forced once more to reschedule. Granny, who'd been planning to go to *Sense and Sensibility* with Chloe, was livid to be dragged into filming the blind Inquisitor's great dialogue with Philip and insisted on upstaging Alpheus by feeding Bonios to his guide dog, who was being played quite excellently by Sharon the Labrador.

Granny's make-up, beetle-browed above black glasses, made him look so menacingly like Gordon Dillon that, after crossing themselves, the crew also gave Lucy a round of applause. Sexton, who'd rushed down from London to have a butcher's at a naked Hermione, felt Granny's makeover was so realistic that they'd better watch out for an injunction from the *Scorpion*.

The power struggle between Granny and Alpheus was so crucial to the plot that it took four days to film, by which time Sharon, egged on by Granny, had chewed up both of Alpheus's blue velvet crested slippers.

Alpheus had not endeared himself to the crew. Regally bidding them all to drinks in the Pearly Gates, leading the stampede, he would grind to a halt just outside the pub to admire the mullioned windows and the variegated skyline of turrets.

'You Brits are so lucky, your history is so old.'

By which time the first round would have been bought, and Alpheus, who had read somewhere that the Royal Family never carry money, would get away with not buying a drink all evening.

'The least often heard words in the English language', grumbled Ogborne, 'are "Thank you, Alpheus."'

'The next least heard words are Alpheus saying, "It's my round,"' said Sylvestre.

Next day, Dame Hermione flew back from New York, but wanting to rest, and refusing to film in the morning, she made Howie ring in to say her throat was still playing up. Rather than waste a tropically heated hall, Tristan therefore shot a little shove-and-grunt scene between Alpheus and Chloe, which, having had plenty of practice, they did quite beautifully.

Once again in seconds, as Oscar ordered his team to rearrange their lights to cast a more diffused, romantic glow, the Great Hall was absolutely packed out. Sexton materialized from nowhere. Meredith was whisking around rearranging pieces of Sèvres on a table beside the bed on which Chloe was now lying on her back, the picture of abandonment. The fact that she had to wear an eye-patch to play the traditionally one-eyed Princess Eboli, somehow made her look even more sexy.

'Don't feedle with those ornaments, please, Meredith,' begged Simone, consulting her Polaroids. 'There were only two vases last time, not that anyone's going to notice.' She sighed.

The trouble with such a hot room was flat nipples. Lucy had to keep darting forward with ice-cubes.

'Sometimes we use Blu-tack,' she told Chloe.

'Do you think my penis is too large?' asked Alpheus seriously.

'Not when Howie's taken off his twenty per cent,' replied Tristan.

Wolfie got the giggles.

'Chloe's chewed off all her lippy,' bellowed an excited Griselda.

'No-one's going to notice that either,' said Oscar, who for once had stayed awake. 'God, look at the light on those pubes.'

'She's like a little Bonnard,' sighed Simone.

'I've certainly got a Bonnard-on,' confessed Sexton, whose red-rimmed spectacles had quite steamed up.

'Hush, or I'll put ice down your trousers,' chided a returning Lucy.

'My mum wouldn't let me do nudes,' pouted Pushy Galore, who was dying to take her clothes off.

'Quiet, please, everyone,' brayed Bernard, whose face had gone an even darker shade of magenta.

'God, this is sensational, Oscar. Dramatize the neck *un peu, chérie,*' murmured Tristan, as Philip's aria poured out of the speakers.

As Chloe raised her head, thrusting out her breasts so that the light caught her rouged, now upright nipples, an approaching Alpheus whipped off his pink and purple dressing-gown.

'Action,' shouted Tristan.

25

Claiming that his bronchitis had turned into pneu-
monia, Mikhail finally arrived and was overwhelmed by
the beauty of Valhalla. A touch of rain had sent the green
flames of the wild garlic sweeping over the woodland
floor like a forest fire. Even Rannaldini's lowering maze
of dark yew had a blond rinse of lemon-yellow flowers.

'You pay me for vorking in such vonderful place?'
Mikhail asked in amazement.

No-one, however, could quite work out whether he
really had been ill or just moonlighting. He had turned
up wearing a black Pavarotti smock, with large pockets
for amassing loot. Maria, in the canteen, soon found her
cutlery disappearing.

Then Mikhail started complaining that he missed
Baby. Alpheus was no fun and far too expensive to drink
with, and he missed his wife, Lara, even more, and kept
hinting that Liberty Productions might pay for a plane
ticket so she, too, could admire the 'vonders' of Valhalla.
From New York, Rannaldini put his foot down. There
was no way he was having Lara and Mikhail stripping
Valhalla of his lovely new pickings.

Less welcome an arrival was Granny's hunky black-
haired boyfriend, Giuseppe, who wasn't needed to play
the ghost of Charles V for several weeks but who'd
rocked up to ogle Tristan's boys and enjoy free booze on
the budget.

'His mausoleum's going to smell worse than the Pearly Gates,' grumbled Ogborne.

Meanwhile, the digging up of the skeletons seemed to have disrupted the household ghosts. The night after Mikhail and Giuseppe arrived, the occupants of the north wing were woken by bloodcurdling shrieks. When a terrified Lucy, a for once quite pale-in-the-face Bernard and an unfazed Ogborne, who was eating a banana, emerged from their cell-like rooms, they found hunky Giuseppe in hysterics. Having slipped Granny a Mogadon, he was just returning from an unspecified location, when he'd seen his own part, the ghost of Charles V, stealing out of a bedroom and creeping away down the corridor.

'He was all in white, weeth a hood over 'ees face,' gibbered Giuseppe.

As Giuseppe's breath rivalled Bacchus's after an all-night bash, everyone assumed he was plastered. Having calmed him down, Lucy tucked him up in bed beside a snoring Granny.

But the following night, as she was wearily drawing her curtains, the windows suddenly rattled, the wind shrieked in the chimney and a ghostly hooded white figure came flitting along the parapets. She had never known such fear – not even a strangled croak would come out of her throat. James the lurcher was no help at all, and only growled if you tried to shove him off the bed.

More sightings followed. Everyone grew increasingly terrified – except Alpheus, who pooh-poohed any suggestion of spooks.

'I'm sure these apparitions would disappear if you guys went to bed sober for a change,' he added pompously.

The weather, although nearly May, was still freezing. After supper the following night Alpheus, mindful of colds, locked his bedroom windows and drew his curtains against draughts. He had just mounted his exercise bike, with the *Don Carlos* score on a nearby music stand so he could study tomorrow's scene, when a chill breeze ruffled the pages. Spinning round Alpheus found the windows still firmly locked.

Suddenly the room felt clammily damp and cold as if he were in an underground cave. Next moment a window behind him had blown open and the heavy dark green velvet curtains were billowing into the room. Outside Alpheus could see the cliff of wood disintegrating, thrashing and writhing as if caught up in the frenzy of a mighty gale. But jumping off his bike and rushing to the other window, he found the moonlit valley all stillness and serenity. The wispy white clouds were only crawling past the shining stars. Not a silver leaf was moving. Far below, the lake lay as still as the blacked-out window of a limousine.

White and trembling, Alpheus rushed out into the corridor, stumbling along endless dark passages until he reached Rannaldini's study. Rannaldini, just back from New York, was all suavity.

'But, my dear Alpheus, these things happen. Poor monk was rumoured to have hanged himself from the beam een your room. But, then, legend weaves on legend like Mees Havisham's cobwebs in these great houses. I never tell you because you insist on biggest bedroom.'

Rannaldini gave Alpheus a brandy but, despite heavy hints, did not invite him to move into the south wing.

'But my wife, Cheryl, flies in tomorrow. She has a heart murmur. I cannot subject her to this.'

'Why don't you rent Jasmine Cottage?' suggested Rannaldini. 'Just beyond Paradise village, on the opposite side of the valley. Hermione recently 'ave it redecorated. I'm sure she would be 'appy to 'ave you there.'

If Liberty Productions picked up the tab, Alpheus felt he could go with this. A pretty cottage would be a more discreet venue to entice young women, and he had clocked the fact that Tabitha Lovell lived just up the road.

After bidding him goodnight, however, Rannaldini added silkily, 'Eef you must creep down my corridors every night to pleasure Chloe, Alpheus, don't wear that white hooded dressing-gown you stole from the Hilton, Milan. How can my crew and cast get their beauty sleep eef they theenk you are ghost of Charles V?' and grinning evilly, he slammed the door in Alpheus's frantically mouthing face.

In the morning, as he was leaving Valhalla to inspect Jasmine Cottage, Alpheus was somewhat spooked to meet Percy the Parson coming the other way with his Smirnoff bottle of holy water to exorcize a ghost – who was, in fact, himself.

'I wish he'd exorcize Cheryl,' grumbled Chloe, who was getting less and less discreet about her *affaire* with Alpheus.

'What's Cheryl like?' asked Lucy, as she painted a dark brown semi-circle in Chloe's eye socket.

'Short-legged, noisy and goes for the jugular, like a tweed Jack Russell,' said Chloe sourly. 'She's the personification of the word feisty.'

'I hope you two don't come to feistycuffs,' giggled Lucy.

Cheryl, when she arrived, was enchanted by Jasmine Cottage, which had a modern kitchen, a power shower, a charming garden with a waterfall and a swing hanging from an ancient apple tree. On her first evening, a mischief-making Rannaldini invited her to supper and to see the rushes, which, of course, included Chloe and Alpheus's spectacular naked bonk. This put Cheryl into orbit. Hermione, incensed that Chloe looked so good, vowed to steal Alpheus from her.

Later Alpheus, turned on by the rushes and feeling it might be expedient to pleasure his wife on her first night – after all, she had intimate knowledge of all his tax fiddles and could turn nasty – suggested they christen the big brass bed at Jasmine Cottage.

It was not a success.

Stoking away, Alpheus's notion of himself as the great lover was shattered by Cheryl yapping shrilly, 'You don't need to go on all night, Alpheus. I'm not Chloe, you know.'

Nor were tempers improved by the driest spring on record. Rannaldini's streams were all disappearing. Blossom whipped off by the bitter east wind fell down the ever-widening cracks in the paths. On the parched sunny slopes, saplings shrivelled and died in their cardboard tower blocks and poor bluebells faded and curled over without ever reaching their sapphire splendour. There was less and less grass. Lucy watched the lambs skipping after Rannaldini's groom, Janice, as she brought them hay each morning.

Tristan was anxious to dismantle the set in the Great Hall and move outside, but he still hadn't shot Hermione's nude scene with Alpheus. On the morning it was scheduled, Hermione rang Tristan herself because Howie was in Tunisia.

'I can't hear you, Hermione.'

'"The voice,"' whispered Hermione sententiously, 'she hasn't woken yet. My body tells me I haven't had enough sleep. I'll do my love scene tomorrow afternoon.'

Spitting, Tristan ordered Wolfie to ring up Alpheus and get him in to do a couple of cover shots. But when Wolfie called Jasmine Cottage, an irate Cheryl told him that Alpheus had left for the set two hours ago. As a result, Cheryl was soon yapping up Rannaldini's drive, and seeing Chloe coming out of the *omnia vincit amor* gates on her way to the post office, blacked her eye with her new crocodile handbag.

This caused huge consternation. Chloe had a starring

role in the garden scene the day after tomorrow. The chorus, Flora and Mikhail, who'd nipped off to Prague for the weekend, were all due back for it. Tabitha had already booked some polo ponies.

'You could change Chloe's eyepatch to the uvver eye,' suggested Sexton.

'*Non!*' cried Simone from Continuity in outrage.

'Could you hide it with make-up, Lucy?' asked Tristan.

'Not for a few days. The eye's much too bloodshot.'

Only when Tristan suggested she come out later for a consoling dinner did Chloe stop sobbing into his shoulder, and rush off to Make Up beseeching poor Lucy to streak her hair for this exciting date.

Cheryl, meanwhile, was roaring round Valhalla in search of Alpheus. She was soon joined by forty members of Dame Hermione's fan club who'd won a *Daily Express* competition, entitling them to a day on the set of *Don Carlos*, and who'd just arrived by bus. Because Hype-along, the press officer, was frogmarching Baby through a series of interviews in London, Wolfie was deputed to show them round.

As they passed the mobile canteen, wafting forth an enticing smell of *boeuf Provençal*, one of the fans asked about the dear little house next door.

'It was a hunting lodge for Act One, but in the end we never used it,' explained Wolfie.

Throwing open the door, he thought for a moment two of his father's prize pigs had pushed their way inside. Then, to his horror, he realized he had caught Alpheus and Hermione *in flagrante*.

Cheryl was about to black Hermione's eye with her crocodile handbag, when Hermione rose to her feet, wrapping a white Hilton dressing-gown round her goddess-like form, crying, 'Cheryl, my dear, calm down! Alpheus and I were only rehearsing for tomorrow after-noon. No-one should act a scene without rehearsing.'

Such was the steamrolling force of Hermione's personality, they were all silenced. The fans went off murmuring reverently that Dame Hermione was such a professional, particularly when she ordered 'bubbly' on the budget for them all at lunch.

Everyone except Chloe and Cheryl was in stitches over the whole affair. The crew wanted to know if Alpheus had a crown on his cock. What, however, a blushing Wolfie reported back to Tristan and Sexton was that Hermione had pubes bigger than Brahms's beard.

'I think she ought to trim it before she does a nude scene. Papa could have told her,' Wolfie blushed even deeper, 'but he's away.'

'How about Mr Brimscombe?' grinned Sexton. 'He'd love to do it wiv a Strimmer.'

'Alpheus can tell her,' said Tristan. 'I'm busy. You brief him, Sexton.'

Sexton, however, pussyfooted so much around the subject that Alpheus went the whole hog and Hermione rolled up on the set the following afternoon with a totally shaved bush. This caused more rage and hysterics.

'Perhaps it was fashionable in the sixteenth century,' said Sexton hopefully.

'We're filming in modern times,' snapped Tristan. 'Get her some false pubes,' he ordered Lucy.

'It's called a merkin,' volunteered Granny.

'Hardly a word that occurs in crosswords,' giggled Meredith.

'During the film of *Carmen*,' said Griselda eagerly, 'when Lilian Watson shaved her armpits by mistake, Make Up had to hold up shooting for two hours while they stuck on individual hairs.'

'Oh, I couldn't,' said Lucy aghast. 'I've just spent even longer covering Dame Hermione with body make-up.'

'Rather like varnishing the whale at the Natural History Museum,' said Meredith sympathetically.

'We'll just have to shoot her from the back,' said Tristan, who was torn between tears of despair and helpless laughter, particularly when Hermione summoned him and Wolfie to her caravan to ask if they thought her breasts were too large.

'You could always get some smaller ones from Props,' said Wolfie gravely, and both men had to flee clutching their sides.

The set was absolutely crowded out. Mr Brimscombe, binoculars hanging from his scrawny neck, was selling tickets at the door. Ross Benson, who'd been smuggled in by a returned Hype-along to do an in-depth piece, fell off a rafter, fortunately landing on the great four-poster. As he was very handsome, Dame Hermione looked very excited. Tristan, however, flipped.

'Clear the set! Clear the fucking set!'

'Please don't bother,' said Hermione graciously.

'Where am I going to hide my microphone?' grumbled Sylvestre, who usually had to drop it down Hermione's cleavage.

'Up her ass,' volunteered Ogborne.

'Quiet, please!' roared Bernard.

'Lucy,' howled Tristan, then lowering his voice. 'Can you do anything about the blue veins on her boobs?'

Lucy darted forward with concealer, murmuring, 'Don't you get nervous about taking your clothes off in front of all these people?'

'Indeed not.' Hermione looked amazed. 'A woman should be proud of her body.' Then, in indignation, 'Why is that man reading *Dogs Today*? Very discourteous of him. Oh, it's you, Meredith. I suppose you don't really count.'

Bernard grabbed Tristan's camera script to conceal a huge hard-on.

'We're turning over,' he said hoarsely.

'Action,' shouted Tristan.

'Christ, Alpheus isn't having to act in this scene at all,' hissed Sylvestre to Wolfie, a few moments later. 'He's bigger than a fucking Thermos.'

'Hermione ees supposed to be gritting her teeth,

239

Uncle Treestan,' whispered Simone, 'but she look as though she enjoy every minute.'

'Cut,' said Tristan, then to Hermione, 'Your husband is virtually raping you in this scene, *chérie*. Could you possibly act a bit more upset?'

'There are beings, Tristan' – roguishly, Hermione quoted him back at himself – 'who are born for others, who are quite unaware of their own egos. Elisabetta had far too perfect manners to upset her elderly partner by showing him she wasn't having a good time.'

Tristan was defeated.

'Okkay, okkay.' He sighed.

They'd just have to film her even more from behind.

'I'd take a wide shot on this one,' he told Valentin.

'One could hardly do anything else.'

Oscar, slumped over the camera ostensibly checking the lights through his eye-piece, was actually asleep.

'Talk dirty to me, Alpheus,' murmured Hermione, who was used to being turned on by Rannaldini's crooning obscenities.

'Unless Sexton pays me cash like you,' murmured back Alpheus, 'I may have difficulty meeting next year's tax bill.'

Chloe was utterly mortified. Alpheus had been pompous and self-regarding.

'But I thought he loved me and would shelter me through life like a great tree,' she told Tristan, as she toyed with her scallops Mornay in the Heavenly Host that evening.

'Plants growing in shade miss out on sun and rain,' said Tristan.

Chloe's breasts leaping out of that crimson dress had the same springy texture as the scallops, he decided.

'You and Baby are stealing the show,' he went on, filling up her glass. 'You'll get your revenge on Hermione when the reviews come out. You're so beautiful, Chloe.'

Chloe glanced complacently at her reflection in a nearby mirror. Lucy's streaking was so subtle. The dark glasses over her blackened eye showed off the tilt of her nose and the luscious curves of her smiling crimson mouth. She must buy Lucy a box of chocolates tomorrow.

Back at Valhalla, a weary Lucy finished writing the day's notes and stuck in Polaroids of a naked Hermione and Alpheus. At least she hadn't had to powder Alpheus's cock. And Chloe's lower lip was rather thin so she'd had to extend the natural line along the bottom with a lipbrush and fill in quite a large gap. But the end result had been heavenly, particularly in that incredibly skimpy dress. Tristan had reeked of Eau Sauvage and even put on a suit.

Out in the park, as the orange glow of sunset died away, the occasional bleat of a lamb and the deep-throated reassuring rumble of its mother reminded her of Cumbria and made her long for tumbling grey streams, geometric walls and mountains rising out of the mist. Why did one feel most homesick when one was miserable?

As Tristan walked Chloe back to the north wing, she cursed herself for wasting so much of dinner bitching and talking about herself. She wasn't used to dining with a good listener. The lamp over the doorway shining through the clematis cast a leaf pattern on Tristan's face. From the sides of his nose past his beautiful big mouth, two lines dug trenches that had not been there in January. *Don Carlos* was taking its toll.

'Your suite or mine?' she whispered.

There was a long pause. An owl hooted.

'Darling Chloe.'

'Are you gay?'

The leaf pattern quivered as he shook his head.

'Is there someone else?'

'Something else. Rannaldini's back tomorrow. I have two, three hours' work to do.' Then, when Chloe looked sullen, 'My father die last year. Your scene with Alpheus was so like his paintings. Give me time, Chloe.' He kissed her cheek.

As he wandered off into the garden, rain dripped through the wood like some Chinese water torture. The constellation of the Virgin was chasing Leo the Lion across the sky. When push came to shove and grunt, he didn't want to sleep with Chloe, who, as she undressed, felt it would have been quite easy to get over Alpheus if Tristan had made a pass at her.

26

Away from home for so long, people started to lose their moorings, groups formed and re-formed, cabals sprang up, feuds and jealousies flourished, as husbands, lovers, children were – sometimes gladly – forgotten. Poor Rozzy Pringle, working flat out in both Wardrobe and Make Up and sending most of her wages home, couldn't forget Glyn, her horrible husband, however, because he was always ringing up to bombard her with complaints and demands.

'When he's ratty,' sighed Rozzy, 'I can never tell if he's been dumped by one of his girlfriends or his business is in trouble again.'

'No work and all play makes Glyn a kept boy,' observed Meredith disapprovingly.

Everyone loved Rozzy, who seemed to love everyone, even the lascivious Mr Brimscombe, who spent hours discussing plants with her and even gave her access to his tool-shed. Lucy had filled a window-box outside her caravan with love-in-a-mist. Rozzy remembered to water it, and took James for walks when Lucy was too busy.

Rozzy loved everyone, but most of all she adored Tristan for his kindness when her voice gave out. She was always shoving buttered croissants and big cups of *café au lait* into his hands. Lucy had to curb tinges of irritation – after all, Rozzy fussed over her too.

Wardrobe had its own Bendix to wash costumes. Rozzy put in Lucy's clothes and occasionally dragged Tristan's favourite peacock-blue shirt off him when he became too obsessed with work to change it. As Cheryl had become extremely bolshie, Alpheus crinkled his eyes in the hope of getting his washing done too, but drew a blank.

Mobbing up Bernard was a favourite location pastime, but Rozzy stuck up for him too. Bernard had insisted on his own little office, facing south between Wardrobe and the smoke-filled ant hill of the production office. Here, he could work out tomorrow's movement order in peace and complete the *Figaro* crossword, which was faxed over to him every morning. On the door was a notice saying: 'First Assistant Director. Please Knock.'

So Baby knocked when he went past.

'Come in. What can I do for you?' asked Bernard.

'Nothing at all. It says, "Please Knock", so I did.'

Bernard was apoplectic, particularly when Baby did it each time he went past, and the habit caught on with everyone else.

They were all giggling about it in the canteen one lunchtime when Rozzy lost her temper.

'Bernard's a darling,' she shouted at them. 'You only dislike him because he's good at shutting up chatterboxes.' She glared at Baby and Granny. 'And he refuses to reschedule because *someone*', she glanced reproachfully across at Chloe, 'wants to buzz off and sing *Carmen* in Paris.'

'Who wrecked their voice in January singing all over Europe?' snapped Chloe. 'I suppose you and Bernard have the screaming hots for Tristan de Montigny in common.'

'*Parlez pour votre* self,' drawled Baby.

Then Chloe went as crimson as her lipstick because Bernard was standing in the doorway. The dreadful silence was only interrupted by the clatter and chatter of

244

the canteen staff washing up. But Bernard was oblivious of Chloe. Crossing the room, he kissed Rozzy's hand.

'Thank you, Madame Pringle. May I buy you a drink?'

With fractionally warmer weather filming moved outside to Rannaldini's garden, which had reached a pitch of late spring perfection. Tristan decided to kick off with a returning Mikhail singing a beautiful aria to Hermione. Alas, Mikhail's English had been so incomprehensible, the taxi driver picking him up at Heathrow took him to Rugby rather than Rutminster. Mikhail rang in in tears, saying he couldn't reach Valhalla before early evening.

Reluctant to waste Hermione, who'd already spent three hours in Make Up bullying Lucy, Tristan decided to shoot a later scene in which Philip finds Elisabetta unattended, and sacks her favourite lady-in-waiting, the Countess of Aremburg. This was the non-singing part in which he had cast Rozzy, which would at least get her name on the credits. Rozzy was only required to burst into tears, but she was dreadfully nervous even of this piece of mime, particularly as Rannaldini had just returned from Tokyo and was scowling from a new chair with 'Executive Producer' printed on the back.

Being called at such short notice, Rozzy had had no time to wash her hair – which Lucy was able to hide under a very pretty, short, curly wig – or to remove a few hairs from her chin and upper lip.

'Some Immac will take them off in a trice,' said Lucy soothingly.

'We haven't got time,' quavered Rozzy.

'Course we have.'

'Lucy,' screamed Hermione.

'Don't leave your old bags unattended,' quipped Meredith, as Lucy belted off to Hermione's caravan.

'I've nicked a toenail,' moaned Hermione, 'and it's sticking into my big toe. Have you got a plaster?'

'Only to put over your mouth,' muttered Lucy.

'Are you nearly ready, Luce?' Wolfie appeared at the door. 'My father's about to boil over.'

As a result Lucy only had time to put a bit of slap on Rozzy and pray that the dark base would hide any hairs, before Sylvestre arrived to mike her up.

Alas, poor Rozzy, struck down by nerves, fled to the honeywagon, from which, because naughty Sylvestre had not switched off the mike, the whole crew could hear the sound of Mount Etna erupting.

'Mrs Pringle's got the runs,' giggled Pushy Galore.

'Pity she's not playing for England,' sighed Ogborne. 'They're fifty-two for four.'

Even Bernard was smiling. Everyone, however, managed to compose their faces as Rozzy arrived on the set, except Hermione who, with merry laughter, proceeded to explain the joke.

'That's enough, Hermione,' snapped Bernard, seeing Rozzy going crimson. 'Rozzy looks beautiful, and the hair is very nice.'

'That style makes you look years younger,' conceded Hermione, 'but you're a little too red in the face.'

'Probably a hot flush,' sighed Rozzy.

'Oh, no, dear, you're well past that.'

'Let's go for a quick rehearsal.' Tristan came off his mobile to Aunt Hortense. 'Rozzy, you look wonderful.'

'He could make a warthog feel like Helen of Troy,' grumbled Pushy.

I'm Elisabetta's lady-in-waiting, I ought to be playing the Countess, she thought furiously as, with the rest of the ladies of the chorus, she bobbed around in front of a hedge of white roses trying to get into shot.

' "Countess," ' sang Alpheus sternly, ' "at daybreak you will return to France." '

'Burst into tears, Rozzy,' shouted Tristan.

Rozzy's only problem would have been holding them back any longer. Particularly when Hermione repeat-edly stroked her face as she mimed her consoling aria and, between takes, loudly advised Rozzy to invest in some decent electrolysis.

'It's well worth it at your age.'

Tears of such humiliation had gushed out of Rozzy's eyes that Tristan was genuinely able to congratulate her on a wonderfully convincing performance, which didn't cheer Rozzy up one bit.

Happily, Hermione's comeuppance was in train. Oscar, who was not the most famous director of photography in the world for nothing, had decided to avenge both Chloe and Rozzy.

That evening, as everyone poured into the viewing room to watch the rushes, all that could be heard was Hermione's agitated squawking. Having lit her from beneath in her nude scene with Alpheus, Oscar had made her bottom look enormous.

'The great globe itself,' said Granny, in a sepulchral whisper.

'You should have reduced it with a darker base, Lucy,' giggled Meredith.

'Any moment, David Attenborough will pop up and lecture us *sotto voce* on the mating habits of the hippopotamus,' cried Baby, in ecstasy.

Shouts of 'My bottom is not that big, my bottom is *not* that big,' were drowned by cheers, particularly from Chloe, who gave Oscar a big kiss.

'What are you doing after this?' she murmured. 'I owe you.'

Tristan laughed, but was cross with Oscar because they ought to reshoot. He was overruled by Sexton and Rannaldini, who both liked big bums and small budgets.

'Do you know the meaning of the word "callipygean"?' asked Sexton cosily, as he tried to bear Hermione away for a consoling drink.

Hermione shrugged him off. She wasn't going to let such a common little man take advantage.

Alpheus had laughed as heartily as anyone over Dame

Hermione's humiliation, until Rannaldini sidled up to him.

'May I be honest, Alpheus? You look in great shape in those nude shots.' Alpheus preened. 'But in future I think you should leave off the false nose. It looks a leetle grotesque.'

Later, on the terrace, oblivious of an exquisite coral sunset, Hermione and Alpheus could be seen berating a sleeping Tristan.

Sexton was not cast down by Hermione's rejection. He had just come back from Cannes where, showing a ten-minute trailer of Chloe and Alpheus in the sack in order to sell more distribution rights, he'd had to massage even bigger egos than theirs. Now he retreated to the production office and continued four different deals on four different mobiles. 'I may look calm,' he was fond of telling people, 'but I'm not.'

Poor Hype-along Cassidy was not feeling calm either. Controlling the publicity was a nightmare. Hermione, incensed that nothing about herself had appeared recently, was unaware that her sacked make-up girl had just dumped in *News of the World*: 'How I Concealed Dame Hermione's Turkey Neck, and How She Ate Technicians for Breakfast.'

Hype-along's rise at dawn on Sunday mornings to empty the village shop of papers was becoming a common occurrence. He'd also had terrible trouble with Baby, who, when he'd taken him up for interviews in London, had fallen asleep over drinks with the *Guardian*, and on the way to lunch with Lynn Barber had jumped taxi to buy clothes in Jermyn Street and not been traced till the following day.

Saddest of all, Tristan, the person to whom everyone wanted to speak, was so violently anti-press he wouldn't give interviews at all. Hype-along, however, was working towards a quiet lunch at the Old Bell with Valerie Grove of *The Times*.

*   *   *

'I think Oscar and Chloe are an item,' Griselda told everyone, as Chloe looked more and more magical in the rushes and Oscar slept even more during the day.

But Chloe was not out of the woods. Baby was watching porn on the Internet one afternoon when up popped a teenage Chloe, cavorting with a black girl and a goat.

'Goodness,' gasped Lucy, when Baby rushed in to tell her. 'Was the goat female?'

'I saw its udder shudder. In mitigation, it did appear to be having a good time.'

'I do hope Rannaldini doesn't know about it,' shivered Lucy. 'I'm sure he'd use it against her.'

Someone was pinching clothes from Wardrobe, especially ties. Griselda and Simone, whose continuity was being screwed up, went out to the Heavenly Host to drown their sorrows and asked Lucy to join them, which at least gave Lucy a chance to quiz Simone about Tristan.

'What's his auntie Hortense like?'

'A battleaxe, who demand the whole time,' sighed Simone. 'And not at all motherly to Uncle Tristan. When she drop him as a baby in drawing room, she ring for maid to pick him up.'

Then Simone added slyly: 'Valentin, Sylvestre and Ogborne wanted to crash dinner tonight, Lucy. They all fancy you, but they know you only 'ave eyes for Uncle Tristan.'

'That's ridiculous,' spluttered Lucy, sending her glass of red flying. 'Of course I don't.' Then, as she frantically mopped up with her pink scarf, 'I wouldn't dream—'

'Dream is perhaps the only thing you should do,' said Simone gently. 'I love my uncle Tristan but he is very damaged.'

Terrified by the ghostly sightings inside Valhalla, Lucy had taken to sleeping outside in her make-up caravan, which seemed less claustrophobic than those little cells and long, dark, spooky corridors. But returning from the Heavenly Host, as she scuttled past silent generators and empty dark-windowed Hair and Wardrobe departments, she wasn't sure. It would be so easy for a ghost to leap out from behind an empty lorry. Even the moon and the stars had deserted her.

As she approached her caravan, still upset by what Simone had said about Tristan, she froze at the sound of pitiful, anguished sobbing. Oh, God, was it the ghost of Caroline Beddoes, mourning her lost love, the blacksmith?

'You might at least try and look fierce,' she hissed at James, who'd stopped in his tracks with his head on one side.

The sobbing grew more pitiful. Lucy's Dutch courage evaporated.

'Who's there?' she quavered, as she unlocked the caravan door, screaming as a grey shadowy figure loomed over her.

Then, as she fumbled for the light switch, she heard James's bony tail whacking against the open door and Rozzy's choked voice saying, 'Don't turn it on, I look so terrible, and I don't want any of the others to know.'

'Whatever's the matter? Let me get you a drink.'

'I don't want one.'

Lucy did. As she fumbled her way to the fridge, Rozzy was racked by a fit of coughing. Then it all came tumbling out. She'd been to the doctor that evening to hear the result of some tests, and been told she'd got throat cancer.

'Oh, Rozzy.' Lucy collapsed on the bench seat opposite.

'There are lots of things one can do,' wept Rozzy. 'Voice boxes, treatment, operations and things, but my career's finished. I'll never sing again. Even worse, we're so broke, Lucy, and I'm all we've got to live on. I feel the prison doors clanging shut on a solvent future.'

Lucy was devastated.

'You'll be able to earn money as a PA. Everyone thinks you're brilliant. You must get a second opinion. The Campbell-Blacks and Rannaldini have a brilliant private doctor, James Benson.'

'I couldn't possibly afford him.'

'I can,' said Lucy stoutly, as she took a bottle out of the fridge. 'You've been so good to me.'

As soon as she'd poured Rozzy a drink, Lucy wrote her out a cheque for six hundred pounds. After all, she got paid at the end of the month.

Later, refusing all Lucy's entreaties to sleep in the caravan, Rozzy insisted on dragging herself back to the cells.

'I don't want people suspecting anything.'

'You must tell Glyn.'

'I can't.' Rozzy started to cry again. 'He'll be so cross with me. Thank you, Lucy, for being such a friend.'

Lucy didn't sleep all night, thinking of a ravishing voice that would sing no more, like a nightingale being strangled. She had been sworn to secrecy, but Tristan, seeing her red eyes next morning, wheedled the truth out of her and was equally horrified. Pretending he'd no idea that Rozzy was ill, he casually asked her out to dinner. Inevitably Rozzy asked Lucy to do her make-up.

'I can't let Tristan dine with an awful old hag.'

At the Old Bell, away from gossips, Tristan told Rozzy he'd been asked to direct *Der Rosenkavalier* at Glyndebourne. 'Eef your voice is rested enough, I would like you to sing the Marschallin. It won't be for two years.'

It was lucky they were sitting in a dark alcove so no-one could see Rozzy weeping again. Tristan knew she would never be able to take up the offer: she might be dead in two years, if, as Lucy suspected, she had secondaries elsewhere, but at least it would give her hope.

Next day Rozzy was beside herself. 'I never dreamed Tristan thought that much of me,' she kept saying to Lucy, who was bitterly ashamed to find herself feeling irritated.

27

At the end of May, the weather finally gave way to heat-wave. Rozzy coughed more in the dry, dusty heat and grew thinner, her adoring eyes growing bigger in her shrunken face as she gazed at Tristan. Bernard gazed longingly at Rozzy, but even on the hottest day he wouldn't take off his shirt in case it dented his authority. He encouraged Wolfie to do the same.

For the first year ever, Rannaldini didn't sprinkle his lawns, so they would look more parched and Spanish. He allowed Mr Brimscombe to water only selected plants: the rest could die of thirst, thus realizing his plan of a Buckingham Palace sweep down to the lake, which was getting perilously low.

Again, despite delays, rows and nightmarish re-scheduling, beautiful scenes were being shot, particularly of the great duet in which gallant Posa defies Philip II on the subject of religious persecution. Here, he so captivates the King, he is nicknamed 'the King's Favourite' by the entire court. It became a running gag on the set that anyone singled out by Tristan became '*le favori du roi*'.

Playing Posa movingly, however, was not enough to Mikhail, who was getting bored. Paradise was a lovely little village but he wished there were more of it. He was also frightfully jealous that Baby was about to have a shove-and-grunt scene with Chloe.

The occasion, shot in the cow-parsley in the shade of a huge lime to blot out the burning sun, was not without incident. They were just about to turn over, when Lucy hissed, 'Cover up, Chloe, *nous avons* company.'

It was Percy the Parson, pretending to be bird-watching.

'Obviously looking for great tits,' said Ogborne as, with great presence of mind, Wolfie whipped off his dark blue polo shirt and pulled it over Chloe's head.

The beauty of his young, broad-shouldered body was lost on no-one. Simone immediately took a Polaroid.

'Oh, hunky, hunky dory,' sighed Baby.

'I've never been topless before,' joked Wolfie, to hide his embarrassment.

'It's Baby the vicar's mad about,' hissed Chloe, as Percy raised his binoculars to peer through an elder bush. 'Better slip a dunce's hat over his cock.'

'My cock is not a dunce.'

'May I have this dunce?' asked Meredith, who shouldn't have been there either, as there were no sets to dress, and everyone collapsed with laughter.

Precious shadows drained away until at last Percy moved on.

'Get Wolfie's shirt off, Chloe,' yelled Tristan. 'Christ, I feel like Icarus about to melt,' he added, taking off his director's cap to mop his brow with his arm.

'At least you don't have to sustain a hard-on,' grumbled Baby.

'Dong Carlos,' said Chloe.

They had all corpsed once more when Tabitha thundered round the corner on The Engineer, who shied violently and nearly unseated her. The sight of Tristan, a half-naked Wolfie and all the crew leering joyfully at a naked Chloe and Baby, additionally put her into orbit.

'You disgusting perve,' she screamed at Tristan, 'turning yourselves on making revolting porn movies.'

Swinging The Engineer round, she galloped off in a cloud of dust.

'Pissed as usual,' drawled Baby. 'I dropped off a cheque for her husband last night. Even Sharon was drunk.'

'Don't be a bitch, Baby,' said Lucy furiously.

'Shut up, all of you,' shouted Bernard, seeing how upset Tristan was.

But the fun had gone out of the day.

As Chloe walked into the canteen Wolfie handed her a big glass of iced lime juice.

'Oh, you angel,' said Chloe, taking a great gulp. 'Will you marry me when you grow up?'

'I'm afraid there's rather a long queue,' piped up Meredith. 'I'd like a very small prawn salad, Maria darling.'

Maria, the cook, loved watching the French crew. She loved the sensual way they tore apart their bread, and undressed their prawns with beautifully manicured fingers, knotting their napkins round their necks to protect their perfectly ironed shirts, propping their knives and forks up on their plates, savouring what they were eating, drinking each glass of wine slowly and reflectively, chattering all the time.

Tristan, although he often forgot to eat, would make love in the same leisurely fashion, imagined Maria. Happily married, with a baby on the way, she could still allow herself to daydream. She had been to the hospital for a scan the day before and proudly produced a photograph of the baby.

'Oh, how lovely!' cried Lucy ecstatically. 'Look at its nose, and its head and little legs.'

'Rather like E.T.' Meredith took the photograph gingerly as if it were a newborn baby.

'What a little angel,' said Oscar, who was the proud father of five.

'Hello, Tab,' shouted Griselda, as Tabitha half sheepishly, half defiantly, sidled into the canteen and dropped her bag on an empty table. 'Come and look at this sweet little babba.'

'Oh, no,' Lucy muttered. But it was too late.

As Tab gazed at the photograph, tears trickled down her cheeks.

'It's adorable,' she whispered. Next moment she had fled.

'What *is* the matter with that girl today?' grumbled Ogborne.

'Someone's left a bag,' said Simone, who noticed everything.

Inside were only a tattered Dick Francis, a bottle of Evian, a Coutts Switch card and photos of Isa, Sharon and The Engineer.

'It's Tab's,' said Wolfie.

'Not the sort to bother with a compact, lipstick or even a comb,' said Chloe dismissively.

'She doesn't need to,' Wolfie was amazed to hear himself saying.

Behind his smooth, broad, fast-browning back, Meredith and Baby exchanged glances.

'Do you think he and Tab are going to be the next item?' Griselda whispered excitedly to Simone, who was suddenly looking very sad.

Tab refused to answer her telephone but, seeing her dirty green Golf outside Magpie Cottage, Wolfie decided to return her bag in the tea-break. Through the car windows, he breathed in great wafts of wild garlic pestled by rain and the soapy smell of the hawthorns. In the lane up to Magpie Cottage, light brown puddles reflected hedgerows and overhanging trees like an album of sepia photographs.

Tab's lawn was blue with speedwell. A few white irises were fighting a losing battle with the nettles round the egg-yolk-yellow front door. The reek of more wild garlic from the woods behind didn't altogether disguise the stench of unemptied dustbins. No-one answered the bell, so Wolfie let himself in.

Tabitha, cuddling Sharon on the sofa, was wearing a pale green vest, a bikini bottom, dirty gym shoes and was watching racing on television with the sound turned down. Her face was deathly white, except for her reddened eyes, but nothing could take away the beauty of her long pale legs.

'What are you doing here?' she asked.

Sharon, who had better manners, jumped down and brought Wolfie a small rug, revealing a pile of dust. Wolfie handed Tab her bag.

'I brought this back.'

'Thanks.' Staggering to her feet, kicking an empty half-bottle of vodka under the sofa, antagonism fighting with loneliness in her eyes, Tab asked him if he'd like a cup of tea.

Wolfie followed her into the kitchen and nearly fainted.

'I'm sorry.' Tab smashed a cup, as she tried to get the kettle under the tap in a hopelessly overcrowded sink. 'I only tidy up before Isa comes back.'

She had cut herself on the cup. Tugging off a piece of kitchen roll, Wolfie wrapped it round her finger, then started to load the contents of the sink, mostly glasses, into the dishwasher, which was empty except for a shoal of silver on the bottom.

'How's your marriage?' he asked.

'A bed of roses.'

Wolfie looked sceptical.

'With the thorns sticking upwards,' said Tab.

'You could stop drinking.'

'I don't drink at all, I've given up.'

'What's this, then?' Wolfie produced the Evian bottle out of her bag.

Tab brightened. 'I'd forgotten that. I think we're out of tea-bags.' Fretfully she opened a cupboard and a lot of pasta packets descended on her head. 'Oh, Christ, we'd better have a slug of that instead.'

But before she could grab the Evian bottle, Wolfie had emptied it into the sink.

'Whydya want to waste perfectly good alcohol?'

screamed Tab. 'Now what am I going to do?'

'Go to AA.'

'One is supposed to meet rather nice men there. I might find a new husband.'

'I'll take you along. There must be a Rutminster branch. I'll check out the time of the next meeting.'

'Just stop it,' Tab flared up again.

Hearing a patter on the trees outside, Wolfie glanced across the valley at tassels of rain hanging from the clouds. They wouldn't be shooting for a bit.

Why had she been so upset at lunchtime? he asked, knowing the answer, but feeling she needed to talk.

'It reminded me of my own baby,' muttered Tab. 'Isa won't discuss it – won't really discuss anything. Then I got a letter from Mummy this morning, raving about my brother Marcus's recital in Moscow. And how charming Alexei, Marcus's lover, was being. I bet she drives him crackers, and the mean old cow's locked her bedroom door so I can't help myself to her stuff.'

Wolfie laughed but, noticing Tab shivering, unearthed a bottle of orange squash, poured an inch into a mug and switched on the kettle as she talked.

'Even if everyone else thought I was a nightmare,' Tab was saying, 'I was always convinced I could whistle Daddy back. Marrying Isa was the easiest way to hurt him. Christ, I need a drink.'

Wolfie poured the boiling water on to the orange squash.

'Have this instead.'

'And another thing,' Tab was pacing round the kitchen, 'everyone cooing over the photograph of that baby reminded me how jealous and awful I was when my stepsister Perdita arrived, and even worse when Daddy and Taggie adopted Xav and Bianca. I tried to be good, but I wasn't.'

As she hung her blonde head, she reminded Wolfie of the cowslips fading in the valley.

'So did I,' he said roughly. 'I was Papa's first child, and

now I have seven stepbrothers and sisters, not to mention Little Cosmo, and a pack of illegits, and I wanted to kill each one when it arrived. I remember thinking, When will Papa ever have the tiniest bit of love or time left for me?'

'You do make me feel better,' sighed Tab. 'If Mummy suddenly gets pregnant we can drown our sorrows.'

As she took a sip of orange squash listlessly, Wolfie noticed how thin her arms were. 'When did you last eat?'

'Dunno.'

The telephone rang.

'You answer it.' Tab led him back into the sitting room.

If it were Isa, it might make him sit up, but it was Bernard breathing fire.

'Gotta go,' said Wolfie, putting down the receiver, then blushing. 'Would you like to have dinner tonight?'

'Men don't ask me out.'

For a second Wolfie thought Tab was going to cry.

'You're like a very rare and beautiful orchid,' he stammered. 'People feel they ought not to pick you.'

'That's nice.' For a second Tab examined Wolfie's dark blue eyes, matching his polo shirt, his square-jawed, slightly old-fashioned Action Man features, his reddish complexion turning brown. He would make a good, dependable friend.

'I'd like to,' she said.

'I'll take you to Shako's.'

'We'd never get in.'

'Wanna bet? There are advantages in having a famous surname. We can take your dustbins to the tip on the way.'

'Oh look! There's Daddy.'

Tab lurched towards the television, turning up the sound and fingering her father's face. Wolfie and he were both tall and blond but it was like comparing a cob with a thoroughbred.

Rupert had just paid seventy-five thousand to make a late entry in the Derby.

'That's a lot of money,' John Oaksey was saying. 'You must be sure Peppy Koala'll do well.'

'Very,' said Rupert.

'Oh, my God.' Tabitha had turned as pale green as her vest. 'If Peppy Koala wins, Isa will murder me.'

She rang at nine o'clock just as Wolfie was leaving Valhalla, her voice slurred.

'I'm sorry, I can't make it.'

'Course you can, I've already left.'

The heatwave chugged on. Between filming, people played croquet and tennis, swam in Rannaldini's beautiful pool, got lost in the maze and helped Granny knit squares of his patchwork quilt. The hawk-eyed Simone went round routing out sunbathers because a tan screwed up continuity. Rozzy watered dying plants, sewed thousands of seed pearls on an ivory satin dress for Hermione to wear at Philip II's coronation and kept wonderfully cheerful.

Dr James Benson had been so kind to her, she told Lucy with passionate gratitude. He was such an attractive, sympathetic man. Whenever Rozzy had to disappear for treatment, Lucy covered up for her, explaining she'd had to rush home to deal with some domestic problems. Lucy spent much of her spare time surreptitiously making Rozzy a wig.

As befitting an international maestro, Rannaldini jetted in and out criticizing everything and everyone, slowing down filming, when it was already disastrously behind schedule, and sending costs spiralling. Rumours of the runaway budget were sweeping Europe and Hollywood. Tristan had already ploughed in five million and seen it vanish, mostly in Meredith's decorating costs. It was as though Rannaldini had thrown petrol over the notes and set fire to them. But Tristan couldn't stop to worry about money: finishing the film was all that mattered.

Alpheus, too, was making no attempt to keep down the budget. Having finally screwed a Jaguar out of Sexton, he now wanted a runaround for Cheryl.

'He's already giving *her* the runaround,' observed Baby, as every day, wearing face masks, Alpheus and Pushy jogged bouncily off into the yellowing park.

Poor Cheryl spent a lot of time spying up trees and was mistaken for a member of the press by Mr Brimscombe, who removed her ladder to much squawking.

Hermione insisted on her limo to and from River House being on permanent standby. She also demanded unlimited champagne, and fresh flowers each day, both in her caravan and on her sunhat. She still thought Sexton was a nasty, common little man for curbing her expenses – everyone knew caviare, like seminal fluid, was good for the vocal cords.

Nor was Sexton setting a very good example. His worries about the budget had not deterred him from employing a ravishing new production secretary called Jessica, on the flimsy grounds that her telephone manner kept the backers sweet. Clearly she had not been hired for her typing. Copies of her first memo from Sexton – 'Please will all the cast assemble for a publicity shit in the Great Hall at twelve moon' – were already circulating the unit.

28

After a nice break with George, Flora was back to accompany Chloe in the Veil Song. For this Tristan had introduced a chorus of ladies-in-waiting, picked from the prettiest extras who would be seen poring over *Tatler*, and playing bridge and tennis. Eboli – or, rather, Chloe – would dazzle in tennis whites. Flora, as the Queen's detective, would flirt and strum Chloe's racquet like a mandolin.

Flora, terrified of acting, was further demoralized to discover her old enemy Serena Westwood, the record producer, had rolled up to see how filming was going. Even with temperatures in the nineties Serena, in an apple-green suit, looked as though she'd just come out of the fridge. She had also brought four-year-old Jessie, who Little Cosmo promptly pushed into the lily pond. 'Uncle Roberto' had regrettably displayed a similar lack of chivalry towards Jessie's mother: he had dropped her after the recording and refused to answer any of her telephone calls.

Lunching in the canteen, Serena and Helen, who had no idea that Serena had had an *affaire* with Rannaldini, which she was frantic to re-ignite, were joined by Hermione in her big straw hat decorated with yellow roses. The three women were all old flames of Flora's George and, not realizing Flora had wandered in, were loudly agreeing how attractively macho George was, and how anyone so rich and powerful could free himself in five minutes to marry Flora, if he really wanted to.

'How old is George?' mused Serena.

'About a year younger than me,' said Helen. 'We used to laugh about his being my toy-boy.'

Hermione, as Rannaldini's long-term mistress, detested any suggestion that Helen might be attractive to other men.

'When were you fifty, dear?' she enquired beadily. 'Was it in '94 or '95?'

Helen choked on her spinach and bacon salad. 'I am not forty-four yet, Hermione,' she said furiously.

'Aren't you, dear?' said Hermione blithely, then peering into Helen's face. 'Those chandeliers Meredith installed are quite lovely but not very flattering if you're heavily lined. After the movie, I'd encourage Rannaldini to return to more subdued lighting.'

A hush had fallen on the canteen. Glancing round, Serena saw Chloe killing herself and Flora looking extremely unhappy, and hastily asked after George.

'He's working in Germany,' mumbled Flora.

Serena raised eyebrows plucked thin as the new moon.

'Is that wise?'

'My Bobby's in Australia,' chipped in Hermione, 'but we have a relationship of trust.'

Grabbing a Mars bar and a packet of crisps for Trevor, Flora retreated, chuntering, to Make Up to find Lucy also going spare. On the premise that she adored children, little Jessie had been dumped on her to stop her prattling during takes. Jessie, having up-ended Lucy's make-up box, was now trying to rouse James from his siesta by tickling his long nose with a powder brush.

'He's going to take her hand off in a minute.'

'Let Trevor do the honours,' said Flora sourly. 'He loathes children. Oh, hell, Rannaldini's just rolled up in that flash orange car. He'll be wearing white polo-necks soon and combing his hair in little tendrils over his forehead.'

Sleek, suntanned, satanic, Rannaldini promptly decided the Veil Song needed gingering up with a spot of sapphic necking between Flora and one of the ladies-in-waiting.

'Who shall we choose?' murmured Rannaldini. 'Chloe, perhaps? Although maybe even randy little Tebaldo wouldn't risk jumping on the King's mistress.'

Running his eye lasciviously over the chorus, he noticed Pushy bobbing around in rose-red gingham, like an apple under a waterfall, and beckoned her over.

Even Lucy couldn't calm an hysterical Flora as she applied designer stubble to her ashen cheeks. Flora took Foxie, her puppet fox and adored mascot, everywhere with her. But this time, she wailed, Foxie must stay in the caravan with James and Trevor, in case he became corrupted.

'Foxie's face must be turned to the wall.'

The light was ravishing. A rare downpour had brightened the late spring greenery. Unearthly white lilacs wafted forth heavenly scent. A froth of cow-parsley merged into the rose-tipped barley.

Then, as Chloe and Flora sang about the randy King trying to seduce a veiled beauty, Flora had to act out the scene with Pushy.

'Just a quick snog.' Tristan patted her padded grey linen shoulder.

I cannot go on, thought Flora after they had notched up twenty nightmarish takes, because she was groping Pushy with all the enthusiasm of one de-fleaing a rabid dog. Even the cuckoo mocked her from a nearby ash grove.

'"Ah, weave your veils, fair maidens,"' sang the chorus, as they swayed about desperate to get into shot.

Taking a sadistic pleasure in how much this must be

hurting Serena, Helen *and* Hermione, Rannaldini kept strolling over to show Flora exactly how the pass should be made, which Pushy clearly adored, judging from the way she giggled and wriggled beneath his wandering hands. He would then seize Flora's hands and slap them like a weatherman's suns on various embarrassing parts of Pushy's anatomy.

'Maestro Rannaldini gives off enough electricity to make the generators superfluous,' said a disapproving voice. 'More cheerfully, Australia are two hundred and fifty for no wicket.'

It was Baby eating a large strawberry ice.

'Remember the times I've had to snog Dame Hermione,' he whispered to Flora. 'Just shut your eyes and think of income.'

Then, when she didn't laugh, he grabbed Foxie from Lucy's caravan, and clasping his furry puppet paws together, kept raising them above his head like a cheer-leader.

'It's no good crying,' hissed Rannaldini, as a tear trickled down Flora's cheek.

The reek of decaying wild garlic, indistinguishable from the breath and armpits of the crew, was making her feel sick. How dare those three witches, Serena, Helen and Hermione, sit there despising her? How dare Wolfie fill in his lottery tickets?

Oh, darling George, prayed Flora, come to my rescue.

And suddenly Flora's prayer was answered as George, unable to resist checking how shooting was going, ruined the first perfect take by noisily landing his heli-copter in the next field.

'We'll go again,' shouted Tristan.

Storming through the buttercups, terrible as an army with banners, George saw that devil incarnate Rannaldini and that smooth bastard Montigny, his peacock-blue shirt flapping against his lean, taut, dark gold body, and Wolfgang, blond as a Nordic god, and Baby, a laughing Cupid, and hundreds of smarmy Frogs leering over his darling Flora as she groped some ringleted tart.

But he misread the excitement on their faces as desire, when it was, in fact, delighted anticipation that someone might at last be going to take out Rannaldini. Either way George flipped. Bellowing at Tristan, sending cameras and crew flying, ordering Flora off the set, George grabbed Rannaldini by his white sharkskin lapels, threatening to bury him, until Clive and his pack of heavies dragged him off.

Analysing it afterwards, Flora wondered guiltily if it had been because George was looking so uncharacteristically red-faced and sweaty, and because his wool suit – it had been cold in Düsseldorf first thing – suddenly looked too tight for him, but irrationally she also flipped.

'I can't walk off in the middle of a take, it's totally unprofessional,' she screamed. 'It's only a grope, you bloody Victorian prude.'

'Pack your stooff, we're going,' yelled back George.

'We are *not*.'

Flanked by bodyguards, Rannaldini went on the offensive.

'Didn't you 'ear the lady?'

As George swung around the hatred so distorted his face that Flora thought he was going to kill Rannaldini.

'I'll get you, you wop bastard!' he bellowed. Then, without a backward glance, he stumbled off in the direction of his helicopter.

'And you're not having custody of Trevor,' Flora screamed after him.

'Why don't you go into the diplomatic service, Rannaldini?' sighed Baby.

'Who do I have to sleep with to get off this movie?' wailed a shaking Flora.

Tristan laughed, then told her how sorry he was.

'I'm going to London tonight, I'll take you somewhere fantastic tomorrow evening.'

After that Flora completed the scene in one take.

Baby, not unpleased by the turn of events, also comforted Flora. He would buy her dinner tonight and then, if she still needed to drown her sorrows, they would go on to Ogborne's birthday party.

29

Rolling up at Magpie Cottage to take Tabitha to Ogborne's party, Wolfie was horrified to go slap into Isa, unexpectedly returned from Australia. The odds on Peppy Koala for the Derby had been shortening alarmingly. Rannaldini was furious at losing the colt and, not wanting to lose him as an owner or Tab as a wife, in no particular order, Isa had decided to stay awake and attend the party to protect his property.

He had missed Tab's birthday at the beginning of June, but had brought her back more Quercus, the sweet, lemony scent he loved. It smelled wonderful on her just bathed body, but it didn't match up to Wolfie's present: a short, sleeveless, pale blue suede dress from Hermès, held up on one slender shoulder by a silver chain. It was also a reward: Tab hadn't had a drink for three weeks.

She looked so beautiful, Wolfie could hardly breathe, particularly when she flung her scented arms round his neck, whispering it was the loveliest dress she'd ever had. Isa was looking extremely wintry.

Over at Ogborne's party, which was taking place around Rannaldini's swimming-pool, a relay race, crew against cast, was in deafening progress. The crew was tipped to win, because Rannaldini, a powerful swimmer who wanted to show off his rippling muscles and flashy crawl, had graciously joined their side.

'Bernard looks more like a walrus than ever,' Chloe whispered to Simone, as the crew were held back by the first assistant director's ponderous breast-stroke.

Lucy, due to take over from Bernard, quivered on the edge of the pool, dying to hide her white body under the water. Having spent so much time on location in hot countries, however, she swam very well. Spurred on by the sight of Rannaldini, the crew's last swimmer, poised to plunge into ferocious action, she streaked up the pool to roars of applause.

'Bravo, Lucy.' As she lurched forward to touch the brass rail, Rannaldini's mahogany body flew over her head. Alas, Alpheus, the cast's last swimmer, had had an Olympic trial and emerged like an otter at the other end, beating an enraged Rannaldini by yards. Vowing to take both Pushy and Cheryl off Alpheus, Rannaldini stormed off to change.

There was a chorus of wolf whistles as Lucy climbed panting out of the pool. 'Pity you're always hiding that gorgeous body under a shirt and jeans, Miss Latimer,' yelled Ogborne, who was now wearing Hermione's rose-trimmed sunhat on his shaved head. Already drunk, he was doing very well for presents.

Tab gave him a purple and white striped shirt from Harvie & Hudson, confessing that in her drinking days she had bought it four sizes too big for Isa.

'Thank you,' said Ogborne, kissing her. 'Pity you're off the booze. I was hoping to get a job carrying you home after parties.'

Tab giggled. All the men had gasped when she'd rolled up in Wolfie's blue suede dress, then sighed in disappointment to see a lowering Isa in her wake. Chloe, however, spotting fresh talent, sidled up to Isa.

Alpheus, the hero of the evening after his winning swim, was having a wonderful time. Pushy, who he'd pleasured earlier in the long grass, was looking very lovely and so was Serena. But no-one outshone Tabitha. He was just edging towards her when he choked on a shrimp vol-au-vent. His wife, Cheryl, had swept in, a vision in cream lace, showing even more boob than Pushy.

'You never told me you were coming,' he hissed.

'You never asked,' hissed back Cheryl.

'Meesus Shaw, you 'ave never look more enticing.' Rannaldini, equally radiant in pale beige linen, clicked his fingers for Clive to bring Cheryl a glass of Krug. 'Let me show you my garden.' Then, seeing Serena moving in on him, desperate for a showdown, he grabbed a swaying hunk with fretted black Charles II hair. 'Serena, my dear, you must remember Granny's partner, Giuseppe,' and shoving them together he whisked Cheryl into the shrubbery.

'Where's Tristan?' asked Tab, who wanted him to see her in her beautiful new French dress.

'Gone to London,' said Simone. 'In a way it's easier when my uncle is not here – the women don't compete for him, the men with him.'

Tab didn't think so at all and was very disappointed. 'That Giuseppe,' she stormed, turning to Wolfie with all the disapproval of the reformed drinker, 'has just thrown up in Rannaldini's delphinium bed and blamed Maria's paella.'

The party roared on. Ogborne, Sylvestre and even newly married Valentin were trying to get off with Jessica, Sexton's ravishing new production secretary. Chloe was finding Isa desperately heavy-going.

'Why are you known as the Black Cobra?' she asked.

'Because I'm lethal.' Isa yawned and looked at his watch: he still hadn't made his number with Rannaldini.

Neither had Serena. Desperate to win back Rannaldini, she flirted more and more outrageously with Giuseppe, until Granny, knitting quietly away under a walnut tree, wanted to plunge his needles into Rannaldini's heart for setting the whole thing up.

The evening's main topic of conversation, however, was George Hungerford's flying visit, and whether Flora should have entered into the spirit of her part. Most of the crew said they would have been only too happy to grope Pushy. Soon Hermione was loudly putting her oar in.

'I cannot understand why Flora Seymour made such a fuss. I have often made love to young women on stage.'

'Can you get me some comps in the front row next time you're at it?' called out an excited Sexton, to guffaws all round.

Hermione flounced off. Trust such a common little man to lower the tone.

Emerging stars reflected milkily in the silken green water. The party was growing more raucous. Those with good bodies had started skinny-dipping.

'Those roses need watering,' said Valentin, emptying a bottle of red over Hermione's sunhat, which was still on Ogborne's head.

'Where's Flora?' asked Simone.

'Having dinner with Baby at the Pearly Gates,' said Lucy.

'No, she isn't, they've just arrived,' crowed Griselda, as, followed by Trevor the terrier, Flora and Baby drifted hand in hand through the buttercups. 'I always said those two were an item.'

'Oh, Grizel, when will you learn?' sighed Meredith.

Ogborne, dripping red wine, and more delighted to have a stale Pearly Gates Scotch egg from Trevor than a magnum of Moët from Baby and Flora, patted the bemused little dog over and over again.

'It's the fort wot counts, Trevor, my lad.'

A snake in the water caused shrieks of horror, particularly when Baby fished it out by its tail and killed it with one crack on the side of the pool. It turned out to be an adder.

'People eat snake in Australia,' he informed his admiring audience. 'It tastes just like fanny.'

'How would *you* know?' asked Ogborne pointedly.

'My brother told me,' said Baby, to howls of mirth.

'Baby is *so* attractive,' sighed Simone.

Crashing around, like a fretful moth, searching for Rannaldini, Hermione perked up when the singing started and she won first round in the not-so-friendly fight to hog the microphone.

'Someone to Watch Over Me' was soon blasting squirrels and pigeons out of the trees within a half-mile radius.

Baby, after several snorts of cocaine, was in a wicked mood, his eyes glittering, his bronze curls tangled round his handsome face. Griselda was thumping him on the back for being exactly the right weight at the moment, when Hermione charged up to them.

'Please protect me from that common little man.'

'Which one?' Griselda stared around.

'Sexton,' hissed Hermione.

'Oh, right,' said Baby thoughtfully. 'Not many people know Sexton went to Eton.'

'Eton,' said Hermione incredulously. '*Eton?*'

'Certainly did. Sexton thought he'd get on better in the film business if he acquired an East End accent, so he took elocution lessons.'

'He's so modest, he doesn't like to talk about his very grand family,' murmured Griselda.

Five minutes later, she and Baby were crying with laughter as they watched Sexton, looking as delightedly bewildered by Hermione's unexpected attentions as Trevor had over Ogborne's Scotch egg.

'You're not to tease,' Hermione was telling him roguishly. 'One can always tell an Etonian from his air of quiet authority. I expect you played cricket against my very good friend Rupert Campbell-Black, who must have been at Harrow at around the same time.'

Baby was so entranced he could hardly be dragged away to sing 'A Nightingale Sang in Berkeley Square' with Granny and Mikhail.

'Oh, I love this tune,' sighed Flora.

She was just wondering where George was when Baby sang, 'And when you stopped and smiled at me,' and, looking straight across at her, jolted her with a lightning bolt of desire.

The moment the song was over, Baby launched into 'Waltzing Matilda' and, watched in amazement by the entire party, seized Flora's hand and danced her off into the park, round and round under the stars through the foam of cow-parsley.

They were both so drunk they nearly fell over one of the set designer's pots of paint near the cloisters. Seizing his brushes, they were busy writing 'Death to Rannaldini', with cackles of laughter, on the chapel walls when they saw evil, leather-clad Clive gliding up on the right and hastily changed it to 'Death to Racism' before running away.

'"Gee, it's great, after staying up late, walking my Baby back home,"' Flora's piercingly sweet voice echoed round the valley, as she bore Baby up the valley to her parents' house, Angels' Reach, because she'd promised to feed Charity the cat.

'What was Rannaldini like in bed?' asked Baby.

'A genius. Mesmerizing, imaginative, with immense concentration, but utterly depraved. He'd have taken me down to hell.'

To their right was a long lake, even shorter of water than Rannaldini's. White daisies spilt over a low stone wall, lilies poured forth scent out of a tangle of weeds.

'What was his watch-tower like?'

'The top floor's all bed with a mural of wildly applauding crowds in evening dress.'

'We'll have applauding clouds,' murmured Baby, idly stroking the nape of Flora's long neck beneath her short back and sides.

Oh, help, thought Flora, I want to sleep with Baby so badly but it's a cul-de-fucking-no-sack.

Ahead, stone angels stretched up from each corner of the roof, plucking star daisies out of a grey suede sky. In protest against their being so late, Charity the cat had left a small disc of sick on the hall floorboards. Baby most resourcefully scraped it up with his platinum Amex card.

'Seriously good pictures,' he said, drifting from one big underfurnished room to another, as Flora opened a tin for Charity and a bottle of Moët.

'My father owns a gallery.'

'Where is he?'

'In London and up to no good, probably. He's very attractive.'

'Like his daughter,' said Baby. He led her out into the garden, waltzed her round and round until the stars joined in the dance, and they collapsed on the dewy grass, their hearts hammering.

For a second, Baby laughed down at her, his bland, brown, unrepentant face irresistibly young and beautiful, caught in the lights from the house. Then he kissed her.

Rigid with shock, Flora clamped her mouth shut, but such was the darting insistence of his tongue that her lips soon opened, and she was kissing him back with ecstatic enthusiasm.

'I thought you only liked men,' she gasped, when she finally drew breath.

'No more Mr Nice Gay,' crowed Baby. 'I take the best of both sexes, and you are definitely the best. I fancy you absolutely squint-eyed.'

'You're drunk.' Flora made a last attempt to keep control, but as he rolled her towards him to unzip her dress, the warmth of his body melted her resistance.

274

'I love George,' she mumbled, into his smooth, scented shoulder.

'George has gone off like a prawn in the sun. Deserves all he gets. Oh, you little beaut.'

Baby was a master of the tease. Running his fingers round the side of one nipple until every nerve of her breast was crying out, stroking her belly over and over again, letting his hand creep up her inner thighs, just stopping short of her clitoris, until she was screaming to have his cock inside her, and even then he was totally in control.

When Charity came out, mewing in outrage that plastered humans had mistaken Pedigree Chum for Go-Cat, Baby just laughed and said, 'Cattus interruptus.'

He was so relaxed.

There were daisies and little shimmering moths all over the lawn and stars all over the sky. Gradually they seemed to merge.

'I'm having *such* a heavenly time,' mumbled Flora, 'but I'm far too drunk to come.'

'Wanna bet.' Sliding out of her, turning her over, Baby kissed each bump of her backbone, slowly, slowly progressing downwards.

'Oh, my God! Oh, my God!'

'Yes, I thought you'd enjoy that.'

'Do I taste of snake?' mumbled Flora.

'No, only of Paradise.'

'How d'you know so much about women?' asked Flora, as they lay back, stupefied with pleasure, on the grass.

'I used to be married.'

'What?' Flora sat bolt upright.

'To a singer.'

'Why did it break up?'

Baby took a slug of Moët. 'She asked me what I thought of her in the Verdi Requiem. I was foolish enough to tell her. She never spoke to me again.'

'Did you mind?'

'Nope.'

'Isn't it rather immoral, pretending you're gay when you're not?'

'Certainly not. However would I get rid of all those ugly cows if they suspected I was heterosexual?'

'You are seriously degenerate,' said Flora, as they fell asleep in each other's arms.

30

Waking cold, stiff and horribly hung over in the morning, Flora was demented. How could she have done this to George? He'd never forgive her if he found out. Rannaldini had spies everywhere and was bound to tell him. 'I'm being punished for shortchanging that cat,' she moaned, as she crunched around on the Go-Cat the furious Charity had up-ended all over the kitchen floor.

'I will take care of you,' said a totally unfazed Baby.

But when Flora returned, crawling with embarrassment, to her dressing room at Valhalla, she found her puppet fox had been cut to tiny pieces. Flora went berserk. She had had Foxie since she was a baby. He had always brought her luck. Without his protection, George would never come back. And who could have cut him up? Rannaldini, Helen, Hermione and Serena all hated her, so did Wolfie and probably Pushy, Bernard and Sexton, after yesterday's débâcle. Or perhaps some admirer of Baby's, outraged she'd got off with him last night. It was all dreadfully frightening.

Everyone was very sympathetic, particularly Rozzy, who gathered up fragments of orange fur and said she'd soon sew Foxie together again.

'Rozzy's so lovely,' a tearful Flora told Baby. 'If only she could get rid of that horrible husband and find some heavenly lover.'

'Hard to kiss a woman whose mouth's always full of pins.'

Flora was far too miserable to have dinner with Tristan that night.

Tab, too, was absolutely miserable. Isa was back in Australia so Wolfie came and watched the Derby with her at Magpie Cottage. Then she had the exquisite but agonizing pleasure of seeing Rupert and his entourage in their grey top hats streaming, solemn as warlords, into the paddock to watch Peppy Koala saddling up.

'Look, there's Lysander, and Declan, Daddy's partner,' she told Wolfie, 'and Billy Lloyd-Foxe, who was his great show-jumping mate, and Ricky France-Lynch and Bas Baddingham, his old polo friends.'

'Who's that blonde?' asked Wolfie, thinking she was beautiful.

'My half-sister, Perdita, uptight bitch. That's her husband, Luke Alderton, he's a saint. Heavens! Marcus has flown back from Moscow. That must be Nemerovsky, his boyfriend. Look at the stupid poof showing off,' Tab added furiously, as a smiling Nemerovsky waved his top hat to acknowledge the cheers of the crowd. Wolfie, who'd been at boarding school with Marcus, thought how happy he looked.

'Here comes Taggie,' hissed Tabitha, as her stepmother, ravishing in a fuchsia-pink silk suit and a big violet hat, was towed into the paddock by a thoroughly overexcited Xav and Bianca.

'Bloody hell.' Tab took a long slug of Perrier, splashing her face. 'Children shouldn't be allowed in the paddock, particularly loose,' she added angrily, as Xav and Bianca rushed forward to hug Peppy Koala. 'And that geek with his hat on the back of his head is Peppy's owner, Mr Brown.'

Mr Brown apart, thought Wolfie wistfully, they were the most glamorous, self-assured bunch: Tab's world. How presumptuous to hope he could ever be part of it.

'God, what a beautiful horse.' Another slug of Perrier spilt over Tab's face, as Rupert's jockey, wearing Mr Brown's colours, bright blue dotted with white stars like the Australian flag, mounted a dancing Peppy.

The little colt gave all his supporters a heart attack by dawdling at the back until the last furlong then, putting on a staggering burst of speed, he bounded past the toiling field to win by three lengths.

Having screamed her head off with excitement, Tab proceeded to sob so wildly Wolfie couldn't help her.

'I miss them all so much. Mr Brown refused to give Peppy to Isa because he thought Isa was cruel to me. That's what Isa will never forgive.'

Neither did the Derby result please Rannaldini. How could Isa have let Peppy Koala slip through his fingers?

To goad Tab, Rannaldini summoned her to his study a week later to watch a big Australian race on cable. Isa was riding a dark brown mare, who won as effortlessly as Peppy Koala. As usual, he was mobbed by groupies. Tab, on the other hand, was more upset to see his deadpan face break into a smile as Martie, his allegedly ex–girlfriend, looking scruffier and shinier than any of the grooms, ran forward to hug him after the race.

'Very well ridden,' said Rannaldini softly, 'but he could spend a leetle more time in England training my horses.' Then, seeing Tab gnawing her lower lip, 'And I don't think he is paying you quite enough attention, my angel, to justify a free rent in that lovely cottage.'

'Put him in the debtor's chair. Where is it by the way?'

'Somewhere much more exciting. Remind me to show you some time.'

But Tab had fled sobbing from the room.

Tristan, meanwhile, was spending more and more evenings in Lucy's caravan. He was obviously not sleeping and everyone was draining him with their in-securities and petty rivalries, as he heroically battled to keep within budget and Rannaldini at bay. He was trying to smoke less, which made him very uptight and, unwillingly yielding to Hype-along's pleas, he had finally agreed to talk to Valerie Grove of *The Times*, in the hope that some good publicity might calm the backers.

In the past he had stuck up for Rannaldini, but as Lucy cut his hair for the interview he repeatedly returned to the attack.

'He's like evil octopus with tentacles everywhere.'

Thinking how thickly and beautifully Tristan's hair curled into his neck, Lucy struggled against the temptation to stroke it. Then he nearly lost an ear as he switched to the subject of Tabitha.

'Rannaldini is so crazy about her, he inveigle her into marrying that absolute shit, Isa Lovell. Now he plays games with her like Iago. She came out of his study crying this afternoon.'

Lucy fought despair. Thank God Rozzy had rolled up with a bottle to cheer Tristan up. Rozzy was relieved that she only had a hundred or so more seed pearls to sew on Hermione's coronation dress.

Next morning Lucy was terrified to discover slug pellets in James's water bowl. Perhaps someone had just missed the window-box or perhaps, she thought wryly, people were jealous because Tristan spent so much time in Make Up – but it was only because he was desperate to talk about Tab.

She had further evidence that afternoon, when Hermione, who she was making up for her great renunciation scene with Carlos, announced she'd heard a horrid rumour that Tristan was queer.

'Of course he's not,' exploded Lucy.

'Well, that's what they're implying. Silly, really,' Hermione gave her horrible little laugh, 'that with so many pretty women to choose from, Tristan's spending his evenings with . . . and also that make-up girls usually stick to their own kind and drink with the sparks and the chippies.'

Then, seeing Lucy's face, she added, 'But I stuck up for you, Lucy. I said you had quite a warm personality and, anyway, beauty is in the eye of the beholder. Oh, Belgian chocolates!'

Lucy was about to snap that they were a thank-you present from Tristan for cutting his hair when Hermione opened the box and found one white truffle left.

'My favourite,' she cried. 'Although I've already got a handsome hubby, and a thousand a year wouldn't go far these days.'

She was just about to eat it, when Lucy snatched away the box. 'James loves white truffles,' she insisted, and opening the amazed dog's jaws, shoved it into his mouth.

Hermione was furious.

'When you think of Flora and that wretched terrier, and Tab drooling over that Labrador,' she said beadily, 'it is extra*ordinary* how women who cannot get it together with a man become dependent on a companion animal.'

James spat out the white truffle.

'Bloody chippies,' exploded Lucy.

Meredith's carpenters, building a cathedral for the *auto da fe* and banging away all morning, had given her a blinding headache.

She was so cross she gave Hermione a parsnip yellow complexion, ageing grey shading, hideous violet eye shadow and a wonky lip-line. Hermione was so busy reading about her health in the *Daily Mail* that she didn't notice.

Tristan did, however, and remonstrated sharply with Lucy.

'Well, if she was about to give Carlos the push and she loved him to bits, she would look grotty,' shouted back Lucy.

'*Ma petite.*' Tristan looked at her in amazement. 'This is first time I see you angry. You are so sweet,' and he ruffled her hair.

'Patronizing bastard,' muttered Lucy.

She was so fed up that she knocked back nearly a bottle of white at lunchtime, and stuck Colin Milton's bald wig on back to front. Colin was so taken by the sight of himself with a youthful fringe of grey curls nestling on his eyebrows that he would happily have let it stay. Tristan, however, went ballistic, and yelled at Lucy to stop taking the piss.

31

The *auto da fe*, which means Act of Faith, is one of the most terrifying scenes in all opera. Heretics in dunces' caps are paraded through the streets by their executioners and followed by sinister black-cowled monks who, with the courtiers and ladies-in-waiting, take up their seats round the funeral pyre.

A newly crowned Philip comes out of the cathedral and repeats his coronation oath to defend the faith. The scene ends with his dreadful words, 'And now on with the festivities!' The masses are then entertained not by fireworks but by the heretics being burnt at the stake.

Lasting twenty minutes in the opera, even Tristan's pared-down version took eight gruelling days to shoot. The harrowing nature of the subject exacerbated Rannaldini's sadism. Meredith and his chippies had only just completed their ravishing cathedral façade, looking on to the east courtyard, when Rannaldini swept in on the first day of shooting and pronounced it utterly suburban: 'Just like a Weybridge *hacienda*. Are we going to have chiming doorbells, celebrating the burning of the heretics?'

Meredith promptly burst into tears. It took all Tristan's tact to stop him resigning. Lucy had visions of being asked to streak Meredith's hair for yet another dinner at the Heavenly Host. Fortunately Sexton rocked up and told Meredith he thought the cathedral was just beautiful.

'And he ought to know,' whispered Hermione reverently. 'Sexton did go to Eton.'

Hermione was also delighted that, after weeks of work, Griselda and Rozzy had finally sewn the last seed pearl on her ivory satin dress. Her first appearance wearing it that afternoon caused gasps of wonder and genuine applause from the crew.

A second later Rannaldini had erupted on to the set, and everyone glanced at the sky in excitement. Then, to their horror, they realized that what they had imagined as the patter of rain was the scattering of thousands of pearls, as Rannaldini ripped off the dress, and stamped it into the dust with his suede boots. Hermione, in her petticoat, screamed and screamed. Oscar crossed himself. It was like seeing a Velazquez slashed in the Prado. Tristan grabbed Rannaldini in white-hot fury.

'What the fuck are you doing? That was the most beautiful dress I ever see.'

'Elisabetta must wear scarlet,' yelled back Rannaldini.

'At her husband's coronation?'

'To symbolize in Philip's crazy mind she has been unfaithful.'

'All those pearls, all those pearls,' whispered Rozzy, who'd done nearly all the work.

A devastated, hysterically sobbing Griselda had to be carried off the set by a buckling Lucy and Simone. Everyone was outraged. They loved Griselda: indefatigable, gossipy old trout. They knew she was good. The crew would have walked out if Rannaldini hadn't built massive penalty clauses into all their contracts. Instead they went slow, with Oscar waking up to relight every ten minutes.

All the crew were putting in impossibly long hours, but no-one more so than Wolfie. Once again, his greatest headache was stopping Pushy Galore appearing in everything. Having waved a flag as a member of the *hoi-polloi* and simpered as a lady-in-waiting, Pushy was determined to star as a heretic, and was utterly incensed when Tristan chucked her out.

'You wait till Ay tell Sir Roberto.'

Fortunately Rannaldini had flown off to Vienna and was not expected back until the evening. Pushy was even crosser when Tristan chose Tab instead. She would look so touching, a dunce's cap on her blonde head, her deadpan face smudged. Tab was terribly excited; Wolfie less so. Supervising the filling of petrol cans with water, he couldn't bear the thought of her beautiful body being torched.

The drought was so terrible, it was as if Meredith had carpeted the surrounding fields brown. Wild flowers that had survived were a quarter of their usual height. Wolfie disappeared in a cloud of dust as he drove his Land Rover round the park. All the cast complained non-stop about not being able to breathe. Wolfie could have burnt the lot of them on the bonfire.

It was the last set-up before lunch as, surrounded by leather-clad paparazzi, with Tristan's four black cypresses in the background overseeing things, Granny as Gordon Dillon took up his position on the battlements of the cathedral. While the heretics were tied to the stakes below, shredded piles of the *Scorpion* were thrown under their bare feet.

'As people in the sixteenth century flocked to see heretics burn, today we devour the papers and gloat over reputations being destroyed,' explained Tristan. 'Think of the poor Duchess of York.'

'Think of Chloe in a week or two,' murmured Flora to Baby.

Out in the park, through the heat haze, they could see Chloe, ravishing in palest pink, having her photograph taken for the *Scorpion*. Hotfoot from a very promising *Samson and Delilah* audition, she had returned to Valhalla for an in-depth interview with Beattie Johnson, the *Scorpion*'s most dreaded columnist. Beattie had written to Chloe direct, claiming she was a long-term fan of Chloe *and* the opera.

'I can handle the press,' Chloe had told Hype-along haughtily when he expressed horror at the planned interview.

Having read Chloe's cuttings and a page-long synopsis of *Don Carlos* in the limo driving down, Beattie Johnson was highly diverted to see the identical twin of her notorious boss, Gordon Dillon, on the battlements and was now shredding reputations, 'off the record, of course', with Chloe.

Lucy, who'd already had to make up Chloe as well as the cast, was having a day from hell. The gruesome concept of an *auto da fe* upset her dreadfully. Her passport had gone missing and she'd spent two hours looking for it. Her back, from so much bending, was killing her. She'd have gone straight to James Benson, if she hadn't given more money to Rozzy who'd been in tears all morning. This was because, after a weekend at home, Rozzy had forgotten Flora's newly repaired puppet fox and done a U-turn only to find her horrible husband Glyn and his glamorous housekeeper, Sylvia, opening a bottle to celebrate her departure.

I can't go on shoring everyone up, thought Lucy in despair.

Having not had any breakfast, she was feeling faint and decided to grab a salad from the canteen, where she found Chloe and Beattie Johnson, two glamorous blondes, sharing a bottle of Muscadet.

'Bernard, the first assistant, has a thumping great crush on Rozzy Pringle,' Chloe was whispering.

'Who's she?'

'Oh, Beattie,' giggled Chloe, 'you must have heard of Rozzy. She's so refined she pees eau-de-Cologne.'

Both women shrieked with laughter. Lucy's blood started to boil.

'Here comes Tristan,' hissed Beattie. 'You must introduce me.'

She's got the hard, set little face of a terrorist waiting to lob a bomb into all our lives, thought Lucy.

'I've seen *all* your films,' Beattie was now telling Tristan.

Lucy was on her way out when she heard Tristan, who'd taken an empty seat at the table, explaining the *auto da fe* to Beattie. 'The Spaniards are experts at ritualistic torture,' he was saying. 'Look at the ballet of killing the bull. In the same way, *auto da fe* sets fire to humans in dunces' caps to humiliate and express power of Church.'

'I love Spanish men,' said Chloe, who hadn't been listening.

'Me too,' sighed Beattie.

'Well, you're both stupid bitches,' said a furious voice.

Looking round, everyone was amazed to see a trembling, red-faced Lucy holding a tray, off which a glass of orange juice and a salad were sliding.

'I hate Spaniards. Hate, hate, *hate* them,' she went on hysterically. 'When greyhounds are past their sell-by date in England, they're sold to Spain where they're raced into the ground.'

'Oh, pur-lease.' Chloe raised her eyes to heaven.

'But the fucking Spaniards are too stingy to shoot them or put them down so they string them up in the woods with their toes just touching the ground and have bets on which is going to die first. It takes hours. The poor dogs scream in agony like the heretics. And you like fucking Spaniards?'

The appalled silence was broken by Lucy's salad crashing to the ground, and orange juice spilling all over Chloe's new pink dress. Flora, Baby and Granny leapt to their feet, but Tristan reached Lucy first.

'It's all right, sweet'eart, of course it's terrible, whether it's greyhounds or heretics.'

But Lucy had wriggled out of his arms and, shouting, 'Why don't you have a word with King Carlos? I bet he shot partridge with your father,' she fled, sobbing, back to her caravan.

'Dear, dear,' drawled Chloe. 'When make-up artists start having tantrums, the rot has set in.'

'Oh, shut up,' yelled Flora.

Tristan was about to go after Lucy when Bernard seized his arm and dragged him off to an urgent meeting in Sexton's office. This Tristan did not enjoy. The budget, Sexton told him bleakly, had hit twenty-two million and was still climbing: Tristan must hurry up the crew. After a snide piece in the *Stage*, picked up by the nationals, the backers were getting antsy. Rannaldini must be persuaded to release more money when he returned tonight.

'He won't unless we allow him to do his sodding introductions.' Tristan unwrapped another piece of chewing-gum. God, he needed a cigarette.

Sexton was just saying he couldn't pay this week's wages when Tab barged into the room. 'What's that bitch doing here?'

'Get out,' bellowed Bernard.

'She was Daddy's mistress between marriages,' stormed Tab. 'She nearly ruined him. She stopped him and Taggie adopting babies in England, she got Abby Rosen sacked, and she outed my brother Marcus. She's the most evil woman in the world.'

'Who *are* you talking about?'

'Beattie Johnson, who's interviewing Chloe,' said Tab. 'In that big black bag are a hammer and nails to crucify her victims.'

'That's blasphemous,' exploded Bernard.

'But a shrewd assessment,' agreed Sexton. 'If Beattie stitches us up, the backers really will pull out.'

Tristan wrinkled his brow. 'I think she's a friend of Rannaldini. We'd better throw her out before he gets back.'

He found Beattie buttering up Pushy.

'If you weren't so lovely, people would take you more seriously as a singer.'

'Sir Roberto's always sayin' that.'

'He says you stand out from all the other extras.'

'Ay'm not an extra, Ay'm a featured extra,' said Pushy haughtily.

'Off the record, how well do you know Alpheus Shaw? What a hunk.'

Tristan had heard enough. Beattie was incandescent with rage when he told her that a car, with her suitcases all packed in the boot, was waiting to take her back to London.

'Do not say Liberty Productions does not evict with style,' he added, as he opened the door for her.

Chloe was also insane with anger.

'We hadn't even begun the interview yet. Everything was off the record.'

'Every inch of that evil frame is taped,' said Tristan.

Spurred on by his meeting with Sexton, he returned to the set determined to dispatch the last gruesome seconds of the *auto da fe* in one stint. It was even hotter. Hermione was flushing up in her new red dress from Versace. Flora and Granny sweltered in their dark suits, but not nearly so much as Alpheus in his gold regalia, or Baby, Mikhail and the courtiers in their ermine-trimmed peers' robes.

As Lucy, tearstained after her outburst at lunchtime, rushed round trying to cool people down with a chamois leather soaked in cologne, Baby could be heard grumbling that he'd be barbied without going near any stake.

'If you confessed at the last moment, you could be strangled before you were burnt to death,' volunteered a listless Flora, who hadn't heard from George since her night with Baby.

To capture the intense drama, Tristan was using a crane to film from above, with Valentin and his camera on a tiny platform hanging twenty feet above the funeral pyre. It would be a wonderful shot, tracking over the excited crowd, the bigwigs of church and state in their gilded regalia and the poor, doomed victims. The head of Props waited with his finger on the button of the smoke-machine. The flames would be added later by special effects.

'Take that "I survived Don Carlos" badge off at once, Baby,' ordered Bernard. 'Quiet, please, everyone.'

'OK, let's go for a quick rehearsal,' shouted Tristan, from a first-floor window.

'Shit,' muttered Valentin, who from his platform could see an orange Lamborghini Diablo sneaking up the drive. 'Rannaldini's back.'

'Ignore him,' snapped Tristan.

In moved the paparazzi like a firing squad, their long lenses trained on the heretics. Swiftly the executioners chucked petrol cans of water on the shredded *Scorpions*, then flicking on their lighters pretended to set fire to the damp newsprint.

'Cue for smoke,' yelled Tristan, and a white cloud engulfed the heretics. 'Excellent, let it clear,' he shouted, 'and we'll go for a take.'

Adjusting his director's cap to a more military angle, Tristan felt a surge of power as he looked down at the huge crowd. He *was* a general commanding a mighty army. The landscape shimmered with heat-haze, a hot breeze ruffled the red-tipped barley into flickering flames. He was just shuddering at the thought of Tab's body being burnt to death when he was roused by a dreadful screaming. And fantasy became reality as the shredded newspaper beneath her stake burst into flames, and flared up around her. For a moment, everyone was motionless with horror. Then, as the screaming grew more terrified, Tristan leapt straight down into the smoke, miraculously landing safely on the stony courtyard.

'It's all right, *chérie*.'

Diving for the rope tying her to the stake, aware of flame caressing his chest, his long fingers somehow managed to untie the knot without fumbling. A moment later he had dragged Tab to safety.

Beating out the flames snaking up her yellow heretic's robe, feeling no pain except that of frantic worry, he dragged the peer's robes off a horrified extra and rolled Tab in them. It was over in thirty seconds.

Next moment, Wolfie, who'd been watching from a second-floor window, hurtled into the courtyard, yelling, 'Is she OK? Get the paramedics, for Christ's sake.'

The front of Tab's hair, her long blonde eyelashes and her eyebrows were singed, there was a terrible stench of burning, but she didn't appear hurt, only dazed and terrified as she collapsed sobbing wildly into Tristan's arms. As Tristan clutched her to his sweat-drenched shirt, examining her face for burns, kissing her frizzled hair, crooning in rapid French that she mustn't be frightened, the extras, thinking it was part of the plot, led a round of applause. As he ran into the courtyard, and sized up the situation, Rannaldini's face was shrivelled into a mask of evil.

'Who left petrol in that can?' he screamed. 'Someone has tried to murder my daughter.'

'They were all filled with water,' stammered an aghast Wolfie, 'I checked them.'

'Well, heads will roll.' Everyone retreated as Rannaldini glared round.

Tristan promptly called a wrap for the day. 'I'm taking Tabitha home.'

'You can't,' muttered an appalled Bernard. 'All these extras, a full cast, we've got hours of light left.'

'I don't geeve a fuck. Oscar can take over.'

'Tabitha will stay at Valhalla. Her mother will look after her,' snarled Rannaldini, 'and you can carry on.'

'No!' Tab was hysterical. 'I want to go home with Tristan.'

Even Griselda was roused from her despondency over Hermione's wrecked dress. 'I always said those two would end up together,' she hissed to a boot-faced Alpheus. 'At least they're the same class. Here you are, darling.' She slipped Tab's short red shift over her head, sliding it down her body as she removed the heretic's robe. 'Go home and have a heavenly tryst with *triste* Tristan, and boo sucks to sodding Rannaldini.'

'That little madam gets everyone nice,' said Baby sulkily.

A stricken Lucy fled to her caravan. A stunned Wolfie kept repeating that there had been no petrol in the cans. Rozzy had mindlessly collapsed into Rannaldini's executive producer's chair, tears streaking down her face.

'Tristan could have been killed.'

'You're so wet, my dear Rozzy,' sneered Rannaldini, 'you could have put the fire out yourself. Clive?' He clicked his fingers for his shadow, then dropping his voice: 'Follow the two of them, see what they get up to.'

32

At Magpie Cottage, Sharon the Labrador, singing in delight, welcomed Tristan by bringing him a pair of Tab's knickers.

'You sing better than Hermione.' Tristan stooped to pat her.

Tab laughed, then gave a sob and fled upstairs to examine her naked lashless face in the bathroom mirror. Five minutes later Tristan found her shaking uncontrollably, rubbing toothpaste into her blanched cheeks. He was amazed, then touched when she refused a glass of brandy. 'I promised God I wouldn't and He – admittedly helped by you – has just saved my life.'

On the bed, Snoopy gazed up from one of her pillowcases, dinosaurs from the other. Tristan had just persuaded her to lie down on the Peter Rabbit duvet when the doorbell rang.

'Tell it to go away,' pleaded Tab. 'Don't bang your head on the beam going down.'

It was James Benson, the smooth family doctor who had been summoned to so many Campbell-Black and Rannaldini crises in the past. Agreeing with the paramedics that Tab was unhurt but deeply shocked, he gave her a shot.

'You'll be fine, sweetie. You're a lucky girl. It would

have been a tragedy if that lovely face had been spoilt. Where's your husband?'

'In Australia. Tristan saved my life. Will you see he's OK?'

Downstairs James Benson produced some very strong painkillers. 'You've come off worse than she has,' he said, as he accepted a large brandy. 'Thank God she's off the booze, but she's not in good shape. She was clinically depressed after she lost the baby in March, and she burst into tears when I said I'd seen Rupert last week. I'd give the old bastard a ring – I'm convinced he's missing her as much as she's missing him.'

'It's all Helen's fault,' exploded Tristan. 'Bloody woman doesn't give a stuff about Tab.'

'That's not fair,' said James Benson sharply. 'I first treated Helen when she wasn't much older than Tab. She was the loveliest thing I ever saw, and sweet too. If she hadn't been a patient, I'd have made a serious play. Rupert was away when she nearly died having Marcus, he was even more humiliatingly unfaithful to her than Rannaldini, if that's possible. Between them, they've done for her.'

Tristan was amazed by the venom in James's voice, but Tabitha was his only interest. 'What about Isa?'

'Cold fish, corroded with moral outrage against the Campbell-Blacks. He'll never forgive Tab. Sooner she's out of this marriage the better.'

Tristan was pacing the room, clearly desperate to be left alone with Tab. Leggy and effortlessly elegant, despite his dusty espadrilles and dirty frayed white shorts, he reminded James of a heart-throb admired by his own generation: Gérard Philippe.

'I know it's none of my business,' he drained his brandy, 'but she's very vulnerable.'

Having let the doctor out, Tristan noticed a framed photograph on the desk of Isa smugly riding in the winner of last year's Gold Cup. Parking his green chewing-gum on his rival's face, he belted back upstairs.

'I'm going to make you a cup of tea.'

'Hot sweet tea!' mocked Tab. 'I'd rather have hot sweet Montigny. Please don't leave me.'

'I won't.'

He was touched to see Schiller's *Don Carlos* beside Dick Francis on the bedside table.

'I'm trying to educate myself,' she muttered.

'Are you sure you're not hungry?'

Tab shook her head. 'Sharon probably is.'

'I feed her. I give her sheep chops I find in fridge.'

Tab giggled. 'Flora and Baby call Griselda: Lady Caroline Sheep. I'm sorry I'm holding up your film, but it was so cool you telling Bernard and Rannaldini to fuck off, and leaving three hundred and fifty extras and Dim Hermione all cooling their heels because of me.'

Tristan lay on the bed beside her.

'Am I squashing you?'

'Not enough,' mumbled Tab.

Tristan could feel the faint down of her leg against his. He thought she'd fallen asleep, then her hand crept into his.

'Are your poor burnt hands agony?'

'Not when you hold them.'

The smell of wild mint and meadowsweet was drifting in through the window. Outside, wild roses cascaded over dark green trees like a William Morris wallpaper. As Tristan lay up on his side he thought he had been caught up in some time warp. Without her lashes and eyebrows and with her extreme pallor and her hairline temporarily singed back an inch, Tab had become a sixteenth-century beauty, Elisabetta, or even Eboli. Her forehead was as white as the moon, her lashless lids like magnolia petals.

James Benson's painkillers had begun to kick in. Bending back his hand as though he were drying his nails, because his palm was still very sore, Tristan ran the inside of his wrist up the red chiffon dress, feeling the concave belly, the soft swell of breast, only to be halted by a rock-hard nipple.

As he bent over and kissed her, Tab gave a gasp and kissed him back in ecstasy, breathing in a faint tang of Eau Sauvage, and the mint of his chewing-gum, burying her fingers in his thick silky hair, feeling his big bumpy head, so different from Isa's, which was as narrow as a weasel's.

'I have longed for you,' murmured Tristan, laying his cheek against hers, 'ever since I saw you at the traffic-lights in Rutminster drinking vodka, Sharon across your thighs instead of a safety-belt. Straight away I want to be safety-belt that protect you,' he smiled down at the malevolent little eyes and great gnashing teeth on the pillowcase beside her, 'even from dinosaurs.'

'The first time I saw you I thought, Jesus! Although it was probably "Jeshush" because I was so pissed. I asked Lucy as she made me up if she'd seen that fantastically gorgeous man downstairs and she laughed and said yes, but I'd have to give all that up now I was getting married.'

'Did you marry Isa because you were pregnant?'

'No,' confessed Tab, gently pulling fragments of singed hair from his chest. 'I never do anything because I ought to, so I put you on hold until I galloped round the corner and saw you all ogling that naked bitch Chloe. God, I was cross, but ever since then I've looked forward more and more to seeing you on the set. It's as though you've got a halo. You're the only person I notice.'

'What about Wolfie?'

'Sweet, but too straight and he doesn't have a halo.'

Even though Tristan's hand was stroking its way very slowly down her body, setting her completely adrift, she had to know.

'Everyone on the unit spends their time speculating about your sex life,' she said falteringly. 'A celibate

Frenchman is a contradiction in terms. There must be someone.'

Outside a blackbird was singing, a dog barked in the valley. Sharon barked back.

'Not any more,' said Tristan, as his hand now crept up slender thighs, honed by years in the saddle.

'Please wait!' begged Tab. 'There isn't someone like Isa's girlfriend in Australia, waiting to rear her hideous head in a month or two? I couldn't handle it.'

'Hush.' As he shut her mouth with his, Tristan's fingers edged under her knicker elastic into the tightest, stickiest hollow. 'Oh, *ma petite.*'

Wriggling out of his arms, Tab leapt out of bed. Like a poppy shedding petals, her red dress slithered to the floor.

Tristan had lost enough weight for her to tug off his shorts without unzipping them. Next moment she was on top of him.

'*Venez* inside *moi, toute* sweet.'

Tristan did just that. As he thrust up inside her, he was briefly conscious of a delicious slipperiness, of muscles closing round him like a fist, and Tab moving, fluid as a dancer. Then he trembled violently, cried out and came.

'Oh, fuck, fuck, fuck, I'm so sorry.' He buried his face in her shoulder. 'I should have held out. I am weemp, but you are so lovely, I was lost, I am so sorry.'

'Don't be.' Tab kissed him over and over, her tears soaking his shoulder. 'It's so gorgeous to be wanted so much. Isa times it like a race. Conserve the energy, push through the gap.'

'I love you totally,' said Tristan, as he slowly returned to earth.

Assuming sex was over for the day, Sharon galumphed into the bedroom, landing between the lovers, and was disappointed to be firmly told by Tristan that it had only just started.

Hazily watching his dark head between her legs, as his long lazily lapping tongue drove her through repeated hoops of ecstasy, Tab was inclined to agree with him. And those lovely endearments he kept murmuring in French. It's like Sharon being talked to by me, she thought. She doesn't understand what I'm saying, but she knows, by the tone of my voice, it's adoring.

'That was the best sex ever,' she said, flopping back on to the pillow. Then, terrified it might only be a one-afternoon stand, she glanced sideways, trying to memorize his face for ever, noting the dark brown curls, straighter since the moisture had dried out of the earth, the big, slightly twisted mouth, the sallow complexion, now burnt dark gold, the long slightly snub nose, thick curly eyelashes that would never need mascara, black rings beneath the hollow eyes.

'When you 'ave finish staring,' said Tristan acidly, 'I have first grey hairs at twenty-eight. It is abomination.'

'You've been working too hard.'

'No, I worry you will never love me. Oh, my angel, what a lovely life we'll have together.'

Tab froze. 'D'you mean that?'

'*Absolument.*' Tristan took her hand, tempted to slide off her wedding ring. 'James Benson wanted me to call your father.'

Fuck, he'd ruined everything!

'Don't interfere.' Tab hissed. 'It's nothing to do with James! Christ, why is everyone—?'

'Not everyone, hush.' Gradually, he calmed her.

'I can't cope if Daddy hangs up on me. I don't want to lose face.'

'No-one would want to lose one as beautiful as yours.' Tristan ran a finger down her cheek.

'Am I really beautiful?'

'Oh, my darling, you are also genius,' he added lovingly. 'I never had horses more better organized on a shoot.'

'Will you tell Isa?' Tab sat up in excitement. 'He thinks I'm a total failure.'

298

'Isa's over.'

'I know I go on about him,' confessed Tab, 'but he's tougher to kick than the booze. I don't love him but him having this other woman hurt almost more than losing the baby.'

'My poor darling.' Tristan kissed her forehead, then her Greek nose and then her luscious, loving mouth. 'We will have lots of kids. But I will always adore you the most.'

Kissing his fingers, tasting traces of herself, Tab examined his signet ring. On it was engraved a snake coiled round a column.

'I can't read the motto.'

'Basically it say, "Don't disturb the Montigny snake, or he'll come and get you." He can see off a Black Cobra any day.'

Having taken Sharon for a run, Tristan left Tab, when she was nearly falling asleep. He had missed a half-day's filming, and had several hours' work to do.

'Come back later,' begged Tab.

'If you promise not to wake up.'

Suddenly thunder rumbled round the valley like a roused guard dog.

'Poor James, he'll be terrified,' said Tab.

'Poor Lucy.' Tristan thought of her anguished, disintegrating face in the canteen.

Outside the front door, white rose petals snowed down on them. As he kissed her goodbye he felt his soul, like those of the heretics, being drawn up to heaven.

Bats flitted across a rising yellow moon, as he floated back to Valhalla trying to keep the silly grin off his face. Overhead, proud and defiant, strode the constellation of Hercules. As Tabitha loved him, he could dispatch thirteen hundred labours. Suddenly he was singing, 'I am Carlos, and I love you, yes, I love you,' at the top of his voice. He was so happy he walked straight under a ladder.

On his bed lay a fax of his interview with *The Times*. He had been very taken by and had got mildly tight over lunch with Valerie Grove, who'd written it. She had described him as the complete Prince Charmant, with naturally aristocratic good manners and a haircut that could only have come from Paris.

Tristan smiled. He must show Lucy that bit.

The piece mentioned his 'close friendship' with Claudine Lauzerte, and said that the word on the street about *The Lily in the Valley* was that it would be both smash hit and artistic triumph.

'Is This the Greatest Montigny of Them All?' said the headline. Below was a big picture of himself. Flanking it were smaller pictures of Étienne, and Tristan's older brothers, including an incredibly rare snapshot of Laurent, who had looked so like Che Guevara.

'One reason I make *Don Carlos*', Tristan was quoted as saying, 'was my brother Laurent die twenty-eight years ago, blown up in Chad fighting injustice, like Posa. His death broke my father's heart. I wanted to give him my own memorial.'

Étienne would have gone ballistic at the mention of Laurent. Tristan hoped the crescendo-ing of thunder wasn't his father smashing furniture in heaven.

But it seemed a lovely piece. Perhaps he was being too harsh on the press in *Don Carlos*. They weren't all bad apples like Beattie Johnson. But his head was too full of Tabitha.

He wished his mother, who had been only two years younger than Tab when she died, was alive to celebrate with him. Idly he switched on his machine.

'Dearest boy.' It was Rannaldini at his most silken. 'However late you get in, pop down to my watch-tower. We must talk.'

Bloody hell, thought Tristan, as he pulled on a pair of jeans. He hoped Rannaldini wasn't going to be insanely jealous.

33

The moon, pale and sinister as Rannaldini, kept vanishing behind fluffy sable cloud. A witch's trail soared straight through Hercules. A chill breeze ruffled the leaves as Tristan walked through Hangman's Wood. The stench of decaying wild garlic was stronger than ever.

Rannaldini, waiting in the watch-tower doorway, was wearing a black crew-necked sweater that gave him a vaguely ecclesiastical air.

'How's Tab?' he asked, as he led the way to the glowing red sitting room on the first floor.

'Very shaken.'

As Tristan collapsed on a pale-grey sofa, his tummy rumbled. The last thing he'd eaten had been one of Rozzy's croissants at breakfast, and he didn't remember finishing it. The vast Armagnac Rannaldini handed him would go straight to his head. 'She's OK,' he went on, 'but we must tell the police. It can't have been an accident, and about Flora's fox being cut up. Tab was so brave,' then, unable to help himself, 'and so adorable.'

Rannaldini had gone very quiet, frowning as he paced up and down, trampling on the red roses that patterned the faded Aubusson carpet.

'I have been sad recently that you and I have so often come to blows,' he said gently, 'but we only fight because we so passionately want *Carlos* to work.'

'Of course.'

'But I never stop loving you, Tristan. You are still my little godson.'

Rannaldini's voice was so hypnotic. Perhaps he should do those introductions after all, thought Tristan.

'And I love you,' he stammered. He felt very happy that everything was falling so wonderfully into place. But Rannaldini went on pacing.

'There is . . .' he began. 'No, I cannot.'

'Go on,' urged Tristan.

'There is secret I prayed I would never have to tell you, but as very close friend of your father . . .' He paused.

Tristan went cold.

'Have you never wondered why Étienne neglected you and never loved you?'

Tristan winced.

'All the time,' he said wearily. 'Laurent died, I suppose. I lived. Laurent was my father's favourite son, then Maman committed suicide. Maybe it deranged him. On his deathbed, he was rambling on that my father was my grandfather. I didn't know what he was talking about.' He shuddered, remembering Étienne in the huge bed, with the determinedly cheerful nurse siphoning off the fountains of blood.

The moon, like a Beardsley rakehell, was leering in through a high window covered in a black lacing of clematis, whose quivering shadows in turn cast an illusion of mobility on Rannaldini's cold, impassive face.

'Your mother was most stunning woman I ever meet. Turn round. I don't think you ever see painting your father did.'

Tristan leapt to his feet. Behind him on the scarlet wall was a small oil of a young girl, her naked body as white as Tab's but far more softly curved and passive. She leant against a dark green sofa. The young Rannaldini, black-haired, black eyes glittering with lust and power, was stripped to the waist in tight breeches and boots. He had a hunting whip in his hand, and had coiled the long lash round the girl's neck. There was an expression of terror and wild excitement on her face.

'Maman,' stammered Tristan, finding himself blushing in horror and sick, shaming excitement at what was clearly one of his father's masterpieces.

'It is called *The Snake Charmer*,' purred Rannaldini. 'The texture of her body is quite extraordinary. I shall miss her dreadfully.'

'What d'you mean?'

'The Tate and the Louvre are planning a huge Montigny retrospective. Your beautiful mother will tour the world and take her place in the pantheon of women who inspired great artists.'

'*Non!*' cried Tristan, in outrage. 'For God's sake, Rannaldini.'

He wanted to throw his shirt round Delphine's naked body. Dragging his eyes away, he collapsed, trembling, on the sofa, fumbling for a cigarette.

'She certainly inspired your father,' began Rannaldini softly. 'What Étienne did not know was that her father, Maxim, your grandfather, was a thug, brutish, utterly unstable, his sole passion his daughter. He was obsessed with her. Delphine only went out with me,' idly, Rannaldini flicked a speck of dust from a bronze of Wagner, 'to escape him. For the same reason, she marry your father. Maxim, her father, was so crazed with jealousy he wait till she and Étienne return from honeymoon – which had not been a success, the marriage hardly consummated. Étienne fly to Australia for two months to fulfil commission.'

Rannaldini paused, his face full of compassion.

'My conscience torture me. Should I tell you this?'

'Go on, for fuck's sake.'

'A week later, Maxim roll up at empty house and rape her.'

Breath swamped Tristan's chest, his heart had no room to beat.

'By horrible luck, she became pregnant.' Rannaldini

admired his expression of genuine concern in a big gilt mirror. 'But she was too terrified to tell Étienne so she passed the baby off as his.'

'I don't believe you,' croaked Tristan, his legs shaking with a violent life of their own. 'Why didn't she have an abortion?'

'She was so young, a strict Catholic, and terrified of it coming out that her father was clinically insane, that people might commit her because she was insane too, that Étienne might kick her out, back to Maxim.'

'You could have helped her,' spat Tristan.

'My poor boy, I was in Berlin. I knew nothing. After you were born, Delphine sink into depression and reject you. Your father was too devastated by Laurent's death to give her any support. Then he do sums. You are large, healthy boy, not premature. He furiously cross-question your mother. She collapse from guilt and weakness and tell him everything, then take her own life. That was the dreadful irony.' Rannaldini's eyes were velvety dark as pansies with sympathy. 'That Laurent, the flower of the Montignys, was dead . . . and you . . .'

'A little incestuously conceived bastard,' said Tristan, with a dry laugh horribly reminiscent of Étienne's death rattle, 'was alive.'

'I am so very sorry,' murmured Rannaldini. 'Étienne was never able to speak of Laurent again.'

'What happened to my . . .' Tristan couldn't say father '. . . to Maxim?'

'He go off his head with grief when Delphine die. He was committed and die shortly of 'eartbreak in the asylum.'

'It's not possible.' Tristan winced as he put his head in his sore hands, but it was nothing to the pain in his heart. 'My grandfather was my father. Oh, Christ.'

Rannaldini put a caressing hand on the boy's rigid, shuddering shoulders. 'My poor child. Knowing all this, I deliberately take interest in you, hoping to give you back some of the love that deserted you.'

The wind had risen, frenziedly shaking the trees. Rose stems scraped at the windows, lacerating each other with their thorns. Rannaldini was trampling over the Aubusson roses again.

'But, when cheeps are down, Tabitha is my daughter.' He sighed. 'I see the longing in your eyes, but she is better off married to Isa, even if he is Rupert's deadly enemy. She needs babies. Marcus is homosexual. There is little likelihood of you fathering healthy kids. You are three-quarters Maxim, remember.' Rannaldini watched the boy shove his fists in his ears, trying to shut out the horrors. 'One day, Tabitha will be reunited with Rupert. He would not be 'appy with some unstable, misshapen offspring.'

'Like the *vrai* Carlos,' whispered Tristan bitterly.

Picasso's one-eyed girl over the fireplace had the same Greek nose as Tab.

'Tonight I find her.' Tristan's voice broke. 'I love her, Rannaldini.'

'There is only a couple of weeks left of filming. Everyone fall in love on location. Chloe and Oscar, Alpheus and Chloe, Baby and Flora, Sexton,' Rannaldini gave a wry shrug, 'and 'Ermione, Sylvestre *et tout le monde*. 'Ave you also not notice the way your niece Simone gaze at my Wolfgang?'

Tristan was too shocked to take in any of these pearls, gleaned from Rannaldini's monitors.

'You will soon forget her.'

'Never.' Tristan's mind was reeling.

Not only was he not a Montigny, but his identification with *Don Carlos*, because the Inquisition had murdered his Montigny ancestor, was a sham.

'No wonder my father – Christ, I mean Étienne – sneered at my obsession with the family. No wonder his lip curl when kind people say I inherit his talent and paint with light. Not one drop of Montigny blood – oh, Christ.'

Then another devastating hammer-blow struck him.

'If I am not Montigny, I have no claim to any of Papa/Étienne's money. I have handed eet over to production. I am a thief.'

His voice rose, his eyes rolled crazily. As he jumped to his feet, he caught sight of Étienne's painting. For a second Rannaldini was alarmed he was going to tug it from the wall and smash it.

'Calm down. No-one has discovered secret in twenty-eight years. Why should it come out now?'

'But I will be living a hideous lie.' Tristan turned, pleading, back to Rannaldini. 'How can I be sure? Everyone says I am all Montigny.'

'Adopted children pick up parents' mannerisms.'

Tristan slumped on the sofa. 'Why did Étienne keep me?'

'Guilt that he'd pushed Delphine over the edge, and after all his boasting to his friends that he fathered beautiful son in his sixties he was too proud to admit you weren't his. But you should be proud of yourself,' continued Rannaldini warmly, 'knowing 'ow much you've achieved from such unpropitious beginning. But I beg you, never have cheeldren. Have a vasectomy at once. Perhaps, one day, like Rupert, you can adopt. Maybe a geneticist would say you could produce normal children. But you must not risk it with my Tabitha. She was so devastated to lose that baby.'

Tristan gave a groan that was almost a howl. '"The knell of all our hopes has sounded,"' he mumbled. '"The dream that has faded was so fair."'

'"Oh, dreadful cruel fate."' Continuing the quote, Rannaldini stroked Tristan's hair.

'Oh, Rannaldini, are you quite sure?'

'My dear boy, if only I weren't.'

From his desk he took a dark red Bible, and from between its gleaming gold pages drew out a yellowing letter. Everything was familiar, the beautiful black script, the thick paper with the serrated edges, the Montigny crest of the chained snake, the little drawing of the entwined lovers in the top right-hand corner, that he'd so often seen on letters sent to his brothers but never to himself. Étienne had written,

My dear Rannaldini,
Thank you for all your understanding and kindness. Without these, I doubt if I would have survived. I cannot imagine a crueller betrayal, but I must accept that Tristan is the product of this obscene incestuous union. Delphine took the easy way out, so I am forced to bring up the boy, although it will be a constant reminder of the foul nightmare of his conception. I can never bring myself to love him.

Unable to read more, Tristan thrust the letter at Rannaldini and stumbled out into the woods. Cannoning off trees like a drunkard, longing to uproot them and build his own funeral pyre like Hercules, he reached the park where he wandered, sobbing, 'Oh, dreadful cruel fate,' over and over again.

At dawn he chucked his signet ring into the lake. Would that it could have been himself but the water had almost dried up in the drought. Beautiful, pale, like a sadistic marquis, totally untroubled and unmarked by his night of vice, the moon on its side lay over Rannaldini's woods.

The rising sun was already gilding the little wood that formed a halo round Magpie Cottage. His halo had gone. Tristan longed to level with Tab, but the truth was too hideous and he couldn't bear to read the sickened distaste in her eyes, or to listen to her lame excuses as she backed off. She needed perfect children to carry on the beauty of her family. She deserved only the best.

Tab had waited up all night. When he told her he wasn't coming back, her howled 'Oh, no!' were the most agonizing words he'd ever heard.

'It's not anything you've done, my darling. It's my fault. You're married. Try and make a go of it with Isa.

I'm no good to you. One day I'll explain.' Then, when there was total silence, 'Tabitha?'

'I've just lost another father,' whispered Tab, and hung up.

Lucy didn't want people to hear her crying, so as soon as shooting had finished the night before she retreated to her caravan. James, who was upset by tears, curled himself into the tiniest russet ball on one of the window-seats, letting out occasional deep sighs to rival Rannaldini's.

At first when Tristan hammered on her door, she thought he was drunk: his shirt and jeans were ripped, his face was covered in scratches, his eyes rolled wildly. He was shaking so violently that she wrapped him in her duvet. As he sobbed his heart out, gabbling in French, often quoting *Don Carlos* and occasionally laughing inanely, he was difficult to understand, but gradually she pieced together what Rannaldini had told him.

Lucy was furious.

'The bastard.' She handed Tristan a cup of black coffee into which she'd poured a miniature Drambuie. 'He knows you're bats about Tab, and Tab is bats about you.'

Oh, why was she cutting her own throat?

'He's jealous you saved Tab's life and she was so frantic for you to take her home. You're a Montigny, sure as *oeufs* is *oeufs*. I can tell by your bone structure and your mouth and the height of your eyes in your face. Why don't you nip back to France and ask Auntie Hortense?'

'*Non, non, non.*' Tristan shook his head back and forth. 'It's all in the letter. I am very fashionable, incest is hot, as Sexton keeps saying.' His wild laughter turned into sobs.

Sitting down beside him on the bench seat, Lucy gathered him up, stroking his hair, trying to still his desperate shuddering.

'I love Tab so much, Lucy. Last night she was Holy Grail in my arms.'

'I know, I know.'

Even a worried James leapt down, and nudged him with his long nose.

'Dear James.' Avoiding his sore palms, Tristan smoothed the shaggy head with the side of his hand. 'I can't stop thinking of that monster raping my mother. She had no-one to turn to. If only she'd had an abortion.'

'No!' shouted Lucy, clutching him even tighter. 'That would have deprived the world of a fantastic director.' She gave a sob. 'People forget you're only twenty-eight, and you've kept this bloody great show on the road. You're exactly the same person today as you were before Rannaldini told you all that junk. It's what you are that matters.'

'But what can I do about the money I put into *Carlos*?'

'Nothing. Your fat-cat brothers aren't exactly skint. *Carlos* is going to be such a smash hit you'll easily be able to pay them back afterwards.'

'"You have the heart of an angel,"' quoted Tristan wearily. '"But mine sleeps forever closed to happiness." Promise you won't tell anyone.'

He refused to be comforted.

Tab was equally distraught. She had been offered a glimpse of Paradise. What was it about her that no-one could love?

Rannaldini moved in swiftly. 'My poor child, but you know Tristan's track record. He cannot commit himself. He 'ave you so he dump you.'

Wolfie was more hands-on. Woken by a pitiful telephone call from Tab, he hunted down Tristan as he was leaving Lucy's caravan, and sent him crashing to join the debris of cigarette butts, skeins of hair and cotton buds on the grass outside Make Up.

'How dare you lead her on, you smarmy Frog?' Then,

as Tristan staggered to his feet, Wolfie hit him again.

Hearing the din, Lucy emptied James's water-bowl over Wolfie.

'Stop it, you revolting bully.'

Slumped against the steps of Lucy's caravan, Tristan told Wolfie he had never meant to hurt Tab, but he had learnt something last night that meant he was useless to her, or to any other woman. When he wouldn't explain what it was, Wolfie stormed off unconvinced.

By this time heads, including Meredith's and Rozzy's, both in rollers, were emerging from windows so Lucy patched Tristan up, dressed his hands and sent him back to the set, where he heroically carried on directing. But everyone noticed he wasn't all there and the spark had gone. Soon rumours were flying around that he'd blown Tabitha out, that she'd blown him out, along with all the old chestnuts that he was gay, impotent, violent and incapable of commitment.

Rozzy was angry and hurt Lucy wouldn't confide in her.

'I thought we were friends. Can't you trust me?' Then she stormed off, when Lucy couldn't.

It really irritated Lucy, the reproachful way Rozzy instantly topped up James's water-bowl and tested the earth of her plants whenever she came into the caravan. Even more maddeningly, there were tears in Tristan's eyes later that afternoon, when he told Lucy that 'Knowing we are haemorrhaging money, Rozzy offer to work for nothing. She is so sweet.'

'Sweet,' agreed Lucy, bitterly remembering James Benson's bills. Even darling Rozzy's getting on my nerves, she thought, in despair.

But that evening, as she put a patch of a greyhound's head over one of the rips in Tristan's jeans, there was a knock on the door. It was Wolfie, looking desperately tired.

'Sorry, I flipped this morning. We had a whipround for the greyhounds in Spain.' He handed her a jangling brown envelope. Inside was nearly three hundred pounds.

'Oh, Wolfie.' Fighting back the tears, Lucy hugged him. 'Come in. Oh, thank you ever so much.' As she poured him a glass of wine, she said she couldn't tell him what Tristan had found out, but if it were true she understood why he'd had to dump Tab.

'She is destroyed.'

'So's Tristan. He needs you.'

She also didn't want to upset Wolfie by letting on to him the part Rannaldini had played.

From then on Wolfie carried Tristan, which aroused the enmity of Bernard, Oscar, Sexton, even of Rannaldini, and most of all the women, because he was so clearly now *le favori du roi.*

34

June melted into July. The birds fell silent. The heatwave intensified. Legend had it that when the ponds of Valhalla dried up, the head of the house would die. Hoovering up shrivelled petals on the burnt lawn, Mr Brimscombe noticed the dangerously low level of the pond near the rose garden and moved the gasping carp to the mere beside the maze. He was just making a note to fill up both from the house mains, when he was called away to round up the cows who, in search of grass, had forced their way into the woods near Rannaldini's watch-tower.

'We'll have to raise the voltage on the electric fences,' Rannaldini told Tabitha.

'Pity Mummy can't do that to keep *you* in.'

'Stony limits cannot keep in love, my darling.'

Tristan missed Tab desperately, but they were still so frighteningly behind schedule and over budget that he plunged into work, driving himself and the crew to a point of collapse.

He was incredibly forgetful, not finishing sentences or remembering names. Before, he'd kept the whole script almost to the line in his head; now Wolfie had to remind him what scene he'd shot an hour before.

His nights were racked by drenching sweats, and hideous dreams of rape, torched flesh and a black cobra curling evilly round the neck of Tabitha, who would suddenly become his lovely, naked mother. How could he blame Maxim for brutal, incestuous lust, when he was tortured himself by the same shaming desires for Delphine?

Often he was seen wandering round Paradise at dawn, muttering, 'Rannaldini doesn't know what he's doing.'

He was still stonewalling about the introductions. The plot was now so cartoon simple he felt that constant reappearances by Rannaldini, explaining what was going on, would hold up the action. It would also mean agonizing cuts of other stuff, paring people like Colin Milton, Granny and Giuseppe down to nothing.

Not up to a tussle, however, he agreed that the Great Hall should be turned into an opera-house with a royal box. Rannaldini would then sweep in in his tails to conduct his overture.

Only two incidents marred the filming of this opening. Meredith was sacked because a falling piece of scenery missed Rannaldini by inches and Lucy, after everyone had raved that her make-up of Granny and the characters in the royal box would win her an Oscar, found an adder coiled in her make-up basket. A terrified Lucy told only Baby, whom she had to make up immediately after her discovery.

'Must have crawled in by itself.' Baby tried to cheer her up. 'Adder in the basket's better than chicken.'

Tristan had already shot two endings: Schiller's, in which Philip hands Carlos over to the Inquisition, and Verdi's, which has the ghost of Charles V, played by Granny's boyfriend Giuseppe, emerging from his tomb (which looked, according to Granny, like a 'public lavatory in Morocco') and drawing a terrified Carlos inside.

Rannaldini now insisted on a third – with the principals of Act V on stage singing the last minute of Verdi's version, then the film ending with himself on the rostrum acknowledging the ecstatic applause of the audience. The lighting rehearsal on his snow-white shirt-cuffs alone went on all morning. Griselda was then sacked because after twenty-nine fittings, he was unhappy with the cut of his tail-coat.

Rannaldini was even angrier that Giuseppe, thinking he wouldn't be needed, had buggered off without permission to sing on a cruise ship in the Bosphorus.

'Get heem back by tonight,' screamed Rannaldini.

'Quite right,' said Granny approvingly. 'Show him who's Bosphorus.'

Granny was in a much happier mood. He had finished his patchwork quilt, darling Rozzy was sewing the pieces up for him, and it would look beautiful on his and Giuseppe's bed. Tristan, heeding a word from Lucy that Granny was worried about work, had spoken to him about a future role as the wonderfully comic Baron Ochs in *Der Rosenkavalier*.

The day that Tristan shot Rannaldini's ending was also Mikhail's thirty-fifth birthday. Having been bumped off in Act IV, Mikhail was not needed and had been happily getting himself and everyone else plastered all day, except Lucy, who was still shocked by the adder and who had to stay sober because she had the loathsome task of making up Rannaldini. She had never met anyone so vain. He wanted bronzer, blusher, white on the inside of his eyelids, mascara, eyeliner and shading, and it took her hours to get his glossy pewter hair just right.

Familiar with Lucy's body from the relay race and his monitors, Rannaldini kept making suggestive remarks and, when she was trimming the hair in his nostrils and terrified of nicking him, putting a warm, caressing hand between her thighs.

Meanwhile, word was whizzing round the set that Mikhail had been so stoical about missing his wife, Lara, that as a birthday surprise – and sod the budget – Sexton was flying her over from Moscow to emerge from Mikhail's birthday cake later that evening.

As Lucy was darkening Rannaldini's eyebrows, Wolfie popped in with glasses of champagne from Mikhail. Rannaldini refused. He never drank before a concert, so Wolfie left a single glass on Lucy's table and told his father he was wanted on the set in two minutes.

Rannaldini was intensely sexually excited at the thought of being on camera. As Lucy removed the pale blue overall and was nearly asphyxiated by Maestro, his aftershave, he rose, a magnificent figure in white tie, black cummerbund embroidered with a silver skull, and beautifully cut black trousers.

He had other sexual games planned for later in the evening, but as Lucy put back the tops on her bottles, he couldn't resist putting a hand up her skirt.

'I know you want Tristan,' he purred, 'and he loves only Tabitha, but don't be sad, Lucy, you have interesting body, and eef I give you few lesson, you could be very passionate.'

His probing fingers wandered upwards.

Utterly revolted, Lucy leapt back, jolting the table, spilling the champagne. The next moment she had slapped Rannaldini's face.

'I don't care if you fire me,' she said furiously. 'And I'm not toning those down,' she added, as her finger-marks reddened on Rannaldini's cheeks.

Rannaldini laughed, smelling his fingers in ecstasy. Shrugging on his new coat, the poetry of whose cut was undeniable, he adjusted his gardenia, picked up the glass of champagne and raised it to his lips as he strode towards the Great Hall. But before he could take a sip, Hermione's top E, as she warmed up in her dressing room, had shattered it. Rannaldini's smile broadened. He had been right not to drink.

'Maestro Rannaldini,' tiny Simone stepped bravely into his path, 'you were not wearing cummerbund with death's head in opening shots.'

'When did continuity take precedence over aesthetic consideration?' said Rannaldini haughtily. 'The skull forecasts death of Carlos and Elisabetta,' and, shoving Simone out of the way, he strode on.

Half an hour later, Baby was tempted to walk out. Hermione had obviously persuaded Rannaldini to substitute a different take of the last duet to the one on the cassette, which he had been sent. On that one she had had a distinct wobble. Now, over the speakers, she sounded wonderful and he distinctly off.

Fucking bitch! Baby wanted to kick her on the ankle as he gazed soulfully into her eyes.

'Farewell, my son, farewell for ever,' sang Hermione.

One camera was trained on Rannaldini. A second, up on a crane, kept cutting from stage to royal box to enraptured crowd. Suddenly Philip, the Grand Inquisitor and a pack of paparazzi in leather, their long lenses raised like machine-guns, charged in. Philip had just grabbed Elisabetta, when the ghostly presence of Charles V slowly emerged from his tomb.

Giuseppe has got back after all, thought Baby, in surprise, as his glorious rich voice poured out of the speakers like the expensive red wines of which he was so fond. As the rest of the cast fell back in terror, Rannaldini whipped the orchestra through the last deafening chords, but as the ghost put out his hand to seize Baby's, Baby crashed to the ground in a dead faint.

'Pissed again,' said Ogborne.

'It was a ghost, a real ghost,' protested a terrified Baby, when he came round. 'He cast no shadow on the wall, and his hand went straight through mine.'

'I told you never to touch spirits,' chided Granny.

No-one, on the other hand, had seen Giuseppe arrive or leave.

Returning to her caravan still shuddering from Rannaldini's grope, Lucy found that the spilt champagne had burnt a hole right through the red checked cloth to the table beneath. Someone was trying to kill either her or Rannaldini.

She gave a shriek as a tall figure loomed out of the darkness, but it was only a hollow-eyed Wolfie. Was she coming to Mikhail's birthday party? Lucy was knackered, but she loved Mikhail. Hoping a few drinks might dull her sense of foreboding, she decided to pop in for an hour, and went slap into a full-dress row.

Chloe and Mikhail had both had tip-offs that they'd landed the parts they wanted in *Samson and Delilah*. A plastered Mikhail was just kissing Chloe in congratulation, covering himself in crimson lipstick, when – with fiendish timing – Rannaldini urged Mikhail's newly arrived wife, Lara, to peep out of her bedroom window for a sneak preview of her beloved. Her reunion with Mikhail was therefore most acrimonious, and no-one emerged from any birthday cakes.

Lara kicked off by slapping Mikhail's face so hard he fell in a nearly empty fish-pond. She then turned on Chloe. 'You are scarlet voman I read about in *Evening Scorpion* on vay down.'

'Oh, Beattie's piece must have come out,' said Chloe, in excitement. 'If you've got a copy, I'd love to see it.'

So Lara slapped Chloe's face as well. Chloe's squawks, however, were nothing to her hysterics when she tracked down the *Scorpion*. Beattie had portrayed her as a ruthless careerist and husband-snatcher, and quoted all the bitchy remarks Chloe had made off the record, including the one about Hermione farting every time she hit a top note.

'Delilah was an absolute cow,' said Baby reassuringly, 'so you'll only have to play yourself, Chloe.'

Chloe fled sobbing to her room. Mikhail, trailing muddy pond weed, stormed round Valhalla trying to find Lara. Everyone, as a result, was very wary of a grungy crone in granny specs and flowing black robes, who was reverently being hawked round the party by Hype-along as Eulalia Harrison of the *Sentinel*. Eulalia was doing an in-depth piece on the whole production that would redress the harm done by Beattie. Helen, who loved the arts pages in the *Sentinel*, had even given Eulalia a bedroom in the south wing.

Eulalia had already cornered Flora about her famous mother. 'Perhaps you could spare me a moment in the foreseeable future to discuss Mother's new album and your début in *Carlos*.'

'I'd like that,' said Flora. 'The album's great, and thank goodness you reminded me, I promised Rozzy one for her horrible husband's fiftieth birthday. He's a mad fan of Mum's.'

'We all are,' said Eulalia reverently.

Even buckets of wine couldn't make the party gel. There was no birthday boy to blow out the thirty-five blue candles on the big chocolate cake. People loved Mikhail and hated seeing him so hurt and humiliated on his birthday.

It was eerie in the shadowy garden: owls hooted, moths scorched themselves on flambeaux, gasping un-watered plants failed to revive in the cooler night air. Baby's protestations that Charles V had been a real ghost began to stack up, as Granny, summoned to take a call from Giuseppe, found him still on his troop ship in the Bosphorus.

In Bernard's office, Tristan, Oscar and Valentin were still wondering after Baby's fainting how much of tonight's film they could salvage. Having raved over Granny's patchwork quilt, which was on display and lighting up the summer drawing room like a rain-bow, the rest of the guests had spilled out into the garden.

Sexton, who was heartbroken that his plan to bring Lara over had misfired so tragically, had arrived with Hermione, who having heard about, but not yet read, Beattie's piece was delighted at Chloe's discomfiture. Considering herself an expert on the subject of the press, she decided to charm the grotesque Eulalia Harrison. After all, the *Sentinel*'s circulation nudged the *Guardian*'s.

'Have you heard my latest CD?'

'I have indeed,' said Eulalia, in her refined ultra-intellectual Islington twang. 'I am a long-term fan, Dame Hermione.'

'Then you shall come to luncheon at River House.'

Determined not to fall into Chloe's trap of bitching up others, Hermione beckoned Lucy over.

'This is my personal make-up artist, Lucy Latimer. You'll want to talk to Lucy about me, and probably to our Woman Friday, Rozzy Pringle. By the way, Rozzy, my rose-lined green cloak has a tear. Rosalind's very nifty with a needle, Eulalia.'

'And a great singer,' said Lucy defiantly.

'Come and meet Sexton Kemp.' Hermione took Eulalia's arm. 'Sexton went to Eton, you know.'

'Bitch, bitch, bitch!' said Lucy, to Hermione's broad departing back. 'Omigod,' she screamed, as a ghostly apparition appeared unexpectedly out of the ebony depths of the maze. 'Oh, thank goodness it's you, Alpheus.'

'Either of you two seen Cheryl?' An enraged Alpheus glared towards the terrace where Rannaldini, still in his tails, the skull leering from his cummerbund, was now standing.

'How dare he say artistic consideration come before continuity?' fumed Simone, as Rannaldini clapped his hands and announced the cabaret.

Earlier in the shoot, after a particularly trying day, Meredith and Rannaldini had joined Tristan in his caravan and, over a bottle of whisky, they had discussed everyone. Rannaldini had taped the conversation and now relayed it on speakers around the house and garden.

Clearly Tristan had been enjoying the catharsis of a really good bitch. The sound of his laughter, which had not been heard since the *auto da fe*, drew the outside revellers in round the terrace.

Having mimicked most of the cast, particularly Pushy and Alpheus, Meredith had savagely taken the piss out of Sexton, but his venom had been reserved for Hermione, as the wife of Bob, his long-term lover. Tristan had defended her manfully, only when Meredith started impersonating her in a screeching falsetto could he be heard crying with helpless laughter.

Initial guffaws from the guests quickly faded into appalled embarrassed silence. Sexton looked as though he was going to cry.

'I never knowed I was that common.'

No-one dared look at Hermione, who for once was lost for words.

As Tristan wandered into the party, Rannaldini could be heard saying on the tape, 'Do you theenk we should replace Hermione?'

'Superfluous Harefield,' giggled Meredith. 'Well, Pushy's already sung her top notes, so why not get some pretty actress, half her age, to play her on film?'

'With an ass a quarter the size,' Tristan had suggested, to shouts of mirth.

'Turn that bloody thing off,' howled the real Tristan, and his hands were round Rannaldini's neck. 'I keel you, you bastard.'

If Wolfie, Bernard and a racing-up Valentin hadn't pulled him off, he would have strangled Rannaldini. 'D'you want to screw up everything we achieve, you fucking madman? Let me get at heem,' he snarled, struggling to break free of their clutches.

'My dear boy,' sneered Rannaldini, straightening his collar, 'how very excited you're getting over a bit of fun.'

A second later, everyone was distracted by Hermione screaming.

'It isn't true about my top notes?'

Sexton was about to protest that of course it wasn't, but Pushy was too quick for him. 'Ay'm afraid it is,

Hermione,' she said smugly. 'Roberto couldn't bear you to sound less than perfect.'

Screeching that she would get both Pushy and Rannaldini, and never work with Tristan again, Hermione flapped off towards River House, so like a great goose that everyone expected her to break into flight.

'Shame the river's too low for her to drown herself,' sighed Baby.

But her departing screech was interrupted by a far more pitiful sound. In the summer drawing room, Granny was crouched weeping over his patchwork quilt, which had been slashed into such tiny pieces that, unlike Foxie, it couldn't be sewn together again. Like eaglets fluttering round a mother bird with an irrevocably broken wing, Lucy, Baby and Flora surged forward, frantic to comfort him, but Granny refused to let Tristan call the police. 'No, no, nothing can bring it and my darling boy back again.'

Ten minutes later, utterly unmoved by such tragedy, Pushy returned from cleaning her teeth in Helen's bathroom (after all, it would be hers soon) and, sidling up to Rannaldini, asked if it were too early to slope off to the watch-tower.

'Frankly it is,' smirked Rannaldini. 'Because I 'ave subsequent engagement,' and singing, 'Life is just a bowl of Cheryl,' he disappeared into the dark.

Ten minutes later he let himself into the watch-tower.

'My darling,' he crooned to Mikhail's Lara, who Clive had just smuggled down a newly strimmed ride. 'Don't spoil your lovely eyes with tears. Suffering will make your wayward husband sing even more beautifully, and you will have a night to tell your great-grandchildren about.'

Then, as a feisty blonde in a foxglove-pink and purple dressing-gown came down the spiral staircase, 'I don't think you know Cheryl Shaw.'

35

The next two and a half days, thank God, were rest days. Tristan had a big press screening of *The Lily in the Valley* in Paris on Saturday night, and then a lunch party for Aunt Hortense's eighty-sixth birthday on Sunday. Night-shooting would start on Monday evening.

Roused early on Saturday morning from the same hideous nightmare, Tristan found his light on and Rannaldini standing in his bedroom doorway. With his bare muscular chest soaring out of tight black trousers, he was hideously reminiscent of himself in *The Snake Charmer*.

'If I have any more hassle from you,' Tristan reached for a Gauloise with a shaking hand, 'I'm taking my name off this film.'

'What name?' taunted Rannaldini. 'You're not a Montigny any more. In fact, your lack of roots is showing, my dear.'

Tristan felt churning black loathing. Unless he jumped to Rannaldini's tune, the bastard would tell the world Étienne wasn't his father.

'Hurry or you'll miss that plane,' smirked Rannaldini, 'and do give my best to Claudine Lauzerte.'

Strolling down the landing, Rannaldini was greeted by his cat, Sarastro, mewing with rage. Stooping to stroke him, Rannaldini found his white fur drenched. How could this be, when it hadn't rained for weeks? Out of the window, through the pre-dawn half-light, he saw Rozzy with a watering-can, like a nurse in the trenches, trying to bring succour to his dying plants.

Padding downstairs out into the garden, he caught her so red-handed, she dropped the watering-can.

'First, you water my cat, next my flagstones.'

'I'm terribly sorry, Rannaldini. I'm so shortsighted I mistook poor Sarastro for some white violas.'

'Rozzy, my dear,' said Rannaldini silkily, 'I had such an interesting session with James Benson yesterday.'

The colour stole from Rozzy's cheeks as though she was bleeding to death.

Flora woke when the sun was high in the sky to find Baby had already left. It was too hot to wear anything but cotton, so she wandered out to the facilities unit in her white nightie. As Trevor rushed reproachfully around lifting his leg on wheels and guy ropes, she could hear Meredith's voice issuing petulantly from Make Up.

'How can I expect darling Sexton to re-instate me, when Rannaldini plays that loathsome tape?'

'Baby sent his love, Flora, and said he'd be back some time on Monday,' called Rozzy, as she emerged from Wardrobe clutching a large Harrods bag. 'I've got the remains of Granny's patchwork quilt in here,' she added conspiratorially, shoving it into the boot of the car. 'I'm going to try and save it.'

'Poor old boy,' said Flora sadly. 'I bet Giuseppe's doing more cruising than singing in the Bosphorus. Although I can't really believe Baby saw a ghost.'

She handed Rozzy another carrier-bag. 'I got Mum to sign two photos and her new album for Glyn.'

'Oh, you darling child.' Rozzy hugged her.

'It was the least I could do after you mending Foxie. Are you OK, Rozzy? You look dreadfully pale.'

'I'm fine,' sighed Rozzy. 'I've got to be.'

'Well, don't work too hard. I hope Glyn jolly well appreciates his birthday party.'

'You look pretty pale too,' Rozzy called after her. 'Why don't you ring your nice George?'

An almighty bang made them both jump. Wolfie, who hadn't put a foot wrong throughout the shoot, had been bullied into filling up Alpheus's Jaguar from Rannaldini's petrol pumps. Catching sight of Tabitha leaving Magpie Cottage, however, he had driven slap into Bernard's Peugeot. This gave Alpheus the excuse to storm upstairs to Rannaldini's study where he found his executive producer signing fan mail.

Alpheus flipped. Not only was his Jaguar totalled but how dare Rannaldini also lie to Cheryl that he'd been humping Pushy, Chloe and Hermione? Cheryl was threatening to divorce him and expose him to the tax-man if he didn't accede to her outlandish demands.

'And she wants custody of Mr Bones, the family dog,' Alpheus shouted finally.

'I am not surprised.' Admiring his beautiful hands, Rannaldini picked up a nail file. 'Eef Mr Bones can hold down job worth two hundred thousand dollars a year on your books *and* bite the postman, he's quite a find. I 'ave to confess I find that emerald stud in Cheryl's *labia minora* quite enchanting, but I think she has the 'ots for Mikhail, so I suggest you get it insured before they get together.'

'I'll get you, Rannaldini . . .'

Alpheus's bellows of rage could be heard all over Valhalla.

Flora had just screwed up enough courage to punch out George's number when Rannaldini catfooted up, suggesting a walk round the garden. Flora was so depressed she thought Rannaldini would be better than no-one to talk to. She was wrong.

As they reached the pond near the rose garden, Rannaldini said, 'I wonder when Baby will tell his little friend Isa that he's just tested HIV positive.'

Flora stopped in her tracks, breathing in a sudden stench of fox. 'How d'you know?'

'I recommended him to a doctor,' said Rannaldini smoothly. 'The poor boy only heard this morning. He's demented, and so must you be, my darling.'

'Are you sure?'

'Well, if you swing all ways and sleep around as much as Baby does, it was only a matter of time.'

'Oh, my God.' Flora slumped on a stone bench.

Trevor had disappeared after the fox. In the almost non-existent water of the pond, a couple of carp gasped and writhed. Then, from his inside pocket, Rannaldini produced an even worse horror.

'What will George theenk of these pretty pictures?'

Flora gave a groan because the top one was of Baby making love to her on the lawn at Angels' Reach.

'Give them to me,' she screamed, snatching the poly-thene folder.

'Have them.' Rannaldini gave a sigh of delight. 'I have the negs. They should make George relinquish his plans for a Paradise bypass. And, eef not, Gordon Dillon will adore them.' And whistling 'This is my last, my finest day,' Rannaldini sauntered back to the house, pausing only to switch on his mobile:

'Bussage, my dear, can you ring Fleet Water Board and get them to fill up the lake and the ponds?'

Flora whimpered with terror. Baby, who'd been mys-terious about his weekend plans, always switched off his mobile. There was no way she could call him and check the truth. Looking round, she saw that Trevor was tossing something in the air.

'Stop!' she screamed.

But by the time she had got there it was too late. It was a little black mole, probably in search of water. Lost above ground, blinded by the sun, the earth was baked too hard for him to tunnel to safety. There was something so pathetic about his tiny pink hands. Sobbing helplessly followed by an insufficiently contrite Trevor, Flora set out to find a spade to bury him. She felt she had bypassed Paradise for ever.

Entering Valhalla, Rannaldini had bumped into his leading mezzo.

'"Dear Chloe, how blubbered is thy pretty face,"' he quoted, in amusement.

'It's all because of Beattie's horrible piece,' sobbed Chloe. 'Howie's just rung in his undertaker's voice saying I haven't got Delilah. Even worse he says the money's on Gloria.'

'She is a newer face, my dear. Your voice is not really strong enough to fill the Garden. The last thing we need is terrible reviews for *Delilah*, just as *Carlos* is previewing.'

Chloe was the second person in twenty-four hours to slap Rannaldini's face.

And now he was in his watch-tower, working on his memoirs, the evil smile playing constantly over his lips. Pushy had left several furious messages on his machine. Having had access to helicopter, orange Lamborghini Diablo and Rannaldini's bank balance while they'd been having an affaire, she was now feeling the draught.

Rannaldini took her next call.

'You promised Ay'd be the next Lady Rannaldini.'

'You were queen for a night, my dear Gloria. Poor Eboli only had two minutes of bliss. You had two weeks. Count yourself lucky. Now, pees off.'

Rannaldini turned back to his memoirs. What a lot he had on the rest of the cast.

That very morning, poor, silly Granny had been so unhinged that Clive had snapped him doing something very stupid in Rutminster. There was no way Hype-along would be able to buy all the nationals once the story broke. And what a lot too he knew about goody-goody Rozzy.

Then there was Chloe's frolic with the goat on the Internet. And Isa's parents certainly wouldn't want to know what he'd been getting up to with Baby, or Isa what Baby had been getting up to with Flora. How gay was Baby, really? And what a shame Mikhail had lapsed last night. That marriage would take a long time to repair.

Sighing with pleasure, Rannaldini picked up his photograph album. What a lot of beautiful women he'd slept with! There was Flora, a plump, ravishing school-girl, and Chloe, whose skin was white-hot in texture, but who had been almost too easy to bed. And Wolfie's mother Gina, hangdog because she'd loathed being photographed in the nude. Not a beauty but incredibly rich, she had given him his start in life.

Sharing a page were Serena the nympho and Pushy, whose pillow talk had been very limited. Over the page was Beattie Johnson, who was helping him with his memoirs and who knew rather too much about him. Beattie had been a marvellous fuck, his second wife, Cecilia, an even better one. And there was his third wife, plump Kitty, so anxious to please, who had escaped to marry Rupert's friend Lysander. One day he would get even with those two.

Across the centre spread was an emaciated Helen – what a contrast to Hermione: rosy, Rubenesque, prob-ably the most beautiful of them all, and certainly the best in bed. Yesterday he had punctured her self-esteem, but she was turned on by punishment and would soon bounce back.

Before the end of filming he would screw Lucy. She deserved a treat. And what a wonderful evening he had had last night, watching Cheryl and Lara exploring each other's bodies. He'd hardly been able to get a cock in edgeways.

But, flipping through the pages, there were two Everests still to conquer: Rupert's women. There was only a head shot of the divine Taggie, taken at Tab's

327

wedding, but by secreting hidden cameras in both her bedrooms, at Valhalla and at Magpie Cottage, he had some stunning shots of Tabitha, naked, slender and most disdainful of them all.

Rannaldini felt chained to a lunatic by his lust, his cock about to detonate. He had fantasized recently of marrying Tab, and giving her blond, beautiful babies.

But things hadn't gone to plan. Rannaldini found himself increasingly identifying with Philip II. He had 'sought in the vast desert of men, for a friend'. He had found Tristan, but Tristan had flouted his authority and won Tab's affection.

It was the same with Wolfie. Rannaldini had wanted his son back so much, but how could it happen that Flora once, and now it seemed Tabitha, had grown increasingly fond of such a ham-fisted, formal, slightly ridiculous, hopelessly romantic young man.

Tab was infatuated with Tristan, but Wolfie was busy gaining ground. In his son's top drawer, under the lining paper, Rannaldini had found Polaroids of Tab in her dunce's cap. He'd kill rather than relinquish her to Wolfie. Suddenly he had a brainwave and picked up the telephone.

'Clive, I want you to make a trip to Penscombe.'

36

Tab was amazed and touched when Chloe rang her the following day, which was a Sunday, asking her to come to Harvey Nichols' sale in Rutminster. But who was there to buy dresses for? Isa was as cool as ever, and Tristan hadn't telephoned since he'd blown her out. But knowing that he wanted polo in *Don Carlos* and that Rannaldini was baulking over the expense, Tab explained to Chloe that she was going over to Rutminster Polo Club that afternoon, to try and persuade some of the England players, all mates of Rupert, to appear in the film for a crate of Moët apiece.

'Not much of a hardship negotiating with those guys,' said Chloe. 'At least drop in on the tennis tournament later.'

'I can't, Chloe. Evenings are the only time it's cool enough to work The Engineer.'

'Well, look after yourself, little one.'

Tab wiped away the tears. How kind of Chloe to be so solicitous.

Inspired by a fortnight's Wimbledon, and the fact that it was 8 July, the day the real Carlos had been born, the tennis tournament had been scheduled for early evening in the forlorn hope that the heat might have subsided. Alas, it was hotter than ever, with black storm-clouds massing like the Grand Inquisitor's army in the west.

The tennis courts at Valhalla flanked Hangman's Wood. Already the poplars were yellowing and every chestnut leaf was edged with brown. It was so still, the smouldering trees seemed turned to stage scenery. Rannaldini had retired to his watch-tower to drool over the newly arrived rushes of himself on the rostrum. Over and over again the opening bars of the overture, like hunting horns deep in the wood, advertised his evil presence.

To add to the tension, people who had fondly arranged to partner one another weeks ago were no longer on speaking terms. Pushy was playing with Alpheus, which would put Cheryl into orbit, Chloe, a reputed demon on the court, with Mikhail, which would equally enrage Lara.

After Friday's débâcle Mikhail had also decided he loathed Chloe, and rolled up at the tennis tournament swigging vodka out of a two-litre Smirnoff bottle.

'"'Appy birthday, Don Carlos, 'appy birthday to you,"' sang Mikhail, 'And I hop' he had better bloody birthday than I 'ave on Friday.'

'Today', boomed Griselda, resplendent in a vast white tent dress, 'is also the birthday of Rozzy's husband, Glyn, probably an even greater shit than the original Carlos, so horoscopes do work.'

'And it is my aunt Hortense's birthday,' piped up Simone. 'She is terrible tart too.'

'I think you mean "tartar", sweetie,' said Griselda fondly.

'Uncle Tristan is probably still at her birthday party now,' said Simone, glancing at her watch. 'She'll be very angry I rattled at the last moment.'

'You couldn't miss a chance of having Wolfie as your partner,' mocked Chloe, swiping at a passing wasp with her racquet.

Seeing poor Simone – who was unaware that her crush

330

on Wolfie was common knowledge – going absolutely crimson, Griselda said quickly, 'Rozzy's been cooking chicken breasts to be wrapped in smoked salmon, sea trout and raspberry Pavlova for that bastard Glyn all weekend.'

Paid for by me, thought Lucy bitterly.

'Oh, look,' said Meredith, as a black helicopter approached from the south-east and landed on the lawn of River House. 'Hermione has returned from Milan. She's clearly not too mortified to make use of Maestro's chopper.'

Meredith was partnering Flora, neither serious players, particularly Meredith, whose Christopher Robin sunhat fell off if he ran too fast. To everyone's amazement, they took out Mikhail and Chloe, because Mikhail smote every ball into the dark midgy canopy of Hangman's Wood.

'I hop' I break every window of his bloody vatchtower,' he growled.

'Why don't you take up golf?' snarled Chloe, as they walked off the court.

Afterwards they could be heard yelling at each other in the maze, in which they would be filming next week.

'No doubt rehearsing the bit when Posa pulls a knife on Eboli,' said Flora, collapsing on the burnt, scratchy grass to watch Bernard and Jessica, Sexton's beautiful secretary, pounding balls at Lucy and Ogborne, who was still keeping the midges at bay with Hermione's winestained sunhat.

Flora was coming apart at the seams, in floods one minute, screaming with laughter the next. Now she was crying because she could hear Tabloid, the Rottweiler, howling and stuck in baking solitary confinement beneath Rannaldini's watch-tower.

'Why doesn't bloody Clive take him for a walk?'

Then, as the hunting horns from the rushes echoed through Hangman's Wood again, 'If I hear that overture once more, I'll scream.'

The horror of the photos Rannaldini had shown her had now kicked in. She hadn't come on yet. What happened if she was pregnant and produced a little HIV baby? If George saw those pictures, he'd never take her back. Every time a mobile rang, she leapt three feet in the air.

Granny, who was partnering Griselda, was equally suicidal. How *could* he have let himself go in Rutminster yesterday? Every time a car came up the drive, he expected blue lights and sirens. Even more cruelly, an indignant Howie had just confirmed that Serena Westwood was on the cruise ship with Giuseppe. Rannaldini's evil matchmaking had worked a treat. Granny's dreams were now as shredded as his patchwork quilt. But, being Granny, he refused to spoil everyone else's fun, and plucked his tennis racquet like a banjo.

'"He said that he loved her but, oh, how he lied,"' sang Granny. '"Oh, how he lied, oh, how he lied."'

'"And then they were married and somehow she died. Somehow she di-hi-hi-ed,"' joined in Flora.

On three glasses of white, and no food since Friday, Granny was also in a fuck-it mood. His sneaky underarm service was soon whistling over the net. Griselda, galumphing around in her white tent, turned out to have a murderous backhand. To everyone's noisily cheering surprise, they routed the number-one seeds, Alpheus and Pushy.

'Pushy's gone white with rage to match her tennis kit,' muttered Ogborne to Lucy. 'I reckon Alpheus threw that game.'

As Pushy came off the court, Meredith was reading out a *Sunday Times* piece claiming that the coveted part of Delilah had not gone to Chloe or even Pushy, but to Rannaldini's ex, Cecilia. With a frantic jangling of bracelets and earrings, Pushy burst into tears.

'Sir Roberto promised me that part, and he promised Ay could be the next Lady Rannaldini,' she sobbed.

'We've all been promised that,' said a mocking voice.

'It comes after being told we've got the most beautiful voice in the world.'

Abandoning Mikhail, who'd passed out under a weeping ash, Chloe had returned to the court.

'Oh, God,' her smile disappeared, 'here comes Helen and that ugly cow Eulalia Harrison. I gather she had luncheon at River House.'

Pushy's sobs subsided. She longed for an in-depth interview with the *Sentinel.*

But Eulalia, pallid beyond belief, with the evening sun showing up a moustache and a gap of hairy leg between flowing skirts and leather boots, had her sights set higher.

'Chloe Catford,' she cried, 'I was appalled by that drivel Beatrice Johnson wrote about you in the *Scorpion.*'

'The bitch completely misquoted me,' said Chloe, unfreezing slightly.

'That was apparent. I resented the way she trivialized you.' Eulalia's blinking unmade-up eyes behind her granny specs were full of compassion. 'Could you spare me a moment tomorrow?'

'Why don't we do lunch?' Chloe turned to Lady Rannaldini, who had drifted on ahead of Eulalia, clearly reluctant to get sucked into the tennis. 'Hi, Helen, that is a gorgeous dress.'

Helen paused for a second, holding out the mauve silk, patterned with purple lilac and pale yellow honeysuckle. 'Lovely, isn't it?' Then, looking coldly at Pushy, 'My husband brought me back the silk from Tokyo.'

Wolfie and Simone easily dispatched Lucy and Ogborne to reach the final against Granny and Griselda.

'We're going to have trouble beating those two,' sighed Griselda. 'Wolfie plays like Boris Becker.'

'Boris Better. Wolfie's much nicer looking and such a good boy,' said Granny approvingly, as Wolfie topped up everyone's glass and handed round strawberries, giving Simone time to get her breath back before the final. He had lost so much weight, his signet ring kept falling off, so he gave it to Lucy to look after.

As the chapel clock struck half past nine, the finalists took up their positions. Lucy and Simone are so sweet, thought Wolfie, as he jumped from foot to foot on the baseline. Why was he too hopelessly in love with Tab to consider anyone else? Glancing across the valley he felt sick to see a car, looking suspiciously like his father's Merc, creeping stealthily up the little lane to Magpie Cottage. An ace from Griselda whizzed past his ear. He mustn't give in to weakness. If he was incapable of returning Simone's love, he could at least ensure her victory.

'Oh, well played, Wolfie,' said Simone, five minutes later, as he aced Granny for a second time.

Alpheus, sitting away from the rabble on the other side of the court, much envied the way Simone ran around picking up balls for Wolfie. It was high time he had an adoring young woman in his life again. He picked up his mobile.

Moths were bashing against the floodlights. Even Rannaldini's sapphire delphinium bed, the only thing watered in the garden, was losing colour in the dusk. A mobile rang, everyone dived hopefully – but it was for Chloe.

'OK,' she purred, 'terrific. I'll be with you as soon as I can.'

Not having had any exercise, she announced she was going for a jog and, giving Mikhail a kick in the ribs as she passed the weeping ash, disappeared into the darkness. Shortly afterwards, Alpheus muttered about swimming his twenty lengths, drained his glass of Perrier and also left.

'He and Chloe must have started up again,' hissed Flora.

'I hate Rannaldini,' said Pushy.

334

'So do I,' agreed Bernard, stunning everyone, because he never bitched.

'No-one hates him as much as I do,' said Griselda, as she remembered Rannaldini wrecking Hermione's dress.

Mikhail must have been roused by Chloe's kick for suddenly he reared up and sang, '"Thunder rumbles deep in the heavens, a man must die,"' then slumped back to sleep.

Everyone exchanged nervous glances, particularly when real thunder started to grumble round the hills in sympathy. A slight breeze rattling the summer-hardened poplar leaves sounded like rain. Lucy put her arms round a quivering James: she'd have to trank him if the claps grew louder.

'Guess what I had to do earlier today,' she asked the remaining spectators, as the players changed ends. 'Streak Clive's hair.'

'Whatever for?' asked Meredith.

'He had an important date, he said. His bloodless face went quite pink. Actually, he was really sweet and told me about his mum, *and* he tried to pay me afterwards.'

'Must be the first time,' shuddered Flora. 'Clive scares me more than Rannaldini. That black crow's been sitting on top of the cypress for the last two hours. D'you think it's stuck?'

'Its name is Death,' said Ogborne, with a sepulchral laugh. 'Christ, that girl's got amazing legs.'

Everyone turned as Jessica, Sexton's beautiful secretary, loped back from the house.

'You'll never guess what?' she gasped.

'You've been streaking Clive's hair,' said Ogborne.

'I just saw Tristan.'

'Don't be ridiculous,' said Bernard roughly. 'He's in Paris. You've had too much to drink.'

'Keep your hair on, Bernie,' said Meredith. 'Baby saw a ghost yesterday.'

'What was Tristan doing?' asked Flora.

'Nearly running me over, belting down the drive.'

'Must have been someone else,' insisted Bernard angrily.

'I find it a relief Tristan's away,' confessed Flora. 'He's so uptight, and he *was* bitchy on that tape. I always thought he adored us all. Oh, well *played*, Simone.'

Lucy hugged an increasingly trembling James. If only she could explain to the others why Tristan was being so difficult.

'I miss the birds singing at twilight,' she said, looking up into the trees.

'They're all exhausted feeding their young,' said Jessica. 'Mr Brimscombe told me nightingales disappear in July. One morning they're here, the next they've gone, departing silently in the dusk.'

'Like us next week,' said Ogborne.

Burying her face in James's coat, Lucy burst into tears, then leaping to her feet fled into the wood.

37

It was nearly nine and even hotter when Tab got home from working The Engineer. She went straight into the shower, then put on the coolest clean thing in her wardrobe, a virginal calf-length grey cotton shirtwaister, which she had never worn but which her American bosses had given her last summer for her birthday, probably as a hint she might curb her dissolute lifestyle.

God, it was stifling. She was already breaking out in sweat again. In the past she would have got stuck into the vodka, but staying off it seemed to be the only achievement she had to cling on to.

She missed Tristan so dreadfully. But as she breathed in a familiar smell of night-scented stock and philadelphus, she was flattened with longing for Penscombe. Tristan, however, had urged her to work at her marriage. Isa was back in England, and as she expected him home later she opened and applied the chic French make-up Simone had given her for her birthday. Then she drenched herself in Quercus, the disturbing, sweet yet lemony scent which Isa so loved.

Going downstairs she found Sharon panting on the kitchen floor. She was on heat, and most of the local dogs, including James, Trevor and Tabloid, when he escaped from his dungeon, had been hanging round Magpie Cottage. 'At least one of us has got admirers,' sighed Tab.

Listlessly she switched on the wireless. They had all been so caught up in *Don Carlos*, they had forgotten the outside world existed. Then she jumped to hear a soft, gruff, utterly familiar voice.

'One of the children had taken her collar off for fun,' her stepmother was saying.

'Oh, no.' Tabitha clutched herself in horror.

'We were playing Grandmother's Footsteps in the woods,' went on Taggie, 'and suddenly Gertrude had vanished. She's deaf and blind. She must be so frightened.' Taggie's voice broke.

'What does Gertrude look like?' asked the interviewer.

'She's only a little black and white mongrel, but her black patches are mostly white because she's eighteen.'

'A good age,' said the interviewer, 'and your husband Rupert has offered an amazing ten-thousand-pound reward. A lot for such an old dog.'

'She's special to us,' sobbed Taggie. 'She eats Bonios in her paws like ice-creams. She was eating one yesterday, and this magpie, one for sorrow, snatched it away. She'll be so bewildered. We just want to know she's safe.'

'Well, I'm sure with a ten-thousand-pound reward we'll have the whole of England looking for her. That's Gertrude, and the number to ring is . . .'

Tears were flooding Tab's face. She had known Gertrude, Taggie's dog, since she was eight, even before Taggie married her father. Rupert had had to work hard to win over Gertrude.

Gertrude had also starred at Taggie and Rupert's wedding, escaping up the aisle and standing panting between her mistress and Rupert while the Bishop ranted about sexual mores. When anyone had a row at home, Gertrude, the peacemaker, would rush in rattling a box of Bonios. She had so much character.

Oh, poor Taggie, thought Tab. She must ring home at once. It took her three goes to dial because she was shaking so much, then the number was engaged. Feeling the need of Wolfie's solid comfort, she dialled Valhalla.

Seeing Magpie Cottage's number coming up, Rannaldini picked up the telephone. 'My little one.'

'May I speak to Wolfie?'

'He is out. The calls are being diverted to the tower. I've been listening to your poor stepmother on the radio.'

'Oh, God, it's terrible.'

'Maybe not so much. Clive was driving back from Cotchester just now and pick up small white terrier, smooth-haired and with curly tail. Maybe it's Gertrude.'

'Has she got a greyish patch over one eye and on her tail?'

'She has.'

'I'll be over in a sec.'

Telling a reproachful Sharon she wouldn't be long, Tab put on gym shoes so she could run faster.

Outside in the dusk it was even hotter. The once deep and dangerous river was so low she could paddle across it. The lights were on in Hermione's house. She could see Mr Brimscombe still dead-heading roses in anticipation of night filming, and waved as she raced past. From the shrieks issuing from the tennis court, the final was reaching a climax. Someone called out but she ran on.

By the time she reached Hangman's Wood, she was drenched in sweat. She had never visited the watchtower. A combination of Rottweilers and Rannaldini's rapacity had deterred her. No guard dogs patrolled tonight, but racing down a woodland ride, she heard an imperious yap. Blind and deaf, yapping was the only way in the big house at Penscombe that Gertrude could broadcast her whereabouts to the family. Crashing open the door, Tabitha stumbled upstairs.

'Here she is,' said Rannaldini.

The little white dog sat in the middle of the room looking around anxiously with clouded, unseeing eyes. She gave another yap.

Tabitha dropped to the floor beside her.

'Oh, my angel,' and suddenly Gertrude, who had often wriggled under Tab's duvet in the mornings, smelled someone familiar who reminded her of home. She whimpered incredulously, frantically wagging her tail, as she jumped off her front legs, to lick Tab's sweating, tearful face. Gathering up Gertrude, burying her face in her neck, Tabitha also breathed in the smell of home.

'Oh, Gertrude,' she sobbed, 'oh, thank God, Rannaldini. Taggie'll be so relieved. I must ring her at once.'

Her breath was coming in great gasps from running.

'Have a drink,' said Rannaldini cosily, pouring her a vodka and tonic. 'Go on. This is a celebration.'

He reeked of Maestro and wore only Alpheus's coveted purple and pink striped dressing-gown. But Tab was too happy to notice, or that, not wanting to be interrupted, he had just diverted the calls back to the house.

'I shouldn't.' She took a gulp of vodka and nearly choked. 'I've got to drive her back to Penscombe. It's all right, darling.' She dropped a kiss on Gertrude's forehead. 'Can I ring Magpie Cottage and ask Isa to look after Sharon?'

Isa still wasn't home, so she left a message. As she rang off she briefly noticed a disgusting painting of a black-haired Rannaldini whipping some naked tart.

'Wasn't I 'andsome in those days?' he demanded.

'You're better-looking now,' said Tab, but without interest. 'Oh, Rannaldini. Finding Gertrude' – she smoothed the lipstick left on the little dog's forehead – 'gives me the excuse to go home, and maybe Daddy'll be so pleased he'll forgive me. I've missed him so much.'

She had never looked more touching. Two blonde strands, escaping from her black velvet toggle, framed her face. Her eyes shone, her cheeks were hectic red, the innocent grey dress clung to her still heaving breasts and wet body.

'I honestly don't want it.' Leaving the vodka, she jumped to her feet. 'I don't know how to thank you.'

Putting her infinitely precious burden on the floor for a second, she reached up to kiss him on the cheek. Rannaldini breathed in her scent. Next moment he had grabbed her with the grip of a madman. Then the solid wedge of his body hit her, winding her, throwing her on the floor, and he was on top of her. Sending buttons flying, he ripped open her dress, suffocating her with his other hand. She could see the black hairs, feel the clash of the wedding ring he had been given by her mother, against her teeth.

Struggling like a wild cat, Tabitha scratched his face and pummelled his ribs, but lust doubled Rannaldini's considerable strength. As he tore at her knickers, she jerked away her head and screamed.

'You're so beautiful,' hissed Rannaldini, 'but you need to be taught a lesson.'

Ducking her head to avoid him kissing her, she found her lips crushed against his dressing-gown. Then he had rammed his cock into her, not minding if his aim was off centre. At first it buckled against her tightness then, tearing her because of her dryness, forced itself inside.

But Tab's screams, like bats' shrieks, had roused Gertrude, who could also see faint but frenziedly moving shadows. Edging towards the noise, she encountered Rannaldini's leg and plunged her few teeth deeply into it. Rannaldini gave a bellow, and groped for the bronze of Wagner on a nearby marble table.

'No!' screamed Tab. 'Please – not Gertrude!'

Too late, Rannaldini had hurled it, catching the side of the little dog's head with a crack, but still Gertrude the lionheart clung on. Reaching down, Rannaldini grabbed her by the scruff of her neck and flung her against a big carved cabinet. With a sickening crunch and a faint yelp, Gertrude slid to the ground.

Rage gave Tabitha strength. Catching Rannaldini off balance, she wriggled away from him, at the same time shoving his head very hard against the sharp corner of a marble table.

'You've killed her, you murdering bastard.'

Jumping to her feet, she scooped up Gertrude, who was gushing blood from a cut-open head, and stumbled down the spiral staircase out into the dark wood. She could still hear cheers and yells of excitement. If only she could reach the tennis court, but terror, fury and grief made her lose her bearings. Turning left away from Valhalla, tripping over roots and bramble cables, she reached a little clearing and paused, gasping for breath.

'Oh, please, don't be dead,' she sobbed.

But Gertrude lay motionless in her arms. Frantically Tab tried to distinguish the dog's heartbeat above the pounding of her own, but there was nothing. Gertrude's merry, curly tail had wagged its last.

Crying hysterically, Tabitha reached the Paradise–Cheltenham road and a telephone box. Her grey dress was soaked in blood. She had no money and dialled 999.

'Emergency. Which service, love?'

'No, I want you to get this number for me.'

Wolfie's machine was on.

'Oh, Wolfie, help me! Rannaldini's just raped me, and he's killed Gertrude. Oh, please get Sharon from the cottage!'

She heard a deafening crash and swung round in terror but it was only thunder. She clutched Gertrude to comfort her, because the little dog had always been terrified of bangs, but now Gertrude was beyond thunder, shouting, loud music, Christmas crackers, even fireworks. Sobbing and shaking convulsively, Tab jumped in panic as the telephone rang. But it was only the worried operator.

'Can you reverse the charges to my father at Penscombe?'

Gertrude's body was losing its warmth and growing heavy.

'I have a reversed-charge call from Tabitha Campbell-Black. Will you pay for the call?' asked the operator.

There was a pause, then she could hear Rupert's light, clipped drawl. 'Yes, of course. Hello.'

'Oh, Daddy,' howled Tab. 'I've got Gertrude and it's a thunderstorm, but she can't hear it any more because she's dead. I'm so sorry, Daddy, Rannaldini kidnapped her and raped me. Gertrude bit him and saved my life, so he threw her against the wall and killed her. Oh, Daddy.'

It was so heartbreaking, for a second Rupert couldn't speak. Then he said, 'It's all right, darling. Where are you?'

'I'm not sure. In a telephone box on the edge of Rannaldini's woods, about a mile out of Paradise. Oh, Daddy, I'm sorry I didn't save her.'

'If Gertrude saved you,' Rupert tried to keep his voice steady, 'that was the best possible way for her to go. Look, stay where you are. I'll be with you in a trice. But, angel, you're too conspicuous in a telephone box.' He didn't want to terrify her that Rannaldini would soon be after her. 'Hide behind a tree until someone turns up.'

'I'll kill him if he comes anywhere near me.'

Rannaldini fingered the bump on his head where Tab had pushed him against the table, and rubbed his leg, which was still bleeding. Fucking dog. Tab would calm down. He'd buy her stepmother a new puppy. He'd better find her before she caused trouble. Picking up her glass of vodka, he went outside. The wood was very dark. Not a star pierced the leafy ceiling. There was no sign of Tab. As he wandered northwards, blackberry fronds clawed at his dressing-gown, like women always wanting things.

Helen had spent most of the day packing. Everything was such an effort these days. She was off to London first thing and, to her heartfelt relief, Rannaldini appeared to be cooling off the appalling Pushy and had even offered her his helicopter.

For years, Helen had boycotted Rannaldini's watch-tower as a ghastly phallic example of Pandora's box but, overcome by restlessness and curiosity as to whether Rannaldini had really dumped Pushy, she decided to take a late-night walk through the woods. Drawn irrevocably towards the tower, she was amazed to find the door open and lights blazing. On the first floor, she found a glass knocked over, a bronze of Wagner on the floor, a chair on its side, and tidied automatically.

Seeing nothing of interest, except one of Étienne de Montigny's revolting paintings, she retreated to Rannaldini's edit suite on the ground floor where he had been watching the rushes. Here, with pounding heart, she discovered Rannaldini's memoirs: diaries bound in red leather with crimson endpapers and, in a huge scrapbook on the table, beautiful obscene photographs of her husband's women.

There was that slut Flora, and Serena Westwood. Helen gasped with horror. She had trusted and made a friend of Serena. And look at Pushy straddling a sofa in a London flat! No wonder the little tart had treated Valhalla as though she owned it.

As if she were watching some horror film, Helen flicked over the pages faster and faster. Oh, heavens, there was Bussage roped to a bed, like an elephant being airlifted to another safari park. She'd been right all along about her and— Oh, God! Blood seemed to explode in her head. There was Tabitha, naked and, in her lean beauty and her arrogance, hideously reminiscent of Rupert.

But there was worse to come: a photograph of Helen herself across the gatefold, pitifully thin, her hips hardly holding up a suspender belt, her silicone breasts jutting obscenely from a skeletal ribcage.

'I'm going mad,' sobbed Helen.

As if in slow-motion nightmare, she turned to the

diaries, fumbling for the entries where Rannaldini had first met her. 'Prudish, pretentious, silly,' she read numbly. Then on the night he had first made love to her in Prague: 'Used wicked doctor/shy young patient routine. Helen a pushover.'

Reading on she realized that, throughout their courtship, Rannaldini had not only despised her but had been making love to other women, recording conquests even on their honeymoon, and interspersed with all this was his craving for Tabitha.

'She smiled at me today. She was wearing a sawn-off shirt and when she raised her arm I saw the underside of her breast like a gull's egg.'

With a howl of anguish, Helen went on the rampage. Tugging a drawer until it fell out, she found a draft will, dated 8 July. Bussage must have typed it that afternoon. Rannaldini was leaving everything to Cecilia, his second wife, to all his children by her and to that monster, Little Cosmo. Not a cent to Helen or Wolfie.

A flash of lightning lit up the wood as though it were day. A deafening clap of thunder ripped open the valley. Running outside, Helen threw up and up and up. Rannaldini must be stopped from publishing his memoirs, particularly if that fiendish Beattie Johnson had any say in it. Suddenly she heard singing: '*These tears are from my soul.*'

Hermione must be on her way to the watch-tower. Jumping behind a huge sycamore, Helen didn't notice at first the dancing fireflies of a helicopter landing in a nearby field, and men jumping out like an SAS raid and running across the grass.

Rannaldini had found no sign of Tabitha, but the voltage of the vodka he'd drunk and the bump on his head, which was still seeping blood into his hair, were making him dizzy. Wandering back in the direction of the watch-tower, surprised to hear sheep bleating, he was suddenly distracted by someone singing Elisabetta's part in the final duet: '*These tears are from my soul,*' soared the voice.

>*'You can see how pure are the tears women weep for heroes.*
>*But we shall meet again in a better world.'*

He was still a hero in Hermione's eyes. She was show-ing him that no-one could sing the part better, and that she had forgiven him. Her top notes sounded as pure and lovely as they had in Paris, eighteen years ago. Hermione, who had given him more pleasure than any other woman. Why was he squandering his energy on silly young girls? Smiling, he walked down the ride and held out his arms.

'My little darling,' he called out.

38

Despite noisy encouragement from the spectators, Granny and Griselda lost 6–3, 6–4 to Wolfie and Simone. Leaving the others down at the court with plenty of drink, Wolfie loped back to the house to organize supper. In the larder he found a big plate of chicken *à l'estragon*, a ham, an asparagus and avocado salad, a chocolate roulade, a large blue bowl of raspberries, and was just thanking God for Mrs Brimscombe when she hobbled, white-faced and gibbering, into the kitchen. She refused a stiff drink and it was several minutes before she made any sense. She had seen a pale mauve light, she said. 'It came bobbing out of Hangman's Wood, across the big lawn, past the chapel and disappeared into the graveyard.'

'Must have been someone with a torch.'

'There was no footsteps, it went straight through the big yew hedge and a wall. Bobbing and pale mauve it was, Wolfie.' Mrs Brimscombe put gnarled hands, shaking like windswept twigs, to her face. 'Lights like that have been seen in Paradise before, come to guide the dead soul to his grave,' she whispered.

Despite the stifling heat, Wolfie felt icy fingers on his heart.

'It means there's been a death, Wolfie.'

Refusing a lift home, she stumbled into the dark.

Wolfie was terrified. His father never allowed servants to sleep in the house although, to Helen's distress, Clive and Bussage drifted in at all hours. For once, he was relieved to hear old bag Bussage tapping away on the keyboard in her office, and singing, probably on the radio, coming from Helen's little study down the passage.

He must pull himself together and open some bottles. Grabbing a corkscrew from a kitchen drawer, he idly flipped on the answering-machine, and received the full horror of Tab's message, that she'd been raped and Gertrude murdered.

'This time I *am* going to kill my father!' he yelled.

Oh, God, where was Tab? He must find her before Rannaldini caught up with her. The *bastard*! Wolfie dialled 1471 to discover where she'd rung from, then found out from directory inquiries that it was the call-box on the edge of Hangman's Wood. No-one answered when he rang. It was so dark now, between flashes of lightning. He decided it would be quicker to drive, and found himself trying to open the BMW's door with the corkscrew. But when he screeched to a halt beside the call-box, Tab had gone. There was blood all over the floor and the telephone. A terrible fear gripped him. Had that pale mauve light been guiding Tab?

Thunderclouds had blotted out the russet glare of Rutminster, the tiny sliver of new moon had gone gratefully to bed behind the wood. Down at the court, the conscientious, frugal Bernard suggested everyone look for balls, whereupon most people sloped off claiming the need to make urgent telephone calls. Lucy, who had returned after her storm of tears in time to watch the last game and give back Wolfie's signet ring, set off with James clinging to her heels for a last run round the south side of Hangman's Wood.

She soon regretted it. The wood exuded such evil. At any moment she expected dark branches to grab her, or the Hanging Blacksmith to thunder by. She was glad when the path curved and she could see the comfortingly twinkling lights of Paradise village. She was just wondering wistfully how Tristan had coped, knowing he was no longer a Montigny at such a tribal gathering as Aunt Hortense's party, when James bounded forward, wagging his long tail, giving excited little squeaks.

Peering through the darkness, Lucy could see nothing. Perhaps James had caught a white glimpse of Sharon across the valley, but settling back on his haunches, still wagging, he gazed in the direction of the west gate. Perhaps he had seen a ghost. Turning in terror, Lucy raced back to the tennis court, to find Ogborne guzzling the last of the strawberries.

'All sorts of exciting crashing,' bellowed Griselda, emerging from the wood.

'Probably cows,' said Bernard, appearing from a more northerly direction.

'And lots of shooting,' added Griselda defiantly. 'OK, Bernard, it probably was Teddy Brimscombe after pigeon. And a helicopter landing and taking off.'

'I always feel this wood's watching me,' shivered Lucy.

'We're still about twenty balls short,' sighed Bernard.

'Here are two more.' Coming out of the wood, Granny dropped a shocking pink and a lime green one on the pile.

As the chapel clock struck a quarter to eleven, Ogborne filled up everyone's glass.

'What are we going to do about Rannaldini's balls?' he intoned.

'Chop 'em off,' said Granny.

It wasn't very funny but even Bernard was braying with laughter, when Lucy's mobile rang. It was Rozzy. Terrified, as the howls of mirth escalated, that

Rozzy might think people were laughing at her, Lucy spanked the air with her hand to shut them up.

'How did the party go, Rozzy? Really well, judging by the din in the background.'

Rozzy, however, sounded suicidal. After all her hard work to make Glyn's birthday special, Sylvia the housekeeper had given him a single of 'S'Wonderful', and he'd been playing it and dancing with her all evening.

'Oh, poor you, how was the food?'

'They seemed to like it, although Glyn fed his smoked-salmon parcel to the cat, and everyone's plastered.'

Over drunken shouts of 'Happy birthday, dear Glyn', Lucy could hear the strains of 'S'wonderful, s'marvellous'.

'He's a pig, Rozzy. How was your dress?'

Glancing round, Lucy saw Granny and Griselda playing imaginary violins and Ogborne holding his fat sides, and wandered away from them.

Rozzy admitted the dress had been a success.

'You'll see it at the wrap party. Are you having fun?'

'Yes,' lied Lucy.

'I miss you all so much.'

'And we you, Rozzy. Where are you ringing from?'

'Upstairs. I've got a migraine.'

'Not surprising, if they're making such a noise.'

Lucy could now hear roars of 'Why Was He Born So Beautiful?' 'When are you coming back?'

'First thing tomorrow. 'Bye, Lucy darling.'

'She's always been a masochist,' sighed Griselda, when Lucy had recounted Rozzy's tale of woe.

'In the old days, they were known as Glyn and Bear It,' said Granny. 'Mind you, I'm one to talk.'

Lucy's mobile rang and she blushed, feeling disloyal when it turned out to be Rozzy again.

'I forgot to say why I rang in the first place. Can you remind Griselda to get Hermione's cloak out of Wardrobe, or leave me a key so I can mend that tear? I doubt . . .' Rozzy paused to listen to the laughter at

350

Lucy's end '. . . you lot'll surface before the afternoon.'

'Griselda and Granny reached the finals,' began Lucy, but Rozzy had rung off. 'She wants you to get out Hermione's cloak.'

'What a little treasure she is— Whoops, sorry, dearie,' added Griselda, as she cannoned off one of Rannaldini's bronze nudes. 'I'd better fetch it before I get really whistled.'

'Rozzy doesn't sound in carnival mood,' said Granny.

'She'd never have gone home this weekend if Tristan hadn't shoved off to Paris,' observed Griselda. 'Oh, sorry, Bernie, I forgot you had the *chauds* for her.'

Up at the house, unable to find Wolfie, the others were having a rip-roaring party on the terrace.

'Where's Mikhail?' giggled Simone. 'Still snoring under weeping ash?'

'Shouldn't we wake him?' said Lucy.

'Oh, leave the bloody killjoy. With any luck he'll get struck by lightning,' said a newly arrived Chloe, who was looking lit from inside and wonderfully beautiful.

It's the first time I've seen her without bright crimson lips, thought the eagle-eyed Simone. She looks so much softer.

Five minutes later, Griselda tottered in.

'Can't find that cloak anywhere. Madam must have taken it to Milan. Hope she hasn't got it dirty. Here's the key.' Griselda dropped it into Lucy's shirt pocket. 'Rozzy can find it. Why should I bother if I've been fired?'

Alpheus arrived next. He had changed into terracotta trousers and a blue checked shirt, and kept glancing sourly at his watch. Everyone was deliberately staying up late in the hope of waking late to get into the rhythm of night-shooting. But eleven thirty was a ridiculous hour to dine.

'I'm starved. Where in hell's Wolfgang?' he said tetchily.

'Don't tell me the Nazi machine's broken down at

last,' mocked Chloe, ignoring a scowl from Simone.

'I'm off to raid the larder.' Going in through the french windows, Ogborne went sharply into reverse as he met Helen, in her honeysuckle and lilac silk dress, coming the other way.

Pretty woman, mused Alpheus. That would *really* annoy Rannaldini. He was about to offer Helen one of her own drinks when, most uncharacteristically, she poured herself a massive vodka and tonic with a frantically shaking hand.

'Such a fascinating play on Puccini on Radio Three,' she told Bernard. 'I had no idea that he never finished *Turandot* and that Toscanini conducted the première.'

'We won't get any dinner out of her,' murmured Ogborne to Lucy.

'My God!' shouted Griselda. 'Our very own *auto da fe.*'

Swinging round, they saw Hangman's Wood going up in flames and a shower of sparks, like an orange inferno. The crackling could be heard four hundred yards away as parched trees and dry undergrowth submitted helplessly to the fiery furnace. They could feel the heat from where they were standing, as the blaze lit up the entire valley.

'Rannaldini's watch-tower's on fire,' screamed Helen. 'All his papers and compositions will be burnt.'

'Hurrah,' said Granny, pouring himself a drink.

'Probably knew they were junk and set fire to them himself,' crowed Griselda, holding out her glass.

All Rannaldini's evidence against Tristan would be torched! Lucy felt giddy with relief.

'What about the rushes?' asked Alpheus, horrified because he was in them.

'There's a duplicate set at the lab,' said Ogborne. 'Hadn't someone better call the fire brigade?'

Someone already had. With a manic jangling, a fleet of fire engines came pounding up the drive and were soon sending fountains of water into the wood.

*   *   *

Five minutes later, the firemen were joined by an hysterical Flora. Having run through brambles, thistles and nettles all the way from Angels' Reach, she was panting so hard she could only croak.

'What about Tabloid?'

'Keep back, Miss,' shouted a fireman in a yellow tin hat, aiming a huge hose at a blazing oak tree.

'Rannaldini's Rottweiler.' Flora tugged frantically at his sleeve. 'His kennel's under the watch-tower – we've got to get him out.'

'Too late, Miss, place's been torched.'

'He might be alive,' panted Flora in desperation. 'Please! Please!'

Shielding her eyes with her arm, she inched forward, but jumped back as the oak tree crashed to the ground, narrowly missing her and spraying sparks everywhere. Someone grabbed her arm, brushing her down and yanking her to safety. It was several dazed seconds before she recognized Clive behind the blackened face and hair.

'Tabloid!' she sobbed.

'It's OK. I took him back to the yard earlier.'

'Are you sure?' Flora yelled over the crashing and crackling.

She didn't trust Clive.

'Get back, for God's sake!' bellowed another fireman.

For a few seconds, the blaze had been pegged by the jets of water. But as the flames merrily leapt back to life again, Flora, hastily retreating, out of the corner of her eye, suddenly saw a body on the ground.

For a crazed second, she thought it was some leering Silenus, caught catnapping in the wood after a surfeit of dryads. Then, slowly, horrifically, she realized that the lolling tongue, the hideously engorged lascivious features belonged to Rannaldini. Alpheus's pink and purple dressing-gown had fallen open to reveal a mini

353

watch-tower of an erection. Flora began to scream.

'That's Rannaldini! He's been murdered.'

'We have found a body,' admitted the chief fire officer cautiously, 'and the police are on their way. If I were you,' he added to Clive, 'I'd take this young lady back to the house.'

39

People were always screaming at Valhalla, often to the accompaniment of classical music. Cars frequently hurtled up the drive, helicopters landed like swarms of fireflies, shots were heard in the wood. As television was so dire on Sunday nights, many of the inhabitants of Paradise had got into the habit of switching off their lights, turning round their chairs and focusing their binoculars on the great abbey.

Those watching the goings-on on Sunday, 8 July, included old Miss Cricklade who took in ironing, pretty Sally and Betty, the maids who worked at Valhalla, Pat and Cath, two village beauties with crushes on Tristan, and that Paradise worthy, Lady Chisledon.

Having clocked Dame Hermione's return from Milan and been disappointed by no sightings of Tristan on the tennis court, the spectators had assumed the flaming watch-tower was part of filming. But when five fire engines had been followed by Detective Sergeant Gablecross, the area CID man, in his battered Rover, and the we-ay, we-ay, we-ay of a police car with a flashing blue light, they realized something was up.

They were then delighted by the arrival of Detective Chief Inspector Gerald Portland, a local pin-up, who was equally delighted to have just returned from sailing in Turkey with a mahogany tan to flaunt at forthcoming press conferences.

Having seen that Rannaldini had not only been strangled but also shot through the heart, he ascertained murder had taken place and set in motion the wheels of inquiry. No doubt Chief Constable Swallow, a dinner guest at Valhalla, would soon ring Lady Rannaldini to express his sympathy.

In no time, two uniformed police had cordoned off not only Hangman's Wood with blue and white ribbon but also the Paradise–Cheltenham road, which passed the main gates at Valhalla, for two hundred yards in either direction. A uniform car halted and took the names and addresses of everyone entering and leaving.

Watchers all down the valley were even more excited to see men in white hoods, overalls and boots, like astronauts landed on the moon, moving around the smouldering remains under brilliant floodlights. These were the scene-of-crime officers, videoing, finger-printing, taking soil samples, waiting for the fire and ashes to cool, cursing under their breath that the fire brigade, who were more concerned with saving lives than trapping murderers, had drenched the place, hurrying as the storm drew nearer. The pathologist, due from Cardiff in an hour or two, would get soaked.

Up at Valhalla, two uniformed policemen were collecting names and addresses. Within half an hour twenty more were swarming in through the east gate, followed by three times as many press.

Rutminster Police were still recovering from the infamous Valhalla orgy in 1991 when PC, now DC, Lightfoot had rolled up to investigate complaints about noise and only been returned to the station with staring eyes thirty-six hours later.

Rannaldini had been cordially detested in the area. He had bribed too many local councillors in return for planning permission. There were endless rumours of rapes and unnatural practices. Two of the comelier village girls had vanished without trace in the past three years. Dark tales had always come out of Valhalla. To the legends of the Hanging Blacksmith and the Paradise Lad was now added that of the Strangled Maestro.

But despite their expressionless faces as, armed with torches, they searched the sinister house and gardens, nothing could suppress the excitement of the police that this was bonanza time. The eyes of Scotland Yard, Interpol and the world would now be on little Rutminster. Every stop would be pulled out as they worked from dawn to long after midnight to find the killer. This would mean massive overtime to pay off mortgage and overdraft. Neither was the hunt tainted with sick revulsion over some fearful child abuse or loss of innocent life, only incredulity that no-one had murdered Rannaldini before.

Detective Sergeant Gablecross stayed with the body until the scene-of-crime men arrived, then made his way up to the house. He lived in nearby Eldercombe and knew a local network of villains, including Clive, as extensive as the secret passages under Valhalla. A racing fanatic, appalled by Rannaldini's cruelty to horses, he had been trying to nail Rannaldini for years, but it seemed the Grim Reaper had got to the Grim Raper first. Gablecross's primary emotion was passionate relief that overtime from the murder would pay for his daughter Diane's eighteenth birthday party.

The tennis party, meanwhile, had retreated into the Summer Drawing Room.

'This is diabolical,' chuntered Alpheus. 'Rannaldini's name added billions to the film.'

'You and Hermione will get top billing now,' cried Griselda, as she waltzed round the room with Granny.

'"A tombstone fell on him and squish-squash he died, squish-squash he died,"' sang Granny, euphoric that with Rannaldini dead the police might not come and take him away. '"She went to heaven,"' he trilled, '"and flip-flap she flied, flip-flap she flied."'

'For Chrissake, Granville,' snapped Alpheus. 'Most of us find this an unendurable strain.'

A second later, his mobile rang.

'Hi there, who did you say?' Alpheus turned his back on the room. 'The London *Times*? The New York, ah. Well, if it was handled in a dignified fashion. Right, give me your number. There's no need to call my agent, he only handles my performing and recording rights.'

Looking smug, he switched off his mobile.

'As you're about to sing to the rooftops,' giggled Meredith, 'Howie is surely entitled to his twenty per cent.'

'I've had offers from the *Express* and the *Mail*,' said Chloe gleefully, 'and I'm not giving that lazy sod Howie a penny.'

Bernard, a soldier used to death, was amazingly calm. His duty was to keep the film on course. Who would be needed for the masked ball tomorrow? Flora, Mikhail, Baby, Gloria, Hermione (who probably wouldn't be up to it), Alpheus and Granny were on standby and if it rained as forecast they'd have to do cover shots in the Great Hall.

Outside, the police were setting up a major incident van with statement forms, floodlights and its own generator.

'Perhaps its generator will mate with our generator. "Love is in the air,"' sang Meredith.

No-one had thought to dim the chandeliers. Flora sat shuddering on the sofa, clutching Trevor for comfort, working her way down a bottle of white, trying to get Rannaldini's grossly contorted features out of her head. She had never needed George more, but there was no answer from his house or his mobile.With her luck, the photographs would have been delivered before Rannaldini was murdered. She wished Baby were here to cheer things up.

Sylvestre was comforting Jessica, DC Lightfoot Pushy,

who was one moment sobbing hysterically, the next upgrading her parents' house from 192 Station Approach to 'Cherrylands'.

Simone was talking to her mother in Paris. Lucy sat beside Flora, James at her feet, occasionally twitching his toes against her ankle to check she was there. Thank God Tristan was far away in Paris. No-one had had more of a motive.

'Maman was very angry that I didn't make the party,' said Simone in awe, as she switched off her telephone, 'but not nearly as angry as Aunt Hortense, because Uncle Tristan never showed up and Aunt Hortense had dispensed with protocol and put him, as her favourite nephew, on her right. His older brothers, including my father, were very angry. Tristan didn't even telephone Aunt Hortense.'

'Couldn't tear himself away from Madame Lauzerte,' muttered Ogborne.

'Shut up, she's in Wales,' hissed Sylvestre.

'I told you I saw Tristan at Valhalla,' pouted Jessica.

That was why James had leapt forward earlier, thought Lucy, in panic.

'Oh, look, you've spilt your wine over that lovely new settee,' cried Pushy.

'Oh, God, I'm sorry.' Lucy gazed down as the stain, like a dark red jellyfish, invaded the sea-blue silk. 'Rannaldini will murder me.'

'It's all right, dearie.' Meredith patted Lucy's hanging head. 'He's dead now. Run and get some salt, Jessica.'

'And bring me some grub,' Ogborne called after her.

'Ooo, look at that lovely man just come in,' squealed Pushy.

'That's Detective Sergeant Gablecross, our local sleuth,' said Meredith hastily arranging his curls in a nearby pier-glass.

Although his athlete's body had grown too big for his suits, as a result of too many hastily snatched hamburgers and bags of chips, there was an undeniable force about Tim Gablecross. His square, ruddy, freckled farmer's face, with its uncompromising mouth and jutting jaw, was only softened by light brown hair, which waved when it rained, and turned-down emerald-green eyes. These were fringed with such long, curly eyelashes, that as a uniformed officer they had stopped his cap falling over his broken nose. Despite a West Country drawl as slow as the smile that occasionally drifted across his face, he was as tough as a police-canteen steak.

Gablecross's wife, Margaret, was crazy about opera so he instantly recognized Alpheus Shaw and Chloe Catford. No wonder DC Lightfoot was going scarlet as he took down Chloe's name and address. Last time he'd seen her, at the Valhalla orgy, she'd only been wearing Diorissimo. Gablecross also recognized Meredith Whalen, who was local, and Granville Hastings, who was waltzing decorously with Lady Griselda, whom he had often booked for speeding. All three looked as though they'd won the pools.

Flora Seymour, on the other hand, gazed into space, cuddling a terrier and shaking uncontrollably. Gablecross remembered her singing in *The Creation* in the cathedral water-meadows, and knew that she lived with George Hungerford, almost more of a wide boy than Rannaldini.

The only thing he noticed about the others was that they were all pissed and on their mobiles, except Bernard Guérin who came over and introduced himself. Gablecross liked Bernard on sight, finding him ex-army, efficient, practical and with a sense of priorities. Bernard had still failed to contact either Sexton or Tristan, who was probably already on his way back from France. As Bernard clapped his hands, the room fell silent.

'You'll all know by now a body has been found,' announced Gablecross, 'and we are making inquiries. We would like you to co-operate and let us retain the clothes you are wearing or, if you've changed, the ones you were wearing earlier.'

'For you, Detective Sergeant, anything,' smiled Meredith.

Gablecross, who battled constantly against homophobia, didn't smile back.

'A man hasn't asked me to take off my clothes for yonks,' said Griselda, with a shout of laughter.

'The police could use her dress as an incident tent,' hissed Ogborne.

'What happens to our clothes?' simpered Pushy. 'I was hoping to wear this little cardie to an audition next week.'

'They're labelled, numbered and put in brown-paper bags,' said Gablecross.

'You weren't wearing those clothes earlier, anyway,' the hawk-eyed Simone told Pushy. 'Nor was Chloe.'

'Yes I was, smartass,' snapped Chloe, opening her long blue cardigan to show a white shirt and pleated shorts, 'but Alpheus *has* changed.'

'My clothes are back at Jasmine Cottage,' said Alpheus quickly. 'I'll go and get them.'

'A police officer will drive you, Mr Shaw,' said Gablecross firmly.

Ogborne was gazing out on the ever-increasing crowd of media.

'I'm going to film them. Always wanted to be an operator,' he muttered, sliding out of a side door.

'Why are all those men wandering around Hangman's Wood in space suits?' asked Jessica, coming back without any salt.

'To avoid contamination of the body,' explained DC Lightfoot admiringly.

'Would have thought it was the other way round,' said Granny sourly.

'I'll get my job back now.' Griselda collapsed on a sofa, drumming her feet excitedly on the floor like a little girl.

'So will I,' said Meredith. 'I did redecorate this room

361

nicely, didn't I? Those onyx pillars are to die for. Wonder if anyone's told Hermione.'

'Wonder how upset she'll be?' mused Griselda. 'They go back a long way. She probably did it.'

'That singing in the wood sounded almost too good for her,' observed Sylvestre, the constant listener. 'Perhaps Rannaldini had replaced her with some young chick.'

'Then she certainly did it,' said Meredith.

'The murderer is most likely to be a member of the family,' volunteered Jessica, who never missed an instalment of *The Bill.*

'With four wives, eight kiddiwinks, and a million steps and illegits to take into consideration,' giggled Meredith, as he handed Sylvestre a bottle of red to open, 'the police will be spoilt for choice.'

'"He went to t'other place and frizzled and fried,"' sang Granny happily.

Christ, what a bunch, thought Gablecross, and leaving DC Lightfoot and DS Fanshawe to get their clothes off them, went off to break the news to Lady Rannaldini.

40

Detective Sergeant Gablecross found Helen in a terrible state, mindlessly tidying her little study, straightening straight objects, looking around with huge, darting eyes, her grey face such a contrast to the lilacs and honeysuckles blooming so luxuriantly on her beautiful silk dress.

Gablecross felt desperately sorry for her, but with murder it was his duty to zap her and start scribbling straight away. 'I'm afraid we've found your husband's body in the wood, Lady Rannaldini.'

'What?' Helen went utterly still, except for her darting eyes. 'Oh, my God, you don't mean he was caught in the fire? How terrible! They say you suffocate first,' she pleaded.

'No, no, Sir Roberto died from strangulation and gunshot wounds.'

'It wasn't an accident?'

Gablecross could have sworn it was relief that flickered over her face. There was a long pause which he let her fill.

'Is everything in his watch-tower destroyed?'

'I guess so.'

'All his precious compositions,' whispered Helen, a muscle jumping in her freckled cheek. 'His life's work gone! I can't bear it.'

'What were your husband's movements today?'

'He went to his watch-tower mid-afternoon.' She was twisting her very loose wedding ring round and round. 'Earlier I saw him walking round the garden with Flora Seymour, who looked very upset. He also rowed with Rozzy Pringle and Alpheus Shaw – I heard them both shouting, I don't know what about. Artistic people shout all the time.'

A red glass paperweight trembled like a raspberry jelly as she straightened it.

'Then some very important rushes arrived of my husband conducting the first and last scenes in the film, and Mr Brimscombe, our gardener, and Clive, my husband's bodyguard, carried this machine out to his tower so he could watch them. My husband was very particular about how he looked on the rostrum.'

'Did he have anything to eat?'

'He had a late lunch of caviare with blinis and sour cream, and some peaches from our conservatory, taken out to the watch-tower around four.'

'Who would have prepared that?'

'Mrs Brimscombe. Clive would have taken it out. Rannaldini didn't like people . . .' she paused '. . . people he didn't want, to visit his tower. Are you sure he suffocated first, Officer?'

'What did you do this evening?'

'I got my clothes ready for London. I've got several committee meetings and a dinner in aid of the Red Cross tomorrow. Rannaldini's letting me have the helicopter,' she added proudly. 'Then, at nine thirty, I listened to a play on Radio Three about Puccini, by Declan O'Hara's son, Patrick. D'you know his work? It's excellent. Did you know Puccini didn't finish *Turandot*?'

Like a tap whose washer had gone. Gablecross knew she'd give him the whole plot, but he let her run on, captivated by her slight American accent.

'Toscanini conducted the première but only as far as Puccini had written.' Helen's eyes filled with tears.

'Toscanini knew my husband, and rated him very highly as a conductor.'

'Did you leave your room while you were listening to the play?'

'The phone rang in the kitchen around ten past ten. But the machine had picked it up by the time I got there, so I left it. The calls are always for my husband.'

'That was the only time you left the room?'

'Yes, but I missed the end of the play, which was maddening.'

'Did you have any supper?'

'Mrs Brimscombe's so dear, she tried to tempt me with an omelette but I'm afraid I chucked it down the john. It was so hot and I had a headache.'

'You didn't feel like joining the tennis party?'

'I popped down earlier with Eulalia Harrison, a charming journalist from the *Sentinel*, who was actually interested in hearing my views for a change.'

For a second her bitterness at always playing second fiddle showed through.

'But I didn't stay. Frankly, Officer,' she started to shake again, 'I feel like Clarissa Eden. The crew and the cast have been flowing through this place as if it was the Suez Canal for three and a half months. I want my house back.'

'Having seen that lot,' said Gablecross drily, 'I'd feel more like Mrs Noah, frantic for a first glimpse of Mount Ararat.' He was touched by the gratitude that swept her face.

'Oh, you do understand. And now Rannaldini's not going to be here to revel in those big rooms, which have been revamped like Buckingham Palace. This is about the only place that hasn't been Meredithed.' She glanced bitterly round the exquisite little study. 'They do say you suffocate before the flames burn you.'

She was shuddering so violently she had dislodged a false eyelash, a funny thing to wear to listen to the radio on Sunday night, thought Gablecross.

'I keep expecting him to burst in, Officer. He was so dynamic.'

'We'd like you to hand over the clothes you wore today.'

'I haven't changed out of this dress.'

'That's fine. Could you let us have it when you go to bed? I'd also like . . .' he consulted his notebook '. . . to speak to your son Wolfgang, and your daughter Tabitha.'

It was as if he had mentioned people she'd forgotten existed. In a state of grief and shock, people invariably look for others to blame. 'Why aren't they here?' exploded Helen.

'Any idea where they might be?'

'Wolfie was organizing the tennis. How dare he disappear when he should be here for me? Tab's just as thoughtless. My son Marcus is quite different.' She picked up a silver-framed photograph of a beautiful boy seated at a piano. 'He won the Appleton, you know. Marcus would never abandon me at a time like this.'

'Can you think of anyone who might have killed your husband?'

Gablecross let an unbearably long pause elapse, until Helen said in a low voice, 'Tristan de Montigny tried to kill him on Friday night. Hermione, Chloe and Gloria Prescott were all furious they hadn't got a particular part. Particularly Gloria who everyone nicknamed Pushy. My husband's been so kind to her, lending her the limo and the helicopter. She took so much for granted.

'He had that terrible row with Alpheus this morning, and one with Mikhail, and Hermione too. He felt she hadn't sung her part very well. But my husband fights with everyone.'

A moth was banging like a muffled funeral drum against the window.

'He can't bear music to be any less beautiful than he hears it in his head.'

Her mobile rang. Helen snatched it up.

'Rannaldini? It's the *Scorpion*,' she whispered in terror.

Gablecross seized the mobile. 'Piss off,' he roared.

Next moment, two photographers had rammed their lenses against the window. 'Look this way, Helen.'

'Bugger off,' bellowed Gablecross, yanking the dove-grey curtains across their faces.

From now on, the media would move into Paradise waving their cheque-books, like flies round a cowpat, eyes in their backsides, making the work of the police ten times more difficult.

Turning back to Helen, Gablecross caught a glimpse of a photograph, pushed to the back of a shelf, of Rannaldini smiling down at a ravishing girl. She was the spitting image of Rupert Campbell-Black. It must be Helen's daughter.

'How did your husband get on with Tabitha?'

Images of the photographs in Rannaldini's watchtower swam before Helen's eyes, with a naked, scornful Tabitha on the top. As she burst into tears, there was an impatient knock and a tall young man in a dark blue polo shirt and tennis shorts barged in. With his dark blue eyes, gold hair and thighs as strong, smooth and brown as its onyx pillars, the drawing room, leading out on to the terrace, might have been decorated to compliment his handsomeness, but he looked much too large in here. Wolfie disliked Helen intensely for neglecting Tab, but he hated to see anyone in distress.

'What the hell's going on?'

'I'm sorry, we've found your father's body, sir.'

The colour drained out of Wolfie's suntanned face.

'He had a heart-attack?'

'I'm afraid he's been murdered.'

The boy took it wonderfully calmly. Was it something he'd half expected, even longed for? It must have been a terrible burden to have had Rannaldini as a father.

Wolfie turned to Helen.

'I'm so sorry.'

Crossing the room, he hugged her awkwardly, patting her shoulder until her sobs subsided. In reality he was playing for time, his mind racing.

'How did he die?' he asked, still with his back to Gablecross.

'He was strangled and shot.'

Wolfie felt a lurch of fear. Had Tabitha killed him? 'What time did he die?'

'We don't know. The pathologist hasn't arrived yet.'

The police mustn't find out his father had raped Tab. He must remove that tape from the machine in the kitchen.

'Can I get you a drink or a cup of coffee?' he asked Gablecross.

'I'm fine.' Gablecross could see Wolfie wrenching his thoughts into order, he could smell his sweat and see the gooseflesh on his bare legs and arms. 'I'd like a few words with you, sir.'

'Let me just find someone to look after my step-mother,' and Wolfie had bolted.

The kitchen was empty but, to his horror, so was the answering-machine. Who could have whipped the tape? Sprinting down the passage, he put his head round the Blue Living Room door.

'Wolfie!' shouted everyone.

They were all drunk. Who could he trust?

'Lucy,' he pleaded, 'could you look after Helen for me, and ring Mrs Brimscombe and ask her to come and help her to bed?'

'I'm ever so sorry, Wolfie.' Lucy jumped to her feet.

'Perhaps we should ring James Benson,' suggested Meredith.

'He'll be out at some smart dinner party,' said Griselda.

'I'll come and check how she is the moment the police have finished with me,' Wolfie promised Lucy.

'I'm going to fetch you a sweater first,' said Lucy.

368

Gablecross interviewed Wolfie in the kitchen. The boy was now making coffee and wearing a red V-necked jersey, which he loathed because his stepmother Cecilia Rannaldini had given it to him for Christmas.

As if there were never any question that he wouldn't, Wolfie said that he and Simone had won the tournament. Returning to organize supper, he'd found a message from Tabitha, his stepsister, on the machine.

'D'you know where the tape is?'

'Must be still in the machine,' lied Wolfie. 'Tab went home because her parents' dog had disappeared. She's living in one of my father's cottages. As I had a second key, she asked me to fetch her dog and take it back to Penscombe.'

Gablecross admired a screen covered in hundreds of photographs of Rannaldini with the famous.

'Couldn't Mrs Lovell's husband have taken the dog?'

'He's away.'

'Rather inconsiderate of Mrs Lovell to expect you to drive over a hundred miles in the middle of a tennis party.'

'She was distraught about her parents' dog,' said Wolfie quickly. 'It was a very old family pet.'

'Did you see anyone when you first returned to the house?'

'I heard Miss Bussage in her office, and my stepmother's wireless.'

'Did you hear anything unusual?'

'Only Hermione singing in the rushes as I walked back to the house. Sound carries much further on thundery nights. Although . . .' Wolfie wrinkled his forehead, perplexed '. . . I don't remember the bit she was singing being filmed on Friday.'

'What time was this?'

'Around half ten, I think.'

Switching the kettle on to boil for the fourth time, he made two cups of coffee.

'Why didn't Mrs Lovell take the dog with her in the first place?'

'Sharon's on heat. Tab's father has a pack of dogs. Tab hadn't seen him for two years. Probably didn't want to rock the boat.'

'Could a more major crisis have made her rush home?' asked Gablecross.

'A dog going missing is a major crisis in that family,' said Wolfie coldly.

'How long did you stay at Penscombe?'

'Only to hand Sharon over.' Wolfie was treading carefully now. 'Someone had just brought Gertrude – their missing dog – back. She'd been run over so I didn't stop.'

As he handed Gablecross the sugar and a biscuit tin, he could only think of Tab's tearful, choked words when she rang to thank him on his way back to Valhalla.

'Please, don't tell anyone Rannaldini raped me. It would kill Mummy.' He had wanted to drive straight back to Penscombe to comfort her.

'Very attractive young lady, Mrs Lovell.' Gablecross helped himself to a chocolate biscuit. 'Did that cause any tension between your father and stepmother?'

'Don't be ridiculous,' snapped Wolfie.

'It still seems excessive to abandon your guests and drive all that way in the middle of a party.'

'My guests', said Wolfie dismissively, 'have been free-loading here all summer. I felt they could fend for themselves.'

The iron has entered into that young man's soul, decided Gablecross. He's not only madly in love with Tabitha Lovell but lying through his extremely good teeth. Glancing at the screen again, he noticed how colourless the famous people appeared beside Rannaldini. You couldn't fail to respond to the flashing whiteness of the smile, the hypnotic eyes, the un-deniable magnetism.

'Could you come and identify the body, sir?'

'Certainly,' said Wolfie, emptying the rest of his cup of coffee into the wastepaper basket.

They found the forensic team sifting through the ashes, videoing evidence, scattering grey aluminium powder on the remnants of the watch-tower, in the forlorn hope of finding fingerprints. The pathologist, who'd just arrived, was examining Rannaldini's body. Only when the sheet was drawn back did Wolfie's composure crumble.

The strikingly handsome Rannaldini now looked like his *Spitting Image* puppet: a grotesque satyr, swollen almost beyond recognition, blood and saliva dripping from his nose and tongue, lips pulled back in a hideous leer. 'How horrified Papa would have been to be videoed without Lucy here to brush his hair,' said Wolfie, starting to laugh, then finding he couldn't stop.

'It's all right, lad.' Gablecross put a hand on his shoulders.

Alpheus's dressing-gown had fallen open to show the muscular legs. Wolfie noticed the starchy white residue on his father's thighs, the bite on the ankle, and the huge erection stiffening as rigor mortis set in.

'Probably been dead for no more than two hours,' said the pathologist, replacing the sheet.

Gablecross glanced at his watch. 'About half ten, then.'

Blood had blackened the grass, washing away the earth, laying bare the Cotswold stone underneath. Wolfie wondered if someone had mistaken his father for Alpheus. Gripped again with terror that Tab might have killed him, Wolfie lurched away, retching into the brambles. As he returned, wiping his mouth on the back of his hand, he said defiantly, 'I don't care how many people slag him off. He was my father and a great man.'

41

While Gablecross interviewed Helen and Wolfie, Ogborne had joined the mob swarming all over Valhalla, as they filmed, photographed and gabbled into tape-machines, describing everything they could see in the darkness.

Armed with Valentin's lightweight video camera, Ogborne had turned up the brim of Hermione's sunhat like a sou'wester. He was delighted to catch Alpheus leaving in a police car to collect his clothes, combing his rich auburn locks for the television cameras.

'Where are you from?' asked a BBC cameraman.

'Bourbon Television,' said Ogborne.

'Never heard of it. Where're they based?'

'Paris,' said Ogborne, who was now filming the paparazzi, who, like puppies fighting for their mother's teats, were jostling each other to get a close-up of Wolfie, returning stony-faced from identifying the body.

'News travels fast.'

'Director's a Frog, so's most of the crew,' explained Ogborne. 'Huge story for us.'

'We're trying to sign up the mistress,' said a reporter from the *Mirror*.

'Which one?' asked Ogborne. 'He had lots.'

'The big one.'

'Hermione?'

'That's it. Know where she hangs out?'

'What's it worf?'

When two hundred readies had been thrust into Ogborne's hand, he pointed to River House.

'She's very greedy,' he called after the departing reporter. Why in hell hadn't he become a cameraman before?

'Great hat,' said the man from the BBC.

'They're all the rage in Paris,' said Ogborne. 'You can have it for fifty quid if you like.'

Thoroughly overexcited by so many hunky young police officers talking softly into their mobiles and flashing their torches, Clive sought refuge in an ivy-clad ruin near the graveyard to ring Beattie Johnson.

'Rannaldini's been murdered. How much are you going to pay me for the memoirs and the photos?'

'We've already been offered them.' Beattie, like Rannaldini, adored giving pain.

'Shit. By who?'

'Wouldn't you like to know? We'll go with the cheaper. Talk to you in the morning.'

Possibly a million smackers the poorer, Clive switched off his mobile and froze as he saw a torch approaching like a will-o'-the-wisp from Hangman's Wood. Beside him, Tabloid started growling and whimpering. Putting a hand down to quiet the dog, Clive felt the rigid bumps of his hackles. Then his own hair shot on end as he realized that the violet-tinged light was too big for any torch, and that it wasn't attached to any policeman.

Bobbing past him, it went straight through a yew hedge to disappear among the dark holm oaks of the graveyard. Clive couldn't breathe. He felt icy sweat trickle down his ribs under his leather jacket. Even if Rannaldini's body was destined for months in the morgue, the violet light was trying to guide him to the graveyard to join Valhalla's dead. The wind was getting up. Feeling, for once, in need of company, Clive raced towards the house.

*   *   *

Alpheus had just returned with his clothes to the drawing room when Ogborne wandered in, carrying a plate piled high with potato salad and chicken.

'How can you eat at a time like this?' snapped Alpheus, his mouth pursing and watering simultaneously.

'Because it's probably the last time I *will* eat here,' said Ogborne philosophically. 'Sexton had to dip into his own pocket to pay the wages last week, and now Rannaldini's no longer here to fork out.'

'But we're all on contracts,' spluttered Alpheus.

Finally tracking down Sexton on his car telephone, Bernard was able to tell him the sad news. Sexton immediately got the contract out of his briefcase and checked the small print. He then gave a whoop of joy: they were definitely insured against violent death. Without Rannaldini's interference, they'd finish the movie twice as quickly and they could scrap those pompous beginnings and endings, include the polo – and he could be an extra in a Panama hat.

Wally, the chauffeur, looked on in amazement as Sexton leapt out of the now stationary car, did a little dance, punched the air and said, 'Yeah, yeah, yeah.'

'Do we have cause for celebration?' asked Wally.

'We certainly do, tyrant's been toppled.'

Sexton then checked his pocket computer and punched out a number. 'I'd like to speak to Rupert Campbell-Black.'

'He's out,' said a gruff, tearful voice. 'No, no, he's just come in.'

'Yes?' snapped Rupert.

'Rannaldini's been murdered,' said Sexton.

'So?'

'We've run out of dosh, because he was making impossible demands. We've only got a week of night-shootin' left, and then a day or two's polo. Polo's Tabiffa's baby. Shame, if we had to junk it.'

There was a pause as Rupert did some sums.

'I'll come in if I can call the shots.'

'Naturally,' said Sexton.

Hanging up, he did another little dance.

'Turn round, Wally. We're going back to Valhalla. But don't forget, Wally, we was in 'Olland Park all day, wasn't we?'

'Naturally,' said Wally, who also liked the idea of being paid.

Outside in the darkness, an *Evening Standard* reporter screamed as she fell over Mikhail's sleeping body under the weeping ash. 'Sorry, sorry! D'you know anything about this murder?'

'Vot murder?'

'Someone's killed Rannaldini.'

'God is merciful,' said Mikhail and went back to sleep.

The moment he escaped from Gablecross, Wolfie rang Rupert.

'Mr Campbell-Black, this is Wolfgang Rannaldini. My father has been murdered.'

'I know.'

'I thought it wouldn't look good to say he r-r-raped Tabitha, so I said Gertrude had been r-run over and Tab came home to comfort you and Mrs Campbell-Black.'

'Good boy,' said Rupert. 'Well done, and thank you.'

Having given up her clothes, Flora looked like a pre-school boy when she returned in Lucy's striped pyjamas. Trevor lay on the floor beside her, legs stretched out like a frog.

As Clive and Tabloid entered the room, everyone reached mentally for their swords. Clive had been Rannaldini's *éminence grise*, the devil's right hand. For a second he and Tabloid hovered, two dogs without their master.

'A favourite has no friend,' murmured Flora.

Lucy leapt to her feet.

'Sit next to me, Clive,' she said. 'I'll get you a whisky.'

'Fanks, Lucy,' said Clive, a tinge of colour creeping into his waxy white cheeks. 'Fanks very much indeed.'

It was strange that the three fearsome dog rivals for Sharon's paw lay down beside each other without a murmur.

Clive was followed by Mr and Mrs Brimscombe, both looking aged and shaken. Mr Brimscombe had taken off his boots.

'Pooh,' said Pushy, noticing his grimy toenails protruding through the holes in his socks.

Flora jumped up and hugged them both.

'This must be absolutely horrible for you, but don't worry,' she whispered. 'I'm sure Lady Rannaldini'll keep you on. I know Mum would snap you up in a trice if she wasn't so broke.'

Griselda patted the sofa beside her.

'Come and sit down, Mrs B. Fantastic chocolate roulade – I've had thirds. How's Lady Rannaldini taking it?'

'In a shocking state.' Mrs Brimscombe lowered her voice. 'Poor soul keeps crying and laughing. She won't go to bed. I wish Dr Benson was here to give her something.'

She flinched as a flash of lightning pierced even the thickly lined blue curtains, followed by a deafening clap of thunder. Both James and Trevor leapt into their mistresses' arms.

'I expect they'll drag the lake to find the murder weapon,' Jessica could be excitedly heard telling Sylvestre.

'The lake has dried up,' said Mr Brimscombe bleakly.

At first it sounded like applause in extremely bad taste but the clapping grew louder and louder until they realized it was the rattle of rain on roof, window and very dry leaf.

'It's raining,' screamed Flora, running out on to the terrace and thrusting her face up into the deluge.

'Flora, Flora, Flora,' shouted the paparazzi, simultaneously trying to shield their cameras and take a picture.

Everyone's clothes and names and addresses had at last been taken. They could now go home or to bed. Night-shooting would start around six p.m.

'I still haven't been able to contact the DOP, the operator or the director,' Bernard told Gablecross. 'It'll be a terrible shock to Tristan – Rannaldini was like a father to him.'

At that moment, a spectacularly good-looking young man wandered in. Rain had darkened and flattened his hair back from his forehead, throwing his angelic features into relief. A drenched duck-egg blue shirt and white jeans clung to his body. Only under the chandeliers could his grey complexion and red eyes be detected.

Montigny, assumed Gablecross.

'Baby,' cried Flora, shooting in through the french windows into his arms.

'Hi, sweetheart,' said the young man. Then, looking into her anguished eyes, 'Hey, hey, what's up with you?'

'Bad news, I'm afraid,' said Bernard. 'Rannaldini's dead.'

Baby didn't miss a beat. 'About time too,' he said approvingly, and crossing to the drinks tray poured himself a large whisky and soda with a completely steady hand.

'Murdered,' said Alpheus sternly.

'Really?' Baby looked only mildly interested. 'I'll buy whoever did it a huge drink. Miracle it hasn't happened before.'

'At least show some respect for Lady Rannaldini,' spluttered Alpheus.

'"The widow howling for her dead husband".' Baby

dropped his voice an octave to sing Mikhail's line. 'And she's a *very* rich widow now, which should appeal to you, Alpheus.'

'This is Detective Sergeant Gablecross, Baby,' said Bernard hastily, 'who'll want to question you tomorrow.'

'The Grand Inquisitor,' sang Baby in amusement. 'You're so rugged, Sergeant, it'll be a temptation to tell you everything.'

Totally undeterred by Gablecross's black, pugnacious scowl, Baby went on, 'For a start, all these people have a motive.'

'Speak for yourself,' roared Alpheus.

'Undeclared tax and cuckoldry in your case,' drawled Baby. 'Sexual romps with ruminants in Chloe's.'

'I'll kill you!' screamed Chloe.

'Jocking off in Isa Lovell's case. Excessive cruelty in Helen's, excessive cruelty to Tristan in Lucy's.'

'Stop it, Baby,' yelled Lucy, blushing furiously.

Utterly unfazed, Baby turned back to Flora and drew her into an alcove.

'Rannaldini had photographs of us making love on the lawn at Angels' Reach,' she said numbly. 'He was going to blackmail George, and if George didn't back off about the bypass, he was going to send them to Gordon Dillon and, as if that wasn't enough, he said you were HIV positive.'

'Glad he thought I was positive about something. That man was such a liar.' Baby rubbed Flora's hands to warm them. 'You poor angel, what a terrible weekend you've had. But I promise you, I'm clean. I had a medical for an insurance policy last month. And, frankly,' he added, pushing the rain-soaked tendrils back from her forehead, 'we'll finish twice as fast now the bastard's dead. Then I can take you back to Oz, away from all this squalor.'

'It's too late,' sobbed Flora.

Baby pulled her into his arms.

'For God's sake, a man has been murdered.' Bernard tapped Baby furiously on the shoulder.

'May he roast in peace,' said Baby. 'Unless you're going to let me identify the body to make sure the conniving shit really is dead, I'm off to bed. One must always leave a party early to give everyone a chance to talk about one. Come on, Flora darling.'

The rumble of disapproval died on people's lips as Helen appeared in the doorway in a long white nightgown.

'I don't know what to do about locking up,' she told Gablecross, in a high, singsong voice. 'Rannaldini's not back yet and I hate leaving the front door open.'

Next minute, she was thrust aside by Miss Bussage who, having handed over her clothes, was now sporting a man's dressing-gown, slippers and a hairnet that flattened her cropped hair. 'The Maestro may have passed away,' she called out defiantly, 'but his genius lives on. I've got all his compositions and his last will on disk, not to mention a copy of his memoirs and duplicates of all the photographs.'

For a second, Gablecross noticed collective horror on everyone's faces. Then there was a thud as Helen Rannaldini fainted.

42

A strange quiet lay over Valhalla. The deluge had shredded roses all over the lawn and flattened the dreaming spires of Rannaldini's delphinium bed. Mr Brimscombe tugged on his boots and hobbled as fast as possible to hoover up the petals before his master surfaced, then suddenly realized that Rannaldini would never shout at him again.

Waking, also realizing his father was dead, Wolfie was ashamed to feel as if a poisoned spear had been yanked out of his side. Then he blushed with shame and revulsion as he remembered Tab had been raped. He longed to ring her but felt it would only remind her of Rannaldini. Instead he got dressed and set about the long haul of comforting staff and telephoning relations, including Gisela, his mother, in Munich. Rannaldini's body still lay under canvas in Hangman's Wood. They would all feel better when it left for the morgue.

Meanwhile every radio station was playing Rannaldini's music. Howie had been on to American Bravo and instigated a massive re-press of all his records. BBC TV had already announced they would be rerunning Rannaldini's masterpiece, *Don Giovanni*, starring Hermione Harefield and Cecilia Rannaldini tomorrow evening in conjunction with Radio 3. News programmes worldwide led on the murder, showing clips of the *Don Carlos* press conference with Rannaldini and Tristan swearing eternal brotherhood and, to Ogborne's delight, of Alpheus rearranging the police car driving-mirror in order to comb his hair before facing the media.

By nine, uniformed police were trooping in in raincoats to start a fingertip search through a drenched Hangman's Wood. Others were going along the high street and up the drives of the big houses dotting the valley, asking people if they'd seen anything even more extraordinary than usual last night.

As cast and crew woke from fitful sleep to clutch their hangovers, euphoria that the fiend was no more was tempered by fear that his killer was still at large. This was heightened by excitement, particularly among the women, as news leaked out that Rupert Campbell-Black would be pumping in millions to save the film, and henceforth acting as executive producer.

At midday Oscar had arrived from Paris with Valentin and three crates of *rouge*, which might now last until the end of the shoot.

'No doubt Peppy Koala will be telling me where to put my lights,' he grumbled, and, adding that he hoped Rupert's temper was better than his daughter's, bore Valentin off to lunch at the Heavenly Host. There he was incensed to find every table taken by the media, who were equally incensed to be banished outside Valhalla's main gates. The vast crowd there included journalists and photographers jabbering away in every language under the sun, a fleet of television vans, arc-lights, satellite dishes, mobile canteens, a bar and Portaloos, as everyone rampaged through Paradise frantic for stories.

Hype-along, wielding even more mobiles than Sexton, and unusually sombre in a black armband, flowered tie and flared pale blue suit, told the cast and crew that the police would prefer them not to talk to the media.

'Unless they offer you at least a hundred grand,' shouted Baby, who'd just spent a lucrative hour on the telephone to the *Sydney Morning Herald*.

Lucy had been woken within seconds of finally falling asleep by James squeaking excitedly and Rozzy banging on the door, distressed not to be able to find Hermione's cloak.

'And why's the place swarming with police?'

'Rannaldini's been murdered.'

'Don't make stupid jokes.'

'It's true, Rozzy.'

Rozzy was furious that Lucy hadn't rung her before.

'I suppose I'm not important enough.'

'Oh, Rozzy.' Groggily, Lucy switched on the kettle. 'You had a migraine, we didn't want to disturb you.'

Rozzy was really upset – 'Rannaldini was a genius' – and wanted to know all the details. 'How's Tristan taken it?' she asked finally.

'I don't think he's back,' said Lucy.

Should she tell Rozzy about Jessica's sighting and Simone's account of Tristan cutting Aunt Hortense's party? Rozzy got so upset if she were left out.

All day the rain poured down on fans, who poured, weeping, into Paradise to leave flowers wrapped in Cellophane at Valhalla's gates.

'Maestro, take me with you to heaven,' said one card. Many fans also made pilgrimages of condolence to Dame Hermione's gates. Alpheus, dropping off a large bunch of salmon-pink gladioli that the Paradise garden centre were selling off cheap after the weekend, was displeased to see the vast number of young people among the crowds. Rannaldini's popularity had clearly not been on the wane.

Outraged that someone had nicked all her lilies in the night, Hermione arrived, veiled and smothered in black, with her arms full of yellow roses covered in greenfly. As she knelt in prayer for at least five minutes for the benefit of the world's press, she was filled with fury that Rozzy had already left a beautiful bunch of lilies in their own vase of water.

*　　*　　*

As the day progressed and the rain continued to gush out of Valhalla's gargoyles, to the worry that they wouldn't be able to film outside was added the fear that Tristan had done a runner.

'We can't stop production. This picture's costing thousands of pounds a day,' Sexton told Gablecross and the couples of plain-clothes men and women who'd arrived to question everyone on the unit.

'Understood,' said Gablecross. 'You carry on. Where are you planning to shoot?'

'If the rain stops, on the terrace, then in the maze.'

'OK, I'll move my team in. No-one must go near Hangman's Wood – the area's cordoned off anyway. We'll draw people out as we need them. We also need to fingerprint everyone.'

Gablecross was paired with the most ravishing black girl, wearing a white, tightly belted trenchcoat, whom he introduced as DC Karen Needham.

'Want to work in movies?' quipped Sexton, as he ushered her into his office.

DC Needham giggled. Gablecross looked boot-faced and asked Sexton what he had been up to last night.

'Dining at my house in town, then driving back to Valhalla,' lied Sexton happily, as DC Needham started scribbling in her notebook. 'Me and my driver, Wally, had just stopped for a sandwich and some petrol around one o'clock. We've got all the receipts. When Bernard rang me wiv the sad news, we agreed I should be the one to tell Dame Hermione.'

'What was her reaction?'

'Gutted. She and Rannaldini go back a long way.'

And up a long way, thought Gablecross irrationally, remembering the rampant cock.

'How did she spend the evening?' he asked idly.

'Several people heard her singing in the wood around the time of the murder.'

'Must have been a tape or the rushes. Dame Hermione came 'ome from Milan around seven thirty,

383

watched *Pride and Prejudice* on the telly. A Jane Austen freak is Dame Hermione. What the hell's happened to Tristan?' he added, with unusual irritation. 'The fucker's always turning off his mobile because he wants to think.'

Driving towards Paradise through the deluge Tristan noted spiky conkers on the horse-chestnuts and a tangle of purply-blue cranesbill and pink willowherb on the verges, echoing Alpheus's dressing-gown. Rounding a corner, he suddenly saw a flotilla of pizza cartons, plastic coffee cups, fag ends and beer cans hurtling down the overflowing gutters towards him, and went slap into a rugger scrum of paparazzi, shouting, scribbling, banging tape-recorders and lenses against his windows. Tristan ducked in horror. Had his hideous secret been rumbled?

The policemen on the gates refused to admit him until he had given them his name and address. As he stormed up the drive, police and Alsatians were weaving in and out of Hangman's Wood. Ahead, the German and Italian flags drooped at half mast. Gripped by a terrible fear that Tab had taken an overdose, Tristan dived into the house. Two minutes later he stormed into Sexton's office.

'What the hell's going on? They've dismantled the Great Hall and the royal box, and we haven't reshot. What's that fucker Rannaldini up to now?'

Tristan had triple bags under his cavernous bloodshot eyes, his lank, damp hair looked as though it hadn't seen a comb for days. The buttons of his faded peacock-blue shirt were done up all wrong. He had only slotted his belt through one loop of his jeans, which were far too loose. He was frantically chewing gum. He looked wild, angry, dangerous, a tramp off the street, reeking of sweat and sex.

Gablecross opened his mouth, but Sexton was too quick for him.

'Rannaldini was murdered last night.'

Tristan's suntan seemed to drain into his black stubble leaving his face dirty grey. 'Oh, *mon Dieu*, who killed him?'

'That's Sergeant Gablecross's job,' said Sexton, almost too cosily. 'Let me introduce him, and his charmin' sidekick, DC Needham.'

Tristan nodded then sat down in one of Sexton's leather armchairs. In an instant his face was wet with tears. 'I cannot believe it. Rannaldini was father to me. Often I wish him dead for fucking up my movie, but he was great man. You are not having me on?'

Mindlessly parking his chewing-gum on the front of Sexton's desk, he groped for a cigarette, then dully slapped his pockets. 'I lose my lighter. When did he die?'

'Around ten thirty last night.' Sexton reached forward with a match. 'Someone torched the watch-tower.'

For a second Tristan's face, like Lady Rannaldini's last night, showed a flicker of something other than horror. Had he also skeletons? wondered Gablecross.

'Everything was destroyed,' confirmed Sexton.

Tristan breathed in smoke so deeply he almost choked, then opened his eyes in horror.

'He didn't die in fire?'

'No, he was strangled and shot,' said Sexton quickly.

Shut up, you fat git, thought Gablecross furiously. Let me get at him before he organizes his alibi.

But Tristan had jumped to his feet, pacing round the room, firing all the same questions, not taking in any of the answers. Someone had sewn a patch of a greyhound's head on the back pocket of his jeans.

'I told Detective Sergeant Gablecross we'd be shooting in the maze when the weather's cleared,' interrupted Sexton.

This pulled Tristan together, as the drug of the film kicked in.

'I'd like to ask you a few questions, sir,' began Gablecross. Karen Needham whipped out her notebook.

'Got to have a shower,' murmured Tristan and, before they could corner him, was out of the door.

Twenty minutes later, showered, shaved, reeking of Eau Sauvage and looking again like Calvin Klein's favourite model, he had disappeared into the production office with Sexton and a euphoric Bernard, delighted to be needed and included again.

'Rannaldini would have wanted us to carry on,' were Tristan's first words. He then ruthlessly scrapped Rannaldini's opening and closing scenes, save for a fleeting glimpse of the inhabitants of the royal box, of Gordon Dillon and of Rannaldini briefly exuding magnetism on the rostrum.

'Then we won't have to reshoot the ending Baby screwed up.'

'So that means five days' night-shooting in the maze and on the terrace, weather permitting,' counted Bernard on his big red fingers. 'Followed by two or three days' polo, which means we could wrap by Wednesday the eighteenth.'

Tristan glanced at Sexton in excitement.

'Can we afford polo?'

'Rupert Campbell-Black', said Sexton carefully, 'has agreed to bail us out.'

Tristan's outraged '*Non*' was as loud as the shot that killed Posa.

'*Non, non, non*! How did this happen?'

'I phoned him,' said Sexton simply. 'It's all very well you 'avin' lah-di-dah views about artistic integrity but without him I can't pay any more wages. I had nowhere to go, like a fart in tight jeans.'

'What's in it for Rupert?'

'Money, and Tabiffa sobbing her little heart out if we cut out the polo scenes. She's persuaded all Rupe's toff friends to appear for a crate of bubbly apiece or some-fink.' Sexton turned the screw blithely. 'Tab knew how much you wanted polo.'

'We can't have Rupert involved,' said Tristan mutinously, 'not after what happened with Tab and me. He must want to kill me.'

'You wasn't mentioned. I don't fink he knows. You wanted your flick saved, you ungriteful bastard.'

The row was interrupted by Griselda barging in, brick red with hangover but in tearing spirits. 'Hello, Tristan, isn't it awful and a relief about Rannaldini? How was *The Lily in the Valley*?'

'OK,' said Tristan, in a surprised voice. It was as if she were asking about some event that had happened centuries ago.

'We've got a problem,' went on Griselda. 'Hermione's in the first set-up this evening, and her pale green cloak's missing from Wardrobe. Her maid swears Madam didn't take it to Milan.'

'Since Meester Campbell-Black is bankrolling us, you better send Rannaldini's Gulf to Paris to fetch another,' said Tristan bitchily.

'They'll have to make a new one,' protested Griselda.

'And I don't fink Rupert will like us squandering his dosh,' said Sexton, in alarm.

'You sort it out, Grizel,' said Tristan. 'Hermione won't be fit to work tonight, we'll shoot her later in the week and concentrate on Chloe, Mikhail and Baby in the maze this evening. I'd better go and see Hermione.' He leapt up restlessly. 'How's Wolfie taking it?'

'Immaculate, coping wiv everyfing,' said Sexton admiringly. 'Helen's in a bad way, can't stop crying.'

'Probably suspects she's been cut out of the will,' said Meredith, protecting his curls with a pale blue umbrella as he scuttled in to discuss the evening's sets. 'Hi, Tristan, you missed all the fun last night. The rain's stripped off all the rose petals in the centre of the maze. We'll have to use potted ones. Have you met butch Sergeant Gablecross yet?'

'All *flics* are pigs,' said Tristan bleakly.

*   *   *

All over the unit, people gathered, whispering in sodden huddles. Alpheus was incensed that, owing to Hermione's compassionate leave and the scrapping of the scenes in the Great Hall, he and Flora had been told to push off until the end of the week.

'I've never known such lousy scheduling,' he fumed. 'I'm never working for Montigny again.'

'He could hardly have foreseen Rannaldini's murder,' snapped Bernard.

'He threatened to kill the guy on Friday night,' snapped back Alpheus, and stalked off to grumble to Sexton about his totalled Jaguar.

'Don Carless,' giggled Flora.

Out of his caravan window, Tristan watched the deluge lay waste to Rannaldini's domain. Once proud delphiniums prostrated themselves on the paths, their petals swept away by the racing muddy water. Torrential rain was bouncing a foot off the hard ground, rattling on the caravan roof like a firing squad.

Could Rannaldini really be dead? Tristan had visions of his godfather hobnobbing with Wagner and taking the heavenly choir apart. Perhaps Étienne was already introducing his old friend to the sexiest angels.

'Can we have a word, sir?'

It was Gablecross and the ravishing Karen Needham.

'I'm busy,' snapped Tristan, as he dialled Oscar's number. 'Can you and Valentin film the bashed-down delphiniums?'

'How was your screening?' asked Karen, perching on the window-seat, and picking up Saturday night's glossy brochure of *The Lily in the Valley*. 'I think Claudine Lauzerte is the most beautiful woman in the world.'

'I also. Now, if you'd excuse me . . .'

'Could you tell us where you were last night?' Gablecross sat down beside Karen.

'I have no time now.'

Exhausted, shocked, obsessive or just plain arrogant, thought Gablecross. Bloody Frogs! They were just like public-school boys, not in any way superior, just assumed they were.

'With such a high profile,' said Karen sympathetically, 'you must get really twitchy before a film comes out. Not just about the critics savaging it, but because the journalists get the opportunity to pick over your private life.'

Tristan looked into her kind, beautiful eyes, longing to lay his head on her trenchcoated breast and sleep for a thousand years.

'I have to rise above the parapet,' he confessed, 'and geeve interview because so much money and people's careers are involved. My father was well known in France.'

'I loved his early paintings,' said Karen, 'the ones of the Garonne.'

Gablecross looked at his running mate with reluctant respect. Tristan was thawing by the second, but froze up instantly when Gablecross asked him when he had returned from Paris. 'I drive through Channel Tunnel yesterday.'

'At what time?'

'Mid-afternoon.'

'If you could let us have your ticket? Then what did you do?'

'Always, as film is ending, I need to psych myself into next one, which will be story about Hercules. At the end, he is given poison shirt by jealous wife and, in his agony, tears up forests and builds his own funeral pyre. I need woodland location so I go to Forest of Dean and drive around for hours, thinking, and sleep in my car.'

Gablecross, if he lost a couple of stone, would make a good Hercules, thought Tristan idly. As he talked, he had been opening his post, systematically binning the letters and even a new cheque-book, and smoothing out envelopes on his blotter.

'Can you tell us exactly where you spent the night?' asked Gablecross.

Tristan ignored him. 'Did you study my father's paintings at school?' he asked Karen, as she retrieved his letters and cheque-book from the bin.

But when she said she had, he gazed at her dumbly, unable to remember what he'd asked. Then his mobile rang.

"Ello, *si*?' Having jumped on it, he immediately shoved Karen and Gablecross out of the caravan, slamming the door in their faces.

Resourceful Karen, however, who had attained A levels in French as well as English and Art, had deliberately left her notebook behind.

'What was he saying?' asked Gablecross, after she'd retrieved it.

'He was talking very fast, but the general gist was that he wouldn't say anything, and no-one had seen him arrive or leave and he'd speak to whoever the person was later.'

'Well done,' said Gablecross grudgingly.

43

Spirals of white mist drifted across the valley, like ghost priests hurrying to welcome Rannaldini to the other side. On the steps outside the house, Gablecross was assuring Wolfie that his father's body would soon be off to the morgue, when a convoy of Fleet Water Board lorries came splashing up the drive. Instantly, like a malignant crow in her black suit, Miss Bussage swooped out of the front door down the path flanked by lavender bushes.

'Take it away,' she hissed at the first driver. 'You're too bloody late. The Maestro wanted his ponds and lake filled up, but he's dead, so we don't need you any more.'

'Yes, we do,' shouted Wolfie, following her out through the *omnia vincit amor* arch. 'Forecast says the heatwave's coming back. I'm head of the house now,' he added coolly, 'and no ponds are drying up on me.'

Then, turning to Mr Brimscombe, who was rubbing his green fingers in glee that at last someone was taking on Bussage:

'Please show the drivers where we need the water.'

'You're not the head of the house,' Bussage exploded with rage. 'I typed his last will. He left everything to Cecilia, and her family. She was the one he loved, who got the part of Delilah. Not a penny to you or your boring mother, or that gold-digging Helen or her slut of a daughter.'

In daylight, Wolfie could see the scurfy grey roots of Bussage's oily dark hair, her malevolent little eyes, her open pores.

'You're fired, you *disgusting* bitch,' he said furiously.

'You can't fire me!'

'I bloody can!'

Dialling the car pool, he ordered a driver to take Miss Bussage to her sister's house in an hour.

'It'll be a pleasure,' lisped Clive.

'That'll give you time to pack,' Wolfie told her. 'We'll send the rest of your stuff on later.'

Reaching inside his blazer pocket, resting his cheque book on his knee, he wrote her a cheque.

'That's six months' salary. Consider yourself lucky.'

'I'll fight you through the courts.'

'Feel free.'

Short of chaining herself to the balustrade, there was not much Bussage could do. Returning to her office, where she had reigned supreme and, for a while, experienced true love, she took the disks of Rannaldini memoirs and envelopes containing the most salacious photographs out of a filing cabinet and locked them into her briefcase, then went down to the cottage to pack.

'Surely my father should go in an ambulance,' protested Wolfie, as Rannaldini's body was carried on a stretcher across yellowing lawns to a black mortuary van.

'It's considered unlucky to carry a body,' said Gablecross gently. 'Ambulances only take the living.'

As the mortuary van doors opened, Miss Bussage came out of Valhalla. Having loaded up her bags, Clive waited, smirking, by the limo. Saying goodbye to no-one, Bussage handed her card to Gablecross. 'I'll be at this address, I'd like to set the record straight.'

'I'll be in touch.'

On the steps outside the *omnia vincit amor* gates, Baby, Flora, Granny and an ashen Wolfie watched, with mixed emotions, the black van rumbling down the drive.

'He was charismatic, glamorous, fearless,' began Flora slowly, 'a brilliant musician and the greatest conductor in the world.' Her voice broke.

Wolfie's face wobbled for a moment, then he put an arm round Flora's shoulders. 'Thank you,' he mumbled.

And instinctively Baby launched into the heartbreakingly beautiful lament which he and Alpheus had sung over Posa's body.

A few seconds later, Granny had joined in, singing Alpheus's part, his clear voice ringing out less powerfully than Alpheus's but with far more feeling. ' "I have cast this man of pride and passion into the tomb," ' he sang.

'You should have played Philip,' whispered Flora taking his hand.

Bernard had tried to persuade Rozzy to join him for a late lunch, but she wanted to pray for Rannaldini in the chapel. Gablecross found Bernard tucking into a large steak, *pomme frites* and half a bottle of *rouge* in the canteen, and started grumbling about Tristan's lack of co-operation.

'He's only a boy,' protested Bernard. 'He's had a bloody awful life, but the last six months have been the worst. Rannaldini was a monster. Tristan doesn't mean to be rude, but the film comes first.'

'How long have you known him?'

'I've known the family for thirty years.'

Breaking up a French loaf with those big red hands, which would have no difficulty strangling anyone, Bernard told Gablecross about being in the army with Tristan's brother Laurent.

'Tell me about the tennis match.'

'Stormy.' Bernard smiled, showing his rocking-horse teeth. 'Women at the end of a shoot, all probably having their periods at the same time, all crying. Chloe and Gloria furious a part had gone to Rannaldini's second wife, Lucy missing Tristan, Flora missing George

– they'd had some row. Mikhail upset about his wife, Griselda and Meredith upset Rannaldini had sacked them. Alpheus cross Wolfie had smashed his Jaguar and Rannaldini wouldn't give him another. Granville Hastings upset his boyfriend was on some troop ship. Wolfie in love with Tabitha, Simone mad about Wolfie.'

'No-one very happy,' said Gablecross who, without realizing it, was steadily eating Bernard's chips. 'Rannaldini was wearing Alpheus's dressing-gown. Could someone have meant to kill him?'

'Possible.' Bernard tugged his moustache. 'Nice guy, Alpheus, but somehow more unpopular than Rannaldini.'

'Think any of them could have killed Rannaldini?'

'All of them. It was the worst shoot I've ever been on, something had to give. Rannaldini needled Tristan crazy. Tristan adores that little madam, Tabitha. Rannaldini put the boot in there.'

'Tell me more,' said Gablecross.

Having averaged a couple of hours' sleep and half a bottle of gin a day over the past week, Baby looked frightful.

'You could drive to Rutminster on my red veins,' he told Lucy, as she got to work with her paintbrushes and pencils, smudging, moulding, embellishing, only half listening to the interminable news bulletins and the chat between Baby and Flora, who had sought refuge in her caravan.

'Hermione, Helen and Gloria are all seeing bereavement counsellors,' said Flora.

'Then why can't I?' grumbled Baby.

'You loathed Rannaldini,' chided Lucy.

'I know. But I adore talking about myself.'

Noticing Flora was trembling again, Baby put a hand on hers.

'It's OK, sweetheart. Rannaldini was murdered for revenge or to stop him doing something even more unspeakable. Now he's out of the way there's no need to murder anyone else.'

'There is, if someone's still got the memoirs and the photos,' shivered Flora.

Next moment, they were distracted by John Dunne's voice on the wireless. 'The music world is in shock and mourning today for Sir Roberto Rannaldini,' he was saying. 'We have on the line someone who worked with Sir Roberto for many years, the great diva Dame Hermione Harefield.'

'Turn it up,' beseeched Baby.

'Roberto Rannaldini was a great conductor, a father figure, and the closest possible personal friend.' Hermione's voice throbbed with emotion. 'He had an amazing gift for recognizing genius in the young. Nearly twenty years ago he cast me as Elisabetta in *Don Carlos*, the part I am singing at the moment. After that first night I well remember Rannaldini saying, "You have the loveliest voice I have ever heard, Dame Hermione." No, I tell a lie, I wasn't a dame in those days.'

The inhabitants of Lucy's caravan were clutching their sides, when Hermione was interrupted by an impatient clicking on the line, and a shrill voice saying, 'Get off the fucking line, Mum. I gotta ring Ladbrokes.'

Little Cosmo, who had smashed his mobile in a fit of temper that morning, wished to use his mother's telephone. To accompanying squawks, John Dunne could be heard saying firmly, 'I'm afraid we've lost Dame Hermione.'

Miss Bussage enjoyed the journey to her sister's house. If, as promised, she had become the fifth Lady Rannaldini, she would have travelled always in a limo, although she would have preferred that leering scoundrel Clive to have worn his chauffeur's cap.

She had no regrets. Valhalla without Rannaldini would have been like lemon and black pepper without oysters. Anyway, whichever newspaper eventually bought the memoirs would give her enough to live on comfortably for the rest of her life.

When she arrived, she couldn't resist getting out the floppy disks and the photographs so she and her sister could have a gloat together. Only when she tried to print out the disks did she find they'd been switched for blanks and the dirty pictures all replaced with a pile of Rannaldini's fan photographs. Her howl of rage could have woken Rannaldini in his chill chamber in Rutminster Mortuary eighty miles away.

44

With all the rescheduling, Gablecross and Needham were anxious to interview the released singers before they dispersed. They caught Alpheus by the pool, bronzed and glistening from his daily twenty lengths.

What a hunk, thought Karen, feeling herself blush as Alpheus's wet hand held hers a fraction longer than necessary as he crinkled his eyes at her. 'I don't know if policewomen are getting younger, but they're sure getting more beautiful.'

'You sure keep in shape.'

'There's no excuse for singers to gain weight,' said Alpheus, lovingly drying his rippling muscles.

'What were you doing between nine thirty p.m. and eleven thirty yesterday?' asked Gablecross sharply.

'Finishing off a tennis match.'

'I bet you play real good,' said Karen admiringly.

'I used to be rated in the top fifty.'

As he vigorously rubbed his hair, Alpheus was frantic to sculpt his waves with a blow-dryer, but didn't want to appear a cissy in front of Karen.

'I can only give you a few minutes, Officer,' he said. 'I've shifted a recording to Milan tomorrow and Lady Rannaldini is kindly lending me the Gulf.'

'Why did you throw the game?' asked Gablecross.

'I had a delightful but not very strong partner, and my mind was on other things.'

'According to our information, you left around nine thirty and didn't stay to watch the finals.'

'I didn't want to catch cold.'

'In ninety degrees?'

'To be truthful,' Alpheus pulled a face, 'I was choked about not winning. Singers are overly competitive.'

After that, he said, he had swum his twenty lengths in the dusk. 'Then I jogged back to Jasmine Cottage, showered, changed, then called my agent Christopher Shepherd of Shepherd Denston. My *Carlos* contract promised to release me by 8 July. I wanted him to pacify the record company and negotiate a few days' vacation with my wife before I start *Don Giovanni*.'

'What time did you ring him?'

'Around ten thirty, I guess, but it won't show on the phone bill. My agent and I have a code. I let the phone ring four times so he knows it's me and calls me back. He takes twenty per cent of my earnings so he can pay for a few calls.'

'May we have your agent's number?'

Karen had studied body language. Alpheus was clearly nervous, the way he kept fiddling with his hair.

'How did you get on with Rannaldini?' she asked.

'Between great artists there is a bond,' said Alpheus firmly.

'You were overheard having an argument on Saturday morning.'

'Of course we fought – artists do. I was angry he had favoured Granville Hastings, not a great voice, on the tape. Rannaldini wanted to justify his decision to employ him. All conductors do this. My powerful instrument can stand it,' said Alpheus pompously. God, if he didn't get to a blow-dryer soon, he'd have an Afro.

'Is it true you were close to your tennis partner, Gloria Prescott?'

'It is the duty of the established singer to encourage talent,' said Alpheus. 'It's even more gratifying when a fine voice belongs to a charming young woman.' He winked at Karen.

'We've had information you argued with Rannaldini about her, and about the attention Rannaldini was paying to your wife.'

'Rumour, rumour. If you say good morning round here people think you're in a relationship. Little minds have little else to do than fabricate stories about the famous.'

'Why did you move into Dame Hermione's cottage?'

'To spend quality time with my wife. We're big animal people. Mr Bones, our German shepherd, pines without her. We can't bring him here because of your goddam quarantine laws so Cheryl never visits for more than a week.' That should endear me to a traditionally dog-loving English cop, thought Alpheus sourly. 'When Cheryl is here, we like to be alone,' he went on, 'and, frankly, not having been to an English public school like you, Officer,' Alpheus crinkled his eyes again – let's flatter the square-faced bastard, 'I found the dormitory atmosphere at Valhalla claustrophobic, so Dame Hermione, a good friend, lent us Jasmine Cottage. Now, if you'll excuse me . . .' Alpheus smothered himself in a white towelling bathrobe.

'Have you any idea who might have killed Rannaldini?'

'Must be an outside job. No-one involved in this movie would want Rannaldini off the credits.'

'You wore a pink and purple dressing-gown to play Philip.'

'Sing Philip,' said Alpheus fussily.

'D'you know where it is?'

'In Wardrobe, I guess.'

'Rannaldini was wearing it when he was murdered,' said Gablecross.

Clearly this jolted Alpheus: his wedding-ring glittered and quivered as his shaking hand moved through his hair. Had Cheryl taken the dressing-gown from the back of the wardrobe at Jasmine Cottage, he wondered, and given it to Rannaldini, who'd always coveted it?

'D'you think someone could have mistaken Rannaldini for you?'

'I have no enemies,' said Alpheus coldly.

'Alpheus Shaw claims to have no enemies,' said Gablecross.

'Nor has he many friends,' said Flora. 'But I mustn't speak ill of the alive, in case you take it down in evidence against me.'

They found her slumped in Lucy's caravan, watched beadily by Foxie, her puppet mascot, and Trevor the terrier. She was three-quarters down a bottle of white and was reading a small, leatherbound book in bad light. She looked wretched, deathly pale and red-eyed.

'I suppose you're not allowed drink. Would you like a cup of tea?'

'We've had about a gallon each,' said Gablecross sitting down opposite her. Karen edged wide-eyed towards Lucy's make-up table.

Tipping the spine of Flora's book, Gablecross saw it was *Macbeth*.

'Enjoying it?'

'Suits my mood,' shivered Flora.

'"And wither'd murder"' she read out, '". . . thus with his stealthy pace, With Tarquin's ravishing strides, towards his design Moves like a ghost." Can't imagine anyone withered or ghostly being strong enough to murder Rannaldini.'

'Rage and adrenalin', pronounced Gablecross, 'give the smallest, frailest person strength.'

'That puts little Meredith in the frame,' said Flora. 'He's never forgiven Rannaldini for calling his *auto da fe* set suburban.'

'Fond of him, were you?'

'Rannaldini? No, I loathed him. He seduced me

400

when I was sixteen, then dumped me. But it's still a shock.'

'What were you doing between nine thirty and eleven thirty last night?'

'Getting pissed, mostly. Then I went home to feed the cat. My parents live next door – you can see the stone angels through the trees. I hadn't realized how dark it was so I skirted the rose gardens, the maze and the stables and ran past our pond on the right.'

'Who saw you at home?'

'Only the cat, who's not great on alibis.'

'Did you notice anything unusual on the way?'

'Like Hermione praising another singer?' Flora topped up her glass. 'Sorry, silly joke. I heard her singing Elisabetta's last duet. Might have been a CD or a tape. There were lights on in River House and Magpie Cottage, I heard sheep bleating – they always bleat when anyone comes through Hangman's Wood, hoping it's the shepherd with their hay. The grass is so poor.'

'Live at home, do you?' asked Gablecross, who knew the answer.

'No, I live with George Hungerford – at least, I did until recently. I was going to marry him.' She accepted one of Gablecross's cigarettes with a shaking hand.

'I'll pay you back. That lipstick really suits you,' she added to Karen, who put it down hastily and picked up her notebook.

Flora dolefully relayed the drama of George landing his helicopter in the middle of her snogging scene with Pushy.

'He went ballistic, I told him to fuck off,' she said, finally and sadly.

'So George has landed his helicopter here before?' said Gablecross quickly. 'Didn't you notice one landing last night around ten thirty and someone running towards the watch-tower?'

Flora's eyes flickered in horror. 'It couldn't have been George,' she whispered. 'I'm sure he's in Germany.' She kept fiddling with her mobile to make sure it was switched on.

'How did you get back to Valhalla?'

'I drove. It was dark by then. It gets very creepy – funny things have been happening recently.'

Topping up her drink, she listed Granny's patchwork quilt, the adder in Lucy's make-up box, slug pellets in James's water-bowl, Tab nearly burning to death in the *auto da fe*.

'Why didn't anyone call the police?'

'We were so desperate to finish the film – the budget was spiralling like Rannaldini's staircase – that we avoided anything that might hold it up. Oh, I forgot. Foxie', she waved her puppet fox, 'was cut to pieces. I was so lucky, Rozzy Pringle spent hours sewing him together, like surgeons in casualty labouring through the night.'

Taking Foxie from her, Gablecross examined the joins.

'Can I borrow him?'

'No!' Flora snatched him back. 'I need the luck.'

Outside a huge rainbow reared up on the other side of Paradise.

'It's stopped raining. Let's go for a walk.'

Hearing the word, Trevor ran yapping out of the caravan. Flora followed him, carrying her glass and Foxie. The fingertip team, who'd been struggling through Hangman's Wood all day, were drenched, pricked, lacerated and stung. Handlers patrolled the edge of the trees.

'Aren't they sweet?' sighed Flora, as their Alsatians strained at their choke-chains barking at Trevor, who yapped back, dancing just out of reach. 'Think of those brave pointed noses sniffing out clues.'

'We use dogs more to intimidate the public,' confessed Gablecross. 'Not very reliable at finding things.'

'I did a dog-evading course once,' volunteered Karen.

'I hid in a badger set, covered myself with twigs, and a bloody great Dobermann came up, peed on me, then passed on.'

'Pissed on.' Flora started to laugh, then shuddered.

'Look, there's Clive, no doubt flogging his story, which must be horrendously steamy, to that disgusting crone, Eulalia Harrison from the *Sentinel*. When did Rannaldini actually die?'

'Hard to be accurate. Bodies cool very slowly on a hot night.'

'What happens if you don't find a body at once?' asked Flora, as they splashed through puddles the colour of weak tea.

'Flesh gets eaten by foxes and badgers.'

'Now I know why you didn't want any lunch,' Flora told Foxie petulantly.

'The eyes go first,' added Gablecross. 'Crows peck them out.'

'Oh, my God.' Flora started to tremble. 'Rannaldini had wonderful eyes, conductor's eyes. He could transform an orchestra just glaring at them.'

She leapt as her mobile rang.

'George!' she gasped in ecstasy, then slumped. 'Viking, how kind, if you're sure it won't be too much trouble. I'm too pissed to drive, I'll get a taxi.'

'That's one of my exes, Viking O'Neill,' she told Gablecross listlessly. 'I'm going to stay with him and his wife for a few days.'

'Just leave us the phone number and address.'

The chapel clock struck seven thirty. The deluge had swept cypress twigs on the paths into long brown snakes. The rainbow was fading. As they moved through the yew rooms of Rannaldini's garden, the rain had dusted and polished the nude nymphs lurking in every corner. There would be no-one to fondle them now.

'What happened when you got back to Valhalla?' asked Karen.

'I saw the watch-tower on fire, and thought of Tabloid

trapped in his kennel. So I left Trev in the car on the edge of the drive and hurtled through Hangman's Wood.'

'Risky under the circs, whole place ablaze.'

'I got to know Tabloid well, when I was sleeping with Rannaldini.'

'You didn't notice anyone in the woods?'

'Only firemen and Clive – God knows what he was doing. There was a disgusting smell of burning feathers, probably Rannaldini's mattress going up. Safety regulations weren't his forte.'

'Could you describe his tower for us?'

'Well, the top floor was all bed, with an appallingly narcissistic mural round the walls of an audience in evening dress, cheering him on to intenser orgasm. The next floor down was all dark blue jacuzzi, the next was a red-wallpapered pouncing chamber, full of low sofas and bowls of exotic fruit on marble tables, and a Picasso on the wall.'

'You don't know where he kept his safe?'

'Nope.'

'Or where he worked?'

'On the ground floor. He had an edit suite.'

'Was that where he did his composing?' asked a scribbling Karen.

'Decomposing now.' Flora giggled, then began to cry. 'I'm so sorry.' She groped for a piece of orange loo paper. 'Jokes are the only way I can cope.'

'It happened when my nan died.' Karen put an arm round Flora's shoulders. 'It's a typical reaction to shock.'

'Rannaldini never took you into any torture chamber?' asked Gablecross.

'He didn't need a chamber,' said Flora bleakly. 'His presence was enough.'

They had reached a balustrade looking over the fast-filling mere. Reaching behind a cascade of bright pink roses for a tin of fish food, Flora chucked a handful of pellets into the water. Goldfish, lying still as autumn leaves, burst into activity, but a huge black fish, ten times their size, suddenly swam to the surface, ravenous mouth not only devouring the pellets but ready to swallow anything alive that got in its way.

'Just like Rannaldini,' shivered Flora. 'Don't ever kid yourself he was a victim. We only met up, after he chucked me, because I sang in *The Creation*. He took me back afterwards to the watch-tower, then beat me up because I wouldn't stay the night. You can see why George hated me being around him this summer.'

' "Let us forget the universe, life and heaven itself!" ' A ravishing voice floated across the hot, muggy air. ' "What matters the past? What matters the future? I love you." '

'It's Baby,' sighed Flora, collapsing on a stone bench in ecstasy. 'Doesn't he make even the hair on your legs stand on end?'

'Was George jealous of Baby?' asked Gablecross idly.

'Oh, no,' stammered Flora. 'Baby's just a friend.'

'Are you sure you didn't go to the watch-tower to get these back? They were in Rannaldini's dressing-gown pocket when he was murdered.' Gablecross splayed out the photographs on the bench like a poker hand. Next moment the ground was covered in fish pellets and Trevor had rushed forward to hoover them up.

'Oh, God,' whimpered Flora. 'Baby comforted me after George and I had our screaming match.'

'So you took him home?' Gablecross pointed to a shadowy angel in the background.

'I thought he was gay. By the time I realized he wasn't, it was too late.'

'Seem to be enjoying yourself.'

'Oh, I was, hugely.'

'Was Rannaldini blackmailing you?'

'He threatened to give them to George or the *Scorpion*.'

'Did you burn down Rannaldini's watch-tower?'

'No, no,' protested Flora. Huddled on the stone

bench, she burst into tears again. 'I love George so much. I keep seeing Rannaldini in the wood, sneering even in death. What'll they be doing to him now?'

'Cutting him up, weighing every organ.'

'They won't find a heart.'

'Did you kill him?'

'No, but I wanted to. I must get a taxi.'

They were interrupted by retching. Trevor had thrown up all the pellets back into the mere. Instantly, the great black fish swarmed up to the surface and swallowed the lot.

'Yuk!' screamed Flora. Snatching Trevor and Foxie, she fled towards the house.

'Poor Flora,' said Karen indignantly, as she and Gablecross made their way through the twilight towards the maze. 'I'm sure she didn't do it.'

'In the right place, at the right time, with the right motive.'

'She's terrified, isn't she? Mind you, I'd be terrified of losing a lovely rich bloke like that.'

'Not so lovely,' said Gablecross grimly. 'What's carving up our Flora is panic that George has done it.'

45

Night brought terror. The famous Valhalla Maze, planted in the eighteenth century, towered twenty feet high and extended more than a hundred yards in diameter. Even in daylight, people got lost for hours but now round every twist and turn of the ebony ramparts the murderer might be lurking.

While Carlos sang of his ecstasy that at last his beloved Elisabetta had summoned him by a letter signed 'E' to a midnight tryst, Chloe as Eboli, the real writer of the letter, was being tracked through the maze by Tristan and Valentin on the crane. Racing to meet the man she believed loved her, Chloe paused to spray on scent and rearrange her breasts in the low-cut taffeta.

Like all newcomers, Gablecross and Karen Needham were drawn to the fascination of film-making. From the terrace, they could see not only the singers, almost sanctified by their wonderful costumes – Chloe in her crimson ball dress, Mikhail and Baby in dinner jackets – but also the great paraphernalia of crew, cables and lights, with Bernard barking out instructions and Tristan completely absorbed, despite the tragedy that had broken over his head, encouraging, bullying, shouting 'Cut!' over and over again.

Now he was patiently explaining the plot to Mikhail.

'This is turning point of play. Once Eboli realize Carlos loves the Queen, she will shop them to the King.

Posa realize that not only will his beloved friend Carlos be burnt at the stake for cuckolding the King, but all his plans for liberating Flanders will go up in smoke so he moves in to silence Eboli.'

'I won't need to act at all.' Fingering his flick-knife Mikhail glowered at Chloe.

The crew glanced round nervously. Their instinct was to huddle together, but in doing so, could they be standing next to the killer?

As Tristan filmed an apprehensive, excited Baby in the centre of the maze, Gablecross and Karen buttonholed Chloe in her caravan. Her beauty was heightened by Lucy's make-up and the crimson dress, which matched her sly, smiling mouth and showed off her smooth golden shoulders. One eye was hidden by a black patch. The other glittered like a yellow tourmaline.

'Traditionally Princess Eboli was blind in one eye,' explained Chloe. 'Baby strokes my face in wonder then realizes, as he reaches the eye patch, he's declared passionate love to the wrong woman.'

As Chloe snuggled into a blue-checked armchair, sipping bottled water, and rotating a slender ankle to prove her long skirt wasn't concealing tree-trunks, she seemed to glow with inner happiness, not entirely in-duced by a long lunch with Eulalia Harrison.

She was devastated by Rannaldini's death, she told Gablecross. He had been wonderful to her. She had spent Sunday afternoon at Harvey Nichols' sale trying on hundreds of things but not buying anything. She had been furious to be knocked out of the tournament. Mikhail simply hadn't tried.

'Afterwards I dragged him into the maze, hoping to sober him up enough to rehearse tonight's big scene, but we rowed because I wouldn't go back to Valhalla and sleep with him. Like all men, he was incensed that Lara, his wife, had rumbled us, but still wanted to carry on the *affaire*. He passed out at about nine o'clock under a weeping ash.'

'How did Lara rumble you?' asked Karen.

'Rannaldini was Lord of Misrule on Friday night. He dragged Lara all the way from Moscow, then deliberately arranged for her to catch her husband kissing off my lipstick. Even worse, he relayed over the speakers a tape of Tristan and Meredith bitching about everyone, particularly Hermione. Tristan went berserk and tried to strangle Rannaldini.'

As she talked, Chloe kept stretching like a cat, hollowing her belly in ecstasy. As she looked up under her eyelashes at Gablecross, he found himself squaring his shoulders.

'A crow with a sore throat has better intonation than Dame Hermione,' went on Chloe, 'but she didn't deserve that humiliation. And by playing the tape Rannaldini completely destroyed Tristan's street cred as a nice guy.'

'D'you think he killed him?'

'Possibly. Rannaldini was a deal-maker, Tristan a dream-maker. It was inevitable they'd fall out if they worked together. According to Simone, Tristan cut his aunt's eighty-sixth birthday party in Paris so he could have got back. I always suspected he was one of Rannaldini's illegits. Rannaldini was far nicer to him than to Wolfie. On the other hand, Tristan could be gay, and in love with Rannaldini. Only that could explain how their relationship survived such fearful rows.'

'You reckon?' Gablecross tried to hide his interest.

Karen's eyes were on stalks as she scribbled frantically to keep up.

'Well, Tristan's incredibly buddy-buddy with his foppish French crew. And he's taken all the attractive women in the cast out to dinner but never lifted a finger. Serena Westwood, who's beautiful, had a next-door room to him in Prague. Not a pass was made.'

'Didn't he like Tabitha Campbell-Black?' piped up Karen.

'So did Rannaldini, bats about her.' Taking another slug of bottled water, Chloe told them about the newspapers flaring up under Tab. 'That was probably the first murder. If Tristan hadn't dragged her free, she'd have burnt to death – and good riddance to most people, she's such a brat. Anyway, they fell into a showy clinch, and he whisked her home, leaving Ranners foaming at the mouth and Tristan's admirers ready to slit their throats. But during the night something happened. Perhaps he couldn't get it up, perhaps Rannaldini put the boot in, but the next morning he blew her out. The atmosphere was terrible. Wolfie's had to carry Tristan ever since.'

Chloe smiled wickedly.

'What other soap updates would you like? Flora had a schoolgirl crush on Rannaldini until he dropped her from a great height. This summer he dropped Gloria, Hermione and Serena and didn't provide parachutes for them either, and he was atrocious to Helen, always flaunting other women. Any of that lot could have done it.

'A lot of people', Chloe pondered, 'might have bumped off Rannaldini for being horrible to Tristan, who does inspire devotion. I'm sure Bernard's a closet gay and in love with him. Rozzy Pringle's got a real old lady's crush, posies in his caravan, darning-needles at the ready. And Lucy Latimer, our make-up artist, as they like to be called, shakes so much if Tristan drops into her caravan you risk getting your eyes gouged out with a mascara wand. Lucy's one of those plain women men leave children and dogs *with* rather than wives *for*. Anyone else?' Chloe glanced up at the telephone list beside the mirror. 'Most of the Frog crew were in Paris on Sunday night, but are quite capable of putting a cross-Channel hex on Rannaldini. Mikhail's a kleptomaniac – removes your earrings when he makes a pass and never gives them back.

'Wolfie's cute. He arrived carrying a torch for Flora,

410

but transferred his affections to the brat. Pushy Galore – that's what we call Gloria Prescott – heard Wolfie threatening to kill Rannaldini around ten forty-five on Sunday night. I should wear a chastity belt when you interview Pushy, Detective Sergeant. She's into hunks.'

Looking up from her shorthand notebook, Karen said tartly, 'Alpheus Shaw told us Gloria was a delightful young woman and a lovely singer.'

In a second, Chloe's look of amused composure was wiped off her face. 'Alpheus Shaw – "Offshore", to his accountant – is a serial adulterer,' she hissed. 'He'll have to quarter his consumption, if he's going to play Don Giovanni with any conviction. I don't know who had the bigger ego, him or Rannaldini. But Rannaldini was so incensed that Alpheus beat him at swimming he seduced Alpheus's ghastly wife Cheryl and, playing Leporello, listed every woman Alpheus had been up and down to this summer, which included Hermione *and* Pushy. Alpheus has also been up to one Stradivarius of a tax fiddle, putting, among other things, Mr Bones, his German shepherd, on the payroll as his financial manager. Rannaldini threatened to expose him, refused to replace the Jaguar Wolfie totalled, and teased him about his big nose. Oh, Mr Shaw had plenty of motive to murder Rannaldini.'

Slowly the quiver of rage subsided.

'On a happier note I guess we have to congratulate you,' said Karen innocently. 'I'd love to play Delilah.'

Again, Chloe's face convulsed with fury. 'I'd got that part. That bastard Rannaldini, who saw himself as a global puppeteer, pulled strings and got it given to Cecilia, his geriatric ex-wife, no doubt in lieu of alimony.' Again the rage cooled. 'This is all off-the-record, of course.' Chloe smiled sweetly. 'Eboli is *such* a mischief-maker – I was psyching myself into the part.'

'Would you like to make a statement?'

'Perhaps,' teased Chloe. 'Mikhail tries to stab me in

the next scene. Please stick around and guard me, Detective Sergeant.'

As she turned to the mirror, dabbing away a few beads of sweat with a powder brush, Wolfie popped his head round the door.

'Five minutes, Chloe.'

Gablecross consulted his notes.

'At nine thirty you were heard down by the tennis court making a call on your mobile, asking how things were going.'

'To my mother, I always ring her on Sunday night.'

'And you were phoned back at nine thirty-five, and said,' again Gablecross referred to his notebook, '"OK, terrific. I'll be with you as soon as I can."'

There was a pause.

'Sorry to disappoint you, Sergeant. It was Mummy ringing back. We were arranging lunch. I'd be free, because of night-shooting. She was letting me know Wednesday was fine.'

'Could we have your mother's phone number?'

'I think I chucked it. She's touring abroad, and gave me lots of numbers, probably some hotel.'

Karen made a note to follow this up.

'You left the tennis after that?' she asked.

Playing for time, Chloe rummaged in her handbag for a silver scent spray, squirted it behind her ears and into her cleavage.

'Lovely perfume,' sighed Karen.

'I can never remember what it's called.' Chloe turned back to Gablecross. 'I went for a jog round Paradise. The tennis had hardly been arduous.'

'You've been most helpful,' said Gablecross, leaping to open the door.

'"Just a jog at twilight,"' sang Chloe, disappearing into the night.

'That woman is the biggest bitch,' stormed Karen. 'There isn't a member of the cast she hasn't slagged off.'

'But very useful.' Gablecross squinted at his reflection

412

in Chloe's mirror: perhaps he was hunky rather than fat. 'Wonder why she never married?'

'Prefers to be the leisure activity of some guy cared for by a wife,' said Karen dismissively. 'And her alibi is extraordinarily thin.'

46

Shooting was progressing so much faster now Rannaldini was no longer around to say, 'No, no, no,' that Gablecross was anxious to nail Mikhail before he pushed off. He found him in the bar, a great Russian bear, dropping five Alka-Seltzers into a pint mug of water.

'Is my fault.' Mikhail rolled dark eyes to heaven. 'I drink two litre of vodka yesterday, and even vorse, I have munchies ven I vake, and eat jacket potato with baked beans and two sandwiches filled with bacon, avocado and mayonnaise. Now I feel seek.' He proceeded to refute Chloe's story. 'Bloody bitch is bloody liar. I never sleep viz her and spend only five minutes arguing in maze.'

'She said you argued for several hours.'

'Rubbish! I pass out.'

'With respect, sir, you might not have been in a fit state to remember.'

'I remember her going, I pass out under wiping ash, I also have a perfect motive for murder. Rannaldini set up party knowing I'd be kissing everyvun, then he introduce my vife. I love my vife, and he visks her off to votch-tower, and make me cockhold.'

Karen, who was given to laughter, buried her face in her notebook.

'How d'you know Rannaldini took your wife to his

414

watch-tower? Have you spoken to her since then?'

'Of course not.' Mikhail smote his breast. 'Rannaldini visk all vomen to votch-tower. Whoever murder Rannaldini is 'ero. Vork is vonderful. I am booked for *Figaro*, for recording of *Elijah*. Cecilia Rannaldini, who play Delilah with me, who eat bass baritone for breakfast, ask me to stay in Rome.

'But all that is nothing', Mikhail unhooked Gablecross's Parker pen from his breast pocket to sign the bill, 'vizout my Lara. Vot price crocus-yellow Range Rover I just buy if there is no Lara to drive round steppes?'

He would be back on Wednesday or Thursday, he assured Gablecross, when they could talk more. 'OK, Mr Wolfgang,' he added, as Wolfie appeared at his shoulder. 'I come and am quite sober.' He belched loudly. 'I am off to murder Eboli. Votch my knife slide into that bitch.' Then he burst into earth-shattering song, ' "Vot has he said? Unhappy woman, tremble," ' as he strode off.

Gablecross turned to a grinning Karen. 'Nice straight bloke.' He liked men who loved their wives. 'Good-looking, too. Now where the hell did I put my pen?'

Overhead Jupiter danced a stately gavotte with a newish moon. Below the rows escalated.

'The beetch keeked me on front legs,' roared Mikhail.

'I'm not having him brandishing that knife at me,' screamed Chloe.

A white rose in a plant pot flew out of the maze, narrowly missing Gablecross's head.

'Don't worry,' said a soft, sweet voice, 'they're only psyching themselves up to sing. Come and have a nice cup of tea. My name's Rozzy Pringle.'

The Tristan-worshipper, thought Karen.

Back in Make Up, which was deserted because Lucy was on the set, Karen saw that Rozzy had a lovely face but so criss-crossed with lines it was as though some Victorian beauty was peering through a lattice window.

Since her trip home for Glyn's birthday, Rozzy had abandoned her short, becoming curls and regressed to her seventies style of straight hair falling to below her collarbones with a straggly fringe. Her pale pink lips, and big dark-ringed eyes were seventies too, as were the flat shoes, and the bra-less figure in the calf-length floral shift. Gablecross thought she looked like a hippie Deborah Kerr. His wife, Margaret, was a huge fan of Rozzy.

'It was my husband Glyn's fiftieth birthday yesterday,' she confided. Switching on the kettle, she took some slices of chocolate cake from a polythene bag. 'So I've brought back some of his cake. We've been married twenty years – it seems like yesterday. How long have you been married, Officer?'

Gablecross clapped his head with his palm. 'You *must* remind me,' he begged Karen. 'It's our twentieth anniversary on Sunday. Murder inquiries take over, you forget everything.'

'Have you got kids?' Karen asked Rozzy.

'I'd so love to have had,' sighed Rozzy. 'My husband has two from a previous marriage. But how pretty *you* are, child.' Rozzy gazed at Karen in wonder. 'I bet you're hungry. We've got basil in the window-box outside, I'll make you some tomato sandwiches.'

'Piece of cake'll be fine,' said Gablecross, who wanted to start the questions. 'You must be upset about Rannaldini.'

'Very.' Rozzy's eyes filled with tears. 'He had such a dreadful childhood, you know. His father was a German officer, fighting in Italy at the end of the war, his mother an Italian intellectual. They fell in love, Rannaldini was the result. The officer went back to Germany, the Italian intellectual was married anyway to a farmer, but always felt little Roberto had blighted her political career. She was terribly harsh on him.'

416

Putting three tomatoes in a bowl, Rozzy poured boiling water on them. 'Then, when Rannaldini was only in his teens,' she went on, 'he realized his fairy godmother had given him good looks, alarming charm and musical genius. The world was at his feet, and I'm afraid it spoilt him. But underneath he was sick at heart, because he'd had four wives and endless, endless women, but never been able to maintain anything permanent.'

'What about Dame Hermione?' asked Karen.

'They made a huge amount of money for each other,' said Rozzy tartly, 'ditto Cecilia Rannaldini.'

'How'd you know so much about him?'

'We often worked together.'

With the swiftness of the working stepmother, forced to do things in a hurry, while she had been talking Rozzy had made a pot of tea, put milk in a jug, laid out cups and saucers, skinned and chopped the tomatoes, and topped them with basil, salt and pepper. Now she slapped them between slices of buttered brown bread.

'*Voilà.*' She put the plate of sandwiches in front of Karen. 'Please tuck in too, Detective Sergeant.'

Gablecross patted his gut. 'Can't get into any of my suits. Could you describe your movements on Sunday?'

It seemed her husband's birthday party hadn't been much fun.

'I came out of the kitchen and found Glyn kissing Sylvia, our nanny-stroke-housekeeper.' Rozzy's lip trembled. 'Stroke's the operative word. She's very pretty, and it *was* his birthday.'

'This sandwich is yummy. Did you have a lovely dress?' said Karen, longing to cheer the poor lady up.

'Rainbow-striped silk,' said Rozzy, 'I made it myself.'

'What time did the party end?' asked Gablecross, helping himself to a slice of chocolate cake.

'After midnight, but I'm afraid I sloped off to bed about eight. It'd been going since lunchtime. I had a terrible migraine. About quarter to eleven I suddenly

417

remembered I hadn't rung Lucy. We've become such friends on *Carlos*. I was so distracted by the din still going on at our end that I forgot what I'd rung up for, so I called her back five minutes later to remind her to get Hermione's cloak out of Wardrobe. The wretched thing's gone missing. I wonder if Mikhail's whipped it?'

'Can I have your telephone number at home?' asked Gablecross.

'Actually I rang on my mobile. I found Sylvia's things by Glyn's and my bed,' Rozzy blushed scarlet, 'a horrid porn mag and a jar of baby oil, so I took refuge in the spare room, which doesn't have a telephone.' She gazed down at her roughened hands.

'What a bastard.' Karen attacked the chocolate cake. 'I'd have given him a smack in the face for his birthday.'

Rozzy smiled. 'Flora got her mother, Georgie Maguire, to sign her latest album and some photographs. Glyn is such a fan. He was over the moon, until Sylvia gave him a single of "S'Wonderful". He played it all night.'

'What a plonker,' said Karen furiously.

Gablecross shot her a reproving look. He found Rozzy a little too helpful. He knew the type: professional martyr, brave little wife, who hadn't the guts to walk out and who couldn't bear to relinquish public sympathy. Lacking love at home, they embraced the whole world. Husband probably was a shit. Rozzy clutched herself when she wasn't bustling about and blinked a lot. But Gablecross had stopped relying on body language after he'd seen himself on TV, making a statement at some press conference, blinking and twitching enough to be the Yorkshire Ripper.

'When did you last see Rannaldini?' he asked.

'On Saturday morning. He'd caught me watering his plants very early. I couldn't bear the way he let them die in the drought. He pulled me into his study and shouted at me. It didn't last long.'

'He seems to have rowed with everyone recently,' Gablecross said, starting on the tomato sandwiches. 'Didn't he and Tristan de Montigny fight over Tabitha Campbell-Black?'

'I don't know what you mean.' Gablecross had noticed that women's voices grew shrill and men's thickened whenever Tabitha's name was mentioned.

'We gather she was the only woman Tristan showed any interest in.' Gablecross knew it was cruel, but he wanted to test Rozzy.

Rozzy went on pouring tea into his cup until it spilled over.

'Tabitha had nearly burnt to death,' she said sharply. 'She was badly frightened. He was a grown-up comforting a child.'

'Whose fault was it that the newspaper caught fire?'

'Wolfie's. He hadn't checked properly and one can still contained petrol.'

'Could he have tried to kill Tabitha?'

'Of course not, but Tab and Tristan are quite unsuited. He reads Bach cello suites for pleasure in the evening. Tab's thick, insensitive, and arrogant – just like her father. Tristan's interest in her was over before it began.

'Rannaldini gave Tristan a hard time,' went on Rozzy, clearly not wanting to discuss Tab any more, 'but he did love his godson. Tristan and I get on really well too. He's doing *Rosenkavalier* at Glyndebourne and he's asked me to sing Octavian.'

'Who could have killed Rannaldini?'

'I have no idea. Perhaps it was some Mafia plot.'

'When did you come back to Valhalla?'

'Early this . . .' She glanced at her watch. 'Heavens, it's after midnight. Early yesterday morning.'

'How far's Mallowfield?'

'About fifty miles away.'

Seeing his detective constable was falling asleep, Gablecross ate the last sandwich and called it a day.

'What a lovely lady,' sighed Karen.

'Bit too good to be true. We'd better talk to Glyn and check out her alibi, but it looks as though she's in the clear. I wonder how DC Miller got on with Rupert Campbell-Black.'

47

'There are some advantages to this job, if you get to meet Rupert Campbell-Black,' said DC Miller in excitement. 'He's supposed to be the handsomest man in England.'

'Only because he's loaded and owns a bloody great mansion,' snapped DS Fanshawe, slamming his foot on the accelerator as he turned into Rupert's drive in the hope of smearing the rose-pink lipstick DC Miller was applying to her delectable mouth.

The beeches, forming a halo round Rupert's lovely, pale gold Queen Anne house, were already turning. In the park below, beautiful horses with whisking tails had taken refuge from the heat under great bell-like trees. The rim of brown rush above the water's edge showed how much the lake had dropped. A dozen cars were parked outside an open front door, but no-one answered the bell.

'He's not worried about burglars,' said Debbie Miller.

Shuffling down a rose walk, ankle deep in petals, ducking to avoid spiky unpruned branches, they reached Rupert's yard, which was immaculate but deserted except for a comely girl groom, who was reading a handsome chestnut colt his *Daily Mail* horoscope.

'It's Peppy Koala,' said Debbie in awe. 'Oh, can I stroke him?'

'He's almost as good-looking as you are.' Fanshawe, who considered he had a way with the ladies, smiled at the girl groom. 'Where is everyone?' he asked, waving his ID card.

'Down at the graveyard. I'd wait until they come back.'

But Fanshawe was in a hurry, and paused only to take the serial number of the dark blue helicopter parked in a field behind the stables. Beyond a tennis court surrounded by a shaggy beech hedge, under the shade of a huge cedar, half an acre of grass was fenced off, before the land rolled into fields. For generations, the Campbell-Blacks had buried their best-loved animals here.

Grouped round a single grave were about a hundred people – estate-workers, grooms, gardeners, Rupert's ancient housekeeper Mrs Bodkin and her husband – most of whom were in tears.

'That's Lord O'Hara, and his wife Maud in the big black hat,' hissed Debbie, who scoured the tabloids every day. 'They're Rupert's in-laws, and there's Taggie's elder brother, Patrick – isn't he to die for? And his partner Cameron Cook, she makes films, and there's Taggie's sister Caitlin. She married Lord Baddingham's son, Archie, and Billy Lloyd-Foxe, who show-jumps for England, and his wife Janey, Beattie Johnson's great rival. Beattie's already been digging up the dirt down at Valhalla. Next to her, that gorgeous boy who's crying is Lysander Hawkley. Now this is interesting, he's married to Rannaldini's third wife, Kitty – she's the round-faced one comforting him. And oh, look, there's Ricky France-Lynch! Isn't he gorgeous? And his wife Daisy, the pretty dark one, she paints. They must have driven over from Eldercombe.'

'You ought to work for *Hello!*,' said Fanshawe sourly. 'What the hell's going on?'

Edging forward, they caught sight of Tabitha, who looked as though she'd been struck by lightning. A big purple bruise on her left temple and cuts down her right cheek added the only colour to her deathly pale face. She seemed about to collapse, and was being supported by Rupert's head groom, Dizzy. Next to them, with a face of granite, stood Rupert, holding Xavier and Bianca by the hand. In her other hand Bianca clutched a jam-jar full of harebells, scabious and meadowsweet, while Xavier held on to a carrier-bag and a Labrador as sleek and black as his face. A dozen other dogs milled round, snapping at flies and panting but unusually quiet, and on the other side of the fence, in silent sympathy, stood Rupert's great horse, Penscombe Pride, Tiny the Shetland, and several red and white cows.

Taggie Campbell-Black, paler even than Tabitha, biting her lip to stop herself crying, held Gertrude, wrapped in an old orange and blue blanket, in her arms. Dropping a last kiss on her white forehead, she laid the little dog on her beanbag, already in the grave. On a wonky wooden cross, Taggie had written the words: 'Gurtrude, are most preshous treshure, is berried hear.'

No-one had corrected her spelling.

Stepping forward, Xav dropped a packet of Kit-Kats and a box of Bonios into the grave beside Gertrude, then took his mother's hand. Suddenly Bianca ran forward and knelt by the grave.

'If you're just pretending, Gertrude,' she called out, in a shrill voice, 'now's the time to wake up.'

For a second, laughter rippled round. Then Declan O'Hara stepped forward. Known to cry on every possible occasion, today he was dry-eyed.

'We all loved Gertrude.' His deep, tender Irish brogue echoed round the fields. 'She lived with us in London and the Priory opposite for eight years, and then with Rupert and Taggie for ten. But even this year she would struggle across the valley every morning for a Bonio and a bowl of milk. What we will remember is Gertrude's kindness and her merriness, but none of us would have imagined that such a frail body contained a heart as stout as Beth Gelert.'

As Tab gave a sob, covering her face with her hand, Debbie noticed the dark bruises along the side and up the little fingers. She must have fought someone off like a wild cat. For a second, she swayed. As Rupert caught her, she buried her face in his shoulder.

'Nothing in Gertrude's life became her like the leaving it,' intoned Declan. 'She died as one—'

'Oh, for Christ's sake, Declan, get on,' snapped Rupert.

'We will never forget you,' Declan's voice broke, 'and on your grave, with shining eyes, may the Cotswold stars look down.'

There were flowers everywhere. Xavier picked up a trowel to help his father as, with gritted jaw, Rupert heaped powdery earth over Gertrude's body. The moment he'd finished, muttering about organizing drinks, frantic not to break down, he belted back to the house.

'Pity, with such a turn-out, it wasn't video'd,' Declan's wife Maud was saying fretfully.

Slumped in despair, Taggie stood alone by the grave. But as she turned for home, Debbie and Fanshawe pounced. It was a while before she took in what they were saying.

'Tab's had a terrible shock over Gertrude,' she muttered. 'I don't think she can talk to you.'

'She was at Valhalla, yesterday,' said Fanshawe, flashing his teeth. 'We need to ask her her whereabouts. Uniformed police will be along to fingerprint her later,' he added smoothly.

'You'd better come in,' said Taggie.

Tabitha was in an even worse state, shivering on the drawing-room sofa, gazing into space. Debbie noticed her ankles, criss-crossed with red weals.

'I'll ask the questions,' hissed Fanshawe.

'Great turn-out for a little dog,' he began.

Tab looked at him uncomprehendingly.

'Wonder if you could tell us what you did yesterday from eight o'clock onwards?'

'I worked my horse,' said Tab, in a high, jerky voice.

'What the fuck are you doing?' snarled Rupert, as he barged into the room.

'Investigating the murder of Sir Roberto Rannaldini.' Determined not to let nobs order him around, Fanshawe stood his ground. 'We're checking Mrs Lovell's movements, in case she saw anything unusual.'

'She didn't,' said Rupert coldly. 'She came home because Gertrude died.'

'Can we ask her a few questions?'

'No, you fucking can't.' He turned to Tab. 'You OK, darling?'

From next door could be heard voices and the popping of champagne corks.

'Could we ask you a few questions, then?' asked Debbie, smoothing her blonde bob. Rupert really was gorgeous.

'If you want to, but you'd better be quick.'

'I'll do this one,' hissed Debbie, as they followed Rupert into his office.

Debbie was very much into the non-confrontational, non-judgemental police interview. She was unfazed by the fact that Rupert was reading faxes, watching the first race runners in the paddock on Channel Four, and filling in entry forms. At least it meant he was relaxed.

'I'd like you to shut your eyes, make your mind go blank, Mr Campbell-Black, and remember exactly what Tabitha said when she called you last night.'

'I'll shut my eyes if you both will,' said Rupert, a shade more amiably.

'OK,' said Debbie. 'What time did she ring?'

After a long pause, Fanshawe opened his eyes to see Rupert vanishing through a side door. 'Mr Campbell-Black,' he shouted, 'you are impeding a police inquiry.'

'And we are in the middle of a funeral.'

'Only of a dog, sir.'

The fury on Rupert's face made them both retreat.

'We are investigating the murder of Mrs Lovell's step-father,' protested Fanshawe.

'Who was *only* a human,' said Rupert contemptuously, 'and a particularly loathsome one at that. Now get out.'

'Arrogant shit,' fumed Fanshawe as he belted down the drive.

'How dare he talk to us like that. All those upper-class fuckers stick together. Same when Lord Lucan copped it, they close ranks and keep their traps shut.'

'And just think how Gablecross will sneer when he hears we've been thrown out,' sighed Debbie.

48

DS Gablecross was a deep thinker. He rose early, like the sun, moved slowly round examining everything from a different angle, before setting in the west, sleeping on things before he came to a decision. Reassured by his lazy smile and deep, West Country drawl, few people realized the bitterness and frustration simmering beneath the surface.

In the middle eighties, the world had seemed at his feet. A loving wife had looked after him, his three children hero-worshipped him. Working on hunches, playing suspects against each other, he and his running mate, Charlie, had been the most dazzlingly successful villain-catchers in the West Country. Charlie had not been above knocking suspects about. Like a foxhound, he was the kindest animal in the world until he got on to the scent of a quarry.

But then Gablecross's life had changed. His wife, Margaret, had returned to teaching, the implication being that as he was more interested in catching villains than angling for promotion, they could no longer support three children on a sergeant's salary. She had swiftly risen to deputy headmistress of the local comprehensive. She was so conscientious that Gablecross often returned after midnight to find her asleep over reports or exam papers. He had preferred the old days: being greeted by charred steak and kidney and Margaret feigning sleep through gritted teeth upstairs. His children had also become teenagers, questioning his every attitude, and regarding police-men at best as fascist pigs who persecuted blacks, gays, women and teenagers.

Worst of all, last Christmas Charlie had been shot in a drugs raid. His killer had been the brother of a young black guy who had committed suicide after Charlie had forced a confession out of him and banged him up for five years.

But if Gablecross's world had been turned upside down, so had the law. As a result of the 1984 Act, hunches suddenly had to be justified and everything backed up with forensic or tape-recorded evidence. Supposed to make it easier to prove guilt, this gradually took the personality out of investigation and only the safety players prevailed. As a result, Gablecross's battle-scarred contemporaries had taken early retirement or dull jobs in security. But being a hunter was the only thing Gablecross knew.

Surrounded by the fresh-faced young turks of the inquiry team, he felt old, edgy, almost a figure of fun. Particularly, as if to rub salt in the wound of Charlie's death, the dandified ego-maniac Gerald Portland had teamed him up with the only black on the inquiry team, Karen Needham.

Karen, who had watched every instalment of *Prime Suspect*, intended to be the first woman head of Scotland Yard. A dusky Cleopatra, with long shiny hair drawn back in a dark blue bow, she had an undulating body and legs so long they made all skirts look like minis. Whenever she swayed through the incident room, the telephones and word-processors fell silent.

Karen, like Debbie Miller, was messianically into the peace interview. You made witnesses and suspects feel you were fascinated in them and what they had done. You utterly understood their trespasses, whether they had abused a tiny child or bashed up an old lady. Faced with her sweet smile and big kind eyes, everyone sang to the rooftops.

All the young turks told Gablecross he was a lucky sod to be paired with someone so pretty and clever. But Gablecross, who liked women, felt he was being sexist if he told Karen she looked beautiful, and racist if he complained about her slow driving and the even slower way she took down evidence in her clear round hand. Otherwise she had only one drawback: she couldn't contain her laughter, even during interviews, over the absurdities of life.

Chief Inspector Portland was crazy about her. In his most paranoid moments Gablecross imagined their pillow-talk.

'Who would you like to work with, Karen?'

'I'd like to zap that arrogant, geriatric, racist, homophobic pinko-basher Tim Gablecross.'

Gablecross found Portland hell to deal with. One of a breed known as 'butterflies', the handsome Chief Inspector had moved from station to station, upping his status and his salary, ironing out his accent. He had a rich wife, children at private day schools, their photographs prominently displayed on his desk, and an old house outside Rutminster, much modernized and crammed with inglenooks. Portland had been so busy going on courses he had never had time to be a policeman. Although he was a good manager and, out of laziness, able to delegate, he didn't want anyone stealing his limelight. He would have preferred a team composed entirely of keen, deferential youngsters, but to crack this murder and cover himself with glory he needed Gablecross's local knowledge and his genius at nosing out a killer.

Despite a shower, Gablecross felt crumpled and sweaty when he rolled up for the first early-morning briefing on Tuesday. Portland, on the other hand, his chestnut hair matching his smooth brown face, looked as sleek and shining as a new conker. Having hung his coat, with the Cardin label, on the back of his chair, loosened his tie and rolled up his very white shirt-sleeves to show off suntanned arms, he smiled briskly at Gablecross.

'Lady Chisledon phoned to complain you didn't have enough identification, Tim, when you popped in yesterday. Said the photo on your ID card makes you look more villainous than any of your suspects. Suggest you get a more flattering one and stop frightening the witnesses.'

Sitting and standing around Portland's office, laughing deferentially, were the Inner Cabinet. They consisted of two boffins from the incident room, where a Home Office computer was gathering all data on the murder, two reps from the uniformed house-to-house task force, and twelve plain-clothes officers in teams of two. These included Gablecross and Karen, Gablecross's bitter rival, the fit, flat-stomached Kevin Fanshawe and Debbie Miller, who'd fallen foul of Rupert yesterday, the blushing DC Lightfoot, who'd been traumatized by the Valhalla orgy, and the aggress-ive DC Smithson, who was, above all, present and politically correct, sir.

From now on the Cabinet would meet every morning to absorb what had happened the day before. Gerry Portland's job was to read autopsy reports, printouts and statements, corroborate all the evidence and give each team lines to follow.

And then go and sleep on the sunbed, thought Gablecross.

On the wall, beside group photographs of Portland's various courses, was a map of Paradise and Valhalla with Rannaldini's watch-tower, the tennis court and Hangman's Wood ringed in red. A day chart, listing the pairs of the inquiry team and the leads they were following, was flanked by a blow-up of Hype-along Cassidy's photograph of the entire unit.

The meeting began with a debriefing. Some officers had been unravelling the tangled skeins of Rannaldini's last hours, when he seemed to have upset everyone, some talking to the family, others touring the houses of Paradise.

'Problem with this lot, guv'nor,' said Fanshawe, 'is they're used to dodging awkward questions and evading the press. They're lying, but they're all shit scared. They can't believe the reign of terror's over.'

'Won't be when Rupert Campbell-Black moves in,' snapped Portland. He was livid that Fanshawe and Miller had been chucked out. There was no way Rupert was going to walk all over his team.

'You sort him out, Tim,' he added, as a sop to the crack about the ID photograph. 'Nail him when he rolls up to kick ass on the set this evening. Don't let Karen's legs distract him.' As he smiled at her, the politically correct DC Smithson looked boot-faced: only by persistent lobbying had she got the girlie calenders taken down from the male officers' walls.

On their return from Penscombe, Fanshawe and Miller had interviewed Mr Brimscombe. Dead-heading the rose walk, he had seen Tabitha racing towards Rannaldini's watch-tower in a pretty grey dress 'wafting perfume, and all dolled up' for the first time in months. Empty-handed, she had waved and run on.

Several people, according to the house-to-house team, had seen, after ten fifteen, the ghost of Caroline Beddoes, clutching a little dog, with her ripped grey dress soaked in blood. After one sighting, the captain of the Paradise Cricket Club had rushed into the Pearly Gates begging for a quadruple whisky.

Wolfgang Rannaldini had claimed Tabitha went home because her stepmum's dog went missing, said Gablecross.

'Dead now,' said Debbie Miller. 'Kevin and I stumbled on this weird funeral yesterday. Tabitha looked like a battered ghost.'

'Leave her a couple of days till we get the post-mortem, but her alibi looks very thin. Have a look at her cottage,' Portland told Fanshawe. 'Talk to the servants at Penscombe and Valhalla, have a word with Tab's husband. We know Wolfgang switched on the machine at Valhalla around ten forty-five,' he went on, 'and claims she asked him to take her own dog back to Penscombe.'

'Chloe Catford claims Wolfie swore he was going to kill his dad after hearing that tape,' said Gablecross. 'Unfortunately it's gone missing. Wolfie probably whipped it.'

The memoirs and Rannaldini's safe had also gone walkabout. Miss Bussage was the chief suspect in the case of the former, but she certainly hadn't smuggled the safe into the limo when she left.

'Go and see her, Tim,' grinned Gerald Portland. 'You're good with maiden ladies. Ask her if she knows why Rannaldini went to the doctor on Friday, and if she knows the whereabouts of a Picasso and the Étienne de Montigny hanging in Rannaldini's watch-tower. Both may have been torched in the fire, but if stolen, could be a motive for murder.'

Other tasks included checking who had helicopters in the area, other than Rupert Campbell-Black and George Hungerford, and which one had landed beside Hangman's Wood on Sunday night.

Out of the window, through the trees, Gablecross could see the Herbert Parker Hall, home of the Rutshire Symphony Orchestra. He wondered what their boss, George Hungerford, had thought of Flora's and Baby's photographs.

'Hungerford was seen driving towards Valhalla like a bat out of hell around ten twenty-five on Sunday night,' said one of the house-to-house team. 'And Montigny went the other way, only earlier.'

'Tristan was seen at Valhalla by Jessica. God, she's

gorgeous,' sighed DC Lightfoot, 'and by that Russian, Mikhail Pezcherov, but he was too smashed to be trusted.'

'Pezcherov claims he spent five minutes on Sunday night in the maze with Chloe Catford. She says it was three hours,' volunteered Gablecross.

'Time flies when you're enjoying yourself,' giggled Debbie Miller.

Checks would have to be carried out on whether Chloe's mother, Alpheus's agent and Rozzy Pringle had made phone calls when they were said to have done. Lady Griselda, Bernard Guérin, Granville Hastings, none of them fans of Rannaldini, had all been crashing around looking for balls near the watch-tower at the time of the murder.

'Flora Seymour and Meredith Whalen have very thin alibis, but Sexton Kemp looks in the clear,' said Gablecross.

'I spent most of last night trying to pin down Baby Spinosissy-something,' said Fanshawe crossly. 'Dame Hermione was also too upset to speak to anyone, but I'm certain they're talking to the press if not to us.'

'Hermione was heard singing in the wood around ten thirty,' said Gablecross.

'Could have been another singer,' piped up Karen Needham. 'Flora Seymour or Chloe Catford.'

'She's a cracker.' Fanshawe raised his eyes to heaven.

'Or Gloria Prescott,' said DC Lightfoot, 'another cracker.'

'Which one's she?' Portland peered at the blow-up.

'That one. She's blinking but her boobs aren't,' said DC Lightfoot excitedly, and got punched in the ribs by DC Smithson.

'Go and see Dame Hermione, Tim,' said Portland. 'You're good with middle-aged nymphos too, but remember, her alarm's wired by umbilical cord to the Chief Constable's navel, so watch it.'

Gablecross ground his teeth. The rest of the team laughed.

The French crew had evidently been hopeless to interview. Their English, which had improved so dramatically during filming, had deteriorated equally dramatically when confronted by DC Smithson's truculence.

' "I was weeth heem, and he was weeth me and other heems, and heem was with heem," ' snapped DC Smithson. 'They're more obstructive than that appalling Campbell-Black.'

'But not quite as gorgeous,' sighed Debbie.

'We have a host of suspects.' Portland rubbed his hands together. 'Priority is to find the memoirs and Rannaldini's safe.'

'Clive may have got them,' said Gablecross. 'He was whispering to that ugly cow from the *Sentinel* yesterday.'

'Well, nobble him today.'

While Portland gave the others lines to follow, Gablecross's mind drifted back to something old Miss Cricklade, who took in washing, had told him when he'd given her a lift into Rutminster that morning. What with Dame Hermione, Miss Bussage in Abingdon, Clive, if he could catch him, Rupert Campbell-Black on the set this evening, it was going to be a long day.

He was brought back to earth by DC Smithson whining that everyone at Valhalla was a publicity-obsessed nutter.

'Well, as one not unacquainted with the media,' Portland examined his fingernails, 'you have to know how to use them. I suggest we ask the help of Lady Rannaldini to appeal to the nation for info.'

'She was in bad shape yesterday,' said Gablecross quickly.

But Portland wasn't listening. He loved press conferences and publicity. He couldn't wait to wrap up the meeting so he could gloat over the smashing photographs of himself in the morning's papers.

'Doubt if you'd learn much,' Gablecross was saying. 'Certain it's an inside job.'

'I'm the best judge of that,' said Portland coolly. 'Lady R's a lovely lady, she's chairman of Enid's NSPCC committee.'

'She could start by paying more attention to her own child,' snapped Gablecross.

49

Few people had seen inside Hermione's pretty Georgian Mill – which stood, hidden by trees, two hundred yards from the river Fleet – because she was far too lazy and tight with money to entertain.

Gablecross was surprised therefore to find the dark green front door open and his wife's favourite singer standing radiant and smiling in the hall. Only when he'd waved his ID card at her did he realize that he was about to shake the outstretched hand of a replica of Hermione's waxwork in Madame Tussaud's.

'Pack it in,' he hissed, as Karen burst out laughing. 'Show some fucking respect.'

Dame Hermione, veiled and clad entirely in black, lay on a dark red *chaise-longue*, with Sexton and Howie dancing attendance. Hermione had not forgiven Howie for being in the know about Pushy's top notes and espousing her cause as Delilah, and was determined he shouldn't get any cut out of her newspaper deals, offers of which were pouring in from all over the world and being handled by Sexton. Howie, who loathed the country, was equally determined to hang in.

Spurred on by Gerry Portland's mockery and having often been impeded in car chases by Dame Hermione's limo, parked slap across Paradise High Street, Gablecross was determined to stand no nonsense. This excited the hell out of Hermione, who loved her men masterful. Whipping back her veil, she patted the sofa beside her. 'I know we're going to be friends, let's call each other by our given names. Mine's Hermione, and yours is . . . ?'

'Officer,' said Karen tartly.

'Shut up,' snarled Gablecross. 'It's Timothy.'

'Does she have to be in here?' Hermione glared at Karen.

'Yes,' said Gablecross regretfully.

'I've just been talking to my very good friend Chief Constable Swallow,' announced Hermione.

Which, translated, thought Karen, means, 'Mess with me and you're a dead duck.' Looking round the room, she decided, you could fall asleep counting the photographs, paintings and sculptures of Hermione. Magazines with her face on the cover lay on a nearby table. Among the trophies on the shelf was the Artist of the Year award she'd won in October.

'I urged the Chief Constable to call a press conference,' Hermione was now telling Gablecross, 'so I can beseech people to come forward and shed light on this dreadful crime. My son, Little Cosmo, has lost a father, I a cherished friend.'

'Lady Rannaldini might want to do it,' said Sexton, as he whisked out of the room to get to the telephone before Howie.

'Lady Rannaldini has no experience of the media,' said Hermione dismissively.

'Nor is she as universally beloved as you, Dame Hermione,' lied Howie.

'Indeed.' Hermione bowed, then turned to Gablecross. 'I have had a thousand and twenty-three letters already, Timothy, and lost ten pounds in weight.'

Sexton, thank goodness, was as adept at twiddling the knobs on her weighing scales as Rannaldini had been on her recordings.

'I feel I owe it to my public, and to Rannaldini, to appeal to the nation on television,' went on Hermione.

'I wouldn't, Hermsie.' Sexton trotted back into the room and squeezed her hand. 'They always turn out to be the one wot's done it.'

'Sexton, Sexton.' Hermione gave a low laugh. 'How wise you are.'

'It's the *Guardian* on the phone,' whispered Sexton.

'I'll tell them you're out.' Howie leapt to his little feet.

'Out?' thundered Hermione, as if she'd sallied forth on some junket. 'I shall never go out again. I must speak with them, for Rannaldini's sake.' She seized the telephone. 'Mr Rusbridger? Alan? . . . No, my producer has brought me fresh fruit and Belgian chocolates to keep up my strength for the sake of my public.'

'Do you know what Helen is wearing for the funeral?' she asked Sexton, as she came off the telephone five minutes later. 'Could you ask Lady Griselda to pop in this afternoon? I shall wear black, of course, and a veil.'

'Thin enough to show the tragedy etched on your lovely features.' Howie was laying it on with a JCB.

Karen got the giggles again, and had to take her notebook over to the window and gaze at the dried-up river as Gablecross tried to pin down Hermione on her movements on Sunday night. People had seen her returning around eight in Rannaldini's helicopter.

'I had been concertizing at an open-air gala in Milan. Because the proceeds were going towards a new hospital,' added Hermione virtuously, 'I only charged my charity fee of sixty thousand pounds.'

That's more than I earn in four years, thought Karen in disgust.

'Around the time Rannaldini died,' Gablecross pressed on, 'at about ten thirty, several witnesses heard you singing a number from *Don Carlos* in the wood. They said a voice had never sounded more exquisite.'

'Then it must have been mine,' twinkled Hermione.

'Did you walk through the wood on Sunday night?'

'Timothy, Timothy, if I sang *pianissimo* from the garden at River House, my voice would float across to

438

Valhalla, but I didn't go out. It must have been a tape or a CD. Rannaldini had plenty. He was clearly comparing them with the rushes.'

'People have said your voice was unaccompanied.'

'I often sang for him alone.'

'So you didn't leave home at all?'

'Certainly not. I rushed back from Milan to spend quality time with my son Cosmo. I spent the rest of the evening recharging my spiritual batteries. I needed to be fresh for Monday, in case Rannaldini wanted to reshoot Act Five. Or, if he'd carried on with the schedule, I had an important ballroom scene in Act Two, Scene Two. I won't pass for nineteen if I don't get my eight hours,' she added skittishly.

'What else did you do?'

'I was tucked up in bed with camomile tea, like the Flopsy Bunnies,' Hermione put on a soppy face, 'by nine o'clock, to watch *Pride and Prejudice*. It's my favourite novel.'

'Who's your favourite character in it?' asked Karen innocently.

'Emma Woodhouse,' replied Hermione, without missing a beat. 'She's beautiful and headstrong. Fans have often compared us.'

For a second, Karen's eyes met Sexton's. She wondered if she recognized pleading.

'And my husband Bobby rang me from Australia for a chat around ten forty-five,' said Hermione airily.

'Does your husband mind Little Cosmo being Rannaldini's son?' asked Gablecross.

'Not in the least. We have a very close and open marriage, Timothy. Bobby is devoted to Little Cosmo.'

Gablecross couldn't dent her. Rannaldini's playing the evil tape on Friday night, his flirtations with Pushy, Serena, Cheryl, Lara, even Tabitha, his threats to replace her with a younger singer had been all part of a game to goad her into singing more beautifully.

'What he loved about me, Timothy, was my ability to

rise to the challenge. Ours was a special relationship. Are you married?'

'My wife's your greatest fan,' blushed Gablecross.

Surreptitiously scraping a sticker saying 'American Bravo Library Copy, Do Not Remove' from its case, Hermione brandished a CD called *Only for Lovers*.

'What's your wife's given name? I've had two thousand five hundred and twenty-two letters and lost over a stone, you know. I simply can't eat.'

'I've roasted a little chicken for lunch,' said Sexton, bustling in in a striped apron.

'Well, perhaps I could manage a slice,' admitted Hermione, as she wrote her name on the CD sleeve.

Shoulders shaking frantically, Karen was gazing intently at the river again.

'We're off, Karen,' said Gablecross icily.

'Leave the poor child,' cried Hermione. 'She is only weeping, like the whole world, for Maestro's death.' Then, catching sight of Rannaldini's photograph on the CD case, handsome and smiling with his hands on her bare shoulders, Hermione broke into genuine tears of despair. 'You will bring his killer to justice, won't you, Timothy?'

On the way out, Sexton made a brief statement.

'I ought to fill you in on my movements on Sunday night, Tim. Frankly it was Sunday, Bloody Sunday. I 'ad a hellish day trying to drum up money. Rannaldini had fucked us with his delaying tactics, refusing to release any dosh until Tristan gave in to his demands.

'I left London after midnight, shattered. But I wanted to be there on Monday morning in case fings turned nasty after Rannaldini playing that evil tape on Friday night. Anyway, Wally and I was about to come off the motorway wiv only the hard shoulder to cry on, when Bernard rang and said Rannaldini'd copped it.'

'What time was that, sir?'

'One fifteen. I called Rupert Campbell-Black. Luckily

he'd just got back, and agreed to come in and save the movie.'

'Just like that?' asked Karen.

'He's that sort of bloke. Then we belted down to Valhalla, as Bernard and I agreed', there was pride in Sexton's voice now, 'I should be the one to break the sad news to Dame Hermione.'

'Look after her,' Gablecross was amazed to hear himself saying.

'The fat cow's lying through her teeth,' fumed Karen, as they walked back to the car. 'Imagine thinking Emma Woodhouse was the heroine of *Pride and Prejudice*. The only thing the silly bitch reads is rave reviews and the directions on the Prozac bottle.'

'And Sexton had a lot to lose if the film went belly-up,' mused Gablecross.

'And Rupert Campbell-Black had only just come in at one fifteen,' said Karen. 'What was he doing in the meanwhile?' She wished Gablecross would loosen up. As a cop you often had to laugh to stop yourself crying. She wasn't looking forward to him wincing over her driving all the way to Abingdon to see Miss Bussage.

50

Rupert arrived at his first night's filming in a murderous mood. If he hadn't spurned Tab and let her fall among thieves, she would never have married so disastrously. And Rannaldini would never have been reduced to kidnapping Gertrude. He felt directly responsible both for the rape and Gertrude's death, and his brain filled with blood whenever he thought of it.

He had agreed to save *Don Carlos* because he wanted to make a not-so-quick buck and amends to Tab. But talking to her the following day, he learnt of Tristan's treachery and only hung in because of her pleading.

'But the fucker blew you out.'

'I know,' sobbed Tab. 'But I still love him and maybe with Rannaldini out of the way . . .'

She was so near the edge, raging one moment, sobbing wildly the next, or just gazing into space, he didn't want to push her into the abyss.

Over at Valhalla, excitement at his impending arrival had reached fever pitch. Chloe, already buoyed up by fifty thousand from the *Daily Mail*, calls from La Scala and the Opéra Bastille, and the press yelling, 'Chloe, Chloe, Chloe,' whenever she passed, was now squirming lasciviously in front of the mirror in Make Up.

'I want an ace face for Rupert, Lucy Lockett.'

'That *would* be an Everest for you,' said Baby irritably,

as he pored over accounts of the murder in all the papers.

'The prospect of having Tab as a stepdaughter would deter even me,' sighed Chloe, 'but one could always dally.'

'Rupert's mad about his wife,' said Lucy crossly, as she clipped Chloe's fringe to one side.

'That's a nice picture of *moi*.' Chloe glanced sideways. 'What paper's that?'

'The *Scorpion*. They list you as a prime suspect, alongside most of the cast, plus Helen, Wolfie and Tristan.'

'Ouch, care*ful*,' squeaked Chloe, as Lucy knocked over a bottle of base, narrowly missing three thousand pounds' worth of crimson taffeta. 'Don't mention that name in our make-up artist's presence.'

One flare-up was averted by Lucy's mobile ringing, which triggered off another. 'No, I cannot do your roots, Meredith,' shouted Lucy. 'I don't care if Rupert is due later, the cast has priority.'

From an upstairs window, Helen watched the press go berserk at the bottom of the drive as her ex-husband's dark blue helicopter landed.

It was absolutely typical. Not only had Rupert won Tab back, he was now swanning in like a prince, stalking towards the maze, with fat Sexton running to keep up, passing Jessica and Simone, who swung round in wonder. When would Rupert bloody well lose his looks?

'You wouldn't have a moment to pop in and see Dime Hermione?' panted Sexton.

'Not unless you provide guards and a chastity-belt,' replied Rupert.

'Here comes Beauty-with-Cruelty,' sighed Meredith, adjusting the baseball cap now hiding his roots.

The setting sun had lent a warmth to Rupert's sleek blond hair and added a touch of colour to his unusually pale face, but his mouth was set in an ugly line, and the glare he gave Tristan could have halted global warming for several decades.

'It's very good of you to help us out.' Nervously, Tristan extended a hand, which Rupert ignored. This was the bastard who'd broken Tab's heart.

Having nodded curtly at Wolfie, and Lucy, who he knew slightly as a friend of Tab's, and kissed Griselda, who he remembered from deb dances in the early seventies, he said:

'OK, let's get on with it.'

Rupert had never taken on anything he couldn't do. Brilliant at show-jumping, he had been a highly successful, if unorthodox, MP and Minister for Sport, a hot-shot financial director of Venturer Television and now, because he'd learnt patience at last and refused to push horses that needed more time, he was one of the leading owner-trainers in the world. But the snail's pace of filming defeated him. How could you spend a hundred and fifty thousand a day on something quite so ridiculous? The caterwauling from the speakers gave him a headache. The only time that number of people had stood around at Penscombe in the last twenty years had been at Gertrude's funeral.

'What the hell's going on?' he asked Tristan.

'Carlos receive letter summoning him to a rendez-vous. He think it is from his stepmother, who he adores. But it is from his father's mistress, who adores him. So if you imagine your mistress . . .'

'I don't have a mistress,' said Rupert icily.

'*Dommage*,' chorused Chloe and Simone.

The crew grinned.

'Well, imagine your son being madly in love with your wife.'

'Impossible,' said Rupert, even more icily. 'Marcus is a homosexual.'

'Well,' Tristan struggled on, 'Carlos is so carried away with excitement, he declares passionate love to wrong woman.'

'Is he pissed? Then how could he possibly mistake Clare—?'

'Chloe!' interrupted Chloe in outrage.

'Sorry, Chloe for Hermione. Hermione's three times her size.'

Chloe blew Rupert a kiss.

'Why didn't you choose singers the same size?' persisted Rupert.

'They were chosen for their voices.' Tristan was just managing to keep his temper. 'In the dark it is easy to mistake people.'

'It isn't dark.' Rupert glared round at Oscar's lights. 'We could be in Blackpool at the height of the season.'

Later they'd moved on to the trio.

'"Tomorrow the earth will open up to swallow you,"' sang Chloe, scowling at Baby.

'"May the earth open up to swallow you,"' sang Mikhail, scowling at Chloe.

'"If only the earth would open up to swallow me,"' sang Baby.

'Cut,' shouted Rupert.

The music ground discordantly to a halt.

'Tristan is directing this film, Monsieur Campbell-Black,' bellowed an apoplectic Bernard.

'Why do these singers keep repeating themselves?' demanded Rupert sarcastically. 'I thought we were trying to make this film shorter, this film shorter, this film shorter.'

The crew corpsed again.

'The Chief Constable of Rutminster's called Swallow,' said Meredith chattily.

'Shut up, Meredith,' howled Tristan and Bernard.

'And why isn't that camera motorized?' Rupert pointed at a buckling Ogborne, pushing Valentin along the tracks. 'We gave up ploughing with horses forty years ago at Penscombe.'

'Why's that man with a beard sticking a knife into that pretty girl?' demanded Rupert ten minutes later.

'He's a freedom fighter,' hissed Griselda.

'Typical leftie behaviour,' said Rupert scornfully. 'Why haven't you given him sandals and an Adam's apple?'

After Mikhail had offered Rupert a slug of vodka, he decided he was quite nice for a leftie.

There was a sticky moment during the break when a hopelessly goaded Tristan made the mistake of assuming Rupert spoke as little French as his daughter.

'How can that imbecile Sexton have brought in such an ignorant, pig-headed, obstructionist ape?' he stormed to Valentin.

'Because you'd have folded, if he hadn't,' said Rupert coldly.

Like children who behave worse when their mother wants them on their best behaviour, Tristan's cast started acting up.

'"I have stained the name of my mother,"' sang Baby piously, in the middle of a perfect take.

'Vot colour 'ave you stained her?' sang back Mikhail.

'I have stained her Prussian blue-hoo-hoo.'

'Cut!' howled Tristan. 'Cut, cut, cut, you fuckers!' then stopped in mid-blast as a mobile rang.

'Telephones are not allowed on the set,' roared Bernard.

'It's mine,' mumbled Tristan, disappearing into the dark labyrinths of the maze.

The trees on the horizon were still black silhouettes, but colour was creeping into the foreground. Pigeons were cooing sleepily, thrushes repeating phrases like singers, when at four thirty Tristan called a wrap. Despite Rupert's constant interference, a miraculous minute or two was in the can. Mikhail's flick-knife had gone safely back to the props van. Everyone was glad to gather round Maria's barbecue on which tandoori chicken, sausages, and tomatoes stuffed with herbs sizzled enticingly. As an extra treat after a long night, Maria had made a huge bread and butter pudding. Bottles of red and white were on the tables.

Rupert was very hungry, and could have done with a drink, but he was loath to fraternize. Back at Penscombe, his stable lads would be out on the gallops in an hour, he hated to miss anything.

Gablecross, who'd been waiting patiently all night, edged towards him. 'Can I have a word, Mr Campbell-Black?'

'No, you can't,' said Rupert curtly. 'I'm off.'

Despite Rupert's antagonism, Tristan, having heard hideous rumours about Rannaldini and Tab, had returned to his caravan and was taking a huge bunch of freesias from a bucket. Wrapping them in the only pages of yesterday's *Le Figaro* not devoted to the murder, he caught up with his new executive producer as Rupert was leaving the canteen.

'Would you please take these to Tabitha and give her, er, my love?'

Suddenly, in front of the entire unit, Rupert's rage boiled over. 'Not after the way you fucked her up, dumping her the moment you pulled her.'

Tristan was greyer than the pre-dawn sky but he held his ground. 'It is not as you think.'

'Don't tell me what I think, you fucking Frog. I may have made it possible for you to finish your poxy film, because Tab put so much work into the horses, but, believe me, sunshine, it has nothing to do with you. Back off and leave her alone.'

Lucy couldn't bear to look at Tristan, she had never hated anyone as much as Rupert, particularly when he snatched Tristan's flowers to chuck them on the barbecue. But suddenly Rozzy erupted from nowhere.

'Shut up, you fucking bully!' she screamed, grabbing the flowers from him.

Oscar choked on his half pint of red, Bernard on his bread and butter pudding. Everyone who had turned away in embarrassment turned back in amazement. Rozzy swearing?

'You shouldn't judge without knowing the facts,' she shouted. 'If Tristan hadn't risked his life dragging Tab from the fire she wouldn't be alive today. Naturally Tab was terrified, and Tristan comforted her. You ought to go down on your knees with gratitude you've still got a daughter, you loathsome brute.'

Rupert looked at Rozzy incredulously. 'My God, the mouse has roared.'

'And how d'you know he seduced Tab?' said Rozzy furiously. 'You've only got her word for it, just as you've only got her word that Rannaldini—'

'Shut up, you bitch.' Wolfie was shaking Rozzy like a rat. 'Take that back.'

Instantly Bernard moved in to separate them, and Rozzy collapsed sobbing in his arms.

'Much more exciting than Verdi,' said Meredith, selecting another spicy sausage. 'Why don't you film this instead, Tristan?'

A piercing shriek from the direction of Wardrobe stopped everyone in their tracks. Wearily putting clothes back on their hangers, Griselda discovered Hermione's new willow-green rose-lined cloak had been delivered from Paris during the night. Assuming someone had signed for it, Griselda had picked up the receipt. On the dotted line in unmistakable emerald-green ink was scrawled the word 'Rannaldini'.

'I know he's alive,' gibbered Griselda as, with purple turban askew, she lumbered elephantine and quaking into the canteen.

'Pissed again,' muttered Ogborne.

But as everyone crowded round, the signature on the receipt, which Gablecross promptly pocketed, was agreed to be perfect.

'Perhaps Bussage is getting her revenge for being fired,' said Wolfie, who'd gone as green as his father's signature. 'She faked Papa's name on enough fan photos and documents.'

But when Bernard rang the messenger, who was speeding towards Dover, he insisted that a gentleman, smelling very strongly of scent and wearing a long black cloak with a turned-up collar, had signed for the parcel. It had been very dark. He had assumed it was one of the cast.

'It must have been the cloak Rannaldini wore to sweep on to the rostrum on Friday night,' whispered a terrified Griselda.

'There's obviously a perfectly simple explanation,' said Rupert, escaping to his helicopter and the safety of Penscombe.

All the birds were singing, the grumbling of the crows in the beeches providing the fauxbourdon, as Simone, Baby and Lucy trailed wearily back to their beds.

'I don't know which is worse,' shivered Lucy, 'a murderer mad enough to dress up as Rannaldini, or the return of Rannaldini himself.'

'I'm sure I saw him yesterday at that blocked-up window.' Simone's pointing finger trembled.

'Well, he made a copy of everything else,' drawled Baby. 'Why not of himself?'

Thank God the sun was rising, shining cheerfully into their faces. Lucy fell into bed but not to sleep. How wonderful Rozzy had been. Oh, why hadn't *she* been brave enough to stick up for Tristan?

51

Having drawn a blank with Rupert, Gablecross was driving wearily out of Valhalla in the hope of a couple of hours' sleep when he noticed lights on in Clive's flat over the stables. Remembering his conversation yesterday with Miss Cricklade, he pulled in.

Miss Cricklade, the local busybody, lived on the west side of Paradise High Street. Between training her binoculars on Valhalla and watching *Pride and Prejudice* on Sunday night, she had seen Clive, Rannaldini's dreaded *éminence grise,* calling on Nicky Willard next door around eight o'clock. He had only stayed ten minutes but, during this time, a little white mongrel had been yapping continually in his car.

'If she went on like that,' Miss Cricklade had told Gablecross indignantly, 'she would have lost her bark, like my Judy did when she went into kennels. I was about to complain when Clive came out and drove off.

'But he was back to see Nicky around nine thirty,' Miss Cricklade had gone on. 'Nicky's mum and dad had gone to Bath for the evening. I gave a scream when I saw Valhalla going up in flames. Next moment, Clive came out of Willard's house like a bat out of hell. I don't think George and Grace Willard would have liked him being there. I don't trust that Clive.'

Nor did Gablecross. He had waived sentences against

him in the past in return for information. Now it was time to call in the marker – particularly as Bussage had implied that Clive knew where Rannaldini's safe, containing a second set of memoirs, was hidden.

He had to lean on the bell for five minutes before he was let in by Clive, clearly furious at the interruption. There was not a speck of dust in the upstairs flat, which was furnished with chrome and black leather. Sado-masochistic literature and videos filled the bookshelves. Posters of muscular youths on motorbikes with tufts of blond hair emerging under bikers' caps adorned the walls. On the mantelpiece was a photograph of a young Clive and a middle-aged woman with pigeons on their shoulders in Trafalgar Square.

Even though it was five o'clock in the morning, Clive was fully dressed in leather trousers and a very white vest, showing off tattoos of bleeding hearts and black widow spiders.

Gablecross realized he must keep his wits about him if this especially slippery fish wasn't to slide through his fingers, and baldly kicked off with the fact that several independent witnesses had reported Clive spending several hours at Nicky Willard's house on Sunday night. Nicky Willard was only sixteen going on forty-five. Unless Clive wanted to be banged up for five years, he had better sing to the rooftops.

Clive promptly played, then handed over the tape he'd stolen from the answering-machine at Valhalla on Sunday night. No wonder Wolfie had wanted to kill his father, thought Gablecross. No wonder Rupert had wanted to kill everyone.

'Where does the little dog come in?' he asked sternly.

Clive displayed uncharacteristic shame. He admitted stealing Gertrude, but hadn't realized Rannaldini would use her as bait.

'Rupert will kill me if he finds out. I want a safe house,' he whined.

451

'He'll certainly rearrange your features. Where are Rannaldini's keys? There was no sign of them in the ashes.'

'The murderer must have whipped them, which means he's got the master key to every bedroom.'

'Good God!'

'More than that. Every room – including the dressing rooms, the caravans and the cottages – was bugged for sound. There were hidden cameras everywhere so he could watch people, or video their goings-on. He had a stranglehold like the Spanish Inquisition.'

Suddenly Gablecross didn't feel tired any more.

'What exactly were your movements on Sunday night?' he asked, as Clive made him a cup of black coffee.

'I delivered Taggie's dog to the watch-tower around eight fifteen, brought Tabloid back here, walked him and Rannaldini's other Rotties and gave them their dinner. Then I went over to watch the box with Nicky around nine thirty. Around eleven thirty we saw flames coming out of the watch-tower so I drove back to see if I could rescue Rannaldini or anything.'

'What's happened to the safe?'

'Dunno. Rannaldini was always movin' it around.'

'Come on. Stealing that little dog, consorting with a minor, d'you want to be banged up for seven years?'

Clive didn't. By that time, Nicky Willard would be twenty-three and have lost his bloom. On the other hand, he didn't reveal all his cards. He had failed to flog the memoirs to Beattie Johnson on the night of the murder because she'd obviously had an offer from Bussage. Unable to get into the safe without Rannaldini's keys, Clive had subsequently ransacked Bussage's files, substituted the blank disks and fan photographs and flogged her set of the memoirs for two hundred thousand to Beattie, with a further eight hundred thousand promised on publication. None of this did he tell Gablecross. But, feeling flush, he

452

admitted, 'quite by chance', that Rannaldini's safe was currently hidden in the priest-hole behind the mantel-piece.

'See? It's 'ollow.' Clive banged a panel, which swung open to reveal a large cupboard containing lots of cobwebs and a large steel box. 'Rannaldini kept it in his indoor school – didn't entirely trust Bussage. I moved it 'ere after the murder.

'It's funny.' Clive poured Gablecross more coffee. 'Since it's been 'ere, I keep thinking the bugger's alive.' With a shiver, he glanced around the flat. 'I'm sure I saw him outside the chapel last night.'

'What did you intend to do with the safe?'

'Hand it in when I got a moment.'

'Very commendable,' said Gablecross sardonically.

Particularly when the bell rang again, and Clive, sulkily, had to admit Bobby Clintock, another of Gablecross's contacts and the best safecracker in Rutshire, armed with rugs and explosives.

At five thirty-five, a loud thud set the horses neighing and the Rottweilers barking in their quarters below.

'Shit,' muttered Clive, peering through the smoke. 'The Montigny's not there, nor the Picasso. Must have been torched in the fire. That's five million up the spout.'

Otherwise they found a lot of foreign currency, enough cocaine to make a snow-dwarf, a print-out of three hundred pages of the memoirs, and a pile of videos and photographs. Pushy Galore straddling a sofa didn't do much for Clive and neither did Bussage roped to the table. Then he saw Chloe.

'Jesus! Expect the goat'll sell its story to *Farmer's Weekly*.'

Poor old Granville Hastings. Gablecross picked up a photo of a devastated-looking Granny. No wonder he didn't want the police called.

Rannaldini must have locked this stuff away on the Sunday afternoon before he died. There was even a copy of his last will, dated 8 July, leaving everything to Cecilia and her children, except for four million each to Hermione and Little Cosmo and a hundred thousand to Clive and Miss Bussage. Nothing to Helen or Wolfie.

No wonder Wolfie had been going to kill his father.

Flicking through a yellow memo pad, Gablecross found notes that Rozzy Pringle had throat cancer, the poor lady, and reminders to contact Rozzy's husband Glyn and also Tristan's aunt Hortense in the Tarn. In a Bible, he discovered a letter in French, on writing paper headed with a crest of a snake and a drawing of two lovers, and shoved it in his inside pocket to read later. Turning, he found Bobby Clintock salivating over Hermione's naked body and Clive drooling over a book of medieval tortures with many of the pages turned down.

'What *was* it with this guy?' asked Gablecross in disgust.

'He was bored with normal pleasure,' said Clive flatly.

'Where was his famous torture chamber?'

'Didn't exist.' Clive's pale eyes flickered.

'Did you take that Rottie away from the watch-tower earlier so you could kill him without it barking?'

'You'll have to take my word on that.'

'Thanks for your co-operation,' said Gablecross, as Clive and Bobby, albeit with great reluctance, helped him to carry the safe to his car.

52

Gerry Portland was outraged when Gablecross emptied the contents of the safe on to his desk.

'Tim-out-on-a-limb again. How dare you go off intimidating suspects and blowing safes? Nothing has been printed.'

'There were two of them, and Bobby Clintock's much bigger than me.'

'You could have torched the evidence. What's the defence going to say to this?' Having bollocked him, however, Portland was soon immersed in the material. 'Jesus! Je*sus*. How the hell did Rannaldini pull birds like that?'

As a result, the morning's briefing was lively, excited and often ribald.

'If you see steam coming out of my ears,' announced Portland, 'it's because Tim's got hold of a copy of the memoirs. We also have the missing tape from the answering-machine at Valhalla.' He pressed the play button. 'Oh, Wolfie, help me! Rannaldini's just raped me, and he's killed Gertrude. Oh, please get Sharon from the cottage!'

Tab's clipped, breathless voice faltered as tears took over.

Despite the sun streaming through the window, a shiver went through the room.

'It was after hearing this tape', went on Portland, 'that

young Wolfgang announced he was going to kill his father. If he'd gone to the watch-tower and read the draft will, he'd have had the added incentive that he'd been disinherited. Rupert also received a phone call from Tabitha a few minutes later.'

'Rupert looked capable of murder last night,' admitted Gablecross.

Fanshawe, who was livid about Gablecross's latest coup, and Debbie Miller had been to Magpie Cottage yesterday. The only unusual thing on Monday morning, Betty had told them, was that Tab's and Isa's double bed had been neatly made. On the other hand, the bathroom had been a shambles. Fanshawe had pocketed a pale coral lipstick, Lancôme's Brilliant Beige, Clinique blusher, base and powder, and a hairbrush full of blonde hairs. Kicked under the bath, perhaps so Isa shouldn't see it, had been the packaging from a newly opened bottle of scent called Quercus.

'Perhaps she didn't want her husband to know she was on the pull,' said Debbie.

Gablecross reported on his and Karen's visit to Miss Bussage. 'The lady was very bitter about her sacking and unashamedly confessed she had meant to steal a copy of the memoirs and photographs. Said she was protecting Rannaldini's reputation.'

'I reckon she was going to flog them,' piped up Karen.

'Certainly enjoyed being flogged,' said Portland, grinning down at the photo of Bussage roped to the kitchen table.

'Disgusting,' chuntered DC Smithson.

'Anyway,' went on Gablecross, 'she reckons everything, including the draft will, was switched in the files before she put it in her briefcase, which she did immediately after Wolfie sacked her on Monday afternoon. He allowed her only an hour to pack because she'd slagged off Tab, and she had the key to the briefcase on her. Bussage suspects Wolfie and Lady Rannaldini, because they were both disinherited – and, of course, Clive. But no-one featured in those memoirs would be too happy to have them floating about.'

'The riveting thing she told us', said Karen in excitement, 'was that Rannaldini visited James Benson on Friday to discuss having his vasectomy reversed.'

This made everyone sit up.

'Not the most pleasant or successful of operations,' observed Portland. 'Rannaldini must have been thinking of having more children. Any idea who with?'

'Hardly Lady Rannaldini,' said Fanshawe, who was desperate to regain the ascendancy. 'That marriage was into injury time. Gloria Prescott claims he proposed marriage to her.'

'He was clearly closer to Harriet Bussage than her unprepossessing appearance would suggest,' said Gablecross, 'and he was cuckoo about Tabitha.'

'He was shooting blanks on Sunday night,' mused Fanshawe. 'But one way to torture Lady Rannaldini, Wolfgang, Dame Hermione *and* Rupert Campbell-Black in one stroke would have been to have got Tabitha pregnant.'

As he talked Sergeant Fanshawe was edging backwards so he could look at the photographs over Portland's shoulder. His jaw dropped at the sight of a naked Tab.

'Christ, she's beautiful. Any man would kill for her. Although,' he edged closer, 'judging from that pickie, she and Rannaldini must have been familiar for a long time – the leaves are off the trees. Perhaps she's lying about the rape.'

'May not have known the photograph was being taken,' said Gablecross, and he explained about Rannaldini having every room fitted with bugs, hidden cameras and two-way mirrors. 'Every night he watched his guests in bed on television monitors.'

'Did they know and perform?' mused Portland.

'Can I have a seat in the stalls?' pleaded DC Lightfoot, and was kicked by DC Smithson.

'So the murderer's not only got the keys to every

457

bedroom but the code to every safe, secret cache and priest-hole in Valhalla,' said Gablecross.

'What we've got to establish is, was Rannaldini the murderer's only target? Did he or she kill to stop the memoirs? Christ.' Portland shuddered at a hideously humiliating photograph of an emaciated Helen Campbell-Black. 'Or to steal them from the watch-tower and flog them to the press for some vast sum? Also, with a second set on the loose, stolen from Bussage's brief-case, the murderer may kill again to get hold of them.'

There had been another sighting on Sunday night of Tristan de Montigny, said DC Lightfoot.

'Janice, Rannaldini's groom, saw him sneaking into the south wing in a dark green polo shirt and white chinos around nine ten. But he rolled up at Valhalla the next day in jeans and a peacock-blue shirt, so he changed his clothes for some reason.'

'Who's close to him?' asked Portland.

'Lucy Latimer,' said Gablecross.

'You and Karen go and see her.'

Janice had also volunteered that Tabitha's husband, the Black Cobra, had also, most unusually, rolled up at the yard to look at Rannaldini's horses at around eight thirty, and had received a call on his mobile, DC Smithson consulted her notebook, around nine twenty-five. 'He said, "It's no good, I can't manage it, the coast isn't clear," and rang off. He left the yard around nine thirty.'

'He presumably wouldn't have been very pleased that Rannaldini had raped his wife.'

'Doubt if he'd show it. Cool customer, quite cool enough to murder.'

'You're a racing buff, Tim,' said Portland. 'Go and chat him up.'

'And how did you get on with Rupert Campbell-Black, Tim?' asked Fanshawe, who knew that he hadn't and who was livid Gablecross seemed to be Portland's pet today.

'We couldn't get near him,' said Gablecross tersely. 'Baby Spinosissimo interests me. He's as elusive as Campbell-Black, but all that drinking and extravagant camping it up means something's eating him.'

'Probably Flora Seymour,' quipped Fanshawe, pointing to one of the photographs of Flora and Baby entangled on the lawn at Angels' Reach. 'He's clearly not all gay.'

'Try and pin him down today, Tim,' said Portland. 'And what about Dame Hermione?'

'We couldn't dent her either,' sighed Gablecross. 'Swears she never left home on Sunday night. Claims to have been talking to her husband in Australia while the murder was taking place.'

'Melbourne CID can check that,' said Portland.

'She wasn't watching *Pride and Prejudice*,' protested Karen proudly, 'and I had a word with her maid Ortrud, who detests her, who said Hermione had wild flowers and grass all around the hem of her négligée next morning.'

'Well done,' Portland beamed at her. 'You go and see her, Kevin,' he added, as a sop to Fanshawe. 'She likes charmers.'

'She asked DS Gablecross to call her Hermione,' giggled Karen. 'It was hilarious when he shook hands with her waxwork when we arrived.'

Fanshawe's guffaw was easily the loudest.

I hate that man, thought Gablecross.

Portland was flipping through the photographs, wincing as he came to the ones of Granny. 'Anything on Granville Hastings?'

'He's due back tomorrow,' said Karen.

'And that sexy Gloria Prescott?'

Fanshawe blew a kiss to heaven. 'We had a brief word as she was leaving on Monday, said she was calling her mum at the time of the murder, which checks out. Debbie and I've arranged to see her tomorrow.'

'Lucky sod. And what did Lady Griselda have to

say?' Portland asked DC Lightfoot and DC Smithson.

'She's made a statement,' DC Lightfoot went rather pink, 'that she was looking for "bloody balls" while Rannaldini was murdered or she'd have done the "bloody job" herself, because she was so furious with Rannaldini for ripping up the beautiful dress she'd made for Dame Hermione.'

'Meredith Whalen was even more forthright.' DC Smithson pursed unpainted lips. 'He said why didn't we buck up and bury Rannaldini so he could organize a grand ball for three hundred people to dance on his grave?'

Portland laughed – so everyone else did.

'Has Meredith got an alibi?' he asked.

DC Lightfoot puffed out his cheeks and went even pinker. 'Well, he claims to have sloped off and had a half-hour lovey-dovey chat with his boyfriend, Hermione's husband Bobby, in Australia after he'd finished umpiring the finals – oh my God!'

'You're right, lad,' chipped in Gablecross. 'That was when Dame Hermione claims *she* was having a lovey-dovey chat with Bobby in Australia.'

'Perhaps they were on a conference call,' giggled Karen.

'Melbourne can sort that out too,' grinned Portland. 'Rozzy Pringle, poor lady, checks out,' he went on. 'But why did Rannaldini make a note to ring Glyn, her husband? You and Karen go and see him, Tim.'

'I could have cheered when Rozzy told that MCP Campbell-Black to eff off,' said DC Smithson.

Every surface of Portland's immaculate office was now covered with paper cups and overflowing ashtrays. As other pairs were given their orders, Gablecross fought sleep. Buoyed up by the findings of the safe, the team were now exhausted at having to assimilate so much information and in need of another fix.

It came from the gallant fingertip team who, having crawled through brushwood, brambles and nettles, had finally concluded their search. Their findings had been passed on to the lab to be printed and analysed, but included, said Portland, as he opened an orange file, an opaque glass lighter patterned with lilies.

'Tristan de Montigny was looking for his on Monday morning and he made a film called *The Lily in the Valley*,' said Karen excitedly.

'Good girl. An empty two-litre bottle of vodka. That'll be Mikhail Pezcherov's,' said Fanshawe.

'Green chewing-gum, probably chucked out by some young lady sweetening her breath for a lover's tryst,' went on Portland. 'Vomit containing sweetcorn, scrambled eggs and smoked salmon, a tumbler engraved with Rannaldini's initials and marked with coral-pink lipstick, a handsome gold signet ring, a dark crimson lipstick.'

Chloe, thought Karen, with satisfaction.

Among other discoveries were a blue petrol can reeking of paraffin, several used condoms, a dog lead, a number of green and pink tennis balls and a bullet lodged deep in the ground. Also noted had been a crushed clump of deadly nightshade, hemlock and agrimony.

'We'll provide you with the list.' Portland glanced at his watch. 'That should give you plenty to be going on with.' Then, turning to DC Lightfoot with a sceptical grin, 'Any more on Rannaldini's ghost in the high-wayman's cloak signing Lady Griselda's receipt?'

Lightfoot shook his head. 'Nothing, except we searched Wardrobe and Rannaldini's house. Not a trace of the cloak anywhere.'

'Oooh, how creepy,' shivered Debbie.

'People on the unit think so too,' said DC Lightfoot. 'They're very jumpy.'

'Clive is certain Rannaldini's still around,' volunteered Gablecross.

'They're a bunch of hysterics,' said Portland slowly, 'but we mustn't rule out the fact that the murderer could

461

be impersonating Rannaldini to give himself anonymity and putting the shits up everyone. Now, bugger off, all of you.' He waved the video tapes, 'I'm going to spend the morning at the pictures.'

Then, as everyone shuffled out of the room with their paper cups and ashtrays, he said, 'Mind staying on a second, Tim?'

Fanshawe looked delighted: Gablecross was clearly in for a bollocking. Gablecross thought so too, until Portland smiled engagingly.

'Count yourself publicly reprimanded,' he said, slamming the door. 'But well done, we've made a big step forward. Let's chew the cud and have a decent coffee,' he added, switching on the percolator, 'then go and see what the pathologist has to tell us. Her report's going to be longer than Rannaldini's memoirs. I called off the press conference. You were right. Lady Rannaldini's off the wall, and Dame Hermione wanted to charge twenty thousand for the use of her services.'

53

The post-mortem revealed a wonderfully fit body, showing no sign of ageing, with the huge shoulder muscles of a conductor and an athlete.

'It would have taken a super-strong person to strangle him,' Dr Meadows's freckled face was perplexed, 'or someone fuelled by such a hatred or fear. He died', she consulted her notes, 'some time between ten fifteen and eleven fifteen. There were broken blood vessels and deep tissue injuries to the neck, and whoever strangled him was wearing a large stone or a signet ring, probably on the little finger of the left hand. The stone cut into the flesh and appears to have swung round to the palm side, perhaps because the wearer had lost weight.'

'Check on everyone wearing rings,' said Portland.

For a second, Gablecross had visions of Rupert's big gold ring glinting in Oscar's lights.

'He was shot through the heart by a gun of the .38 type,' went on Dr Meadows, 'but the angle of the exit wound in his back suggests it happened when he was lying down, fired by someone about twelve feet away.'

'At the same time?' asked Gablecross.

'No, I reckon about fifteen minutes after the strangulation.'

'He had lacerations on his face and a big gash on the

side of his head, which suggests he was pushed or fell against a sharp object, or perhaps the murderer hit him with an iron bar or a spade.'

'There was also', she went on, 'saliva on his chest hair, traces of saliva in his mouth, saliva, canine and human blood on his dressing-gown and a bite on the ankle from an old dog with very few teeth. In addition there was perfume and lipstick, human hair and flakes of skin on his dressing-gown, and flakes of skin under his fingernails.'

'Quite a lot of activity,' said Portland.

'There was also extensive bruising on his chest and face, a couple of cracked ribs, semen stains down his left thigh and vaginal fluid on his penis, suggesting brief penetration then ejaculation after the victim managed to struggle away.'

'That figures.' Gablecross and Portland exchanged glances.

'Carpet fibres on the elbows and outside edges of the forearms also suggest that intercourse or rape took place indoors.'

'On the lounge floor of the watch-tower?' suggested Gablecross.

'The rape victim clearly put up one hell of a struggle,' added Dr Meadows, 'but from the colour of the bruises and the drying of the semen – now, this *is* interesting – the rape took place a good twenty minutes before the point of death. As I already surmised, the shooting took place a good quarter of an hour after that.'

'So he pushed his victim on to the carpet,' mused Gerry Portland, 'raped her. Maybe the dog – probably Campbell-Black's dog, Gertrude – bit and distracted him, and the victim escaped.'

'He pursued her into the wood,' said Gablecross.

'And walked some seventy-five yards looking for her – grass seed, enchanter's nightshade and traces of hemlock were all found on his bare feet and dressing gown,' volunteered Dr Meadows. 'There was no evidence he was dragged outside.'

'Perhaps the rape victim waited behind a tree and surprised him,' suggested Portland.

'Perhaps, but the evidence shows he was retracing his steps, because he fell backwards, as he was strangled, with his feet pointing to the watch-tower.'

'Probably heard Dame Hermione singing,' said Gablecross, putting his palms to his forehead, desperately trying to visualize the whole thing. 'It would be impossible to strangle someone while they were raping you then shoot them as well. You'd have to pull the trigger with your little toe.'

'Another abnormality,' went on Dr Meadows. 'At the moment of death there was extreme sexual arousal but no hint of panic or fear. He was completely relaxed so the murderer appears to have been someone he knew and was delighted to see.'

'Dame Hermione?' pondered Gablecross. 'He'd had a helluva row with her. Perhaps he was delighted she'd rolled up to make it up. Or perhaps he thought Tabitha had forgiven him.'

'Or someone disguised as them,' murmured Gerry Portland.

It would be hard to discern features at that hour of night, thought Gablecross, like Carlos mistaking Eboli for Elisabetta.

'Finally,' Dr Meadows turned over a page, 'Rannaldini's body was near enough to the watch-tower for the murderer realistically to hope he'd be torched in the fire and all the evidence of rape and DNA destroyed with him. There was ash on his body, but no smoke breathed into his lungs, so he died well before the watch-tower caught fire.'

'Which the fire brigade think was started by paraffin around eleven twenty,' said Portland, 'presumably from the blue can found in the wood.'

'From which all the fingerprints had been carefully wiped,' added Gablecross.

'So.' Again the two men gazed at each other.

'If one person had done all these things,' said Portland quickly, 'they would have been raped in Rannaldini's watch-tower, strangled him outside, blasted him with a .38, had a butcher's at the memoirs and decided to torch them as well.'

'They would have to have humped a can of paraffin and a gun into the wood,' continued Gablecross. 'And Mr Brimscombe said Tab was empty-handed when he saw her running towards the watch-tower.'

'Still could have used those hands to strangle him. Or after being raped she could have escaped, run to the phone, alerted Wolfgang or her dad, both of whom could have rolled up separately and taken out Rannaldini.'

'They both wear signet rings on their little fingers.'

'Perhaps Tabitha or someone strangled Rannaldini, found they weren't strong enough and finished him off with the gun.'

Dr Meadows shrugged. 'Possible but unlikely, bearing in mind the time lapses occurring between the two events.'

'Unless someone quite separate from the rape', said Gablecross, 'turned up with a gun, shot him to steal the Montigny, the Picasso and the memoirs.'

'And flogged them both for a fucking fortune. Good thinking. Could be the work of four isolated people, or a gang of people working together. Let's DNA everyone who doesn't check out.'

Portland turned to Meadows. 'You have been a miracle as usual.' He was about to kiss her hand but then, dubious at where it might have been, kissed her freckled, blushing cheek instead.

'You and Karen buzz off,' he added to Gablecross, 'and see what you can find out from Lucy and Baby. Try to nail Isa Lovell and Granville Hastings as soon as possible. I'm off to the one and nines.'

Back at Valhalla, James, no respecter of the rigours of night-shooting, decided that ten thirty was time for a walk and squeaked and pawed the cupboards of the caravan until his weary mistress dressed and took him outside.

Walks, once her favourite pastime, gave Lucy no pleasure now. Every time James froze or dived into the undergrowth she expected the murderer to jump out. Resolutely avoiding Hangman's Wood she headed north-east towards Cathedral Copse.

James, however, decided this was boring and swinging round, totally ignoring Lucy's shrieks, hurtled towards Hangman's Wood, bent on games with German shepherds.

Lucy had no option but to tear after him. Nothing much grew under the towering beeches of Cathedral Copse but in Hangman's Wood, beneath ancient limes, chestnuts, oaks and sycamores broad enough in girth to conceal any lurking killer, thrived a treacherous tangle of traveller's joy, nettles, brambles and goosegrass.

Everything reminded Lucy of death and decay. Ivy hung brown and sere from tree-trunks; moss on the banks was dusty, parched and yellow. Only an occasional torchbeam of sunlight penetrated the tree ceiling pushed down by Monday's downpour. The German shepherds had left, but there were rustlings and bangings everywhere.

'Oh, come back, please, James,' shrieked Lucy.

Then she heard footsteps thundering after her, and broke into a run, tripping over the roots that groped the path like arthritic fingers. They were getting nearer. She let out a scream of terror, then felt a complete idiot as, with lurcher acceleration, which on the hard ground sounded like a herd of buffalo, James shot past her, shimmied round and landed at her feet with nonchalantly wagging tail.

'Bloody dog.' Grabbing his green collar, Lucy shook

it furiously, 'Don't you dare run off like that again!'

Next moment, Karen and Gablecross pounded round the corner. 'You all right, Miss?'

'Fine,' muttered Lucy, in embarrassment. 'James hurtled up and frightened the life out of me. We're all a bit uptight – every shadow seems a ghost.'

Gablecross introduced Karen and said he hadn't bothered Lucy before because she'd seemed so busy, but could he ask her a few questions after they'd checked out the wood?

James had had his breakfast and, stretched out on the bench seat pensively licking liver gravy off his whiskers, had no intention of relinquishing his position, so when Karen and Gablecross appeared Lucy cleared a couple of chairs and switched on the kettle. As she put her brushes and combs to soak in a bowl of Fairy Liquid, she described the tennis tournament. 'I gave Wolfie back his signet ring after the last match,' she said finally, 'then I came back to Valhalla and rang my mother.'

'Everyone seems to have rung their mother,' observed Gablecross.

'It was Sunday night – you feel a bit low.'

'She was pleased to hear from you?'

'Not awfully,' confessed Lucy. 'She was asleep. I hadn't realized it was gone eleven o'clock. Then I went along to the party.'

'Any idea who might have done it?'

'Any of us, I suppose, except Oscar, and Valentin, and darling Rozzy, who was at her vile husband's birthday party,' Lucy got a packet of shortbread out of the cupboard, 'and Mikhail, who was far too hammered to do anything.'

James, who'd been corrugating his long nose in search of fleas, opened a long yellow eye as Lucy took off the wrapping.

'Lovely dog,' said Karen from a safe distance.

'They're known as gazehounds because they hunt by sight rather than scent, and funnily enough when I was taking him for a quick run round Hangman's Wood after the tennis he suddenly bounded forward, wagging his tail as though he recognized someone.'

'Who does he like?'

'Well, Tabitha, Wolfie, Baby, Granny, Flora, Rozzy, of course. He adores Alpheus too. Alpheus loves dogs, and misses his German shepherd, Mr Bones.'

'Tristan?' asked Gablecross innocently.

'Oh yes,' Lucy's voice softened, 'James adores Tristan, but it couldn't have been Tristan, he was in France.'

'Mikhail says he saw him.'

'He'd have seen him in quadruple, he was so drunk.'

Gablecross liked Lucy. She looked so reassuringly normal. Her voice after the initial screaming was so soft, he liked her large sludgy green eyes, and her turned-up nose and big generous mouth, plenty of openings in an open face.

'Rozzy Pringle adores Tristan, doesn't she?'

'Not difficult,' said Lucy quickly. 'He's been so kind to her, and I don't know what we'd have done without her. She sewed up Flora's puppet fox when some fiend cut it to pieces.

'A lot of unpleasant things have been happening,' she went on.

As the kettle boiled and switched itself off, she told them about the slug pellets, and the champagne that burnt a hole in the tablecloth.

'What happened to the glass?'

'It shattered as Rannaldini took a sip out of it. Dame Hermione sang a top note. Rannaldini doesn't normally drink before conducting, maybe Hermione meant it for me and launched into song when she realized he'd picked up the glass. Oh, God.'

'Who brought the glass in?' asked Karen.

'I don't remember,' lied Lucy. 'We were so busy that night. I'd always assumed it was Rannaldini, or Clive on

469

his instructions doing these horrible things, but now . . .' Her voice trailed off.

'People talk to you,' said Karen admiringly.

'Like they talk to minicab drivers and hairdressers,' said Lucy, with a shrug. 'There's no eye-contact. They tend to babble things out because they're nervous of going on the set, and you're not likely to meet them socially after the movie,' she added, with a trace of bitterness, 'so they feel they can let their hair down.'

'Does Rozzy Pringle's husband know she's got cancer?'

'Oh, no,' whispered Lucy in horror. 'Who told you that?'

'We're not free to reveal our sources,' said Gablecross sententiously.

'Oh, goodness.' Lucy collapsed on the bench seat, too close to James, triggering off a low growl and a flash of long fangs. 'Oh, poor Rozzy, she's frantic for people not to know. It could finish her career. I have to cover for her each time she goes for treatment. Oh, please don't tell anyone.' With frantically trembling hands she gathered up the empty blue mugs she'd put in front of Gablecross and Karen and shoved them back in the cupboard.

'Who else knows?'

'Only Tristan. I shouldn't have told him, Rozzy would kill me, but I was so upset. Tristan was wonderful, he offered her a part in *Der Rosenkavalier*, way in the future, which she'll never be able to take up, but just to keep up her spirits.'

'Tristan de Montigny has admitted he was in England on Sunday night,' said Karen, noticing Lucy's eyes darting in terror. 'Said he was looking for locations in the Forest of Dean.'

'That's utterly logical,' gabbled Lucy. 'He hadn't slept for weeks, keeping the whole show on the road.'

'Talked a lot to you, didn't he?'

'Probably because I didn't want to know my motivation for putting on blusher.'

470

'Women got very jealous he spent so much time with you,' persisted Karen. 'But he doesn't seem to have wanted to sleep with any of them.'

'He was too involved in the film,' muttered Lucy. 'Goodness, I've forgotten to make you those coffees.' She switched on the kettle again. 'He didn't want to sleep with me or anyone else,' she stammered, 'because he's in love with my friend, Tabitha, and felt he could talk to me about her.'

'Could he have killed Rannaldini?'

'Certainly not, he adored him,' said Lucy, too quickly. 'He put up with murder – oh, God – from him.'

'Was he in love with him?'

'What a horrible thing to say!'

'You claim he adored your friend Tab, but the night he got off with her Rannaldini made him back off. Any idea why?'

'No,' squeaked Lucy, getting three cups out of the cupboard again with a terrific clatter. Had they found out about Maxim raping Delphine?

'Could Rannaldini have threatened to out Tristan?' asked Gablecross.

'Tristan finds it hard to form close relationships.' Lucy was having great difficulty in unscrewing the Gold Blend jar because her hands were shaking so much. 'His mother died just after he was born, so did his brother Laurent. Tristan's vile father never forgave Tristan for being the one who lived. He was brought up by a hoary old aunt who never praised him. He may have been deprived of love, but he's the kindest, most thoughtful person in the world.' Glancing down, Lucy saw she had emptied the kettle into the full jar of coffee and burst into tears.

'I like my coffee strong,' said Gablecross gently, relieving her of the jar before she scalded herself. The only reason Lucy might have killed Rannaldini, he thought regretfully, was because she was madly in love with Tristan de Montigny. But he still had to go for the jugular.

'Did you know Rannaldini raped your friend Tabitha on Sunday night and killed her stepmother's dog, Gertrude?'

'No, I don't believe it,' gasped Lucy, shaking her head from side to side so the sudden cascade of tears flew around. 'Oh, poor darling Tab. Oh, poor Gertrude and poor Taggie. No wonder Rupert was so upset and horrible last night. If only people knew the truth. That must be why Tab hasn't answered my calls.'

'Could she have led Rannaldini on?' asked Gablecross.

'God, no.' Lucy fumbled for a piece of kitchen roll to mop her eyes. 'She's far too cool, and she simply doesn't need to.'

'We're off to see Baby,' said Gablecross, getting to his feet. 'Any idea where he might have been on Sunday night?'

'None.'

'Why does Chloe loathe him so much?'

'Because he's walking away with the film, and because he, Granny, Flora and me are always giggling in corners. Chloe says we're like a ladies' doubles match and just as boring. I love Baby.' Lucy's voice broke again. 'Beneath that flip exterior, he's determined to become a great singer. He'd only have killed Rannaldini for twiddling the knobs on his recording.'

After they'd gone, Lucy dug out her Switch card – she still couldn't find her passport – and dialled the flower shop in Rutminster.

'Mrs Lovell's a very popular young lady,' sighed the florist. 'A gorgeous-sounding foreign gentleman's just spent a fortune on an arrangement.'

Lucy proceeded to bawl her eyes out, then felt bitterly ashamed. Why wasn't she thinking of poor Tab, who deserved to get together with Tristan again?

54

The heatwave had returned. The catmint round the terrace swarmed with butterflies.

'Red admirals, peacocks, painted ladies of both sexes,' said Gablecross disapprovingly. 'Sums up the lot of them.'

In the summer drawing room they found the biggest peacock of them all. Having abandoned any attempt to sleep during the day, Baby was reading *Viz* and already, at eleven thirty, half-way down a large gin and tonic. 'The Grand Inquisitor,' he sang, 'and DC Needham.' Nodding at Karen, he rose to his feet and fell back again. 'This is the room', he went on, 'to which I am summoned from the polo field for a pep talk from my father. *Plus ça change.*'

Gablecross's lips tightened. 'OK, Mr Spinosissimo,' getting out the word was like navigating a lorry round Hyde Park Corner, 'put that magazine away and tell us what you were doing on Sunday.'

'I went to Oxford. I drove my own car – a red Ferrari – then looked at Magdalen and Christchurch. I checked in at Le Manoir aux Quat' Saisons around teatime. Learned my words for Act Two, Scene Two, which was scheduled for Monday night. I was rather far down a bottle of Krug when I realized I'd been stood up, so I attacked another one. Then I must have passed out.'

'Which room were you staying in?' asked Karen, who was feeling really sorry for him.

'It was called Hydrangea. You'll find it booked under Alpheus Shaw. There's so much press interest in this film, one cannot be too careful.' Then, seeing the disapproval on Gablecross's square face, 'It's a joke, Detective Sergeant.'

'Not a very funny one. How did you pay?'

'With huge difficulty – sorry, another joke, falling even flatter. I paid in cash. I had a win at Ascot on Road Test.'

'A good horse,' said Gablecross, remembering the peace interview technique. 'Did anyone see you arrive?'

'Of course – and leave around two o'clock. I'd sobered enough to drive home. I patted the night porter on the head.'

'Did you stop on the way back?'

'For petrol, I don't remember where.'

'Did you keep the receipt?'

'I guess not. My ambition is to be so rich it doesn't matter if I do.'

'Was there a balcony outside your room?'

'Yes, I went out and practised a bit. Act Two, Scene Two changed Carlos's life – and mine, too, for that matter.' Getting to his feet, Baby poured another gin and tonic for himself, then long glasses of iced orange juice for the others.

'Presumably there was a fire escape by which you could have left and come back,' said Gablecross.

'I didn't check.'

'Did anyone see you during those', Gablecross counted on his fingers, 'nine hours?'

'A waiter brought me the second bottle of Krug – Raymondo, I think his name was. I'd have delayed him if he'd been prettier.'

'What was the name of the lady who stood you up?' snapped Gablecross.

Baby was ashen beneath his suntan, his jaw rigid with

474

pain, but still he joked, 'Even for those eyelashes – really, you must dye them for full impact, Sergeant – I am not going to tell you.'

'You need an alibi,' pleaded Karen.

'I don't care.'

Out in the park, Baby could see a black horse rolling, its back legs whisking from side to side like a bottom-slimming exercise. When it struggled to its feet, grey with dust, much bigger than the horses around it, Baby recognized The Prince of Darkness.

'It was a guy,' he said flatly, 'married, very high profile, wouldn't do either of our careers any good and would create a frightful scandal, which would break his very straight family's hearts.' Then, seeing Gablecross frowning and perplexed, Baby laughed. 'No, it's not Alpheus.'

'You need this other gentleman's corroboration, even if he didn't show up,' said Gablecross mulishly. 'Two bottles of Krug don't constitute an alibi.'

'And a bar of chocolate and some jellybeans?'

'Don't upset the detective,' said Gablecross angrily. 'If you play ball with us, we won't shop you.'

'I can't.'

Seeing the hurt in his eyes, Karen said, 'Were you very close?'

'The closeness, I guess, was on my side. He pleases himself. What pisses me off is I've been had – or, rather, wasn't had on Sunday night.'

'Did you know Rannaldini had two-way mirrors and bugs in every room, even Lucy's caravan?'

'Really?' Baby cheered up instantly. 'No wonder he was so vindictive, after hearing the terrible things people said about him.'

'Any idea who might have killed him?'

'Harder to think who might not – question of bottle.'

'What about Tabitha?'

'Only thing she'd kill for is cruelty to animals, although I gather that Rannaldini killed her step-mother's dog. My money'd be on . . .' Baby looked furtively round the room '. . . our hostess. She'd been cut out of the will. According to Clive, there was a horrific photograph of her in the memoirs.'

Gablecross returned to the attack. 'You weren't meeting Tristan de Montigny?'

'I wish,' sighed Baby. 'Tristan's definitely not gay. He asked me to the cinema and didn't put his hand on my crotch once.'

Karen burst out laughing. Gablecross snorted in disapproval. 'The man you went to meet, does his wife know he's gay?'

'I have no idea.'

'You're lying,' snapped Gablecross. 'It was Flora Seymour stood you up, wasn't it? Because Rannaldini showed her these.'

'Shit.' As Baby gazed at the photographs, he looked shocked for the first time. 'Where did you find those?'

'In the pockets of the dressing-gown Rannaldini was wearing when he was murdered.'

'Does Flora know where you found them?'

'I told her on Monday.'

'Oh, hell, she told me Rannaldini had pictures of us. But she'd shoved off to London by the time I'd come off the set on Monday night. I suppose George Hungerford's seen them by now.'

'Two witnesses saw George in Paradise around ten thirty.'

'Well, there's your murderer.' Baby had regained control of himself. 'They're very good.' He picked up the pictures. 'I must have lost ten pounds and my double chin's gone.'

'Did you really see a ghost on Friday night?'

'No,' confessed Baby. 'I was so pissed off with Dame Hermione masking me. Fainting was the only way to make sure they didn't use that take. I must go and practise.' Wandering out on to the terrace, he threw out his arms and opened his lungs: '"Drunk with love, full of an

476

immense joy, Elisabetta, my dear, my happiness, I await you."'

'What a pity that guy's gay,' sighed Karen.

'As fags go, I rather like him,' confessed Gablecross. 'But I wonder if he really was meeting anyone at the Manoir.'

Meanwhile, news of DNA testing had roused others from their beds in panic.

'It's so definite,' grumbled Griselda. 'I might have pricked my finger when I was turning down that dressing-gown for Alpheus, or put my saliva on it when I broke off the cotton with my teeth.'

'And Alpheus might have left semen stains on it any time as he romped with Hermione, Chloe and Pushy,' said Ogborne.

'Ugh!' said Simone.

'And Mikhail could easily have gobbed on it during the quartet, or Dame Hermione, or Chloe, even.'

'I do not gob,' snapped Chloe.

'Granny and Sharon were in the earlier part of the scene, Sharon slobbers on everyone, bless her,' said Griselda.

'And how many peoples might Rannaldini have bonked in it, since he neeked it from Alpheus,' yawned Sylvestre.

'I cannot find my passport anywhere,' moaned Lucy. 'We've got to produce proper identification. I wonder if my driving licence will do.'

Gablecross was dreading the next encounter. They found Granny gazing wistfully at a strip of wasteground. Covered in thistles, poisonous hemlock, mildewed burdock, gaudy pink willowherb, rusting sorrel, yellowing nettles, it divided the footpath from one of Rannaldini's wonderfully cherished fields of wheat stretching golden to infinity.

'This disgusting piece of land is called a set-aside,' said Granny, his diction as silvery as his hair in the late-afternoon sunlight. 'Unlovable and neglected, just as I feel having been cast aside by my young man.'

Linking arms with Karen on one side and Gablecross on the other, he led them gently into the shade of an elder tree, overhanging and snowing down pale star-shaped flowers on a fallen log, which he brushed clear so they could all sit down.

He was impeccably dressed, Karen noticed, in prim-rose-yellow cords, an off-white linen jacket and a grey silk spotted tie.

'One must always wear a tie,' said Granny, as if reading her thoughts. 'It can double up as a noose, if things get too unbearable. I got my Dear John letter from Giuseppe this morning,' he produced a page of scrawl with a shaking hand, 'saying he and I are finished. He has dumped me after five years for a record producer called Serena Westwood. Just for a contract with Bravo he left me. It's entirely Rannaldini's doing. He knew Giuseppe was greedy, and as my career declined I would be less able to keep him in fast cars and expensive red wine, so he delighted in goading me by introducing my boy to rich, successful young women. It's strange the departure of such a little hustler should cause so much anguish. I want to howl like a dog.'

'I'm very sorry.' Karen took his hand.

Gablecross asked him about Sunday night.

'The tennis tournament was a lark. Gratifying for two old fossils like Grisel and me to get so far, but hard to concentrate with young Wolfgang gleaming like the young Siegfried on the other side of the net. We cheered ourselves up pretending Rannaldini was the ball.

'Afterwards, we got even drunker and I searched for balls with Grisel, Bernard and Lucy, I think. It was awfully dark by then.'

The vibrations in his beautiful voice became more pronounced, as he described the cutting up of his patch-work quilt.

'Ghastly to know someone hates you so much. One thing that has struck me: every time Tristan is nice to anyone – Lucy, Tab, Flora – something horrible happens to them. I was *favori du roi* on Friday. I was telling everyone in the canteen how Tristan had kicked ghastly Howie Denston up the ass for not getting me work, then offered me a dream of a part: Ochs in *Der Rosenkavalier*. A few hours later the patchwork quilt was in ribbons. Only a theory.'

'An interesting one,' said Karen. 'Why didn't you call the police?'

'We were in the middle of a party.'

'Well, next day, then.'

'I assumed it was Rannaldini, and he was quite above the law.'

Gablecross steeled himself. 'Was this the reason?'

For a second, Granny stared at the photographs of himself, it seemed at first, in a giant airing-cupboard. Later photographs showed him shoving loot into a shopping-bag. He gripped Karen's hand even tighter, and started to cry, tears falling quietly in time to the raining elderflowers.

'I'm so ashamed. I don't know what came over me, losing the patchwork quilt, which was pretty, or losing Giuseppe, who was even prettier. He only stayed an hour on Friday night, arrived in a chauffeur-driven limo from the airport, came out of the tomb, made Baby faint – he had that effect on men – then buggered back to London and Miss Westwood, without removing his make-up. I knew it was all up.

'On Saturday morning I went into Peggy Parker's. Clive must have followed me to Rutminster. I only took a couple of double damask tablecloths and some nap-kins. Goodness knows who I was planning to have to dinner. I've never done anything like this before but it'll be all over the papers. Menopausal old queen remanded for psychiatric counselling.'

'I'm sure Peggy Parker won't press charges.' Karen hugged him. 'She's such a music lover.'

'She might ask you to sing at one of her soirées,' said Gablecross drily.

'Prison would be the favourable option.' Granny wafted English Fern, as he mopped his eyes with a pale blue silk handkerchief. 'You children have been so sweet to me.'

'Why should anyone want to kill Rannaldini?' asked Karen.

'For peace,' sighed Granny.

'What a darling old boy,' said Karen, as they trailed back to the car.

'I'll have a word with George Hungerford, when he gets back from Germany.' Gablecross made a note. 'He and Peggy Parker are on the board of the Rutshire Symphony Orchestra.'

'George'll owe you a few favours if he really was in Paradise at ten twenty on Sunday,' said Karen.

55

Having conveniently discarded Debbie Miller and arranged to meet Pushy in the Pearly Gates at lunchtime, Fanshawe found her giving her own press conference to a crowd of reporters. Only his knowledge of the back lanes of Rutshire enabled him to shake them off and find privacy in the Green Dragon at Eldercombe.

Pushy looked enticingly pretty. Her simple black dress clung to her tiny figure, her newly washed blonde ringlets were tied back with a velvet ribbon, but she wore too much eye make-up for real mourning.

'Roberto Rannaldini was the most vital person Ay've ever met,' she confided, as she sipped a Babycham. 'He begged me to be the next Lady Rannaldini, and although he was much too old, Ay felt Ay could grow to love him. Off the record, Kevin, it made folk very jealous.'

Having slipped the photos of a nude lip-licking Pushy straddling Rannaldini's sofa into his hip pocket, Fanshawe asked if Lady Rannaldini had known her husband was having an *affaire* with Pushy.

'Course not. Ay never slept with him. That's why he respected as well as loved me.' Gloria's eyes filled with just enough tears not to swamp her mascara. 'Roberto was so caring. When Ay left a party frock at home, he sent the helly to get it, if Ay wanted to go shopping he lent me the limo, but Ay was careful not to upstage Lady Rannaldini.'

Fanshawe got out his notebook. 'What did you do on the night of the murder?'

'Ay was so choked not to be in the finals Ay went for a walk – it was such a lovely evening. Then Ay came into the house to phone Mum – as Ay told you Ay always do on a Sunday night – because Roberto had urged me to use the Valhalla phones at all taymes.

'Anyway, Ay nipped into Lady Rannaldini's cosy den next to the kitchen to borrow her *Harpers*. Some play about Puccini was on the radio but she wasn't there. So Ay borrowed her handset, Ay know it was cheeky, and settled into the big sofa in the hall between the kitchen and Lady Rannaldini's den.

'It's very spooky, that part of the house. When Ay became Lady Rannaldini Ay was going to whaytewash all that dark panelling. Anyway, Ay'd rung Mum and was still reading *Harpers*, Tabitha's dad and stepmum were in it. Ay don't know if Ay'm telling tales.'

'You mustn't hold back anything that might help us to find your fiancé's killer,' said Fanshawe gravely.

'Well, Wolfie came past around quarter to eleven, Ay'm so little he didn't see me, and he switched on the machine in the kitchen. Next moment he came out, whayte as a sheet. "This time I *am* going to kill my father!" he shouted. There was a crunch on the gravel and he was gone.

'But even stranger, around eleven fifteen – the clock in the 'all had just struck – Ay nipped back to return Lady Rannaldini's handset and her *Harpers*, and it was most embarrassing. Even though I hadn't heard her come back and I was outside the only door to that room all the time, she was back in there. Perhaps she emerged from some secret passage. Anyway, she reeked of paraffin and had torn that lovely dress, and walked straight past me. Next moment I heard her running up the back stairs.'

'That is extremely valuable information,' said a jubilant Fanshawe. 'Would you like to make a statement?'

'If it helps Roberto, of course.'

'I don't think you've met my colleague, DC Miller,' said Fanshawe, beckoning a hovering Debbie from the public bar.

Pushy looked quite hostile until Debbie told her Alpheus had raved about her beautiful voice.

'And I gather you knew Elisabetta's part very well.'

'Backwards. Maestro used my top notes instead of Hermione's in the recording. Her intonation was very suspect.'

'You and Rannaldini had an argument on Saturday morning,' went on Debbie.

'Only a lover's tiff. I was upset his ex-wife got a role I wanted. But Cecilia is a name.'

'People heard Elisabetta's last aria in the wood. They said it sounded miraculous.'

'That must have been my tape.'

'Did you know Rannaldini was planning to reverse his vasectomy?' asked Fanshawe.

'What did I tell you? That was the only condition I'd have made before I gave him my body, I dote on kiddies. Rannaldini and Ay had agreed to be celibate for one another.'

Those were exactly the words she'd told Eulalia Harrison in their in-depth interview yesterday so they must be true.

Having got his statement firmly in the can, Sergeant Fanshawe kept his in-depth question to the end. Was it because Gloria had insisted on celibacy that Rannaldini had been reduced to raping Tabitha Campbell-Black?

In a flash, the innocent virgin became a fishwife.

'The absolute fucker,' screamed Pushy, not minding who heard her. 'We agreed to keep ourselves chaste. I'll have him for breach of promise.'

'These photographs that have come into our possession do suggest your relationship was a little closer.'

'The bastard swore no-one would ever see them. I want my solicitor,' screeched Pushy.

Helen had been ashamed how relieved she was that Rannaldini was dead. No longer did she tremble to hear the front door creaking, and the cat's feet padding stealthily along the corridor. She had been comforted by the flood of letters, many written by authors or television producers seeking her opinion, by the telephone calls fielded by the police and the obituary in *The Times*, which described her as the last and most beautiful of Rannaldini's wives.

On the other hand, she couldn't quite believe the lawyers' assurances that the last will was unsigned and Tab's naked photos danced slyly before her eyes. Then Gerald Portland had telephoned yesterday, asking her to appeal for information in a press conference. Helen had panicked. Faced with a barrage of questions, she'd break down and the truth would come out.

Yesterday, Tuesday the tenth, had also been a terrible day for Wolfie. The cast and most of the crew had taken refuge in their beds, but he, Bernard and the production office had had to work flat out all day in preparation for Rupert's first night on the set.

In the middle of the afternoon, Wolfie had just realized the dustman he'd tipped twenty pounds to take away the empties had been none other than Nigel Dempster in disguise. He was also thinking that if Mr Brimscombe didn't stop moaning about his missing petrol can there would certainly be a second murder, when he was summoned to the house to find his step-mother in hysterics. Perhaps shock had worn off and the loss of his father had kicked in. Despite the heat, he drew her into her study, shutting the door and all the windows.

'Oh, Wolfie, I've done such a wicked thing.'

'It can't be that bad.' Even if she'd killed his father, she'd had enough provocation.

'I burnt down the watch-tower,' then, at Wolfie's look of thunderstruck amazement, 'with paraffin from Teddy Brimscombe's petrol can. The memoirs were so hideous and in the new will he hadn't left me a cent.'

'I'm sure it isn't valid.' Wolfie was amazed Helen had had the nerve. 'The lawyers will sort it out. Papa wasn't ungenerous.'

'Don't you stick up for him! He cut you out too.'

Wolfie winced. 'Did anyone see you?'

'I don't know, I heard Hermione singing, and I ran away. The memoirs were *so* dreadful.' She was shaking so violently, Wolfie was forced out of pity to take her in his arms.

'He said such humiliating things about me, he'd taken nude photographs of me, I looked like a skeleton. I had to stop them being published. Everyone was in them, Chloe, Hermione, Gloria, Serena, who I thought was my friend, that slut Flora!' Her voice rose shrilly.

'I'm sure he loved you best.' Wolfie patted her jagged shoulder.

Like a cat reacting to human warmth, Helen pressed against him. Wolfie longed to pull away; he could feel her rubbery breasts and bony pelvis against him. Her freckles on her deathly white disintegrating face were like flecks of blood on the snow.

'Even Tab,' she hissed, 'naked, whole rolls of film, and she was tarted up in a black G-string in some of them.'

'I don't believe it.' Wolfie leapt away with clenched fists. It was as though she was branding the words on his heart with a red-hot poker.

He wanted to shout that his father had never left Tab alone, but ringing in his ears were Tab's anguished pleas not to tell Helen about the rape.

'Oh, Christ,' he groaned, slumping on the sofa, his head in his hands.

'She led him on,' said Helen spitefully, 'even at our wedding. Look!' She thrust a photograph, which Wolfie

485

had so often admired of late, of a sixteen-year-old Tab smiling into Rannaldini's admiring eyes.

'He'd just bought her a fucking horse,' snarled Wolfie.

'And soon she got a socking great allowance, a cottage and a Sèvres vase, which she smashed. You've no idea how they both tormented me.' Then, when Wolfie didn't answer, 'Please, don't tell anyone I set fire to the watch-tower.'

'I'll sort it out,' said Wolfie wearily.

Knowing that Gablecross and Karen were due to see Lady Rannaldini, Fanshawe, having relayed the dramatic findings of his interview with Pushy to Gerald Portland, then magnanimously and patronizingly passed those relevant to Helen on to his rivals.

Thus armed, on Wednesday afternoon Gablecross and Karen found Helen in her little study, painting a not very good picture of the valley. Was it Freudian, Karen wondered, that she'd left out Magpie Cottage? Gablecross noticed her skeletal thinness, the staring eyes, the deathly pallor, the spread of grey in the fox-red hair, and thought how much she must have suffered. As before, she didn't offer them even a cup of tea.

Two other officers, DC Smithson and DC Lightfoot, he began, had spoken to Mrs Brimscombe.

'She told them', Karen continued gently, 'that you had two dresses made up from the mauve silk, patterned with lilac and honeysuckle. The second one was the one handed in to the police. The first must have been the one you wore earlier.'

'That's rubbish,' stammered Helen.

Mrs Brimscombe says she came down to the utility room after putting you to bed on Sunday night and found the first dress in the washing-machine with all the colours run. "Lady Rannaldini's so particular," she told DC Smithson. "She always insists silks are hand-washed."'

486

'She must have put the machine on herself.' Helen was frantically straightening paperweights. 'She was off-the-wall that night. She told Wolfie she'd seen a purple will-o'-the-wisp bobbing through hedges towards the cemetery. It's supposed to mean death at Valhalla.

'The truth is, Detective Sergeant, when I put on my first mauve silk dress on Sunday afternoon I noticed a rip in the other one.' Helen was talking carefully now, as though she was reciting a poem she hadn't quite memorized. 'So I left it in the utility room for Mrs B to mend. She's so on the blink she obviously thought it needed washing, then panicked because she'd put it on the wrong wash. She was probably terrified,' her voice hardened fractionally, 'thinking I wouldn't keep her and Teddy, now Rannaldini's gone.'

She seemed calmer, but when Gablecross told her Pushy claimed to have smelt paraffin on her ripped dress as she rushed upstairs at eleven fifteen, she lost her temper.

'That evil creature!' she hissed. 'She tried to destroy my marriage, now my husband's gone she's trying to destroy me. She humiliated me in every way, using my phone and my bathroom, pinching the cars and the helicopter when I needed them. How could she think I'd burn down the watch-tower' – her voice rose to a shriek – 'destroying all my husband's precious compositions?'

'Of course not.' Karen jumped to her feet and putting an arm round Helen's shoulders, settled her back in her chair. 'Let me get you a glass of water.'

'They're both lying,' moaned Helen, 'Brimscombe because she's old and confused, Gloria because she's a vindictive bitch.'

'Mrs Brimscombe', Gablecross flipped back a few pages, 'confirms she made you a sweetcorn and smoked-salmon omelette for your tea, the vomit of which was found ten yards from your husband's watch-tower.'

'I never!' gasped Helen. 'I told you, I chucked my omelette down the john. She must have made a second for someone else. Film people are always demanding things.'

But when Gablecross pointed out that they would be able to check Helen's DNA profile, which had been taken that morning, with the saliva in the vomit, Helen caved in and burst into tears.

'I did go into the woods. I so prayed my husband's passion for Gloria was dying out and I wanted to check if they were together. I found myself drawn to the watch-tower around half past ten. The door was open.' Helen was rocking back and forth, clutching herself. 'On his table I found this l-l-loathsome photograph of Gloria with nothing on. I tore it up. Then I heard a noise – I was so upset and so terrified it might be my husband, furious with me for destroying the photo, that I rushed into the wood, and threw up. Then I ran home. It was horrible.' She raised streaming eyes to Gablecross, who grunted sympathetically.

'Did you notice any keys anywhere?' he asked.

'Sure.' Helen wrinkled her freckled forehead. 'They were on my husband's table.'

'That's very useful information,' said Karen, return-ing with a brimming glass, which she placed on the table beside Helen's chair. 'Try to remember,' she added soothingly, as Helen leapt to her feet and shoved a little flowered mat under the glass. 'You were in such a state, Lady Rannaldini, one often blocks these things out. Did you strangle your husband?'

'Oh, no, no,' Helen licked her lips in terror, 'he'd have been far too strong. And I'd never set fire to his watch-tower. Bussage may have taken copies, but all the originals of his compositions and memoirs were there. I admired him so much as a composer. He used to write beautiful letters.' Helen had moved to another table, straightening, lining up, picking up a little ivory fan. 'I remember him quoting Donne: "'No spring or summer beauty has such grace As I have seen in one autumnal face."'

'"Young beauties force our love and there's a rape,"' Karen continued the poem, then raised an eyebrow at Gablecross who nodded.

'Did you know Rannaldini is alleged to have raped Tabitha just before he was murdered?' she asked softly.

There was a crack as the little fan broke.

'She must have led him on,' said Helen, quite unable to control her venom. 'She was always flaunting herself. Omigod,' she looked at them appalled, 'she's got a fiendish temper. You don't think she killed him?'

When Helen had calmed down a little, Gablecross asked if she'd seen anyone else in the wood.

'Promise you won't say who told you.' Helen's eyes were rolling crazily again.

'Of course not,' said Gablecross cosily. 'You've been a marvellous witness.'

'I saw my ex-husband, Rupert,' whispered Helen, 'in the wood with a gun in his hand.'

56

'Jesus, Sarge!' Karen was jumping up and down in excitement as they emerged out of the dark panelled hall into the lavender, yellow roses and falling sunlight of the forecourt. 'Hadn't we better tip off Gerry and go and nail Rupert?'

'Too early, he's at Newmarket, and we'll need far more evidence than a crazy ex-wife's terrified impressions in a pitch-dark wood. She may well have wanted it to be Rupert.'

'Do you think she hates him enough to shop him?'

'Possibly. I think she's pathological where he and Tab are concerned, particularly now she knows Rannaldini raped Tab. I certainly wouldn't rule her out as the killer. Let's go and talk to another side of the triangle, Isaac Lovell, who hates Rupert even more than she does.'

'I'm expecting Isa within the hour,' Janice, the head groom, told Karen and Gablecross when they walked into Rannaldini's yard.

Slim, foxy, knowing, a goer in the sack, Janice was soon confiding that she would happily have murdered her late boss for the way he treated his horses.

'That was his torture chamber,' she added, pointing the yard brush at the indoor school. 'He used to lock himself in with a green young horse, and do terrible things to make them go the way he wanted.'

She had stayed with Rannaldini, she said, because she was so sorry for the horses, and as Gablecross stretched out a hand towards the heads hanging out of the boxes, they all flinched away – except for The Prince of Darkness who, safely muzzled, scraped angrily at his half-door.

'He'll get you with his feet, or crush you against a wall, if he can't use his teeth,' said Janice.

For Sunday night, she had the perfect alibi: a skittle contest, between nine thirty and midnight at the Pearly Gates.

'I was choked when Isa turned up at the yard at eight thirty – I wasn't expecting him. He always slides in, well, like a cobra, never giving you any time to tart up. He's gorgeous, the bastard,' she added to Karen.

'I was dying to get away, but he insisted on looking at every horse, in case they'd lost condition in the drought. We're turning them out just at night because of the flies.'

'How did Isa get on with Rannaldini?'

'Worse and worse. No-one pushes horses harder than Isa. It's an insult to his genius to expect him to flog them home, but Rannaldini wanted more winners. He went berserk when Peppy won the Derby. Last week.' Janice glanced round the yard in terror. 'I can't believe he's not here any more, he threatened to jock Isa off and drop Jake as trainer. That's like an ad agency losing the Coca-Cola account. It would ruin Jake.'

'Was Isa upset?'

'Not outwardly – that's what makes him so attractive, never shows what he's thinking.'

'Not a lot probably – except about horses,' said Gablecross, noticing an empty box with stickers on the green half-doors, saying, 'Champion' and 'World Beater' and 'The Engineer' painted in blue letters above them. The damsel in distress, and now her charger, had fled.

'Rupert Campbell-Black's groom, Dizzy, collected

Engie this morning,' explained Janice. 'Good thing Rupert didn't come. There'd have been bloodshed if he'd seen Isa.'

In the tack room, she handed out chipped mugs of orange squash, and settled down to clean a bridle.

'Isa was paranoid about his private life staying private,' she went on, 'I'm sure Rannaldini hoped to share groupies and experience but Isa wouldn't play ball. He's a terrific stud, but he likes to poach under cover of dark, like a gypsy. He was well pissed off on Sunday night. His mobile rang – it must have been around nine thirty because the stable clock was striking – and he couldn't walk out of earshot because he and I were both in The Prince's box. So he pressed the receiver to his mouth, and muttered that he wasn't going to be able to make it, then he switched off his mobile and said he was off to Magpie Cottage. "You'd better keep it switched off, Casanova," I said to him, "in case any of your ladies ring when Tab's there." He threw me such a filthy look I went cold. He can put the evil eye on you. By the time I'd turned out The Prince, he was gone.'

'What d'you reckon to his marriage?' asked Karen, who was busy taking goosegrass out of the stable cat's tail.

'Pretends he doesn't give a stuff. She's a madam but you can't help loving her and she doesn't deserve a pig like Isa – any more than her stupid, neurotic mother deserved Rannaldini. I heard Rannaldini and Isa rowing again last week, just before he left for Australia. "I'm taking my horses away because you haven't made my poor stepdaughter very happy," Rannaldini was saying, in his oiliest voice, and Isa hissed back, "That's because you want her yourself, you fucker. Well, stay away from her."'

'Perhaps he loves her,' sighed Karen romantically.

'It sounds really weird,' Janice dug her sponge into the saddle soap, 'but because of the blood feud between the Campbell-Blacks and the Lovells, I think Isa feels bitterly ashamed about wanting Tab so much, almost like a paedophile fighting to stop himself jumping on a little kid. So he rejects her. Does that make sense?'

'Utterly.' Karen nodded wisely as the stable cat settled, purring happily, between her luscious thighs. 'A Puritan conscience coupled with an over-aberrant libido seldom leads to an easy love life.'

Gablecross gave her an old-fashioned look.

'Did you see anything unusual on your way to the Pearly Gates?' he asked Janice.

'Only Tristan de Montigny screeching down the drive in that fuck-off car, nearly running me down. Here's Isa! Please don't tell him I've been gossiping – I might want a reference.'

Gablecross had long hero-worshipped Jake Lovell, as a show-jumper then a trainer, and no jockey had captured the public's imagination more than his son. Other riders feared Isa, whispering of the risks he took, how he slithered through gaps of which no-one else was capable, how he hurtled past uttering gypsy curses, turning dark evil eyes on the opposition until it melted away.

But as he got out of a second-hand Merc, chewing gum and dressed in patched black jeans and a nettle-green shirt, dark glasses hiding the evil eyes, he looked harmless enough. About five foot eight, the same height as Rannaldini but half the width, he stood watching them, as narrow and dark as a cypress at noon.

Having taken in Karen's beauty, he ignored her, addressing all his remarks to Gablecross, who immediately softened him up by congratulating him on winning the Grand Annual in Australia last week. Gablecross then displayed so much knowledge about The Prince's form last winter that Isa took him over to be introduced.

Having ruffled The Prince's mane and scratched him behind his ears, Isa removed his muzzle before giving him a Polo. But as Gablecross approached, his equine hero darted huge teeth at him with a furious squeal.

'Shurrup.' Isa cuffed The Prince affectionately on his black nose. In his soft Birmingham accent, he confirmed Janice's statement that he'd dropped in on Sunday night to check the horses and his wife, who he hadn't seen since his return from Australia in June.

'Long time to leave such a beautiful young woman,' chided Karen.

'Times are hard for jump jockeys,' snapped Isa. 'You go where the work is.'

At first he flatly denied taking any calls at the yard.

'We have evidence', Gablecross flipped back through Karen's notebook, 'that your mobile rang around nine thirty, and you cancelled an arrangement to meet someone because the coast wasn't clear.'

'Is that a fact?' Isa was feeling The Prince's legs for swelling. He had a bad habit of galloping round on this hard ground. 'People seem to know more about my life than I do.'

'Who were you talking to?'

There was a pause.

'I don't remember, my mobile rings all day – probably my father, and me telling him Rannaldini was at home and we couldn't remove a horse.'

'Which horse?'

'Sparkling – that grey on the left. Rannaldini had a bee in his bonnet the horse wasn't doing well enough, wanted to give it a blood transfusion before its next race in the autumn. Sometimes it peps them up, more often it wrecks them.'

'Can we have your father's number, so we can check on the time?' said Karen.

Creating a convenient diversion The Prince lunged at Karen's notebook, sending her scuttling across the yard.

'He's ex-directory. I'll get him to call you.'

'How was Mrs Lovell when you got back?' asked Gablecross idly.

'I missed her. She left a message on my machine saying she was going back to Penscombe because

494

Rannaldini'd found her stepmother's dog and she'd be back around midnight.'

'Have you got the tape?'

'Yes, but the message will have been wiped by now.'

'You must have been disappointed.'

Isa didn't answer. His hands tested The Prince's back.

'Your cleaner', Karen peered at her notebook, 'said there was evidence that Mrs Lovell had been, er, dolling herself up, make-up unscrewed, powder spilt on the dressing-table, place reeking of perfume, new dress, packaging and labels on the floor,' Karen was taunting Isa now, 'and, more unusual, the bed was made.'

'First time since we were married,' said Isa.

'Why d'you think she made it?'

'Turning over a new leaf, perhaps. She wasn't domesticated.' He took another piece of green chewing-gum out of his hip pocket.

'Or expecting someone else? What did you do while you were at the cottage?'

'Opened a can of Diet Coke, ate a chicken leg, fed Sharon, read my mail and the racing pages of the Sundays – there was a good piece on the Grand Annual in the *Sunday Express*.'

He bolted The Prince's door and moved on to the grey, Sparkling, who greeted him with evident pleasure.

'I also picked up my washing,' he added bitchily, 'which my wife hadn't touched since before I left for Oz, and took it home to my mother.'

He had been spending most of his time over at Jake's yard because of his father's deteriorating strength.

'He can't look after thirty horses on his own. Baby's horses are here,' he pointed to a bay, and two chestnuts down the row, 'but I'm thinking of taking them back to Warwickshire. The grass is better there.'

'Friend of Baby's, are you?'

'I find horses and ride for him.'

'No idea who he might have been meeting at Le Manoir aux Quat' Saisons on Sunday night?'

'None,' said Isa flatly. 'Our relationship is strictly business.'

'How did you get on with Rannaldini?'

'He was an owner. They're always easier when you win for them.'

'Did you argue a lot?'

'Yes.'

'Did anyone see you leave Magpie Cottage on Sunday?'

'No, but I was back in Warwickshire by midnight.'

'So you had plenty of time to murder Rannaldini.'

'Why take out my most important owner?'

'Because he was intending to take all his horses away.'

'He wasn't. If you've been on this case since Sunday, Sergeant, you must realize Rannaldini was a control freak who tested everyone.'

'Who owns his horses now he's dead?'

'Imagine it's his son Wolfgang, not my greatest fan. He's got a stupid public-school crush on Tab, so that wouldn't be a motive to kill his father, would it?'

'Did you know his last will cut out both your mother-in-law and Tab, so you don't stand to gain a penny?'

'So I was much better off with him alive, wasn't I?'

'Did you know your wife's claiming that Rannaldini raped her on Sunday night, and there are traces of lipstick, perfume and powder on his dressing-gown and his body?'

Isa's face was expressionless, but Sparkling jumped away with a snort of pain, as his fingers tightened on her foreleg.

'I didn't. Rannaldini always had the hots for her.'

'People said she'd never looked more beautiful or excited as she ran towards the watch-tower. Odd she should tart up like that to pick up a dog.'

'She had opened a new perfume called Quercus,' added Karen.

'I gave it to her,' said Isa roughly. 'She knew I was coming round. Has it entered your thick heads that she was tarting up for me, when the loss of her parents' dog put everything out of her head?'

'Did she tell you Rannaldini'd raped her?' asked Gablecross, then swore as they heard Janice calling from the tack room.

'Sorry to bother you,' she smirked. 'But it's Cecilia Rannaldini returning your call.'

For once, Isa had the grace to blush.

'Why's he talking to her?' hissed Karen.

Gablecross shrugged.

'Presumably, as the chief inheritor of Rannaldini's estate, she's his new boss.'

'Quite capable of murdering anyone,' fumed Karen as they left the yard. 'I wonder if that was his chewing-gum found near the body?'

57

Late on Wednesday afternoon, PC Brown and PC Jones rolled up at Lucy's caravan. Tracking down the relevant cast and crew had been a nightmare.

'Miss Lucy Latimer?'

'Yes.'

How nice to see a smiling face, thought PC Jones.

'We've come to give you a DNA test. We'll need identification.'

'That's fine. Thank God, I've just found my passport. I've been searching all day. Would you like a cup of tea? This is James, he won't bite.' She pointed to a shaggy red dog taking up most of the available seating.

'Very nice lady,' said PC Brown, as they ticked Lucy's name off their list twenty minutes later. 'Sergeant Gablecross said she was a cracker.'

'Bit long in the tooth,' said PC Jones, who was all of nineteen. 'Never really fancied older birds, unless they look like Claudine Lauzerte or Joanna Lumley.'

By the time Lucy had finished making up the cast that night, she was really feeling her age, and her back was killing her.

'I'll have to go and see James Benson,' she groaned.

'Let me give you a massage in the break,' said Rozzy, 'might save you the money.'

Lucy stretched on the table, stripped to the waist,

breathing in oil of rosemary, almost falling asleep as Rozzy's wonderful healing fingers crept round the back of her neck, unknotting the muscles. Next moment she jumped out of her skin, as James let out a furious growl, hackles up, long teeth bared. Something loomed in the window. Was it Rozzy's shadowy reflection? Then Lucy screamed as a lens crashed against the glass, and she saw the blurred outline of a cameraman. James continued to bark his head off.

A second later Hype-along barged in through the caravan door, and had used up half a roll of film before Lucy could grab a towel.

'Now I know what you girlies get up to.'

'You bastard,' yelled Lucy.

'Don't do that to us,' chided Rozzy. 'Thank God we've got a guard dog. Good boy, Jamesie.' She held out a hand, but James was still growling and barking.

'You frightened him,' said Lucy indignantly. 'I've got a bad back.'

'And a gorgeous front.'

'Gimme that role of film.'

'Naaah, nice for my scrapbook.'

Hype-along sat down in Lucy's make-up chair and, picking up a powder brush, pretended to mop his brow. 'Give us a drink.'

As Lucy got a bottle of white out of the fridge, he swung round to face them with shining eyes.

'Latest gossip is that Rannaldini had the whole of Valhalla wired up like Fort Knox, and the police have the memoirs, and steam is coming out of Glamour Pants Portland's very clean ears.'

Oh, God, thought Lucy numbly, that's how they knew about Rozzy's cancer. Had Gablecross and Karen already known about Maxim being Tristan's father? Were they flying kites when they interviewed her?

'Now, you're not to spread naughty gossip,' chided Rozzy, taking the dangerously tilting bottle from Lucy, 'or I'll water your flowered tie.'

'Don't be daft!' said Hype-along. 'This is the best fuckin' publicity I've ever had on a film. If *Don Carlos* doesn't earn out in its first weekend, I'm a flying Dutchman.'

Having interviewed so many people in one day and left poor Karen to type up their statements for tomorrow's meeting, Gablecross felt too hyped up to go home and hung around the set, watching, listening and once again failing to nail either Rupert or Tristan, who were still bitching at each other.

For the fourth night running, therefore, guiltily aware that he hadn't rung in, Gablecross drove through Eldercombe village long after midnight. After the splendours of Valhalla and the pretty cottages along Paradise High Street, with their front gardens full of phlox and standard roses, his house on the Greenview estate seemed humiliatingly poky.

Bought on a mortgage back in the seventies, a Hungerford house had been every young couple's dream. Newly painted in pastel colours, with friendly neighbours and the morning sun streaming into a modern kitchen, it had had a genuinely green view across Eldercombe valley to Ricky France-Lynch's house floating in woods like a grey battleship.

But in no time at all developer George Hungerford had started slapping more and more houses around them, blocking out any view, filling the estate with less friendly neighbours, where children took drugs, heaved bricks through windows and resented having a cop living so near.

The value of Gablecross's house had plummeted and a move to a larger one, where the children could have rooms of their own and surrounded by fields, was only looking possible with the added boost of Margaret's income as deputy head.

Tim was proud of his wife's achievement, but he wished the name of the headmaster, Brian Chambers, a smiling leftie with a brown beard who drove a P-reg Volvo Estate, fell off her tongue a little less often. Chambers and Margaret shared a love of opera and swapped CDs. Tim knew he was getting a taste of his own medicine for spending so much time over the years with comely women witnesses. He knew Margaret longed to hear about the goings-on at Valhalla, how she would have given anything to meet Hermione, Chloe, Alpheus and Granville Hastings, but he was still resentful of Brian.

Gablecross thought the pack at Valhalla were crackers and he needed to mull over them with his wife. He hadn't sussed Tristan de Montigny or Mikhail at all. Finding her awake last night, he had asked her if she'd ever heard of Baby Spinosissimo, but at the first 'Brian thinks he's remarkable', he felt himself shutting up like a clam, and the signed CD from Hermione had stayed in the glove compartment.

Difficult crimes always pushed away the rest of Gablecross's life. Over the years, Margaret had learnt to cope with the defensive walls, the pensive silences and the dawn homecomings. Her first pay packet had been spent on a microwave.

Expecting earache, Gablecross was amazed to be greeted by an empty house. Going into the kitchen, he found a tomato salad, a French stick, a quarter of Dutch cheese still in its Cellophane wrapping, and a Tesco's lasagne awaiting him. Against the lasagne was propped a note: 'Five minutes in the microwave, gone to a staff meeting.'

No doubt tucked up in some bar, or worse, with Brian Chambers, thought Gablecross savagely. He ignored the lasagne, making do with a pickled onion, a slice of ancient pork pie and the *Rutminster Echo*, whose first four pages were given over to the murder and, infuriatingly, included excellent photographs of Gerald Portland and fucking Fanshawe, grinning beside Gloria Prescott.

Tomorrow, he must go and see Tabitha, and try to pin

down Tristan. He put aside the paper, and tried seriously to work out who might have killed Rannaldini, but he couldn't concentrate with Margaret still out. It was only when he went into the lounge half an hour later for a large Scotch to calm his rage that he found his wife fast asleep on the sofa, the *Independent* open at the murder.

Fetching the duvet from their bed, he laid it over her. He mustn't forget their wedding anniversary on Sunday.

58

The great excitements of Thursday's Inner Cabinet meeting were, first, that Bob Harefield had been in the air flying to Adelaide on Sunday night when both Hermione and Meredith claimed to have been telephoning him and, second, Mikhail's two-litre Smirnoff bottle contained traces of H_2O but absolutely no alcohol.

'So the bugger was pretending to be drunk the whole time,' chuntered Gerald Portland.

Mikhail had also pretended to pass out under the weeping ash for four hours until an *Evening Standard* reporter tripped over him but, in the meanwhile, could have been quite sober enough to nip into the wood and strangle Rannaldini and, although his English wasn't good enough to understand the memoirs, he could have burnt down the watch-tower after making off with the Montigny and the Picasso.

Mikhail, who also flatly refused to admit he had nicked Gablecross's initialled Parker pen, even when he was caught signing autographs with it in Paradise on Thursday morning, was without contrition.

'I 'ate Rannaldini,' he said, dragging Karen and Gablecross into the Heavenly Host for a late breakfast. 'Whoever kill heem is an 'ero. Eef people think me drunk they leave me alone. After Rannaldini take my

Lara, I do not sleep for twice nights. Of course I drop off under whipping ash.'

'Why was your vodka bottle lying near Rannaldini?' said Gablecross sternly. 'I suppose it sleepwalked.'

Karen, who was deboning Mikhail's kipper, got the giggles.

'You realize you have no alibi.'

'I have no vife either. Vot is life without her? She says I am piss artist, next day I go on vagon.'

'So why was your bottle . . . ?' began Gablecross.

'I go to votch-tower to kill Rannaldini for making me cockhold, but forest fire stop me getting hands on heem. I hope fire does my vork. And now, perhaps, someone will believe I only spend five minutes with screeching beetch Chloe on Sunday night and that I saw Tristan in Valhalla around nine thirty.'

Suspicion, in fact, was hardening on Tristan, who was flatly refusing to have a DNA test.

To stop Rupert throwing his weight around and de-moralizing Tristan even further, Sexton had arranged for him to see a rough cut of the film so far, which Rupert had reluctantly adored. He loved Sharon eating Alpheus's slippers, he loved the hunting and all Tab's horses. He cried buckets when Posa died and, after a long silence at the end, said in a disappointed voice, 'Isn't there any more? Montigny's a shit,' he added, as an afterthought, 'but an extremely clever one. I even forgot they were singing and he's made Valhalla look almost as good as Penscombe.'

Being tone-deaf, however, and unable to appreciate Alpheus's heavenly deep voice, Rupert thought he was the weak link:

'More like the chairman of the local Rotary Club than a king.'

In fact, poor Alpheus had just arrived back from a masterly Boris in Vienna, where he had taken twelve curtain calls.

Why wasn't he treated with more reverence at Valhalla? He'd only popped back, anyway, for a tiny scene praying in the chapel before his coronation, and intended to push off and sing in New York on Friday and Saturday, returning in time for the polo shoot on Monday. But Sexton, on Rupert's orders, refused to let him go.

'You've been overpaid for these extra days, Alphie, so stay 'ere in case we need you.'

Alpheus was hopping, particularly as he'd just read Hermione's interview in the *Daily Telegraph*: 'Now Rannaldini has passed away, it is my duty to shine more brightly as the only star in *Don Carlos*.'

Alpheus was also brooding over the loss of his Jaguar, which a newly steely Sexton was refusing to replace.

At ten thirty on Thursday morning, therefore, Alpheus drew Fanshawe and Debbie into his caravan and confessed he had been withholding information because he wanted to protect his colleagues. After wrestling with his conscience since Monday, he felt he must reveal that, on his jog through the dusk to Jasmine Cottage on Sunday night around ten thirty, he had seen Sexton's maroon Roller parked under Dame Hermione's Judas tree.

Having taken a statement, trying not to betray their glee that they were about to rush in where Gablecrosspatch had failed to dent, Fanshawe and Debbie also, at long last, found a chink in Simone's frantic schedule.

As she stuck Polaroids of Mikhail, Baby and Chloe into a huge scrapbook, she said how furious she was with Chloe.

'How dare she tell *flics* I had said my uncle Tristan never went to Aunt Hortense's birthday party. She eaves-drip my private conversation with Lucy. No-one appreciate pressure in making this movie. Tristan's head was too much in it to go to a party. Can you imagine Beethoven stopping composing Ninth symphony to go to aunt's bunfight?'

Furiously Simone drew a black Pentel moustache on Chloe's Polaroid.

She was very young, Fanshawe told Simone, to have such a responsible job.

'I am Tristan's niece. Everyone theenk *favori du roi* so I must be better than everyone.'

'You notice things?'

'It is my job.'

'Bet you didn't notice ten things out of the ordinary on Sunday night,' said Debbie Miller.

'Bet I did.' Simone covered Chloe's dimpled chin with a black beard. 'Mikhail change his shoes and put on loafers before he finally come into house. And I notice lots about Chloe. For first time she come in without lipstick – always she wears bright crimson colour and she look much better without it. She had also changed her clothes. She still wore tennis skirt . . . but . . . folds?'

'Pleats?' suggested Debbie.

'*Oui, oui*, but the pleats were bigger, and on her T-shirt the blue stripes were paler and wider, but look same.'

'Why?'

'She must have change for a man,' said Simone darkly, 'but didn't want to show it.'

'Well done. Who d'you think it was?'

'Probably Alpheus – they leave at same time.'

'That's six things,' said a counting Fanshawe.

'And Sexton,' Simone giggled, 'he had *reine de pré* in his hair and steeking out of the back of his trousers, and *gaillet* in the buckle of his Guccis and in his medallion.'

Debbie Miller was writing frantically. 'What's *reine de pré* and *gaillet*?'

'Wild flowers.'

'Should have been London Pride,' giggled Debbie. 'He claimed he was in town.'

'Perhaps it was Sexton rolled in the grass with Mees Chloe Super-bitch, that's eight things. And Bernard 'ave ash in his hair, and Helen come in wearing false

506

eyelashes and black pencilled eyebrows as eef she cover up singeing.'

'*Very* good,' said Fanshawe delightedly.

'So Bernard and Helen could have been in the wood,' squeaked Debbie.

'And Sexton up to no good,' shrugged Simone. 'Chloe could also have been with Mikhail or Alpheus, although I think now they both hate her.'

'Who around here wears signet rings or rings on their left hand little finger?' asked Fanshawe.

'Rupert Campbell-Black.' Simone glanced up at the telephone list. 'Granny. Tristan, although he hasn't worn it recently. Now, Sexton is interesting. He used to wear a signet ring on wedding-ring finger, but since 'Ermione thinks he go to Eton, he move it to leetle finger, and it is too loose, so he 'old it on like Prince Charles.

'Valentin, Oscar and Bernard all wear wedding rings,' she continued. 'Griselda wear bloodstone on little finger, 'Ermione often wear big diamond Rannaldini gave her, Gloria like flaunting big sapphire, probably a fake, Rannaldini also give her that too. Wolfie's signet ring keeps falling off because he lose so much weight too, so in the finals he gave it to Lucy to wear for him.'

'Was Lucy there all the time?'

'No, she take James away for queek run. He was whining but she was back before we finish and she give ring back to Wolfgang.'

So both Lucy and Wolfgang could have nipped into the wood and done the business, thought Fanshawe.

'Why d'you want to know?' Simone gave Chloe's Polaroid a squint.

'We have reason to believe the murderer was wearing a big ring when he strangled Rannaldini.'

'Then, it could have been me,' laughed Simone. On the little finger of her tiny left hand glinted an amber in a gold setting.

'That's beautiful,' gasped Debbie. 'Who gave you that?'

'A secret admirer – too precious to tell anyone.'

'You had no motive to kill Rannaldini,' teased Fanshawe.

'Only for putting artistic consideration before continuity,' said Simone, with unconcealed venom.

After all this evidence, Sexton's alibi of speeding in his maroon Roller down the M4, after a weekend of heroically raising money, and Hermione's, of watching *Pride and Prejudice*, ringing her husband Bobby, and spending quality time with Little Cosmo, were looking thin.

Fanshawe and Debbie found Hermione alone and just managing to polish off a large tub of pistachio and ginger ice cream. She had lost a stone and a half, received six and a half thousand letters, she told them, and was ready to return to the set tomorrow because she couldn't let down Rupert Campbell-Black.

Hermione rather liked Fanshawe's sleek dark hair and flat stomach until he accused her of not watching *Pride and Prejudice*.

'Don't be ridiculous, it's my favourite novel. Why isn't Timothy conducting this interview?'

'Nor did you ring your husband.'

'Oh, well, it must have been the day before. When one is jet-lagged and wrestling with artistic problems, time ceases to have any meaning.'

'Evidently. How d'you explain the fact that Mr Kemp's Rolls-Royce was parked under your Judas tree at around ten twenty, and Mr Kemp's clothes, when he finally rolled up at Valhalla some time after two o'clock in the morning, were covered in lady's bedstraw and meadowsweet? In fact, Mr Kemp lied to us about being on the M4 at the time of the murder, Dame Hermione. He was at River House with you.'

If Sergeant Fanshawe had expected a battle of wits he was disappointed.

508

'Indeed,' Dame Hermione bowed her head, 'I must tell you the truth, Officer. Are you married?'

'I have a partner.'

'I am a married woman, but Sexton and I found we cared deeply for each other, and our love tryst occurred in the summerhouse on Sunday evening. Sexton laid down a carpet of lady's bedstraw and meadowsweet, which was what Elisabetta would have lain on in the sixteenth century.'

'Didn't you notice the fire engines and the police sirens and the watch-tower going up in flames?' asked Fanshawe in amazement.

'The summerhouse is behind River House, so one cannot see the watch-tower – and frankly, Officer, we were too busy setting each other aflame.'

Debbie Miller had contracted Karen's complaint, and was laughing so much she had to gaze out of the window.

'Why did you lie about this, Dame Hermione?'

'I couldn't humiliate my husband, Bobby.'

'You and Rannaldini managed to humiliate him for the last few years,' snapped Fanshawe, 'presumably your husband knew which side his bread was buttered when the royalties came in.'

'Unkind, Officer.' Hermione bowed reproachfully.

'Did you know that Rannaldini was planning to have his vasectomy reversed so he could have children?'

'I am not past childbearing age. Cosmo would have adored a little sibling.'

'Numerous independent witnesses heard you singing in the wood on Sunday night, Dame Hermione. I suggest Rannaldini had humiliated you and Mr Kemp intolerably on Friday night. He was about to pull the plug on the sham of your marriage and replace you as Elisabetta with Gloria Prescott. Your career was on the slide, and Rannaldini had plans to marry again and make a total fool of you in his memoirs.'

'Nonsense,' squawked Hermione. 'I insist on talking only to Timothy.'

Fanshawe, however, had the bit between his teeth. 'I think you went into the wood, distracted Rannaldini with your lovely voice, and Mr Kemp did the business, getting his clothes and shoes covered with wild flowers in the struggle.'

'Nonsense, nonsense! You have no proof. It was *my* Bentley you saw in the bushes. Sexton arrived with armfuls and armfuls of lady's bedstraw and meadowsweet . . . the most tender and cherishing lover . . . I shall ring my friend Chief Constable Swallow at once.'

'Where was Little Cosmo while this was going on?'

'Tucked up in bed, of course, where all good boys should be.'

Unfortunately for Sexton, a complaint had just been logged by the incident room from a couple driving towards the M4 around one a.m. last Monday morning.

They had been pushed into the hogweed on the verge by a lunatic overtaking in a maroon Roller, number plate SK 1. To their apoplexy, twenty minutes later, the road-hog had hurtled past in the same Roller but in the other direction going towards Rutminster, and shoving them into the hogweed again.

59

Outraged to learn that Sergeant Fanshawe had made a breakthrough on his patch – bonking on lady's bedstraw indeed! – Gablecross set off for Penscombe, determined to succeed where Fanshawe had failed by nailing Tabitha. Not wanting anyone censoring his questions, however, he and Karen lurked over excellent fish pie in the Dog and Trumpet until the dark blue helicopter had carried Rupert, Lysander and Xavier off to Newmarket.

All round the pub walls were photographs of generations of Campbell-Blacks triumphing at horsy events. Noticing the ferocious intensity on Tabitha's face as she rode a much older and larger boy off the ball in some Pony Club polo finals, Gablecross thought she would have had little difficulty in strangling Rannaldini. One of the specialities chalked on the blackboard was 'Campbell-Black Chowder'.

'What's that made from? Shark and piranha?' asked Gablecross, as he paid the bill.

'No way,' laughed the landlady. 'That's Taggie's recipe. She's the best thing that ever happened to that family. Got her hands full at the moment. Tab's still in shock and won't eat. Floods one moment, shouting the next. Rupert's a continually erupting volcano. Just seen Taggie, dark glasses hiding her poor red eyes, driving off to Cotchester with Bianca.'

Better and better, thought Gablecross. With Taggie out, they must lose no time.

'Shit,' muttered Karen, as she drove up to the gates. 'There's even more paparazzi here than at Valhalla.'

Rupert's beautiful house, pale gold as a drowsy lioness in the burning afternoon sunshine, made Gablecross's Hungerford home seem even pokier. Fucking nobs.

As Ann-Marie, the au pair, knocked nervously on the study door, a shrill voice shouted, 'I don't care what Daddy or Tag say, I'm not having any lunch.'

Having admired Tab's amazing beauty in the silver frames in Helen's sitting room, and without clothes between the pages of Rannaldini's memoirs, Gablecross was appalled by the reality.

Her normally flawless skin was grey and blotchy, the bruise on her cheekbone parsnip yellow, her eyes reddened and staring. The drastic weight loss had given her the prematurely aged look of a terminal anorexic. Her very loose signet and wedding rings clashed as she ran a hand covered with more yellow bruises through her lank hair.

Despite the heatwave, she wore grey cords and an inside-out dark green cashmere cardigan. On a nearby table were a billowing ashtray and a three-quarters-drunk vodka and tonic. All over the floor, open at the murder hunt, were today's papers, which Tab had pinched from the kitchen, despite Taggie trying to hide them. Newmarket was on Channel Four with the sound turned down.

Slumped on a blue and white striped sofa, Tab was flipping through a photograph album. When Gablecross and Karen flashed their ID cards, she said would they please go away. To make up for her mistress's rudeness, Sharon jumped off the sofa, grabbed a lemon-yellow silk cushion and carried it over to Gablecross singing with delight.

'Lovely dog.' Gablecross patted her.

'Lovely flowers,' said Karen enviously. 'You are popular.'

'It's like a funeral parlour. Can you get me another vodka and tonic,' Tab shouted, in a slurred voice, to Ann-Marie.

Mixing tranks and booze, thought Karen, as she clocked a Stubbs of two chestnut mares and a Turner of Cotchester Cathedral against a rain-dark sky on the walls.

'D'you want a cup of tea before you go?' asked Tab.

'We've just had lunch, thanks.' Gablecross nearly shattered his coccyx as he sat down heavily on an ancient beef bone. Removing it from the bowels of the armchair, he placed it on the floor.

Tab went back to her album, patting the sofa for Sharon to sit beside her, exhorting her to admire the pictures of Gertrude. 'There she is at Daddy and Taggie's wedding, and there she is disapproving of Daddy's helicopter. God, she was sweet,' then, in case Sharon was hurt, 'but so are you.'

Having glanced at Gablecross, who tapped his head and mouthed 'plastered', Karen took out her notebook.

At first Tab denied everything, discounting the people who'd seen her racing towards the watch-tower and later weeping bloodstained on the edge of Hangman's Wood. Her fingerprints were all over the telephone box, and on a glass found in the wood, persisted Karen. Her lipstick was on the glass, and her powder and traces of Quercus were all over Rannaldini's dressing-gown.

'Really,' drawled Tab disdainfully, but her hand trembled as she pointed to a picture of Gertrude wearing a green paper crown at Christmas.

'Why did you doll up and put on a new dress on Sunday night?'

'It was an old dress, a present. I hadn't worn it before, because I didn't like it. I'd been riding all afternoon. It was baking, I was expecting Isa, I hadn't seen him for ages, so I tried to look nice. We've only been married six

513

months. Then I heard Gertrude was missing and forgot everything.'

'So you rang Rannaldini?'

'No, Wolfie,' snapped Tab, 'but I dialled the house instead of his mobile by mistake, and it was switched through to Rannaldini, who said he had Gertrude.'

'What a coincidence,' said Gablecross sarcastically. 'So you dolled yourself up to go and see him.'

'No.' For a second Tab closed her eyes, clenching her fists against the memory of a hurtling weight knocking her to the floor. 'But I wanted to get to Gertrude.' She paused for a second, feeling her way. 'She'd cut her paw. Rannaldini didn't want me to take her. He's bats about Taggie and probably wanted to return her personally. So I grabbed her and ran off, but I tripped over a bramble cable. Gertrude hit her head on a stump as I fell – that's why she bled so much. Then I realized she was dead.' There was a rattle of ice as Tab grabbed her vodka and tonic. 'Her grave's behind the tennis court.'

'Why did you leave that message on Wolfie's machine that you'd been raped?'

Tab's eyes flickered in terror, her tongue ran over her gnawed, reddened lips. 'No-one raped me,' she whispered.

'You're lying. Rannaldini had a nasty dog bite, dog hairs and dog's blood on his dressing-gown. I'm afraid', Gablecross gave a sigh, 'the only way to find out the truth is to dig up Gertrude and do a post-mortem.'

Tab caved in completely.

'No, no, please not,' she gasped. 'It'd destroy Taggie. All right, Rannaldini did rape me.'

She was shaking so violently, Karen put down her notebook.

'You're being too rough on her,' she hissed. 'Let me talk to her.'

Pushing Sharon off the sofa, she sat down and put her arm round Tab's shoulders.

'I can't take away the pain,' she said gently, 'but it'll

514

go, I promise. I'm sure you have secrets you never told your mum about, going too far with boys, smoking dope at school. Rannaldini was stunningly attractive.' Karen picked up the *Telegraph* arts page, which had a big picture of him conducting. 'Look at his beautiful hands. Your husband's been away a long time, probably neglecting you.'

Tab's eyes filled with tears. 'Yes, he has.'

'Rannaldini didn't neglect you. He'd given you a wonderful horse, paid for you to go to America, paid for your wedding, given you a cottage and a wonderful job working on *Don Carlos*.'

'I know,' sobbed Tab, 'but – he screwed up my mother, and Tristan's film and I'm sure he screwed up Tristan and me.'

'Only because he wanted you so badly, and you found him attractive. No, let me finish,' Karen was holding Tab's hand and stroking it. 'It was a hot summer evening, you weren't getting it from Isa, you have a bath and wash your hair, you ring Rannaldini, and he suggests you go over, so you put on a pretty dress and make-up for the first time in weeks, and wafting perfume you arrive all hot and excited and Rannaldini greets you wearing nothing but a dressing-gown, but knowing his reputation, you still go in.'

'I wanted to see Gertrude, for Christ's sake.'

'The last telephone call Rannaldini made in his life was to you.'

'That was me,' protested Tab furiously, 'ringing Isa, telling him I'd found Gertrude and was taking her straight back to Penscombe.'

'Thereby giving yourself a pink ticket for as long as you liked with Rannaldini,' interrupted Gablecross brutally. 'Meanwhile, you accepted a drink from him.'

'He thrust a vodka and tonic into my hand.'

'What did you talk about?'

'I said how excited I was to have a chance to go home and make it up with Daddy. Gertrude was in my arms

515

doing a lot of wagging. I couldn't bear to waste any more time, so I put her down, and was just pecking Rannaldini goodbye, when he swung his head so his mouth landed on mine. Then he pushed me to the floor—'

'Why didn't you scream for help?'

'Rannaldini had his hand over my mouth, I saw the black hairs like bristles on crackling.' Tab started to shudder again, her face beaded with sweat.

'You're quite safe,' soothed Karen. 'Sergeant Gablecross and I are here. Ann-Marie's in the kitchen, look, the nice old gardener's outside.'

To Tab, Mr Bodkin seemed miles away, merging into the heat-haze shimmering on the gravel and the smoky-blue trees beyond.

'I tried to bite him, my teeth clashed on his wedding-ring – the wedding-ring my mother gave him, for God's sake.'

'Tell me what he did to you.' Karen was stroking Tab's hair. 'It's quite OK to be frightened.'

Tab described the rape quite dispassionately, breaking down only when she came to Gertrude. 'He hit her with a bust, then threw her against the carved chest. Bastard!' Her voice rose to a scream.

'It's OK to be angry.'

'I pushed him against a table and snatched up Gertrude, who was pouring blood, and stumbled down the stairs into the wood.'

'What happened to your glass?'

'I don't know.'

'It was found by his body.' Gablecross was on the warpath again. 'Sure you didn't kill him because you were so angry?'

'No.'

'Or lie in wait once you found Gertrude was dead, and kill him when he came out looking for you?'

'No.'

'Why didn't you run back to the tennis court where all your friends were?'

516

'I lost my bearings. I was so terrified he'd come after me, I just wanted to get away.'

'How'd you get home?'

'I was waiting by the telephone box. I heard someone singing and footsteps. I thought it was Rannaldini. I ran into the road and a big car coming from Paradise screeched to a halt. I begged the driver to give me a lift. He wanted to take me to Casualty in Rutminster, I asked him to drop me on the road to Cotchester but he swung his car round and took me the whole way home.'

Tab didn't remember anything about the car or the man except that he was kind.

'He wrapped a rug round me and Gertrude – she was bleeding all over the car. He turned the heating up so high he was pouring with sweat by the time we got home.'

'How old was he?'

'Old, at least forty.'

Karen suppressed a smile as Gablecross winced.

'No-one you recognized?'

'No, and he wouldn't come in. I thanked him for saving me, and he said, in this funny accent, "I've got to thank you for saving me from something much bigger," and drove off.'

'Did you notice this picture in the watch-tower?' Gablecross held out a photograph of *The Snake Charmer*.

'Yuk,' said Tab. 'It was on the wall in the sitting room.'

'Are you sure?'

'Quite. Rannaldini pointed it out, saying wasn't he handsome in those days. I told him he looked better now. I wasn't leading him on. It was true. He looked like an Italian waiter when he was young.'

Tab took a slug of her now tepid vodka. Maybe the worst was over. Karen got up and prowled round the room. Gablecross renewed the attack.

'Why did you really kiss Rannaldini?' he asked. 'Did you lure him on to rape you so you had an excuse to strangle him in self-defence?'

'For the hundredth time, I kissed him because I was so grateful he'd found Gertrude. What crucifies me is the thought of her terrible last hours, kidnapped, totally confused and terrified because she was deaf and blind, and then murdered.'

'All very touching,' said Gablecross sarcastically. 'I think you fancied your stepdad something rotten and if, as you allege, this was the first time, how the hell d'you explain these?' Like a straight flush, he triumphantly splayed the photographs in front of her.

For a minute, Tab was speechless as the colour swept her face, merging with the blotches until it was all the same ugly red, as she gazed down at her own lascivious beauty, the half-closed eyes, the curling tongue, the thrust-forward breasts, the pink lips glistening between the long slender white thighs.

'The full split beaver,' said Gablecross roughly.

'My father had a dog called Beaver,' said Tab slowly. Then she flipped. 'How absolutely gross.'

She struggled to her feet to grab the photographs then, finding her legs wouldn't support her, collapsed back on the sofa.

'It's a trick, my head on someone else's body.'

'But in your own bedrooms at Valhalla and at Magpie Cottage,' said Gablecross. 'We checked out the background. You *have* been a busy girl.'

'I have not!' Tab's scream was so raw that Sharon, who'd been trembling and swallowing throughout the interview, crept under the sofa. Her bone was black with buzzing flies now. Gablecross chucked it out of the window.

'I never took off my clothes for Rannaldini,' whispered Tab. 'God, how revolting.' A horrible thought struck her. Perhaps Isa had taken them and given them to Rannaldini, perhaps Rannaldini had hidden in the cupboard, perhaps Clive . . . ? 'Oh, Christ, I swear I never knew they were being taken. Where did you find them?'

'Taking pride of place in Rannaldini's memoirs. Are

you sure you didn't catch a glimpse of them on Sunday night and burn down the watch-tower?'

'No, this is the first time.' God in heaven, why couldn't this sweating, red-faced thug leave her alone?

Karen was flipping through the little cards that had come with the flowers. 'Did you ring anyone else after the rape?'

'No, only Wolfie and Daddy.'

'Not Tristan de Montigny to tell him what had happened?'

'Why ever should I? He was in France.'

'Tristan threatened to kill Rannaldini on Friday. He was seen in Valhalla at the time of the murder.'

Tab started in horror, the colour deserting her face, leaving a grey wasteland.

'If you'd tipped Tristan off Rannaldini had raped you,' accused Gablecross, 'you could have pushed him over the edge. Perhaps he heard your message on Wolfie's machine.'

'No.' Clapping her hands over her ears, Tab frantically shook her head. 'No, no, no!'

'Wolfgang threatened to kill his dad after he heard that tape,' taunted Gablecross. 'Hope you weren't telling porkies. Might 'ave encouraged that young man, even your father, to kill Rannaldini, or did you tell your husband?'

'I didn't.'

'Hello, I'm back. Lovely basket of fruit arrived for you, Tab, darling.'

As a slender, very tall girl walked in, Gablecross leapt guiltily to his feet. This must be Rupert's wife, Taggie. She looked hardly older than her stepdaughter. Unfortunately he was too late to stop Sharon wriggling out from under her chair. Frantically searching around for a present, she snatched Tabitha's photographs off the table, and proudly bore them over to Taggie.

'Drop, Sharon, for God's sake!' Tab stumbled forward, snatching the photographs, then crumpling to the floor, sobbing hysterically. 'They think I killed Rannaldini, that I led him on to rape me. Please don't look at those pictures.'

Seldom had Karen witnessed such fury; a tigress protecting her cub.

'How dare you b-b-bully her after all she's been through, you horrible, horrible beast!' yelled Taggie.

Even Gablecross stepped back.

'You're right, he is a beast,' agreed Karen. Together she and Taggie lifted a weeping Tab to her feet. For a second, she froze, rigid with revulsion, then collapsed weeping in Taggie's arms.

'I didn't want anyone to know about the rape. I wouldn't have blurted it out to Dad or Wolfie. I was just so devastated about Gertrude.'

'I know, darling.'

'I feel so awful about Mummy. She's had such a terrible time with the press over the years. Imagine the f-f-field day Beattie Johnson's going to have when she finds out Rannaldini raped me, particularly if the police say I led him on, and what will the Lovells say? Jake hates me, and Isa's never forgiven me because of Peppy Koala. Oh, Taggie, I've made such a mess of my life.'

'You haven't.' Taggie tugged the red scarf from her dark hair, holding it for Tab to blow her nose on, as if she'd been Bianca.

'You're good, brave and beautiful.'

'Like a beautiful car that doesn't work,' wailed Tab. 'I loved Lysander, Isa and Tristan so much. Why didn't any of them love me? Because I'm bad luck, that's why, and I don't want to bring any more to Mummy. I love her so much too, but she's never rung to see if I'm OK. I expect the police have already told her I pulled her husband. What's she going to think when she sees those pictures?'

What would *you* think if you knew your sainted mother had grassed about your beloved father's gun? wondered Gablecross bitterly.

'What will she say when it all comes out?' mumbled Tab.

'Perhaps it can be hushed up?' Taggie turned beseechingly to Karen.

'Tabitha's been very co-operative,' said Karen, who was feeling thoroughly ashamed of herself.

Taggie turned back to Tab. 'Look, why don't we ask Mummy to stay for a bit?' Her far too kind heart was already sinking as she made the offer.

But a tiny spark had ignited Tab's face.

'Could we? Oh, Taggie, you are kind. I hate her rattling about in that creepy house, stalked by Rannaldini's ghost.'

'And you must open your lovely basket of fruit,' said Karen. 'Mangoes and persimmons. Someone wants you to start eating again.' She handed Tab the tiny envelope.

They were from Wolfie.

'Perhaps he might drop Mummy off,' sniffed Tab. 'I'd love to see Wolfie again.'

60

Gablecross was profoundly depressed. Karen had bawled him out for bullying Tab, Rupert Campbell-Black had lodged a ferocious complaint with the Chief Constable, Gerry Portland was threatening to take him off the case altogether, and he had absolutely no idea who had killed Rannaldini.

It was nearly dark. Walking towards the Valhalla car park he nearly had a fit as he saw a young boy sobbing in Rupert's arms. Then he realized it was Flora, back for a brief appearance as Elisabetta's bodyguard, who'd just been subjected to another short back and sides for the sake of continuity.

'George is a ghastly bore and a pleb, darling,' Rupert was saying, 'and far too old for you.'

'You're older than Taggie, and you're happy,' wept Flora.

'We're not talking about me and I'm certainly not a pleb. George is so insanely jealous, no-one as gorgeous as you stands a chance. If he's kneecapped old biddies in the past, he's quite capable of doing you a mischief *and* putting a contract on Rannaldini.'

'That's what I'm afraid of,' sobbed Flora. 'I love him so much.'

Passing Wardrobe, Gablecross saw Rozzy Pringle getting dress shirts ready for the extras in the ball scene. Looking at the big hot iron in her hand, the scissors and pinking shears hanging from the walls and the safety-pins and needles spilling out of boxes, he thought there were plenty of murder weapons here.

'Sergeant Gablecross,' called Rozzy, blushing slightly, 'you've been working so hard, I thought you might have forgotten your wedding anniversary on Sunday so I got a card and wrapped up some presents.'

'You shouldn't have done that.' Gablecross spoke roughly to hide the lump in his throat. 'How much do I owe you?'

'It's a present – or presents.' She laughed. 'You've been so sweet to us.'

'Not what Rupert Campbell-Black thinks.'

'He's a brute.'

'You've saved my bacon. I *had* forgotten,' said Gablecross gratefully, as he scribbled, 'All my love, Tim,' in a Happy Anniversary card. 'Thanks so much. Every man should have a woman like you.'

'I wish my husband thought so,' sighed Rozzy.

It was a highwayman's night, with racing black clouds and the stars making only cameo appearances, except for blazing Jupiter, still pursuing a glittering yellow half-grapefruit of a moon.

Gablecross couldn't wait to get home to Margaret. He needed to run his latest suspicions past her and have a moan about Karen getting on his nerves. Approaching the Greenview estate, passing the waiters wearily closing up the Chinese restaurant, he reached in the glove compartment for Hermione's CD, saw Brian Chambers's blue Volvo coming the other way, and nearly drove into a wall. Passing his house he saw Margaret in the kitchen in her dressing-gown. She didn't look glammed up. Maybe they'd just had sex, or she knew Brian well enough not to bother too much. Swinging the car round, Gablecross drove over to Rutminster Hall.

He knew, having got away with a solo raid on Clive,

and having received a warning from Portland this afternoon, he was putting his career on the line. But, like a junkie needing a fix, he had to follow his hunch. If George Hungerford had experienced a quarter of the murderous rage he himself had just felt towards Brian Chambers . . . And he was not taking Karen. A tough, uncommunicative businessman would never open up in front of a woman.

Rutminster Hall lay on the other side of town, as far as possible from the Greenview estate. George wouldn't spoil his own rolling hillside with eczema rashes of little houses, thought Gablecross savagely. No lights were on, but music was pouring so loudly out of the speakers that George didn't hear the car coming up the drive. Only people who lived in magnificent parks could get away with playing music that loudly. Only when Gablecross banged the car door did George come racing round the side of the house.

'Flora!' For a second he seemed to disintegrate with disappointment, then seeing Gablecross's ID card, he brusquely invited him in.

'I haven't got long.' It was a lie; he had all eternity to long for Flora.

Gablecross knew George was a mate of the Chief Constable, so he'd better tread carefully. He was also aware that George was a major player in the world property market who had often sailed too close to the wind, but who had shown a softer side as managing director of the Rutminster Symphony Orchestra, where he had fallen in love with its youngest player, Flora Seymour.

This was the man who had ruined Gablecross's view and made the value of his house plummet, but he couldn't hate him because George looked so desolate. Thin, unshaven, black beneath the eyes, he hadn't slept since his row with Flora, and was now, like Citizen Kane, dying of loneliness inside his vast ugly castle.

They sat on the terrace, George with an untouched

whisky, Gablecross with a Perrier. Below them lay new-mown hay like a choppy pale grey sea. Through a gap in the trees, as if mocking them, stood a moonlit temple of Flora.

'Nice place.'

'Morgue without Flora.'

When asked what he had been up to on Sunday, George claimed he had stayed in to watch a video of the orchestra's recent tour of Switzerland. They had played Britten's piano concerto and Glazunov Three. His staff had Sunday night off, so there were no witnesses.

'A helicopter landed in Valhalla.'

'Wasn't mine. Never left its hangar.'

It was no secret, said Gablecross, that George had hated Rannaldini, and had intended to slap a bypass or even a motorway through his land.

'Bastard hated me back. Tried to take over my orchestra, furious that Flora preferred me. Should never have let her get into his clutches. Look what happened! Rannaldini cut her hair, forced her into a man's suit and onto some dyke. No wonder she ricocheted into the arms of that Aussie poofter. Rannaldini set the whole thing up.'

George knew the world was swarming with gays, that it was cool for girls to get into passionate friendships with them. Flora had adored Campbell-Black's son, Marcus. Gays understood women, were more sympathetic. He knew he was hamfisted. Shyness made him inarticulate.

'In theory,' he confessed, 'I shouldn't deprive the world of such a beautiful voice. In practice, I want her home where I can look after her.'

'Same with my wife,' agreed Gablecross. 'All I can say is there's a very, very unhappy young lady at Valhalla.'

'I've been preoccupied,' admitted George. 'I owed forty million to German banks.'

Gablecross agreed it made his two-hundred-pound overdraft seem rather paltry.

'I'm out of the woods now, but I wasn't nice to live

with. I even grumbled about her little dog – miss him like hell, he's so clever. If I came down to breakfast in a tie, he knew I was going to the office and there was no point in getting his lead for a walk.'

'This is *Don Carlos*, isn't it?' said Gablecross, recognizing the music as Philip launched into his great soliloquy.

George nodded. He'd got hooked on it when he was helping Flora learn her part and had identified increasingly with Philip.

But having found a jewel, would he kill someone who'd pushed her into infidelity? wondered Gablecross.

'I'll have that drink after all,' he said. 'Why don't you call her?'

George said he'd been going to ring her on Sunday when a courier had arrived with an envelope: 'Photographs – Do Not Bend.' Heart – Do Not Break.

Inside had been pictures of an ecstatic Flora on the lawn at Angels' Reach with a ridiculously handsome youth with no double chin, beer gut, or grey hairs.

'Shouldn't deprive her of happiness with someone younger.'

'Baby's a charmer but he's very queer,' said Gablecross gently.

'"If you have betrayed me,"' Philip II's voice reverberated round the park, '"by Almighty God, tremble, I shall have blood."'

'What were you really up to on Sunday night?' asked Gablecross.

'I stayed at home.'

'Come off it, Mr Hungerford. You were seen driving through Paradise around ten twenty-five.'

George looked down at the temple of Flora, no longer floodlit, as the moon crept behind a cloud.

'I drove over to Paradise,' he took a slug of whisky, 'saw a light on in Rannaldini's watch-tower. I was going to park my car in the woods above Valhalla and beat Rannaldini to a pulp. Without Flora, I already had a life

526

sentence. But by the telephone box, around ten twenty-five, I saw this young girl, so ghostly I crossed myself. She had blood on her face and all over her dress and she carried a little dog. For a terrible moment, as she ran into my headlights like a moth, I thought it was Flora and Trevor. I just braked in time.'

Gablecross felt a lurch of excitement.

'She wanted me to drop her on the Cotchester Road, but I took her all the way to Penscombe. The dog was dead. I wrapped it in an old tartan rug of Trevor's – poor little thing still bled all over my car.'

'What did she look like?'

'Blonde, about five eight. From her profile I twigged she was Campbell-Black's daughter. I rang the house and said I was bringing her home. She had no idea who I or anyone was. Didn't address a word to me, except to thank me when I dropped her off at around half eleven. I waited till Rupert came out, and folded her in his arms . . . never felt lonelier in my life.'

'See anything else odd on the way?'

'Only a man in a light-coloured bloodstained suit crossing the Cotchester Road, as we drove out of Paradise, but I reckoned by then I was just seeing things.'

The helicopter that landed on Sunday night must have been Rupert's. Christ, what a break! Gablecross knew it was unprofessional but when he'd taken George's statement, he rang Taggie to say they'd identified the man who had brought Tabitha home and it was unlikely that either of them had murdered Rannaldini.

61

Night-shooting on Thursday began with a hefty consumption of porridge, eggs, bacon and sausages. Sugar
Puffs had also rocketed in popularity.

'They are all comfort eating,' sighed Maria, as she
prodded a sizzling leg of pork for the midnight break.
'Frightened out of their wits, seeking the security of
being children again. No, I am sorry, Valentin, pet, you
cannot even have a *vin ordinaire*.'

One of the sparks, drunk last night, had fallen off a
ladder, pulling two huge lights on top of him and
holding up production for an hour. Consequently
Rupert had banned drink from the set and the canteen.
The *entente* had never been less *cordiale*.

All this put a terrible strain on Tristan as tempers
shortened and the crew grew more bolshie from exhaustion. It was impossible to sleep in the day with the
dread of the murderer stealthily letting himself into
one's bedroom. With the short nights, there were
only five hours of real darkness to film two complicated scenes; and with Dame Hermione returning to the
set, they'd be lucky if the camera turned over before
dawn.

Filming had moved to another part of the garden, by
a fountain overlooked by huge sycamores. White roses
swarming over a pergola, shedding an increasing carpet

528

of petals on to the damp grass, were an increasing continuity problem for Simone.

Rupert had already rolled up in a foul temper. He'd had no wins at Newmarket and Helen was coming to stay. He was hopping with Gablecross for upsetting Tab, but even more unhinged by a telephone call from Beattie Johnson of the *Scorpion*, his vicious ex-mistress, threatening to reveal yet another scandal from his past.

'I knew you'd cheat on Taggie in the end, you bastard.'

Rupert was slumped in Rannaldini's executive chair, a straw hat with a Jockey Club ribbon tipped over his Greek nose, venting his spleen on Sexton for agreeing to pay an extortionate sum to Lord Waterlane for the loan of Rutminster polo ground on Monday and Tuesday. Plebs like Sexton were stupidly overawed by titles. Sexton himself was sweating over Fanshawe's visit to River House.

'Police fink we've done it, Rupe.'

Flora, meanwhile, had returned for a last night's shooting, a ghost of herself. Three days in London with Abby and Viking, utterly mad about each other and wildly excited about the fast-approaching birth of their baby, had made her loss of George even more acute. As her eyes were too red and swollen even for Lucy to repair, Tristan had agreed she could be filmed in dark glasses.

Having changed into a rather shiny dinner jacket, her bodyguard's disguise for the ball, she had nipped into the production office on her way to the set in the forlorn hope George might have left a message in the last hour. There was nothing.

Hollow with desolation, she slouched towards the ruined cloisters that flanked the chapel. Broken columns and arches, smothered in ivy and moonlight, cast jagged shadows on paving stones almost worn away by the pacing of monks over the centuries.

Did any of them ever pray for anything as fervently as she was now begging for George's return? Poor God must feel like an undertaker. His services only sought at the death of a love *affaire.*

Then Flora's despair turned to terror as she breathed in indescribable menace. She couldn't move. A scream froze in her throat, she was being suffocated by chloroform. Then she realized it was Maestro, Rannaldini's aftershave, as a figure emerged from the darkest shadows and swept up the cloisters, his black cloak slithering after him like a peacock's tail. In the moonlight, as he opened the chapel door, she could see a pale, cruel, carved profile and a handsome head of pewter hair.

Screaming, Flora fled back to the production office. Thank God, a group was chatting outside.

'I've just seen Rannaldini,' she shrieked. 'I saw him, I swear I saw him.'

Bernard was quite gently telling her she was imagining things, when Valentin, with rare animation, announced that he, too, had seen Rannaldini disappearing into the chapel earlier. By the time he'd woken his father-in-law, Oscar, and they'd screwed up enough courage to follow Rannaldini inside, he had vanished.

'Probably returned to grab the Murillo Madonna,' said Rupert contemptuously. 'There are no such things as ghosts. It is a figment of your feverish Frog imagination. Another reason for not drinking until night-shooting's over.'

'I saw heem,' said Valentin sulkily. 'He had that queek walk with his head thrown back.'

'I saw his cloak slithering,' whispered Flora, who was having difficulty getting her lighter to her cigarette. 'I think he's still alive.'

'Don't be fatuous,' snapped Rupert. 'Rannaldini is dead.'

'How d'you know for certain?' asked Baby, who had rolled up eating a Danish blue sandwich studded with whole garlic cloves to ward off Hermione, Pushy *and* Chloe through the night. 'Did you actually see the body?'

'Wolfgang did,' said Rupert sharply. 'If you've been bullied by some bastard for twenty-four years, you tend to recognize them.'

'Very true,' agreed Baby. 'I couldn't mistake you, and you've only been bullying me since Tuesday.'

Bernard brayed nervously, but before Rupert could retaliate, Baby put an arm round Flora's quivering shoulders and bore her off to his caravan for a large drink.

'Rupert said we mustn't,' said Flora listlessly.

'Fuck him.'

'I nearly did earlier. He was so sweet to me, said George and I are totally unsuited.'

'He's right. Marry me instead.'

'That is the loveliest compliment I've ever been paid,' said Flora, in a choked voice. 'I can't think of anyone I'd be happier with, but I'm stuck with loving George.'

Blowing her nose firmly, she looked up at Baby, worried how grey and pinched he looked.

'Suitably lovesick for Carlos,' said Baby, handing her a large vodka and tonic. 'Dame Hermione assured me earlier that she didn't believe a word of the beastly rumour that I had Aids.'

'Bitch! God, I wish the memoirs weren't on the loose. Every time I open a paper, I expect to see you and me cavorting naked on the lawn at Angels' Reach.'

'Doubt if they'd find space for us, they're so obsessed with Rannaldini.'

The murder was still dominating every radio and television bulletin and every newspaper. Press and police helicopters prowled overhead, giving poor Sylvestre terrible sound problems. There was increasing pressure on Gerald Portland to find the killer. Rannaldini's records were expected to dominate the charts for months to come.

'Very shrewd career move to cop it,' mused Baby. 'Even shrewder if he hasn't. And, talking of dreadful things, I saw Clive in an extremely expensive new beige leather suit, secreting himself into Eulalia Harrison's bedroom just now. What d'you think that means?'

'Something horribly sinister. Perhaps the *Sentinel*'s bought the memoirs.'

Eleven o'clock – it was dark at last. Illuminated by the powerful lights from beneath, like giants with hollowed eyes and great black devouring mouths, Valhalla's trees glowered down. Thunder rumbled behind the black mantle of cloud. Everyone had been ready for hours, but still Dame Hermione had not emerged from her caravan.

Glancing up at the house, Rupert saw one of those aggressive, cropped-haired harpies he used to tangle with when he was an MP, glaring out of an upstairs window. She looked vaguely familiar.

'Where the fuck is Tristan?' he howled.

'Winding Hermione up like Big Ben,' giggled Chloe who, ready and ravishing in her crimson taffeta, was making sly, sliding eyes at Rupert.

'Christ, she's looking good,' muttered Sylvestre. 'Who the hell's giving her one?'

'Valentin, Oscar again, Wolfie, Mikhail again, you again, me again, Alpheus again, Rupert probably, the goat again,' intoned Ogborne. 'God, I could murder a beer.'

Back in her caravan, which, like the canteen, had been towed up to the set, Hermione's determination to look even lovelier than Chloe was not helped by her breaking down every few minutes. 'How could Sergeant Fanshawe think Sexton and I killed Rannaldini? I loved him so much.'

'You are the belle of this wonderful ball,' Tristan was telling her for the hundredth time, 'but you daren't dance with Carlos because all the court is spying on you.'

Tristan looked so strung up and defeated Lucy wanted to kiss away the migraine that was crushing and pincering his tired brain like one of Rannaldini's tortures. But instead she carried on pressing powder into Hermione's forehead, which was wrinkling again.

'You were there, Tristan, when I made my début as Elisabetta in Paris. Rannaldini was my handsome prince, my forbidden Carlos, married to Cecilia – who's now got all the money,' Hermione snorted indignantly. Then, reverting to tragedy, 'Can you believe he has gone?'

Oh, don't cry again, prayed Lucy, who had just added mascara to every single lower lash.

They all jumped at an imperious rat-tat-tat on the door.

'It'll be sunrise in a second,' shouted Rupert. 'What the hell are you doing?'

'Briefing Hermione,' said Tristan evenly.

'Brief is *not* the word. You've been in there two hours.'

'I *am* directing this movie,' said Tristan haughtily.

'Even more deeply into the red. For Christ's sake, move it.'

'Is that Rupert?' cried Hermione in excitement.

'No, it isn't,' said Rupert, running away.

Chloe and Pushy thought this was hysterical.

Despite the delays, everyone clapped dutifully when Hermione finally arrived, because Hype-along had bribed the entire crew with miniature bottles of Jack Daniels – very welcome at a time of Rupert's enforced abstinence.

As Chloe had slagged off Hermione in the *Mail* that morning, and Hermione had slagged off Chloe in the *Telegraph*, and Pushy, in her pink satin, had trashed them both in the *Mirror* ('Roberto's chopper was always at my disposal'), the mood was far from sunny. All three women claimed they'd been 'utterly misquoted' and that Eulalia Harrison would set the record straight when her definitive piece appeared.

Despite her alleged weight loss, Hermione's gold flesh was spilling over the top of her vermilion strapless dress like a cheese soufflé.

'Wonder *bravissimo*,' called out Ogborne.

'Helen could use that cleavage as a cache-pot,' said Rupert.

'Hopefully for a cactus,' giggled Chloe. 'She looks like the town tart with all that slap.'

Realizing that Hermione had resorted to some last-minute blusher, a cursing Lucy rushed forward to tone down her cheeks.

'Leave her alone,' exploded Rupert. 'She's masked for most of this scene.'

At last everyone was in position.

'Quiet behind the camera,' shouted Wolfie.

'Cut,' shouted Tristan, a minute later. 'What is the matter, Hermione?'

'Flora is masking me.'

'I'm guarding you,' protested Flora.

'And why's she wearing dark glasses? So affected and attention-seeking.'

Flora burst into tears.

Rupert turned on Hermione. 'Shut up, you fat cow.'

Hermione burst into tears. Down streaked her mascara from every individual lower lash. Lucy flipped.

'You stupid man, I'll need at least twenty minutes to patch her up.'

Rupert had just fired Lucy for insubordination, when Baby strolled out of the darkness. Unbuttoning his dinner jacket, he flashed a white T-shirt, saying, 'Come back, Rannaldini, all is forgiven.'

There was a horrified silence.

Rozzy, who'd just arrived with beautifully ironed dress shirts for him and Mikhail, gave a gasp of disapproval. 'How could you, Baby? Show some respect for the dead and consideration for poor Wolfie and Lady Rannaldini – and even Dame Hermione,' she added, as an after-thought.

Rupert looked at Baby for a second then, to everyone's amazement, he began to laugh.

62

Beattie Johnson had successfully passed herself off as Eulalia Harrison for nearly a week. Her most pressing problem was what to pack into Sunday's six-thousand-word spectacular for the *Scorpion* and what to hold back for the book she intended to rush out, to be entitled *With a Thong in My Parts*.

The material, based on Rannaldini's memoirs and the dirt she had picked up in the last few days, was God – or, rather, devil – given. She would have loved more time on the piece, but Valhalla gave her the creeps, she wanted to go back to dressing like a human being, and she was terrified that when Clive discovered that out of the promised million he would only get the already paid two hundred thousand, he would come after her with a bicycle chain.

The police also had a copy of the memoirs and were such frightful gossips they might leak some of the juicier material before Beattie got it into the paper. Finally her boss, Gordon Dillon, was clamouring for copy by early tomorrow and she had to break off tonight to dine with Alpheus who, she hoped, would put icing on the more outrageous cakes.

Sighing with pleasure, Beattie scrolled down potential headlines: 'How Fun-loving Flora Swapped Her Dreary Developer For A Tasty Tenor.' 'How Champion Jockey Isa Lovell Swings Both Ways.' 'How Dame Hermione and Alpheus Were Caught *In Flagrante*.' 'How Granny Took a Trip to Parker's Department Store.' 'The Dark Secret of Rosalind Pringle's Lost Voice.' 'How Lust For My Stepdaughter, Tabitha, Consumed Me.' 'The Woman Tristan de Montigny Loves and Why He Must Never Have Children.' (That was a *chaud pomme de terre* and needed to be checked out on a trip to Paris.) 'Why Lady Griselda Never Married.' 'Why Hermione's Hubby Encouraged Me To Keep Her Happy In Bed.' 'Helen Campbell-Black on Tabitha the Tramp and Taggie the Thicko.'

That would put Rupert into orbit, but not half so much as Rannaldini's favourite canard: 'How Rupert, Posing As the Perfect Dad To Adopt Two Kids, Flew to Buenos Aires to Seduce Abigail Rosen.'

Poor saintly Taggie would be *very* upset.

There were darker secrets: the sado-masochistic lengths to which Rannaldini had gone to titillate his jaded palate, the attempt to murder his stepson, Marcus, during the Appleton piano competition.

'You were rotten to your rancid core, Roberto,' crooned Beattie, as she flipped through his photographs of anorexic Helen, Rubenesque Hermione, ravishing Tabitha, and Rannaldini himself with Tristan's mother, Delphine, more voluptuous than any page-three girl. That was a copy of Étienne de Montigny's painting *The Snake Charmer*. Who the hell had stolen the original? The *Scorpion* had reporters looking for it everywhere.

Beattie's favourite was Chloe and the goat. Such a shame that her proposed caption, 'How Public-school Girls Love Their Nannies', was too hot even for the *Scorpion*, and would have to wait for the book.

Outside, in the dark, haunted garden, she could see Tristan talking to Oscar. Her one regret was that, despite sleeping down the landing from him all week, she had neither pulled nor interviewed the gorgeous director.

Her mobile rang. It was Gordon Dillon. Had she any idea who killed Rannaldini?

'None at all, the police are being singularly inept. They think it's some psychopath who'll kill again.'

'Sooner you get that copy filed the better. If you pinpoint the chief suspects, we can run a competition next week asking readers to guess the murderer.'

'We might market a board game like Cluedo, or, "Haven't Got a Cluedo", in Portland's case.'

'You sure no-one's rumbled you?'

'No-one. They're all so self-obsessed. I'm having dinner with the worst.'

'Well, take care of yourself.'

'I've never had a story like this, Gordy.'

Out of the window, she could see the dark rings of the maze and Rannaldini's Unicorn Glade, both places where, in the old days, Rannaldini had laid her. At the centre of the former she could make out the glimmering silver figure of a pawing, snorting unicorn. Nearer, a fountain and a cascade of white roses were illuminated by huge lights.

'"Come, Eboli."' Hermione's voice soared gloriously into the darkness. '"The feast has but started, and I already tire of its joyful noise."'

She'd better organize her own feast, reflected Beattie, which included gulls' eggs, wild salmon, and raspberries and cream. 'With this web, I will snare such a fly as Alpheus,' murmured Beattie, as she put an ice-wrapped bottle of Dom Pérignon into the picnic basket.

She always sweated like a pig as she approached a deadline. What a relief, in her role as grotty Eulalia, that she didn't have to bath or tart up for her date.

Alpheus's long nose was thoroughly out of joint. Having seen a clip of him riding, Rupert Campbell-Black had pronounced he made a sack of potatoes look like Frankie Dettori and refused to let him participate in the polo shoot.

'We can't afford the insurance if you have a fall.'

Nor did Alpheus feel remotely compensated by the

beautiful £3000 suit Griselda had hired for him to wear as a kingly spectator.

Going into the production office on Thursday night, he found it deserted except for Mikhail, four forks sticking out of a dinner jacket pocket, gabbling endearments into the telephone.

'It will not be much longer, my darlink.'

Alpheus, who had picked up enough Russian while singing Boris, pursed his lips. Mikhail was clearly getting over Lara very quickly. Realizing he'd been clocked, Mikhail hastily hung up and clanked off. This left Alpheus to conduct a long telephonic interview with *Le Monde*, until he had made sure that Rozzy had departed carrying Mikhail and Baby's dress shirts, and was able to nip into Wardrobe and appropriate his new three-thousand-pound suit.

Alpheus was pleased about his dinner with Eulalia. A double-page spread in the *Sentinel* would be most useful, particularly if it could be held over until September when he had a Wigmore recital and a new solo album, which would need every help to knock Rannaldini off the number-one spot.

'You must be the handsomest man in opera. If you didn't sing, you could make a fortune modelling,' sighed Eulalia, putting in another roll of film. 'So few men can carry off white suits.'

Having embarked on a rare third glass of Dom Pérignon, Alpheus was feeling romantic and manly. In the dusk at Jasmine Cottage, the dog daisies glowed like little moons. Down in the valley, tractors with headlamps were cutting Rannaldini's hay, blotting out the din made by Hermione and Chloe.

'Turn your head slightly, you've got such an imposing profile,' went on Eulalia, 'I'm sure when the *Independent* described you as wooden last year it was only in the context of a great tree sheltering the whole production.'

She was probably right, reflected Alpheus.

Eulalia, he decided, looked like a fashion model in a left-wing paper, with granny specs dominating a pale, set face, leg and armpit hair marginally longer than the hair on her head and a long floating black dress giving no advance information about the figure underneath. Pushing her on the swing earlier, he had deduced from the dark shadow between her hairy legs that she wasn't wearing any panties.

Unfortunately, from Eulalia's point of view, Alpheus was far more interested in analysing himself and his art and singing snatches of *Don Giovanni* with an engaging smile than in dishing the dirt. He had no idea who Tristan was screwing or who might have killed Rannaldini.

Having spent a further half-hour relaying how he sang his first Philip II, Alpheus leant forward, removed Eulalia's spectacles, told her she had lovely eyes and suggested they try some of that delicious picnic to mop up the Dom Pérignon.

'What a nurturing young woman,' said Alpheus, selecting a gull's egg. 'You've even remembered the celery salt.'

Alas, the totally undomesticated Eulalia had not realized gulls' eggs needed boiling, and the first one Alpheus cracked went all over his new white suit. Eulalia was unfazed.

'Elderflower boiled with hemlock and comfrey will get egg yolk out of anything,' she said and, next moment, had pushed Alpheus back on to the damp grass, released his cock, spread it with celery salt and had her incomparably wicked way with him.

Alpheus had never encountered such vaginal muscles: they were like the strong fingers of some pink-cheeked milkmaid. What couldn't he do with a helpmate of such intellect, who could also cater so deliciously to his physical needs? Under those ethnic clothes and all that hair, Eulalia had a surprisingly lovely body. If she flossed and showered a bit more and wore the right clothes . . .

'Oooooh, oooohooo.' Looking up at the newly emerged stars, Alpheus felt himself ejaculate with all the splendour of the Milky Way. 'That was tremendous,' he said graciously.

Then Eulalia spoilt it all by asking if she was a better lay than Chloe, or Dame Hermione, or Pushy, and if he were screwing her to get his own back on Cheryl for going to bed with Rannaldini.

It is difficult to hit the roof when one is lying under a woman journalist. Who had told her such monstrous untruths? spluttered Alpheus.

'I don't figure the *Sentinel* would be interested in such sleaze.'

He had never cheated on Cheryl. Anyone who implied differently was jealous, probably Chloe, who had become overly possessive when he'd formed a working partnership with Dame Hermione.

'Bollocks, you lying old hypocrite.' Eulalia jumped to her feet.

In her floating black dress, her spectacles glinting evilly in the starlight, she suddenly looked like the Grand Inquisitor. Snatching up a handful of grass and wild-flowers, shoving them between her legs, she ran down the mossy steps to her car.

Going inside, Alpheus discovered his lovely suit was covered in grass stains as well as egg yolk. He was not hunting for comfrey and hemlock at this hour. The grandfather clock in the hall was striking half twelve. Checking the kitchen calendar, which featured a guillemot with a fish hanging from its beak, rather like Bernard's moustache, Alpheus realized it was now Friday, the thirteenth, and shivered.

The only answer was to burn the suit and blame its disappearance on Mikhail, who had admired it hugely. Then he remembered all the photographs Eulalia had taken. Somehow he'd got to stop her using them.

63

When Hermione and Chloe's little scene still wasn't in the can by twelve thirty, a despairing Tristan called a break. He was sure the crew were deliberately going slow. There were dark mutterings as they set off sulkily for the canteen. How could they be expected to flourish on roast pork, minty new potatoes, spring rolls, red cabbage and apple pie and cream without a few glasses of red?

'Just one glass,' Tristan pleaded with Rupert. 'It's getting cold.'

'No,' said Rupert, switching on his mobile.

Immediately it rang.

'Don't want to alarm you, Rupe,' confided an old racing crony from the *Sun*, 'but we're convinced that Eulalia Harrison's Beattie Johnson in disguise.' Rupert felt icicles dripping down his spine. 'Any chance of us getting your side of the Abigail Rosen story?'

'No,' snarled Rupert, and hung up.

No wonder Eulalia had seemed familiar. Over the years Beattie had nearly destroyed him and everything he loved. This time she wasn't going to get away with it. He had never bedded Abby Rosen. He would kill to protect Taggie.

The telephone rang again. Talk of the angel. It was Taggie with brilliant news. Gablecross had found the man who'd driven Tabitha home on Sunday, who could

542

give her an alibi. Rupert had never dreamt he would feel passionately grateful to George Hungerford. 'Whatever happens,' he told Taggie, 'I want you to know I've always loved you.'

Looking up he saw what must be Eulalia/Beattie's window in darkness. It was much colder. Everyone was putting on jerseys. The clapper-loader was changing his board to Friday the thirteenth.

Rupert's friend on the *Sun* wasted no time in breaking the news of Beattie's masquerade to Hermione, who choked on her second helping of roast pork, to Chloe, who went green, and to Flora, who looked about to faint. Soon the rumour was circulating to universal panic: nearly everyone had spoken on and off the record to Eulalia. Suddenly the large police presence, hovering in the surrounding bushes or watching from the top floor of the south wing, seemed totally inadequate.

'Beattie's not answering her mobile,' said a shaken Griselda.

'She was talking to Clive earlier. Probably buying the memoirs for the *Scorpion*.'

Tristan had gone very white but, determined to limit any damage, said that Rupert's friend from the *Sun* had probably been fishing.

'We must stay calm,' he told Oscar.

The crew were sourly drinking Perrier. Mikhail was appropriating more forks. Bernard retreated to a quiet corner of the canteen with a roll, a piece of Brie and his crossword. He was glad there were people around. The park beyond was very shadowy and dark.

Then he gave a gasp as his crossword swam green before his eyes.

'It's been completely filled in by Rannaldini.' His hoarse voice was falsetto with fear. 'Even his Ms are the same, like football posts.' He brandished the pages with a frantically shaking hand, as everyone gathered round.

'*Mon Dieu.*' Valentin crossed himself. 'Where did you leave it?'

543

'On the set – on top of my briefcase, beside Tristan's chair.'

Wolfie had gone dreadfully pale. 'I don't believe it,' he stammered, returning the crossword to Bernard. 'I swear the body was my father's.'

'Of course it was! How often do I have to tell you there are no such things as ghosts?' snapped Rupert.

'I'll take that newspaper, if you please,' said DC Lightfoot.

'Lucy!' cried Simone, dragging Flora into Make Up, pointing to the white strip on her neck above the suntan, which had been revealed by her latest short back and sides.

'That strip shows the executioner where to drop the axe,' sobbed Flora, as Lucy blended it in. 'If Beattie dumps, George and I are finished.'

A worried Trevor couldn't lick away her tears fast enough.

A bored James whined irritably from his bench seat.

'Oh, shut up, James,' wailed Lucy despairingly.

'I'll walk him and Trev for you after the break,' said Rozzy soothingly.

Helen was packing five suitcases of clothes to be unhappy in at Penscombe, when a trembling Mrs Brimscombe rushed in.

'Oh, my lady, they're saying that woman typing next door all week is that Beastly Johnson.'

'Omigod!' Helen clutched a bedpost. Eulalia had been far more supportive than the bereavement counsellor. They had spent hours and hours discussing Helen's hangups about Tabitha, Rupert and Taggie. 'She must be stopped,' she whispered.

Meanwhile, talk of Bernard's briefcase had reminded Rupert his own was still on the set. With Beattie on the prowl, he had better retrieve it.

A chill breeze scattered another snowstorm of petals from the rose arch and shook the pearly drops of the fountain. An owl hooted; ahead a cigar glowed like a tiny brakelight. Then, as Rupert's eyes became accustomed to the dark, his blood ran cold and his heart stopped. For there, on the set, sitting in his executive producer's chair, was Rannaldini. The collar of his highwayman's cloak was turned up, caressing the planed cheeks of his cold, haughty face; his pewter hair gleamed in the moonlight. In a garden heady with the scent of lilies, honeysuckle and night-scented stock, Rupert was suddenly asphyxiated by a waft of Maestro.

'Who are you?' he managed to croak.

But as Rannaldini slowly turned towards him, Rupert bolted. Crashing through the dark garden, hurtling into the canteen, sending cast and crew flying, he rushed up to the bar.

'Gimme a quadruple whisky.'

'Mr Sexton insist no drink.'

'Don't be so fucking silly, I've just seen Rannaldini.'

'Mr Sexton say no drink,' persisted Maria.

'I thought you didn't believe in ghosts,' said a grinning Baby.

Having gone behind the bar and poured Rupert a large Bell's, Wolfie went in search of the briefcase, but when he returned with it five minutes later, he said the set had been deserted.

'Well, there's no way I'm putting up with this sort of thing,' said Rupert shirtily. 'I'll leave you to it,' he told Tristan, who tried not to look relieved. At least, they'd get on quicker.

'I want everyone back on the set by one thirty,' he shouted, as he picked up his mobile and vanished into the darkness.

Beattie returned to Valhalla, kicking herself for wasting time on such a jerk. As she let herself into her suite, however, she found a note, typed on dove-grey production-office paper, shoved under her door. 'Meet me in the Unicorn Glade at one fifteen and I will tell you who killed Rannaldini.'

Beattie wanted to bay like a bloodhound. Hell! It was ten past already. She hoped she wasn't too late. This was going to be the greatest exclusive ever. The scoop *de grâce.*

Quickly checking that no-one had tampered with her machine, she pressed the save button and set out for the Unicorn Glade. Thank God, when she was having an *affaire* with Rannaldini, she had memorized the shortcut through the maze. It was so dark and claustrophobic you could easily lose your bearings. She ran so fast she kept cannoning off the sides, the rough, clipped yew twigs scraping her face and arms.

'Right, left, right,' she panted, 'and right towards the Pole Star,' she could hear the crew chatting as they returned to work, 'and left, right, left towards the great constellation of Pegasus,' and she was out on the other side, leaping in terror as an icy hand clawed her face. Then she laughed, realizing it was only a weeping willow, wet from an earlier shower. Jumping the Devil's Stream, Rannaldini's only spring still flowing, running under a rose arch, she was into the Unicorn Glade.

Based on a fifteenth-century tapestry, hanging in the Musée de Cluny in Paris, this small, exquisite private garden had only been open to outsiders since Rannaldini's death. Filled with scented flowers and herbs, it was populated with little stone foxes, weasels, cats and greyhounds lying down with crossed paws beside rabbits to symbolize that even natural enemies can live in harmony.

Legend had it that the unicorn could only be tamed by a virgin, and in the original tapestry a chaste lady sat in the centre of the garden with the unicorn crouched beside her, his front hoofs on her knee as she stroked his neck.

But, as the joke went, there had never been any virgins

546

in Valhalla, so this touching tableau had been replaced by a lone unicorn, gleaming silver in the starlight as he tossed his head and pawed the grass.

Beattie could almost hear the proud little fellow snorting, as she leant against him to regain her breath. Caressing his smooth back, she ran her fingers up his mane, and his grooved horn, which was raised like a sword on guard. As a child, she had always longed for a pony. Rupert's horses and Olympic gold for show-jumping had been one of the reasons she'd fallen so much in love with him. If he hadn't dumped her, she would never have been bringing the gorgeous bastard down.

Glancing round at opulent shrub roses, towering delphiniums and massed white foxgloves, any of which could conceal the writer of the letter, she was suddenly overwhelmed by a feeling of doom and froze with terror as one of the shadows separated and came towards her.

Then, as the moon emerged from a scurrying black cloud, she saw Rannaldini's face, colder and whiter than any moon, but with eyes crueller and hotter than hell. The dark cloak slid over the dewy grass, as he swept towards her on his way to conduct a requiem.

The words 'I never meant to slag you off' withered on Beattie's lips. She couldn't scream, only retreat, as he came nearer and nearer. Then she tripped backwards over a little stone fox, and felt herself falling. The pain was unimaginable.

64

By three o'clock in the morning the wind had risen, all the crew had put on jackets, and Hermione had grumbled bitterly enough about the treacherous night air to have appropriated Rozzy's dark red mohair cardigan and Bernard's duffel coat.

Noticing Rozzy shivering uncontrollably and fighting a racking cough, Tristan took off his bomber jacket and put it round her shoulders. 'You must take care of that throat.'

In fascinated horror, Lucy watched Rozzy turn her head and drop a kiss on his hand as it rested for a second on her shoulder. Her ecstasy was unmistakable. Earlier in the day, Rozzy had been into Rutminster for treatment for her cancer, but recently Lucy had noticed her poring over the score of *Der Rosenkavalier*, marking in the part of Marschallin with yellow Pentel. Had Rozzy convinced herself she could sing in the opera after all?

Wolfie, constantly taunted by nightmarish visions of Tab being photographed in the nude by his father, glanced up at Valhalla, where chandeliers blazed in nearly every window to create an illusion of a ball in progress. A light was still on in Helen's bedroom. 'She shouldn't be going to Penscombe,' he muttered furiously to Lucy. 'She'll only upset Tab. Christ, I miss her.'

'Poor Wolfie.' Lucy hugged him. 'She'll be back for the polo shoot.'

'When you've finished snogging, Lucy and Wolfgang . . .' called out Tristan, but so acidly no-one laughed.

'Quiet, please,' brayed Bernard.

At three forty-five, Pushy, deciding no-one on the set was paying her enough attention, suggested that as she was *so* much younger than Chloe and Hermione, she and Flora should have a carefree little bop together for the sake of continuity, while the *older* women discussed the ball. 'We did have a love scene earlier,' she pouted.

'No,' cried Flora in revulsion. It was the scene with Pushy that had wrecked her and George.

Seeing Flora about to bolt, and knowing he wouldn't get another night's filming out of her, Tristan told Pushy to pack it in. 'We've got to get this ball scene in the can before sunrise and before Rupert come back and knock our heads together!'

'No way he'll return till Rannaldini's safely back in his coffin,' said Ogborne, in a sepulchral voice.

Three-quarters of an hour later Oscar, pretending to look into his view-finder, had fallen asleep. Flicking his fingers for Ogborne's help, Valentin laid his father-in-law across two chairs. A faint pink flush in a very pale sky heralded the approach of sunrise, pigeons were cooing, blackbirds pecking the lawn for worms.

'Cut and print. Well done, everyone, particularly Chloe,' shouted Tristan. Thank God there were pros like her, who could dispatch a scene in one take. Thank God the deepest anxiety could be dispelled temporarily by a good night's work.

Beyond the set, emerging from the uniform greyness of night, he could see urns overflowing with pink geraniums, white and yellow roses swarming up dark yews and cypresses. Beyond, the tall chimneys of River House soared like pale lupins.

Why aren't I filming dawn? Tristan sighed.

As the crew dismantled the camera tracks, took down lights and prepared the film cans for the courier to take for processing, Lucy wearily removed make-up and wigs, and thought longingly of her bed. Everyone was cheered up by a particularly sumptuous breakfast of fluffy buttery scrambled eggs, smoked salmon and bagels, followed by strawberries and cream. DC Lightfoot, Gablecross and Karen, who didn't want to miss the fun, and half Rutshire Constabulary, who'd been flatfooting round like the chorus of *The Pirates of Penzance*, were soon tucking in as well. Even the French contingent managed to crack a smile when Rupert rolled up with several crates of white and red.

'You can drink yourselves insensible now.'

Having nervously glanced around for Rannaldini's ghost, he dragged a newly arrived Sexton into the production office. Expecting another bollocking about overpaying Lord Waterlane, Sexton was amazed when Rupert announced that George Hungerford was a seriously good guy.

'I fort you loathed him, said he was more of a yobbo than me.'

'Only because he was threatening to ram a motorway up my estate. He's given Tab an alibi and he's offered us his polo field for nothing. And he says we can have the wrap party there too, get us away from Valhalla.'

'What about Lord Waterlane?' asked a wistful Sexton, who'd been invited to lunch at the House of Lords.

'It'll really piss him off, the greedy sod,' said Rupert happily. 'And his vulgar wife too, who was expecting to nail the cast to open her fêtes for the next forty years. Good bloke, George.'

'You are so bleedin' irrational,' sighed Sexton.

'I know how to save money, and I'm also dazzling at playing Cupid.'

Flora, who had changed out of her dinner jacket into a pair of grey linen shorts and a red and yellow striped blazer, looked as young and desolate as a small boy going back to prep school for the second term. Everyone was hugging her, taking her telephone number and saying they'd see her at the wrap party.

'Yes, lovely, I'll be there,' lied Flora, through numbed lips.

She'd send them a crate of champagne – or rather plonk in her new impoverished state – and be at the bottom of the River Fleet by then.

As she walked wearily down to Make Up to collect Trevor, an early bumble bee was burying its face in a dark blue delphinium, the clouds overhead were turning from yellow to pale pink, a black crow swayed on top of one of the Lawson cypresses. In the fields below, black plastic bags of hay lay on the gold stubble like slugs. Any minute Rozzy would rush out and scatter little blue pellets. One magpie for sorrow rose out of the Unicorn Glade.

Even the sight of Trevor, standing on top of James to see out of the caravan window and wagging his tail so hard he nearly fell off, didn't bring a smile to her lips.

As she opened the door, both dogs hurtled down the steps. Having had pees that went on for ever, crapped extensively and examined all the croquet hoops on the lawn to see what foxes and badgers had been about, they belted off, Trevor to woo Maria in the canteen, James to find Lucy.

It was now light enough for Flora to define the stones in the regard ring George had given her on the eve of filming. R for Ruby, E for Emerald, G for Garnet, A for Amethyst, R for Ruby, D for Diamond, spelling the word Regard. At the thought that her darling George would never have regard for her again, Flora collapsed against a huge oak tree sobbing piteously. Everyone swung round, a hush fell at the utter desolation of the sound.

Baby was about to race over and comfort her, when Rupert put a restraining hand on his arm and nodded towards the rose walk where, from arches of acid-green hop fantastically garlanded with a pink rose appropriately called The New Dawn, emerged George Hungerford. He was wearing a dark red polo shirt, dirty white chinos, which looked about to fall down because he'd lost so much weight, and odd shoes. His dark hair was all over the place, and in his hands, in gaudy contrast to Rannaldini's exquisite pastels, was a hastily snatched-up bunch of marigolds, salmon-pink gladioli, scarlet roses and mauve dahlias, which quivered increasingly, like some exotic butterfly.

No-one uttered a word as he approached. Then, in front of four of the finest singers in the world, in a croaky strangulated bass, he started to sing 'Zärliche Libre', Beethoven's little rondo about tender love, which Flora had sung to him so often. He started too high, couldn't reach the top notes and had to begin again. Blood was trickling from hands clutching the roses too tightly. At one moment his voice was so choked by tears he couldn't go on, and the cooing pigeons had to fill in the gap.

Flora appeared frozen to the oak tree; only her knees were quivering as much as George's flowers. Next minute Trevor had erupted jauntily from the maze, nose caked in mud from burying a pork bone, and giving a joyous bark he hurtled across the grass, squashing the flowers as he landed in his master's arms. Once again George nearly ground to a halt, but having dried his eyes on a wriggling Trevor, he managed to falter to the end.

There was a long silence, followed by a burst of cheering and clapping. Swinging round, blinking incredulously, Flora catapulted across the grass, crashing into George's chest. The arm that wasn't holding Trevor and the flowers clamped around her.

'Don't say anything. It's my fault, I'm such a stupid tosser,' mumbled George, as he led her off down the rose walk into the sunrise.

'Oh, how sweet,' sobbed Lucy, running off into the park. Tristan wanted to race after her and apologize for being so sarcastic earlier, but he still had so much to do.

'Why can't *Don Carlos* have a happy ending?' said Griselda, wiping her eyes on a tablecloth.

Even Rupert and Gablecross blew their noses noisily.

'I've always thought Flora a drama queen,' said Hermione sourly.

'Now, now, Hermsie,' said Sexton reprovingly, as he topped up her glass, 'Flora's a sweetheart, and didn't Rupert make a terrific Cupid bringing them togevver?'

Baby, however, who'd been in low spirits all evening, drained his glass of red, turned to Rupert with an expressionless face and said, 'Thank you, Mr Cupid-Black, for ruining the only chance of happiness I've ever had,' and wandered off unsteadily towards the house.

'Another drama queen,' said Chloe scornfully.

'What's the stupid queer going on about?' asked Rupert, in bewilderment.

'Irrespective of his sexual orientation,' said Tristan sharply, 'Baby really loves Flora.'

'At least George and Flora's is one relationship Beattie Johnson hasn't screwed up,' said Sexton. 'What's up for this evening?'

'We'll really have to motor,' Tristan reeled off a punishing list of cover shots, 'and we've got to shoot Alpheus praying before his coronation and Hermione walking up the aisle to join him, and I must reshoot Carlos removing Posa's knife. I've decided it would work better with a gun, and the scene in the centre of the maze didn't work either, too small and claustrophobic. The Unicorn Glade is ringed with yew hedge. We could fake it as the centre of the maze.'

'Let's go and look,' said Oscar, helping himself to a second plate of scrambled eggs for the journey. A yawning Valentin brought a bottle and glasses as well.

'See you in 'alf an 'our, Princess,' whispered Sexton to Hermione, before belting after the others.

A thrush was singing joyfully, 'Night is over, night is over.'

Had Rannaldini deliberately grown roses up his

nymphs to see thorns plunging cruelly into their naked flesh? wondered Rupert. A faun, leering wickedly out of ferns snaking above a water trough, seemed to wink at him.

'What *are* we going to do about that Beattie Johnson?' muttered Sexton in an undertone. If Hermsie found out he hadn't been to Eton, she'd drop him like an 'ot coal.

'Take her out,' said Rupert. 'George has some ideas, we'll thrash it out after this.'

Noticing crows circling like vultures above the Unicorn Glade, he quickened his step, admiring the stone rabbits and hounds frolicking peacefully with cats and foxes amid the flowers. But although the sun no longer cast a rosy glow, the little white unicorn snorting and pawing in the centre had become a strawberry roan, and Eulalia in her flowing black robes, resting against his raised head, had become an hermaphrodite.

As the men moved closer, they noticed an expression of terror grotesquely contorting her features. Then they realized it was her blood streaming over the unicorn's noble head and running in rivulets down his shaggy mane. His grooved horn had pierced through her back and was now rising from her belly like a bloodstained phallus.

'Jesus.' Rupert was the first to speak. 'It's Beattie. She's finally stabbed herself in the back.'

'Are you sure?' drawled Oscar, hastily refilling his glass, draining it, then filling it for Valentin.

'Quite,' said Rupert, lifting her skirt as he had so often in the past. 'Look, there's a cat tattooed on the inside of her left thigh. To get into the part she's even dyed her bush black.'

'And green,' said Oscar, pointing to the handful of wild flowers Beattie had earlier stuffed between her legs.

A little tape-recorder had been attached to her thigh, but the tape had been removed.

'Her spectacles are broken.' Tristan picked up the buckled, paneless granny glasses.

554

The resourceful Ogborne, never without a camera, was taking pictures even of the ashen Wolfgang throwing up into some mauve campanula.

'She's also been shot,' said Sexton, walking round the body. 'There's an exit wound big as a grapefruit on this side. You all right?' he asked a returning Wolfie, who, wiping his mouth on his sleeve, looked terrified and absurdly young.

Wolfie nodded. 'Here's a note.' He retrieved a grey crumpled piece of paper from some catmint.

'Meet me in the Unicorn Glade at one fifteen,' read Rupert.

'I'll have that, if you please, Mr Campbell-Black,' said Gablecross firmly. 'No-one is to touch the body. After we've searched Miss Johnson's room, I'd like statements from all you gentlemen.'

65

As Gablecross and Karen panted up the stairs they were met by Helen in a coffee-coloured silk dressing-gown and a frightful state.

'I haven't had a wink of sleep. Every light in the place has been blazing all night. Liberty Productions are damn well going to pick up the bill. Eulalia's phone's been ringing all night too, and her room's locked so I can't get in to answer it. It's too bad, after all the hospitality we've given her.'

She was even more hysterical after Beattie's door had been broken down to find drink rings and cigarette burns all over the Jacobean furniture, black coffee spilt on the priceless Persian rugs and scrumpled tissues all over the floor.

Gablecross's first impression was that Beattie had done a runner. Except for an ashtray brimming over with fag ends, her desk had been cleared. There was no hard copy, notebooks, floppy disks, tapes of interviews or telephone conversations. All the drawers were empty. In the bathroom, however, was a sponge-bag and a bottle of black hair dye.

As they discovered her computer smashed on the floor, her mobile rang. 'Answer it,' snapped Gablecross. 'Pretend you're Beattie.'

'Hi, there,' purred Karen.

'Where the fuck have you been?' It was the graveyard

tones of Gordon Dillon. 'And where's the fucking copy?'

'What copy?' asked Karen innocently.

'Stop playing games. Six thousand fucking words. I've been trying to get you all night. I hope you locked up the fucking memoirs.'

'What memoirs?' Really, reflected Karen. As a journalist Mr Dillon should know not to use the same adjective more than once on the same page.

'Rannaldini's, for Christ's sake. Are you pissed?'

'There's nothing here.'

'Something must have been saved on the machine.'

'Nothing. I'm afraid the computer's been dropped and its entrails are spilling all over the floor. You could consult them like the Romans did. They might tell you who killed Rannaldini.'

Karen's accent had slipped westward.

'Who the fuck's that?'

'Detective Constable Karen Needham of Rutminster CID,' and ignoring Gablecross's horrified expression and furiously waving hands, 'I'm afraid a body has been found, and Miss Beattie Johnson appears to have been spiked like her rotten copy.'

'You'll get fired,' roared Gablecross.

'No, I won't,' said Karen, who could hardly speak for laughing. 'Gerry utterly loathed Beattie.'

Once again Gerald Portland was absolutely hopping.

'I put twenty men on night duty at Valhalla,' he shouted at the emergency meeting, three hours later, 'and they spend all night drooling over Gloria Prescott, stuffing themselves with roast pork and don't notice a socking great murder two hundred yards away.

'We'll be a laughing stock, and the *Scorpion* will lynch us. They are alleged to have paid a million for those memoirs. They're going to bill that fucking bitch as the greatest journalist since Homer. They're offering fifty thousand for information leading to the capture of her murderer, so no-one will call us any more. Jesus!'

Portland had indeed been no lover of Beattie. While the rest of the media had nicknamed him Pin-up Portland, she had called him Inspector Portly, just because he'd gained a few pounds on a Caribbean cruise, and described his upwardly mobilized accent as 'so camp you could cut it with a Boy Scout's penknife'.

'How come none of you realized it was her?' he shouted at his team.

'Bloody good disguise, Guv'nor.' DC Lightfoot scratched his head. 'Could have sworn she was the spinster maiden-aunt type.'

'I'd forget that line of reasoning if I were you,' snapped Portland. 'Pathologist says she's got a vagina like the M1.'

'I beg your pardon.' DC Smithson pursed her lips as the men grinned.

'So many people have been up and down, stupid, it's very well worn. It's early days, but the pathologist also reckons she was killed between one and two, and had intercourse perhaps half an hour before that. The plants stuffed up her vagina appear to contain some rare specimens.'

'Mustard and cress,' giggled Karen.

'Someone', Portland threw her a look of fond reproof, 'appears to have bitten Beattie's shoulder – we can DNA that. Her specs were broken so we're looking for fragments on the murderer's clothes.'

They had already found the murder weapon, a .22, chucked into the long grass by the Devil's Stream. It had been taken from Props.

'Who has a key?' Fanshawe asked.

'Everyone in that department, but the prop master said the doors are often open all day, it would be easy for the murderer to get a key cut. It's a single-shot gun,' he continued, 'so the killer would not be expecting to miss. It'd been handled in filming during the *auto da fe* by Baby and Mikhail, and covered in their prints which Forensic are isolating.'

It had been a pretty lively evening, according to DC Lightfoot, what with the sightings of Rannaldini and the filling in of Bernard's crossword, which had gone off to the graphologist. As a final act of defiance, one of Rannaldini's cigars had been found stubbed out in Beattie's ashtray.

'Wow,' sighed Karen. 'D'you think our murderer's really dressing up as Rannaldini, and that's what terrified Beattie? She probably wrote worse things about him in her pieces for Sunday than anyone else.'

'Possible,' mused Portland, examining the note again. ' "Meet me in the Unicorn Glade at one fifteen." This was written by someone familiar with a keyboard – it's not a two-finger job.'

'Who would have wanted to murder Beattie?'

'Everyone,' said Portland, with feeling. 'If she had the memoirs, and if she hadn't, they'd all blabbed or been stitched up by her.'

Paddy, Rupert's racing crony on the *Sun*, had quickly been on to Portland, saying he'd tipped off Rupert and all the big names that Eulalia was Beattie just after twelve thirty.

'Sounded like a turkey farm in mid-December,' Paddy had added gleefully. 'Most of them were only too happy to give their side of the story for a consideration. News travels so fast on a film set, everyone must have known Beattie was Eulalia by the middle of the break.'

'Still didn't give them much time to send her a note and murder her before they had to start work again,' said Gablecross.

'If the murderer had a master key,' said Karen excitedly, 'they could have let themselves into Eulalia's room much earlier, discovered she was Beattie and waited till Friday, just before she filed copy, to kill her and whip the piece so they could get hold of as much sleaze as possible.'

'Good girl,' said Portland approvingly.

'Mrs Brimscombe says Beattie went out about ten

thirty,' said DC Lightfoot. 'Murderer could have nipped in then, nicked all the stuff, printed out the piece and left a note under the door.'

'Risky,' said Karen. 'If Beattie returned, found the memoirs and disks missing and the piece run off, she might have smelt a rat or two and not gone to the Unicorn Glade.'

'More likely', said Fanshawe dismissively – anyone would have thought DC Needham was running this meeting, 'the murderer killed her, then returned to her room, fucked the computer, having printed off and nicked Beattie's stuff, then hidden that and returned to the set by one thirty as though nothing had happened.'

'Unlikely it was as early as that,' said Gablecross, who was pissed off with Karen but wasn't having anyone bullying her. 'Sylvestre, the sound man, who can hear mobiles three streets away, heard a scream around one twenty and assumed it was some singer acting up but swears he heard a crash as late as one thirty-five.'

'By which time most of them would have been back on the set.'

'Not Mr Campbell-Black,' said Gablecross darkly. 'He hates Beattie most of all. He pretended to see a ghost and buggered off to visit George Hungerford, or so he says. They came back together, both quite capable of putting out a contract on Beattie. Tristan de Montigny disappeared into the darkness with his mobile.

'Alpheus Shaw', Gablecross pointed up at the unit photograph, 'says he made a few phone calls in the production office, where he was seen by Mikhail, then he returned to Jasmine Cottage for an early night. Baby says he was with Flora.

'Immediately Chloe, Gloria, Hermione, et cetera, learned it was Beattie,' he continued, 'they were trying to get on to her, begging her not to shop them. I imagine those were the phone calls Lady Rannaldini heard through the night. She swears she had no idea that Eulalia was Beattie. I think she's lying. She's now shoved off to Penscombe to stay with Rupert and Taggie. Sexton Kemp rolled up on the set at four thirty.'

'Funny time to be wandering around,' said Fanshawe, who was still hoping to nail Hermione and Sexton for the murder. 'Lucy Latimer spent most of the evening giving Dame Hermione resprays, Rozzy Pringle ferrying clean shirts.'

'Very easy to come and go on a film set.' Gablecross shook his head. 'Never use everyone at the same time.'

'Better search their rooms,' said Portland.

'Can't at the moment.' DC Lightfoot looked at his watch. 'They'll be sleeping. They get wake-up calls around five.'

'Funny old time for Beattie to cop it,' mused Portland, 'missing the nationals.' Then, answering his telephone, 'Great, thanks, I'll be along.' Rubbing his hands, he told his team, 'They've identified the fingerprints on the .22 and the wheel marks in the field off Rannaldini's drive.'

But as Portland left the room, Gablecross followed him into the corridor, looking extremely sheepish.

'Could I have a word, Guv'nor?' Then, pulling a letter and a bit of paper out of his inside pocket, 'I'm afraid in the excitement of blowing Clive's safe, I forgot I'd left this in my other jacket. It was in French. Karen's translated it.'

Having made a statement about Beattie's murder, Helen had left for Penscombe. This in turn left her maids, Betty and Sally, with more time on their hands. They were so terrified of hearing Rannaldini's cloak slithering along the corridors that they always worked as a pair now.

They were concerned about their beloved Tristan. He had always been so courteous and grateful. Filming all night, caught up in admin all day, he looked absolutely dreadful. They had learnt never to touch his papers, but after they'd emptied the ashtrays and removed the cups, chewing-gum papers and glasses on the morning of Friday the thirteenth, they decided to turn his mattresses. No-one deserved a good sleep more. Having worked at Valhalla, Sally and Betty were not easily fazed. They had found strange sex toys in the past, but were truly shocked to discover between Tristan's mattresses a little pornographic painting of their late master, with a long whip in his hand, flicking the lash round the neck of a beautiful girl.

'Never thought Tristan was into SM,' muttered Betty, as they hastily remade the bed.

At lunchtime, Betty had a drink with Fanshawe in the Pearly Gates, and after the second vodka and bitter lemon confessed their finding.

'Blimey!' Fanshawe had never downed a St Clement's faster. Belting back to the house, gathering up Sally on the way, up in Tristan's bedroom, they found the Montigny had vanished.

'I know it was here,' panted Sally. 'We saw the horrible thing.'

'Tristan must've come back, seen you'd cleaned the room, and whipped – pardon the pun – the evidence,' said Fanshawe.

But all was not lost: his eyes lit on a pair of off-white chinos and a bottle-green polo shirt lying newly ironed on the bed.

'When were those washed?'

'First thing Monday morning,' replied Sally. 'We always go round the rooms gathering up the washing. Even on the morning after *he* was murdered, and everyone was flapping around because Tristan hadn't come back, Wolfie said it'd be better if we kept to our routine.'

Gablecross and Karen were both dreading their next interview. It coincided with an unexpected hailstorm, which had sent the press racing for shelter. Lucy's caravan was empty. They found her rescuing a meadow brown from the stony deluge and setting it down under the protection of a hawthorn bush. Her day's sleep had been wrecked by flickering nightmares of Rannaldini, by a restless James barking at prowling police and paparazzi, and by her churning misery that Tristan, as never before, had not apologized for bitching at her.

Her eyes were red and swollen, her skin shiny and unhealthily sallow, her dark brown curls in need of a wash, but her smile was welcoming and she was still, thought Gablecross, easily the most attractive woman on the unit. He and Karen accepted cups of tea, but neither had the stomach for Battenburg cake.

'James hates marzipan too,' said Lucy, going back to sticking Polaroids into a scrapbook with toupee tape.

Initially the questions were innocuous. What had she been doing in the break? Had she noticed anything odd?

'I didn't really have time to notice anything.'

'Sweet little kids.' Karen admired Lucy's nieces round the mirror, as she took out her notebook.

At first when it spun glittering gold on the table, Lucy thought Gablecross had thrown down a coin. Then she realized it was a signet ring. Had she seen it before?

'Of course, it's Tristan's.'

'Motto's in French, know what it means?'

For a second, Lucy looked at the chained, hissing serpent, peering at the tiny words beneath. '"If you disturb the Montigny snake,"' she said slowly, '"the Montigny snake will come looking for you," i.e. "Leave us alone, and we won't hassle you."'

'Rannaldini didn't leave Tristan alone, did he?'

Careful, thought Lucy, not realizing she had stuck Hermione in upside down.

'Take a look at this,' said Gablecross. 'We found it in Rannaldini's safe.'

The same snake crest headed the yellowing sheet of writing paper. Beneath was an exquisite little drawing of two entwined lovers. The writing was so beautiful you were inclined to believe anything it told you.

'My French is hopeless,' she mumbled.

'Here's a translation,' said Karen.

'"My dear Rannaldini,"' read Lucy. As the colour drained slowly out of her face, she forced her other hand to grab and ground the frantically shaking hand holding the letter. 'So it was true,' she whispered, before she could stop herself.

'What?' said Gablecross sharply.

'Nothing,' stammered Lucy. 'That Étienne confided in Rannaldini so much.'

'Come, come. Those two were friends for thirty years, Étienne's paintings are all over the house. You can do better than that. "Obscene incestuous union . . . I can never bring myself to love him." Étienne clearly wasn't Tristan's dad. Was that why Tristan killed Rannaldini?'

'Don't be ridiculous.' Lucy glanced up at Gablecross's square, bullying, ruthless face.

'Why did he lie that he wasn't back in Valhalla on Sunday night? Why's he refusing a DNA test? He was clearly in shock when he finally rolled up on Monday.'

'That was something else.'

'We believe he killed Rannaldini and then Beattie because he was terrified of the truth coming out. His fingerprints are all over the gun that killed Beattie.'

'They can't be,' whimpered Lucy in terror. 'Oh, please, he was in shock *not* because he killed Rannaldini but because, when he reeled home rapturous, goofy from making love for the first time to Tab,' her voice broke, 'Rannaldini sent for him and told him this horrific thing, that he wasn't a Montigny at all, and far, far worse, that his mad brute of a grandfather on the other side, had raped Delphine, his mother, because he was so wildly jealous that she'd married Étienne. The result was Tristan.'

There, it was out.

Karen winced. Gablecross whistled.

'Wow, so that was it. Thank *you*, Miss Latimer.'

'Please don't tell anyone. You forced it out of me,' gabbled Lucy, in desperate agitation. Oh, God, what had she done?

'You know how proud Tristan is of being a Montigny, how naturally aristocratic. He had no mother to bring him up, Étienne was so cold and dismissive, his great arrogant family of brothers all got preferential treatment. Unlike them, Tristan got nothing personal in the will. Being a Montigny was all he had to cling on to.'

She picked up the signet ring.

'Maxim, Delphine's father, was sectioned and a violent psychopath, according to Rannaldini. Tristan's so honourable he felt that as a result he shouldn't have children.'

The hailstorm had turned to rain weeping down the windows. There was such a long pause that Lucy stumbled into more revelations. 'I'm sure Rannaldini made the whole thing up, probably forged this letter. He was crawlingly obsessed with Tab. He couldn't bear Tristan near her – he'd have made up anything to stop him.'

'Probably why Tristan killed him. Why did he lie about bottling out of his favourite auntie's eighty-sixth birthday party?'

'Can't you understand?' pleaded Lucy. 'She wasn't his auntie if he was no longer a Montigny, any more than Simone was his niece, or his brothers his brothers. He'd have felt a fraud at that party.'

'And he claimed to have spent all night in his car.'

'I've told you about that.' Lucy's voice was rising. 'He was exhausted, everyone drains him. This film has been so awful. The next one, now his roots have been severed, was all he had.'

An embarrassed, upset James had curled up almost as small as Tristan's signet ring, which Gablecross was holding up to the light.

'He dropped this beside Rannaldini's body.'

'I don't believe it. He hadn't worn that ring for ages. It was so loose it kept falling off.'

'Beside Rannaldini's *dead* body,' intoned Gablecross. 'The Montigny snake went looking for Rannaldini and coiled itself round his neck until it squeezed the life out of him.'

'No, no!' Lucy clapped her hands over her ears.

'Same reason he stole *The Snake Charmer*.'

'Course he didn't.'

'Betty and Sally found it under his mattress on Thursday. By the time they'd alerted a police officer, he'd whipped it. Rannaldini was going to publish a copy of the painting in his memoirs. Tristan couldn't cope with a pornographic photograph of his mum being on display so he killed Rannaldini and Beattie.'

'No, no.' Lucy burst into tears, head on the table, clenching and unclenching her hands.

'Cooee, cooee,' said a voice.

It was Chloe, avid with excitement, eyes swivelling, reeking of the same beautiful scent.

'I hope you're not bullying darling Lucy, Tim. She's got a long night ahead, and I don't want my lip-liner looking like an is-he-alive, is-he-dead heartrate in Intensive Care.'

Leaving Lucy's caravan on the way back to the car park, both feeling sick, Gablecross and Karen saw a lone figure slumped at a table outside the canteen, and realized it was Wolfie.

'Can we join you?' asked Karen, slipping into the chair beside him.

'You can arrest me if you like,' mumbled Wolfie. 'Why shouldn't I have killed my father? He left me nothing and stole the only two girls I've ever loved.' His teeth were chattering frantically.

'It's all right, lad.' Gablecross patted the boy's shoulder. 'Your dad had cameras and bugs installed in every room, even at Magpie Cottage. Tabitha never posed for him, I could swear it.'

'And', went on Karen, taking Wolfie's hand, 'I'm sure he left you nothing because was jealous of you.'

Wolfie raised incredulous, swollen, bloodshot eyes.

'Because Tab liked you so much,' added Gablecross. 'I read it in the memoirs.'

'Papa was jealous of me?' Suddenly Wolfie was grinning from pink ear to pink ear. 'Because of Tab?'

'Certainly was,' said Karen. 'It was you she turned to after he raped her.'

But Wolfie wasn't listening. 'I don't give a stuff about the money, I can earn my own. Tab's the only thing I care about.' Then, getting to his feet and going, somewhat unsteadily, towards the bar, 'Let's have a drink. The only problem', he added wryly, 'is that she's madly in love with Tristan. Still, it's a start.'

Over in his caravan, Tristan had neither been to bed nor had a moment to rejoice over the ecstatic reviews flooding in for *The Lily in the Valley*.

There had been so much to do. Someone had nicked Alpheus's white suit from Wardrobe. The .22 stolen to kill Beattie had had to be replaced. Helen had gone ballistic about the electricity bill and been ringing all day from Penscombe. Mr Brimscombe had gone equally ballistic because the police had trampled over all his flowers. Rupert and George, who were all buddy-buddy now, kept wanting to have meetings about polo shoots.

He tried to work out tonight's reshoot of the attempted murder of Eboli, an action sequence that required multiple angles and shots so it could be edited to look fast. It would have been complicated even in the Unicorn Glade. This, however, was now gift-wrapped in red and white ribbon and crawling with scenes-of-crime officers, so they'd have to go back to filming in the centre of the maze.

Then there would be several hours spent lighting Alpheus's nose before he prayed in the chapel, but at least that was an interior, which wouldn't be sabotaged by any sunrise.

Tristan was reeling from tiredness. Then another hammer-blow struck: Dupont had rung to say that Aunt

Hortense had been diagnosed with cancer of the pancreas, which could finish her off at any moment. She was heavily drugged and hardly conscious, down at the château in the Tarn.

Tristan was devastated. Hortense might not be his real aunt any more, but she was all he had. He had been saddened and amazed to hear how upset she'd been that he'd cut her party. Perhaps she was a little fond of him, but he had been too traumatized by events to call her to apologize. The moment they finished shooting tomorrow he'd fly out to Toulouse. He felt his world crumbling. If she died before he got there, he'd never discover if Rannaldini had been telling the truth.

'She keeps asking for you,' chided Dupont.

Tristan also felt bitterly ashamed that he wished Hortense had waited until he'd finished shooting to decide to die. Visions of Beattie's stinking, impaled body swam before his eyes. He felt himself retching.

66

'Just like rush-hour on the Piccadilly line,' grumbled Chloe, as most of the unit, including several plain-clothes policemen, squeezed into the centre of the maze. 'Ouch, someone goosed me.'

'Only my brolly, bad luck,' boomed Griselda.

Everyone giggled nervously.

'Quiet, please,' roared Bernard.

Who knew if they were standing next to the murderer? Shirts already soaked in sweat were additionally drenched by the towering rain-soaked yew walls. Even Tristan was wearing his director's cap back to front to stop the drips running down his neck.

'Now I know how labs feel when they're rammed into their kennel after a wet day's shooting,' grumbled Griselda.

'The shooting ees to come,' said Mikhail, admiring his .22.

Everyone else shivered and tried to read Rozzy's copy of the *Evening Scorpion*.

'Killed in Action,' said a huge headline, above an incredibly glamorous photograph of Beattie.

There were endless delays. The moon sailing through an archipelago of angry indigo clouds was making lighting a nightmare.

'Are we going to have problems with those police helicopters?' Tristan asked Sylvestre.

'Music should blot them out but we'll have to watch the long pauses.'

They'd just finished rehearsing when the crush was intensified by Rupert's arrival. As one who believed one should get back on to a horse immediately after a fall, he had dragged along a reluctant, scowling Tab. Wolfie promptly dropped Tristan's shooting script in the mud, which went unnoticed by Tristan, who also felt his heart fail. Tab looked so thin, so pale, so impossibly, ferociously adorable. Griselda hugged her, which made Tab scowl more than ever.

'How ridiculous! We're overcrowded enough as it is,' hissed Rozzy, as she turned over a page of the *Scorpion* to find a large picture, taken years ago, of Rupert arm in arm with Beattie.

'Friend of the Famous,' said the caption.

Having left Tab in the care of an utterly tongue-tied Wolfie, Rupert pushed off to talk to Sexton. The only thing that had driven her out of the house, Tab hissed to Lucy, was the arrival of Helen.

'She insisted Mrs Bodkin unpack for her, then grumbled she couldn't find anything, then pushed Taggie's divine food round her plate all lunch going on and on about Beattie and nurturing a viper in her bosom. Daddy said, "Any self-respecting viper would die of malnutrition trying to survive on all that silicone." He's such a bitch but he does make me laugh. Oh, God, Luce, isn't Tristan divine? I'm not cured at all.'

Glancing surreptitiously across at Tab, Tristan found her gazing at him with such longing it burnt him. He mustn't weaken. If only he could bring himself to explain about Maxim.

'Stand by to shoot,' shouted Bernard.

'We'll have to wait thirty seconds for this cloud, Tristan,' called Oscar, lowering his view-finder from his eye.

'Oh, here's Timothy. I wonder if his wife liked her

present,' said Rozzy, as Gablecross, Karen and two uniformed men with their hats on forced their way in.

'The Grand Inquisitor,' sang Baby. Then, as the music died in the speakers, he launched into '"A policeman's lot is not a happy one, happy one".'

'Hello, Tim,' cooed Chloe, kissing him on both cheeks.

'Tristan de Montigny . . .' began Gablecross, furiously wiping off lipstick.

'Oh, go away,' said Tristan irritably, 'we're about to shoot.'

'Tristan de Montigny,' repeated Gablecross sternly, 'you are being arrested on suspicion of the murders of Roberto Rannaldini and Beatrice Johnson. You don't have to say anything but you may harm your defence if you fail to mention when questioned something you rely on in court. Anything you say may be given in evidence.'

There was a scream from Rozzy, and a rumble of horror that rose to a roar. No, thought Lucy, in dread, I shopped him. Only the people hemming her in kept her from fainting. As chests were thrust out in outrage and the moon went in again, the maze seemed even more terrifyingly claustrophobic.

'You cannot arrest me,' said Tristan haughtily, 'I am making a film, and I have to fly out first thing tomorrow to Toulouse where my aunt is seriously ill.'

And that's the last we'd see of you, matey, thought Gablecross.

'Unfortunately that's irrelevant,' he said. 'You've been arrested on suspicion of murder.'

'At least we finish the scene' said Bernard firmly.

There was a murmur of assent. Gablecross looked round at the solid phalanx of crew, muscular arms folded like a rugger team, blocking any escape, and felt there was no way an English lorry could get through a French blockade.

'Stand by to shoot. Nice and quiet behind the camera,' called Bernard.

Up started the strings, out sailed the moon. Gablecross had to admire the professionalism, particularly Tristan's.

'Roll sound, turn camera,' he said quietly, standing there, as if without a care in the world, never taking his eyes off his singers.

Eboli, with heavy sarcasm, was now attacking Elisabetta's hypocrisy for posing as a virtuous wife when she was all the time having an *affaire* with Carlos, until Mikhail whipped out his .22, spinning it over and over like a hired killer.

The yew walls seemed to expand as people flattened themselves against them. Suppose the gun was loaded? Then Baby leapt forward, squeezing Mikhail's hand like a dog's muzzle.

'Why d'you hesitate?' taunted Chloe, yellow eye flashing.

Everyone jumped as the .22 clattered to the ground.

Lucy felt her eyes filling with tears of despair, as Mikhail begged Baby to hand over to him any incriminating papers he might be carrying to stop them falling into the hands of the Inquisition.

'To you? The *favourite* of the King?' sang Baby, in bitter irony.

It is the only moment in the opera when Carlos doubts Posa's loyalty. Mercifully, no helicopters interrupted the long, long pause. Then, puppy-like, Carlos became all apology, handing over his 'important papers', not realizing he was fatally incriminating his friend, before falling into his arms.

The acting had been so wonderful that for those few moments people had forgotten the murders. As the entire orchestra pounded out the friendship theme, Lucy frantically mopped her eyes.

'I have betrayed my friend,' she thought in agony.

'Cut. That was perfect,' Tristan told everyone. 'Well done. If the gate's clear, print.'

'We'll wrap now, call a weekend break,' said Bernard, who was quivering with rage, 'and by then you'll be bailed.'

'I may not. You, Oscar and Valentin know exactly what to do.' Taking off his director's cap, Tristan plonked it on Bernard's head. 'Now's your chance to play Truffaut.' Then he kissed Bernard on both cheeks, handed him his shooting script and added, with a break in his voice, 'Here are my important papers.'

Finally he turned to Gablecross, mockingly holding out two clenched fists.

'Put on the handcuffs.'

Ogborne and the crew closed in menacingly, but when Tristan shook his head they fell back.

All this was too much for Tab. With a scream of rage, she flew at Gablecross, hammering him with her fists.

'He's innocent, you stupid asshole, Tristan wouldn't hurt a fly. You just need a conviction. Yesterday you thought I'd killed Rannaldini.'

'With some justification,' murmured Chloe.

'Once you get him into that horrible place,' went on Tab hysterically, 'you'll trick him into a confession.'

'*Bébé, bébé*, stop it, please.' Tristan turned back in anguish and pulled Tab off Gablecross. A second later she had fallen against him, sobbing pitifully.

'It's all right.' His arms closed round her. 'I didn't do it, I promise.' For a second, he laid his ashen face against her pale hair and they clung to each other, like souls in torment.

'Mr de Montigny,' said Gablecross, not unkindly.

Tristan searched the appalled, often weeping, faces for one he could trust.

'Lucy, please look after her.'

But as he was led away, Tab had to be prised off by Wolfie.

'He'll be OK.' Lucy made heroic attempts to sound convincing.

'How d'you know?' screamed Tab.

'It's all a terrible mistake,' reassured Wolfie.

'How d'*you* bloody know either?' Tab was about to fly at him, when she caught sight of the photograph of Beattie and her father.

'Stop reading that shit.' She snatched Rozzy's newspaper and tore it to shreds, before storming, like Eboli, out of the maze.

She found her father heaping abuse on Gablecross: 'Tim-Dim-But-Not-At-All-Nice strikes again,' he yelled, then, turning to Tristan, 'Don't worry, we'll bail you first thing tomorrow.'

Having poured so much money into *Don Carlos*, there was no way Rupert was going to lose his director before filming was completed.

'Poor, poor Tristan but also poor me,' sighed Sexton.

They were insured against violent death but not against the director murdering the producer, although it must be a fairly frequent occurrence. He had better get on to the backers to reassure them.

As Tristan vanished into a police car, which in turn vanished under a black tidal wave of press, Hermione could be heard complaining, 'It's very inconsiderate of Timothy. My last night on the set, a most taxing scene. Who will now give me direction?'

'The wrong man's been arrested,' screamed Tab. 'Can't you think of *anyone* but yourself?' She picked up Valentin's discarded plate of porridge and was about to ram it in Hermione's perfectly made-up face when Wolfie grabbed her wrist.

'Pack it in. You're behaving like a stupid child.'

'I'm not stupid. Why don't you do something to help Tristan rather than standing round like a stuck pig?'

After that Rupert took her home.

There was no time to think then until Alpheus and Hermione's little scene in the chapel was safely in the can, but as dawn broke on Tristan's first morning behind bars Wolfie realized Lucy was missing. He found her sobbing in Make Up.

574

'It was my fault he was arrested. I let out his terrible secret.'

She didn't want to hurt Wolfie by revealing his father's part in it, but she had to tell someone she could trust.

Wolfie was totally practical.

'As soon as we get away tomorrow, we're going to France to track down Aunt Hortense and the truth. We'll take the Gulf and leave before anyone finds we've gone.'

67

Gerald Portland had been determined to fight off any takeover by Scotland Yard. 'They hear the West Country burr', he said furiously, 'and think we're turnip-heads down here.'

Pressure from the media and the public, not to mention those viragos in their newly printed 'I loved Rannaldini' T-shirts who were doorstepping Rutminster police station, had been so intense that Portland had rushed Gablecross into making an arrest before he had sufficiently gathered his evidence.

Fortunately, by the time Tristan had been booked in and his clothes, including his beloved peacock-blue shirt, had been whisked off to Forensic, and he'd been forcibly DNA-tested, by having a cotton bud rammed under his tongue, and strip-searched – 'Christ, did you theenk I had Beattie's floppy deesks shoved up my ass?' – it was too late to start questioning him.

Tristan, meanwhile, had been transformed into a snarling wild animal. The final indignity was when he was forced to re-dress himself in the nadir of chic – a papery white boiler-suit.

'I am totally eenocent of murder, but not for much longer,' he yelled, as the custody officer rammed him in a tiny cell with only a single mattress on a low, flat board for a bed and one small frosted-glass window. But at least it had its own bog, and he was so exhausted and so relieved not to have to brief Hermione that not even the arrival of a caterwauling drunk at three in the morning – which he thought, for a hideous moment, might be Mikhail – roused him for long from the best night's sleep he'd had in months.

Prisoners must be checked every twenty minutes. The hatch on Tristan's door was going up every twenty seconds, as women officers and secretaries made flimsy excuses to visit the cells. Winnie, the Polish cleaner, only four foot ten, who had once cornered an escaping serial killer with her Squeegee mop, was continually standing on top of her upturned bucket to peer in.

'He's getting better viewing figures than *Four Weddings and a Funeral*,' grumbled DS Fanshawe.

All this at least gave Gablecross a chance to work out his line of questioning, and gain three hours' sleep beside a tight-lipped Margaret before a quick briefing of the Inner Cabinet.

'We think we've got our man,' announced Portland. 'Application has been made to the French justices to search Montigny's flat in Paris. Police have already raided his rooms in Valhalla, where they found a packed case so he may have been going to do a runner.'

Then, turning to Gablecross and Karen, he said sternly, 'Just remember Montigny's got to cope with what he's done. Don't try to traumatize him any further. You're not there to trick him, just unlock his memory. Never underestimate the blackest villain's longing to be thought well of so don't be judgemental or hostile. Are you hearing me, Tim? All you want to know is what happened and how it came about.'

'Let me get at him,' muttered Gablecross.

'Get us a curl of his hair, Karen,' whispered Debbie Miller.

Karen was terribly nervous. It was the first time she'd had to interrogate a murderer. The minute they'd exhausted a forty-five-minute tape, Gerry Portland would seize a copy for a listen. It was suddenly so set in stone. It scared her that, as the interviewing officers, she and Gablecross had priority and could order members of the investigating team to follow up leads for them.

But Karen was not as nervous as Tristan when he woke up and reality kicked in. It was not just backs-to-the-wall but shoulders rammed against the skeleton cupboard, the lock of which Gablecross would soon be relentlessly picking. Christ, he had so much to hide. How could he hold together a brain disintegrating like a paper handkerchief in the bath?

He had refused a lawyer. There was no way he wanted grey, desiccated Dupont jetting over at thousands of francs an hour, crying crocodile tears, then telling his brothers, and all Paris, 'Now I know why Étienne rejected the boy . . .'

All Tristan wanted, for the moment, was a telephone, nearly giving the duty officer monitoring his call a coronary as he broke into rapid French to find out how last night's shoot had gone.

Surprisingly well, according to Bernard. They'd finished all the cover shots and Rupert's briefing of Hermione – 'Walk up the sodding aisle and kneel down beside that American dickhead' – had been terse but effective.

Bernard admired Rupert more and more, particularly when this piece of information made Tristan laugh, but only until he'd asked for news of Hortense.

'Drifting in and out of consciousness, but sinking fast, I'm afraid.'

'I've gotta get out of here,' raged Tristan.

'Don't worry. Rupert's been on to the French Ambassador and the Home Secretary half the night. Are you OK, *mon enfant?*'

'Well, no-one's tugging out my toenails or threatening to burn me at the stake.'

He had regained his cool by the time he entered the interview room, which was windowless, oblong, furnished with only a square black table and chairs and, he remarked, almost as minimalist as his flat in Paris.

Karen giggled, Gablecross rolled up his sleeves, loosened his tie and switched on the tape-machine, which clung to one of the cracked walls like a leech.

To relax him, Karen at first asked him about his childhood, drawing him out on hoary old Hortense, on the hostility of his father, on his admiration for Laurent, the freedom fighter, who never squealed under torture, and on Rannaldini's affection, which had done so much to dispel Tristan's sense of failure as a son.

Then, making sterling efforts not to sound hostile, Gablecross switched to the day of Rannaldini's murder, and Tristan told the same story, how he'd returned in the middle of Sunday, driven round the Forest of Dean looking for locations.

'In particular the final scene, when Hercules rip up enough oak trees to build his own funeral pyre.'

'Like films about fires, do you?' asked Gablecross casually. 'Have you any idea how Rannaldini's watch-tower caught fire?'

'I tell you, I was miles away in Dean Forest.'

He had bought a half-bottle of brandy at an off-licence, he added, but had lost the tab, and had slept in a field.

'I need peace. For three months, to avoid importuning courtiers, I scuttle down passages like Louis XIV. I was unhappy with Rannaldini's opening and ending. They were too self-indulgent. I needed to plot my campaign.'

'What was the field like?'

Tristan shrugged. 'Just a field.'

'What were you wearing when you came through the Channel Tunnel on Sunday?'

Careful, thought Tristan. 'A blue shirt and jeans.'

'How d'you explain this, then?'

Karen produced an *Evening Standard* photograph, obviously snapped by some fan, of Tristan in a bottle-green polo shirt and off-white chinos outside his car in Dover.

'Maybe I was wearing that. I don't notice clothes. I search for trouser for five minutes yesterday morning before I find I had them on.' Tristan smiled helplessly – the lovable eccentric.

Gablecross wasn't beguiled.

'Betty says before you left for Paris on Saturday you were looking everywhere for that blue shirt, which Sally, knowing it was a favourite, had whipped to mend a rip in the shoulder and sew on more buttons. She left the shirt washed and ironed on your bed on Sunday morning. On Monday morning before you got back it had gone, and both Sally and Betty found your white chinos and green polo shirt in the dirty-clothes basket.'

Tristan raised his eyes to heaven. 'They drag clothes off me – Rozzy too. They 'ave millions of clothes to wash, how can they remember the days?'

'You didn't drop into Paradise to change?'

'Certainly not.' He daren't light a cigarette in case his hand shook.

But just as Betty and Sally had lovingly chronicled the progress of his clothes, so two village groupies with binoculars had seen his dark blue Aston parked in a secluded field down Rannaldini's drive. Wheelmarks had been found here. Traces of similar plants, hemlock, water dropwort and lesser rosewort, had been found on Tristan's wheels.

'They probably flower in Dean Forest,' said Tristan vaguely, as he started to sketch Karen. The damson bloom of her skin, even under the fluorescent light, was exquisite.

'The lesser rosewort is only indigenous to Rutshire,' snapped Gablecross.

Round and round went the wheels of the tape, taking down evidence to be used against him. Underneath the outward languor he's shit-scared, thought Gablecross.

Tristan expressed no surprise that his prints were all over the murder weapon. 'I was unhappy with the scene I'd shot. Earlier we use knife. While everyone sleep on

Thursday afternoon, I took gun from Props, and try out hand movements in front of big mirror in my room. Having replaced it and the key, I type memo on Production writing paper saying I need .22 as well as Carlos's important papers for reshoot on Friday night and leave it in Jessica's in-tray.'

At first Tristan deflected every question coolly. He was enchanted by the recovery of his Lalique lily-patterned lighter which, he explained, had been a present from the crew after *The Lily in the Valley*, and which had vanished from his desk last week, and his signet ring, which he'd lost on the night of the *auto da fe*. 'I lose weight. It must have slipped off.'

He's lying, thought Gablecross. There was no way that shiny ring had been exposed to the elements for nearly three weeks.

'Both lighter and ring were found near Rannaldini's body in Hangman's Wood,' he said.

Careful, thought Tristan, for the hundredth time.

'I must 'ave dropped them when I went to see Rannaldini previous.'

'You often walk in the woods?'

'Of course. I am man in love with the dark. I spent my childhood in cinemas or watching videos with curtains drawn.'

'Your crème-de-menthe-flavoured chewing-gum was also found near the body.'

'Anyone could have peenched that. I leave packs everywhere. My dear Detective Sergeant,' Tristan yawned so hard he nearly put his jaw out, 'I have been working on film about murder for nearly a year. I am not so stupid I litter possessions round Rannaldini's body like Millais' *Sower* and leave my prints all over murder weapon. Someone is framing me.'

'Any idea who?'

'Probably Rannaldini from the grave.'

At one moment, he nearly fell asleep. 'I am bored

talking about myself. Can't we talk about you, Sergeant, or more excitingly you?' He smiled at Karen, who blushed.

Despite the overwhelming evidence, she kept praying Tristan hadn't done it. He was so glamorous – she admired the flawless bone structure beneath the smooth olive skin, the curls dark as winter dusk, the greyhound grace exaggerated by the ten-pound weight-loss. And he was so polite, opening doors when she went out, leaping to his feet when she came back. When he wasn't pacing up and down, he was drawing or scribbling. 'Why d'you keep making notes?' she asked.

'To stop me going crazy. I am in last stage of making film. It's like a marathon winner being dragged away ten yards from the tape. Worst still, greatest scene in *Don Carlos* takes place in prison. Eef only I had had these experiences to draw on when I direct it. The claustrophobia, moths concussing themselves against overhead light, the tiny cell that makes Carlos's dungeon look like Trafalgar Square. How much more realistic would I have made the Grand Inquisitor?' He glared at Gablecross, who, refusing to rise, proceeded to take Tristan in minute detail through the early hours of Friday the thirteenth.

'What did you do during the break?'

'Caught between Hermione and Rupert, with everyone rowing and running off on wild-ghost chase, I have 'orrible migraine and need strong pills to zap it. I go back to the house. Even more 'orrible I see Eulalia 'Arrison approach down south-wing landing. Since she arrive she hassle me for interview and plus, so I leap behind big cupboard.'

'You should have told her *you* had a migraine,' said Gablecross sardonically.

Tristan almost smiled. 'She goes into her room. I hide in mine and take pills. They were called Imogram.'

'You didn't call anyone?'

'Certainly not.' Tristan steeled himself to look Gablecross in the eyes.

Making a note to check the lack of calls with his mobile company, Karen asked what had happened to the rest of the Imogram.

'In my room, or maybe I put them in jeans pocket. I heard Eulalia leave room some time after one, then I must have dropped off, because a crash wake me, like medicine cupboard falling off wall. I looked at my watch, realized to my horror it was two o'clock less twenty-five minutes and race back to the set.'

'There is evidence, intercourse took place before Beattie died. Did you give her one?'

Like James emerging from the lake, Tristan gave an exaggerated shudder: 'It would have been easier to kill than fuck her.'

The tape ran out.

Every time there was a break, one tape was sealed, untouched, in case it was needed in court. Knowing Portland would be listening acutely to the other, Karen was relieved she wasn't interviewing Tristan alone. Hearing his heartbreakingly husky voice, she increasingly couldn't concentrate for wondering what he would be like in bed. Imagining that wonderful sulky mouth kissing hers, the long powerful body crushing her own: violent images. God, she must pull herself together.

His body language told her nothing. He sat very still, never pulled faces, fiddled with his hair, licked his lips or blinked. Even in that white paper boiler-suit, he looked like a hopelessly glamorous intern in a hospital soap. He had drawn a beautiful picture, turning her into a fawn, and was working on a cross-looking warthog.

'What were you asking me?' he drawled insolently.

Was he really so tired that he forgot a question before he could answer it, she wondered, or was he playing for time?

68

At mid-morning on Saturday, Wolfie popped into Rutminster Police Station, bringing Tristan a running order for Monday's polo shoot and a sprig of honeysuckle from Lucy.

Hearing, during a break in interrogations, that he'd been in, Gablecross had huge delight in ordering Fanshawe and Debbie Miller to drive out to Valhalla and check a few of Tristan's statements with Wolfie.

Rolling up at Valhalla, however, a fuming Fanshawe and Debbie were greeted by Rozzy, devastated about Tristan's arrest, and begging them to take a posy of gentians, a picnic of quiche, chicken breasts, peaches and a Thermos of 'proper' coffee back to the station for his lunch.

'I can't get away, Sergeant Fanshawe, I have to dog-sit for Lucy.'

James, looking unbelievably boot-faced, was taking up Wardrobe's entire sofa.

'Where's Lucy gone?' demanded Fanshawe.

'Away with Wolfie,' said Rozzy, in a worried voice. 'She wouldn't tell me where but she's taken her passport.'

'Everyone on the unit has been ordered not to leave the country,' said Fanshawe, in outrage.

Even a furious Oscar and Valentin had had to forgo their Bastille Day jaunt.

'I begged her,' wailed Rozzy. 'Oh, when are they going to let poor Tristan out?'

'When he starts levelling with us,' said Fanshawe. 'You've no idea where Lucy's gone?'

'To have a nice break with that yummy Wolfgang,' giggled Debbie. 'Gablecross will be choked – he thinks she's gorgeous.'

Outside Rutminster Police Station, television vans and the cars of the press, desperate for news, clogged up the weekend traffic like autumn leaves. Time had ceased to have any meaning. Tapes and breaks came and went. Antagonism intensified between Gablecross and Tristan, who had drawn a whole family of bullying warthogs. In the airless room the shadows deepened beneath all their eyes. Gerald Portland, still listening to the tapes, was stepping up the pressure.

'Show him his dad's letter, ask him about the Montigny. Tell him we can't find any migraine pills or memos about pistols in anyone's out-tray, and if that doesn't work, tell him they've trashed his flat in Paris and found some interesting stuff.'

Karen switched on the tape again.

'Have you seen this painting before?' She waved the photograph of *The Snake Charmer*.

'Just beautiful.' Gablecross examined Delphine's naked body.

'Give me that!' howled Tristan. But as he dived across the desk Gablecross's pudgy fingers closed over the photograph. 'Not so fast, baby boy. Betty and Sally found the original under your mattress on Thursday.'

'For Christ's sake, what more lies are they going to tell? I never saw that painting except in Rannaldini's watch-tower. In film we are making, Philip search for letters under Elisabetta's mattress. If I was going to steal painting, I would hide it somewhere more subtle.'

'Rannaldini was going to publish the photo. It says

"Chapter Four, Myself When Young" on the back. Wonder if he gave her one. You didn't want a porn pickie of your mum doing the rounds, did you?'

'Of course I fucking didn't,' shouted Tristan, draining a paper cup of black coffee as if it were whisky, and fumbling for a Gauloise.

'Tabitha Campbell-Black was distraught when you were arrested. Why did you blow her out the morning after you got off with her? Was this anything to do with it?'

As Gablecross threw down a copy of Étienne's letter with the crest of the chained serpent, Tristan let out a hiss far deeper and more venomously fearful than any snake.

'Rannaldini disturbed the Montigny snake, didn't he?' persisted Gablecross. 'Was that why you went looking for him? There were signet-ring marks on his neck.'

'I told you I lost it ages ago.'

'D'you know what this is?'

'A letter from my father to Rannaldini.'

'But was he your father? What does he mean about your being the product of an "obscene incestuous union"?' Gablecross lingered brutally on the words. 'And saying as a result he could never love you.'

'I've no idea.' Shaking violently, Tristan stubbed out his hardly smoked cigarette. His face was fog-grey, his eyes darting with terror. Karen longed to take his hand.

'Was that why you cut Auntie Hortense's party – because you weren't a Montigny any more?'

'No!'

'Was your mad granddad your father? Was that the secret Rannaldini had discovered?'

'Who told you that?' Tristan went berserk, lunging across the table, catching Gablecross by the shoulders, shaking him. 'Who fucking told you?'

The duty officer would have intervened at this juncture if he hadn't gone flat on his back, slipping on

Winnie's over-polished floor outside the interview room.

'Stop it,' shouted Karen. 'She didn't mean to blurt it out.'

'She?' For a second Tristan froze, then releasing Gablecross's shoulders, he turned on Karen. 'Which she?'

'We don't reveal our sources,' she mumbled, jolted by the horror and incredulity in Tristan's eyes.

'It was Lucy. She was the only one who knew.'

'She was only trying to explain why you were so traumatized,' stammered Karen.

'You stupid bitch,' sighed Gablecross.

Tristan slumped on his chair. 'How could Lucy?' he repeated dully.

It was as though Horatio had betrayed Hamlet, or Posa his beloved friend Carlos. After that the fight went out of Tristan.

'Rannaldini showed me the letter,' he told Gablecross, 'and I lose everything. I look at great beech trees posed like divers on edge of Cotswold bank. I ask myself how they stand so towering and beautiful they can hold up the sky. It is because their roots like steel pipes go deep into the earth. Rannaldini sawed through my roots that night.'

Putting his head in his hands, he groaned. 'He wreck my picture, he wreck any hope with Tabitha, he want to publish disgusting painting of my mother. For God's sake, I thought he loved me.'

Karen fought back the tears.

'He was jealous,' said Gablecross gently, echoing the words he had said to Wolfie. 'He treated you appallingly.'

Glancing up in anguish, Tristan noticed for the first time the understanding and compassion in Gablecross's eyes: the 'long-headed legend'.

'You were doing a public service, lad, ridding the world of Rannaldini,' went on Gablecross, almost caressingly.

There was a long pause, just the faint whisper of the turning tapes and the sound of a late-night drunk kicking a beer can along a pavement. Then Tristan realized he was being set up.

'I am not that public-spirited,' he said flatly, and continued to deny everything.

'If you're not prepared to help yourself . . .' snarled Gablecross.

As his cell door banged and he was left alone with the script of *Hercule*, which he would never now make, Tristan was kneed in the groin by desolation. He thought of Aunt Hortense gasping her last, of sunflowers, cicadas, frogs and tractors, their lights going back and forth like low shooting stars in the night. He'd never see her or France again.

The honeysuckle was filling his cell with sweetness, like Lucy's slow, shy, warm smile. Since he had been in prison, the thought of her had kept drifting into his brain like an aria. Now he couldn't trust her any more. With a sob of despair, he picked up the sprig of honeysuckle and ripped it to pieces.

69

Lucy was speechless with admiration for the way Wolfie calmly hijacked Rannaldini's Gulf and, ignoring furiously waving policemen and ground staff, flew off to the south-west of France.

'I learnt to fly before I could walk,' he explained. 'Grisel saw us leaving so the whole unit will think we've sloped off for a dirty weekend.'

'Cause a lot of gossip.'

'Let it,' said Wolfie cheerfully. 'Might make Tabitha jealous.'

Valhalla had been hot, but the Midi seemed a hundred times hotter. The wind, blowing like a hair-dryer about to fuse, whipped Lucy's curls into a frenzy.

'Now I know how a frozen chicken feels when it's shoved into the microwave,' she grumbled.

Stupid from lack of sleep, she was passionately grateful for the cool efficiency with which Wolfie hired a car, located the village of Montvert and booked into its best hotel, appropriately named La Reconnaissance.

Having departed in such haste, Lucy was dismayed she hadn't packed deodorant, a hairbrush, or base to tone down her shiny, increasingly flushed face.

'At least we'll get a decent dinner this evening,' said the ever-practical Wolfie, who was consulting the menu and the wine list as she came down. 'And there's the château,' he added, pointing up at the disdainful back of a large grey house nestling in woodland on top of the hill.

'The Montigny family never forgave the villagers for burning the place down during the French Revolution,' said Lucy, as they got back into the hired car, and she eased her bare legs gingerly on to the scorching leather seat. 'When the family returned from exile, they pointedly built the new château facing away from the village and overlooking the Pyrenees. Oh, what a sweet dog. Can I ring Rozzy to ask if James is OK?'

'Certainly not. She'd want to know where we were and promptly grass to her friend Gablecross. We don't want Interpol muscling in. Anyway, we'll be back tomorrow.'

As Wolfie swung off the main road and headed for the mountains, Lucy groped for her dark glasses to ward off the dazzling golden glare of the sunflower fields.

'Am I too under-dressed?' she asked nervously, glancing down at her orange T-shirt and grey shorts. 'Hortense sounds a martinet. Tristan says she's been having little heart-attacks for ages, growing more and more eccentric. She used to play golf with the Duke of Windsor and once smashed a Louis XIV chandelier demonstrating some iron shot. Evidently she cuts up *Le Monde* every morning and lays all the stories she wants to read on chairs so no-one can sit down.'

'She'll need a fleet of sofas to accommodate the coverage of Tristan's arrest,' said Wolfie.

'Probably been kept away from her, if she's so ill. I do hope she'll see us. Tristan also said she was terribly mean. The estate's next to a golf course, and she rushes out, grabs any lost balls and wraps them up for her nieces and nephews for Christmas. Tristan realized she was losing it last birthday when she sent him a blackboard with the letters of the alphabet round the frame.'

Wolfie stopped Lucy's rattling by asking her irritably if she remembered everything Tristan had ever told her.

'Probably.' Lucy flushed an even more unbecoming shade of red.

Wolfie noticed the anguished way she glanced at every farm-building they passed as if she was expecting some horrific content of battery hen or veal calf.

'Oh, no,' she wailed, as he slowed down behind a lorry, 'they've got lambs in there. I bet they haven't been watered for yonks.'

Nearly removing the side of the hired car, as he short-ened her misery by overtaking the lorry, Wolfie snapped that she'd got to toughen up.

'You can't suffer for every squashed earwig in this world.'

'Hortense suffered,' protested Lucy. 'She claimed that the best years of her life were spent fighting for the Resistance, despite being captured and tortured by the bloody Krauts— Oh, Wolfie, I'm sorry.'

'I'm used to it,' said Wolfie calmly. Then, catching sight of two fat men towing trolleys and sweating in plus-fours, 'Here's the golf course, and there's the château.'

To repel intruders, two hissing stone Montigny snakes were chained to the pillars on either side of the big iron gates. Ahead at the end of an avenue of limes and flanked by ancient arthritic oaks stood a grey, square house with its pale grey shutters closed against prying eyes and the afternoon sun.

The good news was that all Hortense's greedy relations had temporarily pushed off to another family house in Brittany to celebrate the sixty-fifth birthday of Tristan's eldest brother Alexandre, the judge. With them, leaving the coast even clearer, had gone the even greedier Dupont, who was already carrion-crowing at the prospect of a large cut of Hortense's estate.

The bad news was that Hortense, who'd kept such iron control of her life, was now lying upstairs under a mosquito net, morphinised up to the eyeballs, recog-nizing no-one.

'Yesterday, she was convinced the Bolsheviks had taken over the château,' sighed Florence, the kind, plump housekeeper, who was almost as old as her mistress. 'Today the Nazis have moved in, and she's back in the Resistance. So I'm afraid you won't be very welcome,' she added apologetically to Wolfie.

'But Tristan could be in prison for life,' begged Lucy. 'The police think he killed Rannaldini to stop him spreading some vicious tale about his parentage.' If she hadn't seen a flicker of fear in Florence's faded grey eyes, Lucy might not have persisted. 'Hortense is the only person who might know the truth,' she went on. 'Please let me stay in case she regains consciousness.'

Florence was wavering when there was an imperious skidding crunch in the gravel and Rupert, resplendent in a pale yellow suit and grey striped shirt, emerged from a cloud of dust and a hired Mercedes. Apparently unaffected by the heat, he made Lucy feel plainer and hotter than ever.

'What are you doing here?' she snapped.

'Resisting arrest, disobeying the orders of Gablecross, casing the joint. *Bonjour*, Madame.' Slipping into effortless French, Rupert turned all his charm on Florence.

Absolutely bloody typical, fumed Lucy. She'll take one look and roll over. But fortunately it seemed that Aunt Hortense loathed men, particularly those who looked like blond Luftwaffe pilots, almost as much as Germans. Rupert was sent packing as summarily as Wolfie.

Lucy, who was allowed to stay on for a little while, couldn't hide a suspicion that both men were glad of an excuse to escape.

'We'll go back to La Reconnaissance and chivvy ambassadors,' said Rupert, sauntering towards the Mercedes. 'Join us for dinner if you can get away.'

'We'll leave everything in "your loyal hands",' quoted the ever-pragmatic Wolfie, clearly delighted at a chance to ingratiate himself with Tabitha's father.

Frantic with thirst, Lucy gulped down a whole jug of *orange pressé*. Heat was coming in great waves through the kitchen window. Only endless sprinklers kept the

592

garden green. Beyond, like purple shagpile, stretched fields of lavender.

Once the maid had disappeared to shop in Montvert, Florence relented and got out the family scrapbooks she'd kept since Tristan was a little boy. It wrung Lucy's heart to see him always hovering at the edge of family groups, like an outfielder desperate not to miss a smile that miraculously Étienne might one day throw him.

At least the later scrapbooks were crowded with Tristan's cuttings. Florence had already pasted in the marvellous reviews of *The Lily in the Valley*, dominated by the luminous beauty of Claudine Lauzerte.

To stop herself falling asleep, Lucy begged to be given a tour of the house. Downstairs big high rooms papered in cranberry reds, Prussian blues and deep snuff browns were the ideal setting for the Impressionist collection, acquired ahead of fashion in the late nineteenth century, and for Étienne's great powerful oils, but not to lighten the heart of a little boy. Everywhere frayed tapestries of hunting scenes hung above cabinets lovingly painted with fruit, flowers and birds. Leggy gold tables and chairs seemed poised to race through the french windows into a park shimmering with heat-haze. You couldn't see the mountains for dust.

The great hall housed the family portraits.

'That was Louis who died at Crécy, and Edouard who was wounded at Agincourt, and there's Blaize,' Florence ran her finger inside the frame to test for dust, 'who died in Spain on a secret mission. He was murdered by the Spanish Inquisition.'

Lucy peered at Blaize in excitement. Handsome, hawk-faced, with dark cynical watchful eyes, he was definitely a Montigny, and one of the reasons Tristan had embarked on *Don Carlos*.

'And there's Henri, painted by David,' said Florence proudly, 'Such a great general that Napoleon coaxed him out of exile to fight at Austerlitz and Borodino. The Montignys have always been a great military family.'

Soldier-citizens of the world like Posa, thought Lucy.

'Tristan's brother Laurent was brave, wasn't he?'

'More hotheaded,' said Florence, somewhat dis-approvingly. 'A *pied-noir* builder fell off a ladder here one day. Madame Hortense rang six doctors but none would treat him. Laurent jumped in the Jeep, drove to the nearest, put a shotgun to his temple, and didn't remove it until he'd come back and set the leg.'

'How romantic,' sighed Lucy. 'No wonder Tristan hero-worships his memory. Why isn't there a painting of him?'

Florence glanced round nervously.

Laurent's portrait had hung in the hall, she admitted, smiling a welcome to everyone coming through the front door. But Étienne was so devastated when he was killed, the painting was locked away with everything else in his room.

'But surely after Étienne's death . . .' protested Lucy.

'He left instructions in his will that the door was to remain locked.'

'At least let me look at Tristan's room.'

'It was very small.' Florence looked unhappy. 'When Tristan went to university Étienne turned it into an *en suite* bathroom.'

Don't show your anger, Lucy had to keep telling herself.

'There *should* be a portrait of Tristan. He's the hand-somest of the lot,' she said crossly.

In answer Florence looked up at the gilt Montigny snake chained to the lintel. '"Seek not to disturb the serpent,"' she whispered, her face creasing into a hundred folds of anxiety.

'I'm only seeking to disturb the wretched thing', Lucy was nearly in tears, 'because I want to find out the truth. Tristan was desperate to question Hortense about his parents, but he was too busy with *Carlos* to fly out, and now it may be too late.'

'It was a secret, Madame swore to Étienne she would

take to the grave.' Florence glanced up at a gold Empire clock, which featured Neptune brandishing his trident. 'The nurse will be going in ten minutes. You can sit with her instead of me.'

Aunt Hortense had blurred, weather-beaten features and wild white hair, like a gargoyle caught in a snow-storm. She lay without covers, her long nightgown rucked up to show purple bruised shins and a plaster on every toe. Beside her on the bed were two marmalade cats and a tiny brindled Italian greyhound, which one of her gnarled, ringed, gardening-begrimed hands repeat-edly caressed.

Opposite the bed, filling the wall, was a ravishing Rubens of milkmaids tending a herd of paddling red cows and chatting up a swain driving a horse and cart.

'We hung it there last week,' whispered Florence. 'Madame wanted something beautiful to look at.'

To the right hung a small photograph of a young Hortense being handed the Croix de Guerre for her courage during the Resistance. With her boyish brown curls, her deep-set dark eyes and quick smile, she bore an uncanny resemblance to Tristan.

Perhaps? wondered Lucy. But Hortense would have been too old at fifty-five. Could she have had an illegiti-mate daughter? She must have a story to tell.

In moments of consciousness, Aunt Hortense played *la grande dame* for all her worth. 'I wouldn't dream of discussing family matters with a complete stranger,' she told Lucy coldly.

'I just wanted to talk about Tristan.' Carefully Lucy explained the situation. That Tristan had been arrested for two murders that he hadn't done.

Hortense, however, was only interested in why he hadn't come to her party. 'I broke totally with protocol and put him on my right and had to talk to air all lunch. I suppose his film and Claudine Lauzerte were more important.'

595

'He sent you a lovely present,' said Lucy, recognizing Rozzy's gift-wrapping on the Louis XV desk. 'You haven't even opened it.'

'Why d'you stick your nose into everything?' snapped Hortense. 'Are you a journalist?'

'Tristan stayed away from your party because he felt a fraud,' said Lucy desperately. 'Rannaldini had just told him he wasn't a Montigny, that Étienne wasn't his father at all.'

Stammering, Lucy went through all the palaver of Maxim being so jealous of Delphine marrying Étienne that he'd raped her. For a second, Hortense's eyes opened a centimetre like an old crocodile.

'Really?'

'So Tristan's father was his grandfather, and on his deathbed Étienne kept rambling on about fathers and grandfathers.'

'We once had a footman called Maxim,' confided Hortense.

'Oh, for God's sake,' exploded Lucy.

There was a knock on the door, the nurse was back to give Hortense a shot.

'Oh, please don't,' cried Lucy in despair. 'She'll go even more doo-lally.'

'I will *not*,' said Hortense tartly. 'I'll have you know, young woman, I'm in considerable pain, and there's no need to shout.'

Lucy fought sleep. It was still unbearably hot and the scent of jasmine growing up the still warm walls was almost sickly. The melon frames gleamed in the moonlight. She watched the tractors, hung with lamps, going back and forth, labouring to get the harvest in before next week's forecast storm. The combines roared so loudly it was like working in a munitions factory, grumbled Hortense.

Down in the village they were celebrating Bastille Day. Fireworks rose and fell against a pearly grey night; Lucy could hear the accordion playing 'La Vie en rose'.

Glancing at Hortense, she noticed tears trickling down her wrinkled cheeks and took her hand.

'I'm so sorry to hassle you. Could Rannaldini possibly be Tristan's father?'

'I wouldn't put anything past that devil, always hanging round Delphine like a wasp round a melon.'

'Or Bernard.'

'Have you seen the ghost of the Montigny snake yet?' said Hortense, as she drifted off to sleep.

70

'At last I've found someone I can charm,' announced Rupert.

The proprietor of La Reconnaissance had sloped off to a Bastille Day party, but his busty, henna-haired wife had taken one look at Monsieur Campbell-Black, personally cooked him and Wolfie *foie-gras* pancakes and miraculous *coq au vin* and unearthed several bottles of the best claret Rupert had ever tasted.

For five hours, he and Wolfie had not drawn breath, not chivvying ambassadors but discussing everyone on the unit, and particularly the polo shoot. They had enjoyed a glorious bitch about Isa and Helen, and Rupert was touched by the way Wolfie's rather solid face lit up whenever Tab's name was mentioned. Now they had moved on to Tristan and a large bottle of Armagnac.

'I'm sure he's not Papa's son.' Wolfie decided against a second piece of Camembert. 'If Papa had fathered such a genius he could not have resisted boasting about it. Also Papa was half German and I don't think Tristan's got any German blood. With him one thinks of the shifting subtlety of composers like Ravel and Debussy rather than heavyweights like Brahms, Beethoven and Bruckner.'

'Does one?' yawned Rupert. 'I wouldn't know. I suppose Rannaldini could have made up the story about

Maxim years ago just to crucify Étienne. He was such a manipulative shit.'

'He could have,' reflected Wolfie, filling their glasses. It was a relief to talk about his father objectively: people always pussyfooted round the subject.

'Why are you actually here?' asked Rupert suddenly.

'Because I owe Tristan,' replied Wolfie. 'My father fucked him up and I've got to find out the truth. And because I adore Tab.' Wolfie's drunkenly crossed eyes filled with tears. 'And I can only compete with Tristan when he's no longer crippled by this awful stigma. It's like fighting a man with both hands chained behind his back.

'Anyway,' Wolfie smiled slightly, 'Tab told me not to hang around like a stuck pig, and get Tristan out of prison. And also I really love the guy, he's so great to work for. You feel like a dry leaf suddenly swept up by the warm south-west wind of his enthusiasm. I couldn't go back to straight law again.'

'Hum,' said Rupert. 'Did you kill your father?'

'When Tab told me he'd r-r-raped her I wanted to, but it seemed more important to find out if she was safe.'

Wolfie longed to ask if Rupert had killed his father. He felt the man was quite capable of murder but also had enough sense of fair play that, if he had killed Rannaldini and Beattie, not to want Tristan to take the rap.

Was that why Rupert was so sure Tristan wasn't guilty? On the other hand, had he come down here to check out the Montignys as suitable in-laws for Tab, or was he merely a commercial animal in search of his director?

'I know Tabitha loves Tristan,' Wolfie added wistfully, 'but I'm in that state of love so well described by Stendhal, "utter despair poisoned still further by a shred of hope".'

He is a clever boy, thought Rupert, probably too clever for Tab.

'Tab's not perfect,' he told Wolfie. 'She's got my terrible temper, she can be an appalling drama queen, and she doesn't have the greatest sense of humour.'

'Nor do I,' sighed Wolfie. 'People always tell me I'm too serious. I've heard all those jokes about slim volumes containing two thousand years of German humour.'

'I like Krauts,' said Rupert. 'I knew a lot on the show-jumping circuit – good blokes, feet on the ground but knew how to party.'

Getting up, he wandered unsteadily over to the window, unzipped his flies, peed into the garden, causing scuffling and angry mewings from Madame's two cats, and only just zipped up in time as a besotted Madame returned with an even more ancient bottle of brandy. If Monsieur Campbell-Black would come into the back room, Tristan's arrest was on the late-night news.

Clips were being shown of Valhalla, of Rannaldini conducting, of Tristan arriving at the police station and of Étienne in a big straw hat painting in the château gardens. When Hermione appeared, opening her big eyes and saying she had every confidence because her very good friends Chief Constable Swallow, Rupert Campbell-Black and Sexton Kemp were now at the helm, Rupert and Wolfie collapsed with howls of drunken laughter.

'I'm suffering from Dutch Helm Disease,' said Rupert, pretending to fall over.

'Poor old Tristan, but bloody good publicity,' said Wolfie wiping his eyes.

'Christ, she's beautiful,' sighed Rupert, as Claudine Lauzerte was shown talking to Tristan on the set of *The Lily in the Valley*.

'*Très jolie, très chic,*' agreed Madame.

'Oscar's lighting helped,' said Wolfie quickly. 'Tab's much more beautiful.'

'So's Taggie,' admitted Rupert. 'Even so, I wouldn't

mind having Madame Lauzerte as my luxury on *Desert Island Discs*.'

'Thank you,' said Wolfie, as Madame filled up his glass. 'I should like to pick up the tab on this,' he told Rupert firmly. 'I should like to pick up Tab any time,' he added.

Perhaps he did have a sense of humour after all.

'You have a very charming son,' Madame told Rupert skittishly. 'It is rare for fathers and sons to get on so well.'

'Very,' agreed Rupert, then turning to Wolfie, 'If Tristan had really loved Tab, he wouldn't have backed off after a one-night stand. I don't believe in that kind of sacrifice.'

'Yes, you do,' said Wolfie resolutely. 'Tab told me you backed off for nearly a year because you didn't feel you were good enough for Taggie.'

'Maybe I did.' Rupert scratched his head in pleased surprise. 'Maybe I did. And, talking of self-sacrifice, why's Lucy here?'

'Because she wants to slay the dragon of this frightful calumny,' said Wolfie. 'And unconsciously in the hope that Tristan will be so touched by her enterprise and nobility, he'll realize she's the one he loves not Tab.'

'He won't, unfortunately. Men don't love buckets like that, just for their virtues.'

'Lucy's not a bucket,' protested Wolfie. 'She can look gorgeous.'

Rupert raised a sleek sceptical blond eyebrow.

'I wouldn't ask you to shoot on a cocks-only day,' he drawled.

'Telephone,' called out Madame.

It was Lucy.

'Any progress?' Wolfie asked her.

'None.' Lucy lowered her voice. 'She's a stubborn old bat. She wouldn't squeal when the Gestapo tugged out her toenails and she's not likely to tell me anything. She was wandering so badly this evening that she insisted on having the blackout put up in her room.'

Hearing a burst of music, Wolfie looked round and saw Madame was teaching Rupert the can-can and started to laugh.

'Do you want us to come and get you?'

'Neither of you sounds capable,' snapped Lucy, then after a pause, 'I'm sorry, it's been a long day, but Florence is letting me stay the night. She made me a gorgeous Gruyère omelette and opened a bottle of Sancerre. I just wish . . . Are you OK, Wolfie?'

'Hunky-dory. Thingsh will be better in the morning. Goo' night, Lucy.'

Lucy couldn't remember ever being more tired. But just as she was about to fall into the arms of Morpheus she thought of Tristan in his small cell, and how much she would prefer the arms to be his. By this time, Morpheus had retreated in a sulk, and Lucy was left to agonize until four in the morning, when the roar of the combines and the waiting started again.

She went downstairs and raided the family albums, poring over photographs of picnics, balls and shooting-parties, of weddings and christenings, when the limes in the avenue were only shoulder high and the jasmine round the house wasn't planted. Étienne was everywhere, always surrounded by adoring women, while Hortense and his three elder sons looked on, stolid and disapproving. But she found no sign of Laurent, unless he was that beautiful young man with the lively, restless, not-very-happy face to the rear of one group, gazing down at a girl whose slim back was to the camera and whose long dark hair was tied back with a scarlet ribbon.

Around ten on Sunday morning Lucy was toying with a croissant, black cherry jam and coffee so dark brown it reminded her of Tristan's eyes, when a bell jangled in the kitchen.

'I'm plunged in pitch darkness, I don't know if I'm alive or dead,' said a querulous voice over the intercom. 'Will someone immediately bring me a cup of tea?'

'Let me take it,' Lucy begged Florence.

*   *   *

'Haven't you gone?' snapped Hortense, as Lucy opened the shutters.

'Not yet. I haven't got what I came for.'

'I suppose you're in love with my nephew like the rest of them. You're certainly no oil painting.'

'Just as well, judging by some of the oils downstairs,' said Lucy. 'I'd hate to be as fat as the Rubens nude or as bloated as that Francis Bacon cardinal.'

Aunt Hortense gave a snort of laughter.

'Does Tristan love you?'

'No, a great friend of mine, a most beautiful girl.'

'*Bien élevée?*'

'Very, and she adores him.'

'Married, I suppose.'

'Not acutely. She's got a horrid husband and Rannaldini told Tristan he couldn't marry her because he wasn't a Montigny, and because of his bad blood because Maxim had raped his mother.'

Carefully, laboriously, Lucy went though the whole story until Hortense said sharply, 'You told me all that last night.'

Lucy raised her eyes to heaven.

'But you haven't told me whether it's true.'

'I swore to my brother Étienne never to discuss the matter.'

'But it's so unfair to Tristan.'

'Life has always been unfair to Tristan. He was such a sweet little boy – I was far too strict with him. I didn't want him to grow into a cissy. I knew women, and possibly men, would spoil him later.'

There was a patter of feet as the little Italian greyhound scampered in, leapt on to the bed and covered his mistress's grey, wrinkled face with kisses.

'Still they love you. I've spoilt my animals so dreadfully. What will become of them when I'm gone?'

'Tristan would look after them if you got him out of prison. Who is Tristan's father? If it wasn't Rannaldini could it be Oscar, or even Bernard Guérin? He and Tristan are incredibly close.'

'It's a secret I'll take to my grave.'

'You're not going to your grave. Let me wash your hair.'

'Whatever for?'

'I'm a hairdresser!'

'And you have designs on my nephew!'

'Don't treat my head as though it was a glass bauble,' snapped Hortense, a quarter of an hour later. 'Give it a good hard rub.'

Despite pointing out that the fluffy fringe over her forehead was very common, Hortense was grudgingly delighted with the result, even making Lucy hold up the mirror at the back where a pink bald patch had been covered over. Afterwards she let Lucy make her up.

'They'll be doing that to me in my coffin very soon,' she added.

'Don't be so macabre. Do you want me to come back and do it for you then?'

'Not if you make me wear that lipstick. I look like a Jewess.'

Lucy giggled.

As soon as Florence had gone off to church, Hortense decided she'd like to give her make-over an outing and announced she wanted to pay a visit to her brother's grave.

'It's horrendously hot.'

'A good dress rehearsal for hell fires.'

'And I don't think you're well enough.'

'I'm the best judge of that.'

Everywhere outside was evidence that Hortense had lost her grip on the place. A jungle of plants, their huge leaves pressing against the glass, was struggling to get out of the conservatory. Ivy throttled the shutters. An emerald carpet of algae covered the moat. Grass had grown over the stepping-stones of the path leading to the fields of lavender.

But if Étienne had painted with a palette, and Tristan with light, Hortense had created as dazzling effects with plants. As Lucy wheeled her down the garden, she pointed out some pale yellow hollyhocks with pink centres.

'Those came from Monet's garden at Giverny.'

Like a brass section about to explode, to the right was a proud clump of Regale lilies.

'Pick them for my brother,' ordered Hortense.

Rozzy would do her nut, thought Lucy, as she laid the lilies across Hortense's knees.

'What a pity we couldn't have used this for Charles V's tomb.' She sighed as they approached a splendid mausoleum.

'"Étienne Alexandre Henri Blaize de Montigny, 1905–1995, painter,"' she read out in a shaky voice.

Although Étienne had died eight months ago, there were as many flowers outside the tomb as at Valhalla. Pilgrims, acolytes, students and admirers came from all over the world and, denied access to the château, paid homage at the grave.

'Now leave me,' said Hortense. 'I'll call you when I want to go back.'

The noonday sun was punishing. Beads of sweat were breaking through Hortense's make-up, red lipstick was escaping down the lines round her mouth as Lucy wheeled her back.

'Those lilies were struck down in their prime, like Laurent,' reproved Lucy. 'Why didn't they fly his body back and bury him here?'

'Because he was blown up,' said Aunt Hortense tartly.

'By his own side, Tristan told me,' persisted Lucy. 'Why didn't Étienne insist on an inquiry? He had the clout.'

'Would that have brought Laurent back?'

As Lucy eased Hortense back into bed, her flesh felt as soft as marshmallow.

'Was Étienne buried or cremated?' she asked.

'Buried, of course.'

'Great,' crowed Lucy. 'That means his body can be dug up and DNA-tested to see whether he's Tristan's father or not.'

'How dare you suggest that, you conniving hussy?' gasped Hortense hoarsely. 'Coming in here, stirring up trouble.' Then, after an eternal silence, she seemed to cave in. 'All right, Étienne wasn't his father. Now are you satisfied?'

'No,' stormed Lucy. 'I'm not leaving till I know who it was.'

But Hortense, whether deliberately or not, had fallen asleep.

After that Lucy lost any sense of time. As night fell and lightning flickered round the hills illuminating the clouds, she made one last attempt.

'Please, please, Tristan can't marry and have children if he believes a psychopath rapist was his father. He needs a family of his own so badly to give him the love none of you provided. All he ever did was try to please Étienne.'

The clock ticked, the cicadas chirped, Lucy longed to pick up La Grande Mademoiselle's velvet-handled musket, which Hortense kept always by her bedside, and empty it into her.

'I have nothing to say.'

But as the nurse frogmarched Lucy out, Hortense called after her, 'Goodbye, Miss Latimer. Don't forget to put your name and address in the visitors' book.'

'I bloody well won't,' shouted Lucy. 'What d'you want me to say – that you're a stubborn old bitch who, through your pigheadedness, sent Tristan to prison for life?'

She wept all the way back to the hotel. 'I handled her all wrong,' she told the chauffeur. 'If, by any chance, she changes her mind, here's my mobile number.'

She found Wolfie only just recovering from last night's excesses. Rupert had flown home. All she knew was Tristan would be charged in court tomorrow.

71

Back in Rutshire, as Gablecross and Karen were tied up full time with Tristan, other detectives took over their leads. Fanshawe had never been happy with Chloe's alibi about jogging round Paradise in the dusk. She would also have more to lose than most, if Beattie had dumped about her in the *Scorpion*.

So, late on the afternoon of Saturday the fourteenth, Fanshawe and Debbie went over to Valhalla and found Chloe working out in the gym. She was wearing shorts and a pale blue sleeveless T-shirt. Fanshawe, having gone into a frenzy of hair-smoothing and tooth-licking, couldn't keep his eyes off her glistening cleavage and her smooth buttocks, continually on display as she stretched and twisted at the bars.

'Sunday was a sad day for me, Sergeant,' she told him soulfully. 'After a long *affaire*, Mikhail dropped me because his wife found out.'

'Your mother phoned you from abroad at around nine thirty.' Fanshawe frowned at his notes. 'You were going to find out where she was staying.'

'I completely forgot. I'll do it tonight.'

'Then you went for a jog round Paradise.'

'I was depressed, the tennis had hardly been taxing.' Shoving her fists into her armpits, Chloe rotated her elbows so her breasts thrust forward. 'I jogged over the River Fleet up past Magpie Cottage. I wanted to see if

Tab was in. She'd been terribly down since Tristan blew her out. How's he bearing up, by the way?'

Such was Chloe's egoism, it was the first time she'd thought of Tristan. At least, as he'd been arrested, this must only be a routine call.

'We haven't heard,' said Debbie.

'Poor Tristan,' said Chloe lightly. 'Anyway, Tab was out so I jogged back through Paradise. I like street-lights at that hour.'

She extended a smooth, brown foot under Fanshawe's nose as though she was expecting him to kiss it.

'Mr Brimscombe claims he saw you running from the tennis court into Hangman's Wood,' said Debbie, not without pleasure, 'then coming out from a different, northerly direction five minutes later and disappearing into the north wing. He says you came out of the north wing fifteen minutes after that, smelling of perfume and toothpaste. An expert on floral scents, he thinks the perfume was the same he smelt earlier on Tabitha.'

The change in Chloe was phenomenal. Suddenly she was a snarling, cornered vixen. 'Disgusting old lech! Brimscombe's always spying on me.'

'What was the name of your perfume?'

'People are always giving me perfume,' said Chloe hysterically. 'I think it's called Quercus.'

'Why did you go into the wood?'

'I don't remember.'

'Going to kill Rannaldini, were you? Traces of Quercus were found on his dressing-gown.'

'I d-d-don't believe it.' Chloe clung to the bar for support.

'The fingertip team found your lipstick, Fiery Fuchsia,' persisted Fanshawe, 'fifty yards from his watch-tower.'

She's guilty, guilty, guilty, thought Debbie in elation. She could smell Chloe's sweat turning acid. For a second, Chloe's eyes darted towards the door, then she slumped to the floor.

'All right, you win. I went to Magpie Cottage to meet Isa Lovell.'

There, it was out. Fanshawe and Debbie both looked shocked.

'I don't feel guilty,' said Chloe defiantly. 'That marriage is fucked. Tab's been lusting after Tristan all summer. It was Isa, not my mother, who rang at nine thirty to say Tab was taking some dog back to Penscombe and the coast was clear. I intended going straight to Magpie Cottage and darted into Hangman's Wood to put on lipstick and scent, then I thought better of it. I hate being hot and sweaty so I made a detour through the wood where the tennis party couldn't see me – they're such horrendous gossips. Back at the house, I showered, brushed my teeth, changed into almost identical clothes, so people wouldn't suspect anything, and jogged over to Isa's.'

'What time did you arrive?'

'Around ten.'

'See anything out of the ordinary?'

'I was *far* too excited.'

'What time did you leave?' asked Debbie.

'About eleven ten, I guess. Isa didn't want me to jog home in the dark so he dropped me off half-way up the drive, then drove home to Warwickshire.'

So that puts her and Isa in the clear, calculated Fanshawe, in disappointment, unless they had got rid of Rannaldini together.

'Oh, yes,' Chloe smiled spitefully, 'something significant *did* happen. Alpheus rolled up in a white suit in the middle, he was clutching white lilies like the Archangel Michael and started singing "La ci darem la mano" under our bedroom window. Isa poured a bottle of red over him and told him to fuck off. Such style.'

Despite repeated calls to the Home Secretary, it didn't look as though Tristan would be bailed even after his court appearance on Monday. As everyone in the unit was hanging about on Sunday, having been forbidden to leave the country, Sexton, Oscar and Bernard decided to push on and film the polo scenes at George Hungerford's. This had been kept from Tristan until Griselda rang the police station, late on Sunday morning, and chivvied the custody officer into asking Tristan if he wanted the ponies' bandages to match the players' shirts.

Tristan went berserk. 'They cannot shoot polo without me.'

But when he tracked down Bernard, he was even more upset to discover Rupert, Lucy and Wolfie had all done a runner.

'We cannot film without Lucy,' he yelled. 'Who will make up Granny and Mikhail? Who will disappear Baby's double chin and Alpheus's nose?'

'Rozzy's offered,' said Bernard fondly.

'Don't be so fucking stupid.'

How *could* Lucy bugger off like that? raged Tristan. She had left him no message since the now torn-up sprig of honeysuckle. The final straw was Gablecross popping in, all dressed up for his silver-wedding lunch, to put him through the mangle again. Not only had he blocked Rupert's application for bail, he announced bullyingly, but Interpol had broken into Tristan's flat in Paris, found some very interesting material and were about to blow the safe.

'W-h-a-a-a-t?' howled Tristan, his fingers clamped round Gablecross's neck once more. 'You bastard!'

'Don't be stupid!' screamed Karen, leaping forward to prise Tristan off. Feeling the shivering rigidity of his body, seeing the madness in his eyes, there was no doubt he was capable of murder.

'When are you going to tell us the truth?' asked a somewhat shaken Gablecross, straightening his unusually smart blue silk tie.

Tristan collapsed in his chair. Suddenly it came spilling out. 'OK, I came back to Valhalla. I need my address book to call an actor, Colin Firth, to see if he was interested in playing Hercule. I parked the Aston in a field off the drive, I didn't want to be pestered. I sweat like a peeg, so I had a shower.'

'And changed back into your favourite peacock-blue shirt and jeans.' Karen couldn't contain her excitement.

'*Oui*, and then I buggered off to Forest of Dean.'

'Did you call Colin Firth?'

'*Non.*' And beyond that he wouldn't budge.

'He can bloody well appear in court tomorrow,' said a furious Gablecross, as, armed with Hermione's CD and Rozzy's cards and presents, he set off to his anniversary party.

He had looked almost attractive, conceded Karen grudgingly, as she wandered round the incident room, gazing at the map of Valhalla, flipping through statements, looking for silly little details in the jigsaw puzzle. As a detective you had to keep pushing yourself beyond the point you were able or wanted to go, continually asking how, when, why?

Even in the group photograph of the unit, Tristan looked sad. There were enough tears in those haunted eyes to put out any funeral pyre. Why was he so sad?

Karen glanced through the Sundays, which had all led on Tristan's arrest. Rannaldini's fans were still streaming into Paradise. A lynch mob had tried to burn down Tristan's caravan. Portland had put a uniformed man outside. The *Scorpion* had bussed down a lot of actors clutching more tulips in Cellophane, and photographed them weeping and pretending to be Beattie's fans. Much was being made of Tristan's cutting Hortense's party, his rows with Rannaldini, his callous dumping of Tabitha, the raid on the Paris flat. Tristan's family had all said, '*Je ne dis rien*', but Alexandre, the judge, huffing and puffing with disapproval, was expected to fly over for the court hearing tomorrow.

In the *Sunday Times* there was a big piece by George

Perry describing Tristan's ever-flowering genius, and comparing Claudine Lauzerte with Garbo.

'Oh, what a beautiful woman,' sighed Karen, admiring Claudine's huge, languorous eyes and the thick, dusky hair.

Madame Lauzerte, went on the piece, was currently filming in an adaptation of Rose Macaulay's novel, *The World Is My Wilderness*, in Wales. Why should Tristan need an address book and clean clothes to drink brandy in a field? pondered Karen. Who was he gabbling in French to on the telephone when he came back after Rannaldini's murder? The incident room was having difficulty in tracing the owner of the mobile as the number was unlisted. How could such a devastating man have had no suspicion of a relationship – except for a disastrous skirmish with Tabitha – for the past three years?

Karen picked up a telephone. 'How would you like that drink?'

Ogborne, having read down the right side of the Heavenly Host menu all summer and chosen the most expensive food, was so fat he could only fit into tracksuit bottoms. Undaunted, he met Karen at the Old Bell in Rutminster during the break.

The willows trailing in the river Fleet were already turning yellow; holidaymakers were hanging over the bridge.

'Shooting polo's been a shambles,' confided Ogborne. 'Mikhail's fallen off three times. All he's interested in is getting his new crocus-yellow Range Rover resprayed before he goes back to Russia – I'm sure it's nicked. Tab has been yelling non-stop. With no Tristan to smarm, charm and calm, and no Rupert, Lucy or Wolfie, we might as well have stayed at home. How's Tristan? Bet he's enjoying the peace. He'll be auditioning for *Hercule* soon, so they can send potential leading ladies in with his caviare every day – can't be bad.'

'Is Claudine Lauzerte going to be in *Hercule*?'

'I'm sure. If Tristan had had his way, she'd have played Elisabetta, but she's even older than Dame Hermione.'

'Did she give him that peacock-blue shirt and jeans he never takes off?'

'Dunno,' said Ogborne, going vague. '*Secrets and Lies* is on at the Odeon. Fancy going to see it this evening?'

'I might. Did the crew give him a Lalique lighter covered in lilies at the end of the shoot?'

'Naah,' said Ogborne. 'Bit upmarket for us.'

Karen thought she'd better offer some plums of gossip.

'We'll be getting the DNA results tomorrow or Tuesday, Tristan's as well, if they pull their fingers out,' she said. 'Botanists in Forensic are frightfully excited. Among the plants shoved up Beattie's vagina', she lowered her voice as the couple at the next table stopped talking, 'was a really rare white rock rose and an even rarer relation of the monkey orchid, the chimpanzee, which hasn't been found in England for fifty years.' She collapsed with laughter. 'So there's added pressure to locate their place of origin.'

'Shouldn't fink they needed any potting compost up Beattie's snatch,' grinned Ogborne.

'What's Claudine like?'

'Well,' Ogborne deliberated, 'Valentin described her as a bourgeois 'ousewife whose face had been touched by the finger of God.'

'Did anything happen between her and Tristan?'

'I gotta go back to the set. You coming to that movie?'

'Yeah, sure.'

Ogborne glanced round furtively.

'Tristan was giving Madame Vierge direction one day,' he murmured. 'She was in costume, long-sleeved purple dress, little lacy gloves. Tristan was squatting down, holdin' her hands, talking intensely, as he often does with Hermione and Chloe, or even Baby and Mikhail, but I noticed his finger was caressing the gap between her sleeve and her glove.'

'I'll see you outside the Odeon at the start of the big film,' said Karen.

She was not at all pleased when a call on her mobile asked her to whizz over to Penscombe to investigate the whereabouts of Rupert Campbell-Black. Interpol had had no success in finding him, so Gerald Portland wanted her and Gablecross to pump Taggie.

Neither of them talked on the drive. Karen's head was full of Tristan and how to prove his innocence. Gablecross was feeling beleaguered. All his Brownie points over Hermione's CD and Rozzy's presents had been cancelled because he'd had to leave his silver-wedding lunch in the middle of the speeches. Nor would Margaret ever forgive him for snatching up the pink roses and silver foliage, sent by her sister and Australian brother-in-law, to hand over as a peace-offering to Taggie after his mauling of Tabitha last Thursday.

'No-one's got any right to live in such a big house,' fumed Karen, as she pressed Rupert's doorbell with unnecessary force. 'This place would make a wonderful hospital.'

Xavier and a pack of dogs answered the door. For a second he and Karen gazed at each other. Then he said, 'My mother can't be disturbed, she's crying. My sister Bianca is comforting her.'

What a beautiful child, thought Karen, wondering how he fitted into such a privileged white right-wing environment.

'Why's she crying?' she asked.

'Because her dog died. Shall I give her those flowers?' Xav eyed the pink roses in Gablecross's hand.

'No, we'd like a word with her.'

'She's down at the graveyard,' explained Xav. 'I'll take you, if you promise not to upset her. My father left me in charge.'

Karen's disapproval evaporated when Xav introduced her to Peppy Koala on the way. She had won twenty-five pounds on him in the police sweepstake and bought a ribbed scarlet sweater, which she had worn to dramatic effect at the local disco.

'When did your dog Gertrude die?' asked Gablecross, admiring the handsome glossy chestnut.

'Tab brought her home on Sunday night. I woke and looked out of the window. She had blood all over her dress. Daddy went off in the helicopter earlier.'

'Did he?' Gablecross stroked Peppy Koala's sleek, arched neck only a little faster.

'He took his gun because he was so angry.'

'When did he get back?'

'Before Tab. When she arrived with Gertrude, Daddy went out and hugged her. He hadn't seen her for years. She cries a lot and looks past you. Gertrude's funeral was the next day. Mummy won't cry in front of Tab, but Tab's gone to polo today. Daddy promised us Gertrude has gone to heaven, but Bianca's worried Rannaldini's gone there too and might hurt Gertrude again. But Daddy said Rannaldini would be sitting in a bonfire with demons sticking these into him.' As he closed Peppy's half-door, Xav tapped a pitchfork leaning against the wall. 'Tab's mother's staying too. She's a drip. Daddy hates her.'

'Are you sure your father took the helicopter on Sunday night?'

'I said so, didn't I?'

'Where's he now?'

'Abroad, to find out more about Tab's boyfriend who's in prison.'

Out of the mouths of babes and sucklings, thought Gablecross in jubilation.

They found Taggie planting heartsease and polyanthus round Gertrude's grave. Bianca was helping her with a toy trowel. Both children were dispatched to the kitchen to organize cups of tea.

The moment Gablecross laid the roses beside Gertrude's wonky cross, Taggie started to cry again.

'I'm so sorry.' She collapsed on to the grave of Rupert's great Olympic horse, Revenge. 'But Gertrude was with me the whole time before I married and when I lost the babies, and when Beattie Johnson dumped twice. I thought she'd be jealous when we adopted Bianca and Xav. We had to leave her for six weeks when we went to Bogotá, but beyond the odd sniff, she loved them, finished up the food they didn't like. She always kept a biscuit hidden in her basket so she could rush out and eat it very slowly in front of the other dogs. I'm sorry.'

Taggie raised streaming eyes to Karen and Gablecross. 'She was such a mascot. I live in such a lovely house, but it seems so empty without Gertrude. I feel our luck's running out.'

'No, it isn't,' protested Karen, putting an arm round Taggie's shoulders. 'You've got everything to live for. Those kids are so cute.'

'It's probably because Rupert's first wife's staying,' confessed Taggie, wiping her nose with the back of her hand and covering her face with earth. 'She keeps saying Gertrude "had a good innings", like some stupid cricketer. Oh, God, I'm being a bitch. Lysander, Rupert's assistant, has an incredibly clever, handsome headmaster father, who's coming to supper tonight. He and Helen can quote poetry at each other.'

The afternoon sun peering through a lime tree showed up her dreadful pallor.

'Mrs Campbell-Black,' said Gablecross, feeling a louse, 'I know this is distressing, but Beattie Johnson's last call on Friday night was to your husband. According to Gordon Dillon on the *Scorpion*, she had some dirt on him and some other woman while you've been married.'

Taggie looked up in bewilderment, Karen in horror.

'Your husband was overheard telling Beattie he'd bury her. He left the set at midnight. An hour and a half later she was dead. Have you any idea of his movements that night?'

Taggie almost fell off Revenge's grave, frantically

617

digging a hole in the still iron-hard earth with Bianca's trowel.

'He was so pleased George Hungerford had given Tab an alibi,' she mumbled, 'he rushed off to persuade him to get back with Flora.'

'He hardly spent all night playing Cupid,' said Gablecross sarcastically. 'Are you worried your husband might have killed Rannaldini and Beattie?'

'Of course he didn't,' gasped Taggie. 'Oh, bugger.' In her violence she had snapped the little trowel in two. 'Oh, poor Bianca, of course he didn't.'

A witness, went on Gablecross relentlessly, had seen Rupert taking a gun and leaving Penscombe by helicopter. A helicopter had also been seen landing at Valhalla and two men running into the wood near Rannaldini's tower. Another witness had seen Rupert with a gun in his hand.

Taggie sat back on her heels, mouthing in horror.

'He had plenty of motives.' Gablecross ticked them off on his fingers. 'Tab being raped by Rannaldini, Gertrude being killed, Rannaldini arranging for Tab to marry Lovell, Rannaldini trying to murder your stepson Marcus.'

'Rannaldini did that?' whispered an appalled Taggie.

'And your husband had more than enough reason to kill Beattie. Where is he, anyway?'

'Abroad,' said Taggie numbly. 'He didn't leave a telephone number.'

'Oh, come on, Mrs C-B. Your husband wouldn't cross the lawn without leaving a phone number.'

'How's Tabitha?' asked Karen.

Gablecross, like a hound tugged off the scent, kicked her ankle.

'Better, I think.' Grateful for the distraction, Taggie planted a polyanthus upside down. 'Wolfgang's been so wonderful to Tab. He keeps ringing to see if Helen's OK. Helen's convinced he fancies her, but I'm sure he's only hoping to get Tab. Oh, help, I'll be punished for being a bitch again.'

Gablecross returned to the attack. 'What time did your husband leave the house last Sunday?'

'I don't remember, I was so upset about Gertrude.' Taggie began to cry again.

As the stable clock struck five, Xav and Bianca came round the corner carrying a trayful of tea in which floated three cups and some melting chocolate biscuits. They'd been joined on the way by a beautiful young man and a Jack Russell, who was rough-housing noisily round the graves with Xav's black Labrador.

'How dare you bully my mother?' said Xav in outrage.

'Whatever's the matter?' asked the beautiful young man in horror.

'It's all right.' Taggie mopped her eyes on her T-shirt.

'I'll give you a pound each if you go and find my cigarettes,' the young man told Bianca and Xav. 'Now, what the hell's going on?' He turned furiously on Gablecross.

'He thinks Rupert murdered Rannaldini and Beattie,' sobbed Taggie.

'Right.' The young man squared his shoulders. 'My name's Lysander Hawkley. I'm Rupert's assistant and it's time I made a statement.'

'It's nothing to do with you,' pleaded Taggie.

'I was with Rupert last Sunday,' went on Lysander, 'when Tab rang and said Rannaldini'd raped her. We took the helicopter. Rannaldini, incidentally, is the most evil person in the world.'

'How d'you know, sir?'

'He was married to my wife Kitty for five years, nearly destroyed her. I had to give her a lot of therapy when we were first married,' Lysander added solemnly. 'Anyway, Rupert swore he was going to kill Rannaldini, and I wanted part of the action. We landed in the park just after ten thirty. We couldn't find Tab, but about ten minutes later we stumbled on Rannaldini lying on his back in the middle of the wood. It was a bit dark for sunbathing.'

'How did he look?'

'Not well. He'd been strangled.'

'Was he dead?'

'Very, so Rupert emptied his gun into him.'

'What kind of gun?'

'A .38. He bought it in Bogotá when he adopted Xav and Bianca. It's got a silencer on it, and it sounds like a wet fart. If I'd had a gun I'd have done the same thing. As it was I kicked Rannaldini very hard in the ribs. We didn't hang about. We'd already tried to find Tab but the telephone box was redder inside than out. Rupert was going bananas with worry, then Taggie rang him to say someone with a Yorkshire accent was bringing Tab home.'

'And you're prepared to sign a statement that's what happened? You're not just making this up because Rupert's your boss?'

'No. I'm far too stupid to do that.'

Over on George's polo field, they were coming to the end of a long, shambolic day. Valentin had just filmed Baby hitting a ball around and being drooled over by Chloe and a lot of groupies. The sun was setting; they were waiting for the gate. Baby had moved away from the others under the shade of a huge sycamore tree and was sharing a Kit-Kat with his weary chestnut mare. Anything to do with horses reminded him agonizingly of Isa. They had not spoken since the night of Rannaldini's murder, but would have to soon, about the future of Baby's three racehorses.

At least a couple in the next-door room at Le Manoir aux Quat' Saisons had come forward and confirmed that they had heard Baby singing on the balcony between ten and eleven on the night of Rannaldini's murder.

'We thought, Oh, my God,' they had said. 'Then, once he opened his mouth, we sat back and enjoyed it. Is he going to be the next Domingo?'

So Baby had an alibi. On the other hand, the police had found the bottle of Quercus he had left behind in his bathroom at Le Manoir so he wasn't altogether in the clear.

'You know Isa?' A voice interrupted Baby's thoughts. It was Chloe, who'd been in a strange, excited mood all day.

'He's my trainer.'

'I was with him the night Rannaldini was murdered. We've been having an *affaire*.'

'You what?' Baby's pony, picking up the sudden tension, tossed up her head and pulled away.

'I confessed it to Fanshawe, who has such a divinely uppity bum in that grey tracksuit,' went on Chloe. 'I felt awful shopping Isa but I needed an alibi. The police know I was in the wood earlier because I dropped a lipstick, and they've found the scent Isa gave me, called Quercus, on Rannaldini's dressing-gown. Baby?'

Seeing his horrified face, Chloe launched mockingly into Eboli's lines:

'Oh, heavens, what thought makes you blench stock still,
Your word freezing on your lips?
What ghost rises in between us?'

Then, when Baby still seemed incapable of speech, she asked plaintively, 'Will Tab go berserk, and d'you think Isa'll back me up?'

Baby reached up a hand to scratch his restless pony behind the ears. 'Good girl,' he murmured affectionately, 'which is more than can be said for you, Chloe. You're a whore.'

'That's unkind,' pouted Chloe. 'I have to have a man in my life.'

'Have someone's husband, you mean.'

'Tab was keen enough to get her long claws into Tristan.'

'Tab was lonely and neglected.'

'You've never stuck up for her before. Loosen up, Baby. What will Rupert do?'

'Give you a medal. He loathes Isa. Isa, on the other hand, will go apeshit.'

'Isa's bats about me,' said Chloe defensively, then leapt back as, for a terrifying second, she thought Baby was going to hit her with his stick.

'"Bat" is the operative word,' said Baby harshly. 'Isa's a bloodsucker. He's got a perfectly good mistress, called Martie, bankrolling him in Oz. He didn't break up with her when he married Tab, who turned out to be not rich enough because Rannaldini wouldn't help out. I bet Isa suggested you buy some horses for him to train.'

Then, ignoring bellows from Bernard that the gate wasn't clear, Baby vaulted on to his pony and galloped off in the direction of Valhalla.

It took Chloe some hours to trace the ex-directory number of Jake Lovell's yard.

Having gone to bed early, Isa was woken not by the news of a sick horse, which he would have understood, but by Chloe in hysterics.

'Who the hell's Martie?' she screamed.

'My business partner.'

'A bit more than that.'

'Well – it's all over anyway. Who told you about her?'

'Baby. I told him about us.'

Isa sat bolt upright. 'You what?'

'The police found my lipstick near Rannaldini's body and Quercus on his dressing-gown. I needed an alibi.'

'Well, I'm not giving you one, you stupid bitch. Anyone who kisses and tells deserves all they get.' And Isa hung up.

72

Tristan paced in torment up and down his baking, airless veal crate of a cell. The light was fading outside his frosted window, but he could see nothing except the inside of his own heart. He knew that a gentleman never named the women he had slept with. Montignys didn't fuck and tell, as Rannaldini had, although Étienne had fucked and painted enough.

For the last three years he had been having an *affaire* with Claudine Lauzerte, so discreetly that not even Rannaldini's secret service had rumbled them. He had fallen in love with her back in 1977 when she'd joined their table, the first time Rannaldini had taken him to *Don Carlos*.

His dream had come true in 1993 when he'd cast her as the object of a young man's adoration in *Le Rouge et Le Noir*. As she had grown in beauty under Oscar's lighting and his direction, so had their passion for one another. At first she had held off. Only when he had found her sobbing wildly over a newspaper report that he was sleeping with some starlet had he broken down her defences and they'd become lovers.

But at what price? Claudine's husband Jean-Louis, the appropriately named Minister of Cultural Affairs, was universally acknowledged to be a brute.

And that was another reason why Tristan had identified with Carlos. He had experienced all the hell of loving a married woman, with a stern, undemonstrative, unfaithful yet possessive husband. He could never drop in on Claudine unannounced, never expect her to ring him in case the telephone number showed up on a bill closely scrutinized by Jean-Louis's accountants, never ring her at home in case one of the spying servants answered. Nor could he write because Jean-Louis or his secretary, also a spy, frisked the post.

As Claudine became even more adored because of Tristan's films, and was voted the Most Admired Woman in France, Jean-Louis's jealousy increased, and so did the interest of the press who followed her every move.

At first she had been reckless and while they were on location spent all night in Tristan's arms. This had compensated for the endless taunts that he was a closet gay, impotent, incapable of sustaining a relationship. He had also had to endure the hostility of beautiful women like Chloe and Serena, who couldn't understand why he rejected their advances, not to mention the endless matchmaking of his brothers' wives.

He had prayed Claudine would leave Jean-Louis and move in with him or, better still, marry him. He didn't give a toss about the twenty-four-year age gap. Sometimes, when life became unbearable, she had come near to it.

But just before Étienne's death, one of Claudine's friends had rung to say a newspaper was on to her and Tristan and about to blow her saintly Madame Vierge image sky high. Claudine had no desire to relinquish the moral high ground, so she had retreated into her arid marriage. Gradually, for Tristan, hope had died, but he couldn't stop loving her.

Until suddenly he had been jolted by Tab, and believed, by some miracle, there might be life and love after Claudine. But Rannaldini had promptly stamped on that flower.

In his most despairing thoughts since then, Tristan

had dreamt that Claudine, having four children of her own, might not mind that he couldn't give her children. He had so longed to see her again at the screening of *The Lily in the Valley*: he knew Jean-Louis was in Tuscany and was devastated when she'd failed to show up, on the excuse that filming commitments in Wales were too heavy.

He had forced himself to go to Hortense's party the next day, but the sight of numerous Montignys, a tribe to which he no longer belonged, milling around the lawn – Aunt Hortense in navy blue pinstripe, the Croix de Guerre in her lapel, his self-regarding brothers and their braying wives, and the smell of crayfish drifting over the white rose hedge – had sent him fleeing back to Valhalla.

Here he collected the address book with Claudine's telephone number in Wales, showered, changed into the peacock-blue shirt and the jeans she had given him, and on which Lucy had put the patch of a greyhound's head, and set out for the sleepy village of Llandrogan.

He had rung from Valhalla to say he was on his way, his mobile cutting out before Claudine could say no. He had driven like the devil and arrived while she was getting ready, her hair, which she hadn't had time to wash, still in rollers, with only one eye made up and her tummy still blown out from an early supper.

As he bounded upstairs like Tigger, she had sent him down again to pour himself a huge drink, which, by the time she had joined him, had become two. She had looked so exquisite, he had swept her back up to bed, which had not been a success. He had come instantly. In the old days, he would then have made love to her with his tongue and his hands, until he was raring to come again. Now he sensed her relief.

'It couldn't matter less, *chéri*, we're both exhausted. I have lines to learn and I've got to get up at six. I'm not as young as I was.'

It was a far cry from *The Lily in the Valley* when they had made love all night, and the violet shadows beneath eyes softened by happiness had only enhanced her haunting beauty.

Claudine herself, that Sunday evening in Llandrogan, had suddenly felt too old and set in her ways. Reason has reasons the heart knows nothing about. She didn't want him to stay the night. She longed to take off her make-up and cover her face with skin food. Worry about the lurking paparazzi would keep her awake when she needed to look good on the set, and if she fell asleep she might snore.

When Tristan told her about the problems with Rannaldini, she had been unsympathetic. All directors became increasingly twitchy as the end of a shoot approached. Unable to bear it any longer, he had dropped the bombshell that Maxim was his father. To his amazement, she wasn't very interested.

'The aristocracy have always been irregularly conceived, *chéri*. My sister wasn't my father's daughter. I'm not sure I was either. Jean-Louis's father was a naughty old boy too. Whenever we go shooting on the estate I notice how the beaters all look like Jean-Louis.'

'For Christ's sake, it's not the same. My grandfather was a psychopath who raped my sixteen-year-old mother, so I'm three-quarters his mad, tainted blood.' Tristan had wanted to hit her, but had shaken her instead.

'Stop it, you're hurting me,' she had cried.

And what the fuck d'you imagine you're doing to me? thought Tristan.

'I cannot have children,' he said bleakly.

Claudine had shrugged.

'There are too many children in the world. They're nothing but trouble. Marie-Claire is threatening to marry a *pied-noir*. Patrice is divorcing. Béatrice is pregnant by her Egyptian boyfriend. Jean-Louis is out of his mind with worry.' Then, seeing Tristan's blackening face, 'Anyway, *chéri*, you have elder brothers, it is not as

626

if there's any need to carry on the Montigny line.'

When he tried to explain, he knew he was boring her. He would have liked to have left then, but he had drunk too much brandy, and was too tired so instead he had crashed out on her bed. She had shaken him awake at three thirty. It would soon be light.

'I'm so terrified of the English press – they're everywhere.'

It wouldn't do to forfeit being the Most Admired Woman in France, thought Tristan savagely.

As he had driven away from Llandrogan into the desolation of dawn, and pulled into a field to sleep, he had been reminded of the time he had broken the news of Maxim being his father to Lucy and how she'd given him black coffee, laced with Drambuie, wrapped him in her duvet, held him shuddering in her arms and listened and listened, and how her hair was the same soft brown as rain-soaked winter trees.

Coming back to earth, still pacing his cell, he remembered how on the day after the murder, for the first time in months, Claudine had actually slipped into a telephone box in Llandrogan to ring him, pleading with him not to use her as an alibi. She must know he'd been arrested, but she was clearly not coming forward to save him. There was no light in the little frosted window. And no dawn for him.

As Karen walked into the Pearly Gates with Ogborne after the cinema, Jessica dragged her outside into the drizzle.

'I found this in my bag. I wrote Oscar's mobile number on the back of it on Thursday. It's a memo from Tristan to Bernard and the props department, saying he was planning to reshoot part of Posa and Carlos's pistol scene in the Unicorn Glade on Friday night, and he would need the .22 out of the props cupboard. Is it important?'

Karen didn't even notice the drizzle become a down-pour.

'Yes, it is,' she said joyfully.

'And, by the way, Mikhail's looking for you,' said a relieved Jessica. 'He's in the production office.'

Karen found Mikhail utterly despondent about his crocus-yellow Range Rover.

'I telephone ten garage today and ask how much they charge for bottle-green blow-job. They all shout 'orrible things and hang up.'

'I think you mean respray.' Karen had only just contained her laughter, when Mikhail said he wished to make a statement.

'I took the Montigny from the votch-tower and I borrow lighter with lilies from Tristan two or three days earlier. I must have dropped it in the wood. I went there to kill Rannaldini about ten forty-five, but he was already dead, strangled and shot. I also must confess I actually make friends again with my wife, Lara, on night before murder. When Rannaldini took her to votch-tower for bonk, he boast Montigny painting on wall was vorth three million. Finding Rannaldini dead, I took painting instead.'

'What did you do with it?' Karen's pen would hardly write for excitement.

'Hid it under Tristan's mattress for safe-kipping.'

'Whatever for?'

'Tristan wasn't bonker like Sylvestre or Alpheus and wouldn't squash painting. But when I go to remove it on Friday morning it had vanish . . .'

Mikhail was amazed but greatly cheered when Karen gave him an ecstatic hug. Gablecross was never going to speak to her again, but she was more and more convinced Tristan was innocent.

The Llandrogan Badger Action Group held their monthly meetings at the Leek and Grasshopper hotel on Sunday nights. The badger setts along Chantry Wood were the pride of the area, and at least forty badgers were known to travel nightly through the wood, over Jackson's Meadow, skirting Catmint Cottage, down to the stream which divided the valley.

In summer months, the Action Group (or BAG, as they liked to be known), anxious to observe the badgers' habits and protect them from baiters, fierce dogs and even fiercer farmers concerned about bovine tuberculosis, set up a camera to record these nocturnal perambulations and their time and date.

On Sunday, 15 July, Gareth Stacey, BAG's bearded secretary, who spent a lot of time in the field and who stank worse than any badger sett after a rhubarb raid, was about to give a slide show of this month's findings.

'Come on, buck up,' grumbled Major Holmes, the village bully, who didn't care much for badgers but longed to get stuck into the wine and light refreshments that followed.

'It's like magic,' said pretty Tracey Birkett, who taught at the local primary, 'that the brocks don't know we can see them all lit up.'

Out went the lights. Click, click, went Stinker Stacey. On the screen a stout female badger appeared, looping the loop.

'Upside-down,' barked Major Holmes.

Click, click, the right-way-up badger was followed by a barn owl, Lady Wade-Williams's Burmese cat, a couple of cubs, then a huge bull badger, who produced roars of applause.

This woke up Keith, the junior reporter on the *Llandrogan Echo*, furious at having to cover the event when he could be in the pub, and who in the dark couldn't keep himself awake gazing at pretty Tracey Birkett.

Click, click, click, click.

'Look you, Gareth,' said Merv the milkman, 'we have an intruder.'

'By Jove, we do,' said Major Holmes.

As Stinker Stacey repeated the slide, everyone could see a tall dark man in a peacock-blue shirt, jeans and loafers coming out of the wood.

'He's yummy,' sighed Tracey.

'Wouldn't mind having a teddy bears' picnic with him,' said Mrs Jones, the local baker, with a cackle.

'Looks familiar,' said the Vicar, cleaning his glasses.

'It's Lady Wade-Williams's handyman – he's always on the poach,' said Merv the Milk.

The handsome intruder was followed by several rabbits, a fox, more badgers – two of them humping to loud cheers – and Mrs Owen's Jack Russell on a late-night spree.

'There he is again,' said Jones the baker, in excitement.

'Got one of them greyhounds on his back pocket,' said Merv the Milk.

'Lovely bum,' sighed Tracey Birkett, earning a look of reproach from the Vicar.

'He's some actor chappie,' said Major Holmes. 'Seen him before.'

'No, he isn't.' Keith the reporter snatched up the evening paper and thrust it into the beam of the projector. 'It's that Froggy they've arrested for murdering Rannaldini.'

'The time was three forty a.m., ninth of the seventh, ninety-six,' read out Tracey Birkett.

'The murder's supposed to have taken place between ten and eleven,' said Keith, who was now leaping up and down in excitement. 'Turn back to the first slide of him.'

Click, click, click, click, went Stinker Stacey.

Everyone peered forward in excitement.

'Ten fifty p.m. on the eighth of July. Bingo!' yelled Keith in jubilation. 'He couldn't have done it. It's a good hundred and fifty miles from here to Paradise. Bloody hell! What a scoop.'

Even the Vicar forgave such language.

'Golly,' said Tracey Birkett. 'He must have been going into the back gate of Catmint Cottage to see Claudine Lauzerte. Didn't they make a film together?'

'It's him, all right,' said Stinker Stacey. 'We'd better go to the police.'

'It's him all right,' said DC Beddoes of North Wales CID. 'Must have nipped into Catmint Cottage, given Madame Lauzerte *un, deux et trois*, and nipped out again. Puts him in the clear. Couldn't have strangled Rannaldini. You told anyone else?'

'Only the *Daily Mail*, but it's too late for tomorrow's paper. Story'll break with a bang on Tuesday.'

'Madame Lauzerte's not going to like it,' said DC Beddoes, disapprovingly. 'Terrible thing. She'd have let him do life.'

'Must love her not to squeal,' sighed Keith. 'What a story. Froggy would a-wooing go.'

Even when Gablecross and Karen confronted him with the evidence of the Badger Action Group, Tristan still defended Claudine.

'There was no *affaire*. I worry about film. She and her husband were friends of my father. She was like mother to me, we just talked last Sunday.'

'At eleven at night?' chided Gablecross. 'And five hours later you're seen coming out – long time to read the meter. Anyway, the French police have blown your safe and found Madame Lauzerte's letters, which are not those you'd write to a son.'

Even the news he was free to go didn't cheer Tristan.

'Her name must be kept out of the papers,' he pleaded.

'Might have been if you'd levelled with us in the first place. Migraine on Thursday night indeed! When you were nearly three-quarters of an hour on the phone to her.'

631

'Trying to reassure her the story wouldn't come out,' said Tristan despairingly.

'Terrific for her street cred she's been pulling such a gorgeous young guy,' sighed Karen.

Over at Valhalla, a devastated Baby had, like Tristan, paced his room most of the night. How could Isa have stood him up for someone as two-faced and trivial as Chloe? Monday's dawn and his heart were breaking simultaneously as he went out into the park. Torrential rain washed away his tears and the remnants of Rozzy's make-up, which hadn't been nearly as flattering as Lucy's. Having caught and loaded his three horses into one of Rannaldini's lorries, he set off very slowly, stopping every few minutes in case rage and shock made him drive into a wall.

Rupert's house was ash blond in the early-morning sunshine. His dark woods lay as still as possible, like shaggy dogs knowing their coats will be too hot later in the day. As Baby rumbled into the yard, Rupert had just flown in from France. He was talking to a ravishing youth and to Dizzy, his comely head groom, who were both about to ride out. One beautiful horse after another, like a conjuror's silk handkerchiefs, was emerging from the boxes.

Still in his polo gear, his face grey against his crimson shirt, Baby jumped down from the lorry.

'D'you want to train my horses?'

'I'd be delighted,' said Rupert. Then, as he gave the ravishing youth a leg up, 'I don't think you've met my assistant, Lysander Hawkley.'

'Hi,' said Baby, looking Lysander up and down. 'Paradise *was* in Rutshire, but it appears to have moved.'

'Let's unload your horses,' said Rupert, 'and then come and have breakfast.'

*   *   *

This latest development enraged Isa. How dare Baby team up with Rupert! Had he neatly forgotten he owed Isa for the last quarter?

'I owe you nothing, you little toad. If you breathe a word of complaint, I'll tell your father-in-law you were shagging Chloe the night of Rannaldini's murder. Then I'll tell the world how white you bled me.'

73

Gerald Portland's gameplan was in tatters. A mob of reporters had fought their way through the deluge into the Rutminster courtroom, or failing that had ringed the building, spilling down adjacent lanes like the water hurtling down gutter and pavement. They had already written their intros about the Fall of the House of Montigny and the most deadly snake of them all. When news leaked out that Tristan had been freed, they immediately charged off to write bitchy pieces about utterly incompetent West Country police wasting public money and being no nearer to finding the killer. The *Scorpion*, who'd already set the headline 'Beattie's Butcher' over a snarling photograph of Tristan, changed it to 'Thickos' in even larger type and decided to launch their poll asking readers, 'Who Killed Beattie and Rannaldini?'

Only the *Daily Mail* rubbed their hands over Tristan's secret tryst with Claudine and pored over copy and head-lines for tomorrow's paper in a security block. The rest of the media took off like starlings to Rutminster Hall to harass the polo shoot, where they were furious to find that George's security guards kept them outside the front gates and that Rupert, still a chief suspect, had gone racing.

'We've become a laughing stock,' shouted Gerald Portland, who'd specially put on a new lilac-striped shirt to wow the press and felt it was utterly wasted on his Inner Cabinet. They would have to re-examine all the suspects.

A terrible weariness came over his utterly weary team.

Even people who'd covered for each other, like Tab and George Hungerford, or Rupert and Lysander, or Griselda, Granny and Bernard, who'd all claimed to be searching for balls together in Hangman's Wood, could be lying. Chloe claimed to have seen both Alpheus and Isa, but neither of them had seen her. Hermione was still sticking to the story that she'd been in bed with Sexton. Meredith, Simone and Pushy had no-one to vouch for them at all, neither did Wolfie and Lucy, who'd pushed off abroad and, so far, neatly evaded Interpol. Even those with cast-iron alibis away from Valhalla, like Rozzy, Oscar and Valentin, would have to be checked out again.

There was a lot of money on Lady Rannaldini, who none of the investigating team liked very much. Bearing in mind that she claimed to have seen Rupert around ten twenty-five, but Lysander had sworn that he and Rupert didn't discover Rannaldini's dead body until they first approached the watch-tower as late as ten forty, meant someone was lying.

'If Rannaldini was happy and excited at the moment of death, as the PM revealed,' mused Karen, 'the murderer must be someone he was thrilled to see.'

'Which certainly wasn't Rupert, Wolfie or Alpheus,' chipped in Debbie, 'but most likely Hermione, Bussage or Tab.'

'We'll wait for the DNA results before we tackle Tab again,' said Portland, who didn't want any more earache from Rupert.

DC Lightfoot, who'd fallen asleep with his head on the edge of Portland's desk, was gently shaken awake and dispatched with DC Smithson to Rutminster Hall to try to find out if Alpheus and Mikhail had been telling porkies. Fanshawe and Debbie were given the task of re-interviewing Hermione and then Lysander on the timing of his and Rupert's raid on Hangman's Wood.

Gablecross and Karen, who were right at the bottom of the list for letting Tristan off the hook and hassling Taggie Campbell-Black, were allotted the dreary task of trailing over to Mallowfield to interview Rozzy's feckless husband. Gablecross was in despair. Only Karen's enterprise had proved Tristan's innocence. His loathed rival, Fanshawe, was poised to make a strike and Margaret wasn't speaking to him because he'd left the anniversary party so early.

As she had also refused to make him any breakfast, Gablecross popped into the Paradise village shop to buy several Yorkie bars to misery-eat on the way to Mallowfield. Ahead in the queue, he saw Little Cosmo Harefield shoving some photographs and a letter into a large brown envelope. As Cosmo stopped to rest the envelope on a pile of *Rutminster Echo*s, Gablecross noticed he was addressing it to the editor of the *Sun*.

'Please register and express this on my mother's account,' Cosmo told Eve, the proprietor, grandly.

'What have you got there, sonny?' demanded Gablecross.

'Nothing,' lied Little Cosmo.

'Let me look.' Grabbing Little Cosmo by his T-shirt, Gablecross relieved him of the envelope.

'Gimme that, you bugger,' hissed Little Cosmo, trying to knee Gablecross in the groin.

Two photographs got slightly torn in the scuffle, but were still clearly discernible as Hermione and Sexton on the job.

In custody, and possession of one of Gablecross's Yorkie bars and a cup of black coffee, Little Cosmo thawed a fraction.

'Obviously you were upset about your dad's death.'

'Very,' sighed Cosmo.

His father, he grumbled, had divided his inheritance between Cecilia, his ex-wife, Cosmo and all his step-siblings, except Wolfie. This meant Little Cosmo only ended up with four million, which was quite insufficient, after estate duty, for a growing lad, particularly one intending to own racehorses. Cosmo had therefore decided to augment his income.

'Give us a fag,' he added, looking longingly at Gablecross's pack.

Gablecross, however, was not going to risk it, in case Cosmo's mother's friend, the Chief Constable, walked in. He and Karen then learnt that on the night of Rannaldini's murder, Hermione's notion of 'quality time' had consisted of shoving Little Cosmo upstairs with *101 Dalmatians* and a jar of humbugs. Regarding this as insufficient, Cosmo, who had inherited his father's specialist interest, had borrowed his mother's camera and crept across the lawn to the summerhouse. Peering through the windows, he had discovered and photographed his mother and Sexton romping on their carpet of lady's bedstraw. Cosmo liked Sexton and thought he would suit very well as a stepfather. Luckily for his mother and Sexton, Cosmo had taken a mid-shoot break for sloe gin and smoked salmon, and unintentionally recorded both ten twenty-five and ten forty on the large clock on the summerhouse wall.

Although this gave Hermione a vagina-tight alibi, Gablecross had ticked off Little Cosmo roundly for shopping his mother at a time of mourning.

Hermione, who'd just endured another most un-chivalrous grilling from Fanshawe and Debbie, was extremely displeased to see DS Gablecross and Karen.

'I didn't do it, Timothy.' She opened her eyes very wide. 'Why should I want to murder Little Cosmo's father?'

She might, however, feel like murdering Little Cosmo, said Gablecross, spreading the photographs on the table in front of her.

For a moment Hermione was lost for words, then her face lit up. 'But, Timothy, these are quite beautiful. Far more flattering than anything Valentin or Oscar could produce. I never knew my son was so talented. They compare very favourably with the work my good friend Patrick Lichfield did for the Unipart calendar. Such a lovely texture.' Hermione ran her finger over her naked body. 'And I look so fragile beside Sexton's manliness. Even in his birthday suit, Timothy, you can tell an Old Etonian by his commanding air.'

Hermione was so carried away, she didn't notice Karen doubled up with helpless laughter as she fled from the room. Gablecross, chewing his lip, just managed to keep a straight face. 'But Cosmo was sending these pictures to the *Sun*, Dame Hermione.'

'Very enterprising. I told Cosmo he wouldn't get a penny until probate came through. I know Higgy will adore them. We could even try Charles Moore on the *Telegraph*, such a charmer. That one of me on my own is so lovely, Serena could use it on the next CD. Bravo, Cosmo.'

'You're the kiss of death,' Gerry Portland chided Karen and Gablecross, as they gathered round his office table later that morning to admire the Live Sexton Show, as it was now called.

'Moment you start interviewing a perfectly legit suspect – Tristan, Rupert, Hermione – an alibi comes jumping out of the woodwork. I suppose we can assume she was unlikely to have jumped out of bedstraw to murder Rannaldini.'

'It would have taken her at least a quarter of an hour even to run from River House,' said Gablecross, 'and if she'd been out of breath, she couldn't have sung Elisabetta's last aria so beautifully.'

'She's got a marvellous body,' said Portland, 'and knows a few tricks for an old 'un.'

'Hermione agrees with you,' said Karen, who was still laughing.

'I hope the lad isn't too traumatized.'

'Camera's only thing likely to be upset,' said Gablecross. 'That boy's more evil than his father.'

As a result Gablecross and Karen didn't reach Mallowfield until teatime.

Having admired the grandeurs of River House earlier, Gablecross's first angry impression was that Rozzy, as a well-known and much beloved singer, ought to be living in a better house.

Clearly no-one had been watering the garden during the drought or washed the milk bottles, sour and queuing up outside the door. The carpets were thread-bare, the paint peeling. Flowers Rozzy had obviously arranged beautifully for Glyn's party the Sunday before last had shed their petals on dusty surfaces. There were no portraits or photographs of Rozzy, even in her radiant youth. Any cups or awards she'd won over the years had been hidden away. The colours were beautiful, but Gablecross had the feeling, looking at shelves denuded except for cards, that most things of value had been hocked.

He was further irritated to find he quite liked Glyn, who had an unlined face, a beer gut, and who was eating pizza, drinking his way down a pint mug of red, and watching Rutshire bowl out Oxfordshire. Half rising to his feet, he apologized, but without much conviction, for the bottles still littering the place from his party.

'Know I ought to make a trip to the bottle bank but it's easier to bung the dustmen, and they always come before I get up. Tend to let things slide when Rozzy's away. But Syl will have the place like a new pin for when she comes home – on Wednesday, isn't it?'

Sylvia, the housekeeper, was extremely pretty with big blue eyes, a shiny red bob and a regulo-nine smile, which could be turned off as quickly. She was obviously better at keeping herself beautiful than the house. Karen understood why poor Rozzy had sleepless nights over Sylvia.

'Have a drink,' urged Glyn. 'Both of you can't be

driving. Get some glasses, Syl, love. How's it going at Valhalla?'

'Must be spooky,' shuddered Sylvia, as she reluctantly left the room.

'I gather you had a wonderful birthday party,' beamed Karen, who found herself sitting very far forward in an armchair stuffed with tapestry cushions.

'Wonderful,' agreed Glyn. 'Syl wanted to help. But Roz insisted on doing everything. Loves to feel needed. I wanted to get in caterers,' added Glyn expansively. 'Roz wouldn't hear of it. We never save any money. Ex-wife costs a bomb, two kids at boarding-school.'

'When do they come home?' asked Gablecross.

'Wednesday,' said Sylvia, without enthusiasm, as she returned with a jug of orange juice, cans of iced beer and another bottle of red.

So Rozzy'll be back to look after them, thought Karen crossly. You wouldn't put yourself out for anyone.

'Did Rozzy enjoy the party?' she asked.

'Frankly, the old girl has been working so hard on *Don Carlos*, and worrying about the film's budget and our budget, and tidying and cooking, she retired to bed with a migraine.'

Bet that was diplomatic, thought Karen, accepting a glass of orange juice. Perhaps Rozzy'd caught hers from Tristan.

'What time did she go to bed?' she asked, getting out her notebook.

'Ooo, if we're going on record, we'd better check our facts,' said Sylvia skittishly. 'Around, er . . .' She glanced at Glyn.

'Eight thirty,' said Glyn. 'Loads of people were still here. I checked she was asleep at nine thirty. Syl checked her at ten, I put my head round the door about ten thirty and eleven.'

Those up to no good check all the time, thought Gablecross.

'I finally went to bed around midnight,' boasted Glyn,

reaching for the corkscrew to open the red. 'Tripped over the landing carpet, woke Rozzy up. She came out looking all in.'

Sylvia got up to put on a record.

'What did Rozzy give you for your birthday, apart from the party?' asked Karen.

'She got me a signed copy of Georgie Maguire's latest album, and a signed photo,' said Glyn. 'Syl loves Georgie too, don't you, Syl?'

'S'wonderful, s'marvellous,' sang the record player.

'Lovely single, isn't it?' said Glyn fondly. 'We played this and Georgie's album all day.'

'When did you cut your cake?'

'Around eight, I should think. There were still people here at midnight – I left them to it.'

'Your wife made two calls to Valhalla during the evening.'

Glyn laughed. 'She likes to check up, always checking up on me.' He winked at Karen who didn't wink back.

'Why didn't she use the house phone?'

'She was in the spare room – doesn't have a phone. We often sleep in separate rooms. I tend to snore, particularly when I've had a few. The spare room looks north over the back of the house so it was a bit quieter during the party.'

'You ever meet Rannaldini?'

'Sir Roberto? Only after performances in the old days. Charismatic bloke.'

'Think of any reason why anyone should kill him?'

'I could have done a few years ago – he was always jumping on Rozzy.'

'You didn't tell me that,' snapped Syl.

'Why should Rannaldini have made a note to ring you the day he died?' asked Gablecross.

'Me!' said Glyn somewhat flattered. 'I've no idea. Perhaps Rozzy's singing hadn't been up to scratch, or she might have overtired herself. She's always been delicate.'

She obviously hasn't told Glyn about the throat cancer, thought Gablecross. He ought to mention it, instead he said, 'Perhaps her GP could shed some light. Can you let me have his name?'

'Of course. I know she was worried about the young chappie directing it.'

'That is the most loathsome creep,' stormed Karen, as she drove through the dripping dusk. 'Bernard would make Rozzy much happier.'

But Gablecross was talking on his mobile to the incident room.

'Interpol had a tip-off that Rupert was staying in Montvert,' he told Karen as he switched it off. 'Casing the Montigny joint presumably, but when they rolled up at the hotel early this morning the bird had flown. Another couple who sound suspiciously like Wolfie and Lucy, who also stayed there, gave them the slip. Rannaldini's Gulf, on the other hand, has been clamped at Toulouse airport. Now, what the hell can that mean?'

'That at least Lucy's safe, Sarge,' said Karen, patting his arm.

74

Very early that Monday morning, Lucy had been woken by a telephone call from Wolfie.

'We gotta move it. Two plain-clothes men are downstairs looking for Rupert. Madame didn't tell them we were here, but suggests we leg it as soon as possible out through the back garden.'

Wolfie was just gathering speed down the high street, when a loitering gendarme mistook his blond hair and suntanned face for Rupert's, and whistled up his mate to give chase. Wolfie, who drove almost as fast as he flew, had no difficulty shaking them off. The airport was in sight, they could see Rannaldini's Gulf jet merging into the heat-haze on the runway, when Lucy's mobile rang. When she switched it off thirty seconds later she was as pale and trembling as a white poplar.

'Hortense has changed her mind, but we've got to hurry. Dupont and the rellies are expected back before lunch.'

Lucy's heart sank when a waiting Florence said Hortense didn't want to see them. She led them upstairs and, with a lot of cursing, unlocked a bedroom door. As the door creaked reluctantly open, she stood back.

'Madame said you'll find all the information you need in here. You're to be locked in for security reasons. Press that bell when you want to be let out.'

At first it was a question of not choking to death. As

their eyes grew accustomed to the dark, it was plain that nothing had been touched for years, possibly centuries. By yanking open the shutters, Wolfie triggered off an avalanche of dust. Cobwebs, woven on top of cobwebs and dotted with flies and wasps, formed net curtains across windows and in corners.

On the walls, a little Van Gogh and several of Étienne's enchanting drawings of dogs fought for space with school and army photographs and peeling posters of Jane Birkin, Juliette Greco and Bardot. Astérix leered up at them from the yellowing duvet covering the bed in the corner.

A half-full bottle of brandy, Roget et Gallet cologne, LPs of *Sergeant Pepper*, the Stones and Manfred Mann, hairbrushes, their silver backs blackened, *Esquire* and *Playboy*, *Paris-Match* and *Shooting Times* were all jumbled together on the shelves. Newspapers on the table, faded to the colour of weak tea, were all dated 1967.

'What the hell's all this about?' asked Wolfie, trying to open a window.

'Must be Laurent's room,' pondered Lucy. 'Florence said Étienne never allowed anyone in here after his death. But I still don't see.'

Leaning against the wall was a gold-framed portrait. Wiping away the dust and grime with her T-shirt, Lucy gave a gasp because a younger, happier, bolder Tristan smiled back at her. Then her heart stopped as she noticed the now-towering trees of the lime walk then only reached his shoulders, and that he was the same young man who'd been staring down at the girl whose long dark hair was tied back with a scarlet ribbon.

'This must be Laurent painted by Étienne,' she said, in excitement. 'God, he's good-looking.'

Wolfie, rooting round a desk, had found a pile of letters.

'These must have been sent him when he was in the army in Chad. "My darling, darling Laurent,"' read

Wolfie. 'Sounds exciting. And here's another pile with West African stamps on them.'

Swinging round Lucy knew, even before she saw them, that the letters would be tied together with scarlet ribbon.

'Give them here.' She snatched the package with a shaking hand, and, tearing open the top one, read, '"My darling angelic Delphine,"' and knew everything.

'Oh, my God, listen, Wolfie. "Don't be frightened," Laurent writes. "I'll be home in two months to take care of you. Is our baby still kicking in your beautiful belly? If it's a boy let's call him Tristan, but he's not going to be destined for tragedy, only joy." God, they got that wrong. Then Laurent goes on, "I love you so desperately. Don't worry about Papa. I just can't bear to think of you in the same bed as him or even that he's your husband. I know it's important not to humiliate him, that this should never have happened, but the fact that you and I love each other is all that matters."

'Oh, God, Wolfie.' Lucy looked up in horror. 'Poor Étienne, cuckolded by his own son.'

'Like Philip and Carlos.' Wolfie shook his head in bewilderment.

Lucy skimmed the rest of the letter. Laurent had been full of plans for the new life he and Delphine would start in Australia with their baby. He'd get a job, and they'd have love to live on.

'Here's a letter from Delphine to him,' said Wolfie, 'dated November the fourteenth. That must have been just after Tristan was born. She's enclosed a little pencil drawing of the baby, look.'

'Oh, how sweet.' Lucy mopped her eyes. On the back she recognized Étienne's elegant handwriting: 'Tristan Laurent Blaize, a beautiful boy, one hour old.'

'I thought you'd like to see your son and heir,' Delphine had written. 'Isn't he adorable? Étienne is so proud of his imagined offspring. I feel so guilty. Oh, Laurent, please come home, he's nagging me to have sex again. I can't bear him to touch me.'

'Here's an even earlier one,' interrupted Wolfie.

'"Darling Delphine, it's the best news in the world you're pregnant. It seals everything. Let me finish my stint here, there are things I must do."' Wolfie looked up at Lucy. 'That must have been for the rebels. "Then I'll come home and take you away, you will divorce Papa and marry me. Everything will be very simple." Christ, little did he know.'

'Here's another horrible one,' cried Lucy, in distress, smoothing out the letter, holding it up to the dim light from the windows. 'Must be early in her pregnancy, she sounds just like Elisabetta. "Étienne made love to me outside today. I noticed his grey eyebrows and chest hair, the liver spots on his hands, the pleats in his flesh, when he raised himself on his wrinkled arms. Oh, Laurie, I know he's your father but he revolts me."

'I can't read any more.' Lucy thrust aside the letter. 'Étienne was a vain old goat, but he must have been crucified by the son he adored, then constantly re-minded of this betrayal as Tristan grew more and more like Laurent. And that', Lucy choked on the swirling dust in the excitement of her discovery, 'was what he was rambling on about on his deathbed, trying to tell Tristan that he was his grandfather not his father.'

Wolfie was neatly stacking the letters and tying up Laurent's with their scarlet ribbon.

'If Tristan is Laurent and Delphine's son,' he said soberly, 'he's not only a Montigny, but can marry and have children by whoever he likes.'

Lucy's hair was white with dust, her face filthy and streaked with tears. 'So we found out what we came here for,' she said slowly, then realizing the full implications: 'Oh, Wolfie, I hope it works out for you.'

Hortense burst out laughing when she saw Lucy's dusty hair. 'You look older than I do. I hope you were surprised by what you discovered.'

'Stunned.' Sitting on the bed, Lucy took Hortense's hands. 'I'm sorry I was so horrible yesterday. I'm terribly glad for Tristan, but those letters are appalling. I understand totally why you didn't want it to come out. Poor Étienne. But why did someone as gorgeous as Delphine marry such an old man in the first place?'

'Rannaldini encouraged her,' said Hortense. 'She was a bit of a "raver", I think it's called, and wanted to escape from her strait-laced family. Maxim detested Rannaldini and that's why, in revenge, Rannaldini reinvented him as a sex-crazed rapist. Rannaldini persuaded Delphine of the doors Étienne would open, of the exciting life she would lead among the famous, how she'd be immortalized in his paintings.'

'But what about Maxim?'

'I always suspected', Hortense lowered her voice conspiratorially, 'that he wasn't Delphine's father. Her mother had an *affaire* with some actor called Sammy somebody. They were all Bohemians,' she added with a sniff. 'Maxim certainly doted on Delphine and immediately recognized Rannaldini as a rotter. He was even more distraught when she married Étienne, a notorious womanizer, even older than himself.'

'So he wasn't sectioned as a mad psychopath?'

'Certainly not, he went a bit dotty at the end, as we all do, and died in a perfectly respectable nursing home.'

Thank goodness Wolfie was downstairs, not hearing more evidence of his father's fearful lies.

'What happened to Laurent's mother?'

Hortense stroked her little greyhound reflectively.

'She was Étienne's third or fourth wife. Played bridge all day and, when Étienne pushed off, graduated to gin. Tripped over a black Labrador coming out of her bedroom in the dark one night and broke her neck falling down the stairs. Wonderful way to go.'

'So that disposed of one granny,' giggled Lucy. 'I don't mean to laugh, the whole thing must have been terrible.'

'Terrible. Étienne was so excited about his new baby, then a fortnight later we heard Laurent had died in some explosion – friendly fire, it's called. Étienne was inconsolable, so was Delphine, naturally, which touched Étienne because he felt she was sharing his unhappiness and at least they had a new life to look forward to together.

'Then Laurent's things were sent home, with all Delphine's letters and, cruellest of all, Étienne's little drawing. Étienne went on the rampage, found all Laurent's letters locked in her jewel case, and nearly killed her. Next day she took an overdose, sent me a note begging my forgiveness and asking me to bring up Tristan.'

A farm dog bayed down in the valley. The little grey-hound pricked up its velvet ears and stretched.

'Everything was locked in Laurent's room just as it was when he went off to Chad. Everyone thought Étienne was heartbroken, but it was the far more painful heart-break of betrayal.' Hortense lay back exhausted, her face very grey. 'I probably shouldn't have told you.'

'You should. Tristan has to know, so he can under-stand Étienne and forgive him.' Then, as she heard wheels on the gravel, banging doors and voices outside, 'I must go.'

'Dupont et cetera must be here,' grumbled Hortense. 'They'll be devastated I'm not worse. You'd better escape out the back.'

'I've been doing that all day. Look,' Lucy plumped up Hortense's pillows, 'I wish I didn't have to go. It's been a privilege . . .'

'Don't go all sentimental on me,' snapped Hortense. 'Look after my boy.' She handed Lucy a square package that felt like a picture. 'Give this to him. You've got all the letters, haven't you? Show them to him when the time is right, but don't let them fall into other hands.'

'You'll see him again,' said Lucy reassuringly.

'Hurry,' gasped Hortense. 'The others will try to stop you.'

Still Lucy lingered, then tugging off her gold locket, she hung it round Hortense's neck.

'There's a lovely dog inside,' she stammered. 'He'll bring you luck.'

'I'll need it where I'm going,' said Hortense wryly. 'There's no return ticket.'

'D'you think Tristan will fire us?' asked a worried Lucy as Wolfie considerably shortened the hired car's life, jolting it over dusty cart-tracks.

'Hardly, he's still in prison.' Wolfie swung into the road to the airport. 'Don't worry, we'll be home by the tea break.' Then, seeing the crowd of gendarmes round the Gulf, 'On second thoughts perhaps we won't. I'd better drive.' He swung the car round again.

'We can't leave the Gulf,' said Lucy aghast.

'It's Cecilia's now. At least I've flown it over half-way to Rome for her.'

'But it's nearly lunchtime, we won't get home until early tomorrow morning.'

'Or until tomorrow midday, if we stop somewhere nice for the night. You've pulled off a miracle and we're going to celebrate.'

75

The moment he was released on Monday morning, Tristan showered away every speck of prison dirt and drenched himself in Eau Sauvage. To match his mood, he then selected black jeans, a black shirt and, because the temperature had dropped fifteen degrees, a dark brown cashmere jersey he'd never worn before.

Pale and more shadowed than ever under the eyes, he had shed another half-stone in prison, and looked as dramatically elongated and demon-haunted as an El Greco saint.

To forget the horrors of prison and to blot out the even more nightmarish prospect of the *Mail* outing him and Claudine tomorrow, Tristan, as was his custom, plunged into work. But as he hurtled the Aston towards George's house, his dreams of using a polo match under a burning sun as a ritualized symbol of conflict were shattered. After a night of torrential rain, George's polo field was as full of lakes and as green as Ireland. His only compensation was driving through a huge puddle and drenching the paparazzi hanging around outside George's massive electric gates.

Inside, it was difficult to distinguish the massive police and press presence from George's heavies and the fleet of extras who'd been bussed in to act as policemen, paparazzi and Philip's bodyguards.

Behind the house, which crouched ox-blood red and

elephantine on a hill, a stretch of park had been levelled into a polo field surrounded by huge bell-shaped trees now dark and swollen with rain. Overhead, like a flotilla of battleships, hung charcoal-grey clouds.

On the edge of the field, outside a yellow and white striped tent, whose roof was buckling under the downpour, a small band in red uniforms was dispiritedly wringing out their instruments. Seeing his arrival, the commentator stopped telling the shivering extras in their flowery dresses and pale suits that the gallant Marquis of Posa had just scored a goal, and welcomed back 'our director', Tristan de Montigny.

Tristan was in no mood for pleasantries. Ignoring the ripple of applause and the large 'Bienvenu, Tristan' banner, he drove over to the unit, where the place was under water and in uproar, because neither Lucy nor Wolfie had turned up. Tristan was appalled. It was like coming home on a bleak winter night to find the pipes frozen and the central heating kaput. No-one had seen them since Saturday morning.

'I know they'll be found face down in a field,' sobbed Simone.

'Don't be fatuous,' snapped Tristan, who'd gone cold at the same thought.

All around him singers, who'd been soothed and flattered by Lucy for the past three months, were having tantrums and making fearful fusses about catching cold. A fleet of make-up artists had been bussed in anyway to handle all the extras. The most experienced, hijacked to look after the stars, must have graduated from the set of the Hammer House of Horror.

Granny looked about as menacing as a Brylcreemed Barbara Cartland. Tab, Pushy and Chloe had vermilion lips and black-ringed eyes like Brides of Dracula. Mikhail's drink-reddened face clashed horribly with his crimson polo shirt.

'Why isn't Lucy here to sort out my bags and my double chin?' grumbled Baby, who, having played polo until the stars came out with Rupert's cronies then pigged out on Taggie's sea trout, three helpings of loganberry torte and copious glasses of wine, was now trying to alleviate his hangover with a massive gin and tonic.

Alpheus was so furious that Griselda had hidden his noble brow and chestnut locks under a straw hat with a Blues and Royals ribbon that he'd surreptitiously fed the offending headgear to Sharon and Trevor, who'd rushed on to the field noisily tearing it to shreds.

Nemesis had struck swiftly. The new make-up artist didn't have Lucy's blow-drying and colouring skills, and Alpheus ended up with corkscrew curls the colour of mango chutney and looked like Paddy Ashdown in a Shirley Temple wig.

Simone was in hysterics that any continuity had been shot to pieces. 'How could Lucy do this to us?' she stormed.

'Manage without her,' snapped Tristan.

Nor had Tristan dreamt, as the day progressed, how much he would miss Wolfie to field telephone calls, to keep track of his belongings, and control the extras. Rupert had high-handedly sent over a couple of his grooms with all his dogs, and all his polo-playing friends' dogs because they all wanted their dogs in the film and because one always sees lots of dogs at polo. The dogs proceeded to fight and bark and mount each other. Rupert, meanwhile, had buggered off to a race meeting at Ayr.

'I vish his bloody daughter had gone too,' grumbled Mikhail.

One of the first sounds Tristan heard and ignored was Tab, yelling her head off in true Campbell-Black fashion. She was desperately nervous about making her polo film début playing against world-class players, even if she had known them since she was a child. She had wanted to look ravishing for Tristan's return, and been turned into the Town Tart by this ghastly make-up. It was all Lucy's fault. And where was utterly bloody Wolfie to hold her hand, find her whip and absorb abuse like a punch bag?

Even worse, as Mistress of the Horse, she felt it her duty to see the singers played properly. Baby was good, but Mikhail had an unnerving habit of dropping his reins and swinging his stick round with both hands like a Tartar warlord as he thundered down the field.

'For Gawd's sake, watch him,' Sexton pleaded with Tab. Having insurance claims already on a murdered producer and a recently absentee director, he didn't want Mikhail taking out Ricky France-Lynch the England captain, or his forwards Seb and Dommie Carlisle.

Mikhail was sulking because George's open house had suddenly become closed when one of Georgie's heavies had caught him sidling out with a little Watteau and a Sickert under his polo shirt.

'I know the murderer's still at large,' giggled Flora, 'but Mikhail seems to be taking bulletproof vests to extremes.'

She still looked haunted and desperately tired as she and George hardly left each other's side. As soon as the wrap party was over, they were off to Cornwall with Trevor.

Everyone was relieved to have moved away from Valhalla's dark mazes and haunted cloisters. Rannaldini's doomladen overture, pouring out of the speakers, however, was a constant reminder that his killer had not been caught.

The violence of the polo was equally unnerving, ponies thundering over grass as slippery as buttered spinach, sticks clashing, balls hurtling like cannon shot, often into the crowd, players deliberately colliding. The ponies kept jumping out of their thin thoroughbred skins and taking off, because the cast, upstaging each other, continually broke into snatches of their next opera or song cycle to prove there was work after *Carlos*.

'Telephone, Tristan,' shouted Bernard.

It was Claudine in hysterics. It was all Tristan's fault, for barging into the cottage in Wales, the police had already been round, her maid was threatening to dump to the *Express*, and Jean-Louis to divorce her.

And she would have let me swing, thought Tristan savagely. He remembered Gablecross telling him that in big murder cases several marriages always broke up.

Couldn't he get his friend Rupert Campbell-Black to pull strings and stop the *Mail*? wailed Claudine. Tristan said he'd try and hung up.

'I don't want to be bothered with any calls,' he ordered Jessica, who was nervously standing in for Wolfie.

While they were waiting for the cameras to reload and reposition, he finally got through to the château. Hortense was obviously a little better, as she was in a meeting, unable to be disturbed. Tristan might not have been so sanguine if he'd known with whom. He left a message with Florence that he'd be down on Wednesday after the wrap party.

When they broke for a late lunch, Jessica said a French lady had rung five times on the unit mobile.

'*Non, non, non*,' howled Tristan, as it rang again. 'I can't talk to anyone.'

Next moment he had been buttonholed by Alpheus, complaining about both Tabitha and the make-up artist, and Chloe complaining that Baby was being gratuitously offensive, and had nearly ridden his pony over her.

They were soon joined by Pushy.

'Could we have another make-up artist? I know I can look prettier than this, Tristan.'

God, he missed Wolfie to send them packing. Leaving them, in mid-bellyache, on his way to his caravan, he passed Jessica telling Bernard that Lucy expected to be back by mid-morning tomorrow.

Tristan swung round in fury. 'Lucy rang? Why didn't you put her on?'

'You didn't want any calls.'

'I didn't mean Lucy, you stupid bitch. Get her back at once.'

'I didn't take her number,' stammered Jessica, appalled by such unaccustomed rudeness.

'You bloody idiot.'

Jessica burst into tears.

Tristan couldn't remember being so angry. All he had wanted during his lunch break was to pour out his heart to Lucy about the horrors of prison and the difficulties of filming polo. Also, because Lucy had been so wonderfully comforting when he had found out Maxim was his father and had been forced to give up Tab he felt he should perhaps have provided the last piece of the jigsaw, and levelled with her about Claudine. He wanted to explain, before Lucy read about it in tomorrow's *Mail*, that the love that had obscured his vision for the past three years had suddenly been blown away like mist at sea. But if Lucy wasn't getting back till mid-morning, it would probably be too late.

'Oh, you're wearing my sweater. It really suits you.'

It was several seconds before Tristan realized the happy voice belonged to Rozzy, who was looking really pretty. All the lines in her face seemed to have ironed out. He'd forgotten she'd given him this jersey.

She tried to cover up for Lucy, which was difficult when James shot out of Wardrobe and did four pirouettes, nearly strangling himself on his lead, because he too was pleased to see Tristan. Then he slunk back in despair because he wasn't with Lucy.

'I've had to tie him to the table leg because he keeps following me on to the set.'

'Poor old boy.' Tristan unclipped James's lead. 'Where the hell's your mistress?'

'She'll turn up,' said Rozzy. 'I've got a surprise for you,' she added, leading him towards his caravan. 'Which did you like best, my *tarte aux oignons* or the quiche Lorraine?'

'They were both marvellous,' mumbled Tristan, who'd been far too uptight to eat anything in prison. 'My God!'

For a second he thought he'd let himself into the wrong caravan. There were vases of wild flowers everywhere.

'Marjoram, honeysuckle, scabious, forget-me-not, bellflower, thyme, wild basil and those dark purple bugle-like flowers are called self-heal. I picked two vases of them, because I know you will heal after your horrible experience.'

'You're so kind,' muttered Tristan, breathing in the honeysuckle, which reminded him of Lucy's lone sprig in prison.

How dare Rozzy ponce up his caravan! All the books and magazines had been straightened. All the notes secured under a paperweight. The floor was hoovered, even the windows cleaned, so everyone could see when he was there. He wanted to scream.

'It's very kind, Rozzy.'

'It's been a pleasure.' She added playfully, 'I've made you a sort of brunch. I know how strong you like your coffee. Sit down and relax. I've made you an omelette and Mrs Brimscombe picked me these with the dew on them this morning.'

'Rozzy, please.' Tristan opened his mouth in protest, and Rozzy popped a raspberry into it.

'Anyway,' she added, as the rattle of rain on the roof increased, 'you can't film at the moment.'

'You're incorrigible.'

'I'm not taking "*non*" for an answer.' Rozzy got a couple of croissants out of the microwave, and dropped one on his side plate.

For a second, Tristan was tempted to pour out his problems. But Rozzy had enough troubles of her own.

Having cut him a slice of omelette, primrose yellow and oozing herbs and butter, she poured him coffee and orange juice, and shoved the butter plate against his side plate. As she reached behind him to get the pepper-pot out of the cupboard, he felt her breasts brush against him and had to steel himself not to flinch. Rozzy put a hand on his shoulder.

'You're so tense, I'll give you a massage later.'

Suddenly the caravan seemed tiny. James, sulking on the sofa, was no chaperon. Next moment Rozzy's hand had clenched on his shoulder as the rain rattle on the roof was augmented by a rat-tat-tat on the door.

'I am *not* going to let people hassle you,' hissed Rozzy.

'Hi, chaps, that looks scrummy.' Griselda's green and purple striped turban came round the door.

'I'm trying to persuade Tristan to eat,' said Rozzy evenly.

'Don't force the poor boy. Nice to have you back.' Griselda added to Tristan, 'We've got a problem. Alpheus's white suit has been nicked for the second time. I've ordered another from Paris because he won't wear a blazer. But if you could wait to shoot his little scene until midday, by which time Lucy should be back to fix his face. I wondered if we could ask her and Wolfie to make a detour through Paris to pick up his new suit.'

There was another knock. It was Bernard this time, wanting a word with Rozzy.

'I do hope they've had a nice jaunt,' said Griselda, slapping unsalted butter and strawberry jam on a croissant, as Rozzy ran down the caravan steps to the shelter of Bernard's yellow striped umbrella.

'Wolfie's such a smashing chap,' went on Griselda, with her mouth full, 'and had such a bad time with his father copping it, and Lucy's such a lovely girl, but lonely in a way.'

'What the hell are you talking about?'

'Wolfie and Lucy went off in the Gulf on Saturday morning. Makes a jolly good passion wagon. Always thought they fancied each other.'

'Don't talk such fucking rubbish!' yelled Tristan,

walking out of the caravan, slamming the door behind him.

Jumping off the sofa, James tried to follow him, scraping his long claws against the caravan door and whining.

'Hum,' said Griselda, helping herself to a slice of cold omelette. 'Tristan seems to miss Lucy almost more than you do, old boy.'

Half-way across the field, Tristan found he was still clutching one of Rozzy's rose-patterned cups. Next moment Alpheus had descended from one side, Mikhail from another, Pushy from still another.

'Tabitha has been so rude to me,' they shouted in unison.

'I wish I cared,' snarled Tristan.

After two and a half days of Gablecross's interrogation, he could cope with scenes only if he were making them. He'd been so worried that finding out about Claudine was going to break Lucy's heart, and now she'd buggered off with Wolfie and clearly couldn't give a stuff.

'"What news from the court in France, that lovely country of elegant ways?"' sang Chloe to his departing back, and everyone giggled.

Then Tristan watched Saturday night's rushes, which he thought were quite awful and said so. Oscar and Valentin, who'd worked very hard and been rather proud of their efforts, looked utterly deflated.

'What has got into our boy?' sighed Oscar. 'The *flics* obviously put him through it.'

They had all been ecstatic about Tristan's release, but instead of acknowledging their cards and welcome-home banner, he'd just stalked in and criticized everything.

'I'm not working with that fucker any more,' said the crew and cast in unison.

Two things relieved the impasse. The rain stopped,

and Bernard frogmarched Tristan into his now empty caravan and bawled him out.

'You're behaving like a spoilt child. Everyone's jumpy. You're meant to reassure them – and as for bullying poor Rozzy,' Bernard went an even deeper shade of burgundy red, 'when she spent so long mucking out your caravan and praying for your release in the chapel.'

After that Tristan settled down, forgot his problems, and filmed mêlées, skirmishes, and Baby exchanging sizzling eye-meets with groupies and chucking down his stick in fury when Philip ordered him off the field.

It was still gloomy and overcast, however, and the only patches of sky blue were the opposition's shirts, which must have been specially chosen by Griselda to bring out the colour of Tab's furiously flashing eyes. Riding wonderfully wildly and as fiercely as the men, a blue toggle holding back her hair and showing off her glorious jawline and cheekbones, she seemed to be goading Tristan to watch only her.

But Tristan found his eyes drawn to the ponies, glossy black, dark brown, silver-grey, gleaming bay and chestnut, so polished and rippling with fitness. They were so helpful, so responsive, so neat and athletic, so gallant and outwardly unfazed, despite being sworn at and clouted round their delicate heads and legs by sticks and balls. They reminded him of Lucy.

When rain stopped play again, he locked himself in Bernard's caravan and watched a rough cut. Gradually his confidence came back. Tomorrow they had only to film Baby careering down the field, shoving his pony against Tab's, pushing her off the line of the ball to score the winning goal. This would be followed by Alpheus in his splendid white suit summoning Carlos inside for an already-filmed pep talk: a light day's shooting, which should be over by two, giving them time to tie up any loose ends before the wrap party in the evening.

Tristan felt an almost Christ-like elation that here

were the makings of a great film, which even Rannaldini would have been proud of. The old monster looked divine on the rostrum, thanks to Lucy's make-up. She really did deserve an Oscar. And darling Rozzy had been wonderful in her crying scene with Hermione. Christ, he'd been a shit to her after all she'd been through. He'd better go and apologize.

The film had been so dark, particularly in the last terrible scene, that he was amazed to come out to a watery orange sunset, dancing midges and house-martins swooping on insects. People were gossiping outside their tents and caravans. But as he paddled across the drenched field towards Wardrobe, he heard a bloodcurdling scream, followed by a dreadful howling.

Racing through the puddles, his heart thumping, he leapt the four steps up to the Wardrobe caravan. Steeling himself for more unimaginable horrors, he found James shuddering in the far corner, and Rozzy crouched on the floor keening. In the first crazed second, he thought that she had knocked over Lucy's blue bowl of pot-pourri. Then, drawing nearer, he saw the petals were tiny pieces of silk, as though someone had shredded the rainbow.

'Oh, my God,' groaned Griselda, behind him. 'It's her wrap-party dress. She's spent months making it from fragments of silk.'

It had literally been cut to ribbons.

'Why should anyone hate me so much?' wept Rozzy.

'They don't. They love you.' Pulling her to her feet Tristan took her in his arms, stroking her hair, feeling her tears drenching the jersey she had given him.

A hovering, desperately concerned Bernard produced a brandy, which triggered off a terrible fit of coughing, reminding Tristan once again how ill she was.

'Don't cry, *chérie*, I'll buy you another dress.'

Within seconds, relieved that something at last had happened, twenty police, led by Fanshawe and Debbie, had surrounded the caravan. They were disappointed the crime was going to be hard to date.

'I hung the dress in the back of the cupboard, when I came back after Glyn's birthday party exactly a week ago,' gasped Rozzy, between sobs.

Debbie took her hand. 'Who knew it was there?'

'Lucy, Grisel, Simone, I don't know.'

As the shredded fragments were shoved into a plastic bag for Forensic, Debbie gathered up a handful. 'Silk isn't torn or severed, looks as if it's been chopped up by big pinking shears.'

And Tristan shivered, as he remembered the speed with which Lucy often cut up James's liver with a big pair of scissors, claiming he hated it in lumps. Oh, God, it couldn't have been Lucy.

Two policemen were left to guard Wardrobe. Everyone else drifted away, leaving Rozzy with Tristan whose hand she still clutched. To make a break, he crossed the caravan to comfort James, who only betrayed his upset by a frantically shuddering body.

'You still haven't eaten,' gulped Rozzy. 'Let me make you supper.'

Feeling an absolute rat, but unable to cope with her dark anguish, Tristan pleaded exhaustion.

'I'll collapse if I don't crash out. I've got to hold the centre tomorrow. Your dress being cut to bits is bound to freak everyone out, then there's the wrap party. Forgive me,' he said, as her tears started to flow again. 'I'll buy you dinner next week, and please go and get yourself a new dress tomorrow.'

Reaching in his back pocket, he gave her three hundred pounds, then a hug. Outside he found his hovering, desperately worried first assistant director.

'Try and comfort her,' he begged, then his mind careered off. 'In case Lucy doesn't get back in time to make up Granny, can you ask Berman's to put a monk's black robes with a pointed hood in a taxi first thing?'

*   *   *

'What d'you think to that?' asked Fanshawe.

'Ugly,' said Debbie. 'Such a nice lady. Who'd deprive her of a lovely dress when she's got so little?'

'Might be someone with an ancient grievance because she had such a beautiful voice. We should recheck those ladies who might have been singing in the wood. Chloe, Gloria, Hermione, even Flora, and all the soprano extras.'

Debbie sighed, then said, 'She was evidently in Tristan's caravan for twenty minutes this morning. He was so sweet to her tonight. Could it be the murderer not being able to bear him being nice to anyone?'

76

Back in his caravan, soaked to the skin, Tristan realized he was out of whisky, which would not have happened if that little traitor Wolfie had been here. Nor would a pile of post, rising almost to the ceiling, have been left unopened. Without Wolfie and Lucy, he felt totally defenceless, particularly when there was a knock on the door, and a reporter from the *Scorpion* barged in, brandishing a bottle of champagne to celebrate his release. Having seen the first edition of the *Mail*, she wondered if they could have a word about Claudine Lauzerte.

'Madame Lauzerte's been having her gâteau and eating it, according to her maid, who's dumped in the *Express*, and who is very much on your side, Tristan.'

'Fuck off,' howled Tristan, as she held out her tape-recorder.

After that the reporters descended like a pack of wolves. Tristan thought they would rip him to pieces. Fortunately George's heavies were even better at man-handling the press than bribing planning officers or kneecapping little old sitting tenants, and had soon escorted Tristan to the safety of George's drawing room.

'Stay the night,' said Flora, handing him a quadruple Bell's. 'Most of the unit seem to be. They're too scared to go back to Valhalla.'

Tristan didn't need any persuading. He went straight to bed and fell into a dreamless sleep.

*   *   *

Alpheus was sweating. His American agent had been unable to produce any record of calling him on the night of Rannaldini's murder, and both Chloe and Isa had seen and heard him singing outside Magpie Cottage. On Monday morning, therefore, he had had the humiliation of giving a disapproving DC Smithson and a smirking DC Lightfoot a revised version of his movements on the night of Sunday the eighth. He had indeed jogged home from the tennis but, on seeing a light in Magpie Cottage, had decided to call on Tabitha.

Having showered and changed into the first white suit, he had nipped into River House to pick Tab a posy from Hermione's 'well-stocked garden'.

What he did not reveal was that as he was breaking off Hermione's lilies, he had been transfixed by the sight of his co-star, re-enacting their great shove-and-grunt scene in the summerhouse with another, and stayed and watched them for a minute or two. Burning with lust, he had set out for Magpie Cottage, and told Smithson and Lightfoot, who should have stopped grinning like a jackass, that he had indeed sung a favourite aria under Tab's window, and received a bottle of red wine over his white suit. 'I couldn't see who had thrown it.' Alpheus was damned if he was going to give Isa and Chloe an alibi.

He also admitted that next morning he had bagged up the wine-soaked suit and given it to the dustmen. Unfortunately, charred fragments of the second, gulls' egg and grass stained, white suit, together with white rock rose and chimpanzee orchids, identical to the ones used by Beattie to plug herself, were found in the garden at Jasmine Cottage. Suspicion was therefore heavily on Alpheus.

Alpheus's day had not improved. He was furious about his Shirley Temple curls and Rupert not allowing him to play polo.

If the third white suit didn't arrive in time, he would

be forced to wear some tacky blazer, and Tab had been so rude. He was furious with himself for still fancying the brat rotten. Even worse, the DNA tests were due back tomorrow, which would certainly identify his semen, and Lord knows what else, inside Beattie.

Returning to Jasmine Cottage after filming, he poured himself a rare whisky, and jumped nervously as the doorbell rang. He hoped to God it wasn't any more grizzled lady botanists rolling up to revere the chimpanzee orchid. It was very dark outside and at first he thought no-one was there. Then, looking down, he saw Little Cosmo.

One of Cosmo's best buys, acquired for 20p at the Paradise Conservative fête, had been a second-hand Scout uniform, in which he always dressed when he was collecting house to house for himself.

For 50p, Alpheus allowed Cosmo into Jasmine Cottage to clean his shoes. Once inside Little Cosmo produced his favourite photographs of Alpheus outside the summerhouse watching Hermione and Sexton, with twelve lilies in one hand and an enormous hard-on in the other.

When Alpheus tore up the photograph, Cosmo, echoing his late father, replied that he had the negs.

'Let us do a deal,' suggested Cosmo. 'I'd like cash before I hand over the negs. Otherwise I thought I'd offer copies as going-away presents at the wrap party tomorrow night.'

Considerably richer, Little Cosmo left Jasmine Cottage. Closing the gate behind him, he broke into Elisabetta's last aria in a flawless treble, then pedalled off on his bike into the gloom with a maniacal cackle. Alpheus gave a shiver. Could Little Cosmo have murdered his father and Beattie to gain control of the memoirs?

Having been too tired to draw the curtains, Tristan was woken at four by Pegasus, Aries and Taurus, a veritable zoo of brilliant stars, blazing in through the big square window, and a silver glow in the east. Switching on the wireless he learnt of storms causing havoc to flights and cross-Channel ferries. He hoped a returning Wolfie and Lucy would be struck by lightning or horrendously seasick. Then he remembered despairingly that he was still Maxim's bastard son without any money, and that in a few hours the world would be picking over his *affaire* with Claudine. Perhaps her husband would call him out and he would die impaled on a sword, like Beattie on Rannaldini's unicorn.

His musings on the ruins of his life were interrupted by a forecast of a beautiful day with temperatures in the nineties. Opening the window, he breathed in the smell of meadowsweet and wet earth, and felt a warm breeze caressing his skin. Then he noticed the cathedral spire, black on the horizon as the Grand Inquisitor's pointed hood, and remembered he had only one day left to make a great film.

Oscar was aghast to be woken so early. Anticipating a light half-day's shooting, he and Valentin had been out on the toot. On the bedside table was a half-eaten Parma ham and artichoke baguette, an empty Moët bottle and a glass of red wine in which several moths had drowned. By hastily pulling up the duvet over Jessica's russet curls, Oscar revealed her bright mauve toenails.

'It's going to be a scorcher,' announced Tristan. 'And we are going to reshoot all yesterday's scenes.' Then, cutting short Oscar's stream of expletives, 'We can do it if we really motor. I want polo under a burning sun as a contrast to the hunt in winter. Jessica has booked everyone's plane tickets and tomorrow they will disperse, not necessarily to the right place,' Tristan waggled Jessica's left foot, 'but to different parts of the world. This is our last chance. Tell Bernard to round everyone up, I want to start shooting by nine.'

'This is the last time I work for you,' said Oscar, draining the glass of red, moths and all.

By a miracle, René, the finest make-up artist in France, who had made Claudine look so delectable in *The Lily in the Valley*, had yesterday been discovered to be available. For a fat fee and a favour to Tristan, and an even fatter fee from *Paris-Match* for an interview on his day's work, by eight o'clock he was busy transforming hung-over geese into swans.

By nine o'clock, by even more of a miracle, all Tristan's troops – in various states of disarray – including Rupert's polo friends, had assembled on George's field for a pep talk. Giving them no time to gossip over the *Daily Mail* or let the Alka-Seltzers melt in their glasses, Tristan quietly told them exactly how much they had to get through, and how long they could allow for each set-up.

'This is the clock,' he pointed to the big, tickless clock that timed the polo chukkas at the end of the field, 'this is the schedule. There will be no tantrums. We are going to concentrate and get it right on the first take.'

Surreptitiously reading the *Mail*, folded to the size of a CD case, Oscar's eyebrows were getting nearer and nearer to his widow's peak.

'No wonder Tristan was uptight yesterday,' he murmured to Valentin. 'And where does this put Tabitha?'

'Oooh!' squawked Jessica, looking over Oscar's shoulder. 'You're in the paper, Tristan, "Froggy would a-wooing go". What a gorgeous picture of you, and oh, my goodness—'

'Put that away and just shut up.' Tristan's voice wiped any incipient grins off people's faces.

'I would, dearie,' whispered Meredith, stemming Jessica's protest with half a buttered croissant. 'He's not as sunny as usual. Have a read in the break.'

'There will be no breaks,' said Tristan icily.

'We've got our director back,' muttered Ogborne to Bernard. 'At least on a polo field there won't be any pretty ornaments for Meredith and Simone to fight over.'

'Except the players,' giggled Meredith, gazing in wonder at Rupert's friends, Ricky France-Lynch and the Carlisle twins.

Oscar glanced round at rain-fluffed, already turning trees, at the emerald-green pitch, the wonderful view, dotted with russet villages, fields striped where the hay had been cut, and pale gold where the wheat ripened, the blue curve of the river Fleet emerging from the mist, and sighed with pleasure.

'Tristan was right to reshoot. But what the hell is Rupert going to say?'

'Of all the fucking two-timing shits,' roared Rupert, brandishing the *Mail.*

'Whatever's the matter?' said Taggie, aghast.

'Montigny's been screwing Madame Lauzerte for the past three years. They only released him from gaol because he was caught bonking her in Wales the night Rannaldini was murdered.'

'Oh, the beast,' wailed Taggie.

'And all the time he's been two-timing darling little Tab. I never liked him, poncy intellectual, you can't trust the Frogs. And he had the gall to summon her onto the set by nine o'clock. She mustn't see the *Mail,* it'll break her heart.'

Tristan was very white when he came off the telephone to Rupert.

'He's one to talk,' said Meredith indignantly. 'There was a frightful scandal some years ago when it came out that he'd been rogering Amanda Hamilton, who was not only aeons older than him and the wife of the finance minister but also liked being spanked. Rupert's conveniently forgotten all that. Don't let it faze you.'

'I won't,' said Tristan.

He knew exactly what he wanted, rattling out orders like a Kalashnikov, driving everyone. Seldom had there been such tension on a film. But despite police everywhere and a murderer in their midst, by one thirty they had beaten the clock by one minute twenty seconds. They had shot mêlées, cavalry charges, throw-ins, and polo groupies slavering over Baby chucking down his stick. The temperature was rising steadily, the grass drying off fast. Mist swirled upwards all over the park. At any moment the puddles would boil over. The extras, even if they did all look like Claudine Lauzerte, had co-operated all the way; the discipline of the crew, despite thumping headaches, had been superb. There was just Alpheus's little scene and Tab's big one when she rode Baby off, and they could wrap.

'Claudine's pompous husband is close friend of Papa,' Simone whispered to Griselda. 'Should I accept huge sum for interview with the *Daily Express*?'

'Of course, sweetie. Imagine Tristan and Claudine being an item. Jolly humiliating for little Tab to lose out to a woman nearly three times her age.'

Tab, the only person not co-operating, was in a worse mood than yesterday: sending Alpheus and Bernard flying with her pony, and yelling at Wardrobe because her polo shirt had suddenly become too loose, her toggle too shiny, her hat too big and her boots too revoltingly new.

She had also refused to let René make her up – 'I don't want to look like bloody Claudine Lauzerte' – even though René was raving over her beauty.

'Look at the length of her nose and the eyes, and the moulding of her face. She must steal the show.'

'That's another reason for wanting to murder her,' said Chloe sourly. 'I think we can take it she's read the *Mail.*'

Now Tab was bawling out the props department.

'You've put out the wrong fucking saddle for my pony. Mine's got a blue and black check saddlecloth. None of this would have happened if flaming Wolfie had been here.'

77

Wolfie and Lucy learnt in St Malo that Tristan had been released, and duly celebrated. The following morning, they caught the early boat. While Lucy was buying a large bottle of Femme for Rozzy for looking after James, Wolfie picked up the *Mail*, turned green and hastily hid it. The bastard, he thought furiously. How could Tristan have done that to poor, darling Tab? He must get home and comfort her.

Having dumped the hired car at St Malo, they took a taxi back to Valhalla. To steady her nerves, Lucy took increasing nips from a bottle of brandy she'd bought for Tristan. Last night she had written him a long letter, explaining everything she had learnt at Montvert and then sealed it into a huge brown envelope, which contained all the other relevant material. Then she wrote 'Tristan de Montigny, Private and Confidential' on the outside. She had also washed her hair, shaved her legs, bronzed them with Piz Buin. Then, in a St Malo boutique, she had spent too much money on a lovely short-skirted sleeveless dress in wild rose pink and on a sexy sophisticated scent called Fracas to wear at the wrap party.

Now she could only think, In a few minutes I'll see Tristan and I'll die of excitement, but after tomorrow I won't see him any more, and I'll die.

At Valhalla she was disappointed to find no James in

her caravan. Rozzy must have taken him on the set. Unzipping one of the bench seat cushions, she hid all Tristan's parcelled-up papers and paintings inside. It was so hot, she changed into her new pink dress, took another slug of brandy and, because of her shaking hands, rather over-drenched herself in Fracas.

Someone had taken Wolfie's Land Rover over to George's house, so instead he grabbed Rannaldini's pearlescent orange Lamborghini, which looked much in need of a jaunt. He whistled as Lucy jumped in beside him.

'That dress is sensational.'

George's gates were so swarming with police and press, Wolfie had to produce his passport.

'Why did you and I go through all that,' he asked wryly, as he stormed up the drive, 'just to enable two people we're absolutely crazy about to end up together?'

'At least we'll be giving Tristan the best wrap-party present ever,' said Lucy, raising the bottle to her lips. 'Thank you, Wolfie, for everything. It's a pity', she added wistfully, 'you and I don't fancy each other.'

'I've known more unlikely things,' said Wolfie, pulling up on the edge of the field. Thinking how pretty she looked with her pale cheeks flushed and her pink dress showing off her long legs, he amazed himself by taking her in his arms and burying his lips in hers.

'Wow,' gasped Lucy, when he finally let her go. 'You are the most terrific kisser.' Pulling his blond head down, she kissed him again.

Unfortunately pearlescent orange Lamborghini Diablos are very noticeable, particularly with Meredith turning pale and crying out to everyone as they re-assembled after the break:

'My God! Rannaldini's car's just rolled up on the opposite side of the field.'

Most people were therefore vastly relieved when,

instead of a black-cloaked ghost, Lucy and Wolfie, hastily wiping off lipstick, emerged giggling from the Lamborghini.

'Must go and find James.' Lucy set off unsteadily towards Wardrobe.

'Must go and make my peace with Bernard,' said Wolfie, setting off nervously towards the set.

Heavens, there were a lot of police around. The extras in the stands, Granny in his press box, the marquees, the band were all massed on the south side of the field to allow the camera team in their car to race unimpeded up and down the north side.

'Wolfie!' bellowed Mikhail, cantering up on a smart bay pony. 'How vas your dirty veekend?'

Everyone screamed with laughter and surged forward, tripping over cables to hug him. It was just the tension-breaker they needed.

'Have a drink,' said Ogborne, thrusting a beer can into Wolfie's hand. 'Thank God you're back to defuse Tristan and Tabitha.'

On cue, up thundered Tab, leaping off her pony and pummelling her way into the crowd.

'Hi there,' mumbled Wolfie, turning very red.

Next moment he'd turned even redder, as Tab whacked him viciously across the face with the palm, then the back of her hand.

'Bastard!' she screamed. 'How could you leave everyone in the lurch and let Tristan down like that? How am I expected to organize the ponies on my own and star in the film? You've let me down as well. I hate you.' She was about to slap him again when, seeing how handsome he was, even with his navy blue eyes watering with pain, she burst into tears and pummelled her way out of the crowd again.

'Don't worry, Wolfie.' Griselda clouted him on the shoulder. 'There isn't a soul she hasn't bawled out – girl's suffering from post-Tristan tension.'

Lucy, meanwhile, was waiting for a rail of dresses or one of the trestle tables covered in pastel-covered shoes suddenly to take off towards her as a tethered James bounded forward in rapturous excitement. To her horror no dog materialized.

'Where's James?' she asked Rozzy, after she'd hugged her and handed over the bottle of Femme.

'In your caravan. He's not? Then he must have jumped out of the window. Mrs Brimscombe's Cindy's on heat. He'll turn up.'

'Why didn't you bring him?' asked Lucy, trying not to sound panicky or accusing.

'He ran on to the field after a squirrel yesterday, and nearly brought down one of the ponies. Tristan banished him,' said Rozzy, slightly defensively. 'He wouldn't eat or settle while you were away. Then he got all excited on Sunday night when I said, "Mummy's coming home," but when you didn't, he gradually lost heart.' Then, seeing Lucy's anguished face, Rozzy added hastily, 'Don't worry, I'm sure it's some bitch.'

'Lucy,' yelled Griselda, rushing up with an armful of polo boots, 'thank God you're back. Dear old René's taken over and made everyone including Mikhail look like Claudine Lauzerte. Can you do Granny first, Alpheus second?'

'I daren't tread on René's toes,' said Lucy in horror.

'Well, for a start you've got to do something about Alpheus's hair.'

'He's now called Surly Temple,' said Baby, leaning down from his pony and hugging Lucy. 'We have missed you.'

'I must find James, and Tristan and Tab to explain,' muttered a distracted Lucy. Then, catching sight of a pile of tack on a nearby table, 'That's Tab's saddle, the one with the blue and black check saddlecloth.'

'Well, I'm not giving it to her in her present mood,' said Rozzy. 'You take it, Lucy.'

As she carried the saddle past handsome players on their shining ponies and breathed in the intoxicating smell of old leather, dung, sweating horse and expensive aftershave, and heard the thundering of hoofs, the bagpipe skirl of excited neighing and the chatter of the crowd accompanying Rannaldini's overture, she realized how right Tristan had been to want polo to kick-start the film.

Next moment, Granny had erupted from the press box, tearing off his hot black inquisitor's robes to roars of applause and revealing an elegant body adorned only by lavender silk boxer shorts.

'Lucy, Lucy, I'm roasted alive in these clothes. Please turn me into Gordon Dillon again.'

'Serve him right for burning all those heretics,' giggled Meredith. 'I must say the old dear's kept his figure.'

'Hello, Lucy, how was my beautiful France?' shouted Oscar.

'Lovely,' shouted back Lucy, embarrassed but touched as everyone gathered round.

Everyone, that is, except Tristan, who by sheer will-power had driven his army on through the morning. Victory had been in sight. Now anarchy had broken out as all the troops deserted their posts to welcome Lucy. Nor had his temper been improved, on looking through Valentin's long lens, to see Wolfie and Lucy in an orange Lamborghini and a passionate embrace.

'Monsieur de Montigny, could I have a word about Claudine Lauzerte?' asked Lynda Lee-Potter, who was snazzily disguised as a policewoman.

'Not a single syllable. I talk enough to the *flics*,' snarled Tristan. 'Get back to fucking work,' he roared at the crowd around Lucy.

Her cheeks were flushed, her eyes sexily smudged, her long legs smooth and brown below the clinging pink dress. Moving closer Tristan caught a whiff of brandy, which annoyed him almost as much as the Fracas wafting muskily from her hot, excited body, instead of the usual sweet, delicate Bluebell.

The diatribe pouring forth was mostly in French, but Lucy got the gist: that Tristan felt she had been totally irresponsible; that she had wrecked yesterday's shoot by buggering up any hope of continuity, and had now come back to rot up this one. Totally appalled that a mouth that was made for kissing, drinking red wine and quoting poetry should be shouting such terrible things, Lucy remained speechless.

'Couldn't you have waited two more days to push off on your dirty little weekend?' howled Tristan. 'Get out, you're fired.'

'You've got it wrong,' stammered Lucy, 'We only went to France to—'

'I don't want to know,' interrupted Tristan. 'Collect your cheque from Production and get out.'

'You ungrateful bastard!' screamed Lucy. 'After all Wolfie and I have done for you.' And still clutching Tab's saddle, she fled back to Wardrobe.

'Whaddja do that for?' Baby turned furiously on Tristan. 'You'll have a strike on your hands.'

'Strike and you won't be paid a penny!' yelled Tristan. 'Get back on that pony, and you get back into those black robes,' he roared at Granny, then scowling round, 'Where's Wolfgang, so I can fire him?'

'Too late,' sighed Meredith happily. 'Grisel's just dispatched him to Bristol airport to collect Alpheus's suit.'

'Tristan's just fired me.' Lucy stumbled into Wardrobe, sobbing helplessly.

'Oh, darling,' cried Rozzy, putting down her steam iron to hold out her arms. 'I'm so sorry, don't cry. He'll calm down. He's just got so much on his plate.'

'He's still an ungrateful bastard. He's convinced Wolfie and I have been bonking all weekend, when we've been working our backsides off proving he can marry Tab after all. I don't know why we bothered.'

'Have you told him?' Rozzy handed Lucy a wodge of Kleenex.

'No, Wolfie can.' Then, hearing Tab yelling outside, 'Oh, God, I've still got her saddle, I can't cope with her bawling me out as well. You give it to her. I must go and find James. Hell, I haven't got a car.'

'Take mine,' said Rozzy.

Tears blinding her, Lucy somehow reached Valhalla. She was so furious and upset, she went straight to the production office and wrote a furious letter to Tristan.

'This is to let you know you're a Montigny and can marry your precious Tabitha and be happy after all, you ungrateful pig. Don't be horrible to Wolfie. I'm going to give all the papers and photos and things you need for proof to Rozzy.'

Having printed off the letter, she wrote 'Dearest Tristan' at the top and 'your loving Lucy' at the bottom, and streaked the ink with her tears.

She was shoving the envelope into Tristan's pigeonhole when she caught sight of a ravishing photograph of him on the front of the *Daily Mail*. How young and carefree he looked. She was just tearing it out, when she noticed the pictures beneath: one of Claudine Lauzerte, and another, slightly blurred, of Claudine with her hair – rather too long for a middle-aged woman, some would say – streaming down her back, as she kissed a beautiful dark-haired boy, who was fingering her cheekbones in wonder. Their eyes were shut but their long, long eyelashes tangled.

Lucy gave a moan. Slowly, agonizingly, she read the copy and understood why Tristan had never made passes, why he disappeared to his room early but never seemed to sleep much, why he was always so sad, the prince with the heavy heart. And how ludicrous had been all those speculations that he was impotent or terrified of women or in love with some smooth, older man, like Cary Grant in *To Catch a Thief*, when all the time he was sleeping with the most beautiful woman in France.

How idiotic for Lucy herself to pretend she had thought of anyone but him since December or that every drop of make-up, every false eyelash hadn't been put on his singers to please him. It had been the best make-up she had ever done because it had been an act of love. She had only gone to France in the faint hope that Tristan might realize he loved her not Tab. But all the time neither Tab nor she had been in the frame. How he must have loved Claudine not to betray her.

I love him, she sobbed in a frenzy of despair. No pain could be more unendurable. But there could be. When she got back to her caravan there was no James to whack his tail against the walls and squeak with joy.

Neither the police nor any of the local rescue kennels had news of him when she rang in increasing panic. With a shiver she remembered the gypsy encampment outside Paradise, which had moved on since she and Wolfie had left for France. Maybe they had stolen James, or he had gone back to his own people to die.

Noticing Rozzy's end-of-shoot presents, all beautifully wrapped in purple paper and shocking pink ribbons, Lucy was creepily reminded of Alpheus's dressing-gown. Weeping with despair she plunged into the woods in search of James.

Back at Rutminster Hall, Gablecross and Karen had watched the filming of Baby's winning goal. Now the crew was setting up for Baby's and Tabitha's ride-off. Looking round at the ravening media baying for blood and the massive police presence watching from the house or mingling with the extras or hiding in the trees that surrounded George's increasingly churned-up polo field, Gablecross felt a growing unease.

'All this attention only exacerbates the problem,' he

muttered to Karen. 'Murderers get off on it. They're turned on when they read about themselves. It pushes them into overdrive. But, even more ominously, Tristan and Madame Lauzerte have shoved our killer off the front pages. The only way he can get back again is to commit another murder. He's outwitted a massive international murder hunt, but ultimately he gets his biggest buzz out of someone knowing exactly how clever he's been. Which means he'll have to kill again, so that beforehand he can boast to his victim how he did it.'

Karen shivered. The polo had been so glamorous, she had hitherto thoroughly enjoyed herself. Several photographers had taken her picture. The dashing Carlisle twins had asked what she was doing later. Glancing round, she said, 'We've got an almost full cast of suspects.'

'Except Wolfie and Lucy,' replied Gablecross, whom Interpol had alerted of their arrival in England.

'Hello, Tim, hello, Karen.' It was Rozzy with two cups of coffee, 'I gather you went home yesterday. How did you like Glyn?'

'Very much,' lied Karen.

'He's a charmer,' said Rozzy wistfully. 'Was Sylvia much in evidence?'

'No,' lied Gablecross.

'I hope you'll catch the murderer today,' Rozzy lowered her voice, 'because we're all dispersing tomorrow. I'll miss you both so much.'

'The feeling's mutual. Have you seen Lucy?'

'She was here,' confided Rozzy. 'She and Wolfie went all the way to France to clear Tristan's name and the beast has gone and fired her. The poor darling's rushed off to Valhalla in floods.'

'Sorry to hear about your lovely dress,' said Karen.

'Horrible, wasn't it?' For a second Rozzy's eyes brimmed. 'But Tristan, who's a darling, when he's not being a beast, gave me some money to buy another so I rushed into Rutminster first thing.'

'Find anything nice?' asked Karen.

'In Peggy Parker's, of all unlikely places. I thought she was all Lurex and sequins.'

Gablecross looked at his watch. Tristan and Oscar were still fussing over lights. Anxious to get going before their ponies became maddened by flies, Ricky France-Lynch and the Carlisle twins were pointedly hitting balls to one another.

'Ouch,' yelled Sexton, as one hit him on the ankle. 'Ow, Christ, 'ere comes trouble,' he added as, parting crowds and crew like a flea comb, Rupert stalked up to Tristan.

'Have you got some sort of death-wish?' he hissed. 'How dare you reshoot everything when we're so pushed for time and money? And if you think I'm going to put a farthing into your crappy production after the way you screwed up my daughter! Why didn't you level with her that you were regularly ramming ten inches of Parisian sausage into that geriatric Claudine Lauzerte? Amazing you could get in for the cobwebs. Don't clench those Frog fists at me! You haven't got a *jambe* to stand on.'

Rupert seized Tristan's arm and was clearly about to thump him, when Sexton bravely interceded.

'Look, Rupe, we all know you're fired up, but we are against the clock, so why don't you castrate and incinerate Tristan and tug out his toenails after we've wrapped?'

Valentin burst out laughing. Rupert was dickering whether to deck Sexton and Valentin as well, when everyone was distracted by the arrival of Hermione, flanked by outriders, waving graciously from the back of an open limo. Like gulls following a plough, a flock of paparazzi had crashed the party in her wake.

'I have come to stand by my director, Tristan de Montigny, in his hour of need,' she was loudly confiding to hundreds of black tape-recorders. 'My heart also goes out to Claudine Lauzerte, and her husband Jean-Louis, the Minister of Cultural Affairs, at this difficult time.'

'Were you aware, Dame Hermione, that Tristan was having a far from cultural *affaire* with Madame Lauzerte?' shouted James Whitaker.

'Below the belt, James,' said Hermione reproachfully.

'Tristan certainly was,' said Adam Helliker, to howls of mirth.

'Are you in this scene, Dame Hermione?' asked *Classic FM Magazine*.

'Indeed,' Hermione inclined her huge flamingo-pink picture hat, 'but only as a face in the crowd.'

'You can't, Hermsie.' Seizing her hand, Sexton helped her out of the limo. 'The point of this scene is that Carlos is ordered by Philip to dump his polo totties and marry an unseen Frog princess, namely you. It blows your cover if you're seen in the crowd.'

'But polo is international,' pouted Hermione. 'It would be logical for Elisabetta to jet down for a chukka or two.'

'God in heaven.' Tristan clutched his head. 'We'll have to shoot round her.'

'Now where is my son, whose photography . . .' Hermione turned back proudly.

But Little Cosmo had jumped limo and was ringing Ladbrokes, who were taking bets on who had killed Rannaldini. Cosmo was gratified that his mother was 10–1, but decided to put a couple of hundred each on his stepbrother, Wolfgang, and Meredith, his putative father's boyfriend, neither of whom appeared to have any alibi.

The burning sun was boring through Tabitha's hat. At any moment she'd burst into flames. Having screamed at everyone on the set, she was now leaning against her pony, a beautiful grey gelding called The Ghost, unable to mount until her missing saddle turned up. Flora, who'd been gossiping to Baby, came over with a glass of iced orange juice.

'Gee, thanks,' said Tab listlessly. 'You are lucky

keeping Baby as a friend. Tristan won't even speak to me. Even George seems to like Baby now.'

'George now knows that Baby's only a friend, and that his heart lies entirely elsewhere,' said Flora, then realizing what she'd said, added hastily, 'Oh, look, Granny's back in the press box in his black robes. Such a surreal, sinister touch.'

'Last time I acted with Granny I was nearly burnt to death,' shuddered Tab. 'Oh, my God,' she whispered.

For there, away from the crowd, his glossy black hair gleaming, his shadow as misshapen and knowing as a Velazquez dwarf, the personification of darkness in that burning afternoon sun, stood Isa.

'What the hell are you doing here?' croaked Tab.

'Come to wish my wife and my old friend good luck,' mocked Isa, never taking his eyes off Baby.

Oh, help, thought Flora in terror. Isa's the one. He's just the right height to pass himself off as the ghost of Rannaldini and he exudes such evil.

Up galumphed Griselda, oblivious of any tension.

'I've found Tab's saddle, at last. It was under a table,' she shouted, as she handed it to Rupert's groom, Dizzy, who slapped it onto The Ghost, tightened his girths and pulled down the stirrups.

'He's ready, Tab,' she cried.

But Tab was gazing up at Baby, who'd gone even whiter than she had. 'So you're the one Isa loves,' she whispered. 'No-one fucking told me. You bastard, Baby!'

'*Dépêchez-vous*, Tab,' shouted Bernard.

'How long's it been going on?' hissed Tab. 'Before our marriage, I suppose. You'd like me out of the way, wouldn't you?' She was taunting Baby now.

'In your present mood, anyone would,' snapped Baby, gathering up his reins.

'Isa probably wants your horses back,' hissed Tab. 'My father won't want to train them when he hears what you've been up to.'

Picking up the vibes, Baby's mare nearly took off.

'Come on, Tab, everyone's waiting,' chided Dizzy, giving her a leg up.

Rozzy rushed forward to give her boots a last polish, Griselda tucked in her shirt and smoothed down her breeches. René took the shine off her nose with a powder brush.

'Your collar's sticking up, Tab,' cried out Simone.

'A little piece of hair's come loose from your toggle,' cried Rozzy.

'Oh, fuck off, the lot of you,' screamed Tab.

'Cool it, Tab,' yelled Ricky France-Lynch.

'Please don't shout,' grumbled Dommie Carlisle, 'I've got a bloody awful headache. Shouldn't have spent last night shagging someone called Pissy or Cushy.'

Ogborne revved up the car. Valentin in the passenger seat could see through his long lens the players shouting at each other, the ponies' legs a jumble against the pink faces and pretty clothes of the excited crowd. Rannaldini's overture was echoing round the field.

'Quiet, please, everyone,' yelled Bernard. 'We're turning over.'

Clocking the loathing on Baby's face, Tab panicked.

He's going to kill me, she thought, but it was too late.

As Ogborne trod on the accelerator Tristan, in the back of the car, had shouted, 'Action'.

Ricky France-Lynch stroked the ball to Baby, who hit it perfectly, galloping after it towards goal. Too fast, thought Rupert, in sudden terror, as Tab came thundering in at an angle to push him off the ball. But Baby's pony held firm, and dapple-grey and chestnut shoulders met in a shunt so forceful it took both horses off the ground in a cloud of dust, but gave Tab the slight advantage to stroke the ball back up-field to safety.

'Wonderful,' breathed Tristan. 'Keep rolling.'

But as Tab leant over, putting her whole weight on her right stirrup to take the backhand, the leather gave way like a broken arm. There was no way she could save herself. She was toppling over. Next moment the ground came hurtling·up to meet her.

The crowd gave a collective scream of horror.

Fuck, I wonder if we've shot enough, Tristan was horrified to find himself thinking, particularly when Tab remained in a huddled heap.

The Ghost was running around trailing his reins. Ambulances and police cars were careering across the field. Baby was instantly off his pony, pleading as he knelt down beside Tab.

'Oh, angel, I'm sorry, please be OK.'

But Tab didn't move, whiter than the burning sun above. From the horrible angle of her head to her body, Baby knew she had broken her neck.

Rupert, who'd vaulted on to someone's pony, beat the police cars and ambulances. 'Turn that fucking music off! Why'd you have to hit her so hard?' he yelled at Baby. Then, catching sight of his motionless daughter, he dropped to his knees beside her. 'Oh, my Christ.'

Her stirrup, with its broken leather, was still attached to her foot.

Driving back with Alpheus's suit, taking a short-cut through one of George's side gates, Wolfie heard a wail of sirens. Through a screen of hogweed, blond grasses and mauve willowherb, he saw an ambulance belting towards the main gates.

Abandoning the Lamborghini in the gateway to the field where all the unit was parked, he tore after the ambulance, which was temporarily trapped behind a hay lorry.

'Who is it?' he begged a cameraman running in the other direction.

'Campbell-Black's daughter. Looks nasty.'

Catching up with the ambulance, Wolfie drummed his fists frenziedly on the back door until it opened a fraction.

'You can't come in,' said an ambulance man, putting his head out.

'I bloody can. What's the matter with her?'

'Are you a relative?'

'Brother,' gasped Wolfie.

Seeing his blond hair and normally ruddy face now as white as Tab's, they allowed him in, then were slightly startled when he began gabbling away in German, beseeching Tab to live.

78

Wolfie was magnificent. He comforted and found cups of tea for his sobbing stepmother and, later, for a stunned, horrified Taggie. He conjured up a large whisky for Rupert and, by acting as mediator, defused the situation when Rupert's explosions of rage looked like antagonizing the hospital staff.

He also remained icily calm when the specialist listed the terrible alternatives so he could translate the details – albeit watered down – to the others, who were too shocked to take them in.

Tab had been rushed into Intensive Care, where X-rays had mercifully ruled out a broken neck or a fractured skull. But they would have to watch out she didn't develop a subdural oedema.

'What the fuck's that? Can't you speak English?'

The specialist's lips tightened. 'A blood clot inside the cavity of the brain, Mr Campbell-Black. We'll keep examining her pupils for signs of bleeding under the skull.'

'And if you find them?' Wolfie's voice shook only slightly.

'We'll whizz her straight off to a neuro-surgeon and drill straight through the skull.'

Helen's sobs redoubled.

'She'll be all right.' Wolfie put an arm round her shoulders.

'How d'you fucking know?' snapped Rupert. 'And how long before we find out?'

Du lieber Gott, beseeched Wolfie, for the thousandth time, don't extinguish something so vibrant and lovely.

He had never seen anyone so pale. Against Tab's face, the white sheets, spattered with blood from another nosebleed, seemed warm as ivory. Nothing could be more inert than her little hand, which lay in his as cold and as still as a pebble on the shore. Helen, snivelling gently, was holding the other hand. In the corner sat a motionless Taggie and a silent Xavier, who had insisted on coming but who looked absolutely frozen with shock. Rupert, pacing up and down outside, was the first to see Fanshawe and Debbie.

'Whaddja want?'

'How's Mrs Lovell?'

'Unconscious.'

Fanshawe steeled himself.

'I'm sorry, sir, but I'm afraid we're treating her fall as attempted murder.' Then, seeing the fury in Rupert's face, 'Her right-hand stirrup leather was cut through, probably with a penknife.'

'And that happened in a place crawling with cops! Why the hell should anyone want to kill Tab?'

Fanshawe refrained from pointing out that Tab had achieved an all-time high in bloodiness over the last few days.

'That's what we're trying to find out, sir. Can you remember who was near her while she was mounting? Nicking the leather would have only taken a couple of seconds.'

'Dizzy, my head groom, saddled the pony,' said Rupert, 'but she's been with me for ever. She adores Tab. Also,' Rupert screwed up his eyes, 'Dizzy gave her a leg up so no weight would have been put on the leather. Grisel brought the saddle over. Grisel's an old softie – she wouldn't hurt Tab. There was that make-up poofter, René, and Simone, she's a duck, and Rozzy, that drip who's bats about Tristan. Isa, her bastard of a husband was there, Baby, Mikhail. Everyone, really.'

'Lucy Latimer was holding the saddle when Tristan sacked her,' said Debbie, 'but she's done a bunk, evidently searching for her dog.'

'We gather Mrs Lovell was upset because someone put the wrong saddle on her pony,' added Fanshawe, 'and there was a long delay before Lady Griselda discovered the right one under the table in Wardrobe.'

'Tab's saddlecloth is a very distinctive blue and black check,' said Rupert. 'Everyone on the unit would have recognized it and known Tab would be wanting it later.'

'So the murderer could have cut the leather much earlier.'

'And will strike again. He's tried to kill Tab before,' snarled Rupert. 'Why the hell haven't you put a hundred men round this hospital?'

Tab was in a twilight of pain. Black clouds whirled before her eyes, then became smoky grey mist but, as if they were thick elasticated cobwebs, try as she might she couldn't struggle through them. Ahead shone a blinding light. Perhaps she was dead and had reached the other side. To the right she could make out a shadowy angel with a clipboard, who was ticking people off as they disappeared into the light. Tab was frantic to go through too. 'Gertrude,' she croaked, 'I must say I'm sorry to Gertrude.'

'She's not here at the moment.' The angel consulted the clipboard. 'And we're not ready for you either. There are people on earth who need you.'

And Tab had groaned as the mists came down again.

But suddenly they were clearing again and she could see Wolfie sitting on a chair. He looked so sad, but try as she might she couldn't call out to him. Not even when a little white dog with a black patch trotted into the room.

Gertrude, Gertrude! Again Tab tried to speak, but no

words came out. After licking her hand, the little white dog trotted purposefully over to Wolfie, and nudged his knees until he bent down and picked her up. Having licked his face, which seemed to be glistening with tears, Gertrude curled up with a contented sigh on his knee.

Once again, Tab battled to speak, but the mists descended blacker than ever. Then they cleared and Gertrude had gone. It was the most enormous struggle but finally she managed to whisper, 'Wolfie, I'm here.'

Next minute her hands were seized and Wolfie was gazing down at her, trying to stop more tears pouring out of his reddened eyes, even more unable to speak than she was.

'Oh, Wolfie,' she whispered, 'Gertrude's ghost came in and jumped on your knee. She was so happy to be there, I know she was telling me she's forgiven me, and you're the one, and everything's going to be all right. Oh, Wolfie, you have got a halo. I love you so much.' Her voice faded as she drifted off to sleep again.

Wolfie stumbled into the corridor where he found Rupert.

'She came round.'

'Thank Christ! Did she make sense?'

'Not at all. She was gabbling on about Gertrude's ghost. Then she said she loved me.' His voice broke. 'She must be delirious.'

Next moment, he had collapsed on the sofa, put his head in his hands and burst into agonizing sobs. 'I'm so sorry to be a wimp, Rupert, but I thought she was going to die, and I love her so much.'

'I know you do,' said Rupert, in an unsteady voice. 'But she's going to be OK.'

Tab's first question when she came round was 'Why did you go to France?'

'Because you told me to.'

'And why have you been crying?'

'I was worried.' Then, steeling himself because he felt he must level with her, 'Tristan backed off from you earlier in the summer because he'd been told by my father that there was bad blood in his family and he should never have children. Lucy and I went to France to prove it wasn't true so now he can marry you, if you want him to.' He took her hands again.

'You and Lucy went all that way.' Tab's forehead wrinkled trying to understand. 'So you're not in love with Lucy?'

'Of course not.'

'Why were you kissing her, then?'

'There's nothing wrong with *your* memory,' said Wolfie, trying to smile. 'We were comforting each other. We thought you loved Tristan.'

'I've been so jealous,' mumbled Tab. 'This is seriously embarrassing, but once you'd gone away I realized it was you I loved, not Tristan. He's so ratty and obsessed with his film. I feel safe with you. I've wanted to kill Lucy for the last few days.'

Wolfie was struck dumb again as the colour flooded his incredulous, bewildered, hopeful face.

'Your father?' he mumbled. 'He'd never approve. I'm three-quarters Kraut, a quarter Italian, a Rannaldini, and a disinherited one at that.'

'That doesn't matter a stuff. Dad really likes you.' Tab stretched up her hand to touch his face. 'You're much more his cup of Earl Grey than Tristan. He loathes intellectuals.'

'How d'you feel now?' Wolfie trapped her hand, covering the palm with kisses.

'My head aches, but my heart doesn't any more.'

'You mustn't try to talk.'

'I don't want to talk, I want to kiss you.'

I shouldn't be doing this to Tristan, thought Wolfie, but he bent his head and very gently kissed her dry lips, which immediately opened.

'Stop that at once, you must *not* excite the patient,'

said an outraged nurse, who'd bustled in with a torch to check Tab's pupils.

'Yes, he must.' Tab's hand clamped round Wolfie's neck. 'It's exactly what she does need.'

Outside, Rupert, trying to get through to Gerald Portland, had to cope with another casualty. This time it was Xavier, sobbing his heart out. Rupert was touched. Perhaps, at last, his son was mellowing towards his step-sister.

'It's all my fault,' wailed Xav. 'Tab was so horrible this morning, I prayed she'd die.'

For a second Rupert had difficulty in keeping a straight face. 'It seems you didn't pray hard enough,' he said gravely. 'She's getting better by the minute.'

'Will she be coming back to live with us?' Xav asked gloomily.

Looking through the glass into Tab's room, Rupert could see Wolfie taking off Tab's wedding ring and throwing it in the bin. 'I rather doubt it,' he said.

'D'you think her horrible mother could go and live with them both?'

Five minutes later, walking at speed along the corridor, Tristan went slap into Rupert and steeled himself for more abuse. But Rupert seemed in an excellent mood.

'She's come round. Go and say hello.'

As Tristan tiptoed in, Wolfie slid out without a word. Outside he leant his hot forehead against a cool corridor window, raising two sets of crossed fingers to the skies.

'My poor darling, 'ow are you?' Tristan took Tab's hand.

'OK.' She forced herself to look at him. After a day in the sun, he was going brown again. She'd forgotten how handsome he was. 'Look,' she muttered, 'I know I threw myself at you. Wolfie told me why you backed off, but you mustn't feel guilty about Claudine because I'm in love with Wolfie.'

Tristan noticed her ringless finger and her mud-splattered face. Only the ticking clock broke the long, long silence. 'I know you are.'

Looking up, Tab was amazed to see happiness and sweetness in his face.

'Darling Tab, you gave me the most beautiful night of my life.'

'I thought I was so in love with you.'

'And I with you, and I still think Wolfie is the luckiest guy in the world.'

'You shouldn't look so relieved,' grumbled Tab. 'It isn't very flattering.'

'It isn't very flattering that your father looks ecstatic as well. I'm sorry, *chérie*, I've been like a bear with a hurt head and you had that 'orrible fall.'

'Wolfie thinks you'll be cross with him.'

'*Au contraire.* I come not for Wolfie's blood but his car keys. When he saw ambulance, he leave Lamborghini across gateway so the unit cannot get in or out. His burglar alarm is going off every second so Sylvestre is going ape-sheet. Worst of all, Alpheus's suit is locked inside so we cannot film last scene.'

The moment Tristan returned to the set an anxious Rozzy asked after Tab.

'Out of danger,' said Tristan happily, 'and absolutely crazy about Wolfie, which lets me off the hook.'

'Oh, I'm so pleased for them both,' sighed Rozzy, taking Alpheus's suit from him. 'I wonder if it needs a press.'

'Don't bother,' said Tristan. 'Oh, Rozzy, I was such a bastard to Lucy earlier. Now I'm worried stiff. Someone tried to kill Tab, they slashed your dress yesterday, the murderer's on the rampage, and Lucy's not answering her mobile.'

'Leave a message on her bleeper.'

'I've been leaving them all day. I need her to make up Alpheus. We can cover his Shirley Temple curls with straw hat, but only Lucy can give those commonplace features an air of nobility. And to tell the truth,' confessed Tristan wryly, 'I shouted at her because I miss her so much.'

'I'll find her.' Rozzy patted his shoulder. 'Don't worry.'

79

Rupert managed to catch the five fifty news on a hospital television. That pompous ass Gerald Portland was giving a press conference at Rutminster police station. He was flaunting a purple spotted tie with a purple striped shirt and kept smoothing his chestnut hair for the cameras.

'We are treating this incident as attempted murder,' he was telling the rugger scrum of reporters. 'But happily I can confirm that Tabitha Lovell is no longer in a life-threatening condition.'

After that, Portland's emergency meeting of the Inner Cabinet was most embarrassingly interrupted by an apoplectic telephone call from Rupert. 'I merely said she was no longer in a life-threatening condition, Mr Campbell-Black.'

'Don't be fucking stupid. The person who's just tried to kill her for a second time has already killed two people and tried to bump off half a dozen more, and is still on the loose. If that isn't fucking threatening her life, I don't know what is. All you overpaid cretins do is waste tax-payers' money chasing the wrong people.'

'We are about to make an arrest,' said Portland huffily.

'Well, until the killer's behind bars, I want a dozen men guarding Tab at the hospital – and while you're on, never, never, never wear spots with stripes.'

'Bastard!' Portland slammed down the telephone.

But nothing could dent his euphoria. The DNA testing had at last produced a match.

'Who is it, Guv?' begged DC Lightfoot in excitement.

Gerry Portland turned to Gablecross, not without a certain satisfaction. 'I'm afraid it's your girlfriend Lucy Latimer, Tim.'

'I don't believe it.'

'Nor do I,' said Karen indignantly.

'She never had a cast-iron alibi,' went on Portland. 'She was allegedly walking that dog when both Rannaldini and Beattie copped it, and her DNA profile showed up in Rannaldini's saliva and in the bite on Beattie's shoulder. She was carrying Tabitha's saddle when Tristan fired her – that probably pushed her over the top. And her fingerprints and fibres from Tab's stirrup leather were found all over the penknife on her key-ring, which Kevin and Debbie', Portland grinned at Fanshawe and Debbie, 'unearthed from a bin-bag outside Wardrobe. Latimer must have been frantic to get rid of it.'

'The murderer must have stolen her keys,' snapped Gablecross, who had only recently come off the telephone to Wolfie. 'Why should Lucy want to kill Tab when she'd just come back from France, where she'd specially gone to clear Tristan's name so he could marry Tab?'

'Very subtle,' said Fanshawe nastily. 'After such altruism, no-one would suspect her of murdering Tab. Then she could have Tristan for herself. Her total, total obsession is behind the whole thing. You and Karen were the first people to suss how crazy she was about him.'

'Then why did she kill Rannaldini?' demanded Karen.

'Because he was going to tell the world Maxim was Tristan's father,' explained Gerald Portland. 'She killed Beattie for the same reason. Rannaldini had humiliated her by making a pass at her – it's in his memoirs. Psychopaths can't stand being belittled, and Rannaldini was also threatening to tell Tristan she was crazy about him. She tried to kill Tab because she couldn't bear her to have Tristan.'

'Doesn't add up,' muttered Gablecross.

''Fraid it does,' said Fanshawe patronizingly. 'Everyone Tristan favoured got warned off. Granville's patchwork quilt, Flora's fox, poor Rozzy's dress cut to ribbons, putting petrol in the water cans, all the work of a mad person.'

'What about the adder in Lucy's make-up box?' pleaded Karen.

'A plant – made her look like a victim, same as showing Tim the burn from the poisoned champagne on her tablecloth. She's diabolically clever, like all psychos. She failed twice with Tab, but she'll strike again.'

'I swear she hasn't done it.'

'The DNA's conclusive, Tim. It's always the quiet ones,' said Portland, not unkindly. 'Latimer spent so much time making other people beautiful, but they got the clapping. For the first time in her life, she's got a bigger audience than they ever will.'

Then he turned briskly to Fanshawe and Debbie. 'Go and pull her in. Well done, both of you.'

'Where is she?' asked Gablecross dully.

'Searching the Valhalla woods for her dog, but we've got tails on her and she keeps ringing to check if he has been handed in. Next time we'll nail her. You and Karen better go and keep an eye on Tabitha at Rutminster General, Tim. We don't want any slip-ups.'

The ultimate put-down, thought Gablecross savagely, the hound demoted to guard-dog.

Lucy had been searching for hours, shouting herself hoarse, running herself into a state of collapse. To add to her frustration, her mobile wouldn't work in the wood so she had to keep returning to the house or the Paradise–Cheltenham road to ring the police and the local dog sanctuaries.

Purplish-black clouds were massing on the horizon

and the wind had risen, tangling her hair. After yesterday's downpour, the woodland floor was impossibly slippery, her legs were lacerated by bramble cables and nettles, her face and arms scratched, her knees bruised and bleeding where she had continually fallen over. But she felt no pain except desolation.

'James, James.' Her voice echoed mockingly back at her. The hot heavy air carried every sound except a joyful bark. To the clay shoots banging away in anticipation of 12 August was added a rumble of thunder. Untranquillized, James would bolt half-way to London. Returning to the road once more, she punched out the number of Rutminster police station.

'It's Lucy Latimer again, ringing about James, a big red shaggy lurcher. He slipped his collar so he hasn't got a name tag.'

'Who did you say?'

'Lucy Latimer.'

She could hear a hand thudding over the receiver, then a man's voice, calm but quivering with excitement. 'Where are you, Lucy?'

'To the north of Hangman's Wood.'

'Come back to the big house.' Then, after a pause, 'We've got good news for you.'

'Oh, my God! He's red and shaggy.'

'That's the one. Meet us at your caravan, Lucy.'

Crying with relief, her loafers squelching in sympathy, Lucy ran all the way. Oh, please, please, please, let it be James. An extraordinary garish light was gilding the wheatfields, turning the Valhalla lawns a Day-glo emerald. Silver streams were hurtling down the valley into an ever-rising lake. Outside her caravan beside the love-in-a-mist, a bowl of food she'd left to tempt James was so heaving with maggots she nearly threw up. She was about to chuck it out when, glancing into her caravan, she saw that her suitcase had been opened, her drawers up-ended and her bag emptied on the table.

Tristan's papers, she thought in horror. Leaping up the steps, unzipping the bench-seat cushion, she sighed with relief. The parcel was still there. She must lock it safely in her make-up box, but where were her keys? Normally they hung on a hook beside her nieces' photographs.

'Lucy Latimer,' yelled a voice.

'James, where is he?' croaked Lucy as, still clutching Tristan's parcel, she bounded down the steps.

DC Miller had never confronted a murderer before. This one certainly looked crazy: muddy and blood-stained, with scratches on her arms and legs, a torn dress, hair like an electrocuted bird's nest and frantically heaving breasts.

'Oh, please, give me back my dog,' gasped Lucy.

Then police were fanning round her, and Lucy caught a glimpse of handcuffs, or was it a gun in Fanshawe's hand?

'Lucy Latimer,' he said triumphantly, 'we are arresting you for the murders of Roberto Rannaldini and Beatrice Johnson, and the attempted murder of Tabitha Lovell.'

'Wha-a-a-t?' whispered Lucy. 'You tricked me. You haven't got James at all. Bastards!' Her voice rose to a scream.

Seeing a gap to the left, she shot through it. Terror gave her feet wings – she had not run for Cumbrian Schoolgirls for nothing. She also knew Valhalla better than any of the police. Racing across the facilities unit, jumping box hedges, running towards the car park, for a second she left whistles and baying Alsatians behind, then went slap into Rozzy.

'Darling, whatever's the matter? I've been looking for you everywhere.'

'The police! They think I'm the murderer,' sobbed Lucy. 'Oh, Rozzy, help me, I didn't do it.'

'Of course you didn't. How ridiculous!'

'I can't let them arrest me until I've found James.'
Lucy took off across the grass again.

'You certainly can't. Funnily enough, I keep hearing
squeaking. I just wonder if the old boy's got himself shut
in somewhere. Clive's back. He might have been poking
around, and left a door open.'

'Oh my God, Clive stole Gertrude! He might steal
James!'

'I can't keep up with you,' gasped Rozzy. 'I've got a
stitch. I know where you can hide.' She tugged Lucy
behind a yew peacock as a cursing, sweating Fanshawe
pounded past.

Grabbing Lucy's hand, Rozzy led her through iron
gates across the east courtyard in through the back door
along endless dark passages, then up shiny polished
dark stairs into Rannaldini's study, which had a musty,
neglected smell. There were no fan photographs
stacked on the big oak desk now, no-one to encourage
Don Juan, astride the lady of the manor, in the Étienne
de Montigny on the right of the fireplace.

Rozzy went straight to the left of the painting and
started to tap the panelling.

'What are you doing?' asked Lucy, through desperately chattering teeth. The heavy velvet curtains were
drawn but outside she could hear shouting.

'Looking for the priest-hole. I'll find it in a second.'

'Please hurry,' begged Lucy.

'Rannaldini showed me,' Rozzy gave an almost coy
giggle, 'when we once had a little fling, and Cecilia, his
then wife, came home unexpectedly, but he swore me to
secrecy. Now how does it work?'

'Pur-lease,' beseeched Lucy. The raised voices and
excited barking were getting nearer.

'Got it.' Suddenly, with an arthritic creak, the panel
swung back to reveal a big dark cupboard.

'I don't want you to be done for aiding and abetting,'
gibbered Lucy. 'Oh, Rozzy, you do believe I'm innocent?
I adore Tab.'

'I know you do.' Dropping to her knees, Rozzy reached inside the cupboard and removed the floor-board. 'Get inside, *quickly*. What's that you're clutching?'

'Oh, golly.' Half inside the cupboard, Lucy realized she was still clinging on to Tristan's parcel, and gave a sob.

'"The heart that loves you will never be closed to you,"' she stammered. '"Here are my important papers." Oh, please, guard them with your life and see that Tristan, and no-one else, gets them. And if I'm arrested and he comes back,' Lucy's voice cracked again, 'please take care of James. Production's got my wages, that should keep him going for a bit.'

'Don't worry about anything.' Taking the parcel, Rozzy leaned inside to kiss Lucy's muddy, tearstained, quivering cheek. 'Good luck, pet.'

Wriggling down through the hole, Lucy groaned as she landed on some rubble, wrenching her ankle.

'Hush, someone's coming.' Rozzy picked up the floor-board. 'See that sticking-out brick – no, to the right of it. If you press that, a door swings open to a secret passage down to the lake, but don't use it unless you have to. I'll put the police off the scent, then find Sergeant Gablecross, who'll spring you the minute the coast's clear. Never fear, Aunt Rozzy's here!'

In slotted the floorboard above Lucy's head, leaving her in total darkness. Then she heard the panel in Rannaldini's study creaking shut and was overwhelmed with terror.

How could they think she was the murderer? Had she been wise to trust Rozzy, who must have had one hell of an *affaire* with Rannaldini to know all those things? Would Rozzy leave her boarded up for ever like the Canterville ghost? Would Aunt Hortense ever forgive her if Tristan's papers fell into police hands? At least Tristan should soon pick up the note in his pigeon-hole. Oh, God, she mustn't go to pieces.

Leaning against the wall, she regained her breath and

steadied herself, then pressed the brick and sure enough a door creaked open. Feeling her way round the walls she found an opening, but it was only four feet high and very narrow. The air smelt damp and musty. She screamed as something wet, furry and cold scuttled over her foot. She would have stayed put rather than embark on the dark journey if she hadn't heard the faintest whining.

'James,' she called out, not daring to shout, in case she could be heard in the study or out in the garden. There it was again, the faintest whimper.

'Oh, my poor old boy.'

She crawled along, jagging her scratched, bleeding hands and knees even more on the rocks, giving little screams as icy water dripped on her head and slimy walls grazed her sides. She only kept going because of the whining and because, as the passage jinked and twisted, she would have got stuck if she'd tried to turn round.

Just as her eyes were getting accustomed to the dark, it lightened ahead. A clap of thunder rocked the tunnel like an earthquake, followed by another even more deafening. The whining grew more frantic.

'Oh, please,' she prayed out loud, 'please don't let James have broken anything. I'll never be able to carry him back to safety. I'm coming, my angel!' she cried.

She could hear rushing, pounding water. She must be near the lake. The roof was getting higher: soon she'd be able to walk. Then, as she took another turn, her blood froze to a thousand degrees below zero. Her hair shot on end. Her heart stopped as, like dreadful chloroform, she was asphyxiated by the stench of Maestro. Glancing ahead she saw the back of a black figure, terrifying in its utter stillness. She couldn't move, she couldn't cry out. Then she heard the snake-crawling swish of a cloak on the rocky floor, and in the dim light could make out the silvery hair, the cruel, arrogant profile, the burning eyes, the evil smile as he turned slowly towards her.

Oh God, was Rozzy in league with Rannaldini?

James gave another agonizing howl as though someone was torturing him.

'No, Rannaldini,' croaked Lucy. 'Don't come near me. Don't hurt James. Oh, please, no,' and hit the rocks with a dull thud as she fainted.

80

It was the last set-up of *Don Carlos*. Flocks of birds and a
pink and yellow hot-air balloon were drifting up from
the Bristol Channel. On the horizon an orange sun,
striped with black stratus clouds, waited like a curled-up
tiger to erupt over the horizon.

'Tristan's a cool customer,' Grisel muttered to
Simone. 'If he'd had a suitable stand-in, he'd have reshot
that ride-off straight away.'

Tristan was now calmly briefing Alpheus. 'You don't
have to look heavily disapproving, just a flash of outrage because your son is suddenly attracting the best
girls.'

'Quiet, please,' shouted Bernard, for the hundredth
time, as an incredible tension spread through the crowd
round camera and actor.

'Mark it,' shouted Bernard.

'Scene two hundred and fifteen, take six,' shouted the
clapper-loader.

'And action,' shouted Tristan.

Happily, at that moment Alpheus caught sight of
Little Cosmo, showing some photographs to a giggling
Jessica, and had no difficulty looking outraged.

'Cut,' shouted Tristan in delight. '*Formidable*, Alpheus.
Just check the gate.'

Simone pressed her stop-watch. Total silence fell. Two
hundred yards away uniformed police could be seen

examining the cordoned-off area in front of the far goal posts where Tab had had her fall.

The gate was clear.

'Shall we say it now?' went up the chorus.

'*Oui*,' said Tristan.

'It's a wrap,' yelled everyone, whooping and cheering.

'I wanted to say it.' Simone's dark Montigny eyes filled with tears.

'*La fin, la fin*,' said Griselda, blowing her nose noisily.

Solemnly Tristan shook hands with Bernard, Oscar, Valentin, Sylvestre, Ogborne, followed by the crew. Then they all posed for a last photograph, taken by Hype-along, already resplendent in a pink seersucker suit for the wrap party.

'Have you heard from Lucy?' Tristan asked Bernard yet again.

'No, but I'm sure she'll turn up later.'

Over at Rutminster police station, Gerald Portland was going ballistic. 'How could twenty-four of you lose Lucy Latimer? What the fuck am I to tell the press? They're all outside.'

After consultation, however, he decided to put a massive guard on George's house and go ahead with the wrap party.

'Try to contain people in the walled garden,' he told his men. 'If Latimer's that obsessed with Montigny, she'll roll up to kill again. We've got her handbag, her passport, her car keys, she can't get far.'

Down the road at Rutminster General, Gablecross was striding up and down the foyer, muttering, 'I'm not a fucking guard-dog.' Charlie, his old running mate, would be turning in his grave. The hospital was swarming with press.

'Come on, Tim, who's done it?' asked the *Mail on Sunday*.

'Not at liberty to say.'

'Rutminster Constabulary, and Sergeant Gablecross in particular, can't even catch the clap,' yelled Rupert, dummying past the waiting journalists and racing for the front door.

Seeing Karen joining in the laughter, Gablecross turned on her in fury. 'And you can bugger off down to the station and flash your tits at Andy,' he roared, 'in case anything interesting's come in with Lucy's stuff.'

'Stop putting me down. It's not my fault I'm not Charlie,' sobbed Karen, and sending a nurse and a trayful of medicines flying, she ran out into the street.

'Anything interesting on Lucy Latimer?' she asked five minutes later, allowing herself a languorous flutter of the eyelashes.

Andy, the exhibits officer, had in the past lost a lot of sleep over Karen. Making sure no-one was around, he muttered, so she had to draw close to hear him, that a rude letter from a bank manager had been found in Lucy's handbag. 'She's very overdrawn, and the bastard seems relieved funds are coming in at the end of filming. We've also got some bank statements.'

'What's she been spending her money on?' Karen brushed her breasts in the cream shirt against Andy's arm.

'Sends two hundred and fifty a month home to her parents,' said Andy, consulting the statement. 'Subscribes to a number of animal charities, but most of it seems to have gone to someone called Rozzy Pringle. She's given her nearly three grand in the last two months.'

Karen whistled. Could Rozzy be blackmailing Lucy?

Parker's department store in the high street was having an after-hours preview of new stock for account

705

customers. Heading for Evening Gowns, Karen tried on a spangled horror in shocking pink.

'That looks gorgeous,' said the sales girl truthfully, who was used to Peggy Parker's friends, who needed a shoehorn to get into a size twenty. 'You part of the *Don Carlos* crew?'

Karen shook her head. 'But I know a lot of them shop here.'

'We had that Rozzy Pringle in last Thursday,' said the girl wistfully. 'Bought a floaty grey Belinda Belville dress.'

'Are you sure it was *last* Thursday?' squeaked Karen.

'Quite sure. It was my afternoon off. I always miss the celebs.'

Karen was fighting for breath by the time she reached Gablecross, who was hovering outside Tabitha's hospital room. 'Sarge, you'll never guess. Lucy's given huge sums of money to Rozzy, and Rozzy bought her wrap-party dress on Thursday afternoon, the day she claimed to have been going to the doctor. She must have slashed her rainbow dress yesterday to avert suspicion.'

For a second, Gablecross digested this: Rozzy was such a lovely lady too. 'Doesn't make her a murderer,' he said. 'She needn't have cut up her dress. Cancer makes people behave strangely – but good girl, well done.'

Blushing with pleasure, Karen peered into Tab's room, where she could see a smooth, rakishly handsome man shaking Wolfie by the hand. 'He's nice.'

'James Benson, the Campbell-Black and Rannaldini family doctor,' said Gablecross. 'Charges a fortune for being fazed by nothing.'

James Benson was smiling broadly as he came out.

'Not much to worry about there,' he told Gablecross, 'although young Wolfgang must have had a harrowing afternoon. Never a dull moment with that family. I delivered that little tearaway nineteen years ago. Glad she's found the right bloke at last.'

'Wolfie's a good lad,' agreed Gablecross.

'Very good. Needs a big family to cosset him and Tab needs guy-ropes.'

'Could we have a word?'

James Benson looked at his watch. 'I've got two patients to see, Tim, and I'm due out to dinner at nine.'

'Won't take long. This is my colleague, Detective Constable Needham.'

James Benson smiled in delight. 'Oh, well, then I'm sure I can spare a few minutes.'

He led them into the Consultant's office.

'I wonder if we can find some sherry – it's been a long day. How can I help you?'

'D'you have a patient called Rosalind Pringle?'

James Benson stopped in his search. 'Funny you should ask that. Rannaldini wanted to know the same thing, the Friday before he died. Came to see me about having his vasectomy reversed, said he'd heard I was treating her. Take a seat both of you,' he went on, as he perched on the arm of a sofa. 'Said I wished I had been, always thought Rozzy Pringle the most dishy lady, got all her LPs, used to hang round the stage door at Covent Garden when I was a student at the Middlesex. Funnily enough she's exactly the same age as I am. Rannaldini'd heard a rumour she'd got throat cancer. I said I hoped not, tragedy to wreck that heavenly voice, but that I'd never treated her for that or anything else. Funny, I'd forgotten all about it, until you reminded me.'

'You've been incredibly helpful, sir,' said Gablecross. 'If you'll forgive us.'

'That means not only was she bleeding Lucy white under false pretences,' bleated Karen excitedly as they ran down the stairs, 'but she could have sung Hermione's last aria in the wood.'

'Still circumstantial,' panted Gablecross. 'Not going to cancel out a DNA profile.'

But popping into the incident room at the station, they learnt that Rozzy's local doctor had confirmed he had no knowledge of her having cancer.

'Have they brought Lucy in yet?' asked Karen.

'She gave them the slip,' sighed the Custody Officer.

Immediately the smile of satisfaction was wiped off Gablecross's face.

'The stupid fuckers!'

'I thought you'd be pleased, knowing she's your pin-up.'

'You thought bloody wrong. She'd be safe in custody. If she's on the loose, she's in terrible danger. Come on Karen.' Gablecross raced towards his car.

'Ought we to tell Gerry Portland?'

'Certainly not, we're going to show him and Rupert Campbell-Black we can catch villains.'

But the tale of murder twists and turns. Wolfie, working a sixteen-hour day for the past three and a half months, was unused to so much happiness. He still couldn't believe Tab was going to be OK and all his, at the same time. Every sound seemed to threaten the head that he loved. So he swore as his mobile rang.

It was Rozzy in tears.

'Oh, Wolfie, they're trying to arrest Lucy.'

'Whatever for?'

'Killing your father and Beattie, and trying to kill Tab.'

'That's ridiculous,' said Wolfie appalled. 'Look, Tab's asleep, I'll go into another room. We're not supposed to use mobiles in intensive care, it buggers up the equipment. Get onto Rupert, he'll vouch for Lucy's innocence, so will Gablecross. He's in the hospital somewhere, I'll go and find him.'

But as Wolfie ran down the poorly lit and deserted corridor, Isa appeared from the Emergency Stairs at the other end, carrying a bunch of blood-red roses.

708

Having not been clocked by Gablecross and Karen as they rushed out of the front door, Isa had had no difficulty getting past the uniformed policemen guarding the lift. After all he was Tab's husband and the champion jockey and had given them an excellent tip for Goodwood.

'Hello, my darling,' said Isa softly, as he catfooted into his wife's room. 'Time you and I had a little talk.'

81

News either travels faster round a film crew than the
fleetest greyhound or it never leaves the starting gates.
No-one, even two hours into the wrap party, was aware
that Lucy was now prime suspect and still evading a
massive murder hunt. But they knew Tab's fall had not
been accidental, and the presence of policemen everywhere, frisking still arriving guests, taking their cars
apart, murmuring into radio mikes, added to the
general edginess. Guests had spilled out into the walled
garden, where the scarlet and orange rambler roses
clashed less gaudily by night. Beyond lay shadowy
shrubberies, but there was no incentive to escape into
the bushes with someone who might be the killer. The
revellers clung close to the house in the light cast by
George's big golden windows, discussed in lowered
voices who might have tried to bump off Tab, and leapt
if someone touched them accidentally.

Maria had excelled herself with a huge cold turkey
and salads, laid on a side table in George's big drawing
room. But everyone was too hot and jumpy to eat – as
to fear of the murder was added fear of tomorrow,
when they would no longer be a close-knit community.
How would they cope without Lucy to listen to their
problems or Sylvestre to mend their hair-dryers or
Hermione to bitch about? So they all kept busy filling
their Filofaxes with names and addresses they probably

710

wouldn't be able to put faces to in a week or two.

'Do drop in at Cherrylands, if you're ever in Surrey,' Pushy kept telling everyone.

Revellers even fell on the suntanned neck of Granny's ex-boyfriend, Giuseppe, when he had the temerity to roll up with Serena Westwood, who was flashing a large ruby engagement ring.

'What is the French for arsenic and strychnine?' murmured Granny, who pointedly ignored them both.

'Arsenic and strychnine,' said Oscar, waking up to slot another Gauloise into his jade cigarette holder. 'Malevolence is universal.'

'The point of a wrap party', announced Ogborne, who was motoring down his second bottle of Moët, 'is to make your number with the director and producer so they'll employ you again, then get rat-arsed and pull as many women as possible.'

'I've pulled them all anyway,' said Sylvestre.

'You never pulled Simone,' taunted Valentin.

'Unsimple Simone.' Sylvestre glanced across the room. 'She looks pretty in that flowered dress. Maybe tonight is the night.'

'I'm saving myself for my beautiful wife,' said Valentin. 'The only woman approaching her is Tabitha, and Rupert and lucky Wolfgang will put the biggest guard round her tonight.'

Oscar had fallen asleep again on the sofa, his head in Jessica's lap. Tristan's boys were very happy. They had worked hard and been well paid. Tomorrow they would go home to even better food, August in the country, then start work on *Hercule* in a few weeks.

Only Bernard was sad. After tonight he wouldn't see Rozzy. He had had an original La Scala poster of *Don Carlos*, with Callas singing Elisabetta, framed for her as a wrap present. She was blow-drying her hair when he dropped it off. The hot blast swept the tendrils off her face, emphasizing the good bones but also the wrinkles on which one could play noughts and crosses. I would love her when she grew old, he thought despairingly.

Knowing singers love singing, George had booked a trio from the Rutminster Symphony Orchestra. Installed at the end of the big drawing room with a crate of red, they were now accompanying Alpheus. '"Some enchanted evening,"' he sang, crinkling his eyes at Serena. He'd missed out on her during the recording but had always thought her very lovely.

'It isn't enchanted at all,' said Pushy fretfully. 'No Wolfie, no Mikhail, no Rupert or any of his tasty polo friends, and George, although perfectly gracious, would clearly far rather be alone with Flora. And none of those hunky PCs are allowed to dance with us, and where on earth are Sexton and Tristan?'

'They've got an awful lot of loose finishes to tie up,' explained Simone.

'It's called "supervising the winding-up of production",' said Flora who, as the thunder grew more ominous, was trying to get a tranquillizer down a panting, shuddering Trevor, 'which, in Sexton's case, is probably a euphemism for pleasuring Dame Hermione.'

'And it's no party without Lucy,' said Jessica indignantly, looking at the mountain of presents piling up for her on the table. 'I got her a little silver lurcher brooch from *Past Times*. I did want to see her open it.'

'I got her a little eighteenth-century drawing of a greyhound,' pouted Meredith. 'I wanted to see her open it too.'

'Why the hell did Tristan fire her? Here he is at last,' said Jessica, wriggling out from under Oscar's head. 'I'm going to give him a piece of my mind.'

'You won't have much left, then,' snapped Chloe, who was feeling utterly miserable. She was thirty-six. There was no man in her life. And she had not merely lonely hotel bedrooms but also a solitary Fulham flat to look forward to. How could Isa have dumped her?

The only bright spot, she told Flora, was four performances of *Salome* in Vienna.

'Brilliant casting,' said Flora enthusiastically, 'it's so rare to have a Salome whose veils people really want to come off.'

'Chloe's an old hand at taking off clothes,' drawled Baby, who was missing Isa, jolted by Tab's fall and extremely drunk. 'Is there a goat in *Salome*? Has anyone seen Chloe's video? It's called *No Kidding*.'

'Shut up, Baby,' muttered Flora.

'Look out!' yelled Valentin.

For Chloe had grabbed a carving knife off the table and jumped on Baby, screaming, 'Take that back, you little fag-fucker.'

The band stopped and a gasp of horror went round the room.

'Was that why you killed Rannaldini and Beattie? To shut them up?' taunted Baby and, showing surprising strength for someone so languid, yanked the hand holding the knife down to thigh level.

'No, I did not,' shrieked Chloe.

For a few seconds, they struggled in a deadly embrace, eyes filled with loathing six inches apart.

'You fucked up me and Isa,' hissed Chloe.

'Correc-*shon*. You fucked up *me* and Isa.'

'You and Isa?' whispered Chloe in horror. 'I don't believe it, you bloody liar. I'll *kill* you.'

Tangled in the folds of her mesh dress, the knife quivered like a trapped fish.

'George!' screamed Flora.

But as he raced in through the French windows, Hermione made her entrance from the hall with her head held high.

'Good evening, everyone.' Then, catching sight of Baby and Chloe locked in their dance of death, 'Good gracious, I had no idea you two were an item.'

For a second, Baby's face twitched, then Chloe corpsed too, and they had collapsed in helpless laughter.

713

'I'll have that,' said George, as the carving knife thudded on to the autumn-leaf-patterned carpet.

'We'd better have another bottle and compare Black Cobra bites,' said Baby, ruffling Chloe's hair.

'I'll never understand singers,' sighed Ogborne, piling on a second helping of strawberry Pavlova.

'Gifts for all, gifts for all,' cried Hermione, beckoning in Sexton, who was buckling under a log basket of presents.

'How exciting,' squeaked Jessica, tearing off the paper. 'Thank you, Dame Hermione.'

'What have you given us?' asked Grisel.

'Calendars,' smiled Hermione.

'How clever of you to get next year's so early,' said Pushy. After all, she might want to work with the old boot again.

'They're this year's,' said Grisel in outrage. 'And it's half-way through July.'

'No-one's interested in dates,' said Hermione airily. 'Particularly if one's bookings extend beyond the millennium, as mine do. What matters is the lovely photographs.'

'What are they of?' asked Ogborne.

'Why, me, of course. Next year, I'm hoping to show some of Cosmo's *oeuvre*.'

'"There is nothing like a *dime*,"' sang Sexton, as he bopped happily with Hermione. 'I love you, Hermsie.'

'D'you feel you can truly care for Little Cosmo?'

'I love 'im already,' said Sexton truthfully. 'He's so sharp, I'll be able to veg out in his pram while he goes to the office for me.'

A tranquillized, cross-eyed Trevor was now lying in Flora's arms like a baby.

'Why are you looking so cheerful?' she asked Meredith.

'Tomorrow I'm flying to Oz.'

'To meet up with Hermione's husband, Bobby?'

'But not for much longer.' Meredith nodded at a bopping Hermione. 'It looks as though Madam is at last going to give Bobby a divorce.'

'I'm so pleased.' Flora kissed him on the cheek.

'Come on, Meredith, on your feet,' boomed Griselda.

'New trousers.' Halting in mid-bop, Hermione looked beadily at Grisel's Day-glo pink harem pants. 'I'm sure you'll find them very useful.'

'Useful for getting the entire harem in there as well,' murmured Flora to Simone, who, in her pretty flowery dress, was leaning against the wall, sipping iced water.

'I think Griselda's days of promiscuity are over,' said Simone gravely. 'I want you to be the first to know, Flora, that Grisel and I are an item.'

Flora nearly dropped Trevor.

'Was that why you got over Wolfie so fast?' she squeaked.

Simone nodded. 'I have never been so in love in my life. We are flying down to the Tarn to meet Mama and Papa tomorrow.'

'Will they approve?'

'They will probably feel Grisel is a little old for me. She's six months older than Mama, but once they meet her . . .'

'Have you told Uncle Tristan?'

'No, he doesn't take much on board at the moment.'

Having immediately crossed the drawing room to admire George's Picasso when he arrived, Tristan had hardly moved.

Normally at wrap parties he felt elated and disembodied: if someone rolled back the stone, he wouldn't be there. But tonight there was no elation. His mind kept slipping into reverse gear as he bitterly castigated himself for being so brutal to Lucy. He wanted to drive over to Valhalla and find her, but having just arrived, he couldn't abandon his cast and crew, who had endured so much.

Normally also at wrap parties he felt like a prince on

a walkabout with everyone shaking his hand and thanking him for a wonderful shoot. But tonight, although no-one was openly hostile, he could feel their reproach, as palpable as the ever-increasing mountain of presents for Lucy on the polished table beside him.

'What's the matter with you all?' he snarled at Valentin.

'People may not want to work on *Hercule* unless you hire Lucy again,' snapped back Valentin. 'She was so good at calming down singers, and Oscar reckons she's the best he's ever worked with.'

'That's because the lazy sod gets more sleep if he doesn't have to spend hours adjusting lights to compensate for the inadequacies of some make-up artist,' said Tristan sourly.

'Why d'you have to fire Lucy?' demanded Ogborne, his mouth full of Danish blue.

'Oh, for Christ's sake.' Tristan turned away and, for the thousandth time, punched out Lucy's number.

'Don't bug the guy,' Sylvestre chided the rest of the crew. 'You all seem to forget that while he was losing three crucial days' filming he was in prison on a murder charge, being put through the mangle by the *flics*. He's entitled to the odd tantrum.'

'The Vodaphone you have called is not responding,' the operator was now telling Tristan, 'please try later, please try later,' until he wanted to wring her neck and hurl his mobile through George's huge window-pane. If only Wolfie were here, he'd have found Lucy.

'You'll never guess,' hissed Flora to Baby, 'Grisel and Simone are an item.'

'Good God, d'you think she takes her turban off in bed?'

'"You're lovely to look at, delightful to know and heaven to kiss,"' sang Alpheus, as he foxtrotted past with Serena.

'"He said that he loved 'er, but, oh, 'ow he lie, oh, 'ow

716

he lie, oh, 'ow he lie,"' sang Giuseppe in Granny's ear. 'Serena is *so* boring. I want to come back, I miss you.'

'Well, you can't,' said Granny, with decreasing conviction.

'Howie get me *Don Giovanni* at La Scala,' murmured Giuseppe, 'so I can take you on long holiday and pay for all things. Please, Granville.'

'Oh, my dear boy.'

'Excuse me, Granville.' Hermione was scrabbling like a terrier in Lucy's pile of presents. 'I've forgotten Maria. D'you think Lucy'll mind awfully if she didn't get one of my calendars?'

'I expect she'll live,' said Granny.

Tristan shivered. 'I'm not sure she will. I am bloody worried, Granny.'

'Monsieur de Montigny,' said the editor of *Classical Music*, who'd disguised himself as a waiter, 'about Claudine Lauzerte?'

'Who?' said Tristan, as though he was dredging up some long-abandoned wreckage from the bottom of the sea.

'Could we have a word?'

'The word is "*Non*",' snapped Tristan, shoving dancers aside, until he reached Bernard. 'For Christ's sake, try Rozzy again. Ask her if she's seen Lucy.'

'Where's Mikhail?' grumbled Baby. 'I want to sing the Friendship Duet with him.'

'Perhaps he's eloped with Rozzy,' giggled Simone.

It was Mikhail's last night in the capitalist sweet shop. As a going-home present for Lara, he had decided to remove the Murillo Madonna from the chapel. But finding Valhalla awash with police when he returned home after the final wrap, he decided to sleep until things quietened down.

Waking just after eleven, he took a considerable swig from his hip flask and set out. The house was sculptured grey in the moonlight, a sudden chill wind sent the cypresses hissing like snakes. Sliding through the shadows, Mikhail passed two nervously patrolling uniformed policemen and wished he had had slightly more to drink.

He froze at the sound of more footsteps. Slow, lonely, then quickening, coming relentlessly towards him, from the swirling mists emerged a black-cloaked figure gliding down the cloisters, then disappearing through the chapel door. Frantic for company, Mikhail fled in terror back to the production office, but found it totally deserted – everyone must have left for the party. Deciding this was very unPosa-like behaviour and ghosts couldn't produce footsteps, he crept back again.

The chapel was unlocked, no-one appeared to be inside. Feeling his way along the smooth edges of the pews and then the choir stalls, guided by the light of the rising moon now spilling like milk, then like royal blue ink, now like red wine through the stained-glass windows, he reached the Madonna. How beautiful she was, more radiant than any moon. How she would enjoy an exciting jaunt to Moscow.

Mikhail got out his screwdriver and pliers. Somehow she must come off the wall. But as he started to tap and feel round her gilded frame, he nearly jumped through the vaulted roof.

The panel to which she was attached had swung open, revealing utter darkness, a horrible smell of Maestro and footsteps echoing far in the distance. Climbing inside, running a shaking hand round to the left, Mikhail found a key. Someone had been stupid or careless enough to leave it in a lock. Turning it, he felt a door open; groping inside, he found a light switch, and nearly fainted.

He was in a tiny cubby-hole. All round the walls were grotesquely graffiti'd photographs of Tabitha, Flora, Claudine Lauzerte, Granny, Beattie, Hermione and Rannaldini. Ears had been lopped off, squints and beards added, and everything smeared with blood and excrement. But interspersed with these

718

horrors, beautiful and immaculate, were pictures of Tristan at all ages.

Also hanging from hooks were wigs, pewter grey, blond, dark and light brown, and Hermione's apple-green cloak with the pink rose-lined hood, except bloodstains were now rose-patterning the green as well. The table was piled high with body-paints, knives, ammunition, huge, cruel scissors, a half-full bottle of Maestro, videos, tapes, tape-recorders, Rannaldini's cigars, bottles marked 'poison' and cans of petrol. On top lay a ripped-open brown-paper parcel marked 'Tristan de Montigny, Private and Confidential'. And against the table, a going-home present for Lara for the taking, was the Montigny *Snake Charmer*. Beside it, the floor was littered with fragments of cut-up photograph.

Mikhail was nearly gagging on the stench. Who could do these sick things? Grabbing the painting, he nearly dropped it, as a voice snapped, 'What in hell are you doing here? I wouldn't do anything silly, sir,' as Mikhail lunged forward to grab a knife.

Mikhail had never dreamt he'd be pleased to see a policeman. Karen, who was following Gablecross, thought Mikhail looked like a bear raiding a larder. Then she saw the walls behind him and had to clap her hands over her mouth.

'I find vicar's hole full of interest,' announced Mikhail.

'How the fuck did you get in here?' Shoving him out of the way, Gablecross took in the contents of the table. 'Jesus!'

'I enter chapel to pray my vife will return,' said Mikhail piously, 'I just examine vork of art when wall open.'

Lying bastard, thought Gablecross.

'Look, Sarge, here's a parcel addressed to Tristan – in Lucy's handwriting,' said Karen, in excitement. 'And there's a wig exactly like Rozzy's hair and one like Hermione's. Why should anyone want to pass themselves off as Rozzy?'

They had been unable to track her down in Make Up, and she wasn't answering her mobile.

'She must be on the way to the party, unless the murderer's got her too . . . Oh, God.'

Crouching down on the floor, Karen gathered up fragments of photographs, horribly reminiscent of Rozzy's cut-up dress.

'Let's go,' said Gablecross. 'Put that painting down, Mr Pezcherov.'

Outside, having alerted two of the uniformed officers to keep an eye on the cache, Gablecross took the wheel and they set out for the wrap party.

No wonder he complains about my slow driving, thought Karen, as they hurtled through overgrown tree tunnels, down narrow lanes where great banks of elder and wild rose obscured any views of things coming the other way. Black trees and telegraph poles flew past the window.

Karen was being thrown from one side of the back seat to the other, as with the light on and a road map on her knees as a table, she tried to piece together the shreds of photograph.

'It still points to Lucy,' she said sadly, as they shot past a sign saying four miles to Rutminster.

'Why?' snapped Gablecross.

'These cut-up photographs are all of Rozzy. Perhaps Lucy couldn't stand Tristan giving Rozzy all that money for a new wrap-party dress.'

82

Lucy regained consciousness into darker nightmare. She was trapped in a chair, her wrists clamped to its arms by what felt like iron manacles padded with velvet, her ankles and knees similarly secured to the chair legs so her thighs were forced humiliatingly apart. This must be the debtor's chair in which Rannaldini had once imprisoned Tab. The room was cold and dreadfully airless. It smelled like a slaughter-house, of blood, sweat and fear.

As her eyes grew used to the dark, she realized she was in a large steel container. She and the debtor's chair were on a lower level in a kind of pit. Up some steps, on a higher level, stood an imposing carved armchair – like a bishop's throne – a bed and a dressing-table pushed against the wall. From the only wall that wasn't mirror, dully gleamed a highly sophisticated collection of whips and knives.

Then she heard hoarse, unearthly screaming. It was several seconds before she realized it was coming from herself. Shuddering with horror, she pieced together earlier events, Tristan firing her, the police arresting her, Rozzy hiding her in the priest-hole, then Rannaldini's utterly terrifying ghost, or had it been Rannaldini himself? Thank God, Rozzy would seek help and could be trusted to give Tristan his important papers.

Then she remembered James's cries growing more

and more piteous. Someone must have tortured him. She started to cry, but as her eyes and nose streamed she had nothing on which to wipe them. Her ankle ached where she'd twisted it, her legs throbbed with nettle stings and, in the mirror opposite, her dim reflection showed her face, arms and legs cut even more to pieces from stumbling down the stony secret passage. She looked like a victim of Third World brutality.

Glancing at the whips and knives, she knew the churning fear Carlos and Elisabetta must have felt, aware that torture awaited them. The light was too faint to read her watch. She tried to pray. Rozzy wouldn't let her down. But as the hours crawled by, and she grew colder and more dehydrated, her legs racked by agonizing cramps, hope faded.

She must have nodded off. She was woken by terror beyond imagination. Instead of her own reflection, glaring evilly back from the mirror was Rannaldini. Maybe she had died, or her mind was slowly unravelling. Then he was gone, and her blanched, bloodstained, lacerated reflection gazed back at her again.

There was a creak. Jerking her head round as far as it would go she saw a steel panel on the upper level slide back and there was Rannaldini, a monstrous black vulture, poised to swoop down and tear her apart.

'No, no, please not.' Her screams echoed round the chamber, then died on her lips. As the steel door clanged shut, off came the cloak, the pewter wig, the mask. Lucy breathed in a heavenly waft of Femme and wept with relief.

'Oh, you angel, thank God.' Then the questions poured out in a hoarse gasping rush. 'Are the police still looking for me? Have you found James? Did you give Tristan the parcel? What a brilliant disguise! You fooled everyone.'

As Rozzy flicked on a side light, and arranged her newly washed hair, Lucy saw she was wearing a beautiful dove-grey chiffon dress and long grey gloves.

'Please unlock this horrible chair,' she begged. 'What time is it? Where am I?'

'Nearly midnight. You're in Rannaldini's torture chamber.' Rozzy's voice was strangely high and hard. 'Quite the Grand Inquisitor's adventure playground, isn't it? Soundproofed like a recording studio, so no-one can hear the screams.'

'What d'you mean?'

Little by little, terror was taking over again.

'Rannaldini brought the pretty ones down here,' mocked Rozzy.

'I don't understand.'

Both of them jumped as the telephone rang. In an instant Rozzy had grabbed her mobile, whipped a gun out of her bag, and running down the steps, rammed the muzzle against Lucy's temple.

'Don't make a sound,' she hissed.

Rigid with horror, Lucy could hear Bernard's bray so close she could have reached out and stroked his glossy black moustache.

'I've been delayed again, Bernie darling.' Rozzy's voice was caressing. 'Lucy? I haven't seen her.' As Lucy gasped, the gun was rammed harder into her head. 'She must have pushed off home to Cumbria. One more pressie to wrap, then I'll be over. No, no, dearest, you've been drinking – at least, I hope you have. I'll make my own way. Keep the champagne on ice.'

Flicking off her mobile, Rozzy peered at the buttons for a second before pressing one. 'I'll turn it off altogether,' she said chattily. 'We don't want to be disturbed.'

Retracing her steps up the stairs, she placed the gun and the mobile on the dressing-table. 'That was Bernard. The silly old fart was looking for you.'

'You're the murderer,' whispered Lucy.

'I thought you'd never guess,' said Rozzy acidly. 'The whole world is searching but no-one has a clue.'

'And I gave you Tristan's papers.'

Lucy's chattering teeth became a terrible shaking, jolting her body like an earthquake. 'Please let me have your cloak for a second. I'm so cold.'

'Poor child,' said Rozzy sympathetically, then suddenly burst into maniacal laughter. 'You'll be burning hot where you're going. Where were we? Oh, yes, in Rannaldini's torture chamber. He strapped them just where you are, in the debtor's chair.'

What had Gablecross told her? Lucy tried to marshal her crazed thoughts. With psychopaths you had to be passive, respectful, admiring.

'I can't believe you killed Rannaldini.' Every word had to be forced out. 'You're far too slight and, anyway, you were in Mallowfield.'

'Since I'm going to kill you in a minute I'll tell you while I do my face. Now, are you sitting comfortably?'

Settling down on the bed, Rozzy calmly took a tube of moisturiser out of her make-up bag.

'I killed Rannaldini,' she said dreamily. 'He put me down so much he deserved it. It was so easy to slip away from Glyn's party, I pretended I had a migraine. The land slopes up steeply behind our house – such a small drop on to the lawn from the spare-room window. Everyone was too drunk to notice my car had gone. I drove to Valhalla and parked up a little pebbled track in Paradise woods. Then I climbed over the west gate into Hangman's Wood.'

'So James did see you. He wagged his tail and peered into the gloom. Oh, Rozzy, where is he?'

'Don't interrupt,' hissed Rozzy. Then, giving a mirthless laugh, even more sinister than her mad cackle, she went on, 'I saw that tramp Tabitha staggering out of Rannaldini's watch-tower. Got her comeuppance at last. No-one heard her screams. They were too busy cheering on the finalists. I wore Hermione's green cloak. Pretending it was Granny's cut-up quilt, I'd smuggled it out of Wardrobe on Saturday.' With an adoring smile, Rozzy was smoothing base into her face and neck.

'Wandering up one of those rides like the rays of the sun, I saw Rannaldini wearing Alpheus's smart dressing-gown. He was out looking for Tab. So I launched into Elisabetta's last duet.'

The next minute Lucy thought her eardrums would rupture as Rozzy's voice exploded like an atom bomb in the tiny room.

'You can sing,' she gasped.

'I always could, as soon as I recovered from the laryngitis I had at the recording.' Rozzy rocked with obscene laughter once more. 'Pretending to have cancer was such an easy way of milking you. Unfortunately Rannaldini bugged your caravan. The Saturday morning before he died he told me he'd seen James Benson and was going to expose me as not having cancer at all.'

'But I gave you so much money,' said a shattered Lucy. Then forgetting for a second not to be judgemental, 'This ought to be called the creditor's chair.'

'Don't you cheek me,' screamed Rozzy.

Grabbing one of the knives, she ran down the steps, eyes rolling, teeth clenched, and drew the blade along Lucy's cheek. 'It was you who told Tristan I had cancer, you meddling bitch, because you didn't want him to give me any work. Shut up!' she yelled, as Lucy tried to protest.

Then sauntering back up the stairs, Rozzy used the knife to sharpen an eye pencil as she continued her story. 'Catching sight of Hermione's cloak, enchanted by how much his mistress's voice had improved, Rannaldini strode down the ride, took me in his arms and kissed me. As he broke away, my hands closed round his neck.' Rozzy's voice trembled with excitement. 'His last words were Carlos's "Dear God, it's not the Queen." I saw the terror in his eyes, and felt his windpipe give. God, I enjoyed that. Hell!' She had snapped her eye pencil, and began to pare away the wood again.

'How could you, Rozzy?' whispered Lucy, then, hastily

forcing herself to sound admiring, 'Rannaldini was as strong as an ox.'

'I hated him so much and I was wearing Tristan's signet ring for luck. Tristan had given it to me as a keepsake. My hands are smaller than his – it must have fallen off.'

Lining the knife up carefully beside her mobile and the gun, Rozzy drew a dark line along the top of her lashes with an utterly steady hand.

'It was like Piccadilly Circus in Hangman's Wood that night. Having killed Rannaldini, I was about to whip the memoirs from the watch-tower, but I only had time to snatch his keys, when a helicopter landed and Rupert Campbell-Bastard came running into the wood, shortly followed by Mikhail, who stole the Montigny. Then I ran back to the west gate, shoved the bloodstained cloak in the boot and called you.'

'But you were at Glyn's party,' protested Lucy. 'I heard everyone singing "Happy Birthday" and "Glyn's a Jolly Good Fellow".'

'I taped it when Glyn cut his cake much earlier,' said Rozzy. 'I only had to slot the cassette into the car stereo. I rang you twice – the second time to remind you about the cloak – and established the perfect alibi. I drove home singing my head off. I didn't even have to climb back in through the window. I'd put a pillow in my bed, and a melon inside the wig you so caringly made for when my hair fell out from the chemo – "You'll look just as beautiful, Rozzy", you patronizing cow.' The sickening little-girl voice soared to a scream and exploded into gales of terrible laughter.

'I walked upstairs to the spare room.' Rozzy clutched her shaking sides. 'Glyn and Sylvia were having a fuck in the "master bedroom", as the common little slut insists on calling it. Naturally they didn't notice my return. There are pluses in having an un-uxorious husband. Ten minutes later, Glyn came out on to the landing to check I was asleep and tripped over the carpet.'

Gradually the laughter ebbed away. More terrifying were the uncharacteristically foul language and the mood-swings. Beth in *Little Women* one moment, Lady Macbeth the next.

'Clever to murder Beattie,' mumbled Lucy. 'She was such a bitch.'

'And so short-sighted. Never once asked me for an interview, when I've got the most beautiful voice in the world and wonderful stories of all the greats I've sung with. And Beattie was gagging for Tristan. Shit.' Rozzy's mascara wand had slipped, leaving a blob on her cheekbone. 'She bought the memoirs from Clive, you know, who stole them from Bussage. Beattie was going to expose Tristan as being Maxim's incestuous bastard. Why didn't you tell me about that, Lucy? That wasn't friendly to have secrets.' The voice was hard and cruel again. Lucy steeled herself as Rozzy picked up the knife, but for the moment her venom was concentrated on Beattie.

'I didn't want Tristan exposed. I didn't give a stuff that Maxim had fucked his own daughter because Tristan and I never want children. But I do fancy being Madame de Montigny.' Rozzy removed the blob of mascara with a cotton-bud. 'It has such a charming nineteenth-century ring, like a novel by George Sand. Perhaps I should have asked you to do my eyes.' Meditatively Rozzy admired her reflection.

'You look stunning,' stammered Lucy. Praise her, keep her talking, she told herself. She was racked by cramp in her leg, her eyes watering with pain. 'How did you kill Beattie, with so many people around?'

'Best thing about my job on *Carlos* was that no-one knew where I was supposed to be at any one time. Earlier in the week I'd let myself into Beattie's room and read the filth she intended to publish. The night she was killed and you were so busy brown-nosing Hermione I said I'd walk James and Trevor, but I never did.'

That was why James had made a puddle on the caravan

floor – and I shouted at him, thought Lucy, in anguish.

'Instead,' went on Rozzy, 'I shoved a note I'd typed on the production unit word processor under Beattie's door. Then I dressed up as Rannaldini. I felt so safe disguised as him – even that arrogant shit Rupert bolted like a frightened hare. Beattie was so terrified she backed on to the unicorn. Its horn came up through her belly like a corkscrew,' Rozzy's voice quivered with delight again, 'and her blood spurted out like a fountain. But I couldn't risk her screaming, so I finished her off with the .22 from Props. I had a key cut back in June. I was wearing gloves. See – I can even make up in them now. I'd no idea Tristan had left his prints on the same gun when he'd tried it out that afternoon.

'Still dressed as Rannaldini, I raced back through the night to Beattie's room. There I stole memoirs, photographs, videos and tapes, printed out Beattie's piece to give me all the gen and smashed the computer on the floor.' Rozzy couldn't speak for wild laughter. 'Then I went into the chapel to pray for Beattie's departed soul, and hid everything in my little priest-hole behind the Murillo Madonna.'

'You did all that in the break? You *are* clever.'

'I ought to get the Nobel Prize for ridding the world of those monsters.'

'You ought.' Lucy was casting round frantically for things to ask. 'What about *The Snake Charmer*?'

'I've so often found things hidden under Glyn's mattress,' Rozzy became the tragedy queen for a second, 'that out of habit I often checked Tristan's room. The only thing I discovered was the Montigny, and I knew Mikhail had stolen that so I hid it in my priest-hole. Isn't this a nice lipstick? Revlon's Fire and Ice. It exactly matches this feather boa Tristan bought me. He chose the dress too.

'Oh, I have had fun.' Rozzy's voice dropped to cosy intimacy. 'I devastated that silly old poof, Granny, by slashing his patchwork quilt. I got so many Brownie points for sewing up Foxie after I'd cut him to pieces. And I had so many goes at you, Lucy. Who put the adder in your make-up box? Who poisoned your champagne? I knew Rannaldini didn't drink before concerts, although he lapsed on that occasion. If Hermione hadn't shattered that glass with her top E, he'd have died that evening instead. And I put slug pellets in James's bowl.'

'I thought you loved James.' Lucy made heroic efforts to keep the hysteria out of her voice. 'Oh, please, where is he?'

'I've no idea. I had two goes at that arrogant tart Tabitha. I substituted the can of petrol, I put on gloves to cut her stirrup leather today with the little penknife on your key-ring. Then I dumped the key-ring in Wardrobe's dustbin, which even those dolts from Rutminster CID couldn't miss.'

'You tried to kill Tab today,' cried Lucy in horror. 'That must be her attempted murder they were arresting me for. Oh, God, is she all right?'

'Tragically,' Rozzy paused dramatically, 'she is – the little whore.'

'I still don't understand why the police suspect me.'

'Oh, my child,' said Rozzy gently, as she drew lipstick outside the lines of her mouth, 'because your DNA profile's on Rannaldini's dressing-gown and in his saliva where I kissed him and on the bite on Beattie's shoulder. I just loved plunging my teeth into her, knowing it would incriminate you, and it's in the blood on Hermione's cloak, and your fingerprints are all over Tab's saddle and the penknife.'

'But I never had a DNA test.'

'No, but you lost your passport, remember.' Rubbing cream into her hands, Rozzy clasped them in ecstasy. 'I borrowed it and stuck my passport photograph on top of yours, and when the two flat-footed cretins rolled up at Make Up, I said I was Lucy Latimer, showed them your passport and took a saliva test in your name. I wasn't on the list of suspects due for a DNA test, because the police knew I was in Mallowfield.'

Lucy could take no more. 'That's the most horrible part,' she sobbed. 'I thought we were friends.'

Radiant, smiling, the great diva making her entrance, Rozzy glided down the steps and stroked Lucy's hair. 'You poor darling,' she said, in such a sweet, sad voice that Lucy knew the whole thing had been a bad dream. Then Rozzy grabbed her hair, yanking it back until she screamed.

'You stupid bitch! I did love you until you started meddling. Why did you go to France to free Tristan? He'd have been so much better off in prison, safe from all those drooling, ravening bitches. I'd have visited him every week.

'Why didn't you and Wolfie take me with you? You deceitful cow, sucking up to his family.' Rozzy's eyes were glittering, foam frothing along her mouth, mad laughter echoing horribly off the walls. 'I know you're crazy about Tristan,' Rozzy was hissing in her ear, spraying it with saliva, 'but having spent his life surrounded by beautiful people, how could he settle for someone as plain and common as you?' Seizing Lucy's face, Rozzy wrenched it towards the mirror. 'Look at yourself, you ugly bitch!' As Rozzy slapped her face back and forth, Lucy felt blood trickling from her nose to join her tears, choking her.

'I suppose he was kind to you,' said Rozzy reflectively. 'Kindness is such an aphrodisiac to ugly women. What would the Montignys think of you?' she added mockingly.

'I got on with Aunt Hortense,' gasped Lucy.

'She must have been appalled. A hairdresser with a broad Cumbrian accent! I'll teach you to have ideas above your station, Miss.'

My station, thought Lucy, in crazed anguish, is Carlisle. Above the town soar the mountains, olive green, filled with lakes, criss-crossed with stone walls.

She'd never see them again. And she'd never see her darling mum and dad, or her sister, or her little nieces – and they'd be told she was a murderer.

Rozzy was back at the table, spraying Femme between her breasts and legs.

'What did you do with Tristan's papers?' whispered Lucy.

'I'll burn them when I get a moment.'

'I promised Hortense he'd get them,' said Lucy despairingly. 'At least give him Étienne's self-portrait and Laurent and Delphine's letters. Then he'll understand why his mother copped out and why Étienne rejected him.'

'Don't tell me what to do!' snapped Rozzy. 'Tristan needs love and understanding.'

'He needs roots,' sobbed Lucy. 'Hortense'll tell him the truth.'

'I think not.' Rozzy rose to her feet, Lady Macbeth's presence dominating the room. 'I took your passport to the chemist and bought rat poison.'

'Please, no,' shrieked Lucy. 'Hortense is dying anyway. She's such an old duck.'

'Old dyke, you mean. I'm off,' said Rozzy coolly.

'Don't leave me.'

'You know it all now, sweetie. You've got to die. It's so easy. There are two buttons to flood the torture chamber. As I'm leaving I'll just press the one outside the door,' Rozzy murmured lasciviously, 'and Madame Guillotine over there will slide up and the lake will come pouring in. How convenient of Wolfie to fill it up – and we've had so much rain. It takes five minutes to flood the pit.'

'Please, not,' gabbled Lucy.

Rozzy posed before the mirror, the flame-red boa warming her face, the grey chiffon giving wondrous curves to her slight body.

'You look beautiful, Rozzy. Your eyes are like stars.'

'They're the last stars you'll see.'

'What time is it?' gasped Lucy, trying to cling on to some reality.

'Nearly twenty past twelve. Cinderella shall go to the ball.'

Rozzy dropped her wig and mask, followed by the gun and her mobile, into her bag.

'Shame you haven't time to read in the memoirs about Rannaldini's favourite games, Lucy. Either he'd fuck them in the pit as the water came over their noses so their cunt muscles, in their imagined death-throes, clamped round his cock. President Kennedy pushed whores under the bath-water for the same buzz.' Rozzy smiled, as if she were telling a bedtime story.

'Or he'd sit up here watching them drown, then press a button to release them from the debtor's chair, so they floated choking upwards. But in your case, Miss Goody Two Shoes, I won't press that release button till tomorrow.' Rozzy's face contorted with hatred. 'And you'll float out into the lake, not pretty like Ophelia, but bloated and smelly with wrinkled fingers.'

'The police'll know I've been strapped in.'

'No, they won't, those manacles are very soft. Rannaldini knew about hurting people without marking them. And they'll find your sweet little suicide note. I tore up your last letter to Tristan – "your loving Lucy", you presumptuous bitch – and retyped it: "Dear Twistan . . ."' it was Rozzy's obscene baby voice again, '"I'm sowwy I killed all those people and did all those wicked things, but I had to be *favori du woi*." Well, I'm *favori du roi* now,' added Rozzy viciously, 'and I'm excellent at forging your signature. I've done it on enough cheques.'

Lucy flipped. 'How dare you write a suicide note on my behalf?' she yelled. 'I'd never do that, because of James.'

'James is dead,' said Rozzy indifferently. 'I didn't tell you because I didn't want you snivelling while I did my make-up. He whined so much I let him out on the motorway.'

Lucy rolled her head in agony as she remembered James pirouetting with joy or leaning against her or darting off with a biscuit, or sitting quietly enjoying the rain after a heatwave.

Pressing the button so the steel door slid back, Rozzy flung on Rannaldini's cloak and escaped quickly, in case Lucy's howl of desolation reached the outside world.

'I'm doing you a good turn,' she called back softly. 'According to Schiller, "the peace of death" is the only escape from the pangs of unrequited love.'

As one steel door clanged shut, the metal guillotine keeping out the lake slid upwards and water started to trickle in.

83

Back at the wrap party, it was ten minutes to twelve. People had anaesthetized themselves with drink against the terrors and were now dancing. But a shiver went through the room as Clive strolled in, holding a bunch of white lilies. Here was Rannaldini's hitman, who knew far too much about all of them, as difficult to ignore as a mamba sliding across the floor.

'Where's Gablecross?' murmured Clive to DC Lightfoot.

'Guarding Tabitha Lovell at Rutminster General.'

'He isn't. I just called there.'

'Where the hell have you been anyway?' demanded DC Lightfoot. 'Everyone wants to question you.'

'That's why I haven't been here. Where's Lucy?' Clive's pale, lashless eyes flickered round the room. 'I bought these flowers for her. Always liked Lucy. No-one streaked my hair better. And there's tasty Tristan.'

Tristan was smiling for the first time that evening because Hype-along had just presented him with an album of stills through which Tristan was flipping with exclamations of delight. There was Baby looking romantic, and Mikhail heroic, and Hermione naked and enormous from behind, and Oscar asleep, and Rupert narrow-eyed and mean in his executive producer's chair.

'Thank you, Hype-along, it's all here to remind me,'

said Tristan, kissing his press officer on each sideboard.

On the last page, finding two photographs stuck in side by side, he gave a gasp of pleasure. In the first Lucy, naked except for a pink towel, was stretched on a table with Rozzy massaging her shoulders. In the second, she had reared up in alarm, gorgeous breasts flying.

'Look at Lucy's boobs, everyone,' shouted Ogborne, who was peering over Tristan's shoulders. 'How d'you get her to do that, Hypie?'

'Banged on her caravan window after dark.'

As people crowded round, Tristan seized the album, not wanting everyone to drool. Then his heart stopped as he noticed the venom on Rozzy's face as her fingers closed round Lucy's neck.

'Oh, my God.' Glancing up in horror, he saw Gablecross and Karen running through the door. 'Where's Lucy?' he yelled.

'I hoped you were going to tell us that,' said Gablecross.

'*Regardez.*' Tristan thrust the photograph album at him.

For a second, Gablecross studied the two pictures, then he drew Tristan into George's study next door.

'Where the hell is she?' asked a grey and shaking Tristan.

'She was last seen around seven thirty outside Make Up,' said Karen.

'Then she evaded arrest and ran off into the garden,' added Gablecross.

'Arrest?' snarled Tristan. 'Whatever for?'

'Hanging on to my lapels won't do any good. Just let go,' said Gablecross irritably. 'Lucy was arrested for the murder of Rannaldini, Beattie and the attempted murder of Tabitha.'

'That's crazy! Lucy couldn't kill an earwig.'

Gablecross explained that her DNA profile matched up. 'Since then she vanished into thin air.'

'And James?'

'Not a sign,' sighed Karen.

'Someone's either hiding her, she's hiding out in the wood, or the murderer's got her,' said Gablecross. 'It would help if Rozzy turned up.'

'Oh, my Christ.' A distraught Tristan was pacing up and down, thinking and thinking. 'And they've searched Valhalla?'

'Everywhere.'

Next moment, Griselda rushed in, shaking with horror.

'Tristan, Karen, Sergeant Gablecross, listen to this horrible message on my machine.'

Griselda was followed by Flora, George, Bernard and Simone. Her hand was trembling so much they had to endure several seconds of whirring speeded-up chatter before she found the right place on the tape. The voice on the machine was so high and terrified at first no-one recognized it.

'Please let me have your cloak for a second, I'm so cold.'

'Lucy,' gasped Tristan, looking round with desperate bloodshot eyes.

'Poor child.' At first the second voice was sympathetic, then it burst into gales of dreadful crazy laughter, then became chillingly hard and cruel. 'You'll be burning hot where you're going. Where were we? Oh, yes, in Rannaldini's torture chamber. He strapped them just where you are, in the debtor's chair.'

'That's Rozzy's voice,' said Bernard hoarsely.

George put an arm round Flora's shoulders.

Tristan jumped to his feet. 'Do something, for Christ's sake.'

Gablecross raised a shaking hand for silence, as Lucy, in a high, terrified voice, spoke again: 'I can't believe you killed Rannaldini. You're far too slight and, anyway, you were in Mallowfield.'

'Since I'm going to kill you in a minute,' it was Rozzy's

736

voice, amused bitchy, 'I'll tell you while I do my face. Now, are you sitting comfortably?'

'What time was that call made?' barked Gablecross.

'Someone called me before that,' said a trembling Griselda.

'It was me playing seely buggers.' Simone had gone scarlet. 'I rang you on the upstairs phone, Grisel, around twelve less ten minutes.'

As if trying to help the police with their inquiries, the clock on the mantelpiece chimed midnight.

'So it could have been as little as ten minutes ago,' said Karen, making lightning calculations.

'I don't understand why those obscene outpourings are on my machine,' wailed Griselda.

'You're in her memory,' said Bernard, who'd gone as grey as Simone had scarlet. 'Rozzy's as blind as a bat. I called her just after eleven forty-five to ask if she'd seen Lucy and check when she was coming over. She probably meant to switch her phone off after that, not wanting to be interrupted, and pressed your number instead.'

'We've got to get Lucy out.' Tristan was suddenly roused from shock. 'Where the fuck's the torture chamber?'

'I can show you,' said a soft voice.

Clive was hovering in the doorway. Never can so many people have been pleased to see him. He was still clutching Lucy's lilies.

Pray God, they aren't destined for her grave, thought Tristan in horror.

'If Rozzy slams the door and flicks the switch to let the water in, Lucy's got five minutes at best,' said Clive.

'Take my plane,' urged George.

But as they rushed out of the front door towards the hangar, there was a tick, tick, tick and a judder overhead. Like a troupe of dancing stars, a helicopter landed on the lawn. As Rupert opened the door, his blond hair silver in the moonlight, Gablecross, Tristan, Clive and Bernard, cursing as he stubbed his toe on a

737

reconstituted-stone cherub, raced towards him. But Karen outstripped them.

'Quick,' she panted. 'It's Lucy, in terrible danger. We've got to get to Valhalla and rescue her.'

'The Famous Five,' drawled Rupert, glancing at the others behind her. 'That lot have as much chance of rescuing anyone as Mr Blobby.'

'Oh, for Christ's sake!' howled Tristan.

'Rupert!' came an excited cry as Hermione ran out of the house. 'Now the party has really begun.'

'You're on!' said Rupert, shooting faster than light back into the helicopter. 'As long as Karen can sit on my knee – but I'm not taking that murderer.' He glared at Clive. 'He stole our Gertrude.'

'You must,' pleaded Karen. 'He's the only person who can lead us to Lucy.'

As she wriggled past Rupert to get into the back seat, she felt the hard bulge of a gun, but decided it wasn't the moment to quibble. Anyway, they might need it.

Gablecross, still on the ground and on his mobile, was alerting the uniform boys at Valhalla.

'Whatever you do, don't arouse suspicion. She's mad and extremely dangerous, and she's got Lucy Latimer in there.'

As they flew over a pale lunar landscape, dark grey trees, black houses lit by a molten moon, Clive briefed them in his soft sibilant lisp: 'The torture chamber's fifteen feet from the lake and ten feet below the water level. The moment Rozzy presses the switch, the iron door slides up.'

'I could swim under the guillotine and free her,' urged Tristan, desperate for some action.

'You haven't time. You'd need a blow-torch to saw through the manacles and that wouldn't work under gushing water. The switch to unlock the debtor's chair is unfortunately inside the torture chamber just to the right of the light switch. Rozzy must have a key to the chamber. We've gotta get it off her to get inside at all. And we've only got five minutes. There are three underground approaches to the torture chamber,' he went on. 'One, you can go down on hands and knees from Rannaldini's study but only if you're a slim build, and that takes nearly twenty minutes. Another passage runs from the chapel and takes ten minutes. That's the route Rozzy'll come back up, once she's slammed the door on Lucy. The third, which I don't imagine Rozzy knows about because it hasn't been used for years, consists of steep steps down from the middle of the maze. Takes about four minutes. The helicopter can drop us on the edge. Those steps come out through a side door into the passage which goes up to the chapel, about twenty yards from the entrance to the torture chamber. If someone', Clive glanced round the helicopter, 'could intercept Rozzy as she came out of the torture chamber and lure her past this entrance, at least one of us could run down the tunnel and switch off the water. Then once we'd relieved her of the key, we could get into the chamber and unlock the debtor's chair.'

'I can see exactly why you were Rannaldini's hired assassin, up to every trick,' snarled Rupert. Ahead he could see the lights of Paradise High Street.

'We'll be there in a minute,' said Clive.

'Tristan's got to lure her out,' announced Gablecross. 'Rozzy's absolutely nuts about him.' Then, turning to Tristan, 'You must wait for her to come out, tell her you love her and you're frantic to get her away from the murderer.'

Tristan, who'd been going round every circle of hell, looked at Gablecross aghast. 'I can't tell Rozzy I love her.' With his track record, the gods would punish him for lies like that by not saving Lucy. 'I couldn't convince her.'

'For Lucy's sake, you bloody well can,' snapped Rupert. 'If you hadn't fired her this morning, none of this would have happened.'

'Rupert's right,' begged Karen. 'If you can tempt her out of the way and get her off her guard by indulging in some serious snogging.'

'Fantasize she's Madame Lauzerte,' said Rupert sarcastically. 'You've had enough practice at screwing geriatrics.'

'Shut up,' howled Tristan, seizing and violently shaking Rupert's shoulders so the helicopter lurched as it started its descent.

'Pack it in, you two,' ordered Gablecross.

Narrowly missing the floodlit spire of All Saints, Paradise, flying over sleeping cottages in the high street, and Hermione's house with its tall chimneys, Rupert followed the silver ribbon of the river Fleet and swung left at the glimmer of Rannaldini's lake. Tristan gave a groan at the thought of all that water pouring into Lucy's gasping, choking throat. There was the black dartboard of the maze, with policemen like ants closing in from all sides.

'D'you know the way to the centre?' asked Tristan, as he and Clive jumped down from the helicopter.

'If I concentrate.'

A minute later, they had pounded down a yew corridor slap into a dead end.

'For Christ's sake,' yelled Tristan, doing a U-turn.

For a moment, as they backtracked, Clive lost his nerve, then the helicopter was overhead and a hovering Rupert was aiming a spotlight and leading them to the left and then to the right, backwards, forwards, sideways, across. Perhaps it was God's hand guiding them as well, because Tristan never stopped praying. Then, miraculously, the honeyed scent of philadelphus swept over them. They had reached the centre of the maze.

This time Clive's memory didn't fail. As he kicked the stone alcove three times, it swung sideways and darkness loomed. They could smell damp, rotting wood and weed.

'The steps are very slippery,' warned Clive.

It was like a yew corridor without any ceiling. Clive led the way. Tristan was as soaked with icy sweat as from the dripping walls of the stairway he kept crashing against. Often he was too hasty, and felt himself falling against the snake-like caress of Clive's leather suit. The steps seemed greased with goose fat.

'I haven't got a head for depths,' he confessed, as he battled against an ancient phobia of being trapped underground: an irate nanny had locked him once in a dark cellar.

Lucy was what mattered. Oh, please, God. But it was to Hades, God of the Underworld, he should be praying. Please spare my Eurydice. He kept imagining the water choking Lucy until her generous heart gave out and he'd never be able to tell her how much he loved her. He was losing his balance, about to stumble down into the darkness. Clive was far too slight to support his weight. Then, suddenly, they'd reached level ground and collapsed, thankfully, against a solid oak door.

Behind them, they could faintly hear Gablecross on his mobile. 'Uniform boys have located the entrance to the torture chamber from the lakeside,' he was telling Karen. 'They can't see any sign yet of water being sucked inside.'

'Perhaps Rozzy hasn't left?' whispered Karen hopefully.

'Open the door into the passage *now*,' Gablecross hissed down the stairs to Clive. 'We may be able to pre-empt her.'

The door was warped by damp and opened inwards, after a lot of tugging and kicking.

'Turn right,' muttered Clive to Tristan. 'The passage kinks sharply to the left. Lurk behind there until she comes out.'

Tristan had never known such darkness: the total blindness of the Grand Inquisitor. No-one dared shine a torch in case Rozzy saw a light ahead as she came out, but she must hear the thunderous crashing of his heart as he edged along the wall.

Once she emerged, he mustn't betray his fear. His mouth tasted as acid as a rotten lemon, he was trembling violently, he reeked of sweat, his knees were jumping frantically as he positioned himself round the rocky bend. However could he act well enough to convince Lucy's murderer that he loved her? Then he was aware of dim light. Whipping round he heard a clang of steel, a heavy door creaking shut, a switch being flicked on, followed by arpeggios of crazy laughter. He nearly turned and fled.

'Now!' hissed Clive.

'Rozzy?'

'Who's there?' called out a high, terrified voice.

Tristan could see the outline of a cloaked figure.

'Rozzy, it's me.' His voice, sounding surprisingly deep and strong, seemed to echo round the dripping walls.

But before he could add 'Tristan', he heard a bang and felt an agonizing pain in his right shoulder. She had shot him. Reeling back from the shock, he crashed against the side of the tunnel cracking his head.

'Me, Tristan,' he gasped. Then, righting himself, he stumbled forward. 'Rozzy, are you OK? I've been so worried.'

'Tristan?' whispered Rozzy in horror. 'I thought you were the police.'

As he came towards her, she saw blood seeping into his pale grey shirt. 'Oh, my poor darling,' she cried. 'I'm so sorry, I must bandage that wound.'

She looked so normal, and unusually beautiful, her big eyes so full of concern and tenderness that, for a fleeting moment, Tristan thought they'd all been imagining things. Then, through the dimness, he saw the switch to the right of the door.

'How could I have hurt you?' moaned Rozzy.

'It's nothing.' Tristan moved towards her, then, taking a deep breath, 'The murderer's on the loose. I was so scared for you.'

If he rammed her against the torture chamber door and kissed her, he could surreptitiously reach up and turn off the switch. Unfortunately, she was bearing down on him. 'Let me wrap this round your shoulder,' she tugged off her red feather boa, 'till we reach the outside world.'

As she coiled it round his neck, hanging on to the two ends to contain him, he nearly bolted.

'I've come to take you to the wrap party.' He forced himself to sound light-hearted. 'Everyone's waiting.'

'There's no hurry,' said Rozzy coyly. 'Orphée.'

'There is, because you're in danger.' He seized her left hand and found it empty. The gun must be in her bag, or concealed in the folds of Rannaldini's cloak. 'I love you.' Tristan crossed his fingers as he led her up the tunnel.

'I always knew you did, darling,' said Rozzy adoringly.

As they passed the entrance where Clive and the others were lurking, Rozzy stopped and so did Tristan's heart. 'Look at me,' she insisted.

'Orpheus wasn't allowed to look at Eurydice.' Tristan tried to sound playful.

'Take me away,' begged Rozzy, 'to Paris and then your house in the Tarn. I want to meet Aunt Hortense and see where you grew up.'

If he got his arms round her, he could clamp hers down, but he didn't know whether his right arm was strong enough – it didn't seem to belong to him any more. He felt increasingly dizzy and the feather boa was tightening terrifyingly round his neck. But as he lured her round to the right, he could see Clive stealing, like a ghost, out of the side entrance.

'What's that noise?' she asked sharply.

'Probably a rat – oh, Rozzy.'

She jumped as she heard another footstep, but as she spun round, Tristan grabbed her. 'You look so young.' He took her face between his hands.

'You don't still love Claudine?'

'Of course not,' breathed Tristan. 'I just never in a million years presumed someone as beautiful as you could love me back.'

Utterly repelled, he felt her scrawny fingers, entrapping his neck like a sea anemone, the bumpy ribs, the razor-sharp collarbones, the slack breasts beneath the grey chiffon. By contrast her tongue was bone hard as she rammed it between his lips almost down his throat, and rubbed her body feverishly against his. The sour milk stench of her breath was enough to make him gag.

'Make love to me, Tristan.'

With Lucy drowning? he thought in fury.

Then he felt her clawing fingers tightening round his neck and her big black bag, which was still hanging from her arm, pressing against his chest.

'You're in danger,' he mumbled, dickering as to whether to grab the bag. 'Lucy'll take out anyone I love.'

'Lucy's taken care of.' Rozzy smiled beatifically, and Tristan found himself looking into the eyes of true madness, as Rozzy went into hysterical laughter. 'We needn't worry about Lucy any more.'

To stop her laughter, Tristan kissed her again, on and on as, in frenzied rage, he grabbed her arms forcing them behind her back, gripping her tighter and tighter, until the pain in his shoulder became unbearable.

'Let me go, darling.' Rozzy was laughing and struggling.

Christ, she was strong, as she bucked and writhed against him. He was going to black out, he couldn't hold on any longer.

Then, mercifully, he was aware of shadowy figures approaching and seizing her. But Rozzy had wriggled out of their grasp.

'Bastard! You double-crossed me!' She was ranting, screaming, foaming at the mouth, lunging forward to plunge her teeth into Tristan's chest, trying to knee him in the groin and claw his face, as Rupert and Gablecross dragged her off. It took all their strength to yank her arms back, so Karen could clip on the handcuffs. 'Gotcha!' yelled Gablecross.

As Rozzy's bag fell to the floor, Karen leapt forward and up-ended it. Out fell gun, mobile, mask and wig. Karen pounced on a huge set of keys, glinting in the torchlight.

'Which one belongs to the torture chamber, Rozzy?' she asked gently.

'I'm not telling you,' giggled Rozzy. 'You're too late. The randy bitch'll be dead by now.'

She went into more crazed laughter, which turned into a howl of agony as Rupert seized her arm. 'I'll break it unless you tell us.'

'I can take pain, you bastard, *aaaaaaah*!' screamed Rozzy. 'It's the purple Yale. Christ, let me go!'

'And to open the inside door?' With no compunction, Rupert applied more pressure.

'Ouch! Oh, no!' Rozzy's head fell forward. 'It's the steel one splashed with blue paint,' she whispered.

Rupert raced down the passage to where Clive and Bernard were trying to break down the door. Uniformed police were pouring down the stairs. Everyone was yelling instructions.

Tristan stumbled after Rupert, his shirt totally red now.

Rupert fumbled with the key. 'Give me some light, for Christ's sake.'

Four torch beams found the keyhole.

The door swung open, and a blast of icy wind from the lake slapped them in the face. All they could see in the dim light was churning rising water.

'We're too late,' thought Karen in despair.

Reaching past her, Clive pressed the button. As

Tristan jumped down into the pit, turning the water red with his blood, the manacles sprang back and he groped and found Lucy and with his last ounce of strength dragged her to the surface.

How white and still and dreadfully cold she was.

'Oh, please don't die,' he groaned.

Next moment Rupert, Karen and Clive were in the water helping him lift her on to the bed.

Trying to remember his first aid, Tristan dragged himself up beside her, fighting to stop his lips trembling as he put them on her frozen ones. Oh, God, that the first kiss he gave her should be the last. He tried to breathe in, then collapsed, covering her torn pink dress with blood.

'I'll do it,' said Rupert, gently shoving Tristan out of the way. 'You've lost too much blood.'

'Get the fucking paramedics!' shouted Gablecross.

They all watched, frantically willing and praying, as Rupert breathed in and out.

'Come on, Lucy, don't give up on us,' pleaded Karen.

But after a minute or two, Rupert stopped and for a moment rested his head on Lucy's shoulder. 'I think it's too late.'

'Let me have a go.' Tristan lurched forward, slumped against Lucy, his arms round her. 'Lucy darling, don't leave me, I love you.'

Suddenly she gave a shudder and a gulp, then water gushed out of her mouth, as the paramedics stormed in.

'She's going to be OK, lad.' Gablecross patted Tristan's hand as he was lifted on to a stretcher. 'We'd better get you both to hospital. Of the two of you I'd say you were in the worst shape.'

'Well done.' Briefly Rupert squeezed Tristan's thigh. 'Was Sarah Bernhardt one of your relations?'

'Probably,' said Tristan, and passed out.

*   *   *

'Rosalind Pringle,' said Gablecross, 'I am arresting you for the murders of Roberto Rannaldini and Beatrice Johnson, and the attempted murders of Lucy Latimer, Tabitha Lovell and Tristan de Montigny.' But as he reeled off the names, he had an eerie feeling that the murderer had vanished, and he'd never be able to get a conviction on this discreet, gently smiling, suddenly old lady, who kept nodding and saying, 'Where's Tristan? I mustn't be late – he's taking me to tea with Aunt Hortense.'

84

It was six in the morning when Gablecross received a summons from on high. He had just spent two hours debriefing Lucy and steeled himself now for a mega-bollocking and probably the sack. A couple of hounds catching the fox on their own may be very clever, but it doesn't endear the Master, the whips, the horses and particularly the rest of the pack to them.

'Your behaviour has been utterly reprehensible,' thundered Chief Constable Swallow.

'Tim-Going-Out-On-A-Fucking-Limb again,' shouted Gerald Portland. 'Why didn't you and DC Needham keep in touch?'

'There wasn't time, Guv'nor, and you mustn't blame DC Needham. I chewed her out for not being as good as Charlie but she did brilliantly. She discovered Rozzy had been taking vast sums off Lucy for private treatment for non-existent cancer. Then we found Rozzy's cache – that was a piece of work. There DC Needham discovered some photographs cut to shreds. When she pieced them together, she found they were three passport photographs of Rozzy Pringle. She'd used the fourth on Lucy Latimer's passport, so her DNA profile on Rannaldini and Beattie would show up as Lucy's.

'She confesses most of it on this tape.' Gablecross chucked it down on the table. Then, seeing both Portland and Swallow still looking boot-faced and knowing their weakness for a title, he added, 'It was on Lady Griselda's machine. Karen's still debriefing Lucy. We wanted to get in touch, sir, but at the end we were only playing with minutes.'

'How's Rozzy Pringle?'

'Dagenham.'

'What?'

'Two stops up from Barking.'

'You ought to be fired and probably prosecuted,' said Portland, after Swallow had bustled off importantly into the next room to take a telephone call. 'You left Tabitha Lovell unprotected at Rutminster General. You risked the lives of Tristan de Montigny and Rupert Campbell-Black – no bad thing in itself, admittedly – not to mention that little toad Clive.'

'He did brilliantly,' protested Gablecross, 'performed like a trooper. Pity we can't recruit him.'

'How's Montigny?'

'Only a flesh wound, bullet lodged in the muscle. They're operating now. Rozzy Pringle was so bats about him that he was the only one who could lure her out. He did fantastically too.'

'And Lucy Latimer?'

'I wanted to talk to you about her,' said Gablecross. 'She's outwardly OK. In shock, of course, she had a terrible experience, devastated as well that her dog was killed. We don't want the defence to nobble her, and if the press get onto her the whole case will collapse. She's desperate to get away. I said we might be able to arrange a safe-house for her abroad until after the trial.'

In the next room they could hear Swallow's voice rising.

'All right, all right, Mr Campbell-Black, that's entirely up to the Police Promotions Board. I don't care if you do go over my head.

'Jesus, that bastard gets on my wick,' said Swallow, as he returned very red in the face. 'Now where were we?'

Gablecross was so tired he didn't at first take in that,

in their roundabout way, both Swallow and Portland were congratulating him.

'You saved our bacon,' admitted Portland. 'Not sure how much longer we could have gone on spending tax-payers' money.'

'You've done well, Tim. Better go home and put on a clean shirt before the press conference,' said Swallow. 'And I think DC Needham's going to be every bit as good as Charlie.'

It must be tiredness and the fact that the Chief Constable had never called him Tim before but, for a hideous moment, Gablecross thought he was going to cry.

'I absolutely agree, sir,' he muttered.

Tristan came round to find his room full of flowers and sunlight. His shoulder throbbed, but he could move his arm, and the diamorphine was keeping any pain at bay. Sergeant Gablecross was his first visitor, carrying a bunch of purple chrysanthemums and a brown parcel.

'Where's Lucy?' demanded Tristan. 'Is she all right? I want to see her.'

'She's being debriefed,' said Gablecross carefully. 'She's very anxious you should read this.' He put the packet on the bedside table. 'She handed it over to Rozzy for safe-keeping when she was arrested. Rozzy was intending to burn it. We'll need it as evidence later. The sister said I mustn't stay long. We'll take a statement when you're feeling stronger.'

How beautiful the boy was, he thought enviously. Even when he was running a temperature, the dark hair falling over the white forehead and the flush on the hollowed cheeks reminded you of black trees and snow warmed by a winter sunset.

Tristan, slumped back on his pillows, was constantly reminded of the horror of Lucy's inert frozen body. 'Are you sure she's OK, or as OK as she can be? Is James really dead?'

'We think so. Rupert's going to advertise, so are we.'

'I must get her a puppy.' Tristan turned fretfully to the package. '"Private and Confidential". I suppose that means everyone at Rutminster Police Station's had a look.'

As soon as Gablecross had left a 'Do Not Disturb' sign on the door, Tristan opened the package.

The enclosed letter was headed 'Hôtel de Ville, St Malo', dated 16 July, and smelt faintly of the disturbing, overtly sexy scent Lucy had worn the morning he'd sacked her. Tristan shuddered at the memory.

Dear Tristan [what kind, generous handwriting Lucy had!]

I hope I bring you tidings of very great joy, but the facts are so overwhelming I thought you'd prefer to take them in when you're on your own. Although Wolfie and I can answer any questions as best we can later.

Your aunt Hortense swore to your dad she would never tell the truth, but in the end was persuaded that promises should occasionally be broken.

You truly are a Montigny, Tristan, and Étienne was speaking the truth on his deathbed rambling on about your father being your grandfather. The problem was, Rannaldini got the wrong grandad. Étienne was your grandfather, Laurent your father.

Tristan slumped back against the pillows, reeling from the shock. He read on incredulously:

So in a way Étienne was Philip II and Laurent Posa, a soldier of noble lineage who hated staying idle, so he stirred up trouble in Chad, and got blown up for trying to right wrongs. On the other hand, he was also Carlos because he fell madly in love with your mum. She was just back from a disastrous honeymoon with Étienne, where she'd found she couldn't bear him near her. Laurent came home all suntanned and handsome. She fell madly in love with him

751

and fell pregnant with you, while Étienne was away painting in Australia.

The paper was shaking so violently, he could hardly read, let alone turn the page.

When Laurent died, all his things were sent back. Love-letters from Delphine, plans for naming the baby Tristan, if it was a boy, plans they would run away together the moment he came out of the army, how Laurent wanted to be there when Delphine broke the news to Étienne because he knew what a temper his father had.

The extraordinary thing is that Don Carlos *must be in your genes, because Étienne's humiliation and heartbreak must have been so like Philip's. You can now understand his animosity and harshness towards you. How would Philip have reacted, if he'd been left to bring up Elisabetta's and Carlos's orphaned son?*

All the letters and photos are here for you and, perhaps most important, a self-portrait painted by Étienne the year you were born, just after he found out about Laurent being your father. I think it must be the saddest, most beautiful and humane painting he ever did. Hortense said he wanted you to have it after his death, so perhaps you could understand and forgive him.

The words swam before Tristan's eyes. The whole thing was too enormous for him to take in. His hands were trembling so much and he was so weak, it was a struggle to open the envelope. Letters and photos cascaded all over the bed. There was Delphine, Christ, she was sweet – not at all like the tawdry temptress of *The Snake Charmer,* and so pretty, despite the ghastly high-heeled boots, square fringe and pastel lipstick of the sixties. There was Laurent, so dashing in his uniform, the ideal Monsieur Droit, and the letters so passionate they burnt the page.

Tristan felt rage welling inside him, as he examined the little pencil drawing of himself as a newborn baby. There was pride in every centimetre. 'Tristan Laurent Blaize, a beautiful boy. One hour old,' Étienne had written on the back.

The self-portrait was in bubble wrap. It was small, fifteen inches by twelve, but an undoubted masterpiece. The tears glittered like Rutshire streams as they flowed down Étienne's wrinkles; all the hurt pride and pain was contained in the narrow eyes and the clenched mouth.

'Papa, Papa,' cried Tristan.

Étienne was still his father, and at last he understood everything. What an absolute shit Laurent must have been. If only he could ring Étienne beyond the grave to tell him how much he loved him.

He lay for a long time listening to the wood pigeons cooing and the distant rumble of traffic. But only when he glanced up at the red plastic bag of blood dripping strength and vitality back into his body, did he realize the full implications. He was a Montigny, of the blood, if on the wrong side of the blanket. He was nothing to do with Maxim. He could marry and have children with whom he chose.

Giddy with happiness, he glanced at the bottom of Lucy's letter. 'With all my love', she had written.

There was a knock at the door. Ignoring the 'Do Not Disturb' sign, Wolfie walked in. He was grey with fatigue, but it would have been impossible to find anyone looking happier.

'How's Tab?' asked Tristan.

'Seriously wonderful,' sighed Wolfie. 'Oh, Tristan, I am so lucky.' Then, with typical lack of ego, 'But how are *you* feeling? I hear you saved Lucy's life.'

'You and Lucy give me back mine,' said Tristan, pointing to the letters and photographs strewn over the bed.

Wolfie picked up Étienne's self-portrait. Taking it to

the window he whistled. 'I didn't see that. Christ, it's powerful – Christ-like in a way, carrying that weight of suffering in one face.'

'I can't take it in. Tell me what happened.'

'Lucy did it. She put up with a hell of a lot of stick from Aunt Hortense and eventually won her over. We were summoned back as we were leaving and allowed to go into Laurent's room – which reminds me, I must find out what's happened to Papa's Gulf.'

'Lucy did all that for me?' said Tristan, in bewilderment.

'She wanted you to find happiness.'

'And I fire her because I was furious she let me down, and I back off even last night, because I didn't think . . . I must find her.' Reaching up, he kept his finger on the bell.

'Where is Lucy Latimer?' he demanded, as a fleet of alarmed nurses rushed in.

When he discovered Lucy had been discharged several hours ago, he went berserk, panic-stricken she was dead. He'd forgotten to salute that single magpie that flew past the window just now; he was being punished for pretending to be in love with Rozzy. He was about to pull out all the drips, and leap out of bed, when Gablecross and Rupert came running in.

'Where the fuck's Lucy?' he snarled.

'You must persuade him to stay,' said a worried sister. 'He's running a high temperature and he's lost so much blood.'

'Lucy wanted out, Tristan.' Gablecross sat down on the bed. 'She had a terrifying ordeal. And if the press or defence get hold of her the whole case could collapse. We've found her a safe-house.'

'How can she be safe without me?'

'Very easily,' drawled Rupert.

'Shut up,' snapped Gablecross. 'She'll be quite OK,' he added, prising himself out of the stranglehold of

754

Tristan's good arm. 'But she was insistent that no-one should be given the forwarding address.'

'For how long?' whispered Tristan in horror.

'Nine months, perhaps a year.'

Tristan slumped back in bed, the picture of desolation.

'This is crazy, I need to thank her. I need her.'

'Best thanks you can give her at the moment', said Rupert, who was reading about his heroic exploits in the *Daily Express*, 'is to leave her alone.'

'But I am in a different position now. I thought I was Maxim's bastard child without any money, a maimed being who could not have children.'

'You've hardly got a good track record.' Rupert turned to page three, smirking over the headline: 'Rupert's Kiss of Life Saves Lucy.'

'But she must feel something for me to have gone to France.'

'She was freeing you for Tab,' said Rupert bluntly. 'She didn't know anything about Claudine Lauzerte. That knocked her for six. If I were you, pretty boy, I'd get on with what you're good at, editing our film.'

At that moment an excited nurse popped her head round the door. 'I know you're not taking any calls, Tristan, but it's Claudine Lauzerte on the line.'

'We'll leave you to her,' said Rupert, and sauntered out.

In the corridor, he turned to Gablecross. 'Let the young puppy sweat. Let him find out he's really missing her.'

Rupert was extremely happy. Peppy Koala was favourite for the St Leger. He was convinced he had masterminded Lucy's rescue and produced what was going to be an incredibly successful film. Outside the window, a sea of press and television cameras filled the car park right up to the door.

He was delighted that Xavier had taken a terrific shine

to Karen. This afternoon they were going off with Bianca to choose a puppy for Taggie's birthday.

Rupert was also enchanted with his future son-in-law. All that was needed was to organize a quickie divorce for Tab. Helen didn't seem wildly keen on the idea, she'd always felt Wolfie was *her* admirer and that it was all too close to home. Tab's grandfather, Eddie, wasn't wild about it either.

'How can you marry a Kraut, darling? I spent half the war fighting them in the Middle East.'

The only cloud on the horizon for Rupert was that Bluey, his first jockey, had yesterday announced that he was going to live in America, having conveniently fallen in love with a trainer's daughter. But as one door closes . . .

When Isa Lovell had walked unannounced into his office at Penscombe that morning, Rupert had reached for his gun, which was back in his desk drawer. But to his amazement, Isa held out his hand.

'This feud's gone on too long. I'm sorry I fucked up your daughter because I hated you so much. But it looks as though she's found the right bloke at last. I came to say my father's been forced, for medical reasons, to jack in the yard. He and Mum'll need supporting, so I wondered if you'd like me to come and ride for you.'

It took a lot to silence Rupert. Finally he said coldly:

'We're almost entirely flat here now.'

'I know,' said Isa, 'but yesterday I tried out a mare who could win the National and the Gold Cup.'

Rupert stared at Isa's pale, impassive gypsy face, so like Jake's twenty-five years ago. It must have taken courage to come here. Getting to his feet, he took Isa's hand. 'I'll have to check with Wolfie and Tab, but I've never turned down a good offer or one that might irritate my first wife. And I reckon if you and I joined forces no-one in the world could beat us.'

'Except, perhaps, Little Cosmo,' said Isa drily.

Bernard comforted Tristan the most by putting things in perspective.

'When Étienne sent Laurent into his own regiment, hoping it would straighten the boy out, he asked me to keep an eye on him. I tried but Laurent was bent on bucking the system. They were torturing prisoners in Chad, Laurent hit a senior officer across the mess and there were persistent rumours of anti-French activities. Of course, there was outrage at the time that he'd been taken out by his own side but I think it would have happened sooner or later.'

'I hate Laurent and my mother for what they did to Papa.' Tristan's face was haggard.

'Laurent was the best-looking lad I ever saw,' admitted Bernard. 'He was your father's most adored son, the true *favori du roi*, which made the betrayal much worse. He had all Posa's charisma and courage.'

'And his ruthlessness,' snapped Tristan. 'Pretty shabby cuckolding your own father.'

'He was terribly young, only twenty, and she was sixteen. I loved Laurent,' confessed Bernard. 'I held him in my arms as he lay dying and he said, "Look after my son."'

'So you knew?' said Tristan in amazement. 'That's why you came out of the army, and went into films, and became my first assistant.' His eyes filled with tears. 'You've been my guardian angel,' he mumbled, grabbing Bernard's hand.

'Guardian angels don't have brick-red faces and black moustaches.'

There was a pause. Tristan longed to pour his heart out about Lucy, but felt under the circumstances it was tactless.

'I'm sorry about Rozzy.'

Bernard shrugged. 'I've got a family at home. They've never seemed more precious.'

*   *   *

The Shaven Crown was packed out with members of the Inner Cabinet getting drunk. Gablecross usually felt sad at the end of a murder, even if they'd caught the criminal: it didn't bring back the victims. Beattie had probably had a mother who was fond of her. But it was hard to feel upset about a monster like Rannaldini.

'Well done, Karen.' Gablecross patted her arm. 'My second Charlie.'

Karen's face lit up. But embarrassed, because she felt so colossally honoured, she immediately changed the subject. 'Poor Rozzy seemed such a nice lady. What made her do it?'

'Low self-esteem. Couldn't hack not being loved by everyone. Kill anyone who slighted her. The exposure made her feel important, the centre of attention. She's a singer, after all. Then she got a taste for it. In the end she'd have killed Tristan because he couldn't have reciprocated her love. I'll drive you home,' he went on, seeing Karen suppress a yawn.

It was such a beautiful night. Moths danced in the headlamps. Shooting stars careered across a drained blue sky. The scent of limes drifted through the car windows. Gablecross had dropped Karen off and was turning off the Paradise Road towards Eldercombe. He was just congratulating himself on being home early for Margaret for once, so they could discuss Diane's eighteenth birthday party, which he could easily pay for now, when he heard singing:

'She'll be coming round the mountain when she comes, She'll be coming round the mountain when she comes, Singing ay yay yippy, ay yay yippy . . .'

Some nutter was turning up his stereo at full blast. Next moment a huge maroon Roller roared past, shattering the peace of the evening.

Gablecross gave chase. But every time the road widened enough for him to catch up, the Roller's driver put his foot down, and the laughter and singing grew more raucous. He finally managed to block them in as they swung into River House's drive. Inside he found Hermione and Sexton.

'"She'll be coming round the mountain—" Sergeant Gablecross!' cried Hermione, in amazement. 'We thought you were our good friend the Chief Constable going home.'

Gablecross got out his notebook, and was just pondering whether to book them for speeding, drunk-driving, not wearing seat-belts, or creating a nuisance when Sexton said:

'Come in and celebrate.'

'You both appear to have been celebrating for several hours, sir.'

'Indeed,' Hermione bowed, 'and with cause, Timothy. We want you to be the first to know. We are with child. A sibling for Little Cosmo.'

Gablecross hoped it would be a little brother, or Cosmo would certainly put her on the game.

'We've got a smashin' bottle of Krug in the fridge,' said Sexton cosily.

'Bubbly for the bobby, bubbly for the bobby,' chortled Hermione, as she weaved up the drive.

Gablecross sighed. He obviously wasn't going to get home to Margaret for a while.

85

In a mad frenzy of superstition, Tristan locked himself away editing twenty-four hours a day. Only when *Don Carlos* was finished and an unqualified triumph would he feel worthy of seeking out Lucy. It was an agonizing task because every frame with people in it was a testament to her genius.

How could she have made his cast so beautiful yet so full of character? Hermione looked not a day over twenty-five, Flora disturbingly boyish, Baby so pale, wan and fond, Chloe so languorously seductive, Mikhail so noble, Granny so unrelentingly evil, Alpheus so tortured yet kingly.

'She's actually made that prat look like a gent,' observed Rupert, who popped in most days and got frightfully excited over the special effects. Tristan's filming of the grey, writhing traveller's joy in winter suggested a wonderfully ghostly Charles V.

On each visit, Tristan begged Rupert for information about Lucy's whereabouts. Every day he telephoned Gablecross but met the same stonewalling refusal. Too much money was invested in the trial to allow any slip-up.

Another reason Tristan worked through the night was the bad dreams that racked him if he tried to sleep, of Lucy drowning in a sea of blood, of the painting of Cleopatra and the asp in Buckingham Palace – except it was Lucy's face not Cleopatra's from which the colour was draining.

Having finished editing, Tristan had to bite his nails until he showed the final cut to the press on 11 January and went into even deeper despair that the whole thing was junk.

'You're too close to it,' said Wolfie soothingly.

'But will the man in the street like it?'

'You couldn't get more philistine than my future father-in-law,' confessed Wolfie, 'and he's mad about it. Admittedly, he's convinced he directed the entire film. I even heard him singing "Morte de Posa" in the bath the other morning.'

But Tristan wasn't to be reassured. He was always cold, always miserable. He dreamt of crumpets, big log fires and Lucy winning the mothers' race. The only glimmer of cheer was that *The Lily in the Valley* had been nominated many times over in the incredibly prestigious Academia Awards in Edinburgh, which boded well for the Oscars in February. It was widely rumoured that Claudine Lauzerte would be flying up to Scotland for the ceremony. If so, she must have been tipped off she'd won Best Actress. She wouldn't put her head on the block otherwise.

January 11 and 12 were a hellish two days for Tristan: carrying the coffin at Aunt Hortense's funeral on the Tuesday morning, flying to London for the première and press screening of *Don Carlos*, followed by interviews, which would probably go on all night, with a breakfast script conference for *Hercule* first thing Wednesday morning, then off to Edinburgh for the Academia Awards ceremony.

Tristan arrived at the première in Leicester Square in dark glasses so no-one could see his reddened eyes. He had been icily in control during Hortense's funeral, and only given way to helpless weeping when he'd reached the sanctuary of his room at the Savoy. He had grown increasingly close to her in his frequent visits to Montvert in the last six months, as they had unlocked his past together. Hortense was also his last link with Lucy. He arrived at the première alone, which fuelled the gossip-mongers, who knew he was meeting Claudine tomorrow. Leicester Square, swarming with police keeping back the huge crowds and the paparazzi, was also horribly reminiscent of Valhalla. He longed to bolt into the cinema.

Alas, the red carpet had already been appropriated by Hermione, resplendent in extremely low-cut purple velvet, arm in arm with Sexton, posing for the huge pack of cameras and press photographers, determined even the *Rutminster Echo* should have the chance of a decent picture.

'Hermione.' 'Hermione to me.' 'Big smile, Hermione.' 'Who's your date, Hermione?'

'Why, didn't you know? It's Sexton Kemp, our producer.'

'Look this way, Sexton.' 'To me, Sexton.' 'Sexton.'

Sexton was in heaven. Tristan was going through the roof.

'"Whenever I feel afraid, I hold my cock erect,"' sang a voice in Tristan's ear. '"And whistle a happy tune." Can't you give the old cow direction to move on?'

It was Baby, straight out of an Australian summer, his bronzed beauty enhanced by a dinner jacket with black satin facings, worn with a black silk shirt and a satin bow-tie.

The press were going nuts trying to identify him.

'They won't have to ask after tonight,' said Tristan, as they finally fought their way in. 'Everyone will know who you are.'

More than can be said for you, thought Baby. Tristan had lost so much weight he was almost unrecognizable.

Outside, the press was going into further frenzy, as a blond couple emerged from an orange Lamborghini.

'Must be Chloe Catford,' said the *Mirror*.

'It's Tabitha Campbell-Black,' said the *Sun*. 'Isn't she fucking gorgeous?'

'She's Tabitha Lovell now,' said the *Mail*, 'about to be Rannaldini. She's marrying Wolfie next month. He's the hunk beside her, and here's Rupert.'

A great cheer went up from the crowd.

'Been saving any more lives, Rupe?' 'Put your arm round Taggie.' 'A bit happier.' 'To me, Rupe.' 'Can we have all four of you for a family group?'

'That's quite enough,' snapped an extremely uptight Rupert, shoving them all inside.

After that people arrived in a great rush: Alpheus and Cheryl just on speaking terms, Chloe ravishing in Prussian blue taffeta, Flora and George flashing wedding rings and wall-to-wall smiles for the photographers, Mikhail and Lara in splendid form, until Mikhail caught sight of Alpheus, turned as green as a cooking apple and fled to the gents.

'Russians don't have the big-match temperament,' said Alpheus dismissively.

'Bollocks,' murmured Baby, grabbing two glasses of champagne and handing one to Chloe. 'Mikhail's gone to whip off those priceless diamond cufflinks, which he's just remembered he nicked from Alpheus during the recording. He'll have pickpocketed another pair by the end of the screening. Doesn't Tristan look appalling?'

'Probably sick with nerves,' said Chloe. 'I know I am. The advance publicity's been so overwhelming there's bound to be a backlash. Oh, here's Simone and Griselda who's wearing a dinner jacket. Gosh, they look blissful, and so do Granny and Giuseppe, although Giuseppe's just cannoned off that pillar.'

'Pissed already,' said Baby. 'Who's that stunning guy with Helen?'

'Lysander's father, David Hawkley,' whispered Flora. 'He's a headmaster, a classical scholar and rather glam in a geriatric way.'

'Perfect for Helen because he's just got his K,' boomed Griselda. 'She loved being Lady Rannaldini, but Lady Hawkley sounds even more kosher. I must say, she looks great.'

'Naturally, I'm in mourning for my late husband,' Helen was telling the *Times* Diary. 'The police are still refusing to let us bury him. Have you met Sir David Hawkley?'

Hermione's great white breasts, meanwhile, were nearly popping out of her low-cut dress in indignation.

'Helen's only wearing black because she knows it suits her,' she hissed to Sexton. 'Purple is the colour of mourning. And have you seen how dreadful Tristan looks?'

Everyone was bemoaning the fact that Lucy had been spirited away by the police and would miss the fun yet again.

'*Regards*, some colossal stars must have arrived!' Little Simone was jumping to see over the crowds as a white-hot firework display of flashbulbs exploded up the other end of the room.

'They certainly have.' Griselda lifted her up to have a look. 'It's DS Gablecross and DC Needham.'

'She looks stunning,' raved Simone, 'and the pretty woman with them must be Madame Gablecross.'

'And there's Abby and Viking,' giggled Flora. 'They keep waking their baby up with a torch in the middle of the night to see if it's OK. Must be rather like the Nuremberg trials. Oh, look at my George blushing because Alexei Nemerovsky's remembered him from the gala two years ago. Nemerovsky's Marcus Campbell-Black's boyfriend,' she added to Griselda and Simone. 'And there's Marcus.' Belting across the room, Flora fell into her old friend's arms.

'Goodness, you look well,' they cried in unison.

'I'm so pleased we were asked and not Gerry Portland and the Chief Constable,' muttered Karen. 'It's

764

Detective Sergeant Timothy Gablecross, Mrs Margaret Gablecross and Detective Constable Karen Needham,' she happily told the photographer, who had produced a notebook. 'Nice to see someone, rather than us, scribbling things down. Who's it for?'

'*Tatler*,' said the photographer.

Karen glanced at the Gablecrosses and went off into peals of laughter. 'Portland and the Chief really will fire us now.'

'Any information on Rozzy Pringle's trial, Sarge?' asked the *Sun*.

'Only that it's coming up at the end of April,' said Gablecross firmly.

It was such a jolly party, most people didn't feel nervous until they spilled into the dimly lit cinema.

'How's Rozzy?' Simone whispered to Karen.

'Very, very mad now.'

Tristan, Rupert and Taggie, who'd taken refuge in a side room, slid into their seats at the last moment.

'I'm so nervous for Uncle Tristan,' muttered Simone, catching sight of his grey, frozen face as the lights dimmed.

But she needn't have worried. From the moment the royal family appeared in the royal box, there was cheering and clapping, followed by screams of delighted recognition, at the shot of Granny, as Gordon Dillon, glowering across at them from the opposite box, then a shiver of excitement as Rannaldini swept in.

God, he was attractive, thought Flora, with a shudder, as he tossed aside his highwayman's cloak, brought down his stick and the orchestra exploded.

Then there was the beautiful shot of the armies meeting on the skyline, merging into the hunt streaming down the valley, which in turn merged into the hard colours of heatwave and the violence of the polo, then back to Baby singing in Cathedral Copse.

'Listen to the clapping,' murmured an amazed Rupert to Taggie, as applause broke out again and again, at

Valhalla in the snow and sunset, at Meredith's red drawing room, at the wonderful horses, at Griselda's inspired costumes, and at the end of every aria, but not for too long, in case something was missed.

And the music sounded glorious. 'Who composed this stuff?' demanded a bigwig from Disney at the end of 'Morte de Posa'. 'Can't we sign him?'

Things were also pepped up by the sub-plot of the murders.

'That was just after Tab's leather was cut,' whispered Griselda to Anne Robinson, as Tab and Baby collided in front of the goal. 'And that was when Tristan was arrested,' she added, as Baby, Chloe and Mikhail squabbled over pistols in the maze.

There was an added frisson as Rozzy made her solo appearance, which Tristan had refused to cut.

'"Do not cry, my dearest friend, do not cry,"' sang Hermione, as she stroked a sobbing Rozzy's face.

'Boo,' hissed Baby from the back stalls. 'I'd watch out, Hermsie, Rozzy's probably got a flick-knife hidden in the folds of that skirt.'

There was a long, horrified silence, followed by howls of laughter. There was laughter, too, when Sharon chewed up Alpheus's slippers.

Tristan had been apprehensive about the nude scenes. But they were so magically filmed and lit, so genuinely erotic, and so wonderfully woven into the fantasies of the characters, that everyone loved and clapped them.

Roars of applause and end-of-game whistling, however, greeted Hermione's bonk with Alpheus, and at one moment eager fans started singing, 'England, England,' in time to her bobbing bottom.

'One *is* more popular than the other singers,' whispered a gratified Hermione to Sexton.

But the audience needed these brief moments of laughter to relieve the heartbreak of the story and the horrors of the *auto da fe*. All round the cinema people were hiding their faces as the executioners set fire to the piles of newspaper beneath the heretics.

Tab, who loathed classical music and had intended to neck in the back stalls with Wolfie, except when Sharon or the horses came on, had watched every second.

'Daddy keeps crying,' she murmured to Wolfie. 'Normally he only cries in *Lassie* or *The Incredible Journey.*'

Wolfie was simply dying with pride, because despite the feuds, the tensions and even the murders, Tristan had produced the most beautiful and thrilling film he had ever seen.

The two hours seemed to flash by. Carlos and Elisabetta had bidden their poignant farewells. Then Carlos was led off by Charles V, leaving Elisabetta, looking very like Princess Diana, to face the paparazzi lining up with their long lenses like a firing squad, until she fell to the ground riddled with bullets. Then the paparazzi became the Inquisition in their black habits with Valhalla's four massive triangular cypresses echoing them along the skyline, cutting briefly to Rannaldini on the rostrum, handsome head thrown back, eyes closed, bringing the music to a triumphant close.

There was total, total silence. But as the end titles rolled up, before the lights went on, the cinema exploded. Hugs were exchanged, hands clasped, cheeks kissed, everyone was embracing, jumping up and down, cheering their heads off, as though a war or lottery had been won.

It was no longer a question of whether *Carlos* was going to be a hit, but how much bigger it was going to be than anything in years.

'I must go and congratulate Tristan,' cried Tab, as everyone surged into the ballroom next door. 'He looked like one of his own ghosts earlier. Oh, I wish Lucy was here.'

'No-one is to ask questions about the murders. It's all *sub judice*,' Hype-along was frantically telling the press as they fell on the bar and the food.

Oscar, Valentin and Sylvestre were already getting plastered.

'Well done, well done, *mes amis*,' said Dupont, the Montignys' lawyer, kissing each of them, most uncharacteristically, on both cheeks. 'What a film! Étienne couldn't not be proud of Tristan after that. I must get hold of a tape to show his brothers, but I'd like to tell Tristan personally how much I enjoyed it.'

Tristan's brothers were livid, added Dupont, lowering his voice, because Aunt Hortense, in reverse ratio to Étienne, had left her entire spare quarter to stray dogs and Tristan.

'In his present crazy mood,' sighed Valentin, 'some might say the two were indistinguishable. Where the hell ees he? *Merde alors!* Leetle Cosmo just march in with Pushy Galore. Perhaps he make her next Lady Rannaldini after all.'

The roar of the party and the Friendship Duet pouring out of the speakers made it difficult to make oneself heard.

'Tristan's portrayed the press as so irredeemably bloody,' shouted the *Independent*. 'We'll have to be nice about his picture to redeem ourselves.'

Gordon Dillon, on the other hand, was tickled pink to be portrayed as himself. The *Scorpion* was going to do a big feature, he told Granny, immediately inviting him to lunch in the boardroom.

'Only if Giuseppe can taste the food and drink first,' said Granny drily.

'No chance of your bringing that Lucy Latimer as well?' asked Gordon Dillon foxily.

There was no doubt that Baby had stolen the show.

'What are you doing next?' asked the *Guardian*.

'Fat Franco's broken a rib falling out of someone else's bed,' drawled Baby, 'so I'm taking *Otello* over from him at the Met.'

'Wow, the tenor's Everest,' said *Opera Now* in admiration.

No, thought Baby wistfully, Isa Lovell was the tenor's Everest.

'Did you enjoy shagging Dame Hermione?' asked A. A. Gill.

Alpheus was in ecstasy, with so many charming young women journalists to crinkle his eyes at. He had even hung his dinner jacket over the back of a chair to show off his manly figure. George and Wolfie propped up the bar, getting pissed together, keeping an eye on Flora and Tab in case any journalist asked awkward questions.

'It was the proudest moment of my life', sighed George, 'seeing Tebaldo, sung by Flora Hungerford, coming up on the credits.'

'Hello, Wolfgang. Hi, George,' called Helen. 'I don't know if you've met Sir David Hawkley.'

'Hello, Mummy.' Tab, breaking away from her circle of press admirers, came rushing over. 'It's so cool. Lynda Lee-Potter's coming down to Penscombe tomorrow to interview me and Sharon. *Dog News* are putting her on the cover, and Celia Haddon is going to make her Pet of the Week in the *Telegraph*.' Then when Helen didn't respond, Tab asked lamely, 'Did you enjoy it?'

'Enormously,' enthused Helen, 'Tristan is so clever, and the acting was wonderful. Even Hermione was better than usual. Meredith's sets were surprisingly effective, so was Lucy's make-up and Valhalla looked stunning. Wolfie's also been a tower of strength,' she continued warmly.

'I thought your little yellow Lab stole the show,' said David Hawkley, smiling at Tab.

'When is your baby due, Dame Hermione?' asked the *Sunday Telegraph*.

'Early April,' Hermione put on a soppy face, 'an Aries bairn.'

'Where are you having it?'

'In the Hippopotamus House at London Zoo,' Baby whispered to Flora, 'David Attenborough's on standby.'

'Where are you staying in New York?' Flora asked him.

'With Rupert's younger brother, Adrian, who owns an art gallery and sounds distinctly promising,' confided Baby. 'So tomorrow might be another good day.'

Looking down from the balcony, Hype-along was gratified to see all his stars still ringed, six deep, with frantically questioning press. But they were all waiting to talk to Tristan. Many of them had held their pages and were desperate to telephone their copy.

'Where the hell is he?' asked Hugh Canning. 'It's like *Hamlet* without the Prince.'

Hype-along tracked down Rupert, on a window-seat, talking to Taggie. 'I love you,' he was saying.

'Sorry to interrupt,' murmured Hype-along, 'but you're the only person Tristan might listen to.'

As Rupert fought his way round the edge of the room, he heard Alpheus saying, 'Now where in hell did I leave my dinner jacket?'

At the bottom of the stairs, he passed Wolfie in deep conversation with Helen. 'As you're going to be my mother-in-law for the rest of your life,' Wolfie was saying icily, 'it would be nice just occasionally if you could tell Tabitha how brilliantly she'd done.'

'That's my boy,' said Rupert, patting him on the back.

Rupert found Tristan in a small office gazing out on the passers-by and the plane trees of Leicester Square. His face was orange from the street lights, his shoulders hunched, his desolation palpable.

'You must be over *la lune*,' said Rupert cheerfully. 'You've made a bloody marvellous flick, and the press are all downstairs waiting to tell you so.'

'What is life to me without her?' said Tristan idly.

Next moment he had grabbed the lapels of Rupert's dinner jacket and thrust him against a filing cabinet with the strength of a madman.

'I've made you a fucking fortune, you bastard. I'm not speaking to anyone until you tell me where Lucy is.'

For a moment, Rupert gazed at him, seeing the depths of his loneliness and despair.

'OK. I'll lean on Gablecross. If he tells me, I'll fax it up to the Caledonian tomorrow.'

86

Melanie, one of the Academia Awards publicity team, very young, pretty and silly, met Tristan at the airport and made him feel that by catching the right flight he had successfully landed on the moon.

'It's *so* good of you to come all this way – may I call you Tristan? We all love *Lily in the Valley* so much – we're going to give away little bottles of Diorissimo by the way. It's fast becoming a cult movie with my generation. Madame Lauzerte', she added reverently, 'has already arrived. She asked me to give you this letter.'

She was obviously so dying to know what was in it that Tristan had to sit with his back to the taxi window to stop her reading over his shoulder.

My darling [Claudine had written],
   I am so longing to see you. It has been such a difficult seven months. Jean-Louis is still adamant he doesn't want a divorce, but he has agreed to turn a blind eye to you and me as long as we are incredibly discreet. I am staying at One Devonshire Gardens in Glasgow tonight. You can join me there this evening, without even having to go through Reception. Call me at the Caledonian as soon as you get in. Your loving Claudine

*   *   *

'Which of us is happy in this world?' quoted Tristan bitterly. 'Which of us has his desire, or having it, is satisfied?'

Seven months ago that letter would have orbited him into the seven hundred and seventy-seventh heaven. Now he felt like a small boy being shunted into care.

Melanie had already seen the ecstatic review Alexander Walker had given *Don Carlos* in the *Evening Standard*. Now she was going on and on, reeling off the celebs and incredibly distinguished academics who'd jetted in from all over the world.

'We feel the Academia is more prestigious than BAFTA or the Césars or even the Oscars. Oh, look at those queues for *Don Carlos* already going round and round and round the cinema.'

They had reached the outskirts of Edinburgh, passing square charcoal-grey houses and sooty gardens where the first daffodils were being blown horizontal by the east wind. There was the cardboard cut-out of the castle against an angry sky of racing clouds.

Tristan gasped at the cold as he jumped out of the taxi, but as he scuttled towards the warmth of the Caledonian, he noticed a beggar slouched on the pavement. An empty whisky bottle lay beside him. In an upside-down tweed cap on the pavement gleamed a few coins. But what caught Tristan's already watering eyes was the total despair of the beggar's dog, a very old, lanky lurcher, whose opaque rheumy eyes gazed into space and who, despite his matted russet coat, was shivering uncontrollably. Thinking how uncomfortable the unrelenting pavement must be for his bony hocks and elbows, Tristan handed the beggar a tenner.

'And bloody well spend it on dog food,' he snapped.

At the sound of Tristan's voice, however, the old dog suddenly pricked up his brown velvet ears and staggered to his feet, making little whining noises in his throat. Next moment his long tail was frantically hitting his sticking-out ribs as he lumbered unsteadily forward.

'James,' croaked Tristan incredulously, 'oh, James,' and dropping to his knees, he hugged the dog until he had red hairs like larch needles all over his smart navy blue overcoat. 'We thought you were dead. Where did you find this dog?' he demanded furiously.

'He's not mine,' said the beggar, in a surprisingly educated voice, hastily pocketing the tenner. 'I think he came from some gypsies,' he added defensively. 'He lives in a squat, but we all borrow him. He looked so thin and pathetic all the passers-by used to fork out for him. Now, he's lost heart and doesn't sell himself, and people tend to walk by in embarrassment. We're going to club together and invest in a cute little terrier. Much better returns.'

Tristan rose to his feet, somehow controlling the fury gathering force inside him. 'Go and drink yourself into an early grave,' he shoved a wad of notes into the beggar's hand, 'and give me that dog.'

'Oh, there you are, Tristan.' It was Melanie, braving the cold again in her twinset, short skirt and very high heels. 'You'll be late for pre-lunch drinks. So many people want to interview you,' she went on, through the streaked blonde hair that blew across her mouth. 'Madame Lauzerte rang again, and this', she handed over a fax with an excited little giggle, 'has just come in from Rupert Campbell-Black. He's a cult figure for our generation too. Tristan. *Tristan!*'

But Tristan and James had vanished into very thin air.

87

Lucy's safe-house was a rescue kennels outside Boston. She had begged Gablecross to find her a place where she could put her terrors and utter anguish in perspective by looking after those even worse off than herself. But nothing had prepared her for the sadness of falling in love with one terrified, often dreadfully maltreated dog after another, nursing it back to health only to find it had to be put down after a few weeks to make way for a newer, younger arrival. She was tormented that she had no idea what had really happened to James and, as her longing for him and Tristan grew more desperate, she felt as in need of rescuing as the dogs, and wished she could plunge the fatal needle into herself.

There were moments of happiness when a dog was rehomed, and the other kennelmaids, who seemed to love their work, sensed her misery and were incredibly kind. But she always refused their invitations to come out in the evenings in case she broke down.

She had had little contact with England since she left. Her family had been told nothing except that she was safe. Karen and Gablecross had been over and were now painstakingly piecing together the prosecution's case, but Rozzy had become so mad it seemed doubtful she would ever be brought to trial.

'But don't feel sorry for her,' warned Gablecross.

'She's an evil, cold-blooded psychopath, and clever enough to be faking.'

Constantly, Lucy woke screaming from nightmares of drowning in the torture chamber, of Tristan covered in blood being dragged away from her and, worst of all, of Rozzy's crazy laughter as, like a tolling bell, she listed Lucy's imperfections, 'Too common, too dull, too ugly, too presumptuous.'

As a result, Lucy had steeled herself not to ask Gablecross about Tristan. By now he must have got it together with Claudine or Tabitha, and moved back to his own world.

She had no access to English or French newspapers, but occasionally came across snippets about *Don Carlos*. Flipping through yesterday's *Boston Globe* during her lunch hour on 13 January, she stumbled on a photograph of Claudine and Tristan.

'Scent of Victory Brings Lovers Together Again,' proclaimed the headline to a story that the French film *The Lily in the Valley* was tipped to sweep the boards at the prestigious Academia Awards that evening, which would be broadcast on PBS the following night.

Looking at Tristan's young, happy face as he gazed so proudly down at Claudine, Lucy gave a wail of misery. She had been given a new name, Linda Gilham, a new passport and a new social-security number. Why couldn't someone provide her with a new heart? As she stumbled out into the yard, dogs everywhere started barking their heads off, scrabbling against the wire fencing.

'Oh, shut up,' screamed Lucy, then, knowing she'd been horrible, ran forward to stick her fingers through the wire to be nuzzled and frantically licked.

Like a vicious cancer, her longing for Tristan had grown more unbearable every day. There was no morphine to ease the pain, but as some compensation she could record tonight's awards and play the tape over and over again.

It was her turn that evening to muck out the kennels. Afterwards she went straight into the shower, scrubbing herself clean and washing her hair, which as part of her disguise hung blonde and straight an inch below her collarbone. As she put on a nightie, which Tab had once given her, with a picture on the front of Peter Rabbit eating a carrot, she reflected that Tristan probably wouldn't recognize her now. He met so many people, he might not remember her anyway. At least she had a lovely warm bedsitter, centrally heated against the East Coast winter and with views over the kennels and the park where she walked the dogs for their allotted twenty minutes a day.

She had bought a litre of white and poured herself a large drink to steady her nerves. The sweat was already coursing down her ribs. Over and over she checked the tape was working and that she'd got the right channel.

But in the end the awards passed in a blur. As the cameras roved around the tables, Lucy was conscious of the depressing number of ravishing women. Then she gave a cry of delight, as through a cloud of Gauloise smoke emerged Oscar, Valentin, Bernard, Sylvestre and Ogborne, all getting plastered. But as she searched in vain among the other flushed self-satisfied luncheon guests there was no sign of Tristan or Claudine.

Up and down, up and down, gush, gush, gush, went the winners, thanking everyone from Auntie Glad to the guinea-pig.

'Oh, get on with it,' implored Lucy.

But at last it was Best Actress. In the clips from *The Lily in the Valley*, Claudine looked so beautiful that Lucy groaned. It was impossible Tristan couldn't still be in love with her and, sure enough, it was her name Stephen Fry drew out of the gold envelope.

From an aerial view, the round tables covered in white damask, all with their rings of green Perrier bottles at the centre, floated like water-lilies on the bluey-green carpet, as Claudine glided between them up onto the stage. She was wearing a beautiful suit, the colour of bramble fool, which brought out the violet in her wide-apart eyes. Lovingly stroking her award, which was gold and in the shape of an owl, she murmured a few platitudes only redeemed by the sexiness of her French accent. Although it wouldn't seem so sexy to Tristan, thought Lucy, helping herself to another glass of wine, because he was French anyway. Claudine didn't look a bundle of laughs, nor did she get tumultuous applause. She had lost too many Brownie points not coming forward to save Tristan in July.

Valentin won the award for Best Cameraman. The prize for Director of Photography went to Oscar, who caused huge laughter by being caught fast asleep on camera when his name was read out. But he woke up enough to tell the audience Tristan was the finest director he'd ever worked with.

'Hear, hear,' shouted Lucy. 'But where *is* he?'

The Best Actor Award went to Anthony Hopkins, which was an excuse for another glass of wine, and at last it was Best Director. Tristan was competing with Woody Allen, Stanley Kubrick and Steven Spielberg. Lucy's nightgown was drenched in sweat, she couldn't stop shaking. 'Please make him win,' she prayed, 'so that at least I see him.'

As more clips were shown of Claudine in *The Lily in the Valley*, Lucy hurled a cushion at the television set, narrowly missing her fast-emptying bottle. Julie Christie, just as beautiful as Claudine, was slowly opening the envelope, tantalizing, taking her time.

'And the best director is Tristan de Montigny for *The Lily in the Valley.*'

Lucy's scream of excitement was lost in the roar of applause as the whole audience rose to their feet to pay tribute to the courage with which Tristan had faced his terrible problems in the past year. But Lucy's tears of joy turned into wails of despair as, after a roll of drums, the spotlight once more tracked bloody Claudine coming back through the tables up onto the stage.

And her make-up's been redone, thought Lucy savagely.

Claudine wasn't looking very sunny, however, particularly when there were groans of disappointment and a flurry of booing and shouts of 'Where's Tristan?'

'I am afraid Treestan de Monteegny ees eendisposed,' said Claudine defensively, 'and cannot accept this award. But I know he would thank you all for this wonderful honour. I am so 'appy to accept it on his behalf because he is most wonderful director I ever worked with and the one with the most integrity.'

'Which is more than can be said for you,' shouted a drunken Ogborne.

Poleaxed with disappointment, Lucy switched off the television and threw herself on her bed. The pain was unendurable. Hearing his name, seeing the others in the crew had brought everything back. How could she exist for another second without him? She was crying so hysterically, at first she didn't hear banging on the door.

'Linda, Linda, Linda,' shouted Bella, the senior kennelmaid, 'what in hell's the matter? Please open the door.'

'Go away,' sobbed Lucy. 'Leave me alone.'

'Gee, I'm sorry to bother you, but you know about lurchers and some guy's brought one in. I told him to come back tomorrow, but he seems desperate. I said you'd take the dog's particulars and settle it in.'

'We don't want any more dogs,' wept Lucy. 'It'll mean another one put down to make room for him.'

Wiping her face on the counterpane, seizing a handful of tissues to blow her nose, mumbling that she simply wasn't up to it, Lucy stumbled downstairs into the freezing cold night to discover it had been snowing. The dog pens on either side of the rough track leading up to the check-in office were empty of dogs but blanketed in snow. Snow lay on the roofs of the kennels behind, where she hoped the dogs were sleeping and wouldn't wake up when she installed the lurcher. Newcomers were often traumatized by the din.

Snow, already freezing on the wire fencing and the dogs' nameplates on each pen, reminded her unaccountably of Valhalla. And then she saw him tiptoeing tentatively out of the office, a big grey shaggy dog, and her eyes were full of tears once more because in the moonlight he looked like the ghost of James. He was a little rickety on his legs, but as she drew nearer he suddenly noticed her, stiffened and his tail began sweeping back and forth, almost touching his ears as he broke into a lovely loping canter.

He must be a ghost, he must! But as she ran forward, and he bounded towards her, swifter than eagles, she could see his dark paw prints stretching out behind him in the snow. Then he sank down on his ancient legs, squeaking and pirouetting four times in the moonlight, and, sneezing in excitement, he collapsed at her feet.

Totally immobile for a few seconds, Lucy fell to her knees, hugging him, wailing as she felt the razor sharpness of his ribs and backbone, but all the time his tail beat frenziedly as his long tongue shot out to lick away the waterfall of tears.

'Oh, James darling, how come you're in America?'

Wiping her eyes on his fur, Lucy raced up the snowy path in her bare feet with James bounding beside her.

'It's a miracle,' she screamed, 'someone's brought in my James. Tell me I'm not dreaming.'

Then she heard a voice, the most heartbreakingly husky voice in the world, saying indignantly, 'No, I didn't make myself clear. I want to keep the dog. It is your kennelmaid that I want to rehome.'

'Tristan,' croaked Lucy. 'Oh, Tristan.'

In the doorway to the waiting room her knees gave way, with James's shaggy body the only thing propping her up. As Tristan came through the other door from the general office, she gave a gasp because snow was melting in his hair as it had been on the first day of filming, and because he was even thinner than James and, under the fluorescent lighting, looked greyer and more ghostly than James had in the moonlight.

It must be a dream. Her eyes were so wet and her throat so dry, she couldn't cry out, and neither, it seemed, could he. They just gazed at each other. The only sound was the brisk drumbeat of James's tail against a metal filing cabinet.

'Where did you find him?' At last she stammered out the words.

'In Edinburgh, outside my hotel. Some bastard use him to beg for money. He was so thin I didn't recognize him. He was the clever one who recognized me.'

As someone closed the door discreetly behind him, Lucy's thanks came tumbling over each other. Wiping her eyes and nose on the sleeve of her nightie, she crouched down beside James, clinging to him, kissing him over and over, as he snaked against her in ecstasy.

'I thought I'd never see him again.' Her voice broke. 'Oh, how did you find me?'

'Gablecross finally admit you are here, or I would have arrived seven months earlier.'

Lucy gazed down, thinking how tearstained and soppy and Pollyanna-ish she must look in her Peter Rabbit nightie with her yellow hair in bunches. But Tristan was only aware of her sweet, trembling mouth and the way her cheekbones shone like mother-of-pearl as the tears slid over them. Then, suddenly roused from shock, he noticed her bare feet and how little she was wearing.

'You mustn't catch cold.' Whipping off his coat, he wrapped it round her. Breathing in the tang of Eau Sauvage on the dark blue collar, fighting the temptation to fall into his arms, Lucy collapsed instead on to a leather sofa.

'I didn't wake you?' asked Tristan.

'No, I was watching the Academias. *Lily in the Valley* won everything. You got Best Director.'

'I did?'

'You don't sound very excited. It's a *huge* honour.'

'Other things matter more.'

'How's *Don Carlos*?' Anyone would think she was at one of Helen's drinks parties.

'People seem to like it. Everyone loves your make-up, and have bet you get Oscar.'

Soothed by Lucy's stroking, James had collapsed on the floor, but kept one eye open – after all, his future was at stake. All round the walls hung photographs of beautiful, happy, rehomed dogs, cheek to cheek with adoring but often extremely plain owners. Maybe, thought Lucy hopefully through a haze of white wine, one didn't need to be beautiful to be loved. Then she made the mistake of asking how Tab was.

'Blissful,' said Tristan happily. 'Rupert's revving up for a massive wedding at Penscombe in April.'

How lunatic she'd been to hope. Smoothing the feathers on James's legs, Lucy felt the tears starting again.

'That's great.' Desperately she tried to keep the conversation light. 'I can be godmother to your first child.'

'I'd much rather you were its mother,' muttered Tristan.

But Lucy wasn't concentrating, only noticing that he seemed to be edging across the room towards her, like James trying to get on to her mother's double bed when they stayed in Cumbria.

'Lucy darling, please stop crying,' begged Tristan, 'I can't bear it. Listen to me. Hortense die last week.'

'Oh, no, I'm so sorry.' Lucy looked up in horror. 'She was such a darling.'

'She love you too, and eef you hadn't sought her out, I would never have known I was Laurent's son. That parcel was most wonderful present I ever have. I can never thank you too much.'

'But it's me who should thank you. You saved my life, you brought James back. We'll have to settle abroad,' said Lucy, in a worried voice. 'He'd never cope with quarantine, nor would I.'

Tristan was so close now, she could again breathe in the familiar heady cocktail of Eau Sauvage, peppermint chewing-gum and Gauloise, and her heart started to hammer as his knees brushed against hers.

'James and I had long conversation on the plane coming over.'

Was she imagining it or had his hand just stroked her hair?

'James detest crate I have to put him into,' continued Tristan. 'He didn't believe I was taking him to you. He was so depressed and nervous I had to sit in the hold and hold his paw. It was very uncomfortable for both of us. There were two parrots with us, who both learn to say "I love Lucy" by end of flight.'

Still unable to take in what he was saying, Lucy gave a shaky laugh.

'James want to live in France,' insisted Tristan.

'We don't know anyone in France,' said Lucy, in a choked voice.

'You know me.' Crouching down beside her, Tristan put one hand over her mouth, '*Tais-toi*, my darling, for just one second. Since you go away nothing in my life has been so dreadful. I suffer over Claudine, but nothing to the purgatory of life without you. Those months of filming, you bring such sunshine into my life.'

With the other hand he was now stroking her forehead, fingering her feathery eyelashes, wiping away a fresh supply of tears, running his finger down her nose in wonder. 'You are really real,' he whispered. 'I have nightmares every night that you are dead.'

'Oh, so do I,' breathed Lucy, appalled to find she couldn't stop kissing his fingers.

'Hush, I talk. First, I kid myself you are sweet little sister I never had. When you take care of me after Rannaldini tell me about Maxim, I kid myself you are mother I never had. But then you come back from

France looking so beautiful in that pink dress, and I sack you because I am so white-hot jealous you're having *affaire* with Wolfie, I suddenly realize you are true grand passion I never have. When you nearly died, I died with worry, but when you went away, I died worser.' Tristan removed his hand from her mouth and waited. 'Lucy, *Lucy*. Please look at me and *say* something.'

But she was so stunned by the wonder of his words, she could only stare down and ask herself how the hell Peter Rabbit could stuff his face with carrot at a time like this.

Tristan picked up one of her bunches. 'You look so sexy with blonde hair.' Then a horrible possibility dawned on him. 'There is not someone else?'

'Someone else?' squeaked Lucy incredulously. 'Of course not. I've never loved anyone but you since that moment I saw you with snow in your hair. The Prince with the heavy heart.' Then she remembered the occasion and cried out despairingly, 'But what about Tab and the wedding?'

'What's she got to do with it?' asked Tristan in amazement. 'Tab's marrying Wolfie. Oh, my God, did you think it was still Tab and me? Oh, my poor angel.' Kneeling up, he pulled her against him, feeling the frantic pounding of her heart, as she in turn felt the exquisite pain of being crushed against the hardness of his big gold blazer buttons.

'That's wonderful for Wolfie,' gasped Lucy, 'but weren't you heartbroken?'

'Not in the least. They will have pretty blond babies.'

'And Wolfie'll look after her so well, he adores her so much.'

'Not as much as I shall adore and look after you.' For a second Tristan sounded almost beady. 'And you and I will have lots of babies with dark curly hair, who will be even prettier. I know how you love kids.' He picked up Lucy's hand and kissed each finger. 'As Maxim's son, I couldn't give them to you so I back off. By the time

I open parcel and learnt the truth you had gone. Why did you run away? It broke my heart.'

'I couldn't bear the pain.' Tentatively Lucy's hand crept up to the dark stubble along his jaw. 'I thought you were in love with Claudine or, at least, Tab – that's stiff competition – and Rozzy . . .' Her voice trailed off in embarrassment.

'Rozzy what?' demanded Tristan, forcing her face upwards.

'She, well, she said I was too plain, ugly and common, and your family would be furious. Ouch!' Lucy screamed, as Tristan's hand clenched on her chin, then gasped in alarm because his eyes had become black whirlpools of hatred.

'Eef that evil monster weren't in security prison,' he spat, 'I break in and tear her to pieces. How dare the beetch! You have sweetest face in the world. And my family will love you. Whether you will love them is different matter. My brothers are very pompous. And it's me they are furious with at the moment because Aunt Hortense leave me so much money, and', Tristan smiled suddenly, 'they don't quite know how to handle Griselda. I adore your face.' Very gently he covered it in kisses. 'And now it will grow as familiar as the paintings on my bedroom wall.'

But Lucy wasn't ready for certainty. 'What about Claudine? I read the *Mail*.'

Tristan scrambled to his feet, pulling Lucy up against him. Despite his thinness, his chest was still broad, and his arms incredibly strong as they closed round her.

'I should have level with you,' he muttered, 'my love for her die, the night Rannaldini die. I drive to Wales and find I am chasing dream.'

'Did you see her in Edinburgh?'

'No, I run away. I call her from airport. She was furious. "Are you sick?" she shout. "No," I say, "I am seeking."'

Running his hands deep into Lucy's hair, he gazed

785

down at her. 'You have no need of Oscar's lighting.'

Then, breathing in faint traces of Bluebell, he knew spring had at last returned. As he kissed her Lucy could feel his wonderful big bruised lower lip crushing hers, and his tongue caressing her tongue. Just for a second her eyes flickered open and saw that his were closed in ecstasy, the thick dark brown lashes fanning his beautiful cheekbones. As she swivelled her head sideways so he could kiss her even harder, she felt as though she was being drawn up to heaven like one of Chagall's angels. And what her head still couldn't quite take in, her heart accepted completely, that he truly loved her.

As they broke for breath, she flung her arms round his neck. 'You are the most blissfully gorgeous man who ever walked this earth, and I'm going to love, cherish and adore you for ever.'

'If you don't, I shall be horribly jealous,' said Tristan. 'Even of Pierre Lapin.' He fingered Peter Rabbit. 'Look at lucky him, lying against those wonderful breasts.'

'How d'you know they're wonderful?' mumbled a blushing Lucy.

'I have Hype-along's picture in my wallet. I show it you later. But first you must have this.'

Reaching down to his coat which had fallen on the floor, he took a little black velvet box from the inside pocket. 'Aunt Hortense leave me ring, which once belong to Marie Antoinette. You give me back my name, Lucy, now I want you to share it with me.'

Lucy's hands were trembling so violently, Tristan had to open the box. Inside, like mistletoe berries waiting for kissing lovers, gleamed three pearls.

As a tear splashed on one of them, Tristan said shakily, 'I would be safest, happiest guy in world, if you would wear it always.'

They were brought back to earth by a great snore rending the air. With his future assured, James felt safe to fall asleep.

EPILOGUE

The police had finally allowed Rannaldini to be buried in huge pomp. Unwilling to attend the funeral, Tristan came alone to Valhalla to pay his last respects. It was a bitterly cold, dark afternoon: the east wind howled and lashed the naked trees. A 'For Sale' sign swung dismally outside the main gates.

Tristan went straight to the graveyard. Here, amid a sea of flowers and higgledy-piggledy ivy-clad graves, soared a splendid white marble headstone, on which had already been inscribed the words: 'Roberto Rannaldini, Maestro and Composer, 1949–1996.'

As he stood in the fading light, Tristan relived the past year, remembering Baby serenading Hermione in the snow, Tabitha screaming at the hunt, Granny silencing the rabble with such terrifying authority, Alpheus singing with such kingly anguish, and Mikhail as he lay dying reducing everyone to tears.

Tristan thought of Simone, Wolfie and Bernard working themselves to the bone, of Valentin and Oscar creating radiance even when they seemed at their most languid and inattentive, of dearest Lucy, always comforting and smiling, of Sexton giving him full rein and heroically raising the money, and the rest of the crew backing him all the way despite their grumbling.

But without Rannaldini it would never have happened. Without Rannaldini's kindness and continual encouragement in the early days he would never have emerged from the shadow of Étienne's disdain and become a director. And what would Rannaldini, who had never settled for less than perfection, think of his film, which was now in a little black oblong box for present and future generations to judge?

More important than winning any Oscars, Tristan hoped that, whatever form or being he was now, Rannaldini would be proud.

Strange that one narrow grave could contain so much vitality, strange that so much tragedy and passion should be contained in one small, black videotape, which Tristan now laid on Rannaldini's grave. On top he placed a white gardenia.

But as he stood in silence, he could have sworn a pale violet light, like a torch beam or a peacock butterfly left over from summer, landed on the grave, and danced for a second before disappearing into the earth. He shook his head. It must have been a trick of the light.

Leaving the graveyard, he wandered past Meredith's cuckoo clock lying upside down in the park. The patch of yellow grass beneath Lucy's caravan was green once more, the love-in-a-mist in her abandoned window-box turned to seed pods. Tristan put a couple in his pocket.

Looking over the valley with the ghosts of the past swirling around him, he was overwhelmed by sorrow that *Don Carlos* was over and Rannaldini gone for ever. But as he walked swiftly back to the car park he felt only joy as he switched on his telephone and dialled his future:

'May I speak to Lucy de Montigny, please?'

ACKNOWLEDGEMENTS

In 1985 Robin Baird-Smith, then of Constable the publisher, sent me to Death Valley to write a short book about Patrick Lichfield photographing three ravishing nude models for the 1986 Unipart calendar. As well as Patrick's crew, there was a second film crew videoing the shoot for television. Everyone was obsessed with their own agenda. With temperatures hitting 140°F, the rows were as pyrotechnic as the high jinks. Returning home a wreck, but eternally grateful to everyone involved for such riotous fun, I vowed one day to write a novel about a film crew on location.

The result, fourteen years later, is *Score!*: the subject no longer a calendar shoot but the filming of Verdi's darkest opera, *Don Carlos*, with the resultant tensions leading to murder. Only when I had embarked on the story did I realize that in addition to filming and recording I would need to research opera and the ways of singers as well as the infinitely complicated police procedure of solving a murder. This consequently means a huge number of people to thank for their help. Singers, and those who work with them, seem to have particularly large and generous hearts.

On the filming front, I must start by thanking my dear friend Adrian Rowbotham, an independent director, who not only talked to me for hours, but later nobly ploughed through the manuscript for errors. I am also eternally grateful to the charismatic Peter Maniura of BBC Television, who was brilliant on directing the film of *Dido and Aeneas*, and the ebullient Mick Csaky of Antelope Films, who rolled up to lunch with a complete and marvellously funny brief on how to fund the film of an opera. Mick also introduced me to the divine soprano Susan Daniel, who over many meetings shared her singing experiences, particularly of starring in the film of *Carmen* with Placido Domingo.

Brilliant filming advice was given me by Ray Marshall, Chloë and David Hargreaves and Alison Sterling of Fat Chance Productions, Alan Kaupe, Clifford Haydn-Tovey, James Swann, Nick Handel, Bill and Susannah Franklyn and, in particular, Irving Teitelbaum and Rob Knights, who allowed me to range freely on the set of *Mosley*, the excellent series they produced and directed for ITV. During this time I had terrific conversations with actors Jonathan Cake, Jemma Redgrave and Roger May, as well as Chris O'Dell, the director of photography, Rudi Buckle, sound, Charlotte Walter, wardrobe, Heather Storr, continuity, Shelagh Pymm, publicity, Patricia Kirkman, make-up, and an ace caterer called Melanie.

My heroine in *Score!* is a make-up girl, always the still centre of any shoot, so I would therefore especially like to thank all the make-up artists over the years who soothed and transformed me, as well as beguiling me with anecdotes. They include Maggie Hunt, Valerie Macdonald, Jacqui Jefferies, Becky Challis, Rozelle Parry, Sally Holden, Clayton Howard, Juliette Mayer, Sarah Bee, Jenny Sharpe and Celia Hunter.

Several chapters in *Score!* are set in France. Here I am deeply indebted to star journalist Suzanne Lowry as well as my French publisher, Valérie-Anne Giscard d'Estaing, for thinking up glamorous names; Jonathan Eastwood for being brilliant on French law; Jill de Monpezat for kindly reading the French chapters for accuracy; Caterina Krucker for correcting my French; and my brother and sister-in-law, Timothy and Angela Sallitt, who lived for ten years in a stunning house in the Tarn, and who have been a constant source of information and inspiration.

On the music front, I am quite unable to express sufficient gratitude to Bill Holland, head of Polygram Classics and Jazz, easily the nicest and most generous man in the record business, who not only lent me numerous books and plied me with the relevant CDs, but also endlessly answered my questions, waded through the chapters on recording and finally produced a glorious double CD of the music featured in *Score!*

Bill also invited me to a miraculous production of Berg's *Lulu* at Glyndebourne. Again I am extremely grateful to the then General Director Anthony Whitworth-Jones for letting me wander everywhere, and to Humphrey Burton and Sonia Lovett and their crew at NVC Arts, who were filming *Lulu* for Channel 4, for allowing me to attend production meetings and sit in the control room and beside the cameramen during the performance.

Going back to the seventies, I must thank my friend Guelda Waller for first taking me to *Don Carlos* at the Royal Opera House, thus igniting a passion, which has grown with the years. It was therefore a colossal thrill to be allowed to sit in on Phillips Classics recording sessions of *Don Carlos* in Walthamstow Assembly Rooms in 1996. I would especially like to thank the executive producer, Clive Bennett; the legendary Christopher Raeburn, who produced the record; the mighty Bernard Haitink; the sublime chorus and orchestra of the Royal Opera House, Covent Garden; the beguiling language coach, Maria Cleva; the endearingly laid-back orchestra manager, Clifford Corbett; and the magnificent cast, including Richard Margison, Robert Lloyd, Galina Gorchakova, Robin Leggate and Roderick Williams. I also had particular help from Patricia Haitink, Jan Burnett, the co-ordinator, James Jones, in charge of publicity, and the PA James Ross, a rising young conductor, who talked to me for hours about the opera and made some excellent suggestions when the book was in synopsis stage.

My characters sing a lot in the book. I am therefore extremely grateful first to Theodore Lap and Hugh Graham and secondly to Avril Bardoni for permission to quote from their excellent English translations of the *Don Carlos* libretto, which in Hugh's case was for the 1997 EMI recording conducted by Antonio Pappano, and in Avril's for the programme when *Don Carlos* was performed at a 1997 Promenade concert.

I must thank Ingrid Kohlmeyer of English National Opera and Helen Anderson and Rita Grudzien of the Royal Opera House, who were constantly helpful. I am also indebted to Katherine Fitzherbert, who runs English Touring Opera, which brings such joy to music lovers around the country. Katherine allowed me to sit backstage with the DSM Helen Bunkall at a production of *Rigoletto* and work the lightning flashes. She also invited me to *Werther* followed by a riotous, end-of-tour party. Here I had the luck to meet the conductor Alistair Dawes, then Head of Music Staff at the Royal Opera House, and his wife Lesley-Ann, a singer and teacher, who have since become extremely close friends, letting me sit in on lessons, taking me through the *Don Carlos* score and answering endless questions.

Other singers who have given me wonderful advice include Susan Parry, Penelope Shaw, Andy Busher, Christine Botes, Joanna Colledge and John Hudson.

I must thank my musician friends, who sometimes have rather trenchant views on singers. They include Chris and Jacoba Gale, Ian Pillow, Diggory Seacome,

Luke Strevens, Jack and Linn Rothstein, Lance Green, who thought up the title *Score!*, and his wife Justine, Richard Hewitt and Steena and Marat Bisengaliev.

I have also been royally entertained and enlightened on the subject of opera by dear Sir Ian Hunter, Nicholas Kenyon, Michael Volpe, George Humphreys and Paul Hughes.

As *Don Carlos* in my book is set in modern dress, I spent an utterly magical two hours recce-ing the state rooms at Buckingham Palace for ideas. This was kindly organized by Claire Zammitt. These rooms are only open to the public from early August to early October. My director in *Score!*, however, visits the rooms in early spring, which was the only time it could be fitted into the plot. I hope Her Majesty will forgive the poetic licence.

St Peter's Grange, a beautiful fifteenth-century retreat nestling in the wooded grounds of Prinknash Abbey, Gloucestershire, is the model for the abbey, around which filming and murder take place in *Score!*. I was very privileged to have Father Damien of Prinknash and Peter Clarkson to show me repeatedly over the house and garden and to answer endless questions on its dark and romantic history.

Score! is my first and almost certainly last whodunit. After battling with the complexities of murder, I rate the genius of Agatha Christie and P.D. James even higher than that of Einstein. I would have given up altogether had it not been for the kindness and co-operation of Gloucester and Stroud Police. No matter what hour I rang, no matter how fatuous the query, they entered into the spirit and never failed to provide an answer. Their only disagreement was whether the male member remains erect after the moment of death, Stroud maintaining it did, Gloucester it didn't. Other police officers beguiled me with thrilling tales of murder and later waded through the manuscript for errors. They know who they are and the extent of my gratitude.

Gloucester Fire and Ambulance Services were just as helpful, particularly their assistant divisional officer, Graham Jewell. Gloucester Reference Library kindly checked names for me. The British Polio Fellowship, the British Film Industry and Weatherbys were also always ready with answers.

A writer does not automatically expect kindness from her own profession, but few could have been more welcoming and generous with their time than David Fingleton, Mel Cooper, Charles Osborne, Michael Coveney, Malcolm Hayes, Norman Lebrecht, Keith Clarke and Richard Fawkes of *Classical Music*, and James Jolly and Christopher Pollard of *Gramophone*.

I must also thank the authors of five books which were invaluable in helping me to understand my subject: *The Colin Clark Diaries: The Prince, the Showgirl and Me*; *Ring Resounding*, the marvellous account by the late John Culshaw of the first recording in stereo of Wagner's *Ring*; *The Jigsaw Man*, a study of criminal psychology by Paul Britton; John Baxter's wonderful biography of Steven Spielberg; and the late Sir Rudolph Bing's *Five Thousand Nights at the Opera*.

My friends as usual came up with endless ideas. They include Teddy Chad, Vanessa Calthorpe, Flavia Cooper, Val Hennessey, Huw Humphreys, Annabel Dinsdale, Richard Stilgoe, Graham Ogilvie, Harriet Capaldi, Godfrey Smith and his grandson, Max Cordell-Smith, Louise Naylor, Michael Cordy, Simon Craker, Marjorie and Peter Hendy, Jill Reay, Lizzy Moyle, Rowena Luard, Sarah King, Claire Williams, James and Georgie Carter, Maurice Leonard, Maria Prendergast, Philip Jones, Rob and Sharon Morgan. Alistair Horne and General Sir Peter Davies were brilliant on French soldiering; Peter Davies, the art writer, on French painters; Micky Suffolk on helicopters. Andrew Parker Bowles, Charlie Mann, Charlie Brooks on racing, Astrid St Aubyn and Zahra Hanbury on ghosts, my doctors Graham Hall and Pat Pearson and their staff at Frithwood surgery on medical matters and our vet, dear John Hunter, on animals.

Animals play a hugely important part in *Score!*, particularly the heroine's dog, James, who is based on a shaggy red rescued lurcher of the same name, the adored pet of Alan Little of Gardners. No-one else in the book, however, is based on anyone, unless they are so famous – as David Mellor and Nigel Dempster are – that they appear as themselves. *Score!* I must emphasize is a work of fiction, and any resemblance to any living person or organization is purely coincidental.

I wish I had space to thank everyone who helped me. Those named were usually experts in their own field, but I took their advice only as far as it suited my plot, which in no way reflects on their expertise.

I am extremely grateful to Transworld for publishing *Score!* and to Broo Doherty for working so hard to edit it; to Neil Gower for drawing such a beautiful map; and to my agent Desmond Elliott and his assistant Douglas Kean for all their support and kindness. I'd also like to thank Jo Xuereb-Brennan, who provided marvellous advice when cuts in the original manuscript were asked for.

The real heroines of *Score!*, however, are my five friends, Pippa Birch, Annette Xuereb-Brennan, Anna Gibbs-Kennett, Mandy Williams and Caterina Krucker, who typed the huge manuscript in all its endless drafts and rewrites. I cannot thank them enough for their enthusiasm, industry and advice on everything from polo backhands to pregnancy kits.

I must especially thank my dear PA, Pippa Birch, for looking after me so beautifully, and my cleaner, Ann

Mills, to whom *Score!* is dedicated, who has restored our house to order for the last fifteen years and is simply one of the nicest people I know.

The lion's share of my gratitude as usual goes to my husband Leo, my children Felix and Emily, and my dogs, Hero and Bessie, who have put up with murder, literally, for the last three years, and have been constantly comforting and inspiring.

APPASSIONATA
by Jilly Cooper

Abigail Rosen, nicknamed Appassionata, was the sexiest, most flamboyant violinist in classical music, but she was also the loneliest and the most exploited girl in the world. When a dramatic suicide attempt destroyed her violin career, she set her sights on the male-dominated heights of the conductor's rostrum.

When Abby gets the chance to take over the Rutminster Symphony Orchestra, she is ecstatic, not realizing the RSO is in hock up to its neck and is composed of the wildest bunch of musicians ever to blow a horn or caress a fiddle. Abby finds it increasingly difficult to control her - undisciplined rabble and pretend she is not madly attracted to the fatally glamorous horn player, Viking O'Neill, who claims *droit de seigneur* over every pretty woman joining the orchestra. And then Rannaldini, arch-fiend and international maestro, rolls up with Machiavellian plans of his own to sabotage the RSO.

Effervescent as champagne, Jilly Cooper's new novel brings back old favourites like Rupert and Taggie Campbell-Black and his son Marcus and ends triumphantly with a rampageous orchestral tour of Spain and the high drama of an international piano competition.

Appassionata – the most swooningly romantic and heart-warming novel of the year.

'Triumphant . . . a boisterous tale of sex and Chopin amongst Rutshire folk'
Tatler

'*Appassionata* – the divine Jilly Cooper's latest and greatest novel'
Jane Procter, *Sunday Times*

0 552 14323 5

THE MAN WHO MADE HUSBANDS JEALOUS
by Jilly Cooper

Lysander Hawkley combined breathtaking good looks with the kindest of hearts. He couldn't pass a stray dog, an ill-treated horse, or a neglected wife without rushing to the rescue. And with neglected wives the rescue invariably led to ecstatic bonking, which didn't please their erring husbands one bit.

Lysander's mid-life crisis had begun at twenty-two. Reeling from the death of his beautiful mother, he was out of work, drinking too much, and desperately in debt. The solution came from Ferdie, his fat friend; if Lysander was so good at making husband jealous, why shouldn't he get paid for it?

Let loose among the neglected wives of the ritzy county of Rutshire, Lysander causes absolute havoc. But it is only when he meets Rannaldini, Rutshire's King Rat and a temperamental, fiendishly promiscuous international conductor, that the trouble really starts. The only unglamorous woman around Rannaldini was Kitty, his plump young wife who ran his life like clockwork. Soon Lysander was convinced that Kitty must be rescued from Rannaldini at all costs, even if it means enlisting the help of the old blue-eyed havoc maker: Rupert Campbell-Black himself . . .

'Delicious . . . her bawdy humour shines through at all times . . . almost like an old-fashioned comedy of manners – with dollops of sex . . . settle down and have a rollicking good time. Satisfaction guaranteed!'
Jackie Collins

'Irresistible . . . I devoured it in a day . . . she's on cracking form . . . just read it and enjoy'
Susannah Herbert, *Sunday Telegraph*

'It is a happy, happy feckless romp . . . her fans, who are legion, will love it'
Maeve Binchy, *Mail on Sunday*

0 552 13895 9

PANDORA
by Jilly Cooper

No picture ever came more beautiful than Raphael's *Pandora*. Discovered by a dashing young lieutenant, Raymond Belvedon, in a Normandy Chateau in 1944, she had cast her spell over his family – all artists and dealers – for fifty years. Hanging in a turret of their lovely Cotswold house, Pandora witnessed Raymond's tempestuous wife Galena both entertaining a string of lovers, and giving birth to her four children: Jupiter, Alizarin, Jonathan and superbrat Sienna. Then an exquisite stranger rolls up, claiming to be a long-lost daughter of the family, setting the three Belvedon brothers at each other's throats. Accompanying her is her fatally glamorous boyfriend, whose very different agenda includes an unhealthy interest in the Raphael.

During a fireworks party, the painting is stolen. The hunt to retrieve it takes the reader on a thrilling journey to Vienna, Geneva, Paris, New York and London. After a nail-biting court case and record-smashing Old Masters sale at Sotheby's, passionate love triumphs and *Pandora* is restored to her rightful home.

'Open the covers of Jilly Cooper's latest novel and you lift the lid of a Pandora's box. From the pages flies a host of delicious and deadly vices . . . Her sheer exuberance and energy are contagious'
The Times

'One reads her for her joie de vivre . . . and her razor-sharp sense of humour. Oh, and the sex'
New Statesman

'She's irresistible . . . she frees you from the daily drudge and deposits you in an alternative universe where love, sex and laughter rule'
Independent on Sunday

'The whole thing is a riot – vastly superior to anything else in a glossy cover'
Daily Telegraph

'A wonderful, romantic spectacular of a novel'
Spectator

0 552 14850 4

A LIST OF OTHER JILLY COOPER
TITLES AVAILABLE FROM CORGI BOOKS
AND BANTAM PRESS

THE PRICES SHOWN BELOW WERE CORRECT AT THE TIME OF GOING TO PRESS. HOWEVER TRANSWORLD PUBLISHERS RESERVE THE RIGHT TO SHOW NEW RETAIL PRICES ON COVERS WHICH MAY DIFFER FROM THOSE PREVIOUSLY ADVERTISED IN THE TEXT OR ELSEWHERE.

☐	12041 3	**LISA & CO**	£5.99
☐	14696 X	**HARRIET & OCTAVIA**	£6.99
☐	14697 8	**IMOGEN & PRUDENCE**	£5.99
☐	14695 1	**EMILY & BELLA**	£6.99
☐	15055 X	**RIDERS**	£6.99
☐	15056 8	**RIVALS**	£6.99
☐	15057 6	**POLO**	£6.99
☐	15058 4	**THE MAN WHO MADE HUSBANDS JEALOUS**	£6.99
☐	15054 1	**APPASSIONATA**	£6.99
☐	14850 4	**PANDORA**	£6.99
☐	14662 5	**CLASS**	£6.99
☐	14663 3	**THE COMMON YEARS**	£5.99
☐	99091 4	**ANIMALS IN WAR**	£6.99
☐	04404 5	**HOW TO SURVIVE CHRISTMAS** (Hardback)	£9.99
☐	14367 7	**THE MAN WHO MADE HUSBANDS JEALOUS** (Audio)	£12.99*

*including VAT

All Transworld titles are available by post from:

Bookpost, P.O. Box 29, Douglas, Isle of Man, IM99 1BQ

Credit cards accepted. Please telephone 01624 836000, fax 01624 837033, Internet http://www.bookpost.co.uk or e-mail: bookshop@enterprise.net for details.

Free postage and packing in the UK. Overseas customers allow £1 per book (paperbacks) and £3 per book (hardbacks).